W9-BUK-017

The wounded and dead lay everywhere before them. There was movement on the ground to Rachel's left. The leather of her saddle creaked as she dismounted and knelt down beside a fallen boy. Israel was behind her instantly, grabbing a lantern from a nearby tent, holding it just above her head so she could see.

Dried blood from a deep saber cut across one ear lay thick on the boy's neck. His left sleeve was torn and his arm was still oozing blood. The boy looked up at her face, tawny in the firelight, and at the reflection of campfires glowing in her large dark eyes. Her gathered hair fell long over one shoulder and a strand of it brushed his lips. The moment her soft hands touched the skin of his forehead and arms, tears rose in his eyes and ran down the side of his face. "Oh, thank you, ma'am. Thank you!" Reaching beneath her dress for the edge of her petticoat, she tore it in strips and bound him up.

All night long Rachel moved from camp to camp, Israel beside her, stanching bullet wounds, salving abrasions, always working her way to the rear.

Also by Charles Durham
Published by Ballantine Books:

THE LAST EXILE

WALK
IN THE
LIGHT

Charles Durham

BALLANTINE BOOKS • NEW YORK

Sale of this book without a front cover may be unauthorized. If this book is coverless, it may have been reported to the publisher as "unsold or destroyed" and neither the author nor the publisher may have received payment for it.

Copyright © 1992 by Charles Durham
Map copyright © 1992 by Claudia Carlson

All rights reserved under International and Pan-American Copyright Conventions. Published in the United States by Ballantine Books, a division of Random House, Inc., New York, and simultaneously in Canada by Random House of Canada Limited, Toronto.

Library of Congress Catalog Card Number: 91-92154

ISBN: 0-345-38975-1

Manufactured in the United States of America

First Trade Edition: April 1992
First Mass Market Edition: December 1994

10 9 8 7 6 5 4 3 2 1

This book is for my own daughters,
Deborah and Rebekah, whose hair and
eyes are as dark as Rachel's,
but whose father loves them truly.

... and in memory of
my dear friend, C. E. Griffeth
1923–1991

Acknowledgments

I had help from many friends in gathering facts for *Walk in the Light*. First, I want to express grateful appreciation to my very close friend, Allen Joy, for the loan of his extensive Scottish library. Thanks to the librarians at the Scott County and Garden City, Kansas, libraries—and especially to Jean Long and Earlene Nicholson for their wonderful help with Inter-Library Loan. Thanks also to Elaine Maack, curator of the Quaker Room at Friends University in Wichita, Kansas, for help with early Quaker speech patterns. Dr. Jerry Cashion of North Carolina State Historical Society set my feet in the right direction on several important questions regarding slavery. In a wonderful telephone conversation, Beverly Tetterton of the Public Library of Wilmington, North Carolina, gave me important information about master-slave relationships on Cape Fear during the Revolution. I also wish to thank the Maritime Museum at Beaufort, North Carolina, for their willing assistance.

Where I may have wrongly interpreted information these friends have given me, the responsibility is mine and mine alone. In any case, I offer them my sincerest thanks.

*The chiefest obligation that we have to live as we do arises
from the fact that amongst us are children—those beings of
whom it is said, "Except ye become as little children ye shall
not enter into the Kingdom of Heaven."*

WALK IN THE LIGHT WHILE THERE IS LIGHT
Leo Tolstoy

*Aince mair Jesus spak tae the fowk: "I am the licht o the
warld," he said; "him at fallows me will gang nane i the
mirk, but will hae the lict o life."*

—*John 8:12*

THE NEW TESTAMENT IN SCOTS
A Translation by William Laughton Lorimer

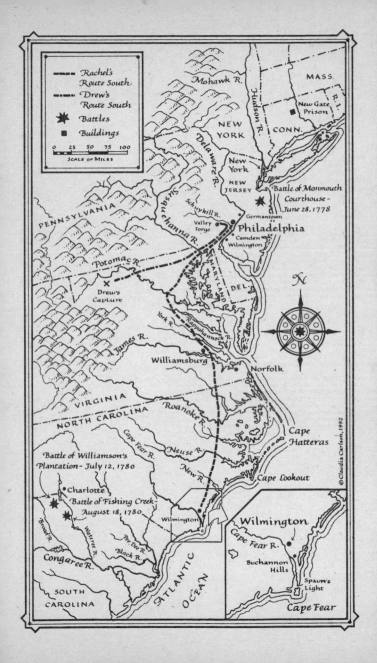

BOOK ONE

The Child
1753-1767

ONE

It was dark morning, the air cold and very still.

In the wide eastern sky, a pink-tinged blue had begun to glow, silhouetting the broad shoulders of the hill called the Great Shepherd of Etive. In the expanse between dark blue of night and promise of day hung the morning star—like a silver lamp waiting to guide in the dawn. At the foot of the Great Shepherd's slopes spread a low, grassy meadow through which twisted a little stream, gurgling and whispering in the darkness. So early was it, one could scarcely see a white mist lifting up from the water, freezing ghostlike on the naked branches. A heavy frost coated everything: the trees, the grasses, the dense thatch of the cottage roof that overhung one small window. One would wonder, looking at the unmortared stone of the cottage walls, how it stayed together, piled as it was, one irregular stone on another. Through the irregular glass of the window, a glimmering lamp cast its yellow light.

Outside, leaning against the rough east wall of the cottage, a man stood, his arms crossed over his chest, gazing upward through a black tangle of limbs against the faint blue. He ran a huge hand over the beard of his face and shook his massive head from side to side. When a man lives this far north, he thought, March is a cold month. Spring's already come to Cornwall. "It would be warmer there," he muttered.

At the sound of the man's voice, a night bird rustled in the trees, and on the meadow's far edge, a young deer started from its bed and swished through the frosted grass.

Then, from behind the man, came a thin cry cutting through loose crevices in the dry-stone wall. A shiver went down his spine. The cry grew louder, more determined. Mingled with the cry was the metallic sound of a clock striking four.

He visualized the scene inside, Bess leaning forward, drawing the child out of her own body, blood on her hands and on the bed. He shivered again. Well, it wasn't the first time she

3

had done it. He could not help her, for he could not stand the sight of blood—not since Culloden, where his father's blood spurt with every beat of his heart from the hole where he had been shot through the head with a British musket ball.

In his mind he heard the guns again, felt the cold rain on his face, smelled the acrid smoke, and heard the shrieks of wounded men. They had fought like devils that day: the MacDonalds, Clanranald, Glenbucket, Glengarry, Frasier, and Stewart. But Culloden Moor had been a poor place to stand; and with the Lowland Scots against them, it had come to worse than nothing. The Highlands were dead now, kilt and tartan gone, and the pipes. They were even forbidden their own language in favor of English.

"Damn English blood!" he swore aloud, and shook his head harder.

The new baby's cry came louder, more insistent than before. It would certainly be warmer in Cornwall, he thought again, much warmer.

An hour later Bartlett Calhoun was riding a fine roan horse over the hill's crest on his way south toward Cornwall, the sun's thin light sparkling in the frost on the limbs and grasses and cottage thatch.

Donald Calhoun—just six years old today—stood mute, watching the top of Bartlett Calhoun's black felt hat disappear. For a long time he stared at the empty space where his father had been. He did not understand, but felt the emptiness of his going.

Donald, a thin, red-haired boy with high cheekbones and vacuous blue eyes, was full of confusion. In a strange way, he had always felt his father liked him, sometimes even that he loved him. Donald was proud of his father, though he did not know just why. As Calhoun had ridden out, he had leaned down in the saddle and tousled the boy's hair with his huge hand. "Good-bye, boy," he had said, and then ridden away, never looking back. How strange it felt to have your father call you "boy," as though he had forgotten your name.

At last Donald picked up a wooden pail, knelt his black woolen trouser knee into the edge of the stream, and casting the bucket with a splash into icy water, let it sink, then pulled it in. As he stumbled back toward the house with the heavy load, his mind was full of his father's going.

Once inside he set the bucket on the slim table near the

door, brushed at the wet mud on his knee, then carried an ancient wooden dipper of fresh water to where his mother lay on her bed against the north wall. He handed it to her gently. He watched, frightened to see how her hands quivered as she lifted the dipper to her lips. Donald did not think of his mother as young, but she was only twenty-four, dark-haired, dark-eyed. The redness of his own hair had come from his father. He was even more alarmed at his mother's face, so pale and wan, for delivering herself of the tiny newborn had drained her of all strength.

She drank down the cold water, handed the dipper to Donald, then lay back with a sigh. Donald fingered its wooden bowl absently, gazing down at the small red face in the crook of his mother's arm. Never had he seen such smallness, a tiny bow of mouth the size of a walnut, a minuscule upper lip that lay over the lower like an exquisite bud, an illusion enhanced by its color, the translucent color of a faded rose. The girl-child's little arms waved in quick jerks, her miniature fingers grasping and flexing in the empty air.

"Rachel's hungry," his mother said softly. Her voice was weary, but smooth and kind as always. Donald's eyes widened and his face grew warm as she pulled aside the soft cloth of her nightdress and gave the baby her breast. The tiny one nestled her face into the breast, and her arms stopped waving.

Bess Calhoun smiled up at Donald, then reached out, taking his hand in hers, squeezing it reassuringly.

He found his voice again. "Is that what you're goin' to call her, Mama, Rachel?"

"Yes." She smiled. "Do you like it?"

"Oh, I do, Mama! I like it lots!"

For a moment Bess said nothing, and a troubled shadow fell across her eyes. Her lips tightened and her pale face turned red. "Daddy's gone?" she asked.

"Gone again, Mama," he replied.

"Well, it's not the first time, is it, Donald?"

"No, Mama, it's not," he said resignedly.

"You'll have to help me, Donald," she said. "I can't do it alone."

"You won't have to, Mama. I'll help."

Donald's throat tightened and he felt a terrible pain about his heart—an emptiness, thinking how alone they were. But instead of crying, he lifted his chin and a look of determination came into his pale blue eyes. Almost like a soldier at "about face," he turned and went to his work. Shortly, a sound of sizzling lifted into the air as he poured fresh batter of barley flour onto the griddle above an open fire. There was no meat in the house—just meal and milk. But he pulled a stool to his mother's bedside and sat down beside her, two plates of freshly baked bannock before them, and two tin mugs of milk still warm from the cow. As they ate he talked of tiny Rachel's perfect features, and how before very long it would be spring and they would need to be getting next autumn's barley crop into the ground.

T W O

THREE years went by, and Bartlett Calhoun did not return.

Then, one warm day when the riven slopes of the Great Shepherd had turned dun and gold with the lateness of the year, and the autumn air was fresh and light, little Rachel sat on a lichen-covered rock at the stream's edge, splashing her feet and laughing as the sun danced among the leaves in the treetops. To her mother Bess the valley was a place of grandeur and aching solitude, but to Rachel it was simply the place of her being. She had been out of the valley only twice, both times to a village near the Firth of Lorn, a long day's walk to the southwest. And even those times she had forgotten.

As they sat by the stream, a breeze gliding about in the treetops above made the leaves flutter alternately green and silver. Rachel noticed such things, from the muttering of the brook to the cooing of the doves in the branches. She looked up, and sensed that the light that danced tremblingly on the faces of the leaves was somehow speaking to her. With joy she splashed the water, kicking up showers of diamondlike droplets that wet her faded blue smock and sparkled in her long dark hair.

Suddenly there was a sound from the tall grass to her right, and she looked around quickly.

"*Dona!*" Rachel cried.

Donald, now a boy of nine, and only a head shorter than his

mother, had done his morning chores and was playing in boy-ish abandon among the grasses on the meadow's edge, his flaming red hair bobbing in and out of sight.

"Dona, I *see* you!" she called out, jumping up from the rock. With a dozen child-sized steps, Rachel plunged into the grass and flung herself down beside him.

Instantly, Donald lay still, his face turned toward her. He smiled, a little breathless, gazing at her from eyes that for all their paleness seemed to Rachel deep pools of blue light. He was not now the thin boy he had been at six. His face was pleasantly full, glowing with boyish mischief. Beneath Donald's left cheek crouched a small bundle of fur, perfectly matched to his flaming cap of curly red hair, and from the fur, two black eyes in a narrow face pled for Rachel's sympathy.

"Ohhh," she said, and with her chubby hand stroked the long nose tenderly. From between curled lips and shining white teeth came a low growl, but she continued to stroke.

"Dona," she laughed, her dark eyes flashing with light, "you look just like Annie." Donald's freckled skin blended with the color of "Annie's" fur.

It was nearly a year since Donald had found the fox in a den across the stream, one of five kits. He had watched the vixen come and go through the winter before, knew when the babies were born; and then, when she did not return for three days, he had gone to the den and heard the kits crying. This was the only one of the litter he had been able to keep alive.

"Annie" was now so tame that she lived peacefully with their black and tan hound, and slept curled up in bed beside Donald, her muzzle pressed behind his left ear.

With Donald's head resting between the fox's long splayed ears, its keen black eyes searched Rachel's face for her intentions.

Donald caught his breath. "We go to the village tomorrow!" he said, and his smile widened to show teeth perfectly white, the two front ones a little larger than the rest.

"Vi'age?" she asked. "W'as vi'age?"

"A place where people live, silly!" He laughed. "We go there every year . . . to buy flour and salt. You're just not old enough to remember."

"I do so 'member!" she said, a scowl crossing her finely formed features. "I 'member *lots*!" She took a swipe at his hair with her small hand. The fox glanced up nervously at her hand

as it swung by. But Rachel brightened again, and the three fro-
licked in the grass until Bess called them in for dinner.

It was early next morning when the four set out for the village,
Rachel riding astride Donald's shoulders, and the fox in her
arms. The hound came happily along, zigging and zagging
about, traveling five miles for their one. It would take three
days to reach the village, which lay outside the valley's northern end and down at the head of Loch Leven.

As they mounted the shoulder of the northern hill, Donald
looked back at their valley home. His heart was beating fast,
not just from the climb, but for pride he felt in his summer's
work. Below them to the right lay the plot he had planted and
harvested. He knew that inside, the cottage rafters hung heavy
with meat he had hunted and smoked. East of the cottage stood
a high and orderly row of peat he had dug with his own hands
from the bog, cut into slabs and stacked to dry. He looked up
at Bess, who was standing behind him, half winded from the
long climb.

"It's good, Donald," she said, laying her hands on his shoulders. "It's very good!"

In the light of his mother's approval, Donald thought his
heart would burst with satisfaction.

After two nights they reached the edge of Kinlochleven, in the
early morning. All along the grassy lane, little bands of children kept running past them to the parish school, a school the
likes of which existed in all Highland towns—and through all
Scotland, for that matter—part of the long shadow John Knox
had cast two hundred years before.

Donald looked wistfully after the children as they passed.
Rachel only stared at them wide-eyed. She could not remember having seen other children before.

But Bess's eyes were on Donald, and she ached for him.
Donald wanted to learn. But their valley was too far from the
school, and she could not spare him. He was nine years old
and unable to read; there was not a single piece of writing in
the cottage for him to learn with. Bartlett had hated anyone
who could read and write. "They think they're God Almighty!" he had muttered.

But Bess could read, and when soon after their marriage he
had discovered her books, he had grabbed them up, carried

them out, and burned them while she watched and wept. It was the first time she had seen him angry.

"No wife of mine is gonna put on damned airs with me!" he had growled.

As Bess watched the children rush along the road to school, it came to her. Why had she not thought of it before? With Bart gone there was no reason for the children to remain in ignorance. Perhaps it had been pride that kept her from asking for the books she would need to teach them. Well, it would stand in her way no more!

"Where are you going, Mama?" Donald asked. They had come to the lane leading to the village kirk, a fine white building of stone with a steeple and a slate roof, and Bess had turned abruptly into the lane.

"For a surprise," she called back over her shoulder. "Wait here and see!"

Donald dropped down in the grass, lay back with his hands behind his head, and gazed down at the village, nestled as it was in a defile of the hills, with the blue ocean lying at its door. Rachel went picking flowers out of the grass, little yellow-petaled blossoms no bigger than the tip of her own thumb.

The village had only two or three streets, bordered on either side by the cottages of poor crofters. A few frame dwellings stood by rather grandly.

As Donald's eyes searched out the village, he was thinking more of his father.

"Why did Daddy leave?" he had asked Bess.

"All Highlanders have wand'rin' in their blood!" she had answered.

Donald raised up and squinted at that blue patch of ocean reaching in among the hills. Is *that* why he wanted to run down the road and find a boat and set out to sea? he thought. Because all Highlanders have wandering in their blood?

Then he heard his mother's voice again—humming a happy melody—and he looked about. Here she came down the lane, her step light, her face in smiles, and in her hands—he could not believe it—a book! No, two books!

"Mama!" he exclaimed, jumping up and running toward her. "Are they ours? Where did you get 'um?"

"Yes, they're ours," she answered. "I begged 'um from the good rector."

"Oh, let me see!" And he grasped at them until Bess thought he was like to tear them.

"Careful," she whispered.

As he took them, Rachel's swarthy face and glowing eyes looked up at him.

"W'as this?" she said.

"Books, Rachel," he answered excitedly. "Books!"

He turned them in his hands. Both were bound in brown leather, dry and chipped at the edges, stamped in what once was brilliant gold, now faded with time and use.

"What do the words say?" Donald whispered.

"This one," Bess answered, "says *Holy Bible*, and this, *The Pilgrim's Progress from this World to that Which Is to Come*." She paused. "Donald," she said.

"Yes, Mama?"

"You're going to read these books."

"I am?" he said breathlessly, his pale blue eyes wide.

"As soon as we get home, we'll begin."

Three days after, they came once again into their valley, this time laden with stores of seed, flour, salt, and the little else they could trade for and carry. But that very first evening, beneath the wavering light of the crusie, Donald began to learn. First came the letters, then the syllables, then the words, until at last he could read.

As months passed by, Rachel watched the drama unfold, lying at the foot of Donald's bed, watching the polished pendulum on her mother's clock flash the light as words from the page came pouring from Donald's mouth: how a boy and a giant fought in a valley—maybe like my valley, she thought—and how a man named Christian made a long journey.

"Where was he going?" Rachel asked.

"He was going to God," Donald answered.

"God?" she asked. "Is God a village?"

"No, silly," he huffed. "God is like a man, a man who lives in the sky. Mama prays to Him sometimes. I've heard her when she didn't know I was around. He's like . . ." Donald struggled. "He's like a father. Yes! That's it! He's like a father. And He's good and kind—Mama says so."

Rachel propped her chin on her palm. "I'd like to meet God," she whispered.

"I said He lives in heaven," Donald remonstrated.

"But He's like a father?" she asked again.

"Like a father," he said.

"Then if I can't meet God, I'd like to have a father," she answered.

THREE

"WHY's the dog howling and barking so?"

"I don't know, Mama," Donald answered. "It's not the same as when a deer comes among the trees."

It was a bitterly cold winter night nine months after Rachel had turned five. In the middle of the earthen floor, on a hearth of sooty rock, a fire burned. A wavering band of smoke went up from the orange flames, some finding its way through the hole in the roof's center, while the rest made a fog among the rafters. The great square beams above glimmered with the varnish of many winters' smoke, glossy and black as volcanic glass.

Somewhere in the roof thatch a mouse rattled the straw, and small bits of grass and dust came floating down. On the thick and aging hand-hewn post supporting the vaulted roof hung an ancient and blackened crusie lamp—nothing more than a little iron pan with a lip on each side in which a wick, four in all, lay in fat, sputtering with a sickly yellow flame.

Rachel was playing near the fire and, strangely, took no notice of the howling dog. In the semidarkness her brown eyes, seeming larger than ever, reflected the light of the glimmering wicks. The yellow fire on the hearth shone on the olive skin of her face and arms. As she played, there were two parts to her story, and she acted both parts, chattering back and forth to herself, sometimes laughing, sometimes directing the play of her imaginary friends, her voice going from high-pitched surprise to conspiratorial tones that were soft and low.

The dog's bark grew sharper and more insistent. Donald went to the window and looked out.

Bess was sitting across the fire from Rachel on the bench of the great old floor loom. Above the loom, suspended on chains from the rafters, hung two more crusies, illuminating the patterned weft of coarse wool cloth that was in the making.

As she wove, the beater of the great loom made its dull thud ... thud ... thud ... a rhythm one could feel through the soles of the feet in the hard earthen floor. Bess's feet worked the treadles and her quick hands threw the shuttle from side to side.

The windowpane was banked with snow, and through the glass above it the slopes of the valley and the limbs and trunks of the trees were glistening white in the light of a full moon. A short distance away, at the meadow's edge, the big dog stood with his head outstretched and hackles raised, alternately barking and howling across the stream toward some object still hidden from Donald's sight. Donald followed the point of the dog's nose until at last, away on the hillside, he saw a dark vertical slash of movement, bobbing from side to side as it advanced through the deep snow.

"Mama, it's a man!" The boy paused breathlessly, and the treadles stopped, Bess holding the shuttle motionless before her. "Now he's crossing the stream, Mama," Donald called across the room. Bess's eyes were wide; she stopped breathing.

The man was coming up the path, the dog nipping and barking violently at his heels, but he came on as though the dog were not there. Then his solid footsteps sounded just outside, stomping of heavy boots, the lifting of the latch; without knocking, the man came in.

He filled the doorway, and the room seemed suddenly far too small. Bess gasped, then sat open-mouthed, unable to utter a sound. Donald had rushed to his sister, a poker in hand, his eyes fixed hard on the huge intruder.

The man had a thick brown beard, full and well-trimmed. His eyes gleamed with intelligence, and his mouth wore the kind of self-confidence that makes the one who wears it either instant hero or villain. Dressed as he was for the cold, he might as well have been a Russian peasant: a fur hat pulled down at a confident angle above his left eye, heavy leather boots into which he had tucked the cuffs of his heavy wool trousers. His bulky wool watchcoat, long and black, hung just above his thick knees.

For a moment Rachel continued to play, willfully oblivious to the man's presence. When at last she looked up, she saw him and smiled. The big man's eyes had settled on her, and he returned her smile.

"And who might *you* be?" he asked. His voice was resonant and deep, like low thunder.

"Rachel," she answered, her voice as confident as his own. Even so, her face was filled with awe at this giant of a man, this godlike figure that filled her doorway. "And who are you?" she ventured.

Bess suddenly found her voice, and it was tinged with keen resentment. "You don't recognize your daughter, Bartlett?" Anger flushed the deep olive of her skin. "But no, you wouldn't, would you? She's the one you couldn't wait around to see." Without taking her glaring eyes from Bartlett's, she said to Rachel, "Rachel, this is your father."

Then slowly, as if entranced by his presence, Rachel rose from the floor, her long dark hair framing her upturned face, and started toward him. Calhoun was stunned when she laid her face against his massive thigh and put her arms as far around his legs as they would go. He opened his mouth, and for the first time in Bess's memory, he was speechless. For a moment he held his hands awkwardly above her shoulders, not knowing what to do with them. Then, recovering slightly, he fingered a strand of her hair, cautiously, as though he was frightened. Then, gaining courage, he spread one great hand and laid it on the crown of her head. Kneeling, he took her in his arms and lifted her up, holding her tightly to his chest. With eyes turned away, Rachel first laid her face against his bearded cheek, then cradled her head in his shoulder. Bartlett stared, his eyes wide with wonder. Donald was astounded, and Bess glared on.

Even in youth, Bartlett Calhoun had been a free-spirited, conscienceless boy. To this, the cruelties of the battle at Culloden had added an air of bitterness, and as he grew older, his character had only grown worse. Bess thought of him as the most unconsciously self-centered person she had ever known.

The morning after his return, the sound of Bess's spoon hitting the side of the mixing bowl as she prepared breakfast woke Bartlett from sleep. Instinctively he had known better than to go to his wife's bed, and had spread his blankets on the floor near the fire. With breakfast over, he was sitting, with elbows planted heavily on the worn oak table, when Rachel burst through the door.

"Come out and play in the snow with me, Papa!" Rachel looked into the big man's face. She was bundled for the cold, and her large eyes danced with joy and anticipation.

He laughed. "After a while, little one." Rachel had never heard such a laugh as his. It was full and rumbling, but hard about the edge. He squeezed her tightly. "For now, go out with Donald and the two of you have a wonderful time!" As she ran out the door, he turned to Bess, and, clapping his hands together in his grandest theatrical fashion, smiled broadly and announced, "Bess, I've come to take you out of this godforsaken valley."

Bess was in the center of the room, bent forward to tend the fire. She did not hesitate for a moment but straightened to her full height.

"And what makes you think I'll go?" she demanded.

"And why not?" he thundered, rising from his chair and beginning to pace out his enormous energy. He went quickly up and down the room, swinging his great arms in wide gestures. "The world is filled with better places. People to see and talk to, things to do! Even a Highland *village* would be better than this valley. Why?" he said, stopping in sudden amazement. "Don't you *want* to leave this place?"

"I'm happy here, Bartlett," she said quietly, sinking slowly onto one of the low wooden stools. She stirred the fire with a crude stick poker, and hot red sparks shot into the air. "The children are happy here, and besides . . . *our* life together—yours and mine—is over." As she gazed at him, her lips drew a thin line of resolution and her hand formed a determined fist in her lap.

He came to her, reaching out to cover her hand with his. He dropped down to one knee so as to look up into her eyes. Then he said quietly, chuckling and shaking his head side to side, "No, Bess . . . I don't think it's over. You've never refused me . . . and frankly, you never will." He grinned lasciviously and his eyes sparkled. He felt her fist tighten beneath his hand. Then he stood.

Her eyes burned into his; but she bit the inside of her lip and made no denial. She wanted to scream, "No, no! It's a lie!" But it was not a lie, it was true. He did indeed have power over her. At thirty-seven he was still a virile and exciting man. But there was more to his power than virility. Even at this moment she wanted him, and had to force herself not to throw her arms around him and let him sweep her off to their bed. He saw it in her face, knew how she was struggling. Abruptly, he reached out and caught her face between his hands, pulling her mouth close to his.

"No, Bartlett!" she whimpered.

He held her and kissed her hard.

Suddenly, something within her caught, like a boat careening wildly down a river lodged against a rock.

"No! I said," and she pulled her lips free, wrenching out of his arms. Insanely, with all her might Bess struck him full across the face. The sharp sound resounded through the cottage.

Instantly Bartlett Calhoun's smile disappeared. For a long moment he did not move, his breath laboring in the loud silence. With fear in her eyes, Bess moved away. As the realization of what she had done sent fear creeping upward through her body, her breathing stopped altogether. Slowly Bartlett's smile returned, creeping over his face, a curl twisting his thick lips. With a sudden movement he wrapped his iron grip around her wrist. Her eyes grew wide and she pulled hard, making breathless little whimpers and lifting her free hand as a shield.

When his right palm fell hard against the side of her head, the room went black and filled with stars.

When evening came and Bess awoke, it was to see Rachel lying curled in the bend of her father's massive arm. Donald sat against the far wall, silently brushing Annie's red fur, refusing to meet his father's eyes. Donald had not embraced Bartlett when he came, and all day long he had refused to speak a single word to him. To speak or be kind to Bartlett would betray the hurt in his mother's eyes. The fox squirmed from Donald's grip and went sniffing into the corner. Donald gazed at the hard earth between his crossed legs.

Rachel looked across the fire to where her mother lay. Rachel was puzzled; such a strange tension hung in the air, no one speaking, eyes avoiding eyes. For the first time she became aware of the sadness in her mother's downcast face, and of something else, a kind of hatred in her eyes. Rachel gazed at the great bruise on her mother's cheek, and at a shining tear that trickled out of her swollen eye. She looked up again at her father's fine, strong features and wondered, How could this be? She had no way of knowing that the simple act of reclining in her father's arm was an act of betrayal. Is Mama bad? Rachel felt a tightness in her stomach. That her mother might be bad was a new thought. She felt the unspeakable strength and hardness of Bartlett's arm beneath her. All the while his wonderful voice was droning on about the places he had been and things he had done. She did not know him, but fathers were strong, and most of all they were like God, and God is wonderful.

But her mother? What was she? Rachel did not know. What was she to do; what else but with all her might cling to them both?

In only two days they moved from the valley. It was very early in the morning, with all they owned piled into a big wooden two-wheeled cart to which Bartlett had harnessed Queen Mary, the milk cow.

Bess's face was downcast and streaked with tears as she climbed submissively atop the load. In her arms she held the most precious of her possessions, the mantel clock her father had given her when she left home. As she held it pressed against her body, somehow it imparted a touch of comfort— a point of contact with a saner, more secure time.

Donald stood beside the cow,. a stick in his hand to guide her. Bartlett reached down from the back of the roan and with one swift motion swept Rachel up to her proud place in front of him. She looked around and smiled. She had no idea what it meant to leave her valley, did not dream the void it would leave, did not understand why her mother's heart should be breaking or why Donald seemed so withdrawn and sullen. She had never been on a horse before, and for a moment she was afraid. But then she felt her father's arm enfolded gently around. He was holding the reins easily between two thick fingers of his left hand, and her with the other. She felt the horse lurch forward as his great heels kicked its sides, watched the cow follow, and heard the wheels of the cart groan into motion behind. The dog, sensing they were going somewhere together, trotted lightly ahead.

"Daddy," she said suddenly, twisting about and looking up into his face. She pointed back. "Daddy, Donald's fox!" The creature sat forlornly in the clearing.

"We're going to the city, Rachel. No place for foxes there. I told Donald to leave it."

"But Daddy!" she said.

"No buts, Rachel," he said. She could feel his deep voice in his belly behind her. "The fox stays!"

Bess could not bear to look at Donald's downcast face. She

stared at Bartlett, half pleading with her eyes, half glaring her hatred. He glared back. "Stay out of this, Bess," he growled.

Donald, with tears running down his cheeks, ran from the cow's side, shouting and shooing the fox out into the tall grass, his heart near bursting. Between his sobs he prayed silently the fox would know how to hunt and fend for itself.

"Go on!" Donald cried through his tears. He waved his hands wildly over his head, trying with all his might to sound threatening. "Awa wi' ye! Awa!" he shouted.

The fox simply sat, chittering in her throat, cocking her head and gazing at Donald. She laid her long ears back and with her forefeet kneaded the ground softly. Then, as the cart groaned ahead, the fox nervously looked this way and that, then darted from Donald's sight and into the underbrush. Donald kept his eyes on their backtrail. He hoped he might see his friend one more time, but more than that, he was looking away to hide his tears.

F O U R

DAY after day they traveled, the big wooden cart jostling through pasture lands and along rutty roads that toughened Donald's feet as he drove Queen Mary. Rachel rocked, tired but contented in her father's arms, silently awed by the distant reaches of the lonely west and the grandeur of the Grampian Mountains. At last they looped the shores of Loch Lomond and descended into the valley of River Clyde.

Late one afternoon, just as buds were bursting and the smell of spring hung heavy in the air, their cart wheels rolled into the west edge of Glasgow. There, in a wide grassy field, stood a deserted cottage, its door dangling on a rusty iron hinge.

"This'll do for a few days," Calhoun rumbled, swinging his right leg forward over the pommel and sliding down with Rachel in his arms. "Donald," he called, "help me pitch a few necessaries off. Rachel," he set her down, "unhitch the cow and lead 'er down to the river to drink."

Donald had said very little since the day they left. He was still silently smarting with resentment at being torn from the peaceful valley, and he was wondering about Annie, if she knew how to burrow and make her way in the wild without him. But he threw down his driving stick and climbed up onto the cart while Calhoun handed Bess down.

Bess looked about. The yard was grown over in tall grass, and a ragged, dirty bed ticking hung limply from the yawning front window. As she stepped cautiously in, peering through darkness to which her eyes were not yet accustomed, a pigeon fluttered wildly down from the rafters and escaped through the door above her head. The floor was strewn with straw, bunched and dirty in places where dogs had obviously bedded down. The smell of the fouled straw cut sharply into her nostrils.

"It'll take some cleanin'," she said, not daring to hint at the revolt she felt in her stomach.

"Then let's get it done!" Calhoun thundered, ducking his head for the low door. He had a canvas roll of belongings thrown across his shoulder.

Bess choked and coughed in clouds of dust as she pushed mounds of fetid straw before her broom. By the time Bart and Donald had emptied the cart, and Rachel had come leading Queen Mary up from the river, the sun was dropping behind the western hills.

Bess had found their three crusie lamps and hung them, one from the middle rafter, the other two in the darkest corners. She fumbled in her apron, found flint, steel, a tin of char, and struck a fire on the little hearth in the center of the room. Soon the lamp wicks were quavering with meager yellow flames. Bartlett Calhoun stood just outside the doorway, the fragrance of his pipe drifting into the room as he sighed a restless sigh.

"Bess," he said, turning about and ducking as he entered. She looked up. His red face appeared jaundiced in the lamplight. "Bess, you and the boy stay here. I'm goin' in to see some old friends."

"And Rachel?" she said, noting he had said "you and the boy."

"I'll take 'er with me."

She glared at him. "Why?" she said coldly.

"Because I want 'er with me; that's why enough." He met her icy glare.

Rachel, worn down from the long journey, was sleeping on

a hastily thrown-up bed on the room's south side. He went to her and shook her gently by the shoulder.

"Rachel," he whispered. "Rachel, wake up."

At this, Rachel opened her eyes slightly and looked up into her father's massive face. "What is it, Papa?" she breathed.

"You an' your papa are goin' into town."

"I'm tired, Papa. Couldn't I stay here?"

"There's some folks I want to see Papa's girl," he said.

And he picked her up, cradled her in his arm, and pressed her head against his shoulder.

The night air was cool as Bartlett saddled the tired roan. With Rachel perched before him, they left the cottage behind and rode to the waterfront streets where the taverns lay.

Under the oily light of streetlamps men and women came reeling out of the darkness and back in again. Music and raucous laughter came pouring through the doors of the ale houses. Never had Rachel heard such laughing, nor seen women reel as they walked, nor men lying in the streets, their mouths wide and arms outstretched. Angry shouts mingled with gales of laughter and the sound of retching assaulted her ears. She pressed hard against her father's belly for protection, then, turning in the saddle and looking up to see if he, too, was afraid, saw his face radiating a dark glow. His even, white teeth shone in the lamplight, and he laughed a deep laugh that made his midsection heave terribly.

"My *God!*" he shouted, snatching his hat from his head and slapping his thigh with it. "This makes me feel *alive!*" His husky voice rang out above her head. Lust for the city shone like fire in his eyes. The blackened night, the people-filled streets, barmaids standing hip-tossed outside tavern doors, gazing at him with bold eyes and unconcealed smiles, the smells of tobacco and gin-soaked air—all of it stirred into blaze the dark fires of his mind. But to Rachel all was a jumble of terror and noise.

Their horse clopped slowly over the cobblestones, jerking sideways and skittering, as uneasy at the strange noises as the child on its back. Suddenly, just as they rode under a streetlamp and the light was full upon them, from somewhere to the right a bold female voice sang out from a tavern door, "Bart Calhoun! Where *have* you *been?*"

Calhoun knew the voice without turning, threw back his head and bellowed out glad laughter as the woman pushed her way through the milling crowd of revelers. When she stood beside the horse, Rachel looked down into the woman's smiling face—a strange mixture of beauty and roughness, which seemed even stranger in the dancing flame light. The woman's cheeks were boldly rouged, the neckline of her blouse scooped dangerously low, and open sensuality shone out from her eyes. As the woman's eyes fixed on her, Rachel began to sob and shrank deeper to her father's belly.

"And what is *this*, Bart?" she asked. The smile softened and a tenderness came into her voice.

"This, Tess," he said with a bow and wave of his hat, "is my daughter, my own lovin' daughter!"

"God!" The woman laughed softly. "Nothin' ever loved you, Bartlett Calhoun," and her laugh faded with pity for the child, "and you never loved nothin'."

At this Calhoun himself threw his head back again and roared with laughter. When his laughter had nearly subsided, he looked down.

"What about it, Tess?" he roared. "Could I find a game here tonight?"

For a moment she didn't answer, so intent was she on the little girl.

"What?" she said at last. "Oh, what a question!" she exclaimed. "Was there ever a night at Horn Pipe Tavern when there wasn't no game?" Then extending her hands upward to the child, "Rax your arms down to Tess, darlin'!"

Rachel looked desperately back to her father, and squirmed as his big hands placed her in the woman's arms. "Let me down," she whimpered frantically, then screamed, "Daddy, take me!"

"Why no, darlin'! Let Tess take you in to meet some friends o' your daddy's." And the woman held her more tightly, pressing her to large unconfined breasts.

FIVE

WHEN midnight came, Rachel lay on a table in the corner of an upstairs room where Tess—a woman with a name so like her mother's, but who was so different—had spread a comforter. The child was asleep.

With three other men, Calhoun sat at a table in the middle of the same room. His billowing white shirt lay open down the throat, exposing a wedge of hairy, bearlike chest. He held a carefully guarded hand of cards before his eyes, and a tightly rolled leaf of tobacco between the thumb and middle finger of his right hand. The sweaty baldness of his head glistened in the lamplight, setting off the deep red of his beard. He was quiet now, studying his hand, puffing deeply on the burning roll of tobacco. He blew a stream of smoke upward without raising his clear blue eyes from the cards. His companions waited for his call.

"Why'd you bring that child here, Bart?" Tess said slowly. She was sitting beside him, her right arm about his shoulder. Her voice was cajoling, and she smoothed the fringes of hair about his wide expanse of baldness. "I'da thought even you'd have conscience enough to keep 'er out of a hole like this."

"You talk like an old woman," he growled, and waved away her question with the hand in which he held the burning roll of tobacco leaf.

"Where'd you get that thing?" she asked, drawing back and choking in the cloud of acrid white smoke.

"Courtesy of the American savage, my dear," he said, still concentrating on his hand of cards. "Their gift to the western world, via the Spanish. 'Cigar,' they call it."

"Well, the bloody savages can have it back if you don't mind!" She snatched it from his hand and in one swift motion threw it out the window. It made a hot red streak into the darkness outside.

Calhoun's eyes snapped and he started from his chair.

21

"You believe in livin' dangerously, Tess." The words came from a man across the table. "I've seen Calhoun here kill for less than that."

"Let 'er alone, Calhoun," said another of the men. "No trouble here tonight."

"No. No trouble," Tess said, smiling confidently down at Calhoun.

Calhoun, wavering, sank gradually back into his chair.

"I expect I know Bartlett Calhoun as well as any of you men," she said.

"A good bit better'n us, I'd reckon," the first man joked dryly. The others broke into laughter.

"*I* sure don't wanta know 'im as well as you, Tess!" The lurid laughter rose again. An appeased smile broke across Calhoun's face. He grabbed Tess and jerked her into his lap.

"We go back a long way, don't we, Tess?" he said, patting her on the hip.

"Clear to the year before Culloden," she answered.

"The year before Culloden," he echoed quietly.

"You were a handsome young soldier," she said, "all kilted in the Calhoun tartan, one o' the best pipers I ever heard."

"It did the Highland cause no great service to be handsome or kilted," he said, an ancient gloom sounding in his voice. He looked down at the wool trousers, gray and dull, that had taken the bright tartan's place. "We should never'a let Prince Charlie lead us into that war."

"You followed your *daddy* into the war, if I remember right."

At the mention of his father, Calhoun muttered under his breath, "Damned old man! Why I followed 'im anywhere I'll never know."

"You trusted 'im!"

"Trusted! I never trusted that old man. When I was a lad o' ten, that old devil sent me up a ladder, and then kicked the damned thing out from under me. I laid there lookin' up at him an' he down at me, and he says, 'See! Don't never trust nobody!' "

Tess roared with laughter and the men snickered. Calhoun looked up at her from beneath his thick brows.

"Well, he got 'is point across," he said. "I've never trusted anybody since that day." Calhoun paused thoughtfully. "But then I did just what you said, Tess . . . I followed 'im into battle. Damn near died with 'im for it, too."

There was a long pause, and Calhoun slammed his cards on the table. "Ahhh! Can't keep my mind on this game. I'm done!"

Without protest the others folded their cards and laid them down. A long silence followed, in which Bart held Tess by the waist and swayed her back and forth on his knees.

"Tell me, Bart." Tess spoke quietly. "Why *did* you bring that little girl here tonight?" Instantly he stopped the rocking. Tess was gazing into the corner where the child lay breathing peacefully in sleep.

"Makes me feel good to have 'er along," he said. "Besides, I love 'er—and she loves me. She's the only thing I ever had that loved me."

"If you say so, Bart," Tess returned, never taking her eyes from the child. "But I don't think you even know what love is!"

It was a month later, when the days were lengthening until the twilight of evening almost touched the twilight of dawn. Bartlett Calhoun, standing in the cottage door, fished a pipe from his pocket, filled it, and ambled out to sit on the grass up from the river, where he could watch the sun linger between the earth and the far western hills. Donald and Bess saw him go, and in a few moments followed.

Donald felt an uneasiness in the pit of his stomach. Things had gone well this month in Glasgow . . . too well, he feared. Big, rough Bartlett had been tender, even loving, to his mother. His voice seemed softer somehow. Maybe it was the way he felt toward Rachel. But how long can it last? Donald wondered.

Rachel, who had been down at the river's edge watching sea birds dive for fish, saw them sitting on the grass and came running. She plopped breathlessly down on Bartlett's right thigh, and he held her in the circle of his arm. Rachel loved the smell of his pipe; the fragrance was rich and had a kind of calming effect on her—a thing Bess sometimes welcomed.

She watched the curls of smoke rising up, saw them dissipate in the evening air, and felt the warmth of his massive chest—a kind of refuge against all danger.

"Look at the sun, Rachel," he said.

She felt his voice rumble within, and lifted her eyes. The sun, red as blood, lay just above the hills. Wisps of earth cloud drifted across its face, and yet its redness burned through.

"Fine sight," his low voice said.

And Rachel, her head leaning against him, nodded. Somehow she knew just what he meant. It was a thing they shared deep inside, an intuitive communion with earth and sky. As the sun's red disk sank lower, and the cool of evening whispered its coming, in the warmth of Bartlett's body a flush of deep security swept over her.

Her arm went about his bull-like neck and she rested her head on his shoulder. She could not have told just why, but within, her heart was happy and at rest.

In spite of his own uneasiness, Donald saw this communion between Rachel and Bartlett and felt a tinge of happiness. He sat quietly, his fingers linked about his knees, eyes lifted up to where sea gulls swept on stiff, pointed wings against the evening blue. There was peace in the air tonight—peace in Bess's relaxed voice and Bartlett's low tones. The gold of the sky, gathering the color of faded rose, was reflected in the waters of the Clyde sweeping by only yards away. The whole land was bathed in that fading glow.

"It's getting cool," Bess said quietly at last. "Time to go in."

But for Rachel the lovely, intimate evening was too delicious to leave. To keep from going in, she began to giggle and squirm, teasing Bartlett into play. She jumped up, circled him while laughing, and climbed onto his shoulders, mussing his hair and suddenly grabbing his pipe from his lips.

He laughed. "Bring it back."

He pulled her over his shoulder to his lap, nuzzling and nibbling at her neck until she giggled and squirmed with delight, squeezing her so tightly it seemed to Rachel that no power in the world could tear her from his arms. He kissed her on the cheek, a soft, fatherly kiss, deep and strong, and her arms circled his powerful neck.

Then she sat back on his lap, facing him, leaning against his raised knees, and began to tease.

"Your beard tickled!" she said, her big brown eyes snapping.

Then she reached out, tangled her fingers in his beard, and lurched back with all her might.

"Owww." Bartlett feigned a howl of pain. Rachel doubled with laughter, then pulled again.

Bess gazed at their play, her young face showing wear even in the subdued light, a fond smile playing about her lips. Donald watched intently. His father had never played in such a way with him, and wondering why, he felt the slightest resentment, but shook it off quickly. Suddenly, Donald felt restless and, getting to his feet, began throwing stones as far into the river as his strength would allow. He threw until his arms ached, and all the while, behind him came the laughter of his sister and father, growing more intense, even frantic.

Now Bartlett held Rachel pinned against his knees with one beefy hand, and with the other swatted her lightly and repeatedly on the cheek. She laughed uncontrollably to see the hand coming again and again, squirming to escape it, and to hear his deep-voiced laughter and taunts.

She found herself suddenly free and swatted back, striking at his hands and then at his face, but her futile blows batted empty air. Again his great hand pressed her back so that she could not rise. Sudden panic leapt up within, and still he struck her.

"Let me go, Papa," she whined in fear. "Let me go . . . please!"

The frantic edge of frustration rose into her head and came out of her mouth in terrified laughter that was quickly changing to helpless screams and tears.

Rachel could see it: from out of his laughing eyes, something perverse and evil shining. Her face felt hot as the blows came again, harder. Then her breath would not come. Under the rapidly falling blows, the roughened skin of her face felt ready to bleed.

"Bartlett . . ." Bess said. She had raised half up from the ground, but the urgency in her voice was tempered with caution. "Bartlett, don't!"

He only laughed that rumbling roar of a laugh, hitting and hitting. Rachel's mouth was open in a taut, silent scream, tears of bitter terror in her eyes.

"Bartlett!" Bess jumped to her feet. "Don't!" She grasped his arm, the fingers of her hands hardly reaching around, and pulled as hard as she could.

"Daddy!" came a shout. And Bartlett looked up. Donald was standing with anger in every line of his face, a large stone in his right hand, his fingers clenched about it so that his knuckles were as white as his face.

"Daddy, let 'er go!"

The grin faded from Bartlett's lips, his face went blank and his hand slowed . . . then stopped altogether. Bess, tears running down her cheeks, covered her face with her hands.

Rachel, struggling to find her breath again, her face torn

with confusion and pain, reached out to her mother, and Bess gathered her up into her arms.

Bartlett's eyes were wide and his breath came deep. Donald thought he saw Bartlett's hands tremble a little as he gathered himself up from the ground, dusted the grass from the seat of his trousers, and headed silently toward the house.

Rachel, hugging her mother's neck with might and main, sobbed uncontrollably, convulsing now and again as her lungs pulled in air.

S I X

FIVE years went by. Today was Rachel's tenth birthday, a shining morning at the end of March, and she was happy.

Bartlett Calhoun was away trading horses somewhere in the Argyll district. Donald, who had finished school last year, was hired out to a sheepman up the road. Rachel—who liked nothing so much as reading, but had come to dislike school and skipped it whenever she could—was home for the day.

Everyone was happier with Bartlett away, which fortunately was often and long. Even Rachel—whose worship for her father had not altogether died—felt that somehow the air was cleaner during his absences.

"I love the new doll you sewed for me, Mama!" The packed earth floor where Rachel sat beside her mother's chair was covered with a rug Bess had woven from scraps. Rachel's feet were curled beneath her, her dark eyes shining. Bess had given her the doll that morning. There was no weariness in her mother's face today, though even Rachel could see how the years were beginning to line the corners of her eyes.

"I made it with love, Rachel." Bess's voice was warm.

Rachel looked up and smiled. Bess dropped her hands into her lap and sighed.

"Ten years old!" she exclaimed. "And how beautiful you've become!" She reached out and fingered Rachel's hair, dark and grown nearly to her waist. Rachel, relishing her mother's admiration, smiled, the white of her perfect teeth contrasting sharply with the swarthiness of her skin.

Suddenly there was the clamor of hoofbeats in the yard, and Rachel looked out.

"Mama," Rachel whispered, "it's Daddy!" She jumped to her feet and, as she ran out to meet him, joyously cried out, "He's come for my birthday!"

By the time she was on the path, Bartlett had dismounted and was striding furiously toward the house. When she saw the darkness of his face, she wished suddenly that she was anywhere but here.

He strode past Rachel without looking down. She watched him disappear through the doorway. What a sudden shadow, she thought, to be cast over the day. She turned and ran in after him.

"Bartlett!" Bess said, and stood to greet him.

"Daddy!" Rachel chorused, running in behind him.

And with no more warning than that, it happened.

In a moment Rachel found herself a limp tangle in a patch of brilliant sunlight on the earthen floor. She looked up. The freshly whitewashed wall that halted her flight was spattered with fresh, red blood, a single drop of which trailed slowly downward over the face of the stones. As it entered the patch of sunlight, the drop shone bright and glistening. In the midst of the stain, bonded to a rough protrusion of rock, clung a patch of pitifully torn skin.

"Dear God!" Bess shouted. "Bartlett, what have you done!" She dropped to her knees beside Rachel. Tenderly she laid back the strands of dark hair sticking to the blood on Rachel's cheek. She looked in terror first at the child and then up at Bartlett.

"Bartlett, why on God's earth?"

Rachel went suddenly limp in her arms, her head pitched at a frightening angle, strands of long, dark hair scattered about over her face. The only sign of life was a faint pulsation in the purple vein at the base of her pale throat. A dark place the shape and size of a big man's hand was rising on her face. Around the mark, her skin was a thick, pasty white.

"Ohh," Bess cried out in paralyzing fear.

Rachel's eyelids began to flutter, almost imperceptably, then she opened them with a wide, wild glaze. Above, the rough unpainted rafters and the darkness beyond them spun around her mother's frightened face. As the room whirled, her stomach cramped, and doubling into a little ball, she rolled to her side. Burning hot fluid rose into her throat and she retched convulsively. She began to softly sob, fearing to wail aloud.

Bess bowed her head in her hands and began to weep. Bartlett stood with his back against the doorjamb, a confused look of disgust on his face.

"Say nothing of this to Donald," he growled. "Do you hear? Nothing!"

"What difference could it possibly make?" Bess wailed. "Do you think your son doesn't know how you treat Rachel?"

He growled under his breath.

"God, give me courage," she pled aloud.

Then scooping the child up in her arms, she swept past Bartlett and carried her to her bed against the south wall. Bartlett turned and stormed from the room. The sound of skittering hooves came through the front window, and Bartlett's voice.

"Not a word of it! Not a word!"

For a long time Rachel lay there, listening to her mother's sighs as Bess stood at the little brown table, working over the noon meal. Rachel's eyes felt swollen, and the skin of her forehead stung like fire, but the pounding inside her head was gone. She clenched her teeth in anger. Why? she wondered, staring up at the underneath of thatch above the rafters. When no answer occurred to her, her anger grew hotter.

Suddenly able to take it no longer, she jumped up, then reeled back, holding her head.

"Rachel?" Bess looked up from the potatoes she was slicing. "Lie there just awhile longer."

"I can't, Mama!"

And she ran out, at the moment that Donald, returning unexpectedly from work, was coming up the dirt path. At sixteen, Donald had grown tall, his arms lank but sinewy and strong. The red of his hair shone brightly in the midday sun. He wore his hair long on the sides and combed it back, braiding it in a queue at the back of his neck. Bartlett said the queue was "putting on airs," and despised it.

Rachel dipped her head, covered her face with her hand, and tried to run past him, but he grabbed her shoulders and shook her sharply.

"Rachel!" he cried. "Stop it!"

She began to sob aloud.

"Rachel, stop cryin' and tell me!"

She dropped her hand.

"Ohh," he breathed.

Where the patch of skin had been peeled from the side of her forehead, a trail of new blood was running down her dark cheek onto the front of her dress.

"What happened?" he said softly.

"I . . . I can't *tell*!" she sobbed.

"And *why* can't you? Why can't you tell your own brother?"

"He *said* I mustn't . . . he said . . . he said . . ." And then sobbing all the more, she wrenched her small shoulders free and went running toward the river.

As Donald Calhoun watched her go, a chill crept into his heart. How much more could she take? Donald knew what Bartlett was doing to Rachel. Rachel must surely understand that he knew. Yet she had become part of this conspiracy of silence. Donald wanted her to speak it out, to lay the blame where it belonged. He wanted her to shout her anger and beat her fists against his chest and take out her rage on him if it would help. But she could not do that—at least, not yet.

Donald thought of the years before Bartlett had come back, when it was just the three of them. What a happy child she had been! He ran a hand through his flaming red hair and shook his head. From the moment Rachel saw her father, she had idolized him. Bartlett Calhoun was a big man, a powerful, unbending force to whom she had clung from the moment they met. But now? Lord, what would this do to her?

For the first time in his sixteen years, Donald wanted to hate his father. Why couldn't *he* be the object of Bartlett's frustration? Bartlett had never acted as though he really loved him. Yet, "A son is a thing of glory to a father!" he often said, always loudly. But Bartlett treated Bess and Rachel like something you wipe your feet on.

It was more than he could bear. The light was rapidly going out of Rachel's young eyes.

Donald turned and entered the cottage. When he hung his coat on the peg beside the door, Bess did not look up from her work, but he could see her shoulders shaking with deep sobs. He came and stood beside her, putting his arms around her shoulders and smoothing her dark hair—hair so like Rachel's but prematurely streaked with gray.

"Did he hurt you, too, Mama?" he asked softly.

She shook her head, not looking up. "Just Rachel," she sobbed.

For a long moment Donald said nothing, trying only to comfort her.

"Mother," he dared at last, "let's pack up and go away where he can't find us—for Rachel's sake."

She turned her face toward him. Her eyes were swollen from crying.

"I can't," she said in a small, weak voice. He looked down at her, pitying her for this weakness. Could this be the strong woman who had raised them in the Highlands? Yes, it was her—strong and resourceful—as long as *he* was away.

"I must tend to Rachel," he said quietly, dropping his arms from about her shoulders. He dampened a clean cloth, rubbed it with a little soap, then took something from the pocket of his coat and went out.

Donald found Rachel beneath the tree down by the river. As he approached, she kept her eyes on her play. Yesterday she had made a house of sticks, and with water dipped from the river, had made mud pies. Now Rachel was serving the hardened pies to her stick people, her movements slower than usual, her face sad. She had stopped crying, but once in a while her shoulders convulsed with a quick intake of breath.

When he was standing over her, she looked up at him with big expressive eyes, and he thought his heart would break.

"Here, darlin'," he said, "let me wipe the blood away," and laid his hand on her shoulder. She leaned her head against him, and tenderly he cleansed the wound and the skin beneath it.

What kind of monster would take a bright, happy child like Rachel and do to her what Daddy has done? he thought.

"There has to be a way out," he mused aloud, but his head hurt trying to think of what it might be. What *was* it about Bess Calhoun that kept her from leaving such a man?

Then, unexpectedly, Rachel spoke.

"Why did he ever come back?" she said softly, her small voice even and strong. His heart skipped a beat, and he held her small shoulders in his hands. To say what she felt—it was at least a beginning.

"Donald," she said pleadingly, "what have I done to Daddy?"

"Nothing, Rachel," Donald answered, "nothing at all."

"But, Donald, I must've . . . and it must've been *bad*. Daddy never beats you, because you're good. Oh, Donald," she said, looking up into his eyes, "I'm going to be so good Daddy will never beat me again!"

Donald knew no answer. It was what Bartlett had taught her, and his own arguments could not change that.

"Rachel," he said quietly, and he pulled her close, "what shall we do? What shall we do?" He gazed into the wide branches of the oak that overspread them. The sun, hovering in the mid-afternoon sky, touched the oak's leaves, and as if in answer to his question, its rays formed a bright, four-pointed star of such brilliance that for a moment he was blinded by it. He held her head to his chest and stroked her hair.

Suddenly, as though just remembering the object in his hand, he held her at arm's length and smiled brightly.

"What's that in your hand, Donald?" she asked.

The sadness of her full eyes tore at his heart, but his smile broadened and, leaping up, he held the object behind his back.

"For me?" she said, her face brightening a little.

"It's your birthday, isn't it?" he said.

"Let me see, Donald." And a little smile spread the corners of her mouth. Donald stepped back, hoping to tease her into life. A small laugh, like the tinkling of a bell, broke from her lips, and she reached for him. He danced quickly back, staying just ahead of her, still holding the package behind his back.

"Catch me if you can!" he shouted gleefully.

Twice he eluded her around the tree.

"You're too *fast* for me!" she said, crossing her arms and stamping her foot petulantly. A mock scowl played over her face.

"All right, all right!" he said, throwing both hands above his head. "I surrender!" And he handed her the package, small and rectangular.

"What beautiful paper!" she cried. "So rich, such a wonderful green!"

Eagerly, she tore a corner of the paper, exposing an edge of bright blue leather incised with a line of gold. "Oh!" Rachel gasped sharply. "Look," she cried. "Oh, Donald!" she shouted gleefully.

Now the paper lay on the ground beside her hardened mud pies. She held the object up, and the sun filtering through the tree limbs glinted from the gold.

"*Gulliver's Travels*, by Jonathan Swift," she read aloud.

"I hope you like it, Rachel," he said softly. "It's not a great lot, maybe just enough to tell you I remember."

With her eyes glistening, Rachel threw her arms around him.

"Oh, it *is* a great lot! And if it weren't, I wouldn't care. All that matters is that you love me. And you always make me know that. But where did the money come from? How could you *ever* afford it?"

Donald's face turned a deeper hue of red. "I laid back a little here and there," he said.

"So Daddy couldn't find it, I'll bet!" Rachel squealed, dancing about with the book clutched tightly to her breast. Abruptly, she stopped and her face fell.

"But I've nothing for you," she said, "and it's your birthday, too."

He smiled and shook his head. "All I want is your happiness," he said.

And laughing together, they ambled arm in arm back toward the cottage.

"But why *Rachel*?" Donald was almost shouting. It was the next evening, and he and his mother had gone down to the river's edge. The days were lengthening now, and the sun was just setting in the far northwest, casting what seemed to Donald and Bess, in their sorrow, a doleful vermilion and orange on the face of the smoothly gliding river.

"Your father is not a predictable man, Donald," Bess answered. Her voice was calm, but hazy with weeping. "I don't know why he does it," she said. The tears began to run again. "And I don't know why I cry so. Good Paul tells us to take such without complainin', to be happy.

"Speak till ither in psaums and hymes an gudelie sangs; sing an lilt tae the Lord in your hairts. Gie thenks at all times for aathing tae God our Faither i the name o' our Lord Jesus Christ."

Donald stood stock-still, his hands behind his back, gazing at her and shaking his head slowly. The evening sun made a halo of his red hair.

"Oh, Mama!" the boy said. "I believe in God, but it's hard for me to look at it so. I can't think He would have a mother take refuge in Him at the danger of her daughter's life and mind! If you don't leave him, it may come to a killin'. I do love my father, but there are days when I truly feel he needs killin'!"

"Donald," Bess said sternly, "whatever happens, do as I've always told you; stay out of his way!"

The boy dropped to his knees before her. She was only thirty-four, but in the years since Bartlett's return her cheekbones had been broken, and her nose, and the marks were there to remain forever. As Donald looked deeply into his mother's eyes, even yet he could see something of her old beauty shining through. Beneath the scars, he thought, she was the same mother he'd always known. The ugliness was his father's hand.

"Why've you stayed with him, Mama?" he asked softly. "Why, after all these years, do you stay in the same house, sleep in the same bed? How can you bear to be near him?"

Bess gazed silently away at the setting sun. After a long silence she spoke the truth. "I don't know," she said.

"Mother," Donald said, hesitating, "now that the old boar's turned on Rachel, we'll never see the last of it." He gripped her hand tightly, as if to force a decision out of her. "Mother, what're you going to do now? Must we keep Rachel where he can always hurt her?"

Bess dropped her head into her hand and began to sob softly, covering her mouth with her handkerchief. "I don't know," she choked. "I just don't know."

SEVEN

"WE'RE movin'!" Bartlett said to Bess one day when Rachel was fourteen. It was spring, and he had just ridden out from town.

"Whatever for?" Bess exclaimed.

Rachel, who had recently discovered Shakespeare, was sitting casually in the open window, absorbed in *Romeo and Juliet*, when her father came in. Her face and form were

becoming the face and form of a woman, and her voice had
the roundness of youth.

The fire of Rachel's love for Bartlett was a bed of gray ash
in which not one coal remained alive. She no longer spoke to
him unless spoken to, and always avoided his eyes.

She had learned to bear the marks of Bartlett's abuse in a
grand, petulant moodiness in which she carried her chin high,
and in the darkness that deepened her already deep eyes.

When he entered and said abruptly that they were moving,
she looked up sharply from her book and listened intently.

"Can't sell the horses I combed out'a the hills last fall," he
growled. "They've got lean through the winter, and I wanta
drive 'um to good pasture. Somewhere up in the Highlands."

"The Highlands," Bess gasped. Rachel shifted her gaze to
her mother's face. Bess's eyes darted about and a smile began
to spread over her lips. "The Highlands!" she repeated. "Oh,
Rachel, did you hear? The Highlands!"

"I heard," she said almost inaudibly, despising to give
Bartlett the pleasure of her approval.

"All Scots have wanderin' in their blood!" Bartlett laughed.

With that, he cracked his whip above the oxens' heads and
the wheels of their loaded wagon began to groan forward. It
had taken only two days to be ready, and once again they were
on the move, this time heading north. Bess sat up on the wagon's board seat, while the others rode horseback in order to
drive Bartlett's growing herd.

The second day, when they had passed Loch Lomond, the
land rose up beneath them. On the fifth day Bess pointed away
to their left.

"There it is," she whispered to Rachel, who was riding
alongside, "there on the horizon, the Great Shepherd of Etive.
When you were a little girl, we lived in the meadow just beneath it."

Rachel's heart ached at the memory, but she said nothing.

On to the north and west they climbed, the tenth day dipping into the fertile valley of the Great Glen, Glen Mor, crossing the river just south of Loch Ness, and ascending into the
hills once again. Their destination, Bartlett said, was the "top
o' the kingdom."

That first night in the higher hills west of Glen Mor, along
the roadside, Bess and Rachel lay together in the wagon,
wrapped in thick blankets and nestled down in straw. Bartlett

and Donald had staked out the animals and bedded down near them.

The entire way, Rachel had avoided Bess. It was a hard thing to want your mother's touch and yet not to want it. She had felt this way for months, recoiling sharply at Bess's approach, and a kiss was out of the question. Even Rachel could not imagine why she felt as she did.

Bess loved Rachel, and the pain at being held at arm's length was almost more than she could bear. As they lay only inches apart in the wagon bed, Bess ventured to reach out and touch Rachel's fingers. To her surprise—and to Rachel's—her daughter did not pull away, but tenderly grasped her hand. There, for the first time since either could remember, they talked quietly.

"Did you ever see the sky so black and deep with stars?" Rachel asked.

"Not since we left the Highlands," Bess answered softly. "It looked like this in our valley."

Rachel smiled in the darkness, remembering.

"Yes," she said, "it did." She paused. "I remember the little stream; it made a laughin' sound . . . and the light on the wet stones was so pretty."

"We were happy there," Bess whispered.

"And the place where we're goin', Mama, will it be as pretty as Etive Glen?"

"Pretty?" Her mother's voice was soft in the darkness. "No, not 'pretty' . . . *grand* is more the word for where we're goin'. A place so wild you'll feel you've come to the edge of the world. It's a craggy land, vast . . . and there's wind." Bess paused as in memory she felt her hair blowing and the cold winter rains in her face. "The winds," she whispered, "so fierce that on the heights, all the saplin's die . . . and the hardy one that lives becomes a poor scraggly thing that grows leanin' to the northeast."

Rachel gripped her mother's hand, warm and now so frail. A tree leanin' before the wind, she thought, a tree like Mama. Alive, yet twisted by the wind! How different Mama had become from those happy times in the valley. The hard winds had twisted her for sure, and in ways that she herself could not tell. It was a disfigurement of mind as well as face. Bess thought that somehow she deserved Bartlett. And since it was right and proper she suffer, she would do it in silence. Her hope for happiness was gone, and in its place she had learned to prefer the certainty of misery with Bartlett Calhoun to the uncertainty of life without him.

"I'm glad to be here," Bess said. "The southern lowlands were not to my likin'. There's somethin' in me that longs for the distant hills where I was born. Even with its rocky ground and poor crofter's cottages, it *is* home, and the wildness feels good. I feel one with the land here . . . and with God."

"Will we ever move again, Mama?"

They could hear the men snoring and the steady clicking of crickets in the grass. Bess paused for a long while and sighed. The stars spread above them in glowing clouds and single white sparks.

"Your father is changin', Rachel," she said. "He's forty-six years old, and life has worn him down. Though he'd never say it, he's terrified that the lusts that make him think he's alive will soon be gone. He can't fool himself into thinkin' he'll live forever. That's the real reason we're movin'. He's goin' back to the place where he was young . . . so he can remember."

"Mama . . ." There was hesitation in Rachel's voice. "Whyever did you marry Daddy?"

Bess smiled in the darkness.

"He was a handsome lad!" she said quietly. "Tall and strong. And when he asked me to go away with him, my feet went right out from under me." She lay quietly for a moment. "I'd not thought of those days for a long, long time.

"He was twenty-five when he rode onto my father's farm. I was sixteen. At first I paid him but little mind, then . . . one day my mother told me never to see him again. From that moment I could think of nothin' except him and bein' at his side.

"When he was young, your father loved the Highlands. He's mostly bluster. He cried real tears when he burned his kilts and threw his bagpipes into the sea!"

"Daddy, a piper?" Rachel asked with amazement. "I've dreamed long of kilted pipers swinging free down the lanes with the drones moaning and chanters skirling. Though I've never heard it, it seems a kind of mem'ry somewhere in my soul."

"When I met him just after Culloden," Bess said, "his pipin' days were o'r."

"Mama," Rachel asked, "where was Donald born?"

"In some little village on the long road between Poolewe and Dingwall," Bess answered, "a year and six months after we married."

"And you don't know the name of the village?"

"Rachel, in the first three years, your father dragged me three times across Scotland, from one coast to the other; wanderin', always wanderin'. I was seventeen the first time. The next I had a babe in arms and it was winter. How the snowy wind did sting and bite! Lurchin' along on the board seat of that ox cart, Bartlett drivin' his horses and sheep before us." She shook her head from side to side. "I knew then the life I'd let myself in for. And by then I knew of his anger.

"For a little while we lived in the Lowlands, at Smailholm just north of the Tweed. There's where he took to racin' greyhounds . . . and to drinkin'. And it was there . . ." She hesitated. "It was there he brought other women to our bed. I cried out against it, but he beat me without mercy."

Bess felt a slight start in Rachel's hand. "Are you asleep, Rachel?" she asked.

"Almost, Mama. I just can't hold my eyes open anymore."

"You didn't hear what I just said, did you?"

"I guess not, Mama," Rachel said, her words slurring.

"It's as well you didn't," Bess whispered. She felt Rachel's hand go limp. Perhaps there would be a new beginning between them, she thought, and watching the night silently deepen overhead, Bess drifted away into sleep.

"If Daddy did nothin' else for me, he taught me to ride!" Rachel called back as she raced ahead of Donald. They had ranged out to find the best track for the wagon to follow.

"That he did!" Donald laughed as he watched the easy motion of her body in the saddle. Rachel rode astride, and as the beast's hooves beat their way along the ridge of the heathered hills, she was perfect grace, a masterful horsewoman . . . and last night, it had come with full force to Donald how beautiful she was becoming.

He reined in and shaded his eyes, watching her ride ahead.

What a wonderful wife she would make for someone, he thought, shaking his head and smiling—a combination of beauty, intelligence, and daring—if . . . if she could erase the scars Bartlett had left on her heart—if she could learn to trust again. The child in her was dead, but the childishness was not.

Bartlett had stolen away her childhood, murdered in cold blood the simple harmonies of her life and home.

"I hate him," she had confided last night as the two walked down to a spring for water. "I hate his foul, whiskey-soaked

breath, and his stupid, stupid ways! If I *could* forgive him for
what he's done to me, how could I forgive him for what he's
done to Mama?" She had stopped on the rocky track, then
turned to face Donald. Her eyes were flaring with contempt,
and the light of the setting sun caught them.

It was then he had seen it for the first time—a beauty he had
somehow been blind to. Her face was a soft oval, her nose del-
icately modeled with slightly flaring nostrils. Her mouth was a
bit overwide, perhaps, but her lips were full, gracefully shaped,
with a pronounced upturn at the corners. She was not yet tall,
but the gentle lengthening of her graceful fingers and the sober
maturity of her dark eyes hinted strongly of the woman she
was to be.

Her eyes—it was Rachel's eyes and hair that set her apart.
They were large eyes, full of light and intelligence, eyes that
snapped with fire when she was angry, eyes that seemed deep
and faraway when she was dreaming.

Her hair reached below her waist—dark brown hair that in
the evening sun glowed a rich auburn, but in near-darkness
seemed black as coal.

"Has he ever loved me, Donald?" her eyes darting. "I once
thought he did," she had said.

"I don't know, Rachel," he answered. "It's all more than I
can understand." He took her hand tenderly.

"I couldn't've survived without you," she said. "We would
have killed each other by now—Daddy and I."

She was right, he thought as she and her mount came racing
back. One or both of them would be dead.

Donald chuckled to himself. At least he could thank God
there had been no fights between them since leaving Glasgow.
Rachel had stayed out of his way; and Bartlett had somehow
been different. Perhaps it was the freedom of the open road
that had sweetened his disposition. Whatever it was, time, like
the earth, had slipped pleasantly past under the feet of their
oxen, and their destination was near.

"The trail goes this way," she shouted, pointing to the northwest.

At that moment the grasses farther along the ridge began to
pitch and bow with the wind, marking the path of a mighty
gust of air as it bore down upon them. Donald lifted his eyes
to the sky and took a deep breath.

"I can smell it!" he exulted.

"What is it?" she asked as she rode in.

"I can smell the ocean," he said excitedly. "It can't be far!"

Two days later, the sun full up in the morning sky, Rachel bounded ahead to the crest of the next hill.

"It's the coast!" she shouted back, standing up in the stirrups and waving her hand. "And the top o' the Kingdom!"

With the sea wind blowing her hair out behind her, Rachel sat on the grassy crest and gazed outward. Dun-colored hills turning green filled her vision, hills with high and rugged shoulders marching away in columns, their sundered and folded sides sweeping downward into a valley. Long and narrow at their feet lay a sheet of blue water winding among the feet of the hills. And beyond, rising so as to appear higher than the valley, was the mighty Atlantic, from whose face rose the blue shoulders of a great island.

"The Atlantic!" Donald exclaimed as he rode up.

"And the Isle of Skye," she said. "And look down there, on the loch's south banks, far over, a village among the trees."

Calhoun came riding up. "There it is," he said in a deep whisper, "the glen of Loch Redfern."

His bold mouth curled in a self-satisfied smile as he leaned forward and rested his elbow on the pommel of his saddle, his eyes scanning the horizon.

Then came the blowing of the oxen and the groan of wagon wheels. Bess sat high in the wagon, too filled with awe to move. Rachel stood down from her horse, her dark eyes searching the inlet's southern shore. She saw picturesque little houses, some clustered among trees, others scattered in the open, and wondered about the people who lived in them and how they would change her life. Donald laid his arm across the back of the nearest ox and his eyes swept the wonderful valley from north to south. It was spring, and on the vast hillsides the coarse moor grass had begun to green. Where the hills folded into crevasses, the turf was fine and sweet, freckled with elegant little flowers, and everywhere the ewes had begun to lamb.

EIGHT

THAT summer was the most peaceful since Rachel's seventh year. The cottage they found was on the upper edge of the village. It was small, but clean and airy, surrounded by a briar-bush hedge, and within the hedge a dozen birches of varying thickness.

Donald found work at the tannery while Calhoun bargained for grazing land and bought sheep. Bess sold her store of weaving in the village, then setting up her wheel and loom, began to spin and weave again. Rachel busied herself about whitewashing the cottage, planting flowers, and meeting the village youth.

Then came the end of August. Last night the first hint of summer's fading had swept in on the wings of a cool northwest wind. Rachel and Bess were out walking in the freshness when something about Bess's face caught Rachel's eye.

"Mama," she said, "are you all right?"

"I'm fine," Bess answered, glancing away from Rachel. "Why do you ask?"

"You're flushed—bright red on your cheeks, but the rest of your face is pale, white as a ghost. And you're breathing hard."

Rachel touched Bess's forehead with the back of her hand. "Why, Mama, you have fever! I'm sure of it. We must get you home."

In the morning, before leaving for the village, Rachel asked, "You're sure you're well, Mama?"

"Completely well!" Bess smiled. "You go along now. They sent up to say the tannery's closed for lack of hides today, so Donald will be with me."

When Rachel was gone, Bess said, "Donald, help me carry the wheel out beneath the trees. I'd like to work in the open air this mornin'. It's warmer there, and the light's better."

The dry-stone-walled cottage sat on a slope high above the

sea loch, and from within the hedge at the east end of the
house one could sit in the shade of birches and look across to
the farther shore. Before the Calhouns came, the yard had been
covered with grass, but now it was bare and hard-packed,
topped with fine gray dust; the work of Bartlett's four chained
greyhounds that lay stretched out in the sun.

The crofters hereabout kept Border sheep, and all summer
long Bess had been carding and dying wool. As Donald carried
the great walking wheel out, Bess came behind him with a basket of wool, dyed red, ready to spin. Donald sat down in the
sunlight against the cottage wall to watch as she worked and
to repair a worn leather headstall.

Bess gave the wheel its first spin, then stepped back, drawing the coarse fibers out and letting them wind. Her long hair,
now broadly streaked with white and tied in back with a faded
yellow ribbon, was nearly as long as Rachel's. As she worked
and as the morning sun warmed her stiffened hands, her bright
eyes gazed about at the blue sky, and a sense of peace came
over her. Then her gaze fell to Donald, his long legs crossed
before him as he drew the thread in and out of the leather. The
sun reflected brightly in his red hair.

"Is this the same child I bundled across Scotland in winter
winds twenty years ago?" she asked, smiling.

"One and the same," he said, looking up and returning her
smile.

"I can hardly believe it," she said. "My life has gone by fast
as a weaver's shuttle."

"In spite of Daddy," he said.

"Yes, in spite of your father."

Donald paused, the needle inserted halfway into the leather,
and gazed up at his mother.

"You like this place, don't you, Mama?" he said. His voice
was fine and masculine. She only smiled. "Let's stay here,
Mama. I know the house isn't much, but the fresh sea air is
good for you."

"Perhaps we can," Bess said thoughtfully. He saw the glint
of hope in her eyes. "But in the end it will all depend on your
father. Remember what's said in the Book, 'Wives, be subjeck
to your guidman, as tae the Lord.' You know, Donald, I've always tried to be subject to your father."

And look where it's got you, he started to say, but just then
a bit of lint from Bess's carding floated near her mouth, and
she breathed it into her throat. Suddenly she began to cough.

"Mama?" Donald said, half rising.

She waved him back, rasping for air, her pale face a threatening red. Donald came to her side. At last the fit subsided. Bess pulled out a simple white handkerchief and held it to her mouth. She lowered it and folded it quickly into her hand.

"Mama!" Donald reached for her hand. "Mama, let me *see*."

She yielded reluctantly and opened her hand. Donald stared down at the crumpled white cloth, then at Bess, alarm in his blue eyes. In the center of the folded handkerchief was a large spot of blood.

"It's nothin'," she said calmly.

"It certainly *is* somethin'," he said quietly. "Mama, I knew you weren't well, but . . . but this?"

He lowered her hand tenderly, knowing what it might mean. Silently, Bess picked up the wool, and gave the great wooden wheel a turn. The spindle whirred softly, drawing out the fibers, spinning them into a long thread as Bess paced back, still coughing slightly. Donald stood, staring and thinking.

"I could listen to the sound of the spindle for hours," she said, trying to distract Donald from his new fear.

Then, suddenly, above the spindle's whisper, a thin, high-pitched shout came from somewhere down the lane.

"Listen," she said, reaching out to stop the wheel. She held her breath, straining to hear. The voices came nearer: two of them, one female, young and clear, the other the voice of a man, deep and bellowing. Was it in anger, or simply someone calling out? Donald walked toward the fence, gazing intently down the road.

A quick movement beyond the tall grass where the road curved, and Rachel appeared, half running, half walking, glancing behind her as she came. Her face was red—agitated and angry—her long hair flowing behind as she strode, her legs straining against her sky-blue dress, its folds billowing behind. Her lips were compressed in a tight pout and bright tear streaks ran down to the corners of her mouth.

When she reached the gate, Donald started toward her.

"Rachel!" he cried, "what's happenin'?"

Rachel, sniffing and sobbing through a deep scowl, neither answered nor broke her stride. Instantly through the gate and past them, she slammed the heavy cottage door behind her.

Then up the road came Bartlett Calhoun, wide-brimmed hat in his hand, his jaw set hard, and bearded face like a thundercloud. On the verge of fifty, Bartlett was yet a muscular man.

There was no stoop in his tall frame, but dark skin sagged beneath his determined eyes. Without a word, he crashed through the gate and made straight for the house.

Donald stepped into his path and lifted his hands. A bolt of fear shot through Bess. Donald was a stripling, far lighter than the outsized man before him. Bartlett brushed him aside.

"Bartlett!" Bess pleaded. "Stop! Please tell me what's wrong!"

Then Donald saw in Bartlett's hand a long-bladed knife and heard him mutter, "Damn little fool! Thinks she's the all-and-end-all!"

"Daddy!" Donald struggled to keep Bartlett from the door. "What's she *done*?"

"Told me to go to *hell's* what she's done," he bellowed.

"Daddy, Daddy! *Listen* to me!" Donald was fighting for time—a moment in which Rachel might do something sensible, like climb out the back window. "Daddy, what did *you* do to make her say a thing like that?"

The big man pushed his son violently, and Donald sprawled against the cottage wall. Bartlett glared at him coldly.

"When does Rachel need *any*thing to be disrespectful to her father?" he shouted. "I caught her comin' down the road, walkin' alongside Timothy MacKnighton, him astride that black stallion, grinnin' down at her and her grinnin' back at him. Him tellin' her he'd never seen hair the likes of hers, and how it shines in the sun!" The word *hair* Bartlett let roll out with a growl. "She's a *child*! He's near a man! I'll make her not so 'lovely' to 'im!"

Donald took a deep breath and put his outspread hands against the big man's shoulders. "What do you intend to do, Daddy?" he said, quietly but firmly.

"She's backtalked me for the last time," he said, spitting the words from between clenched teeth. "I'm goin' in there and cut off that crownin' glory she's so damned proud of!" And he waved the razor-sharp knife in the air.

With a quick twist, Bartlett wrenched away and started for the door, the knife thrust forward.

Suddenly the door flew open—kicked from the inside. Rachel Calhoun stood framed in the doorway, the bright sun flooding her tear-streaked face. Sobs of frustration broke from her lips. In her hands was her father's own long fowling piece, pointed straight at his belly, the hammer at full cock, Rachel's tense finger on the trigger.

The big man stopped in midstep and his eyes went wide.

"No!" her mother screamed. Deftly, Donald stepped between his father and Rachel and, with one quick movement, lifted the gun's muzzle. But the upward swing of the barrel increased the pressure of Rachel's finger on the trigger. The gun boomed, bellowing shot and fire and smoke into the morning air.

Rachel Calhoun would not for all the world have harmed her brother. In the utterly silent moment, while the scene was shrouded in white smoke, she dropped the gun and, with trembling hands, covered her face.

"Donald!" she screamed.

Gradually the smoke faded into the surrounding air. Bartlett Calhoun was standing, his face white as bleached flour paste, eyes wide and thick lips trembling. Bess, rigid beside her spinning wheel, hid her eyes so as not to see.

Donald Calhoun stood staring in empty shock. Through the cloth of his tan shirt a profusion of blood was streaming down, dripping from the fingertips of his limp arm into a growing puddle in the gray dust at his feet. Then his eyes rolled upward, his lids fluttered, his body went limp, and he fell straight, crumbling in a heap. Behind him Bartlett Calhoun stood dazed by death's close pass. Bess ran to her son and knelt over him. Rachel dropped to her knees, her hands shaking violently, her eyes gushing so with tears that she could not see.

Quickly Bess undid Donald's collar ties and pulled the fire-blackened cloth from his flesh. There it was, a bloody hole. A single pellet had pierced his shoulder, just above the collarbone, going cleanly through the thick muscle stretched between shoulder and neck. Bartlett had loaded the gun with large pellets to kill marauding dogs, but the rest of the charge had gone over Donald's shoulder, narrowly missing Bartlett's head. The big man's ears were still ringing from the gun's explosion. Where the lead had emerged from Donald's back, the hole was larger, ragged, bleeding heavily. Bess ripped a puff of clean carded wool in two and stuffed it into the wound. Then she stood, her face flush with indignation.

"Bartlett Calhoun . . ." she breathed through clenched teeth, her hand quavering as she shook it before his face— somewhere inside a dam had broken and the accumulated anger of twenty-one years was in her voice—"if ever you touch her again . . . no, Bartlett, if ever you *threaten* Rachel again . . .

I swear by the God of heaven that some dark night, when you lie asleep in your bed, I will kill you myself!"

Bartlett scowled and his bushy brows narrowed. He looked from Bess to Donald's stony face, and then at last to Rachel, whose eyes still streamed with tears. "All against me," he scowled, then turned about, banged through the gate, and disappeared onto the moor.

BOOK TWO

Drew
1768–1770

NINE

LOCH REDFERN stretches eight narrow miles northeast to southwest from where River Redfern comes down out of the hills of Wester Ross and continues through a narrows to the open sea.

Clustered on the loch's southern shore, the village of Lochredfern stood barely visible among tall spruce and pine. At the upper edge of the village, a wide meadow spread up onto the slopes of Hill MacLaren—more mountain than hill—that towered over all the coastal lands. MacLaren's deeply riven slopes, strewn as they were with rain-rotted boulders, clothed in grass and heather, cast an air of mystery over all that lay below it.

The sun this October morning, breaking over MacLaren's shoulder, flooded the valley with light, turning the ghostly mists that had hovered in shadow into silver. The air became crystalline, tangy cold.

The tan upper meadows, bathed as they were in silver light, shimmered with patches of lavender—the autumn color of heather in bloom. High overhead, thin clouds swept the bright blue, and beneath, the face of the loch roughed before a southwest breeze.

From the broad meadow, a never-failing, spring-fed burn bubbled down, entering the loch to form a narrow inlet too shallow for ships, but perfectly suited for the boats of fishermen—such boats as by midmorning lay about upturned on the sandy shore. The fishermen had taken their catch—cod, haddock, whitefish—and disappeared, leaving only one boat floating in the sheltered harbor.

This boat was like the others, sharp at both ends, a rudder in the stern. Its master sat amidships, dipping the oars, pulling slowly for the open loch, where he would put up the sail.

The sailor was a young man with strong arms and large hands that gripped the oars easily. As he and his boat emerged from the inlet, a light wind ruffled the thick, dark hair on his hatless head, and the little hull began to twist about in the water. He stood, and was just reaching forward to raise the sail when suddenly, from the shore, someone called out to him. For a moment he paused, holding the heavy canvas in his hands, searching the waterside. Then he saw. There on a high bank, almost hidden in the tall grasses, sat a figure backlighted by the morning sun. He shielded his eyes.

Looking down at him was a face he'd never before seen: a smiling face, youthful, with flashing eyes and long dark hair thrown artfully forward over the left shoulder. Above the face was a man's red and blue highland bonnet pulled snugly down at a plucky angle. To his amazement, he saw that it was a girl.

"Aye?" he said, straightening as the boat continued to drift beneath him.

"Where're you goin'?" she called. Her voice was clear and as open as her face, but in tone, lower than he had expected. It was her easy familiarity that surprised him most, for they were total strangers to each other.

From her perch on the bank, Rachel Calhoun returned the sailor's gaze without blinking. What a wonderful face, she thought: young, but dark from sun and weather. And his eyes—clear, so full of intelligence, such a lovely light gray— contrasted with his dark hair. His jaw's a little square, she thought, but his smile is wonderful.

The boat was drifting farther out, and still he stood staring. For a moment she was afraid he would drift away before answering.

"Where is it you're headed?" she repeated.

"Across the loch," he said at last. His voice seemed a little unsure. Then he recovered himself. ". . . and then up the farther shore a ways." A quizzical look came over his face. "You're new here. You've got to be, for I've never seen you before."

She made no answer, purposely leaving him on the tenterhooks of his own awkwardness.

"What's your name?" he ventured.

"Rachel," she answered. "Rachel Calhoun." Still sitting, she had drawn her knees up and was hugging them close. "And yes, I *am* new here about." Her smile broadened. "Now what's *your* name? I've never seen you before, either!"

Suddenly realizing that he was drifting, he dropped the sail and grabbed for the oars. Rachel, making no effort to suppress her merriment, laughed out loud. Embarrassed by her laughter, the young man misstepped, pitching the boat to one side. He dropped down and grabbed both gunnels, sending Rachel into fits of laughter.

He reached for the oars and, pulling the boat closer to shore, gazed up at her, blushing at his awkwardness. For the first time he could see her clearly. What a striking face, he thought, such eyes, the gentle curve of her lips, and the upturn of her mouth at the corners.

And then he remembered.

"I've *heard* of you," he said slowly. "Aye, I *have*!" And he shook his finger toward her in recognition. "*You're* the girl who came near to killin' her brother!"

Like a candle gone out in the wind, the smile disappeared from Rachel's face. Without a word she started up from the tall grass, whirled about, and disappeared over the bank.

"Wait!" he called after her, jumping to his feet. "Wait!"

Silence, but for the breeze in the grasses. On the other side Rachel, instantly angry, was striding away. Whoever he was, he'd no right to say such a thing.

"Rachel Calhoun!" he shouted. "Come back!"

No sound, and then, among the heads of the grasses, her face appeared again.

"Forgive me," he said meekly.

"What right had you—" she blurted.

"Yes! Yes, I'm sorry," he interrupted, throwing up his hands. "It was a rude thing to say."

She lowered her eyes, then raised them again. He saw then that he was forgiven.

"You were right enough," she said, "I *am* the one."

Then he saw them, tears shining in her great brown eyes. "That was stupid of me!" he said quietly. "I shouldn'ta asked. If you'll stay a moment, I'll talk no more about it."

She blinked, averting her eyes, and with the back of her hand wiped the wetness from her cheeks.

"Well?" she asked again, sniffing slightly as her smile reappeared.

"Well what?" he asked.

Her smile broadened, almost as though the unpleasant moment had not intervened.

"I asked you a question," she said. "What is *your* name?"

"I . . ." He was stumbling all over himself again. What on God's earth would make him act so? he thought. ". . . my name is Andrew Wolfe," he said. "And Lochredfern is my home—always has been." He smiled an almost timid smile and then ventured, "But not you, Rachel Calhoun. You're from . . . oh," he guessed, growing playful, "you're from the east, from Perth maybe, or Dundee, or could it be Glasgow?"

"And how could you know that?" she asked curiously.

"Your speech," he said. "You've a Lowland Scot's tongue so broad it'll scarcely fit in your mouth! And besides," he went on, "I know your brother who works at the tannery."

"Donald?" she asked, her eyes growing wide.

"Aye," he said.

The dark hair and light gray eyes were haunting her; and something else about him she could not fasten a name to. Whatever it was, it set her heart aflutter.

"Well, Rachel Calhoun," he said, "if I stay here talking to you, I'll not get back tonight. I must be on my way." He stood again, reaching for the sails.

"Let me go with you," she said breathlessly. It was a wild impulse, but she didn't want him to leave. "I've not crossed the loch before. I've never ever been in a boat. May I go?" There was excitement in her eyes.

"Why . . ." he replied, "you don't know who I am or where I'm goin'."

"Yes I do!" she interrupted. "You're Andrew Wolfe and you're goin' across the loch. I need know no more."

"And what would the townsfolk say if I took you?"

"No one could care less than I *what* they'd say," she answered.

"Well I *do* care," he said, "and I'll tell you what they'd say. They'd say their doctor was keepin' company with a lady much too young for him, one he hardly knows!"

Rachel's eyes widened in mock surprise. "I didn't know," she said. "Please forgive me . . . *Doctor!*"

He began to laugh. "You'll not let me get ahead, will you?"

"Then what would you have me call you?" she taunted.

"Well, Rachel," he sighed, "if ever you and I meet again, you may call me what all others call me. My name is Andrew, and they call me Drew."

"Do you always get your way?" he said as she took his hand and stepped down into the boat.

She smiled. "Usually."

"It's against my better judgment," he said as he helped her to a place by the mast. Rachel ran her hands over the weathered gunnel and the worn seat. Drew's eyes did not leave her, even while hoisting the sail. Her hands were brown and in transition—neither the hands of a child nor yet the hands of a woman. There was something strange about her, but also something warm and alive that pulled at his heart; something that reached out and pleaded to be loved. Perhaps it was that absurd, rakish bonnet, perhaps the eyes, a hint of sadness in them, more than a hint of defiance, and so full of light.

"How old are you, Rachel?" he suddenly dared.

"I'm twenty-two, and how old are you?" she tossed back.

Drew Wolfe threw back his head and laughed aloud. "Twenty-two! You're not a day over eighteen, and you can't tell me you are!"

"Eighteen will do fine," she said, a strange little curve coming to her lips.

"Why, you're not even *that*, now are you?" he asked in amazement. "Truly, I've a *child* on board my boat!"

The curve of her lips deepened into a smile. "And do you expect me to believe you're old enough to be a doctor, Drew Wolfe?"

"You can believe it or not," he said. "But *I'm* the one who's twenty-two."

She looked him all up and down with sly disbelief in her eyes. Then, "And where're we goin'?" she asked, as if to change the subject. The sail filled with wind just as he took the tiller in hand.

"There's a family I must see," he said simply.

As the mast creaked in its step, the boat moved smoothly forward and in an instant was gliding across the water.

The sail billowed out, stretching its seams until Rachel feared they would tear. Drew pulled the sheet closer and closer to the wind, until the boat was skimming the water and standing perilously on its beam.

He watched her carefully. She leaned back, her feet braced on the keelson just behind the step of the mast, gripped the gunnel, and lifted her face to the wind. Not a *sign* of fear, he thought.

"It's wonderful!" she whispered.

"Yes! Yes it is!" he answered.

She laughed brightly, and dipping her hand over the side, the rapid water stung her fingers deliciously, and the boat's sliding motion, the waves breaking over the bow in a fine spray, took her breath. "This is the most exciting moment of my life," she almost shouted.

And before he knew it, Drew Wolfe was laughing as excitedly as she.

The crossing took half an hour, and Rachel was not ready for it to end, but Drew eased sail, and they coasted into a little cove on the northern shore.

"Are you hungry?" he asked, standing, furling the sails. The boat was drifting quietly.

"Starved!" she said.

"There's food," he said, pointing. He jumped ashore, tying a line from the bow to a single post sticking out of the sand. "There in that canvas bag; some cheese, and there's milk in a gourd. Slices of fish liver between oatcakes, and a little jar of foggie-bee's honey."

"How long do you expect to be gone!" she exclaimed, reaching for the bag.

Unceremoniously she opened the string ties, took out the honey jar and oatcakes. He stepped back into the boat, sat down, and waited for her to pass the bag to him. When she did not, he reached for it himself.

As Drew sat chewing on a bite of cheese, he watched her. There's something very like an animal in this child, he thought. She took quick bites, concentrating wholly on her meal. Abruptly, she looked up.

"What?" she asked.

"Nothing," he answered, shaking his head.

Her eyes grew serious and she looked down at the food in her hand. "Why're we here?" she asked.

"Little John Sinclair . . . his father nearly killed him yesterday. Drunk out of his head. He rolled an ox cart over the little boy's body. I came last night. He's hurt pretty bad, but I think he'll mend."

"*Uisque beatha,*" she breathed with disgust. It was Gaelic for "water of life." The English had shortened it to "whiskey." "I know about *uisque beatha*," she said. ". . . one of my own dear daddy's failings." There was an edge of bitter sarcasm in her voice.

"Your daddy's not alone, Rachel. There're more glens and caves in these hills that hide distillers' pots and copper coils than anyone can count. It's a Scots invention. Many a Highlander drinks a quart of it every day—which takes considerable practice."

From the sandy cove a path snaked perilously up the face of a rocky cliff. With Drew going first, they began to climb.

At last they stood on the top of the bluff, where an unhindered southwest wind blew Rachel's hair into tangles. Between the height's edge and a single cottage in the distance stood a small burial ground surrounded by a stone fence. Within the fence was a scattering of headstones, most of them very old, all of them bearing the name Sinclair.

As she walked toward the cottage beside Drew, Rachel looked back over her left shoulder to the west. The inland hills rose up in the distance, an interminable succession of ever-rising blue on the left, and on the right, the sea's dark horizon backlighted by the sun. She listened. Their feet crunched in the dry grass, and the voice of the wind whispered over the face of the ground.

"John will mend," Drew said on their return walk to the cliff's edge. "He only cracked a rib or two. A wonder!"

Rachel said nothing, and for a long moment there was only the sound of the wind and the crunching of feet in the dry grass. Then, "It was the worst day of my life," she said flatly.

"What?" he asked, stopping and turning to her, completely at a loss for her meaning.

"It was the worst day of my life," she repeated, "the day I shot Donald."

Her dark eyes, the lower lids rimmed with tears, looked directly into his, seeming to plead with him, but otherwise there was little expression on her face.

"You don't have to talk about it, Rachel," he said. "I'm very sorry for my words."

"No," she said quietly. "I want to talk about it. I need someone to listen."

The wind whipped long tangles of hair across her face, and she fingered them back. "You tended his wound, didn't you?" she asked him.

"Yes . . . I did. He came to me the next day. But there was nothing more I could do for him. Nothing was lodged inside, and the wound was clean—your mother had poured some of your father's whiskey in it. But he's a very lucky man."

"Aye," she said quietly, "and I'm a lucky young woman—

for I could not live with havin' killed him." The tears broke
over her lids, first the right and then the left, and went rolling
down her cheeks.

"Life has been hard for you," he said, his face filled with
yearning.

"Sometimes," she said, tossing her head a little to one side.
"But the worst of it is, I'm a terrible disappointment to my
mama and Donald. I'm too like my daddy!" she exclaimed,
laughing a little through her tears. "Independent, free, unwillin'
that anybody tell me what to do."

He smiled, nodding his head. "That's easy to see."

"Mama's gotten to be a religious woman—prayin' to 'the
Father'!" There was disgust in her voice. "I've had all the father I can take without goin' and prayin' to another one! Oh,
when I was little, I prayed God would stop Daddy from beatin'
Mama and me. He didn't, and I gave up on prayin' altogether.
I never could stand to be tricked into thinkin' things that
weren't true. Not that Mama was tryin' to trick me, of course;
she wasn't. But I couldn't understand why she believed
somethin' that never worked for her."

Drew nodded his understanding. They had started again toward the bluff.

"I have exactly the same problem with prayer," he said.

"My spirit—if you can call it that—has always loved the
trees and the hills, and the grasses where you can lay down as
if you were on your own mother's breast. When I feel the urge
to pray, that's who I pray to, whatever spirits live in the glens
and moors."

Drew only smiled, but inwardly he marveled at her supersti-
tious nature. They came to the bluff's edge just as the south-
erly autumn sun passed into early afternoon. Its light glittered
on the roughed loch below, and made the faces of all the
southern hills seem dark. Drew reached inside his medicine
bag and pulled out a white cloth folded around more oatcakes,
handing her one.

"Let's rest here at the top of the bluff for a little while," he
said. "I just realized," he added, "your mother doesn't have
any idea where you are."

"No," she chuckled. "No one knows. But it's all right,
Mama's accustomed to it. She can hardly stand what she calls
my 'free-spirited ways.' 'Always strikin' out,' she says,
'hereawa'—thereawa'! God only knows where to.'"

Drew threw back his head and laughed at Rachel's imper-

sonation of her mother—the exaggerated tone of her voice, and
her mouth half full of oatcake. She covered her mouth with her
hand and joined in the laughter.

"I am a free spirit . . . very like my daddy, I suppose—
though I hate to think it."

"Donald says you're a fine horsewoman."

"Ah," she said, picking up a crumb and putting it in her
mouth as she spoke excitedly. "When you put a horse into the
picture . . . well, a horse'll take you anywhere you want to go.
But they are contrary beasts—at least the ones my daddy
keeps—in no way to be predicted!"

A glimmer of understanding came into the young doctor's
eyes and he looked at her keenly.

"Rachel," he said, "I can't help notice how often you mention your father. It makes me wonder if you hate him as badly
as you say you do."

"You'd not wonder if you'd seen me tryin' to kill 'im that
day!" she exclaimed.

He chuckled. "No, I suppose not," he paused, "yet it does
puzzle me."

"Make out of it what you want, Drew Wolfe," she said with
fire in her eyes, "but you can take my word, I cannot *stand* the
man!"

T E N

THAT night, Rachel stood next to her bed in the northeast corner of the one-room cottage, undressing. Bess had just put
down her sewing and was about to extinguish the crusie above
her chair, and Donald had been in bed for an hour. As usual,
Bartlett was away.

"Donald tells me you missed school today," Bess said quietly. There was no hint of recrimination in her voice. She knew
that if Rachel chose to miss school, there was nothing she
could do to change her.

"Oh, Mama!" Rachel breathed in disgust. "You know I can't

bear another word of the Shorter Catechism! Besides, today I did something else . . . something much more interesting."

Bess waited, but Rachel simply lay down on the straw tick and pulled the covers up to her chin. "Good night, Mama," she said.

"Good night, Rachel," Bess said, feeling her heart sink. It was a terrible thing to have Rachel shut her out as she did. Bess reached down, stroked her daughter's forehead, and smoothed her hair on the pillow. Bess shook her head sadly, extinguished the corner lamp, and went to her own empty bed.

Rachel lay in the dark smiling to herself. Sixteen was not too young, she thought. Many a girl in the American colonies marries at that age—even if it's not done in the Highlands. Drew Wolfe was the one. He had to be! Rachel was much too excited to sleep, and when she drifted off at last, a young new face lingered in her dreams.

Meanwhile, the real Andrew Wolfe was out on the hillside above the village, sitting on an ancient rock and gazing into the night sky. The moon was a tawny scythe in the west, almost touching the planet Venus. The air was still and the loch lay like dark glass, reflecting the descending moon and myriad stars. Drew, who loved the dark, was glad for the deepening of autumn. In summer, northern twilight lingered until it touched the morning, so that for weeks on end true darkness never came.

One by one the lights in the village below went out, and an autumn chill crept through Drew's corduroy coat. A strange pleasantness was stealing into his consciousness, something that had been in the back of his mind since returning from the loch's other side, and it made him smile. Rachel's laughing face, a diaphanous image imposed upon the starry sky, was before him, and he could not resist the joy of thinking of her.

It frightened him. He had other commitments, and she was young—a mere child. What was it about her that enchanted him? Yes, that's the word, he thought, she enchants me—as though something about her cast a spell over him. Not even Elizabeth made him feel like this.

Perhaps it was pity he was feeling. The stories making the village rounds about how she had been treated were enough to make a man cry. Some of them he had heard from her own brother.

The air was still, and a meteor flashed across the west, a

bright one plunging down toward the Atlantic. Something stirred in the grass to his right—a field mouse, most likely.

"Why can't I get her out of my mind!" he said aloud, but there was no one to hear. What an indescribably strange yearning it was.

He wanted to help her, to end her sorrows, to give her shelter, to be her champion—perhaps even to love her. A wave of humiliation swept over him then. He put the palms of his hands against his temples and pressed hard.

"I can't *think* like this," he said aloud, the words echoing off the walls of his mind. What would Elizabeth feel if she knew? "I'll never breathe it!"

Then, laughing to himself, he thought of what a bittersweet secret such a love would be. Perhaps by morning the feeling would pass. . . .

"Donald," Rachel said the next morning, "do you know Andrew Wolfe?"

Rachel was at the wooden basin, her hands in the water and soapsuds, washing the breakfast bowls and spoons. Through the window the morning sun poured in, sparkling through a cut-glass pitcher that sat on the sill, making rainbows in the suds. The pitcher was one of her mother's two treasures. The other was the clock ticking slowly on a table against the north wall.

"The young doctor? Yes, I know him," he said.

Donald was sitting in a straight-back chair, leaning his head forward while Bess braided the fiery red hair into its accustomed queue.

"We met months ago at the village dock. He's a good man, well-liked, and for a doctor so young, the town trusts him."

Bess listened quietly and cut a fresh length of ribbon for the end of the pigtail.

"But why?" Donald asked. "Why do you want to know about Drew Wolfe?"

"I met him yesterday," she said in a matter-of-fact kind of way. With her face toward her dishes, Donald could not see her smile, but he thought he heard it in her voice. "He talked to me . . . and I liked him."

"Well . . ." Donald went on. "I know he's the son of the district fox hunter, had an older brother who fought at Culloden and then left Scotland. And I know Wolfe went off to the University of Edinburgh when he was fifteen."

"That takes money," Bess injected.

"Aye, the old doctor who died last summer took care of that well enough." Donald paused, then explained, "But Drew never finished medical school. Too much Latin to suit his taste—always reading but not much doing. Men come out of there and never see a single patient. Figured he'd learn more comin' home and workin' with the old doctor. An' from what I hear, before the old man died, Drew learned his trade pretty well."

Rachel put away the last of the wooden bowls with a clatter, quickly undid her apron, and, with her face flushed, ran quickly out the door.

"Well!" Donald exclaimed. "What got inta her?"

Bess knotted the new ribbon and patted her son's hair into place. "Can't you tell?" she asked. "Your sister's smitten of the young doctor."

Donald chuckled to himself. "She'll get over that quick enough," he said. "In another month or so he's gettin' married."

"Married?"

"An Edinburgh girl," Donald said. "She'll be comin' out soon."

"Well," Bess said thoughtfully, "let's don't burst her bubble today. There'll be time to tell her later."

ELEVEN

RACHEL woke late, just in time to raise up on her elbow and see the light of October's last morning break over MacLaren Mountain. She looked about the cottage.

Alone, she thought. Where could Mama have gone so early?

She turned over, snuggling the thick woolen blanket up about her shoulders. It was delicious to be free! She thought of school and laughed to herself. She was of no mind to go. Bartlett's reputation made the other students regard her with suspicion, and they didn't know what to make of a girl who couldn't stand what she called "the stodgy drone of the class-room" but had read Defoe, Swift, even Locke, and most of Shakespeare. And Bess, sick as she was, needed her about the house. Besides, she had picked up ciphering on her own, and she was full up to her eyebrows with the Shorter Catechism.

With the windows above her bed open, Rachel could see the clear morning sky and feel the air's cold crispness.

"What a dreary thing it would be to clean house on a day like this," she said aloud.

She threw back the covers, and when her feet hit the floor, the cold earth set her dancing. Goose bumps sprang up from head to toe at the touch of the cold washcloth, and before she had finished bathing, her teeth were chattering uncontrollably. She dried quickly with a worn linen towel, roughing her skin till it was red, then pulled on a crisp white shirt, very loose across the shoulders, with a long tail and open collar. With feet and legs still bare, she went to Donald's chest and knelt over it.

Donald had two pairs of trousers and one pair of knee breeches. Poor as he was, these were more than most young men in the village owned. Every day he wore one of the pairs of trousers to work, alternating between them, but the off-white linen breeches he wore only on special occasions. That was good, because Rachel liked to wear the breeches when she rode horseback.

She drew a pair of fresh long worsted stockings above her knees—they felt warm to her legs—and drew the breeches up, tucking the shirt's long tail in and buttoning the band around her slender waist. The small belts just below each knee she buckled as tight as she could to keep the stockings high, and then went to her mirror.

Rachel smiled at what she saw.

"You're more than a little vain, Rachel Calhoun," she said softly to herself. The mirror was an old one chipped about the edges, backed with sun-faded silver—her mother had picked it up a dozen years ago from the roadside where someone had cast it off.

Every morning Rachel would stand here preening, trying her coiffure this way and that, gazing at her own captivating eyes in the dim reflection, brushing her long hair until it glistened even in the meager light of the cottage.

"Rachel!" Donald would tease, "for goodness sake!"

More than once she had turned about. "Would you like this better?" she would say, then stick her tongue out, pull at the corners of her mouth with her fingers, and the two would dissolve in laughter.

There was no such play when Bartlett was home, however. He would snort and mumble in disgust at Rachel's preening, while Donald and Bess smiled behind his back, pleased she could find some rare touch of pleasure, even if it had to be in her own beauty.

Satisfied with her appearance, Rachel quickly made a lunch, hurried out of the house and down toward the pen where Bartlett kept his best horses. She walked briskly, the firmness of her legs hugged by the worsted stockings, the womanliness of her thighs hidden in the bulk of the boy's breeches. The lines of her face were young and clean, the swell of her cheek and roundness of her chin blending into the smooth long curve of her jaw, ending where it met her delicate ear. Her steps were brisk, but not as a boy's would be. Rachel was like a half-grown colt on long slender legs, an illusion made complete by the roanlike color of her hair.

As she approached, a powerful stallion the color of midnight raised his head and huffed a greeting.

"I'll not be takin' you today, Blacky," she said. "You're great fun to ride, but today I want the geldin', for I'm goin' a long way."

The gelding was shorter, not as angular and strong, but he could keep going when the stallion had given out. Rachel fitted the halter to his head, then took a comb from where it hung on a post and began to curry its coat, a coat the color of buckskin. Her perfect teeth glistened white in the morning sun, and her eyes danced under long lashes. Even the movements of her head and graceful neck spoke of vigor and life.

"You like it, don't you, boy?" she said softly. The animal whinnied as if in answer. Not only could Rachel ride, but she had a way with horses that neither Donald nor her father had. They trusted her somehow.

She threw a blanket across the gelding's back and cinched the saddle down—an old saddle her father had had since before she could remember, scarred and scuffed, smelling sweetly of oil and old leather.

"We'll be alone today, you and I," she said. "I've some thinkin' to do."

Rachel was leaning far forward in the saddle as the two burst from the enclosure and up into the meadows. The climb was steep, and by the time they reached the ridge, the gelding was breathing hard. The inner muscles of Rachel's thighs felt weak and giddy, for she had held on tightly with her knees. She stood high in the stirrups and gazed around, scanning the morning sky. The clouds were very high, thin at the edges, like white lace against light blue broadcloth. To the west an eagle wheeled, returning from an adventure over the sea. Directly above, a white gull floated, the edges of its translucent wing backlighted by the radiance of morning sun.

What freedom! she thought as she watched them. Perhaps they were not birds at all, but winged spirits come to call her away. Lightly, she kicked the gelding's sides, plunging down the ridge away from the village.

The gelding settled into an easy lope along a narrow path, trodden for centuries by the feet of foxes and hares and the hooves of deer. The path's faint ribbon wound south, downward, sometimes disappearing behind the swell of a lower hill, reappearing again, winding on, finally to vanish in its own thinness. The hills among which it ran were rolling hills which so strongly suggested the presence of giants, it seemed to Rachel that one must surely at any moment raise its head above the next ridge.

She rode effortlessly and without fear. The sleeves of her crisp white blouse, rolled to just above her elbows, fluttering in the breeze, showed her forearms to be dark from the sun of summer past. She lifted her face to the morning light, and her hair floated out, wonderful amber tints shining.

As they came down into a fold of the hill where a sturdy pair of young birches grew, a covey of quail flushed, their wings whirring. She started at the sound, then laughed at her own fright, and watched as the birds rode on fixed wings, gliding smoothly across the meadow.

The path led on into a wooded glen, which to Rachel's imagination was a dark camp of sleeping soldiers. Beyond the wood, on the shoulder of the opposing brae, stood the walls of an old ruin, a mere dot against the great hill. This was her destination.

As they loped past the wood and started up again, she could see that the old ruins sat on an earthen table jutting out naturally from the hillside. Gray stone walls stood among a scattering of trees—some young, others centuries old—creating a brooding picture that made Rachel slow the gelding and look about with caution.

Many times she had heard of this place in stories told by the villagers. Some said that druids had worshiped on this plot of ground, sacrificing bulls on a flat stone altar. A few hundred years ago, when the land was flourishing, this abbey had been built, but the monks who had inhabited its cloistered walls had long since disappeared and the abbey fallen into decay.

Rachel dismounted and slowly entered the broken enclosure, leading the little horse behind her.

She looked about uneasily. It was told for a fact that on nights of the full moon, pagans still came here, dancing the old druidic dances and calling on the goddess. Even in the full light of day there was a feeling in the walls she could not describe.

The abbey roof was altogether gone. Its walls were mostly intact, massive stone, with projecting stumps of rotted wooden beams here and there. High sculpted arches rose in tiers, one story above another, and wide, empty windows admitted floods of morning light that cast mottled patterns on the floor. One great lower window framed the trees and ocher meadows, while others opened only to darkness. The ancient pavement was covered with centuries of earth and vegetation, grass as high as that on the hillsides, and even trees that reached into the roofless expanse above. The abbey had become a sheltering place for wild things; mud nests of birds hung in crevices, dens for foxes and hares opened into the foundation.

But Rachel, as she walked through the long shafts of sunlight falling through the empty windows onto the grass, felt nothing but peace and sweetness here. What a mystery the abbey was. For the first time she thought of her own life's mystery. Her sixteen years had seemed forever—all of it filled with conflicting emotions. Yet it was not forever, but a speck floating in uncountable eons. Like infinite space between the cold stars on a dark night, time reached forever backward, forever forward, and only now she was beginning to see how small a part of it she filled. Filled? No. She *filled* nothing. Of what value could she be? She did not know, but she *felt* she was of more value than the mere speck of time in which she lived, no matter what her daddy thought.

Slowly she strolled from one pillar to the next—pillars supporting nothing. Then, at the east end of the great nave, she came upon a low central mass of stone and was instantly certain that this was the ancient altar. On its sun-drenched table, overgrown with a thin coat of lichen turned orange and black, Rachel sat down. Minutes before, she had dropped the buckskin's reins, and the horse was wondering about, cropping grass idly. A feeling of weariness came over her, and lying back on the stone face, gazing with dreaming eyes into the open sky, she drifted off into sleep.

It was the light shining on her face that awoke her. The sun was near noon, and this being autumn, lay low in the south. The light was coming through a crack in the edge of a stone casement, an eight-pointed star of great brilliance that made her shut her eyes and look away.

The rays, moving steadily eastward as the sun went west, fell full across Rachel's white cotton blouse and illuminated her face. At the altar's edge, where the ground was moist and covered with thick moss, a tall fern was growing, and across it fell the beam of light, striking its fronds in such a way that only their upward face shone while the rest was left in shadow, making them appear as shining steps on a winding staircase suspended in blackness.

Rachel reached out, touching the fern with the tips of her fingers, making it tremble. The light shimmered. It almost seems to be . . . she thought, searching for words to describe the feeling. "Patches of God light," she remembered Donald saying one day. Oh, Donald, she thought, light is beautiful, but God light? No. She fingered the fern again then lifted her eyes up to where the abbey's southern wall stood, one end broken down. She would climb up on the wall above the countryside and look out.

As she climbed, a bird started from its nest, flew straight down and then out through an empty window, settling at last in a distant thicket. Then, at the top, Rachel stood on tiptoe, searching. Looking westward, she caught her breath.

Beyond the trees was the ocean, nearer than she had ever seen it before. A light breeze smelled wetly of salt, and she could feel the distant, slow roll of the water's gray face. How she wished Drew could be here—together they would go riding to the ocean and stand hand in hand as the breakers rolled in.

Quickly she came down, found the gelding, took him by the reins, and went out. The ocean was not far, but her path was up and down, through hollows and over hills. Of a sudden, all unexpectedly, it lay before her, taking her breath—its blue-gray waves flecking bits of light like diamonds through the air.

"Down," she said to the gelding, urging it forward with her heels.

Once on the rocky beach, Rachel swung her right leg forward over the saddle's pommel and slid down. Off came her shoes, then the garters and long stockings. She stepped shivering into the water, where out a short way the breakers thundered and roared among the rocky barriers, the foam rolling in about her legs. With many a slip she climbed up the wet sides of a large rock and, with the breakers crashing just under her feet, gazed seaward. She wanted to stand and, with her hands in the air, shout with all her voice over the waves, but something restrained her, an awe, a yearning after something she couldn't name. Life was such a bittersweet thing! If there was a God, she thought, this was the kind of ocean He would make, deep and of such a power that no human could think it.

"Question Four . . ." She could not drive the Shorter Catechism question from her mind, force-fed or not. "What is God?

"Answer: God is a Spirit, infinite, eternal, and unchangeable. . . ."

As she saw the ocean's gray face rolling, hearing it thunder, and felt the wind whipping her hair, she could almost believe in that God—a God unlike a man—an infinite Spirit brooding over the face of these waters. An excitement at the thought of being surrounded by such an infinite One surged through her.

Yet the ocean would sooner drown me than bear me up, she thought. And if a beast attacked me on the hills, the earth's breast would drink up my blood as quickly as it would drink showers of rain.

For a while she pondered these things, pondered them till her mind ached with longing. Then she thought of Drew again. He excited her, made her want to be near him, to touch him. Was it wrong to feel this way? No, it wasn't wrong. Tomorrow she would go and find him, would come straight out and ask if he thought he could care for her. Yes, that was what she would do!

Feeling her stomach growl, she realized that she had eaten nothing all day. The cloth bag that held her lunch was gathered at the mouth with a drawstring which she fingered open. Slices of bread, thick with foggie-bee's honey, washed down with cider, wet and fresh and cold—nothing could be better.

The sun had started on its way down toward the sea. If she

did not hurry, the murk would catch her in some hollow and she would never find her way out. Then she remembered there would be a full moon tonight, and there was no cause to hurry.

As the sun sank lower, its brilliance on the waves began to blind her, and she knew it was time to go.

Rachel and the buckskin were halfway between the sea and the old abbey when the sun dropped out of sight behind them. At the same moment, the eastern sky began to brighten.

For an instant Rachel thought the distant countryside had caught fire. Then she saw: it was the moon, orange as a pumpkin, like a living thing lifting up over the next hill.

As they approached through a meadow, the abbey's black silhouette slowly rose against the face of the moon. It was then she heard it, a sound like singing. A tingle ran along her spine as she realized the sound was coming from the abbey.

Who would be in the abbey at night? she wondered, tugging the little horse to a stop. Cautiously she went on, climbing the hill slowly so as not to be heard. The singing grew louder, clearer, but Rachel could not make out the tune. Quietly she reined in the buckskin, coming to stand in a gap of the tumbledown walls.

There they were, a dozen girls, hands linked and dancing in the moonlight about the stone altar on which she had lain this morning. Rachel leaned her forearms against the saddle's pommel, gazing at the skipping girls, all in white, dresses tucked up into waistbands, so that their bare legs flashed white in the moonlight. She was thunderstruck at the sight of the naked legs prancing in time to song.

In the midst of the circle, standing beside the altar, a hooded old woman dipped her hands into a wooden bucket and sprinkled water on the girls as they danced. Faster and faster they went, frantically, until at the very moment when it seemed they could dance no faster, the old woman reached under her garment and drew a long knife, holding its point toward the rising moon.

> "Ancient Mither, who o'r the heather sweeps
> Wi' the voice of the moaning and hurried Wind,
> The licht o' the golden Sun goes down,
> The leaves fa', the warld grows cold.
> I caa you in the ancient wa' intae this circle round,
> Amang these stones, on this thy night

Work thy sacred magic.
Ancient Mither, bring thy sky-force doun."

Rachel's mind was in the circle with the girls, when beneath
her the grass rustled. Out of the corner of her eye she saw
something gray like a hare streak between the gelding's hind
legs. Instantly the gelding bucked, then broke running and
pitching toward the circle of bare-legged girls. The onrushing
scene stopped, the whole throng of girls staring at her as she
came, then dropped their hands and ran screaming in every direction.

The last thing Rachel remembered as the horse pitched was
coming down almost on top of the old woman.

The woman, the dagger still high in her hands, followed her
with staring eyes to the ground.

Rachel had no idea how long it was before she woke, but
when she did, the girls were standing about her, gazing down.

"Ohhh, look at the blud!" they murmured in fright.

Still dazed, Rachel raised her fingers and felt warm blood
running down the side of her face.

"I'm gonna bleed to death," she whispered hoarsely.

But the old woman laid her hand on Rachel's head and began to chant. Her voice no longer seemed old, but strong and
young. Her hood fell back and Rachel looked up into her face,
alight with moonglow—a face as young as her voice, amid
long hair colored like wheat at harvest time. With her hand
firmly fixed on Rachel's head, she said clear and strong:

"An' whan I passed by thee, and saw thee polluted in thine
own bluid, I said untae thee whan thou wist in thy bluid, Live;
yea, I said untae thee whan thou wis in thy bluid, Live!"

Then there was silence. The flow stopped, and almost as one
the girls looking on, as surprised as Rachel, caught their
breath.

"There," the woman said, "now lay easy."

"Do you not understand what they were, girl?" Bess scolded
as she dressed the cut on Rachel's head.

"I know, Mama," she said, but not meekly.

"I've waited up these hours for you," Bess huffed, wetting
a cloth in a wooden basin and dabbing at the dried blood, "and
Donald's still out lookin'!"

"It was that worthless beast of a horse," Rachel exclaimed,

"throwin' me and leavin' me to come home afoot. If the woman and girls had not helped me, I'm sure I'd not've made it, weak as I was."

"Woman and girls!" Bess spat. "They were witches, that's what they were! Tonight's Sow-en, Feast of the Dead, their greatest sabbat. You had no business bein' out."

"Well," Rachel said quietly, "whatever they were, the woman saved my life."

"Aye, that she did," Bess answered. "But if you hadn't been out, you'd not'a needed savin'."

As Rachel lay beneath her window that night, tired and sore, visions of the day filled her head. The bittersweet longing she had felt as she sat on the rock looking out to sea came again. Still she did not know what name to give the longing, but it was very deep, and somehow the thing longed for was carried in the arms of the wind and on the water's waves. It stood in the abbey's black silhouette, and the orange disk of the moon, and in the touch of the young woman's fingers, and the sound of her chanting voice.

Perhaps there was some great mystery behind the world after all. And strangest of all, whatever the longing was, it was greater even than the longing she felt for Drew Wolfe. But she had not forgotten Drew, and tomorrow she would go and find him.

TWELVE

IN spite of all that had happened yesterday, Rachel was out of the cottage and on her way up Hill MacLaren before the sun cleared the ridge. She had put on her light tan dress trimmed in russet and, as she went, had to lift it a little to keep the heather from catching its skirt. The crisp air and anticipation of finding Drew set her atingle with excitement.

According to Donald, Drew Wolfe lived east of the village, halfway up the mountain's slope, in the family cottage with his father. His mother had died six years ago.

At last she saw it—in a wide, grassy meadow marked out by ancient decaying fences. As she came near, Drew was emerging from the door, a leathern bag in his hand. He appeared deep in thought and did not hear her footfall in the grass.

Rachel stood at the corner of the fence, herself unseen, but seeing him as if for the first time.

Drew's face, hands, and bare forearms were naturally fair, but evenly tanned in a way that excited her. His eyes were thoughtful, his lashes long, every feature of his face well-shaped and sensitive. He stood just a little less than six feet, and his billowy white shirt flowed downward from obviously muscular shoulders and arms. The fit of his breeches showed a trim waist; and the calves of his legs—hugged tightly by light green stockings below white linen breeches—gave added grace to his self-confident step.

As she stood there, Rachel tried to memorize every feature of his face. There was a kind of subdued ruggedness to it, and his dark hair and hauntingly clear gray eyes made her heart beat faster. In spite of the morning's coolness, tiny droplets of perspiration stood out on her upper lip. Rachel was not *thinking* anything at all, but bursting with feeling, bathing in the thrill of being close to him again.

She laid her hand on the iron fence rail, overgrown with dried morning glory vines that rustled when she touched them. Startled at the sound, Drew stopped and looked around.

"Rachel!" Instantly his face was alight. "What're *you* doin' way out here?"

"Lookin' for you," she answered happily. The bodice of her dress accentuated the slimness of her waist and flare of her hips. With the morning sun casting auburn highlights in her hair, Drew's first thought was that she had purposely dressed to match the autumn grasses on the hillside. Something about the picture of her standing there by the fence with the great land-and seascape behind her made her seem a beautiful figure out of a painting. And again, as on the day when he first saw her, he was stricken by the wonderful beauty of her face.

"If you're goin' to see the sick, I'd like to go with you," she pleasantly dared.

A cloud of uncertainty passed over Drew's face, and he gripped the bag in his hand a little tighter. He looked away and paused for a long moment. At last he said slowly, quietly, "Rachel, I loved havin' you with me the day we crossed the loch.

And I'd love it again—more than you might know. But if we keep it up, folks will begin to talk. So I think we shouldn't."

She winced with disappointment.

"But Drew," she pled. All her brashness was suddenly gone. She felt desperate, as if he might somehow disappear from her sight forever, and she found it hard to breathe.

"Rachel . . ." he said, stammering. He looked directly into her eyes, and knew instantly he should not have, for his will began to melt within him. "Rachel," he began again, "there's another thing to think of. If your father didn't want you with young Timothy MacKnighton, a boy only eighteen, what would he say to your bein' with me, a young man of twenty-two? No," he concluded firmly, "you're goin' to get us both killed!" He started off down the hill, walking rapidly.

For a shocked instant Rachel did not move, then, running, she fell in beside him, skipping every few steps to keep up.

"But you're a *doctor*," she said, trying to reason with him. "Timothy is . . . well, he's a *boy*; he couldn't take care of me; you can. Daddy would be *glad*."

Her words hit Andrew Wolfe like a hammer. He stopped in his tracks, breathing hard, but not from the rapid descent. Suddenly he realized that everything he had felt about Rachel, she had also felt about him; and that while he was struggling against his feelings, she was not struggling at all. To her the matter could reach only one conclusion. He turned to face her.

"Rachel!" he said. "What're you *sayin'*!"

She stepped toward him, gripping his upper arms. Before he could stop her, her lips were on his. His will disintegrated, and his arms went around her, pulling her closer yet. She was breathing hard when her lips separated slowly from his, melting with delight, tears glistening on her cheeks as she looked into his eyes. With the bare fingers of her right hand, she reached up and smoothed his dark brown hair.

He was deeply shaken. Nervously he looked this way and that over the grassy mountainside. There was no one near. A wide cluster of stunted trees stood between them and the village below, shielding them from any outside gaze. They had not been seen, he was sure of it.

"Rachel," he breathed, "this is insane!"

"No!" she said. "It's *good*! Drew, I need you! You can take me away and give me a whole new life! And oh, Drew," she breathed, "I do love you." And she laid her head on his chest.

He was beside himself. If he told her the truth, what would

she do? She had instantly and stupidly placed every hope of her life in him. He was not to blame for that; *she* was. But he was to blame for not having told her everything from the beginning. He was to blame for not wanting to tell her. He felt his arms involuntarily tightening about her again.

"Rachel! Oh, Rachel!" he said.

He was in a mélange of ecstasy and denial. Then, at last, it all came into focus. He held her out at arm's length and looked directly into her eyes.

"Rachel, listen to me! I understand your wantin' to get away from your father. There's nothin' wrong with that. God knows, if I were in your place I'd want the same. And . . . fool that I am to tell you . . . I never felt drawn to anyone the way I feel drawn to you. But I—"

"Then you feel it, too!" she exclaimed, her dark eyes growing wider.

"God help me, yes!"

"Then why not ask my father for me?" she all but shouted. "He'll give me to you in a minute!"

"Rachel, I—" He stopped, wrestling with some internal thing; she could not tell what, but she could see the struggle in his face.

"Go on," she said, her eyes large with anticipation.

"Rachel, I can hardly bear to tell you," he said, his voice softening. He looked away and at once felt the terrible cowardice of the act. Yet he simply could not look into those eyes and tell her the truth. At last a measure of composure came to him, and he said quietly, "Rachel, in three weeks I'm to marry!"

As Rachel ran down the steepening slope, through her tears she saw nothing but a blur of blue sky and tan grasses. The only sounds were her feet crunching in the dry grass and her own sobbing. Down she ran, down a precipitous hill into a low swale where a stream spread out. The sheltered growth was still green, and the ground spongy and wet, making her stumble again and again. But she plunged on, the high grasses stinging her face as she went. Then, having reached the swale's farther side and coming up onto higher ground, she threw herself down on a great flat rock that overlooked a pond. She had been here before, and had unselfconsciously called the place "Rachel's Pond." A rowan tree growing by the water overspread the rock with its branches, bare in the early autumn.

There she lay, sobbing, throbbing at the pain and anger

mixed together and boiling inside ... the pain of disappointment, and anger at herself for presuming so much, anger at
Drew, anger at life. At last she sat up and, reaching into the
reticule fastened to the waist of her skirt, pulled out a clean
handkerchief which she dipped into the pond's cold water. She
lay back again and folded the wet cloth over her eyes. Now
and then a sob shook her body, and she groaned a little.

"You just can't trust a man," she said in a tear-choked whisper. "I'll never try again! Never!"

The autumn morning was very cool, but the sun climbed
higher and the young rowan's bare branches let its rays
through to warm her shoulders. After a while, overcome by
weariness of spirit, she slept.

It was mid-afternoon when Rachel awoke to find the sun still
high, filtering down, making little patterns of light on her dress
and hands. A breeze sprang up from the northwest and whistled softly in the tree's bare limbs. Her mind felt clearer, and
her head had stopped aching.

"I am a fool," she whispered. "It really wasn't his fault—but
I *do* wish he had told me that first day!" The humiliation was
fresh and strong, stinging like a nettle. She covered her eyes
with her hand. "Oh," she murmured through gritted teeth, "I
don't want to see him again—ever!"

The sun was sinking into a blue bank of sea cloud and the day
cooling quickly when Donald came looking. In his hand he
held a faded shawl. She was sitting on the rock's edge when
he found her, hugging her knees, gazing emptily into the pond.
His approaching steps crunched in the crisp grass with a cadence that told her it was him, and when he laid the shawl
gently over her shoulders, she did not look around.

"Donald," she said, her voice very calm and even, "I made
a complete fool of myself today."

"Drew came and told me what happened," he said quietly.

"Did he tell it where Mama could hear?"

"No," he said. "He came to the tannery. I'm the only one
who knows." Donald sat on the rock beside her and pulled her
head over onto his shoulder. "I'm sorry, Rachel," he said, "so
sorry."

"Donald, I was certain he was the one!"

"You can't come to love someone in just a week's time, Rachel," he said.

"Oh, but you can, Donald. Really you can. And I just don't know what I'm goin' to do!"

"And I can't tell you what to do," he said.

But he sat there with his arm about her shoulder as the evening came on.

"It happened right here," Drew said to Donald Calhoun the next evening. "It hit me that Rachel was talking about marriage, and I stopped to face her. Then . . . Oh," he sighed, looking down at the place where they had stood. "Then she kissed me."

Donald smiled. There were dark circles under his friend's eyes, and his complexion made him appear ill.

"So what are you going to do?" Donald asked.

"Dear Lord," he said, "if only I knew the answer to that! I can't sleep! I can't eat! I get up in the middle of the night and take long walks on the mountain. Yesterday I thought I knew; I told myself that I'd call the wedding off. The next thing, I was saying to myself, 'What kind of fool are you? You hardly know this girl!' " He looked at Donald. "Why did Rachel have to come along just now? Why couldn't it have been three years ago . . . or *next* year? Why now? No one has *ever* done to me what she does. Don't you see how unfair it would be to Elizabeth to marry her, feeling as I do about Rachel?"

"Perhaps not," Donald said quietly. "It's likely an infatuation. It will pass in a few days."

Drew looked about, wildly frustrated. "I wish I believed it would pass," he said. "I can just imagine Elizabeth's face when I tell her. She doesn't deserve to be treated like that. She's a good, steady, responsible girl."

"And very pretty, I hear," Donald said, looking impishly from under his red brows.

"Yes . . . yes, she's pretty," Drew answered slowly.

"But not with a beauty that shines like Rachel's," Donald said. "Is that what you mean?"

"Yes," Drew sighed, "not like Rachel's. And there's not the same exciting childishness about her, the wide-eyed wonder, the adventuresome spirit. I just don't know. My emotions bounce around like an India rubber ball!"

"Well," Donald said in the same slow way, "it's as much Rachel's fault as yours."

"I'm afraid I led her on," Drew answered.

"No you didn't," Donald said. "You just befriended her. She

presumed too much . . . way too much. She's not your responsibility. If she's anyone's responsibility, she's mine."

There was a long silence in which Drew stamped around in the grass, sighing and gazing out over the loch while Donald watched him. Donald was feeling sad for Rachel, but he smiled at the way in which Drew had caught himself on the horns of this dilemma.

"Another week," Drew said, "and a ship will enter that loch from the sea, and Elizabeth will be on board." He looked around at his friend. "What am I going to do?"

"Well," Donald answered, "until you decide, you're not going to let on to Rachel that you've thought of calling off the wedding. She's settled down a little, gotten used to the idea she made such a fool of herself."

"You're right," Drew said, "absolutely right. I'll say nothing to her."

"Myself," Donald said, "I think you should go ahead and marry."

"Because you think this is just an infatuation."

"Because I'm sure of it," he said firmly.

Three weeks later, as Drew stood before the parish rector with Elizabeth's hand in his, he was almost certain he had made the right choice. He had kept his promise to Elizabeth, and he could live by that. He had made his own bed, and it would be a very comfortable bed at that.

THIRTEEN

EARLY autumn had been dry and the tan hills sear, but in late November the weather changed. Cold northwest winds blew in from the Atlantic, bringing clouds and damp cold. Heavy rains beat down, making the short gray days even shorter and long nights longer.

Yesterday, a day in late December, began with chill winds churning the waters of the loch and roaring through the tops of the birches around the Calhoun cottage. There were no stars before dawn, only heavy clouds rushing across the face of the darkness.

It was well after eight in the morning, still dark, since even on clear days in December the sun did not break over the rim of Hill MacLaren until after ten. A few moments ago a soft thud accompanied by a metallic click woke Rachel from an uneasy sleep. For a moment she lay wondering. That was Donald going to work, she thought, the door latching behind him. The fire he had built to cook his breakfast and warm the room cast its flickering light on the wall and ceiling above her bed. The wind whistling and moaning about the eaves made her burrow deeper into the covers.

As she lay listening, Rachel became aware of another sound, raspy and hollow, from across the room. It was Mama, coughing, gasping for air, sighing and moaning a little, then drifting back into an exhausted sleep, every breath wheezing like a blacksmith's bellows.

This spell of sickness had begun a week ago, and every night had grown steadily worse. Rachel lay watching the firelight play on the ceiling, wondering what she could do, feeling miserably helpless.

Suddenly Mama burst into coughing again, and when the fit past, Rachel heard her weeping softly. Yesterday she had spit up a piece of lung. When Rachel had seen the thin bloody sliver, she had been beside herself.

Daddy, Rachel silently scolded, why can't you be here when you're needed! As usual, he was gone, somewhere to the south this time, combing sheep out of the hills.

"Mama?" Rachel called out. "Mama, what can I do?"

Bess opened her mouth to answer, but another spasm of coughing cut her off. At last Bess managed, "There's nothing . . . nothing at all," and the coughing began all over again.

In desperation, Rachel threw back the cover, got up, and threw a wool shawl across her shoulders, shivering in spite of the little fire. There was a pile of dried peat blocks against the north wall. Rachel picked up two of the nearly black bricks, laid them on the blaze, then stepping to the window, she looked out. The faintly lightening sky was mottled with heavy black clouds.

"Rain today for sure, Mama," Rachel said, trying her best to sound light and unconcerned. "I don't know which I would rather have," she went on, slipping from her cotton nightgown, the firelight flickering over the whiteness of her body, "these winters here where we hardly ever see snow, but it rains till the walls grow mold, or the awful cold and snow back east." She pulled an everyday dress over her head, the faded blue one with frayed threads at the neck, slipped it down, and wiggled the bodice into place. "But I think I prefer the wind and the rain. It suits my personality better." She stepped into her only pair of leather shoes. "I like the clouds . . . and the darkness."

She went to her mother's side and knelt down. Bess's hair, streaked widely with gray, was spread in a tangle over her pillow, and there were puffy circles under her eyes. Her breath was foul and her skin pale, except for a bright red patch on each cheek. Even in the light of the hearth fire, Rachel could see the paleness.

She laid her hand softly on her mother's forehead. "You're fevered," she whispered.

"Always," Bess coughed.

Rachel withdrew her hand and stood, looking down, her heart breaking at the sight of her mother lying there. "I'll be back soon," she said, drawing a thick wool blanket about her shoulders.

"Where're you goin'?" Bess managed.

"Out . . . to fetch Drew Wolfe," she said.

"No," Bess started to protest.

"It's all I know to do, Mama," Rachel answered. "I can't stand to see you lyin' there like this. I'll be back as quick as I can."

And without further argument she opened the door to a mighty gust of wind, stepped out, and pulled it tightly closed behind her.

The sharp wind caught Rachel's hair and whipped it about in the darkness. The damp cold swept down the neck of her dress, sending a shiver down her spine. She drew the blanket up over her head, grasping it tightly beneath her chin.

Everything was black, the only visible objects being bare birch limbs tossing against heavy clouds. Up across the meadow came the sound of surf beating on the loch's rugged shore. Carefully Rachel picked her path down the road. Slowly the dark outline of the village trees came into view, then gathered around her until she found herself walking up the shadowy street. The sand, beaten by last week's rains, felt firm beneath her feet. The wind pinned the skirt of her dress against her legs, and her ankles began to sting.

At last she was standing in the deserted, windswept street,

hesitating before the house of Andrew Wolfe. It was a two-story dwelling on a little rise of ground that fell away toward the water's edge. Through a window with diamond-shaped panes a lamp was glowing, the image of its flame repeated warmly in every bevel of the glass. The house had belonged to the same doctor who had taken Drew under his wing. When the old physician, having no child of his own, saw that Drew would take his place, he had left it to him and his bride-to-be. The newly married couple had moved in the day after their wedding. It was a fine house, made in the old way with white-washed stone walls, mortared together, and above, a smooth thatch of rushes which would turn the heaviest rains. There was a great chimney at each end, from one of which was rising a column of smoke.

Rachel stood gazing up at its tall white walls. In the back of her mind she had a vague feeling that had things gone just a bit differently, she might have been living here now as Drew's wife. She shook off the feeling and clutched the blanket tightly. "Well, if I must, I must," she said. Resolutely, she took the first step up the walk and hammered on the door.

When the door opened, a young woman stood framed before her in the doorway. Her face was in shadow, for the light came from within the room, but Rachel had the immediate impression of warmth and kindness. The woman was only slightly taller than she, and very blond. Behind her the room glowed with warmth, and a voice called out, "Who is it, Beth?"

Before answering, Elizabeth Wolfe stepped to one side "Come in out of the wind and cold, dear!"

"No . . ." Rachel stumbled. "I mean, I mustn't!"

"And why mustn't you?"

"I . . ." Rachel could not frame an answer. She had come determined not to like this woman, but she could not help herself, and she was suddenly afraid that Elizabeth would not like *her*. Had Drew told her what had happened between them? What a fool she had made of herself? Had they lain in bed and laughed together at the stupid girl who lived on the village's upper edge?

"*Ra*chel!" Drew had stepped up behind Elizabeth, caught his breath, and for the briefest instant there was panic in his eyes. He hesitated, then stepped aside and motioned.

"Come in, Rachel," he said. But he was afraid, and his heart was beating faster. Why, he wondered, would Rachel come here? Suddenly he was angry. Why would she be so audacious? Had she come to make trouble? With a temperament like hers, she might say something.

When Rachel saw Drew, she felt a sudden flash of heat across her face. But she could think of nothing to do but go in. She steadied herself and stepped through the door.

"Here, dear," Elizabeth said, taking her blanket, "back up to the fire."

"It's Mama," she said, speaking directly to Elizabeth. "She's very sick."

Drew felt instant relief. How perverted I am, he thought; glad for her mother's illness. His own duplicity revolted him.

"What's wrong?" he asked. His voice showed no trace of anxiety.

"Coughin'—*terrible* coughin'," Rachel answered. "And blood. Yesterday Mama coughed up . . . somethin' bloody."

Drew cast Elizabeth a knowing look and reached for the greatcoat that hung on a peg by the door. "I'll go to her," he said quickly.

"I'll come with you, Drew," Elizabeth said, disappearing into the next room. Rachel searched Drew's face for some feeling, some sign that he remembered that day, but there was none.

When Elizabeth reappeared, a hooded wool cape over her shoulders, Drew was looking about the room for his bag of medicines.

"Your bag's over there, beneath the bay window," she said, then smiled at Rachel. "Just a little absentminded for a doctor so young."

As they went out, Rachel fell in beside Elizabeth.

"Do you understand what's wrong with you, Bess?" Drew asked quietly after examining her.

Bess was on her side facing them, pale and sallow, her breathing labored. The straw tick cradled her deeply, and Drew was holding her right hand in his; it was clammy and cold.

"Aye," she answered. "It's consumption."

"That's right," Elizabeth broke in softly as she stroked Bess's shoulder. Elizabeth's lips had a paleness to them, and she had a habit of pressing them together between sentences so that they pursed a little. Even in the dim light her hair glowed like gold. "Look, Drew," Elizabeth said, "how her back is hunched, and in her handkerchief, spittle laced with blood."

"We hardly ever see it out here in these hills," Drew said.

"Bess, you must've caught this a long time ago, when you lived in Glasgow. That's where most cases are—in the cities."

"Why can't I breathe?" she wheezed desperately.

"Scars in your lungs, or fluid," Drew answered.

Elizabeth gazed at Rachel, who was standing on the other side of the bed, watching intently. Elizabeth was a strong young woman, but there were sympathetic tears in her eyes.

"What can we *do*?" Rachel burst out, her voice on the edge of breaking.

"Rest. That's all she can do, rest."

"And pray," Elizabeth said.

"No medicines?"

"Verdigris," he said, "but it'll do her no good now."

"Now?" Rachel said, her voice small and the word drawn out in disbelief.

"No, Rachel," he said, "not now."

"What a lovely girl she is, Drew!"

Elizabeth undid her shawl and laid it across a chair near the fire to dry as Drew closed the door against the bluster. It was nearly noon, and they had just come from the tannery. Donald had to be told that his mother and sister needed him. The wind, rather than diminishing, had increased, and heavy rain had begun to fall. In Elizabeth's mind she was seeing Rachel's face all over again.

"I'm absolutely *taken* by her!" she exclaimed. "Those eyes . . . her very soul seemed to be looking out at us—especially when she was talking to you about her mother." Elizabeth shook her head slowly, and her tone dropped. "She must have a very great heart for a girl so young!"

Drew was laying a new slab of peat on the fire. He made no response.

"Don't you find her an unusually attractive girl, Drew?" Elizabeth said, turning toward him.

Still he made no answer.

"Drew?"

He'd an absent look on his face. But at last he nodded his head. "Yes, Beth," he breathed. "Yes, I surely do!"

Elizabeth continued with confidence. "That girl will need us, Drew."

"Need us?" he said, punching at the fire with a poker. "Need us how, Beth?"

"Her mother's going to die."

"Yes, no question."

"The girl has no other woman in her life. The family's not well accepted here. She's very alone, and needs someone; and there's probably no other woman in town better fit to befriend her than I."

"I don't know, Beth. Surely there's someone . . ."

"But I *want* to be the one, Drew." She paused. "It would do me good to have someone like Rachel to care for. Out here, so far from home, I need her every bit as much as Rachel needs me."

He sighed. "Well, we'll just have to wait and see what happens."

"Always gone when he's needed most!" Rachel spat bitterly.

Instantly Donald caught her by the shoulder and wheeled her around to face him. As he gripped her arm, his light blue eyes flashed with uncharacteristic anger. Rachel compressed her lips until they turned white.

"Let me go!" she whispered, glaring back at him.

Across the room Bess lay in her bed just waking from sleep. It was late evening. Rachel was preparing supper, all the while fuming at her father's absence. Donald jerked his head toward the door and pulled Rachel after him.

It was night again, very dark, the wind howling and the rain falling harder. Outside, the door firmly closed behind them, the two stood against the cottage wall, poorly sheltered beneath the rain-spattered eaves. Only by the window's faint light could they see each other's angry faces. Donald gripped Rachel's shoulders with both hands, shaking her hard. She wrenched violently to free herself.

"What do you think you're doin'!" she demanded between clenched teeth.

But he held tightly, his own jaw set hard.

"She's *dyin'*, Rachel!" he exclaimed.

"I *know* she's dyin'." Rachel raised her voice near to a shout and sudden tears swam in her eyes. "And if Daddy had never taken us to the city, she *wouldn't* be!"

"Don't scream!" he said, and he clamped his hand over her mouth. Immediately she began to claw, trying to tear it away. But Donald's work-hardened strength was much too much for her.

"Get your hand off me!" she managed to say between his

fingers. Nonetheless her voice was lower this time, and Donald released his hold. She had never seen him so angry.

"I'll not have you addin' to her burden now!" he said in a violent whisper. "Oh, what's the use!" he said, then throwing his hands into the air, he turned his back to his sister and dropped his chin to his chest. For a long moment she stood with her arms crossed, breathing hard and scowling at the back of his bowed head. Then she saw it: his shoulders quietly shaking.

"Donald?" she said pleadingly, dropping her arms to her side. Her whole demeanor softened.

"Oh, Donald, I am sorry, *so* sorry!" she said. Now her hands were on his shoulders, and now about his waist. He turned around and they clasped each other tightly, weeping softly.

"Oh, Donald," she said again, "I'm so afraid . . . but Daddy, why *couldn't* Daddy be where he should be, just one time in his life?"

"Daddy is Daddy, that's all," Donald said through his own tears.

"Donald," she said. "Oh, Donald, *please* stop making excuses for him; all my life you've tried to make him out a better man than he is. The truth is that Daddy—"

"Listen!" Donald whispered.

"What is it?"

"Shhh . . ."

And above the wind, through the door, they heard a small voice.

"She's callin' for you, Rachel."

"Yes, Mama?" Rachel said unsteadily. She was afraid Bess had heard the violent words between her and Donald.

"Come sit beside me, Rachel." Bess's voice was weak and small. Rachel looked down on her mother and felt herself trembling. This was her mother's voice, but not her face. Her dark, once beautiful eyes were sunken, her cheeks thin, every trace of prettiness—prettiness in which Rachel had always taken such pride—gone.

Rachel sat down, and almost timidly took Bess's thin hand, holding it tightly, as if to warm it with her love.

"Rachel," Bess said, "don't fret over your daddy's bein' gone."

"But, Mama—"

"Shhh. It doesn't matter, Rachel. I want peace, and with him gone, I can have it."

"Oh, *Ma*ma!" Rachel began to sob.

"No, Rachel! Now listen to me. I have somethin' I want to say—just to you."

Tears were running down Rachel's cheeks, but she paid them no mind, sniffed a little, then swallowed.

"All right, Mama," she said, her voice small and meek, "what is it you want to tell me?"

"Rachel, I've always loved you . . . every bit as much as ever I loved Donald. In some ways, more . . . for women share things men can never know. And you and I have always shared secrets that we've not spoken with our lips, haven't we?"

Rachel laughed a little through her tears, and nodded.

"Dearest," Bess went on—she gripped Rachel's arm with pitiful weakness, her bony hands cold on Rachel's warm skin—"the deepest sorrow I've ever known has been what your daddy has done to you."

"Mama!" Rachel began to cry again.

"Just listen, Rachel," she said. Bess's voice somehow grew stronger as she went on. "The moment you first saw your daddy when you were a tiny girl, you loved him. I couldn't understand why or how, but you did. And, Rachel, in his own twisted way, your daddy always loved you. But he doesn't know how to show it. The way he grew up, the real meanin' of love just never came to him. He had nobody to show him— his mother dead and his own daddy a hateful old man!"

Bess's eyes grew watery and red. She gripped Rachel's hand again.

"Sometimes I wish that old man had never lived!" She paused and with her unsteady left hand wiped her eyes. When she spoke again, her voice was quieter. "But I must remember," she said, "in another way, that old man didn't matter at all. It was my weakness for your daddy that started all our troubles, yours and mine. I should've run away with you in Glasgow. It would've been hard, but we could've gone back to the valley where we were happy. But I clung to the hope that I could yet teach him love and lovin'. As good Paul has told us, 'Gin I speak wi' the tongues o' men an' angels but hae nae luve i my hairt I am no nane better nor dunnerin' bress or a ringin' cymbal.' I wanted to teach him such love . . . but I was wrong; I could not."

Rachel sat silently, the tears coursing freely down.

"But, Rachel," and here Bess's eyes took on a strange fire, "Rachel, the worst he's done is tellin' you you're just like him. It's a lie. And you must promise me now, you'll never believe the lie that you are like your father!"

"I won't, Mama," Rachel vowed frantically. "I'm *not* like him! I'll never be like him, not for one minute of my life!"

Bess smoothed a wide strand of Rachel's hair between her thin fingers. It gave her a kind of peace to feel the rich youthfulness of her daughter's hair.

"Forgive me if I've spoke out'a turn, but I couldn't let it go unsaid. The heartbreak of it is that your daddy never gave you back the love you gave to him. I've seen the disappointment in your eyes a thousand times. He was a light that was never there!" Bess paused, gathering strength. In the silence she continued to let Rachel's hair slip comfortingly through her fingers. "Now I fear you'll spend all your life searching for the love your daddy never gave, some love to light your life."

"Lookin' for love is bad?" the girl said.

"No, dearest; lookin' for love is good, if you don't search like your very life depends on your findin' it. And it's good if you look in the right places . . . and if, once you've found it, you can bring yourself to *believe* you've found it!"

"Mama, I'll *know* love when I find it!"

"Aye . . . at first most certainly. But it's later on that troubles me. Later, when havin' married a man, somethin' rises in you to say that you didn't find it after all. Somethin' *will* say that to you, Rachel. And it'll say it on the very day when the man you find tells you he loves you with all his heart. Somehow you just won't believe it, and you'll take it for a lie. All I'm sayin' is, if he's a good man, believe him, Rachel, no matter what the thing inside you says!"

"Why're you tellin' me this *now*, Mama?"

Bess's tired eyes seemed filled with a cold light. "Because of what you and I both know, Rachel."

Fearfully Rachel asked, "What is it we know, Mama?"

Bess shook her head and smiled ever so faintly. "That I'm dyin'," she said softly.

"No! Mama, you're not!" Rachel grabbed her mother's hand again and held it tightly against her breast. "You're just *not*!"

"But I am, Rachel. And with you near to being a grown-up woman, you'll need to be hearin' all I've said. And Donald . . ."

"Yes, Mama, what about Donald?"

"I've asked your brother to see after you, and I've asked God, too. Together the two of 'em'll show you the way. They'll be a light to you. Please listen to 'um, follow their light, no matter how dark it gets, Rachel . . . your brother's and God's."

FOURTEEN

IT was Monday, the twenty-third of January, 1769. Last night Rachel had hardly slept at all, and at sunup was standing at the north window of the cottage, gazing out. The sky was overcast—a dull sheet of cloud the color of lead, stretching from horizon to horizon. A deep mist had buried the face of the loch and was drifting up onto the mountain, hiding sheep and horses and scattered cottages.

In a little while the iron-throated bell hanging in the tower of Lochredfern's ancient stone kirk would call, and Rachel would go for the burial of her mother.

Two days ago Mama had begun to fight for every breath. Rachel had propped her up in bed, and for a little while Bess had breathed more easily. But then, lying with her head tilted back, Bess's eyes widened into a stare, and when Rachel spoke to her, she did not answer. Donald had run for Drew. He came, bathed her feverish face, but in the end shook his head sadly.

All through that horrible night Bess's breathing had become more and more labored, breaths further and further apart, until yesterday morning, her lungs consumed by disease, she had suffocated and died. This morning they would bury her in the Lochredfern kirkyard.

Then, as if to drive a dagger through Rachel's already suffering heart, last night she heard the gate slam and went to the door. There, coming whistling up the walk, was Bartlett.

"No!" she had shouted, suddenly filled with rage. "Go away!" And she had run out, flailing at him with her fists.

The whistling died on his lips as he caught her arms and held them. She broke down, sobbing.

"Where *were* you?" she pled. "Oh, Daddy, why weren't you here?"

Confused, Bartlett looked past her to see Donald standing in the doorway.

"She's dead, Daddy," Donald said calmly.

"Dead?" he whispered. "Your mother? My Bess? Dead?"

Donald stepped out and gathered Rachel to himself, and as he turned, gave Bartlett a withering look. Bartlett had dropped his arms, staring at nothing. It wasn't until this morning he had returned to dress for the funeral. Few words had passed between them, and he hadn't said where he stayed the night, but at least he was sober.

When the service was over, the kirk doors slowly opened and the black-robed vicar emerged. Behind him came the bearers, a simple coffin carried between them, then Rachel leaning heavily on Donald's arm, and behind them, Bartlett. Bartlett's hat was in his hand and his bald head was bare to the snapping cold. After him came Drew and Elizabeth, with Drew's father and a dozen other village folk who came out of sympathy for Bess and for Rachel and Donald.

At the graveside the vicar, a tall man with snowy hair and a white stock flowing down onto his gown, read from a black book and prayed. Donald was standing with his arm around Rachel's shoulder, and he felt her grow rigid as the vicar prayed the prayer they had heard a hundred times from their mother's lips.

> Our Faither in heiven,
>   hallowt be thy name;
>   thy Kingdom come;
>   thy will be dune
> on the yeird as in heiven.

> Gie us our breid for this incomin day;
> forgie us the wrangs we hae wrocht,
>   as we hae forgien the wrangs we hae dree'd;
> an say-us-na sairlie, but sauf us
>   Frae the Ill Ane.

"Our Father in heaven"; Rachel felt anger boil up in her throat. If there is a God in control of human destiny, she

thought, then he is like Daddy, cruel and unfeeling to let Mama
live and die so.

A soft touch on Rachel's arm made her look about; it was
Elizabeth, tears brimming in her eyes, her pale lips compressed
in sorrow. Rachel buried her face in Elizabeth's shoulder, holding her tightly as the nails were being driven into the coffin lid.
With every fall of the hammer, Elizabeth felt their shock passing through Rachel's body and into her own.

Rachel was kneeling over her mother's trunk later that afternoon, sorting through the meager collection of things in the
upper tray. From above her head the crusie cast down its yellow light. The fire on the hearth had gone out when they had
returned from the funeral, so that the cottage had been cold.
Donald had built it up again and then gone down to the tannery. Bartlett had not come home, so Rachel was alone with
her grief.

She fingered each thing lovingly. There was a miniature
painting on ivory of Bess's mother, a lock of hair from a favorite sister who had been gone for years, a locket, a tarnished
ring, a few old brass coins treasured for some reason that only
Bess had known.

From the wall her mother's shelf clock clicked, then began
to strike the hour. The tone was metallic, but full and pleasant.
One . . . two . . . three . . . four. The short day was nearly over,
the sun already dropped into the sea.

Rachel lowered the trunk lid gently and had just closed the
hasp when the front door latch rattled and the door swung
open. Rachel rose halfway, startled.

"Daddy," she said, "where've you been?"

To her own surprise, there was a note of caring in her voice.
She felt strangely toward him—not so angry—likely because
Bess had loved Bartlett through all his evil ways, and because
with Mama gone, she felt so alone.

"That's the second time in two days you've asked me where
I've been!" he growled. His syllables were slurred and he
steadied himself against the doorjamb.

"Oh, Daddy, no . . ." her voice was pleading, "not drunk today, not the day we bury Mama!"

"What damned business of yours is it if I want to get drunk
on the day your mother leaves me behind?"

Rachel could not bear this mood, not tonight.

"Daddy, I've been thinkin' since yesterday." She dropped

her gaze to the floor. "Daddy, for the sake of Mama's memory, maybe you and I could learn—" A scornful snort made her look up. He was leaning heavily on the doorjamb, his eyes focused on her, a curl on his thick lips.

"I see what you're tryin' to do," he said with a growling laugh. "Now that she's gone, you're scared. Scared who's gonna take care of you . . ."

"No, Daddy. That's not it at all. I'm just remembering when I was very little, and things between you and me were better. And tonight, it's true, I am so lonely. In spite of all, I was hopin' you and me—"

"Lonely! Like hell! If you're lonely why don't you go out and sidle up to young MacKnighton, or," and his voice rose in volume, "or to that young doctor! Yessir, that'd be a catch for you."

"Daddy, how could you *say* that!"

"He'd take care of you real good. He's married, but that shouldn't matter to the likes of you!" And he began to laugh.

His words were like hot coals in Rachel's heart. Without thought, she sprang up, shouting frustration and anger at the top of her voice. She reached around, found the hot griddle over the fire, grabbed it by the bail and threw it at him with all her strength.

Calhoun caught it with his hand, and as the hot iron seared his flesh, he roared with pain. Rachel recoiled in terror at what she had done and, falling back toward the north window, tried to claw it open. His heavy hand fell in a death grip on her shoulder, and she turned to face him, screaming and trying to pull away.

Instantly Bartlett reached for the butcher knife that lay on the table and threw her against the wall. Pain shot through her shoulder as she slid to the floor. Before she could move, he was on top of her, his knees on her shoulders and one beefy hand tangled in her hair.

She tried to fight, to throw him off, but the pain in her shoulders where his knees pressed down was like bolts of lightning.

"I'm gonna teach you at last!" he bellowed, yanking a fistful of hair. She screamed and twisted beneath him. "Nobody here this time to save the mama's girl, is there? Lay still!" he thundered, and struck her across the face. Convulsed as she was with anger and frustration and sobs, Rachel willed herself to lie still lest he kill her. She closed her eyes tightly, clenched her fists, fighting to suppress her screams, whimpering as she felt the fierce pull on her scalp and heard the knife sawing through strand after strand of hair.

It was the same evening, and the wind was howling in from the Atlantic, hurling snowflakes horizontally across the windowpanes of the Wolfe home. The warm south Atlantic currents ran off the northwest coast, making it impossible for snow to gather on the ground oftener than once in twenty years. But the force of the gale made the walls of the house quiver.

Drew was sitting in the bay window of the west wall, leaning his head close to the glass. The draft of air from the cold pane felt good to his cheek. Elizabeth hated the damp cold, so different from the drier cold of the east, and insisted on keeping a roaring blaze in the fireplace. To Drew the room was insufferably hot.

He gazed out into the darkness, watching the snow strike the window, flakes scurrying rapidly across, losing themselves in the darkness again. With his finger he absently traced circles in the condensation on the pane.

Elizabeth sat silently nearby, her sewing laid aside. The candle on the stand shone on her long blond hair, but her eyes had an ominous light of their own. She sighed, rose from the chair, walked impatiently to the front window, and looked out, saying nothing. Drew sensed the tension and looked about. She was standing with her back to him, arms akimbo, taking deep breaths and letting them out in prolonged sighs.

"Say it, Beth," he urged quietly.

It was the cue she had been waiting for.

"Bartlett Calhoun is a snake!" she exploded. "I've never before wished a man dead, but for him I make an exception."

"Do you make *all* your enemies on first impression?" Drew asked, returning his eyes to the window. He smiled at Elizabeth's vehemence.

"Why Bess Calhoun stayed with him all those years, I cannot imagine! The old devil killed her!" she said.

Drew said nothing.

"He *did*!" she said, turning to glare at Drew. "Poor consumptive thing! With the heel of his boot he ground her right into the earth! If he had been mine, Drew, truly I would have killed him."

"He's a big man, Beth."

"No matter. I'd'a thrown a sheet over his worthless head, 'n then beat 'im to death with a board!"

"Now, Beth," he smiled, "you'd'a done no such thing."

"Ah! And wouldn't I, now! Try me sometime, Andrew Wolfe, and you'll see if I would!"

She let out one more sigh and came to stand beside him at the window. The tone of her voice softened.

"Drew," she said, "with her mother gone, Rachel's not safe in the same house with Bartlett Calhoun."

"No," he said quietly. "She's not safe. But it does puzzle me—what makes him take out his bitterness on *her*." Drew paused thoughtfully. "I've never known a brighter girl, or a more comely one. She'll be a fine woman someday."

"Not if *he* can help it," Elizabeth spat.

She placed her hands softly on Drew's shoulders and looked down at him, suddenly overcome with the enormous contrast between Drew and Bartlett Calhoun. She leaned down and pressed her warm cheek to his. "How happy I am you're mine," she whispered.

"That makes two of us," he said, smiling and pulling her down onto his lap. Elizabeth lay her head against his shoulder and looked into his gray eyes. He kissed her softly, lingeringly, and held her close. The wind made the glass of the window hum with its force.

Then, without warning, came a sudden pounding on the front door. Elizabeth quickly stood, straightening her skirts.

"What now?" Drew murmured as he rose from the window seat and reached for a lamp.

He pulled the door open and a gust of cold air roared in. He peered into the windblown darkness. There, within the circle of lamplight cast through the doorway, stood two figures, the taller holding the smaller by his side so closely they seemed one.

"Drew . . ." Donald spoke quietly, calmly, but there was agony in his face. About his shoulders was a badly worn great-coat with broad lapels, and on his head, a faded blue beret. Under his right arm he sheltered Rachel against the cold.

"Donald!" Drew reached out quickly, gripped his friend by the shoulder, and ushered the two inside.

"Donald? Rachel?" Elizabeth said as they came in. "You're both chilled through! Here, let me take that for you, dear." And she reached for Rachel's blanket. Elizabeth saw instantly that something was wrong, for Rachel was looking away, saying nothing, grasping a faded yellow shawl beneath her chin in such a way that it overshadowed her face. "Rachel?" Elizabeth said. "I'll take that shawl and lay it near the fire."

But Rachel pulled away, her face still in shadow.

"Rachel," Elizabeth said in her confusion, "what's wrong?"

"Donald, what's happened?" Drew insisted.

Donald's face grew red and he started to answer, but suddenly could not speak. His lips trembled and his eyes were rimmed with tears. Elizabeth looked at him in alarm. At last Donald turned to his sister.

"Rachel," he said, "let them see."

Donald's very movements were full of intense compassion and tenderness as he knelt before Rachel, gently lifted the tattered shawl, and laid it back on her shoulders. Elizabeth gasped and she covered her mouth with her hand.

"Dear God in heaven!" Drew Wolfe murmured.

Rachel stood at her full height before them. Her chin, lifted with a kind of defiant grandeur, was thrust forward, her teeth tightly clenched in rage. She looked neither to the left nor to the right, but with a cold right eye stared unflinchingly ahead. An angry bruise and purple swelling veined with a network of thin red lines hid her left eye altogether. On her left cheek a bright abrasion ran from the corner of her mouth to just below the wounded eye.

Elizabeth burst into tears. "How *could* he?" she sobbed. "Oh, Drew, how *could* he?" For—more terrible than her bruises—Rachel's long dark hair was gone, and only a mat of short ragged tufts remained.

At last Donald was able to tell the story. An hour ago, he said, with only Rachel and Bartlett in the house, their father had held Rachel to the floor under the rugged weight of his brutal, thick knees, and with his butcher knife, lock by lock, had cut her hair away.

Elizabeth was at once outraged and melting with sorrow. Hot tears blinded her eyes as she faced away from the girl, one clenched fist pressed hard beneath her breast and the other at her waist, every line of her body vibrating with hatred for this man.

"And on the very day when her mother was buried!" she exclaimed.

Drew knelt in front of Rachel, tears swimming as he cradled her face in his two hands. He lifted her chin until Rachel was looking at him with her one good eye. How like a child she seemed at this moment—how strange and far away that foolish moment of thirteen weeks ago.

Rachel turned her eyes away without moving her head, refusing to meet his gaze.

"Rachel," he said quietly, "look at me."

Then, ever so slowly, she turned her eye toward his, an eye so large and deep, so filled with a blend of darkness and light, swimming in tears, that Drew felt his own chin quiver in spite of himself.

"Oh, Rachel," he said. "Rachel, Rachel! God forgive me!"

A tear squeezed from the compressed corner of Rachel's injured eye, down onto the swell of her cheek. Suddenly sobbing, she threw herself against him and buried her face in his shoulder. Drew stiffened as if to withdraw from her embrace, then, realizing that Rachel's need was greater than his fears, he held her close.

"The sconce with the reflector, Beth," he said quietly. She brought it to him, and he shone the candlelight from a polished circle of tin onto Rachel's face, pressing tenderly beneath and above the raw abrasion.

"Nothin' broken," he said. He sighed deeply. "We'll put on a poultice to draw the swelling. It'll heal . . ." Then speaking only to Rachel, his voice became very soft but very strong as he said, "And your hair will grow."

Elizabeth added, "But the *deeper* damage is done . . . the humiliation, the attack. You *can't* erase that."

"Where's your father now, Donald?" Drew asked firmly.

"Passed out on his bed," Donald answered. Having found his voice, his blue eyes flashed and his words poured out in a torrent. "I'd'a died before I'd'a let 'im done it, Drew. Under God, I would've. I sware to heaven, I'd kill 'im for it, but then I'd be in the fire and . . ." he looked tenderly at his sister, "and she—she'd be alone with nobody to look out for her."

"You did right, Donald." Elizabeth was still trembling with anger and compressing her lips tightly. "You mustn't reproach yourself for this. The best you can do now is to keep it from happening again. Donald, you've got to leave Rachel with us."

Before Donald could answer, another voice broke in, firm and cold as steel.

"I'll not be goin' back," Rachel said, "whether you let me stay or not." They were the first words she had spoken.

"Of course you can stay," Donald said, "I can't be beside you forever, and here you'd be safe enough."

"And you, Donald, you'll stay with us the night," Drew said. "You need not go home in this storm."

"I've got to go," he answered, setting his jaw firmly. "With Mama gone, I'm all Daddy's got now to see he doesn't drown in his own vomit!"

FIFTEEN

DONALD turned up the collar of his greatcoat and went home through the driving snow. Bartlett lay stretched out, uncovered on his bed, the room cold. He was snoring so loudly that Donald heard him before he opened the door.

He stirred the few coals remaining on the hearth into life, laid on more peat, then sat on the floor, his hands about his knees, and stared emptily into the fire. Lord, how he wanted to wake up and find this day had been a dream! Or simply drop off to sleep and not wake up at all.

For a long time he sat, the hours passing and the years of their lives parading before his eyes. If only he had taken Rachel and run away when she was seven, she would be a different person now. If only Bess had had the courage to send Bartlett away, if she had refused to leave the valley when he first came back to them. If, if, if . . .

Donald's mind grew numb, his eyes heavy, and he fell asleep beside the hearth. A burst of wind rattling loose thatch on the roof and swooping down the smoke hole above the fire woke him. He looked at the face of the clock on the shelf. Five o'clock, sunrise still hours away. No sooner did he open his eyes than he became aware of a plan that must have formed in his mind while he was sleeping.

He got up, added fuel to the fire, and put a pot of water on to boil. Then he stepped to Bartlett's bedside. Bartlett was sleeping silently now, and Donald stood looking down at him, shaking his head as he thought of the twistedness of his father's life—a man who had laid down the reins of his lusts and let them run where they would. He reached down and shook Bartlett.

"What?" Bartlett slurred. "Who ... whataya want?"

"Daddy, wake up!" Donald said sharply. "Daddy, I think you'd best be up and about. I've somethin' to say to you."

"What in hell ..." Bartlett said. Grumbling to himself, he rose to sit on the side of his crumpled bed. "My damned head feels like there's a hammer inside it!" He swore bitterly, leaning forward, his head in his hands.

"Little wonder," Donald said coldly.

Donald lighted the crusie, measured meal into the boiling water, and set two bowls of corn gruel on the table.

"Come and eat," he commanded.

Without a word Bartlett went unsteadily to the table and sat down. The crusie's trembling frame shone yellow in his bloodshot eyes. Donald pulled up a chair across from him, folded his arms on the table, and stared steadily as Bartlett, making a quiet slurping sound, spooned the gruel into his mouth.

Strange, Donald thought, he looks ten years older than he did yesterday morning before the funeral. At last Bartlett, with the spoon lifted halfway to his mouth and his head bent forward to receive it, noticed that Donald was staring at him. He looked up beneath his bushy eyebrows. Donald's blue eyes were bright with intense purpose.

"What're you lookin' at me like that for?" he said gruffly.

Donald said nothing.

"Well?" Bartlett demanded. "You've got somethin' on your mind. What is it, or do I have to drag it out'a ya?"

"Daddy," Donald began slowly, and his voice was very calm, "unless I miss my guess, there'll be men from the village comin' to see you before the sun clears Hill MacLaren."

Calhoun let the spoon sink back into the gruel as the whites of his eyes expanded. "What for?" he said, his face blanching.

A sardonic smile spread across Donald's lips and he shook his head slightly in disgust. "You really don't remember?" he growled.

Donald rose from the table, went to his own trunk, opened it, and pulled out a cloth bag. He laid the bag on the table in front of Calhoun, who looked down at it, then up at Donald.

"Go ahead," Donald said, "open it."

With his thick fingers Calhoun loosed the drawstring and tugged it open. Reaching in, he pulled out a dark brown mass that appeared almost black in the weak light of the crusie and laid it on the table.

"Hair," he exclaimed dully.

Donald reached into his belt and with one swift motion pulled a long butcher knife and drove its point into the table between Calhoun's hands. Still the man's face was a blank.

"Somethin' about this I should remember?" he said.

"Don't you recognize your own daughter's hair?" Donald shouted at him, half rising and leaning across the table. Bartlett glared back, then picked up the mass and rubbed it slowly between his fingers.

"Rachel's hair?" he said. "What . . ." Slowly the light began to draw in his face. "My God."

"Daddy, I doubt God'll do you much good this time. The men who'll be poundin' on that door in about an hour'll not see much excuse for what you did. . . ."

Calhoun's eyes wandered nervously about the dark room. "They'll not come in this weather," he said weakly.

"Snow and wind won't stop 'em," Donald said. "It was all I could do to keep Drew Wolfe from roundin'um up last night at midnight an' comin' after you."

"The doctor's in on it?"

"He treated her cuts and bruises. That's where she is now."

"Cuts and bruises?" Calhoun's face went whiter than before, and he looked hard toward Rachel's bed. Up until now he had not realized it was empty.

"She'll recover," Donald said, "from the flesh wounds, at least. God only knows what the rest of it'll do to her! But," and his eyes softened a little, "Daddy, I think you'd better get your things together and go."

Calhoun paused, then rose with a lurch. He grabbed his head again, groaning and falling back against the table. Then he recovered and, as quickly as he could, got his belongings together.

Fifteen minutes later Donald followed Bartlett to the stable; he held the lantern as Calhoun fit a halter on the black stallion's head, cinched the saddle down with quick, hard jerks, and threw the canvas sack with all his belongings on behind. Then, with reins in hand, he mounted up.

As he started toward the gate, Bartlett turned his horse and looked down on Donald. Donald held the lantern high, for he wanted to see his father's expression as they spoke their final words. The snow was swirling about Bartlett's face, the force of the wind turning up the brim of his black felt hat, flattening it against the crown.

Calhoun's eyes, though redder now than before, were determined and focused. He looked hard at his son, his thick lips compressed in a straight line. This time, apparently, even Bartlett Calhoun had some dim idea of his guilt.

Donald, his eyes dry and clear, gazed unflinchingly up at him. He felt smug inside, his lips curved in a faint smile. "The weather's in your favor," he said, his words barely audible over the wind. "Folks hereabout haven't seen snow like this in years. They'll not want to follow very far."

Bartlett nodded and dropped his gaze to the ground. For a moment Donald thought he saw a tear in the man's eye, but perhaps it was only a snowflake that had stuck in his lashes and melted.

"Take good care of her," Bartlett said. For once his voice seemed almost humble, and a gust of wind caught his words and carried them away.

Donald lifted his chin in question.

"Take good *care* of her, I said!"

Donald flared inside. How dare the cursed old reprobate tell him to "take care of her"! What did he *think* he had been doing these years? Watching over her, protecting her, comforting her, doing the work of a father! But he only smiled.

"I'll take care of 'er," he said. Then, using every ounce of strength he could muster, Donald extended his hand. Calhoun reached down and shook it—hard.

"Good-bye, Daddy," he said, his voice void of emotion.

Bartlett's lips compressed, then relaxed and compressed again—as though he had been about to say something but thought better of it. Hesitantly he lifted his eyes to the gate that was just coming visible in the gray morning. It had blown open in the night. He set his bearded jaw and, without a word, clicked to the stallion, kicking him lightly with booted heel.

As Donald stood watching him ride out, a wave of immense relief flooded over him.

It was full light when Rachel woke up.

"Where am I?" she wondered hazily. The window was not in its proper place, and overhead, where smoke-blackened rafters should be, was a ceiling, smooth and white. And the bed. She ran her hand over the smooth sheet. The scent of the room was clean and fresh, free of gathered smoke.

Then the fog cleared from her head and she remembered.

"My hair!" she exclaimed aloud, and sat up, feeling with her hands. The short tufts told her it was not a dream. She swung her legs over the side of the bed. "A mirror," she said, looking around. "Where is a mirror?"

Unknown to Rachel, last night Elizabeth Wolfe had removed the large mirror from her room. "It would be too much for her to see herself now," she had told Drew.

A large chest stood against the east wall, across from Rachel's bed. In rapid succession she opened its drawers, rummaging noisily through them. There was a knock on the door.

"Rachel?"

Rachel shoved the bottom drawer closed and held her breath. "Elizabeth?"

"Yes, dear, it's me. May I come in?" And without waiting, she opened the door.

Rachel was standing before the chest. "I was looking for a mirror," she stammered.

"All right," Elizabeth said hesitantly, "I'll get you one."

When Elizabeth reappeared with a hand mirror, Rachel was sitting on the edge of her bed, one leg dangling off, the other tucked beneath her.

"Now, Rachel," Elizabeth said before handing it over, "you've got to remember that your face will heal—"

"Please, Elizabeth," Rachel said impatiently, "just let me see for myself."

Elizabeth handed her the mirror, and as Rachel held it up before her eyes, she winced and a little cry escaped her throat. The flesh around her left eye was puffed tight, and a deep purple bruise stained the entire side of her swollen face. Her chopped-off hair stood out in every direction.

Rachel dropped the mirror as though it was hot and hid her face in her hands. Her shoulders began to heave, and the tears ran between her fingers.

Elizabeth eased down on the bed beside her, handing her a handkerchief and slipping her arms about Rachel's shoulders.

"Go ahead and cry," she said tenderly. "It's a terrible thing your father's done; you've a right to hate him for it."

Rachel wept with great sobs. "Elizabeth," she said, her words interrupted with convulsed weeping, "I'd like to be alone. Please leave."

"You're sure?"

"Yes," she said, clenching the handkerchief in her fist. "Yes, please. I don't want *any*one to see me, not even you."

It was about noon when Donald walked back into the village with the news that Bartlett was gone. Elizabeth met him at the door.

"She's alone in her room," Elizabeth said. "She'll not come out, and she doesn't want anyone coming in. She's absolutely bitter with humiliation."

"Maybe she'll let me talk to her," Donald said.

Elizabeth led him to Rachel's door and knocked.

"Yes?" came a quiet, muffled voice.

"It's Donald," he said softly. "May I come in, Rachel?"

There was silence, then soft shuffling and the slide of a door bolt. He waited a moment longer as Elizabeth retreated into the parlor.

"Come in," he heard her say.

Rachel was sitting on the floor next to the low cased window, looking out into the falling snow. Donald went to her and, kneeling down on one knee, laid his hand on her arm. She didn't move when he touched her, but he felt the current of her anger running through his hand.

It felt good to have Donald's touch, but in her fury she could not let him know. She wanted to throw her arms around him and bury her face in his shoulder, but she could not.

"Donald," she said abruptly, her voice trembling with emotion, "you must never let him near me again! Not ever as long as I live! I hate him, and what I failed at doin' once, I'll try again . . . and this time I'll do it right!"

"It's over, Rachel," he said slowly. "Daddy's gone."

She showed no sign of having heard.

"Did you hear me, Rachel? He's gone."

"Gone where?" she muttered, still staring out the window, her arms folded tightly over her breast.

"God only knows," he said, "but gone away . . . this time for good. It's just you and me now."

"Are you sure?" she asked, looking at him for the first time.

"I'm sure. But Rachel, Daddy was so drunk when he cut your hair, he didn't even know what he'd done. For the first time ever, I think, I saw shame in his eyes. The whole thing terrified him." Donald paused for a moment. "Rachel, I lied to him. He thought every man in town was comin' after him. He lit out in the snow. To tell the truth, Rachel . . . as I watched him go, though I felt relieved, I felt a little sorry for him, too."

Rachel sprang to her feet and turned to face him, fire in her one good eye, her face glowing red.

"There you go again, Donald Calhoun," she shouted, "makin' excuses for him! Why must you? Look at my face! Look at my hair! He's a piteous, hateful man! For once, just once, Donald, be as angry with him as I, and make no excuses!"

Abruptly she turned her face to the window, trembling.

"Rachel?"

"Just go, Donald," she said. "It's gonna be a while before I can get over your takin' his side against mine."

"Rachel, that was not what—"

"Please, Donald. Just go!"

As she stood trembling, watching the snow fall, the door closed behind her. She turned slowly to the dresser, picked up the mirror, and peered into it again. As she looked in disgust at her spiky locks, and with her finger traced the puffy bruise, she felt the anger boiling inside—anger at Bartlett, anger at Donald, anger at Bess and Bess's God.

"Oh, dear, sweet, weak God of my mother!" she said. "What have you to say to me now!"

It was a full week before Rachel returned to the cottage—not because she was unable, but because she did not want to be seen. A kerchief tied around her head hid her shorn hair, but her eye was still purple and swollen. At last Elizabeth insisted she go, and insisted Drew go along to carry her things.

As Rachel and Drew trudged up the hill toward the upper edge of the village, Drew balancing a large canvas bag on his shoulder, neither could think of anything to say. It was the first time they had been alone since that day on Hill MacLaren, three weeks before Drew and Elizabeth were married. When they reached the gate, he opened it for her and set the bag down inside the fence.

"This is as far as I go," he said.

She turned and looked into his eyes. "Because you don't trust me?" she said.

"Because I don't trust myself," he answered.

She looked at him with surprise.

"No," suddenly alarmed, "I shouldn't've . . . please forget I said that," he stammered. "It's just that I can't forget, and I wish I could."

Rachel's expression grew tender and her voice soft. "It's over for me," she said consolingly.

"Is it?" he asked, feeling a tinge of disappointment.

"Yes," she said. "Now, Elizabeth is the best friend I have on this earth, and I'd do nothing to betray her."

"Nor would I, Rachel."

"I know you wouldn't," she said. "You proved your strength to me long ago, and I trust you." She reached out and squeezed his hand.

Rachel watched after him as he disappeared down the road. He had surprised her, saying he didn't trust himself with her; she would have never guessed. As for herself, she had meant every word she said.

For both Donald and Rachel the winter without their mother was lonely beyond expression. Again and again, as she went about her work, Rachel looked up expecting to see Bess at her loom. At times she even heard the thudding of the treadle and the sound of her mother's voice, but her eyes fell only on the cold emptiness of the loom's worn bench, and on the treadle so deathly still, and it pierced her heart like a dagger of ice.

It was not just the loneliness, it was the rape of her tender childhood, and that last terrible act of violence that had torn the fabric of her mind in a way unknown to her before. What could it all mean? What was she to think of herself? Daddy always told her she got exactly what she deserved.

Today—a day in the middle of May—she felt her mother's presence in the room so strongly she could not endure it. She was doing laundry in the old wooden tub when it struck her. She suddenly straightened, wiped the suds from her hands onto her apron, and ran to the door. Once in the open she plunged into the tall grasses above the cottage and turned across the moor toward her pond.

Soon she was lying stretched on her back, alone in the high gentle meadow. The sun was warm, and within reach of her hand the cold water shimmered in the sunlight. Ducks murmured as they fed, quietly paddling in and out of the cattail reeds growing thick around its shores.

This pond was still her favorite of all places. Sometimes in her loneliness she came here, other times she went again to the old abbey; and when she was there within the walls, in her mind she could see the flashing legs of girls dancing in the moonlight, and could feel the spell of the enchantress's words that saved her from death. What of it if the woman sang her song to the moon? If she could not believe in her mother's God, at least Rachel knew that on that night Mystery had touched her.

Timothy MacKnighton had come after Bartlett went away, but Rachel had refused to see or think of him since the day she was shorn ... or was it since the day she had kissed Drew Wolfe? One was vanity and the other devotion, but no matter; she would not see Timothy again—and Drew she could not have.

Above her in the rowan tree, where its branches overgrew the great rock on which she lay, a dozen tiny gray birds with dark brown slashes on their breasts flitted and chirped and played. The tree was just putting out leaves, but already had blossomed with a multitude of little snowy fans.

She gazed up at the playful birds. How peaceful and happy they seemed. Sometimes she watched them in wild flight, and her heart wished to be with them as they swooped and dived and soared.

Rachel reached over the rock's edge and plucked from the pond's surface one small white flower that a bird's play had made flutter down. She was thinking of yesterday and her morning visit with Elizabeth Wolfe. These days she saw Elizabeth often, to walk or work together at sewing and spinning.

How strange, she thought, that Elizabeth seemed to need her as much as she needed Elizabeth. They were two very different women. Elizabeth was older, but not by much, and was beautiful, yet she was blond and Nordic. Rachel was not unaware of her own beauty, but hers was of a darker, Mediterranean kind. She realized how impulsive she herself had become, how brooding, how given to fanciful ideas, while Elizabeth was steady, practical, and methodic. Yet she felt at home with Elizabeth, felt her emotions at the very time Elizabeth was feeling them. Once she had awakened in the night, and somehow *knew* that Elizabeth and Drew were at that moment disagreeing sharply.

As Rachel smoothed the velvety flower petal between her fingers, she mused over what Elizabeth had said to her yesterday.

"What is it I see in your eyes today, Rachel? You seem so far away."

Rachel had answered by shrugging her shoulders slightly and smiling, but she knew it had been a sad smile.

"I love your coming here," Elizabeth had said.

Then she thought of how Elizabeth had reasoned with her so earnestly.

"I'm afraid for you, Rachel," she had said, laying her sewing in her lap and looking at her earnestly. "I'm afraid that either you'll become unspeakably bitter and distrust everyone, or that you will despise yourself and become the slave of some evil man—just as your mother was."

Rachel shook her head and tossed the petal back onto the water. That was just what Mama had said before she died, she thought.

One of the tiny birds lit on a cattail that had burst into a cloud of seed and sat pecking greedily at its perch. A breeze sprang up, ruffling the waters, shaking a shower of white blossoms into the air, some lighting on the water, some along the cattails.

Suddenly she realized that her lonely mood had passed. It always happened that way. If she came close to the earth, it always had the power to heal her mind, and the winds to blow her sadness away.

She sat up and gazed across the meadow where it fell away to the village and then to the loch. Donald would be coming home soon, and she must have a meal for him—not because he demanded it, of course, but because she loved him, and because in more ways than one, she owed him her very life.

SIXTEEN

As the year 1770 dawned, the Highlands were dismal with decayed glory. The marauding English Lion had devoured national pride. Everywhere the young looked, poverty stared at them. Clan life was dead, their lands divided among outsiders. For a clansman, there was no future in the Highlands.

So the exodus continued—men and women going by the

thousands—some to sea, others to Britannia's colonies in Africa and South America. Some thought life in the British army better than this. But for most the great magnet lay to the southwest, in the distant land of North America. From across the North Atlantic the American colonies sang a siren's song, and thousands went after it. And as the glens and braes emptied, those who remained felt a deepening air of perpetual sadness.

In February of '70 a young woman in Lochredfern died in childbirth. Early in March contagion carried away three children of one family, all within a week.

"You did all you knew to do, darling," Elizabeth comforted Drew.

"That's just it, Beth!" he said, pacing the floor of their bedroom. "If I had only *known* more, then I might have saved them! The University of Edinburgh has the finest medical school in Europe, and yet all the time I was there I saw not one dissection, and counted the pulse of not one fevered child! Everything I learned there came from books. Surely, Beth, a medical school can do better than that. What I know, I owe to an old village doctor, and when he died, my training came to an end! All I have to look forward to is slow improvement through trial and error. And think of those who'll die while I'm learning!"

One week from that day, an English ship hove into harbor for repairs, and the ship's crew came ashore, including the ship's doctor. Drew was sitting in a dreary state of mind at a table in the Lochredfern Tavern when they came in. The doctor was a gruff sort, fifty or older, Drew guessed. By a stroke of fate he came to Drew's table and introduced himself. It did not take long for the conversation to turn toward medicine.

"Best place in the world to study," he said, "is Philadelphia Medical College. Founded only five years ago—excellent opportunity! Philadelphia's the second-largest English-speaking city in all the world, and Philadelphia Hospital is one of the best—grand, spacious." The man's voice was coarse and his gestures expansive. "Dr. William Shippen lectures on midwifery and obstetric procedures every week. The town's got dozens of fine medical men more than willing to lecture and take apprentices. Four thousand practicing physicians in the American colonies—only about three hundred from the European universities." He looked sharply at Drew as he spoke.

"Man like you could start pretty high on the ladder over there."

Between the tavern and home, Drew Wolfe's mind was aflame. He stared at the ground ahead of him, mumbling excitedly to himself.

"Mornin', Dr. Wolfe."

"What? Oh, mornin', MacKenzie! Didn't see you."

MacKenzie passed by, and Drew was lost in thought again.

"What a chance!" he told Elizabeth. "I could learn everything there is to know. And comin' from the university, I'd be way ahead o' the game! And Beth," he said, "we'd feel right at home there. Jones says Pennsylvania's a third German, a third English, and a third Scots, full of men and women with names like MacDonald, MacPherson, and Cleary. It would be like goin' home. Whataya think, Beth?"

Elizabeth looked at him in wonder. Obviously he had already made up his mind.

On Friday morning, the first of June, Rachel was in the yard bent over a patch of soil beneath the cottage eaves, spading it for flower planting, when she looked up and saw Elizabeth coming on the run, her face alight with happiness.

"Elizabeth," Rachel called out, pleasantly surprised.

"Rachel!" Elizabeth answered breathlessly as she reached the gate. "Oh, Rachel, I've the most wonderful news!"

Rachel raised up, smiling, wiping her hands on her apron. "Whatever is it?" she asked.

"Rachel," she said, taking Rachel's hands in hers, "Drew has decided to go to America!"

"America!" Rachel exclaimed. She felt suddenly sick. "Why to America? I had no idea . . ."

"He made me promise not to tell until he was sure. He's going to study medicine in Philadelphia."

That night, Rachel could not sleep, and when first light broke, she was standing breathless at Elizabeth's door. She must go with them, she decided. She *must* go to America.

Though she loved the craggy heights of the Highlands, the excitement of winds sweeping in from the sea, the smell of heather in the spring, and the dusky oranges of the widespread hills, Scotland was also the scene of all Rachel's bitter memories. Perhaps in America she could begin again.

* * *

"No!" Drew's voice was firm.

"Don't be a mule, Drew," Elizabeth countered. It was evening, the same day Rachel had told them she was going. The argument had begun at supper and kept up until now as they lay in bed. He had drifted off to sleep once, but Elizabeth had wakened him with a new salvo.

"Drew," her voice had an icy edge to it, "I can't sleep till this thing is settled."

"It *is* settled." Drew was only half awake.

"You can't know what this means to her, Drew," Elizabeth said quietly. "Rachel thinks America would be a refuge for her—away from the place where her mother died, from the place where her father hurt her. Don't you see that it could be a new beginning for her as well as for you and me? How can we deny her?"

"All you say is true, Beth," Drew sighed, fully awake, "but none of it really matters. Donald couldn't part with her. And, Beth, where would the money for her passage come from?"

"There'd be a way," she answered. After a long silence when each could hear only the other's breathing, Elizabeth, staring hard into the room's blackness, spoke again. This time there was anger in her voice.

"Andrew Wolfe, I can't believe you would think of leaving that girl to face her father alone."

"Her father's gone," he answered, his voice thin with frustration.

"But you know perfectly well he's sure to come back!" she said. "And volatile and giddy as that girl is, she'll provoke him to kill her. You just cannot leave her here!"

Drew was feeling desperate. He did not *want* Rachel to accompany them to America, just as he had secretly not wanted her to come and live within the same four walls with them in the winter.

He was afraid of himself in Rachel's presence. No one knew about that morning on the mountain when they had kissed, but he knew. Medicine wasn't his only reason for leaving Scotland. He wanted to put an ocean between himself and this girl.

"Beth," he pleaded, "she's not alone; she has Donald. Don't you see the girl's as dear to me as she is to you? We can do *nothing* more for her—and there's an *end*!"

Drew waited for Beth's reply, but the only sound he heard was her head rolling away from him on her pillow. Soon he dropped again into sleep, but Elizabeth lay thinking. There *was* something she could do; there had to be. But if there was, she must do it on her own.

The infernal stench of the tannery drifted through every door and window in Lochredfern. Changing winds wafted it first to one part of the village and then to another, except when the weather was still and damp, and then it settled, a blanket of smells covering the town.

These thick aromas rose from vats of limewater where hides lay rotting to make the hair "slip," from calf hides curing in a thick soup of pigeon dung, and from great piles of animal hair that stood sogging and reeking until the plasterer could come and cart them away.

Today the big doors of the low stone building stood open to the early morning, pouring out its mixture of rancid odors. Around the yard, stacks of fresh hides stood under sheds, and on a half-dozen racks sheets of already tanned leather lay draped, drying in the sun.

Rachel did not like the tannery, but today, feeling lost and alone, she came to find her brother. As she rounded the corner of the building, her mind was so far away that she barely noticed the horrendous smells.

Her dark hair was still a poor thing compared to what it was before her father butchered it. It had grown to a point below her ears, and she had trimmed it in a bob such as a Dutch boy might wear. Her smooth face gave no hint of the savage bruise her father had inflicted upon her. In stark contrast to the tannery, Rachel's appearance was crisp and fresh in a bleached linen blouse and tan skirt that reached to her feet.

Nonetheless, her spirit was low. As she entered, Donald looked up from his work and saw her lifeless face. He had a long, iron-hooked pole in his hands, and was stirring the mass of limp hides that lay soaking in the tanning vats. His thick leather apron, once a very light brown, was deeply stained with blood and fats and tanning liquor.

"Morning," he said.

She smiled slightly, and then simply stood watching the sinew and muscle of his arms as he hooked the hides and, with mighty effort, turned them over in the thick brown broth.

At last he stopped, leaned on the long pole, and wiped his brow with a stained handkerchief, searching her face. He looked down again at the vat, and for a long moment watched the bubbles rising and breaking on the dark surface.

"Rachel," he said slowly, then paused for want of the right words. "Rachel," he repeated, "I know how bad you want to go to America." He paused. "But do you know, if you go, I'd never see you again."

Her expression did not change. "I know," she said, "and I don't think I could've borne it, to be away from you forever. But I did want so to go!"

"Try to forget it, Rachel," he said with deep feeling. "I'll do my best, poor as it is, to make life better for you, at least until you find someone to take my place."

Rachel looked up and smiled, a quiet and simple smile of gratitude, then started for the door.

"I'm going down to the boats," she said, looking back, her mood a little brighter. "I'll bring you fresh fish at noon."

It was the following day, early in the morning. Donald had eaten his breakfast and was ready to leave for the tannery.

For a moment he stood near the door and looked about him. Yes, he thought, there's peace in this place now, with Mama at rest and Daddy away. He looked at his sister lying in her bed against the north wall, sleeping so quietly.

The mantel clock struck once for the half hour, its lingering mellow tone filling the room. Its hands indicated five-thirty, but the summer day had long since dawned. At these latitudes the sun rose as early in the late spring and in summer as it rose late in the winter. Sunlight was pouring in through the windows—deep-cased windows that made one feel the thickness of the cottage walls.

Rachel had planted morning glories in a window box only a month ago, and now the vines were climbing the little trellis she had made, their large blue trumpets radiant in the sun. He remembered how she had waited months for the seed to come—all the way from London. And her excitement when they arrived. That very day, she had cut a tiny nick in each hard seed case and soaked them in water before planting. Now, with the window box above her bed, each morning when she awoke they were there to greet her in all their wondrous blue.

The sunlight's brightness made the entire room seem beautiful in its simplicity: a freshly swept dirt floor, rough furnishings, and whitewashed walls. Rachel had found the energy to transform this poor place into something their mother had never imagined.

Donald stepped quietly to the bed and looked down on her

face, so peaceful and relaxed in slumber. He understood now that in spite of all Rachel's comeliness, in spite of her fire and intelligence, her emotions often played her false. She was a caring, compassionate girl, but quick to anger, quick to joy—and when her emotions ran high, she often acted without thinking. It was as though there was little that mediated between her mind and her actions.

But as the sun flooded the flowers and illuminated the white linen coverlet that lay over her, he knew that at the core she would one day be an even better woman than their mother, for Rachel had the courage not only to bear a thing, but to fight back. He did not want to disturb her sleep, but this morning he must. He reached down and shook her gently.

She opened her eyes, squinting at the brightness. Then, smiling, she took his hand and squeezed it affectionately, as through sleepy eyes she looked up at the morning glories.

"How lovely!" she said, the huskiness of sleep still in her voice.

"Yes," he said quietly, then paused. "Rachel . . ." There was a note of excitement in his voice. "Rachel, I've got to tell you something that can't wait till evening. I had a visitor at the tannery yesterday afternoon."

Rachel raised herself on one elbow to listen, her eyes filled with curiosity. "Who?" she asked.

"I'll not tell you who," he said, "but this visitor and I—we had a long talk, and I've changed my mind about something very important."

Her smile faded, giving way to mounting interest. She listened intently as he went on.

"This is a lovely place, Rachel. You've turned it into a true home for us." He paused and searched her eyes. "But I see it now; there're too many memories here for either you or me ever to be happy—really happy, I mean."

As understanding flooded in, she felt tears rising in her eyes. Could it be true?

"We should go, Rachel. You and I together, to America."

"Oh, Donald!" she exclaimed. She came up out of the bed, put her arms around him and, laying her head on his shoulder, began to laugh and weep at the same time. He could feel the excitement coursing through her.

"Ohhh," she gasped again, and then, when she'd had a moment to think, she drew back. "But Donald, how?"

"I think I know a way," he said, "my visitor and I." He

smiled conspiratorially. "But I can't tell you . . . there are reasons." He spoke firmly. "Say nothing about it to anyone . . . just trust me."

She gazed into his eyes, trying to find some clue. At last, smiling through tears of happiness, Rachel hugged him again.

"All right, Donald," she said breathlessly, "I'll wait . . . and I'll trust you."

SEVENTEEN

It was a June morning three weeks later, the sun standing high over MacLaren Mountain, and Rachel had just come out of the cottage to look at the sky.

High above, through the leaves of the birches, windblown wisps traced long patterns against the blue—a promise of wind or rain in three days, her mother had always said.

In an idle mood, she ambled about the yard until she came to the place where the hill fell away toward the village. She could see the entire loch from here, from where the river entered to the place where it emptied into the sea. Wind currents playing about the loch's face made patches of shimmering sunlight so bright she had to turn her eyes away.

Then her heart leapt into her throat! For there on the breast of the loch was a three-masted ship resting at anchor! It had slipped in at night by the light of a nearly full moon. She felt her heart skip, and her breathing was fast.

"That *has* to be it," she said aloud. "The ship! *Our* ship, down from the Orkneys!"

How strange she felt, how charged with anticipation! The prospect of America, a place of forgetfulness, a place where the hard, stony memories of childhood would fade away like a Highland mist.

Then, unbidden, another emotion rose in her breast; a petulance, an anger at Drew Wolfe, who would have left her behind. Well, she thought, and she pursed her lips in a little smirk, we'll see, and so will Doctor Andrew Wolfe!

* * *

"The ship is in, Andrew!" He heard the front door slam and her voice from down below.

Elizabeth came running up the stairs, her blond hair bouncing on her shoulders, her skirts flying. Excitement glowed from her bright blue eyes.

"Oh, Drew," she said, "the ship is in!"

Drew Wolfe laid down the quill and, quickly rising from his desk, looked out the upper-story window. He could see it clearly—tall masts and wide spars crossing and recrossing above a sleek, dark hull. At this moment boats were being lowered from the starboard davits.

"That's the one," he said. "It won't be long now; two days, a week perhaps. We'll soon know."

Elizabeth cast her eyes about the chamber where Drew's things lay ready to be packed.

"I know how excited you are about this, Drew," she said as she ambled among the stacks waiting to be put in trunks and boxes.

"But?" he asked.

"But you've seemed quieter yesterday and the day before."

He only shrugged, continuing to gaze out the window, and did not answer.

Elizabeth looked at the stack of books. How he loved his books, she thought, how devoted to his task Drew was, how fervently he had read in order to become a better physician, how he had scraped and saved to buy the best instruments.

She fingered the covers and examined the titles. *Officinalis and Extemporanea: A Complete English Dispensatory, in Two Parts, Theoretic and Practical*, by Quincy; *Miscellaneous Observations in the Practise of Physick, Anatomy and Surgery*, London. She shook her head and smiled, glad these were his to read and not hers. But no matter; his mind was equal to it.

Spread out on a table was an array of instruments: an ivory medicine dropper, numbered bottles and vials, and some instruments that made her shiver: a trephine for boring into fractured skulls, a forked retractor, scalpels, needles for sewing, a saw and tourniquet for amputation, bullet extractors; on and on—so many that as she gazed at them, they lost their individual meaning.

"Beth," Drew said, not turning from the window. There was a question in his voice.

"Yes?" She turned toward him, smiling.

"You've said no more about her."

"About who, dear?"

"Don't play games with me, Beth." He turned to her, an indulgent smile on his face.

"You mean Rachel," she said quietly, dropping her gaze to the floor and smiling.

"Yes—Rachel. It isn't like you to just give up."

"You said we'd reached an end," she answered.

Drew smiled and snorted, then turned back to the window.

When Drew married Elizabeth, he had been sorry to leave his father James, alone on the mountain, but this was much harder, going away, certain they would never see each other again. But Drew's two sisters lived nearby. One had married a tacksman, and the other married Lochredfern's only blacksmith. His older brother Robert was gone.

When Robert was seventeen, he fought at Culloden. That was twenty-four years ago, the year before Drew was born. When Drew was only two, Robert had left the Highlands for America, and settled somewhere in the Mohawk Valley. He had written, then without explanation his letters stopped. It was as though he had simply disappeared from the earth. Most thought he had been killed by an American savage, but James and Flora never knew.

Drew hoped that when the day came for him to leave, there would be no tears, just a quiet resolution. Both he and his father were typical Highland men who hid their emotions, but at heart they were very close. Robert's long-ago disappearance did make it harder, though.

It was early Tuesday morning when Drew trudged up to James's cottage. He entered without knocking and found his father bending over the griddle, preparing breakfast. James was sturdily built, dressed in black woolen trousers and a billowy-sleeved shirt of off-white Osnaburg. His hair was pure white, but he gave the impression of agility and great strength as he rose from the fire.

"The horses fed?" Drew asked.

"Aye. Long before the sun reached the rim."

Two terriers, both with black, wiry hair, square-built and short-legged, were lying beside the fire. One got up and sniffed at Drew's rough brown boots, then, apparently satisfied, returned to the warmth of the hearth. James was fox hunter to the district. When sheep replaced the cattle, fox were a constant nuisance. James kept the gritty, energetic feists to go into the foxes' dens and drag them out.

"I see a ship's dropped anchor in the harbor," James said.

"Yes, sir. She's here." Drew laid his hand on his mother's great old walking wheel and gave it a slow spin. "I went down yesterday and met her master—a man named Hamilton."

"How long's she gonna be here?" James asked as he poured on the batter.

"A week, maybe two. She's old and took damage last week in a storm off Cape Wrath. Got to do repairs."

"Down from the Orkneys?"

"Yes, sir."

"What's she got on board?"

"Wool, barrels of pickled cod, mostly. But a few passengers, too. All of 'em leavin'—same as we."

Here at last was the thing neither man wanted to touch. After a long pause, Drew heard the clank of the chain as his father took the griddle from the fire and the scrape of the knife as he cut the bread.

"Eat with me, Andrew," his father said, then paused and looked up at him. "It may be the last time."

And so the older man poured the younger a fresh cup of warm milk, set the pitcher on the old table, and handed Drew a wooden plate with a wedge of bannock and a thick piece of yellow cheese.

A long silence followed, each man aware of the sound of his own chewing—and aware that after another week, they would never meet again. At last James broke the silence.

"Andrew," he said, "I've been thinkin' of your brother . . . and how when you reach America you could ask after him, and see what you might find."

Drew broke off a small piece of cheese and stared at it for a while before he answered.

"Yes, sir," he said. "I've thought on that very thing. But I'll be a long way from the Mohawk Valley, and it'll be a while before I can do much about it."

"That's sure enough," James answered, "and I'll understand it. Even so, I'd be grateful for what you can do. Somehow it would help me to know what became of him. I'd like to know if ever he married, if maybe he had children, and if he did, how it was that no one ever let us know when he died." There was a long pause, and for the first time in his life, Drew heard James say it. "Robert must've died," the old man said, a tired look passing across his eyes, "else he would've found a way to tell us." Another pause. "You boys have always been so close to my heart, and it's hard to go on, not knowin'."

The old man's last words had been a choked whisper that made Drew look from the piece of cheese to his father's face. James looked quickly down to his plate. Drew did not know that his father could weep, but there was the glint of tears swimming in his eyes now.

"You can count on me, sir," Drew said quietly. "As soon as I can."

James nodded his white head without looking up.

"I'll be grateful," he said again.

Evening of their last day in Lochredfern. All day long, Drew and Elizabeth Wolfe had greeted callers, but Rachel Calhoun was not among them.

"Too hard for her to say good-bye," Drew said to Elizabeth, as he tightened the knot in a rope around a box of books. "I think we oughta go and find her."

"Why force ourselves on her?" Elizabeth asked.

"Because she's pouting," Drew insisted, frowning. Then softening, he added, "And because I'd like to see her one last time."

Rachel was at her spring-fed pond above the village, sitting near the southern shore, on the big flat rock amid tall reeds and overshaded by the rowan tree. She gazed up at the great old hill in whose shoulder the pond reposed. The sun—an hour or more from setting—bathed the heather in soft light, warming the back of her bare neck. Rachel always favored the warm light of evening and morning to the washed-out light of midday.

The air was perfectly still, as without warning a low-flying hawk crested the rise just above her then came low, hovering over the branches of the rowan tree, so near she could see every marking in its feathers, and even the glint in its eye. Breathlessly she watched, and a warm feeling flooded her entire body. The hawk was her friend, a messenger sent by someone from out of space and out of time.

It whistled and wheeled away on slanting wings toward some hidden nest, some repository where her spring clutch waited, and Rachel watched after it, a warm smile on her lips.

The bird's coming reminded her of yesterday, when she had

gone down to the kirkyard. There she had sat at the foot of an ancient spruce near her mother's grave.

"Mama," she had said, "I'm goin' away. I hope you don't mind. Likely I'll never be back." She paused and wiped a tear. "I don't know why I'm tellin' you this. You already know, for you came to me in a dream to tell me I'd be goin'. And it was written in your face that you were glad."

At that moment another hawk, or perhaps this very one, had swooped down between the branches of the trees, calling out as it descended, with a shrill and yet harsh kreee, kreee, kreee, and then had circled her mother's grave again and again and again, all the while calling kreee, kreee, kreee.

Like a thunderbolt in her chest the knowledge had come— Mama had flown away from this place, and this winged one had come as her messenger. She had scrambled to her feet, left the kirkyard, and walked rapidly out across the hillside, filled with ecstasy and certain knowledge that somewhere her mother lived, that she knew, and that she understood her going.

As Rachel looked out across the pond, a pang struck her heart.

"Why should I want so to leave this holy place?" she wondered aloud. "But I do want to leave. I want to cross an ocean, see a new place, leave the old things behind!" Her heart was on tiptoe.

On the pond's water, rippling gold in the lowering sun, three wild ducks paddled softly, silently dipping their heads to feed . . . murmuring as they went. Then, as they swam toward the pond's farther edge, Rachel's gaze was caught by a movement lower down in the meadow. A distant voice broke into her dream.

"Rachel!"

For a long moment she did not answer, then, watching as a man and a woman bobbed higher among the grasses, she smiled to herself.

"Elizabeth," she said, so softly they scarcely heard, "here I am." Elizabeth and Drew came up to the pond's edge where the reeds began. The pond lay between them and Rachel. Drew spoke across the quiet water.

"We've come to tell you good-bye, Rachel," he said.

At the sound of his voice the ducks took alarm, flapped their wings furiously, and exploded from the water, the feet of the hindmost duck dipping once, twice, three times, farther apart with each skip, until they were away, flying low toward the marsh surrounding the lower creek. Rachel's eyes followed their going. Again she did not immediately respond, and then, as if in a muse, said quietly, "This is a *wonderful* place, isn't it? If only I could come here always, every day for the rest of my life." At the end her voice trailed off to nothing.

"Rachel?" Drew was puzzled and hurt. "Aren't you going to tell us good-bye?" Elizabeth smiled slightly.

Then, for the first time, Rachel looked directly at them. Even across the pond they could see how large and clear her dark eyes were. She shook her head with what seemed to be profound sadness.

"No," she said. Her voice was smooth and very full. "I don't want to tell you good-bye. I want to go with you."

Drew said nothing.

"I've heard said," Rachel went on, "that America is a wonderful place, but this pond is so full of peace. I really should stay here."

"Peace is needful for you, isn't it, Rachel?" Elizabeth said quietly, glancing sidelong at her husband.

"Sometimes, Beth"—she had taken for her own Drew's pet name for his wife—"sometimes I just come so unraveled it *hurts*." She straightened her shoulders, looked about, and breathed deeply. "That's when I come here, and the unraveling just . . . goes away."

She's acting! Drew thought. Why, the theatrical little . . . He could think of no appropriate word to finish.

Inside Rachel was smiling, and felt herself on the verge of wickedness. Let him beg for a warm word of farewell; she would not give it!

At last the sun's disk dipped behind the far blue line of islands, and the first night chill dropped down.

"You don't know the meadow very well," she said to them. "You'd better go while there's light, or you're sure to stumble into a bog or ditch."

She saw the puzzlement in his eyes. He looked directly at her one last time, started to say something, then decided it was no use.

"Well," he said awkwardly, "anyway, Rachel, good-bye."

"Good-bye, dear," Elizabeth said, smiling.

"Good-bye, Elizabeth," she said warmly, ". . . and Drew."

Drew took Elizabeth's hand, looked about, and walked away across the meadow.

EIGHTEEN

An hour on board, and all was ready. Drew and Elizabeth were at the rails, silently saying good-bye to Lochredfern forever.

The loch's shining water rippled before the wind, and after days of idleness, common seamen strained against windless arms, the ship's great anchor cable groaning upward. Men aloft on the yardarms released the sails, and the heavy canvas dropped and immediately billowed out with loud snapping thuds. The vessel began to glide, slowly, then more rapidly, until it was plowing the loch's waters earnestly westward.

As MacLaren Mountain faded into the distance, Drew and Elizabeth turned their attention to the deck. Sailors were hurrying about, climbing in the rigging—whistling signals, shouting orders, hauling lines. The barrels of salted whitefish and pickled cod below mixed with the smells of aging wood and oakum-tarred ropes.

Elizabeth watched the passengers who lined the rails, all part of a thin but steady stream flowing out of the coves and inlets of the Highlands since the Clearances were passed. Too many for a ship this size, she thought, old men, small children, some with a lost look in their eyes, young farmers and their wives, two hundred at least.

Within hours *Swan* had threaded the narrows between Loch Redfern and the sea. Isle of Skye lay before them a grayish-blue bank of mountains rising out of the southwestern horizon. The ship bore south through the sounds of Sleat and Rhum. After two days, Tiree and Coll passed to port, and far to starboard the mists over the Outer Hebrides faded behind. The wind was fair, and by noon on the third day only the wild and empty Atlantic lay before them.

Swan was a fourth-rate vessel of three masts, English built, and launched in 1716, fifty-four years ago. She had two decks and a lower hold, could mount fifty-six guns and carry a crew of three hundred. But to make room for cargo, Captain Ham-

116

ilton had cut the crew to fifty, and she mounted only a dozen guns.

At night and in foul weather the passengers packed below deck as tightly as the fish in their barrels, each man, woman, and child in a space scarcely two by six feet—not quite the size of a decent grave. Tools and implements, chests filled with clothes and remembrances of cherished braes and glens, were all stored away in the holds below, along with the fish.

The age and condition of the ship made it instantly clear that this would not be a comfortable voyage. Hamilton said that with the most favorable winds, passage would take seven weeks, but more likely ten, even twelve.

Today, as *Swan* passed from under the lee of the outer island, the north winds hit her, singing and moaning among the rat lines and through the standing rigging, snapping the ragged edges of sails worn alarmingly thin. The ship heeled sharply to port, sending unwary passengers reeling into the rails and unsecured baggage sliding. Then on the wings of the wind came clouds bearing rain. At first the rain pelted the decks lightly, then advanced in great blue curtains of water that swept the passengers down the ladderways and left them huddling cold and wet on the lower deck.

Drew and Elizabeth sat hunched in their billet near the stern where, thankfully, a portside window let in light just behind them. In their westward course, that window would always face south toward the sun. They huddled close in the semidarkness as the rain pounded the upper deck, leaning together against the thick oak slabs of the hull. A press of subdued passengers, murmuring low, lay about them on three sides. Elizabeth drew her feet up beneath their heavy wool blanket and rubbed her toes to drive out the chill.

The beamed ceiling hovered low. Gray daylight filtered down through uncaulked cracks—and rainwater, soaking skin and clothes, ran in little rivers down the sides.

"It's the quarterdeck right above us keeping us dry," Elizabeth whispered to Drew. "Thank God for that."

Drew nodded.

With sickening regularity the ship lunged forward and down, then forward and up, her bow alternately plowing deep into the oncoming swell, lifting nearly free, slackening and plunging, slackening and plunging. The huddled mass of passengers weaved and rolled with the ship's motion.

"And thank God," she said, "for the wall to lean against."

"Hull," Drew corrected. She cut her eyes at him.

"Thank God for the *hull*, then," she said, a trifle impatiently. Then, "Can we do it, Drew?"

"Do what?"

"Make it across this ocean?" The slanting deck pressed them firmly to the hull, while others were hard pressed to keep from sliding into them. On Elizabeth's left an old woman with water blue eyes hunched up against her. Even through their thick blankets, Elizabeth could feel the woman's thinness and the angles of her protruberant bones.

"Nothing else we *can* do," he answered with resignation.

The heat of two hundred bodies warmed the damp air, and the smell of unbathed flesh grew thick. Gray light seeping in through the windows washed across the lower deck in broad, slow sweeps. Somewhere in the dimness on the other side of the deck, an old man vomited and the sharp, sickening smell filled the enclosure. Soon the sound of retching was coming from everywhere. Elizabeth buried her nose in the arm of Drew's coat to filter out the smell.

Evening came on, the light of day faded, and the enclosure grew dark. Just left of where the great shaft of the mainmast pierced the deck, a hatch opened and a young sailor, dripping wet, came down the ladderway with two lighted lanterns in hand. Without speaking, he hung them from wooden pegs driven into two overhead beams, one fore and one aft, where they swung, pouring out a yellow light from their diminishing candles, casting strange moving shadows in and about the unfortunate travelers.

Deeper in the ship, in the forward hold where there were no windows and no passageway to the deck, Rachel lay staring with blank eyes at her own lantern swinging from a wooden peg overhead. The lantern's windows were horn scraped thin, through which the candle flame was only a frosted image, wavering back and forth with the pitch and yaw of the ship. It burned slowly, filling the little billet with the smell of charred wick and melted beeswax. Not a breath of the stale air stirred.

Rachel pulled the blanket up tighter about her chin. At least, she thought, she had not been sick. This miserable hold had tested her for that! And, place of all places on the ship, the bow pitched the highest and went the lowest, forward and up, forward and down continually. I'm a pretty good seaman, she thought, chuckling to herself. She was surprised at how little it bothered her to be alone here. The hardest part was to be shut away from the sun.

Suddenly a mouse darted past. Turning about in the far corner, it crouched and watched her, its eyes like tiny black beads shining in the lantern light. Thank God for mere mice, she thought. Mice over rats any day, and she'd seen only one rat since boarding.

Then she heard it—the clang of the ship's bell sifting dimly through the deck floor. She began to count: one—two—three—four—five—six . . . That was all, six bells. Nearly midnight.

Rachel tugged the blanket off and sat up. She reached for the small hand mirror and brush arranged neatly on the head of a barrel she had made into a dressing stand. It did not take long to brush her short hair. She snorted in disgust. An ill wind that blows *no* good, she thought. Time was when it took an hour to brush her hair.

As she laid the brush aside, there came a knock at the door and a muffled voice. "Rachel?"

"Donald?"

The door opened. "The upper deck's clear," he said, "and the rain's slacked off a little. You could come up for air."

"It's about time," she huffed.

Donald laid a sea cape about her shoulders. It was wool, black and rough, but the heavy warmth felt good. Leaving the lantern behind, they stole quietly up the ladderway onto the deck. The blustery wind felt good, and she breathed it deep into her lungs. The light rain pelted her forehead and cheeks.

"Is it worth it?" Donald murmured as they huddled in the lee of the mainmast. For a moment she didn't answer. "Well?" he asked. Even in the darkness, he could feel the expression on her face.

"Worth this little inconvenience to get away?" she whispered at last. Her voice was determined and husky. "Worth it to get away from Daddy's shadow? Worth it to be going where things *happen*, where people are free to work and determine their own fate?" She paused again. "Yes, it's worth it, worth every minute of it!"

"You're a wee, gutsy thing!" He chuckled and, reaching beneath her cape, took her hands in his, warming them. "And I'm glad of it," he said.

She smiled in the darkness, and laid her head on his shoulder.

"I'm glad you're glad," she whispered. "And I know that when we reach Philadelphia, everything will come together for us. You wait and see."

The night was long.

When the tardy dawn filtered through still-pouring clouds, the lanterns had been cold for hours, the last of night spent in wretched darkness. Not once had the ship's pitch and yaw paused, nor the dripping of the water. From here and there came fits of sneezing; nearby, an infant wheezed with croup. The child's mother was sobbing in terror.

Elizabeth's back ached, and the muscles of her shoulders and legs were beginning to cramp. When her feet went numb so that she could not feel them, she could bear it no longer.

"Drew ..." she whispered. "Drew?"

Slowly he lifted his head from hers. His three-cornered hat was pulled down over his eyes. For hours he had been awake, wondering about Donald, and wondering if he had been wrong in his stubborn refusal to let Rachel come with them.

"Hmm?" he answered.

"Drew, I can't stand this another minute!" she whispered. "I'm going to the head ... then up on deck for a while."

"It's still raining," he said quietly, looking out the window behind him. With the ship heeled to port, the sea was rolling by just below the window. Tens of thousands of small rain-pelt circles marked the water's rushing face.

"Time to change one misery for another," she whispered again, and struggled to stand.

Stretching her stiffened limbs, Elizabeth reached out to one of the ship's great ribs, steadying herself against the sharp angle of the inclined deck. She picked her way carefully through the rumpled sheet of humanity, past the great bole of each mast, beyond the galley with its behemoth cookstove, a great hulk of black iron that mocked them by standing cold and wet. At last she reached the place where the hull narrowed to become the bow. There, built into the ship's side, she found the lead-lined trough where passengers came to relieve themselves. Human waste drained through the gutter and out into the sea below. Cold wind and splatterings of rain whistled up through the scupper holes. Elizabeth sighed in disgust. No curtain or bulkhead screened this seagoing outhouse from crude onlookers. She looked about. A boy of about nine lay on his belly next to his mother, his chin propped on his folded arms. He watched her closely. Elizabeth scowled and waved for him to turn his head. Sheepishly he looked away. The lead lining was cold and wet to her bare skin, and the violent upward pitching of the bow made it hard to keep one's seat. Balance was impossible. Elizabeth was certain there had to be another way, but for the life of her, she couldn't think what it might be.

As Drew Wolfe mounted the steps of the ladderway, his heavy greatcoat pulled high about his neck and his hat anchored firmly, six bells were sounding from the quarterdeck. He opened the hatch and, standing in the ladderway's shelter, took a deep breath of clean air. The cold rain pelting on his face revived him. He felt alive again.

The wind was unabated and the ship was reaching hard. Drew pulled down on the brim of his hat, lest it fly away in the wildly whirling currents. He raised his lapels against the cold and gazed upward through the maze of mast and rigging. Fast-moving gray clouds were skimming the topsails. At a distance, the face of the sea was hiding in the rain. But far to the west, beyond a heavy dark rim of cloud, he caught a glimpse of clear blue sky.

At that moment a sailor scurried past the hatch and through Drew's field of vision. For an unbelieving instant Drew stood in silence, then, grabbing the ladderway rail, pulled himself quickly up onto the deck and, running after the young man, shouted urgently above the wind, "Sailor!"

The youth stopped, hesitated, and turned.

"Donald!" For a moment he could find no other words. "What are you *doin'* here?" he said at last. His voice was stern, more rebuke than question.

His friend's answer was quick and calm. "Leavin' Scotland, Andrew, same as you."

Drew Wolfe's mind was swirling, confusion mixed with rage. He came quickly across the slippery deck, took Donald by the shoulders and gripped them hard.

"And what about your *sister!*" he bellowed. "How could you *leave* her? Have you lost your mind?"

"Is that what you think of me, Andrew?" Donald said quietly. "That I'd go off and leave Rachel behind?"

Wide-eyed and wondering, Drew stood staring intently into Donald's eyes.

"I'm not that kind of man," Donald said. "Rachel's down below . . . in the forward hold."

Drew spun around and, almost slipping on the wet deck, ran for the ladderway, with Donald close behind.

"I know," Elizabeth said when Drew told her.

They were below deck, standing by the mainmast.

"You know?" he said incredulously.

"It was my doing, Drew. You wouldn't've heard of it. It was enough that Donald and I knew."

"What else *could* we do?" Donald asked Drew earnestly. "You mark it! There would'a been a day when Daddy would'a come home, and it would'a begun all over again. She hates him—he would'a been at 'er again, an' she wouldn't'a been able to bear her own life! Do you think she's due no dignity or respect in this world?"

Donald's temper was on edge, his voice rising as he spoke. He could not imagine why his friend could not clearly see that Rachel's entire life was at stake.

"Besides," he went on, "just as much as you, that girl deserves to go where there's a tomorrow." Then quietly, "I'm sorry, Drew, but it was all we could see to do, Elizabeth and I. It was a week ago I went to Mr. Hamilton. We agreed that I would work as a common seaman to earn passage.

"You should'a seen her face when I told her. It's been a long time since I'd seen light like that in her eyes. I knew then I'd done right."

"In any case," Elizabeth said, "Rachel's on board, and now that you know it, there's no reason for her to hide in the dark any longer. I'm going down to her."

That evening, Drew stood alone at the forward rail, gazing into the darkness of the onrushing sea. Behind him the rigging creaked and groaned as the ship lunged headlong through the hollows and swells. He was angry with Donald, angry with Elizabeth.

The crosswind leapt down the neck of his coat, and he tugged it tighter, huffing disgustedly. He had thought he was in command of his own household. Elizabeth had said she trusted him, said he was a paragon of good judgment. But she had gone directly against his will—and what was worse, she had deceived him!

Ah well, he thought, I'll get over it. Have to, or I'll not be fit to live with. But there was the other thing—Rachel. She tugged at his heart so, and more than angry, he felt chastened.

"It was wrong to leave her behind," he mumbled, "absolutely selfish of me. Who do I think I am to try to shape the girl's life like that?" He shook his head. "Not the man I thought I was," he whispered, "that's certain.

"Well," he sighed. "Thoughts are not deeds, and nobody's the worse for it. She'll find someone soon enough, an' then for certain there'll be an end!"

NINETEEN

IT was the sixty-third day of the voyage, toward evening. Two days ago the ship's course had changed. Now they were traveling more south than west, and the sailors had begun to search the horizon anxiously for land.

The wind was steady, the ship running trim with the wheel tied down. About the deck a few scattered passengers were strolling, a half-dozen sailors sitting or checking the trim of the sails.

"Look at 'em," Donald said, pointing midships. "Like they had been friends forever!"

From where Donald and Drew stood near the binnacle where the ship's compass and lamp were housed, they watched Elizabeth and Rachel walking along the deck together in rapt conversation.

"Each so different," Drew said, "yet each needs the other."

"It's hard for me to think Elizabeth needs Rachel," Donald said. He looked around at Drew. The lines of Donald's face were angular and clean, bright in the lowering sun, his red hair aflame and blowing in the wind.

"Oh, Elizabeth needs Rachel, all right," Drew replied. "Something about her that's a comfort to her. Maybe a boldness in Rachel that Elizabeth feels she never had."

"Boldness? Recklessness is more like it!" Donald laughed.

"Maybe so." Drew nodded and smiled.

Near the mainmast, Rachel and Elizabeth were carrying on a conversation of their own.

"But are you sure?" There was great urgency in Rachel's voice, elation in her eyes.

"Yes, absolutely sure," Elizabeth answered.

"Does Drew know?" Rachel cast her glance toward Drew and Donald near the ship's stern.

"No." She smiled. "Not yet. I'll tell him when the voyage is over, when we're settled in. If Drew knew, he'd hover over me till I couldn't breathe." She smiled, then reached out and clasped her hand over Rachel's. "For now," she whispered, "let's just let it be a secret between you and me."

Rachel threw her arms around Elizabeth and held her, laughing.

"Oh, Elizabeth!" she said. Standing back, she placed her hands on Elizabeth's shoulders and looked directly into her eyes. "Thank you!" she bubbled. "Thank you for your friendship. Thank you for *needing* me!"

"And thank you, dear," Elizabeth said quietly. "It seems we each have our needs." Then taking Rachel by the hand, she added, "I admire you so, your life and your fire! I hope our friendship goes on forever."

"It will, Elizabeth!" Rachel's heart was bursting with the warmth and goodness of it. "It will go on forever!"

That night, after darkness fell over the North Atlantic, during Donald's watch, Drew, Elizabeth, and Rachel lined the rail, watching the stars overhead and talking quietly. The night was warm, and with a high sea running, Hamilton had given Donald his first turn at the helm. In the light of the binnacle, the three could see Donald's hands firmly gripping the great wooden wheel, and the highlights and shadows of his angular face.

"He's been a good brother to me," Rachel whispered to no one in particular.

"One of those rare people," Drew responded, "whose motives are absolutely pure."

"Yes." Elizabeth nodded in agreement. "I've never known him to say an unkind thing or even to lose his temper."

"Oh, he gets angry!" Rachel laughed. "At me!"

"At you?" Elizabeth smiled quizzically.

"Yes, at me," Rachel said, grinning sheepishly. "You know how I am, Elizabeth. Headstrong, too much temper, too quick to act. Of course I've seen him angry at Daddy, too. But somehow Donald always felt that Daddy was less responsible for the things he did than I. And so he was more likely to hold me accountable."

Elizabeth searched Rachel's face uncomfortably. Rachel *was* a headstrong girl, sometimes with disastrous results. Hearing Rachel laugh about it made Elizabeth wish the flaw did not amuse Rachel so.

"Donald was angry that night of your mother's buryin'," Drew commented.

"Yes," Elizabeth said. "He was at that."

For a few moments they stood, feeling the roll of the ship on the dark sea and, looking up through the rigging, beyond the sails.

"Can you find the Pole Star?" Drew asked.

"Yes, there it is!" Rachel said, pointing midway between the horizon and the sky's zenith.

"Oh, Drew!" Elizabeth said, suddenly breathless. "Look!"

"What?" the two chimed.

"There, to the west. It's a light!"

At that moment, from high in the rigging, a voice sounded. "Land hoooo!" it cried.

Then came scurrying feet and excited whispers—sailors and passengers scrambling onto the deck and gazing westward. The point of light grew brighter. Someone came up behind the three, but none turned to look.

"The Cape Sable light." The masculine voice of Mr. Hamilton came from over Rachel's left shoulder. "It'll not be long before we make the mouth of the Delaware."

When the first thrill had passed, and the throng had gone back to their billets and stations, Drew and Elizabeth excused themselves and went below, leaving Rachel and Hamilton alone together at the rail.

"The wind's warmer tonight," she said as it blew through her short hair and tossed the billowy folds of her sleeves. But her mind was not on the wind; it was on the glow of the light receding behind them.

"One of the first lighthouses on the continent," Hamilton said. "Stands on a high point of land in the south of Nova Scotia."

"It's beautiful!" Rachel exclaimed.

"Beautiful?" Hamilton exclaimed. "Well, in a way I suppose you might say so—if you've been at sea for two months."

"No," she said, the tone of her voice detached, "beautiful in another way. I can't explain it, but it seems to reach out to me. I never saw the lights on the coast of Scotland, but there's something alluring about it—something wonderful, that one can ride on the heaving ocean and know where the land stands firm."

The point of light disappeared, and out over the water darkness was complete again. Rachel turned back and saw Donald still standing at the helm. How glad she was for him, for life, for the future that lay before the both of them. There is nothing better, she thought, than a good, new beginning!

BOOK THREE

Philadelphia
1770–1775

TWENTY

THE day *Swan* threaded the last bit of her way up the Delaware and docked in Philadelphia, Donald broke the news to Rachel. They had just come up from below and he had set her trunk near the gangplank. Drew and Elizabeth were waiting for her on the quay.

Rachel looked excitedly about. Beyond the waterfront lay the second-largest English-speaking city in the world, far and away the biggest she had ever seen. The waterfront was a bee-hive of activity to the north and south farther than she could see, wharves jutting out into the river and great ships from the reaches of the world.

"Time for you to be goin'." Donald smiled. "They're waitin' for you."

She looked up at him with surprise.

"And what about you, Donald? Where're your things?"

"Rachel . . ." He hesitated, and she sensed something was wrong.

"What is it, Donald? Why do you look so?"

"There's somethin' I've yet to tell you." He paused as her large eyes tried to search out his secret. "My work as a deckhand—it didn't pay for my passage—it paid only for yours."

She caught her breath.

"For my own," he said, meeting her eyes steadily, "I've committed myself to be indentured for four years. Master Hamilton is the broker, and the price for my work will go to him for gettin' me here."

"I don't understand," she said, her face blank.

"Well, darlin', it means two things. First, I can't leave the ship till someone agrees to pay my passage in exchange for my work. And second, till then, I can't know where I'll be goin'."

A tear came up in Rachel's eye. "You mean you may be goin' away?"

"Yes . . . yes, that's exactly what I mean."

"It's simple enough," she said, firm resolution coming to her mouth. "Wherever you go, I'll come with you."

"I hope so," he said, "but I know how you've had your heart set on this city and all its fine ways."

"The city is nothing, Donald."

"And the Wolfes?"

She blanched and for a moment stood in open-mouthed silence.

"The Wolfes," she whispered, and suddenly she remembered Elizabeth's secret. Quickly she shook the question off. "It's nothin' to worry about," she said. "You'll have work here in Philadelphia, and it won't matter."

It was fourteen days later, and a steady rain was falling as Rachel went carefully down the steep cobblestone cartway. Twice she had slipped, almost losing her footing, and it was yet two blocks to the waterfront.

She placed one foot after the other, unconsciously gripping the basket on her right arm until her knuckles turned white. Protecting her from the rain, she wore over her head a twilled woolen shawl—blue and green on a red field, very like the Stuart tartan. The rain soaked through the shawl and touched her ear, sending a shiver down the back of her neck.

From beneath a white linen cloth, neatly tucked into the oak-split basket, the yeasty-sweet smell of fresh bread arose. She was taking the bread—still hot from the oven—with a large wedge of cheese and a jug of fresh cider to Donald.

It had been a long walk from the west side where she lived with Drew and Elizabeth. What a change from Scotland, she thought—the churches, the State House, the schools. A city of thirty thousand, and the town not yet one hundred years old. And all the homes! Even after fourteen days, Rachel still looked about wide-eyed at the houses. Philadelphia was called "The *City* of Homes." Big houses set back among old trees on either side of the street—so unlike Glasgow, that drab old-world town. And how wide the streets! How clean the air! It was wonderful! The only thing to spoil it all was the problem with Donald. As she mulled it over, the shadow on her face darkened.

Down around the curve of Dock Street she came until she reached Penn Street. On one side ran the great Delaware River, and on the other the riverfront buildings squatted tightly to the

ground, some wooden with low, shingled roofs, neatly trimmed
in fresh paint of off-whites and slate-blue-grays, looking out on
the river from many-paned windows which glowed with warm
lamplight.

HARBOR INN, one read, MCDONALD AND SONS—SHIP'S CARPEN-
TERS, said another, and BLUE ANCHOR TAVERN, all neatly lettered
signs overhead. The strong smell of Frampton's Brewery
floated on the wet air. Across the brick walk and cobblestone
cartway countless wharves jutted out into the river. All up and
down the wharves stood ships from American, Continental,
and Caribbean ports. The tops of all the tall masts seemed less
distinct today, faded in the low mists of the heaviest clouds.
Their yardarms, naked and shining gray in the rain, dripped
steadily.

From in front of Blue Anchor Tavern she caught sight of
Swan's masts rising up between Atwood's Wharf and the
Crooked Billet. Soon she stood beside the ship's great hawser,
soggily looped over a stout oak shaft set into the quay's pav-
ing. The current pressed the ship's port side to the pilings that
lined her berth.

Rachel gazed about until she spied him on deck, a single
figure standing alone at the stern rail. Donald had an oiled
leather cloak about his shoulders, and even in the rain his
flaming red hair shone from beneath the dark three-cornered
hat. He seemed to be gazing out over the river toward distant
Windmill Island.

For two weeks she had come every day, and today would be
the last. As the slippery gangway bobbed lightly under her
step, Donald was completely unaware of her presence. Once
on deck, she stood for a long moment looking at his sagging
shoulders, thinking what a forlorn figure he made, standing
like that in the rain. She was overcome to know that he was
going away. For the first time in her life she and Donald would
be apart.

Every day for two weeks prospective buyers had passed up
and down the quay, going from ship to ship, their feet shuffling
like the feet of shoppers examining dry goods spread out in
store windows.

A current of activity charged the American air. The steady
line of men and women with money in their pockets, coming
from everywhere: gentlemen and their wives from Philadelphia, bearded Amish from Lancaster and beyond to Carlisle,

Dutch from Schenectady and Pittsfield and the Mohawk Valley, all with a frenetic desire to produce!

"It's the nature of this place," Hamilton had told Donald, waving his arm wide to indicate the entire seaboard and continent. "These people are free—have been for a hundred and fifty years. No king to stand over them, and freedom gives a man hope. Hope breeds enthusiasm and industry like nothing Europeans have ever seen! There's work to be done, forests to be cut, land to be claimed and farmed, iron for implements, stone and lumber for building—inexhaustible, all for the taking! And the fever is epidemic. You'll catch it before long, boy."

"Workers! The one thing we cannot find enough of!" one man had said to Hamilton as he looked Donald up and down. The man was short, stoop-shouldered, dressed in black, with upper lip and sideburns shaven, but a long beard, white and thin, on his German chin. "You must bring us more workers!" he said.

Yet for all the old man's vehemence, he had no use for Donald. Then, two days ago, toward evening, a big man had ambled up the gangway, looking for Hamilton.

"Understand you've got a Scot for indenture," the man had said.

"You understand right," Hamilton answered.

"I need a man who can read and write, a man to teach the young ones on my plantation—white and Negro—in letters, arithmetic, and history."

"Young Calhoun can read and write well enough. You'll have to talk to him."

The bargain was struck. Hamilton wrote the conditions with a flowing hand—once on the top portion of a sheet and once on the lower. Each man signed both upper and lower parts, and handed the sheet back to Hamilton. With a touch of ceremony, Hamilton folded the paper in halves, pressed the crease tightly, and then tore it along the straight line. But halfway across he tore a notch into the lower half, a "dent" that could be matched only by the protrusion on the sheet's other half. Buchannon took the upper and Donald the lower, and Donald, from that moment on, was in*den*tured.

Donald sat face to face with Rachel in the warmth of Master Hamilton's cabin, her basket's contents spread out before them. The separation hung over them like a cloud.

"I'm afraid I can't think of much to say," Rachel said awkwardly.

Donald looked at his plate and chewed slowly. He could feel the tension brewing in Rachel. It was like the tightening of a rope, a mood that sometimes came over her when she was feeling sorry for herself. She wiped a tear, and her food felt as though it would stick in her throat.

"Why must things always be this way?" she said, sniffling. Then she began to cry. "Why am I always the one left alone? Mama's gone, Daddy's nobody knows where, and you're leaving me!" Her chin quivering, she dropped a piece of bread onto her plate, hid her face in her hands, and began to sob.

Donald's left elbow rested on the table, his forefinger laid loosely across his closed lips. What a sudden change, he thought. Yesterday she had seemed quite glad for him to go, but now . . . she was acting so like a child, it was hard to think of her as the grown woman sitting there before him.

"Rachel . . ." he said softly. "Rachel, you can still come with me if you choose."

"Oh, Donald," she wept, "I just can't. You know I can't. Elizabeth's depending on me! We've become like sisters—and with a baby on the way . . . oh, Donald, I don't know why life must be so cruel! I thought things would be perfect for us here. Why must you go so far away?"

"I must go where I can find work, Rachel. You have your choices to make and I have mine. I know Elizabeth needs you, but . . ." He hesitated.

"But what?" Rachel said, looking up, her large dark eyes snapping fire.

"But . . ." He hesitated again, then blurted, "I don't think Drew really *wants* you to stay."

"How can you *say* such a thing?" Rachel jumped to her feet so abruptly that her chair clattered to the floor behind her. "You only *imagine* he doesn't want me here," she said indignantly.

"Well, in any case . . ." he said, letting the point pass, "I must do what I must do. I could work in a Philadelphia tannery, but this is better . . . easier, and has more promise for you and me both."

"How selfish of you!" Rachel spat the words violently. "Easier for you, perhaps, but what of me, left alone here?"

"Rachel, you're *not* alone!" His red complexion grew redder and his voice rose. "You've the Wolfes, and that's what you wanted more than you wanted to come south with me. You've a fine home in a great city. Why is it Rachel, that you can't see the sorrows of others as clearly as you see your own? Do you think I *want* to leave you? That I want to be away from the sister I've always loved?"

His anger was rising, and Rachel's eyes began to dart about uneasily.

"Why *is* it," she responded in a rising voice, "that you have no *pity* for me? Is it that you hate me, just as Daddy did?"

"*Hate* you, Rachel?" he exploded in frustration and anguish. He got to his feet and began to pace. "How can you even *think* such a thing! There is no one I've loved as I love you. How can you be blind to that?" he shouted. "Why must you resort to such a ri*dic*ulous argument?"

For the first time in his life Donald actually wanted to strike her. He turned away to the cabin window and gazed out, though he saw nothing. He held both hands behind his back, clenching and unclenching his fists. Rachel came quickly around the table and stood directly behind him.

"I'll tell you how I know you don't love me," she said, her voice pitched high and cracking with sobs.

Donald felt he could take no more, but he struggled for composure. Suddenly he raised his hand for silence, and Rachel, seeing the hand quivering with anger, stopped in mid-sentence.

"That's enough," he said in a quiet voice, barely controlled. "What you're saying is outrageous . . . if we go on, we'll get nowhere. Right now I care about only one thing, that you and I part with a feeling of love and happiness between us."

He turned toward her. A wisp of red hair lay over his forehead, and his blue eyes were glazed with tears. Slowly a tired smile appeared on his lips as he opened his arms to her. For a moment Rachel hesitated, then she came to him and buried her face deep in his shoulder. He held her close, smelled the sweetness of her hair, thought of their lives together. How he loved this girl, but what dissatisfactions, what contradictions lay within her!

"I'm so sorry!" she said, her voice muffled in his shoulder. "But sometimes I . . . I almost drown in my own self-pity!"

He felt her shake and knew that she was half crying, half laughing at herself. He lifted her chin upward and looked into her eyes.

"Rachel," he said, "you must always remember. I'm not

your enemy. The only enemy you've ever had was Daddy. But he was just a weak, bull-headed man who's gone from your life forever. If you hate him, he'll not feel it at all, but it'll destroy you. You've got a new life ahead, and you mustn't drag Daddy up onto these shores with you!" He paused, and still holding her chin and looking into her eyes, "Do you understand what I'm sayin', darlin'? Do you?"

Rachel felt her anger fade and an incredible love rising in her heart. She nodded her head, a little laugh bubbled up, and then she began to sob again. Donald held her tightly and wished with all his heart that she would be coming with him. But he knew her devotion to Elizabeth—knew how Elizabeth was counting on her—and with that in his heart, he let her go.

It was mid-afternoon when Hamilton returned with Edward Buchannon, a tall man with a big chest, lean haunches, and an easy manner, his eyes and voice very kind. He took an immediate liking to Rachel.

"Missy," he said, "you should be coming to Wilmington with us."

Donald said nothing. Rachel only smiled and said, "Thank you, but I can't. I've a friend who needs me."

"*I* know what it is," Buchannon teased. "You want a taste of the big city! Well," he added, "you'll always be welcome at Buchannon Hall. You remember that, won't you?"

Then, reaching down, he swung Donald's sea chest to his shoulder with such ease that Donald stood amazed. Arm in arm, Donald and Rachel followed Buchannon to the packet boat.

"I'll write often!" Donald called back as he stepped onto the gangway.

"Donald, do remember how sorry I am for the things I said! I'm the one who's selfish, never you! Do be careful, Donald. I'll come to you someday, if I can."

Buchannon stood at the boat's low rail, smiling, wondering. The hands cast the ship's moorings and unfurled its sails. Too quickly the little vessel was in mid-river, and Rachel was standing alone, the still-falling rain dampening her hair and lodging in droplets on her long lashes.

As she watched the boat disappearing rapidly downriver, she took a deep breath and waved one last time.

Their separation wouldn't be for long, she was sure of it. Important as Donald was, he was not her whole life. She must learn to live on her own. Philadelphia was an exciting place to be, and she would make the best of it.

T W E N T Y - O N E

"WHAT a grand new world!" Elizabeth said one day in early August. She was at her great wheel spinning fresh skeins of wool into thread, working without thought. "I do miss Lochredfern, though, waking up to the call of gulls over a sleepy little loch, the sun rising at mid-morning over MacLaren Mountain."

"It's all so far away now," Rachel answered dreamily as she sat nearby, carding wool, straightening the fibers for the wheel. "It's hard to believe we'll never see it again."

They were in the parlor of the house Drew had leased on their arrival in Philadelphia. The tall west windows were open, and a breeze was bearing the fragrance of roses in from the lawn. The day was hot, but large surrounding trees overarching the house made it cool. A kitten playing on the waxed pine floor pawed at the gauzy curtains, then sat very still, gazing upward at a wire cage where Queen Anne, a yellow canary, sat trilling its song into the mid-morning air.

From where Rachel sat near the window, she could look down the long hill and see the banks of the Schuylkill. The house stood on an oak- and chestnut-covered eminence a little east of the river. Like hundreds of homes on the northern seaboard, it was elegant in its simplicity, with big rooms and high ceilings and light blue woodwork and tall windows with deep casements.

"I do admit," Elizabeth said, as she continued to spin, "the biggest surprise about this place is the heat! In the Isles seventy-five degrees is a warm summer's day, but here, my goodness—eighty and ninety degrees!" Even with the breeze, perspiration glowed above her pale lips, and loose blond ringlets had fallen across her forehead. "I should be thankful not to have to bear it in my later months." She laughed lightly. "Few things are more miserable than that, they tell me."

Rachel stopped carding for a moment and sat looking admiringly at Elizabeth.

"The new dress is just lovely on you, Beth."

Elizabeth blushed. "Well," she said, "it's going to announce to all the world that I'm with child."

It was a common enough dress—a simple red check on polished cotton—but it had an expandable waist that tied in back with a silk ribbon. Elizabeth had just begun to show.

Rachel smiled, gathered up more wool, and began to card again.

"Beth." Rachel was unconsciously using Drew's pet name for Elizabeth. "I've been meaning to ask you." She paused and laid the carding in her lap. "It's about Drew . . . and about me." Her dark eyes seemed puzzled, and she compressed her lower lip thoughtfully, feeling the inner smoothness of it with the tip of her tongue.

Elizabeth smiled, gave the wheel another spin, and let the tug of the spool draw her in. "What about you and Drew?" she asked.

"It's something Donald said before he went away. He said . . . he said Drew didn't want me here. Do you think that's so?"

Elizabeth laid her hand on the wheel, stopped it, and looked directly into Rachel's eyes.

"I've never understood Drew's way with you, Rachel. Like his father, he holds things in and keeps them to himself. Why, he's never said a single word about how I deceived him—and we must admit, Rachel, that's just what it was, deception. And yet he hasn't let it come between us."

"He forgives easily."

"Yes, Drew's not one to hold a grudge. It's one of the very best things about him—though there're so many things I love . . . I'd be hard pressed to name them all." She paused. "As far as his not wanting you here—he *was* reluctant, but he seems glad enough now. Does he make you feel unwanted?"

"No, Drew is very warm to me."

"Then I wouldn't worry over something Donald said. Donald sometimes sees problems where there aren't any.

"Perhaps there *was* something Drew felt about you once— some small thing that rubbed his fur the wrong way—but he's obviously resolved it. No, Rachel, I wouldn't worry. These are

happy days—some of the happiest of our lives—and we
mustn't spoil them imagining things."

That night in her bed, the question lingered in Rachel's
mind. She tossed her head on the pillow, fidgeted with the coverlet, and scant moments later turned over restlessly. Could it
be? she wondered. No. No, not that. She had succeeded in putting that behind her, and surely Drew had done the same. Elizabeth was right; it was Donald's imagination—nothing more.
Suddenly she felt better, and soon drifted off into sleep.

T W E N T Y - T W O

IT was five months later—midwinter, January of '71—and bitter cold. Andrew Wolfe paced before the hearth where a steady
fire blazed. In the near corner, on the lid of the kindling box,
the cat was curled as though in hibernation, its eyes closed and
tail drawn up around its paws and nose. Through the clear
panes of the tall windows, snow flurried softly down and the
stark branches of the trees were still as statues. Back and forth,
back and forth, Drew continued to pace.

Across the room the great oak clock with beveled glass and
shining pendulum began to strike. Drew looked up, glaring in
disbelief. "Ten o'clock!" he exclaimed. "How time drags!"

There was another presence in the room—quiet and unprepossessing: a man just a few years older than Drew, but taller,
thick of body, rocking quietly in a straight-back rocker near the
window. In spite of his stoutness, the figure he cut was clean
and sharp. He wore his clothes well, though they were a half
century out of style: a snow-white shirt with stock, black knee
breeches, black shoes with bright buckles, meticulously polished, and unbound hair that fell almost to his shoulders. When
he spoke, his speech was as out of fashion as his dress.

"Surely thou knowest, Wolfe," he said, chuckling, "that time
hurries for no man!"

"But it's standing still, Israel!"

The big man chuckled heartily. Drew had met Israel Bowman six months ago in Bowman's shop at Black Horse Alley and Second Street. In remarkably little time they had become close friends.

Drew stopped pacing and turned to gaze out the window.

"Rebekah and I have twice been through this." Bowman spoke quietly now. "Both children were born healthy and good. It's in God's hands. Take a long breath, friend, and ease thyself."

Bowman was a third-generation American, the son of a German girl from Lancaster County and an English Quaker from Quakertown. In matters of religion, Fox had prevailed over Luther, and he had grown up in the Society of Friends. When he spoke, Israel used the outmoded singular forms of English address: "thee," "thou," "thy." His Quaker father had drilled into him that under no circumstance should he flatter anyone with the plural "you," thereby implying that he or she was the equal of more than one person.

On the heels of Israel's assurances, rapid footfalls came brushing down the long, straight stairway. Bowman glanced up and Drew turned about expectantly. There, standing midway down the stairs, was Rachel, leaning forward over the banister, her eyes atwinkle.

"Well, Drew Wolfe," her voice was lilting and happy, "I feel sorry for you now. You've got *three* women to keep you in line!"

Before Rachel could utter another word, Drew had flown past her up the stairs, pulling her after him to the room where Elizabeth had just given birth.

Rebekah Bowman, Israel's wife, had just washed the newborn girl and was swaddling her in linen and flannel. She laid the child at her mother's side on the high walnut bed. Elizabeth's head lay deep in a large down pillow. Her golden hair was undone, but Rachel had arranged it artfully in long waves over her shoulders. Elizabeth's face was pale but shining.

Drew leaned down and kissed her. Her lips were relaxed and warm, slightly fevered, but not a matter for his professional concern. He laid his large hand on the small bundle.

"Sabina, after my mother?" Elizabeth smiled questioningly. Her tired eyes beamed with expectation of his approval.

"Sabina," he said with finality, smiling to know how this pleased her. He placed the index finger of his right hand into the baby's tiny palm, and her little fingers shut tight around it.

Rachel stood in the doorway, a quiet smile spreading softly over her face.

That night as she lay in her bed, Rachel Calhoun thought of how good the last six months had been. Donald had written often—just as he said he would—and she herself had become part of a close-bound threesome. This was more like a complete family than she had ever known . . . and today had been the best day of all.

Someday, she thought, I'll have a child—and his father will be as tender and kind as Andrew Wolfe was today. How lucky Elizabeth is to have him! Rachel nestled her head deeper into the goose-down pillow.

It was the end of February, and outside Israel Bowman's shop large flakes of snow were falling thickly. Already a foot of white lay across all Pennsylvania, a storm Israel was sure had deposited snow from Canada to south of Baltimore.

He looked up from his workbench near the front bay window. His full face was topped by his mother's German-blond hair. His eyes were light green, kind, astute. Drew stood with his back toward the room, watching the snow fall gently down, the flakes clinging to the clothing of people passing by. Behind Drew, in the Franklin stove, a roaring fire made its iron sides glow red. Even so, the shop was too cool for easy comfort, and Israel was wearing cloth gloves with the fingers cut off. He always enjoyed the winter. "It's easy for a fat man to keep warm," he said, laughing, "and I like the smell of wood smoke and the sound of crackling wood."

In spite of the Quaker light of peace, Israel was a gunsmith, the best between Philadelphia and Allentown. Firearms, after all, had other uses than war. "Besides," Israel winked, "even a British Regular would reconsider his duty, looking down a three-quarter-inch bore."

Israel's heavy workbench was at the front window, nearest the best light. It mounted a large vise and a wooden rack along the back in which a variety of hand tools were arranged: files, augers, calipers, chisels of various shapes and sizes, all neatly tended and well-oiled for instant use. Along the east wall stood another bench mounded in wood shavings, peelings from a thick maple plank that would soon be the stock of a new rifle.

Back in the dark of the room, candle lanterns hung unlighted from the ceiling beams. Beneath them stood a long machine used for boring, reaming, and polishing handforged barrels. Along the back leaned a row of thick maple planks. Near the front, on the west wall, hung the completed fruits of Israel's labors: a half-dozen well-carved Pennsylvania long rifles, and several pistols on pegs above them.

Israel Bowman was two years older than Drew Wolfe. He had a brisk step and a ready sense of humor. He was a quietly confident man, sure of his own ideas. For a few moments he continued to file away steadily at a lock plate clamped in the vise before him. The light, diffused through the falling snow, was clear and even—good to work by.

"Israel, what more could I ask?" Drew exclaimed. "The finest wife in the world, a healthy daughter, a growing medical practice: as bright a future as any man could want!"

Israel stroked the lockplate with the file a half-dozen more times, then felt the surface with his fingers.

"Oh, thou couldst ask for another daughter, like mine." He paused a moment. "On second thought, don't," and a loving smile crossed his face.

"Don't?"

"No," he said, his voice broken by a chuckle, "with three women in the house, almost never are they all in good humor at once." He laid his file aside and laughed, shaking his head. Drew smiled broadly.

"Even in a Quaker home?"

"Even in a Quaker home," Israel answered. He paused, taking up the file again, and with great care touched up the forward bevel of the lockplate. A seriousness fell across his face. Drew caught the change of expression.

"Something on your mind, Israel?"

"Thy word 'future,' " he said quietly. "Our 'future' is in question, I'm afraid."

"You're seeing ghosts in dark hallways, Israel."

"Ghosts? I think not," Israel answered. "War clouds, rather. This colonial pot we swim in is coming to a slow boil. One of these days there'll *be* war. Thou canst count on it. And, friend, when war comes, *then* where will the future be—thine *and* mine?"

With his hands clasped behind his back, Drew moved closer to the Franklin stove. The stove's front was open and sparks were popping out onto the hearth.

"I don't think so, Israel. If I've the sense of it, the colonists are devoted enough to England—"

"Not all," Israel interrupted. "Look at me, as much German as English. And look at thyself. It's English cruelty that drove thee from thy homeland. For that and a hundred other causes, when was ever a Highland Scot also a lover of England?" Israel stopped, pointed the work-worn file at his friend, and said, "Wast thou not a grown man before knowing 'bloody England' to be separate words?"

Drew chuckled. It was true. "But look back, Israel. Just a short time ago the people of this country fought beside England and took Canada from the French. And *six* years ago— the Stamp Act—all the rabble up in Boston mobbed together and called themselves the 'Sons of Liberty.' And what happened? Parliament *listened* to them, relented, repealed the act! What sense is rebellion against a government like that? And as for the Scots in this country, we all swore an oath of fealty to England. Many of us—despise England as we do—will not break that oath."

Israel snorted. "Most Scots I know would break their oath to England soon enough! And as for Parliament's repeal of the Stamp Act—that seemed good at the time, but in 'sixty-seven they levied more taxes to take the place of the ones they took off . . . and worse, forced us to house their standing army!"

"Well, I'd think we should be able to understand that," Drew answered. "She's protected our interests here. And the Seven Years War left England up to her eyes in debt. Is it not reasonable that we repay what England spent to defend us?"

Bowman laid the file on his work-cluttered bench and looked directly at his friend.

"What is this 'us' and 'we'?" he said. "Hast thou lived here all thy life? I think, Andrew, thou hast many things yet to understand—bigger things."

Drew turned about and opened his hands to the fire. "To a Quaker," he said, "there should be nothing bigger than old wounds healed."

"Ideally," Israel answered, "but mighty tides flow in this country. We—I can use that word better than thou—have always been afraid of the British army. The most formidable fighting force in the world, we've said. But now we've fought side by side with them. We've seen them blunder, even seen them beaten. Sixteen years since Braddock was ambushed on the Wilderness Road! He wouldn't listen when Americans told him he was going about it wrong! Then, with a bullet in his breast, his last words: 'Who would have thought it?' Well, *we* thought it. They can be beaten by men who know how!" Israel gazed intently into Drew's eyes. "And for the first time we understand that!

"*And . . .*" he went on, "we no longer *need* them. The French are gone. There *is* no border between here and Canada. The lands north of the Ohio are there for the taking. Some want even to press on to the Mississippi. There's a thirst to move beyond, to occupy the land, to get at its wealth. And we have only King George to tell us we cannot, him forbidding us to step over his line of 'sixty-three! I myself do not need George Rex to tell me how deep into this continent I can go or how to carry on my trade."

"And one more thing," Israel's pale green eyes locked firmly on the eyes of his friend, "we have had one hundred and fifty years of freedom. We've become a people of our own. We are no longer Englishmen."

With his left foot Drew Wolfe nudged a coal back onto the hearth. "Strong words . . . coming from a Quaker," he said quietly, and quickly changed the subject.

Rachel had had a strange, breathless dream, one that left her afraid and pondering desperately for its meaning.

She dreamed that it was night in an unknown place. She was trudging alone over a causeway bounded on both sides by rough water. From the dense fog ahead, a tall stone keep was emerging, its door standing open to receive her. The tower was built on a rock rising up out of Loch Redfern, its battlement hidden in the fog.

She struggled painfully on against a mighty wind. She was bowed over, and close to her body her hands cupped a tiny light that the wind threatened to blow out at any instant. Everything depended on her keeping the light alive. Suddenly, just as she was nearing the door of the tower, she felt something coming up behind her and, looking back, saw a huge black figure following close. She had to keep the light from going out, despite the wind, despite the darkness, despite all dangers. Then, with the door of the slender tower only a few feet away, she awoke with a beating heart and the back of her neck sweating profusely.

Next morning when she came down for breakfast, she appeared shaken.

"Rachel?" Elizabeth said. "What's wrong with you?"

She plopped heavily into her chair at the table. "A dream," she said.

Drew smiled. "I told you not to eat so late at night."

"Maybe," she said, "but a dream like that has to have a meaning."

Drew chuckled.

"No, Drew," Elizabeth said sympathetically. "Dreams do have meanings—at least sometimes."

Later that day, when they were alone, Rachel confided further to Elizabeth.

"Beth," she said, "I think the light was my awareness of life—very small as yet—and the dark thing behind me . . . I don't know. Perhaps it was my shadow on the fog. Perhaps it was Daddy. Maybe something else."

"And the tower," Elizabeth asked seriously, "what do you think the tower was?"

"I have no idea. Its top was hidden in the fog. But, Beth, I'm sure it was all about something in the future. Whatever could it be?"

TWENTY-THREE

THE first thing Drew Wolfe had done on his arrival in America was to begin his search for his older brother, Robert. Robert had been Drew's fondest childhood idol, and the feeling had never diminished.

But more importantly, Drew was doing it for his father. After all, he had made James a promise. If he could discover what had happened to Robert and what his life had been like before he died, it would help James Wolfe put Robert's ghost to rest.

So Drew had begun to inquire how he might find out about a man who had lived in the Mohawk Valley west of Albany— almost three hundred miles from Philadelphia—in about the year 1749. The answer was always the same.

"Johnson," they said, "William Johnson, King George's superintendent of affairs of the Six Nations. He's lived in the Mohawk Valley since 1738. If anybody'd know about your brother, Johnson would."

So Drew had written. Johnson wrote back to say he had put out inquiries for someone who knew something about Robert Wolfe, but that was five months ago, and since then, nothing. Drew had grown discouraged, yet he still had a little hope that before long he might hear something to pass on to his father.

On the last Thursday of April a late cold snap descended on the valley of the Delaware. The evening air was growing colder as the New York stage rolled into Philadelphia an hour late. Before the wheels of the coach could halt in front of St. George and the Dragon Inn, a middle-aged man emerged from the inn door, throwing a cape around his shoulders as he came. Immediately the driver halooed, bounded down, and, taking off his gloves, shook him enthusiastically by the hand.

As the two men traded laughter, the door of the stage clicked open and one of four passengers climbed out. He was a lean young man, tall, rather handsome, well-dressed. Shackleton the innkeeper eyed him up and down, and as he did, his merriment faded. The young man stood cockily with arms crossed over his chest, looking about—as it seemed to Shackleton—like he owned the place.

"Innkeeper, my trunk!" the youth demanded.

Shackleton, bristling at his tone, turned his back and continued talking with the driver. When he felt a large hand on his shoulder, he looked around to see the young man staring directly into his eyes.

The passenger was a good thirty years younger than Shackleton, and his behavior was an unendurable impertinence. To show his contempt, Shackleton stared coldly into the ice-blue eyes and said nothing.

"I have a trunk on board there," the young man said impatiently. "Take it into the inn for me."

Shackleton waited a long moment before answering. "Somethin' wrong with your back, sonny? You look to be healthy enough a young fella ta me."

"So this inn doesn't give service?"

"Depends on how a man asks for it, I reckon." Then Shackleton turned to the driver again and asked, "What's the roads like 'tween here 'n' New York?"

The young man pulled his trunk from the back of the coach,

perched it easily on his shoulder, and, with a leer of disgust at Shackleton, carried it in.

Once inside, he banged the trunk down on a table and looked around. At the noise, a girl emerged from a backroom door and stood questioningly by the great hearth where a late-season fire was burning. The young man started slowly toward her. His gait was loose and relaxed, and he smiled easily, rubbing his hands together and looking her directly in the eye. She was less than twenty, he judged, not a pretty face, but she had a good shape, and he liked that in a girl. She felt uncertain under his gaze.

"Big town, Philadelphia!" he said, trying to seem pleasant and harmless.

"Yes sir, it is . . . very large," she answered politely.

She picked up a broom and, not taking her eyes from his, began sweeping cinders from the stone hearth back into the fire. "Is there anything I can do for you, sir?" she asked, trying to hide her uneasiness.

"Could be," he said. "I'm from Albany—a doctor. I've heard rumor there's a new physician here, come from Scotland, the Highlands where my own father once lived. I'd like to find him if I could. His name is Andrew Wolfe. Ever hear of 'im?"

As he spoke there came the sound of straining harness and iron-tired wheels beginning to roll on the cobblestone outside. Jacob Shackleton reentered the room just in time to hear the name.

"You lookin' for Andrew Wolfe?" Shackleton asked.

"You know him, innkeeper?"

Shackleton huffed and wished he'd said nothing, but he answered as civilly as he could. "Know 'im well. You'll find 'is house on the west side a town, just north of High Street afore it crosses the Schuylkill."

"All right if I leave my trunk here for a while?" the young man asked, as he gave the girl a lingering appraisal.

"Overnight, if ya like," Shackleton said grudgingly, "but not past tomorrow noon."

"I'll be back for it in the morning," the young man said, and with long strides walked out of the inn.

Drew Wolfe sat back in his chair and gazed across the table, shaking his head in absolute surprise. It was after dark, Elizabeth busy at the hearth with supper. Fifteen minutes ago this young man had come to the door claiming to be the son of his lost brother Robert.

"I can't believe it!" Drew exclaimed. "We never knew Robert had married, much less that he had a son!"

"Well, Uncle Andrew," the young man said brightly, "Culloden threw a mighty scare into my father. He always thought England would hound 'im to death if they could find 'im. It got to be quite a thing with 'im, stayin' out'a reach. He thought maybe they'd trace 'im through 'is letters, and so 'e just quit writin' altogether. It was soon after that 'e married my mother. I was born in 'fifty-one and named for my father. They've always called me Rob."

Drew leaned forward impatiently.

"Rob," he said, apprehension in his eyes, "what became of my brother?"

"He's dead," Rob said bluntly. "Died fightin' beside Herkimer against the Mohawks in 'fifty-eight. Mama died soon after."

It took Drew's breath away. Robert had to be dead, he knew that, but to hear it gave him a chill. He sat stunned for a few moments while Rob rattled on. At last he got hold of his emotions. After all, here was Robert's own son, an unexpected answer to James's desire to know, an answer that came in such a personal way. As soon as Drew had regained his composure, he smiled again.

"And you came here because of my letter," Drew said fondly.

"That," Rob said, "and because it's the best place in the world to study medicine."

"Exactly why *I* came!" Drew suddenly sat forward, amazed at the parallels between the boy and himself.

At that moment Elizabeth broke into the conversation. She had taken a large cut of meat from the spit and was carving it on a platter as she listened.

"Supper's ready," she said, setting the platter on the off-white linen cloth in the midst of four set plates. "I'll call Rachel; she's upstairs rocking Sabina."

Elizabeth went to the foot of the stairs and called in a whisper. In a few moments Rachel appeared and, when halfway down, paused in surprise at the presence of a guest. Drew jumped to his feet.

"Rachel," his gray eyes shone with enthusiasm, "here's someone I want you to meet."

Introductions were made and they sat down, Drew and Elizabeth at opposite ends of the table, Rachel and Rob across from each other. Two tapers in crystal stands lighted the scene. Elizabeth noticed immediately that Rob could hardly keep his eyes from Rachel's face. But then that was little wonder—most young men were stunned at Rachel's first appearance.

"Let me see if I understand," Rachel said with interest, as the platter of roast beef went around. "You're Drew's nephew?"

"Yes, ma'am! Uncle Drew and my father were brothers."

She turned to Drew, obviously elated. "I had no idea!"

He chuckled. "Neither did I."

"And you're from Albany?" Rachel asked, turning to the youth again.

"Albany," he affirmed. "My folks lived in the Mohawk Valley, near a place called Deerfield. Both died in the French and Indian War."

Suddenly, Sabina's frantic cry came to their ears.

"That nap didn't last long," Elizabeth said, rising.

"No, Beth," Rachel said, coming quickly to her feet. "You're weary. I'll bring Sabina down."

Elizabeth sank back into her chair and sighed. "Perhaps she'll sleep well tonight."

"Rachel's a great help, isn't she, Aunt Elizabeth?" Rob said. He had turned in his chair and was following Rachel up the stairs with his eyes.

Elizabeth was startled at the easy way in which he referred to her as Aunt.

"Yes . . ." she said dryly, irritated by his overweening familiarity, "she certainly is a great help."

Drew looked up from cutting his meat to find her looking straight at him, her pale lips compressed a bit tighter than usual. Drew shrugged it off as something he would ask about later.

When Rachel sat back down, she had Sabina expertly cradled in her arms. Again, Rob's gaze was on her. The soft candlelight on Rachel's face made her eyes seem even larger and darker. She smiled at the child as though it were her own, and when she did, the swell of her lips struck him as about the most wonderful thing he'd ever seen.

Rachel felt the gaze and looked up, thinking he was looking at Sabina. She held the baby a little higher so he could see, and found his ice-blue eyes were fixed not on Sabina, but on her own eyes. She gazed back without blinking.

How long had it been since she had felt a man's gaze on her like that? Total emptiness rushed in, then a sickening awareness of how very lonely she was, followed by a great warmth filling her breast.

The warmth rose into her face, and knowing she was blushing, she dropped her eyes.

"So what medical experience have you had, Rob?" Drew broke in brightly, unaware of the unspoken exchange between Rob and Rachel.

"I've been apprenticed to an old doctor for a couple of years now," he answered, "a good one, and I've done well. All the townspeople say I'm already better than the old man."

Elizabeth saw that even while Rob was talking to Drew, his eyes were on Rachel, and a bitter cues came into her mouth. In an instant she saw a dozen cues warning her not to trust Rob Wolfe. Did Drew see them, too? No. Drew was absorbed in having found his brother's son. Elizabeth cleared her throat, but Drew did not look her way.

Perhaps, Drew felt, here was a chance to honor old family ties, to do something for his dead brother by helping his only son.

"You know, Rob," he said, "it comes to me that I might be able to help you get to know the right people so you won't waste time finding your own way. And, if it's all right with Beth . . . and with Rachel—you could stay here with us."

He glanced up at Elizabeth, only to find her eyes burning holes in him and her lips pressed tightly.

". . . at least until you could find something of your own," he adjusted his offer, "or for a night or two."

Elizabeth rolled her eyes up toward the ceiling.

"Why, yes," the boy answered nonchalantly, "I'd be happy to accept your hospitality—as you say, if it's all right with Aunt Elizabeth . . . and with Rachel."

Rachel lifted her eyes from the baby and looked around, puzzled at the expressions she saw about the table: Drew, confounded by whatever it was Elizabeth was thinking; and Elizabeth, obviously put out about something; and Rob Wolfe's continued steady gaze directed at her.

"On second thought," Rob said suddenly, glancing at Elizabeth, "I'll stay only the night. I've enough to get me by until I can begin work. It's very important that I have a place all to myself . . . so I can have the time I need for study. If you're going to take me under your wing, Uncle, I wouldn't want to disappoint you."

"Take him under your wing, indeed!" Elizabeth fumed when Rob had been shown to his room. "If you're not careful, Drew Wolfe, that boy will be taking *you* . . . for a ride!" At a sound on the tread, she glanced up. Rachel was coming down the stairs after putting the baby to bed.

"Well, Beth," Drew sighed, "he *is* my brother's boy, and I owe him something on that account alone. Besides, he's got the intelligence and character to make a good doctor. I could see it in his eyes."

"That's not what *I* saw in his eyes!" Rachel said, laughing lightly. "They're the most gorgeous blue eyes I ever saw!"

"Yes, young lady," Elizabeth said. "*I* saw his eyes, too. And I saw some things in them that apparently neither of you saw! First, Rachel, he didn't take those eyes off of you from the time you appeared on the stair. Second, he's got the very thing in those eyes that can lead a young girl right down the primrose path. And third, Mr. Judge-of-Character," she said, looking straight at Drew, "I don't think he's all that smart, and I don't think he has *any* character at all."

"You're imagining things, Beth." There was an edge in his voice.

"And his calling me 'Aunt Elizabeth'!" Her voice was full of sarcasm.

"Well, you *are* his aunt, are you not?" Drew said.

"I'll need more proof than he's given us so far," she answered with a huff.

"Beth . . ." Rachel cut in pleadingly. "Beth, I think he's very interesting . . . and handsome. He has such lovely blue eyes!"

"Rachel!" she responded.

"Do women really notice a man's eyes?" Drew asked, looking innocently from one woman to the other.

"Of course they do," Elizabeth said, reproving him.

"And a lot more!" Rachel cut in, smiling broadly.

"Rachel Cal*houn*!" Elizabeth was almost beside herself. "I've never *seen* you so! Drew, I'm sorry. I don't know how she could've said such a thing in your presence!"

"What did she mean, Beth?" Drew asked, teasing his wife further. It had become a game now, to see who could raise

Elizabeth to a higher pitch, like two dogs nipping at a cat from opposite sides.

But Elizabeth recovered her wits, and setting her fists on her hips, she made her declaration. "The important thing is what this young *man* means!" she said. "And Drew Wolfe, you'd better know that I'm keeping an eye on him!"

Rachel grinned. "And so am I," she said under her breath.

"What was that, Rachel?" Drew smiled, knowing it for another parry and thrust.

"Nothing," she said, her lips curved into a pursed smile.

"Another thing, Drew," Elizabeth added, "I don't intend to feed him every day. Watch that you don't ask him over more than once or twice a week."

"I promise," Drew said, putting up his right hand as if he were taking an oath. "But Elizabeth, I think you're very mistaken about the boy."

T W E N T Y - F O U R

ANOTHER week passed and the warmth of spring returned. The sun was still high when Rob Wolfe found Rachel in the garden out back of the house.

"Well, hello," he said, his voice seductive.

She looked up from her task to find his eyes on her and, clutching at the throat of her blouse, quickly straightened.

"Pulling rhubarb, are you? Let me help." He stepped forward and bent over the same row, his face much nearer hers than she wanted it to be.

She felt herself blushing again, just as she had the other night. She did not like it when a man's very presence made her blush. She clung tightly to the throat of her blouse, and at last managed to speak.

"The rhubarb's getting too large," she said. "It needs to be pulled—see how big the leaves have grown?" She said this holding up one stalk with its elephantine leaf.

"Did you know these are poison?" he asked, beginning to

pull stalks, breaking off the leaves and putting the stalks in her basket.

"The leaves? Yes, I know, but not the stalks."

"No, but they'd as well be," he said. "Bitterest things I ever tried!"

"Well, silly," she said, "you can't eat them raw!"

"Man never knows how a thing tastes till he tries it. I'll try anything I think might be sweet."

She stared hard at him. He looked up from the rhubarb row and smiled, much too daringly, she thought.

"I think we've about enough," she said. He was pulling one stalk after another. "You know that if you pull them all, the plants will be done for the whole year. But if you leave some, they'll keep right on growing."

"No," he said, "I didn't know. All right." He straightened. "I'm done."

He stripped off the last leaf and placed the stalk with the others. Then taking her completely off guard, with one smooth motion he reached for his handkerchief and also for her hands. Very tenderly he wiped the black dirt that had gathered there. It took her breath away, and she found herself following him as he tugged her toward a little bench next to the garden path.

"You're a beautiful young woman, Rachel Calhoun," he said, placing one of his large hands over both of hers where they lay in her lap. Again the familiarity suspended her breathing, and for a long, awkward moment she could say nothing. "In fact," he went on, "I think you're about the prettiest thing I ever saw in my life."

She was about to answer that she was not "a thing," when the dark brown of her eyes connected with the ice-blue of his, and the words froze on her lips.

"Does Elizabeth know you're here?" she asked.

"No. I didn't go into the house. Just wanted to browse around the hill unnoticed." He gazed about, his eyes taking in everything, the garden, the trees, the lawn that sloped quickly away down to the Schuylkill, the stable and small carriage house. Then he let his eyes settle again on her. "It's a complete surprise to find you here," he lied. "Tell me about yourself, Rachel."

The interest in his voice and eyes seemed genuine. Some young men she had known could talk about no one but themselves. Yes, she thought, Rob was interested in her, and she somehow had the unaccountable feeling that she could trust him.

"There's not so much to tell," she said. "I came to the colonies with Drew and Elizabeth. My mother is dead, and I don't know where my father is. But that's as well; Daddy drove my mother to her death and I hate him!"

She glanced up to find his eyes wide with interest, inviting her to go on.

"I've a brother, six years older than I. He's indentured to a southern planter down on the Cape Fear. It's been ten months since I've seen him, but he writes almost every week. We're very close, he and I . . ." She hesitated. "But apart from Donald, the best friend I have in the world is Elizabeth Wolfe."

"Donald is your brother?" he asked.

"Yes. Yes, Donald is my brother. I guess I didn't tell you his name, did I?" Rachel was gaining confidence now. "But you— what of yourself?" she said.

"Oh," he said, "you already know about as much of me as there is to know—except for one thing."

He paused, looking so intently into her eyes that it took all the will she could muster to keep from looking away. Yet she knew that if she did, she would lose whatever advantage she might have gained.

"What is that one thing?" she ventured, cocking her head as boldly as she could.

"That I've not had a decent night's sleep since I met you seven days ago," he said.

His hand tightened over hers. Suddenly, he saw panic in her eyes.

"You're afraid of me!" he said, feigning surprise. "Now admit it, you are!"

"No!" she lied. "Yes. Yes, you're right. Something about you frightens me, though I can't say just what it is."

"I knew it," he said, his voice quiet, yet firm. "I've seen that same look in the eyes of a pup beaten by its master. What is it, Rachel, that gives you that same look? There must be something. Tell me."

Rachel felt her stomach tighten. How could he come so close to the truth?

"It's all right," he said, his voice soft and soothing, his eyes searching out the contours of her face. "I can see you don't want to tell me. I'd never press you—but if ever you want to talk, I listen well. Do you understand?"

Like a wave it came over her. How could Elizabeth have
misunderstood him so completely? He was full of understanding, of deep insight. He was kind. He was loving and tender.
Abruptly he stood, holding both her hands in his.

"I must go now," he said. "But, Rachel, I'd like to see you
again, if you'll hear to it. It's true, every word I said; I've
tossed and turned every night—and it's all because of you. I'm
a smitten man!"

He laid her hands back in her lap and turned onto the path.
Her eyes followed his slim form as he rounded the corner.
When he was gone, Rachel's heart was beating so hard she
could feel it in her throat.

My! she thought. Her mind was swirling, and she took a
very deep breath as she rubbed the hand he had touched. "Oh
my!" She had to tell Elizabeth about this!

Forgetting the basket of rhubarb he'd set on the bench beside her, and lifting her skirts so that she wouldn't trip, Rachel
ran straight toward the house, then stopped on the low stone
step, her hand on the latch. The blood was actually pounding
in her ears, and she knew her face was flushed.

Biting her lower lip, she stood, wondering. Perhaps she
shouldn't tell Elizabeth after all. Elizabeth had made it plain
she did not like Rob. No, it would only complicate things. She
turned away and walked slowly back toward the garden.

The next day, Rachel went out of her way to go past the hospital, then lingered for a while, hoping to get a glimpse of Rob.

"Rachel!"

She spun around and saw him coming out onto the walk.
Suddenly she felt giddy, and her hands grew warm as she remembered how he had touched them. He was coming rapidly
toward her. Steady, she whispered to herself. Don't act a fool!

"Rachel, what are you doing here?" he asked.

He was smiling that irresistible smile, his eyes alight, and
when he gently touched her arm, her heart doubled its beat.
But on the outside, she appeared perfectly at ease.

"I was just passing by," she lied, nodding to the basket on
her arm, "and I thought of you and stopped." She had indeed
been to the market, but had gone far out of her way to pass the
hospital.

Rob knew this, and his smile broadened. "Wonderful!" he
exclaimed. "May I walk you back to the house?"

A shadow flitted across her face.

"You'd rather I didn't." He smiled understandingly. "Elizabeth doesn't care for me, and you'd rather we weren't seen together."

She nodded. "Yes, I'm afraid you're right," then offered, "but you could walk me to the bottom of the hill if you like."

"Good!" he said, and took the basket from her.

He caught her peeking up at him from under her starched white cap. She laughed an embarrassed laugh.

"You're blushing," he said.

"I am not!"

"Yes you are! Even the tiny lobe of your ear is blushing pink."

She reached to cover the ear with her hand. Her hair had grown down to her shoulders, but today she had it swept and tied at the back of her head. She laughed again and blushed still more. An intoxicating confusion swept over her, an ecstasy, but all too soon they were at the bottom of the hill.

"I'm going to have a house like that one someday," Rob Wolfe said, looking up through the great trees. "Amazing how quickly my dear uncle established himself here."

"Well," Rachel said, "it's not a grand house, just a plain one in a beautiful place. Drew and Elizabeth are hardly rich."

"No, hardly rich, and they never shall be, not the way Uncle Drew handles his accounts."

"Oh? And how would you know about that?"

"Part of learning the trade. He tells me we're men of compassion first, men of business afterward. His books are full of uncollected accounts, and he's been in the country hardly a year."

"Drew *is* a man of compassion," Rachel said quietly. "Material wealth is quite unimportant to him."

"Well," Rob said, taking an expansive breath, "this is the 'land of opportunity,' and I intend to take advantage of it!" Still smiling, he looked down at her and handed her the basket. As he did, his hand purposely brushed hers.

"I've got to be going," he said.

"So soon?" she asked, modestly dropping her eyes for a moment, then lifting them to meet his gaze.

"Yes, I've a lot to do before I can be ready for tomorrow's classes. Uncle Drew has loaned me books, and I've got to go home and bury myself in them."

"Home? Where are you staying?" she asked, knowing how

brazen it must seem. But he seemed pleased, and did not evade the question.

"Down near the docks," he said, "a little room near the water. I love the smell of ships and the sound of gulls calling. Besides," he added, "I've got to spend my money wisely, and the room costs hardly anything."

"Are you eating well?" she asked.

"Oh yes, well enough! And with the meal or two I plan to take here each week . . ."

"You're not eating well!" she said. "I'll talk with Elizabeth about it. And I'll bring a lunch to you every day!"

"Rachel, you needn't—"

"Hush!" she said. "It's all settled. I'll bring you something tomorrow."

As Rachel watched Rob going along High Street, she felt a little flutter inside, not a purely good feeling, but a kind of irresistible elation charged with uneasiness.

For Rachel, the summer was something new.

At last she had found someone to love, someone for whom she had been waiting since the day she'd learned she could not have Drew Wolfe.

Inwardly she now blushed about the episode with Drew. And once in a while the whole incident would come back with startling clarity. Occasionally she wondered what life would have been like with him. She had finally decided that Drew was too melancholy for her. If the two of them were colors, they would be opposite—Drew would be blue, and she would be red. But Rob? His color would be red, too. They were a perfect match. He needed excitement, elation, just as she did.

But there was the problem with Elizabeth. When Rachel admitted that Rob had been courting her, the color had risen into Elizabeth's face, and her pale lips had compressed in anger. She had turned away and found it hard to be civil, going about her work as though Rachel was not even present.

"I will say this now, and never broach the subject again," she said to Rachel that day. "Rob Wolfe is a clever, unprincipled deceiver. You keep his company at your own peril. But you must do what you must do, Rachel, and I'll interfere no further."

So, with Elizabeth's reluctant acceptance, Rachel's summer with Rob had been filled with picnics beside the river, walks along the docks, and excursions into the hills.

It was true that sometimes Rob seemed more adolescent than man, boastful, a little vain—showoffish. And she was surprised at how possessive he was, and yet how free to go his own way. Once he simply disappeared for three days and Rachel had grown frantic. When he returned, he had offered some explanation about wanting to be alone. But he expected Rachel to account for her time.

And there was that strange, strange day in July when Rob had called for her in the afternoon. As they walked down the drive together, she contemplated his admirable face. His eyes were shaped, she thought, like Drew's, and like Drew's, their lightness worked their magic and she felt drawn into them.

She could see as they walked that something was wrong, that his mind was elsewhere, that he was withdrawn, for he did not touch her, not even with a brush of the hand. With every step, Rachel was more aware of the invisible wall between them, and inside, her heart was sick.

At the bottom of the hill she took his hand in hers, but his fingers seemed as lifeless as his face.

"What's wrong, Rob?" she asked pleadingly.

He glanced sidelong at her. "Not a thing," he mumbled.

She squeezed his fingers, but he did not return the gesture.

By the time they came even with the State House, Rachel was feeling frustrated. When they reached the waterfront and he still had not brightened, her breath came fast as anger flared. Rachel stopped, but Rob, taking no notice, walked on.

"Rob," she said angrily.

He stopped, turned about, and looked at her with his ice-blue eyes.

"Rob, I don't know what's wrong, but I don't intend to spend this afternoon with you sulking like a spoiled little boy!"

Rachel stood with her arms akimbo, eyes flashing. She looked him straight in the face, her lips white with resentment. She paused as he stared at her.

"I love you, Rob," she said, "and I'll not have you shut me out! Do you hear?"

He tilted his head to one side and returned her angry gaze. At last he spoke, his words coming slowly. "I don't take to being told what to do," he said. "Are you coming with me or not?"

"Why should I," she said, "when you treat me so coldly?"

Slowly he started back toward her. There were others on the street, and he spoke quietly, his face only inches from hers.

"Well," he said, "are you coming?" He closed one sinewy hand about her right wrist and his teeth were clenched.

She looked down. He was gripping her so tightly the feeling was going out of her hand.

"Rob, you're hurting me," she hissed. "Let go!"

"I said, don't—tell—me—what—to—do!" And he began to twist her arm.

"Rob?" There was alarm in her voice. "Rob, what do you think you're doing?"

Suddenly he took a deep breath and closed his eyes. The viselike hold on her wrist began to relax.

"I'm sorry," he whispered, holding his breath, his eyes still closed. A strange smile crept over his face. "I lost my temper."

"Rob, what *were* you about to do?"

He let go of her wrist. "Let's go," he said, turning away, walking again.

Rachel was beside him, looking up at him and rubbing her wrist. With her mind awhirl and every instinct calling out for love, she refused to admit what had just occurred.

"I'm sorry," he said, "really sorry."

He turned his face away. Rachel wasn't sure, but she thought he might be crying.

"It's all right, Rob," she said, laying her hand on his upper arm. "It's really all right."

In a few minutes' time he was his old self again—light and airy, happy as they walked along the quay looking at the ships, collecting the names of foreign ports. But all the rest of the day she felt a shadow hovering over them.

Later that night, when Rob brought her to the door and walked away, she stood looking after him, wondering.

He's alone and frightened, she thought. Not only do I need him, but he needs me.

TWENTY-FIVE

TRUE to his word, Drew had opened the proper doors to his nephew. Charmed by the young man, he had taken Rob as his own apprentice. But quickly, by the end of the third month, August, all the charm had faded, and Drew understood for the first time what Elizabeth had been saying.

It was a Tuesday morning, and Rob had come up the walkway to the hospital. He had reached out, but the door opened before he touched it. He found himself face to face with Drew.

"You're late again, Rob," Drew said. "I've been here since sunup." He pulled the watch from his waistcoat pocket and clicked the cover open. "It's three minutes of nine. Where have you been?"

His questions were sharp and curt.

"Just overslept," Rob answered nonchalantly. "Important matters kept me up late, Uncle." His tone was light, and he smiled, casting Drew a knowing look. "What poor suffering soul are we off to see this morning?"

Drew neither smiled nor moved. "Your studies kept you up, I hope," he said dryly. He watched Rob's face carefully, hoping the young man would dare to make eye contact with him. "Poring over the surgical books I loaned you, no doubt."

"Oh, come on, Drew!" Rob said, dropping the respectful title and giving his uncle a disdainful look, though still avoiding his eyes. "There're scarcely fours years between us." His tone, suddenly, was confidential. "You're young enough to know what I mean. A man my age has to have a little . . . a little free rein!"

He smiled a conspiratorial smile, and as he spoke, Drew noticed the network of tiny red veins in Rob's eyes, and the dark circles beneath them.

"I was afraid that's what you meant." Drew sighed, his voice sounding weary. "Rob, you may be my brother's son, and you have the mind to become an excellent doctor. But, frankly, I doubt you have the will to get the job done."

Abruptly, Rob's smile disappeared.

"My will to be a doctor," he said, an edge of anger in his voice, "has nothing to do with my private life! I will not make a drudge of myself for anyone or anything!"

For a long moment Drew stood staring blankly, biting his lip. Inside he felt disappointment, even rage, that Rob could have such potential and so little purpose. Worse, he had no conscience. When Drew spoke, it was with great restraint.

"I'd hoped you were more of a man than that, Rob," he said calmly. "The kind of work we do requires the sort who can take himself in hand." He looked his nephew up and down. "And it requires a man who can be trusted—to be sober, to have the right kind of associations. Once the women of this town find you're seeing waterfront doxies in the middle of the night, you'll be through." Drew paused. "Besides that, I've a practice of my own to protect, and I can't afford to play nursemaid to some young fool who won't settle down to work."

Rob's face was growing redder as his uncle spoke, but not with shame. He replied in a loud voice, "Uncle, I think you've said about enough."

"Maybe, Rob. But *you* haven't said *nearly* enough. If you and I are going to work together, you've got to promise you'll stay away from whiskey and your disreputable friends."

"I'll see you in Hell first." Rob's voice had dropped to a forced whisper, his hands clenched into fists; for a moment Drew thought Rob was going to strike him. The boy was taller than he by several inches.

"It's hard to believe I could've been so wrong about you, Rob," he said. "I should've listened to Elizabeth. I'm afraid you and I have come to a parting of the ways."

Rob said nothing, but his mouth tightened and there was hate in his eyes.

Drew ached inside. Had he not tried to do his best by his dead brother? What more could he do now? Nothing, he knew, but wanting to leave the door of friendship open, Drew reached out to give the boy's hand a parting shake. But in a quick movement Rob slapped Drew's open hand, then turned and began walking rapidly away.

"Rob!" Drew called out.

Rob kept going.

"Rob! One more thing!"

Rob stopped, and with his back to his uncle, listened.

"Rob, there's something we haven't settled." Drew's voice was calm and determined, very even. "The most important thing of all."

Slowly Rob turned, and for the first time looked Drew squarely in the eye. A scornful smile spread across his lips.

"And what is that?" he asked emphatically, knowing the answer perfectly well.

"Rachel," Drew said, his eyes unwavering.

Rob cocked his head. "What about Rachel?" he asked. His voice was like oil, and the curl of his smile deepened.

"You're not good enough for Rachel, Rob. I don't want you around her again."

"Well, well, Uncle," he said with all the sarcastic smoothness at his command. "Rachel is what this whole thing is about, isn't it? I should've guessed." He paused as his eyes narrowed. "Tell me, Uncle, do I detect a little jealousy there? Yesss," he hissed, "I knew there was something that I just couldn't quite put my finger on. Tell me, Drew, does Elizabeth know?"

"You young fool," Drew said slowly, measuring every word as he took a firm step in Rob's direction. Now it was Drew's hands that were clenching and unclenching.

"Not so much younger than you, eh, Uncle?" He chuckled.

"Rob," Drew said, fighting to restrain himself, "if you've got the sense God gave a goose, you'll start down that path and never set eyes on my face again!"

The youth smiled. "Or on Rachel's."

"Or on Rachel's!"

"A little unfair, not to give her any say in the matter . . ."

"Rachel's no fool," Drew answered. "When I tell her what you're about, she'll want no more of you."

"And in her devastation," Rob said, "she'll be a ripe fruit ready to fall into your comforting hands."

Drew started toward him, but Rob raised his hand.

"Stay right there, Uncle. I'd be no match for you in a fight—I'll give you that. But," and the oiliness returned to his voice, "you've got your reputation to think of. It wouldn't do for the good doctor to knock down his dead brother's son—not right here on the grounds of Philadelphia Hospital." Without taking his eyes from Drew's, he went on. "You know, Uncle, women who have daughters fear men like me." The smile faded from his lips and his face grew solemn. "And they've good cause—if they prize their daughter's precious virginity. But, Uncle, you're the kind they really should watch out for. The kind that keep their thoughts so well-hidden that no one ever knows what you'd do if you had the chance and the encouragement."

Rob turned away slowly, his eyes riveted to Drew's; then, with deliberate steps, he walked off.

Drew, struggling to breathe evenly, watched him, wishing to Almighty God that Rob Wolfe was dead.

TWENTY-SIX

"YOU'RE wrong!" Rachel cried that evening. "Both of you!" Her eyes shot fire at Drew, then at Elizabeth. Rachel had collapsed on the lowest step of the staircase, her dark face streaked with fresh tears. "You're *wrong* about Rob!"

"With all my heart I wish it, Rachel," Drew said quietly. "I, of all people. But he's not the man I wanted my brother's son to be, and that's that! You'll just have to forget him."

"I will not! You say all these things to make me doubt! You're trying to drive us apart, and I won't let you *do* it!"

"But Rachel, there're other women."

"Never! Never!" she shouted. "Why don't you accuse him to his face? He should be here to defend himself, but you're afraid . . . afraid of the truth, afraid of Rob!"

"Perhaps he'll make it easier by going back to Albany," Elizabeth said quietly. She was standing by the west window, looking out. Until now she had said nothing.

"Back to Albany?" Rachel gasped as she leaned forward. "You think he'll leave—so soon?"

"We can hope!" Drew answered.

"Oh, I won't *let* him go!" she cried. She jumped up and ran toward the door.

"Rachel!" Elizabeth called after her. "Where are you going?"

"To find Rob!" she called back.

"No, Rachel!"

She had reached the porch when Drew caught her and grabbed her arm.

"Beth's right, Rachel. You *can't* go to Rob!"

"Why not?" she demanded, struggling against his grip. "I love him!"

"You don't *love* Rob Wolfe, Rachel!" Elizabeth insisted, taking the girl's hand tenderly.

"How can you *know*, Beth?" Rachel almost screamed, pulling her hand away. Then, suddenly ashamed of the outburst, she buried her face in Elizabeth's shoulder and sobbed.

"Oh, Rachel," Elizabeth said. "Don't you remember your mother's fear that you would find someone like your father—all because of the love your father stole from you? Rob is the same kind of loose, careless young man your father was when your mother married him! Can't you see it, dear?"

Drew, looking on in silence for fear of saying the wrong thing, sank down to the edge of the porch. Rachel was sobbing, her shoulders shaking hard under Elizabeth's clasp.

"It can't be true, Elizabeth! Rob's *not* what you think!"

"Then wait, Rachel," Elizabeth insisted. "Wait for him to prove himself one way or the other."

At that, Rachel's resistance seemed to melt. Elizabeth guided her back into the house and up to her room.

"Do you think she listened to us, Beth?" Drew asked when Elizabeth returned.

"I don't know, dearest." Elizabeth sat down beside him and reached for his hand. The night was cool, and Drew put his arm around her, holding her close.

"That devil of a father follows her yet," he said.

"I'm afraid he'll never let her go, Drew."

"Not until some truly good man shows her what it's like to be loved," Drew answered.

"That's one of the reasons I love you, Andrew Wolfe," she said, shaking her head and snuggling closer. "You're such a fool of an idealist!" She paused. "I doubt Rachel is capable of accepting anyone's love. Before she can, the girl will have to go through the fires of purgatory, perhaps through Hell itself!"

Drew pondered her words.

"And you know, Drew, the most terrible thing about it," she went on, "if ever she finds a good man, and he falls in love with her, Rachel will take him right through Hell with her!"

* * *

Later, unable to sleep, Rachel heard the bedroom door down the hall close behind Drew and Elizabeth, and soon the quietness told her they were sleeping. The house was in absolute darkness as she lay there, riven with turmoil, her thoughts confused. She tried to sleep, but it would not come, and she tossed from side to side in the dark, the hours creeping slowly by.

"How can they be so wrong about Rob?" she whispered. "Is it possible they're right?"

With a toss of her head on the pillow, she cast the thought off. It was enough that she herself be certain about Rob—certain she loved him. Oh, there was a haziness about it somewhere in the back of her mind—something she didn't quite understand. But it was clear that he was handsome, that he was bold. Of course, sometimes he acted like a twelve-year-old, but she was certain that if they were together, he would grow up, that he would settle down to becoming a doctor. After all, how could a man as lonely and restless as Rob ever settle down until he found the woman who was right for him? She was certain that she was that woman.

Why, this very moment she could feel herself in his arms, his large hands pulling her close. Breathlessly, through her gown, she touched the softness of her own body, imagining the hands were his. The memory of his strength, his warmth, and his insistent lips on hers filled all the world.

She *had* to go to him! She *would* go—this very night! She sprang from the bed and pulled open the top drawer of her clothes chest. Then it hit her; suppose Rob *had* left. Suppose she went to his door and found him gone?

She stood in the darkness, frozen with indecision, the rapid beat of her heart thumping in her ears, her mind awhirl. She clasped her head in her hands and sprawled helplessly across the bed. Then she began to weep.

Oh, if he would come to her, if only she could hear his whisper from the lawn below, then she would run down to him, and together they would go away. She rose quickly, went to the window, and searched for him among the trees. Nothing but shadow. It was no use. She fell back to the bed, her head aching with tears.

In her misery, Rachel lost track of time. Then the tiniest sound suddenly riveted her attention. Her eyes went wide in the darkness. She waited—there it was again—like a pebble striking her floor and skittering across the pine boards. She caught her breath—from somewhere outside came a whisper.

Up quickly, Rachel slipped from her bed to the window and looked out. There was no moon, nor any breeze stirring in the tops of the trees. She stood tense, listening as if her life depended on it.

"Rachel," the whisper came. "Rachel?"

"Rob? Rob, is that *you*?"

His whisper was clear and sweet in the night air. "Rachel . . ."

"Yes, Rob."

"Meet me at the bottom of the hill, down by the Schuylkill."

And before she could think, she was dressed and on her way softly out the front door.

Overspreading trees on the riverbank made the darkness complete, and Rachel, running and breathless, stumbled along the path. At last she stood still, afraid to go on. With only the sound of crickets and her own breathing, she stared into the blackness and listened.

"Rob?" she dared softly.

Silence.

Then she heard him sliding down the steep embankment. He had taken the back way! She called again.

"Rob!"

"Rachel!" And a hand touched her arm. "Oh, Rachel!" he said.

Reaching out, she held him close. "They don't want me to see you, Rob," she said, still in a whisper.

"I know that well enough," he said. "Uncle Andrew made that very plain. Oh, Rachel, how I've fought to stay away—but I couldn't do it!"

"And I," she said. "They don't understand you, Rob. They think you have other women. I told them how wrong they are! You've never had other women, have you, Rob?"

"Of course I haven't!" he said, his arms tightening around her. "You're the one—you've captured my heart, and there can never be another!"

"Oh, Rob, I knew it! I knew they were wrong." And she began to sob.

"There now," he said, stroking her hair. "It's over. You'll come with me now, tonight!"

"Where, Rob?"

"I've a room near the waterfront—I been workin' on the

docks. I can get you into my room and the landlord'll never know."

She stiffened in his arms. "I . . . I'd never *do* that, Rob."

"And why not?" he whispered.

"It would be wrong—I can't. My place is with them for a little while longer. And I could never just come to *live* with you, not unless we wed. Besides, I'll talk to them. Perhaps I can make them see."

"You'll never make them see anything!" he said angrily.

"But I've got to try!"

"And if you can't?"

"Then I'll come to you. We'll marry."

Rob Wolfe was suddenly silent, staring into the dark. Marriage? "How soon, Rob?" she asked. There was a plea in her voice. "How soon can we marry?"

"Soon," he said, but the sound of conviction was gone from his voice.

TWENTY-SEVEN

RACHEL climbed the stairs to her room and began to pack her trunk. She included the old leather-bound copy of *Gulliver's Travels* Donald had given her when she was ten, three dresses, and two pairs of shoes, but when she came to her mother's clock, she gazed at it longingly.

"I can't take it," she said in a hollow voice. "Maybe . . ." She rose reluctantly from the stripped bed and stepped into the hall. "Beth," she called, with a note of sternness, holding her chin higher than usual.

"Yes, Rachel," Elizabeth answered from a nearby bedroom. Her voice was flat of emotion, but not condescending.

"Beth, I'm going away. . . ."

"Yes. I heard you packing." She paused, and stepped half into the hallway. "I'm sorry, Rachel. Truly you'll never know how sorry I am."

There were tear marks on Elizabeth's cheeks, her pale lips

paler than Rachel had ever seen them. Suddenly Rachel could find no words, and the two stood in long, heavy silence. There was a window at the end of the hallway, the evening sun pouring in, casting a bright but melancholy light on the walls and on their faces.

"Beth," Rachel said, "it's wrong to ask favors of you now . . . but I have one I must ask."

"Yes?" Beth regarded her with curiosity.

"Mama's clock. I can't take it with me. It would take too much space in my trunk, and . . . and I'm not sure where I'm going."

"You've no place to go?" Elizabeth said pleadingly.

Rachel hesitated and looked down at the floor. "I have a place," she said. Then looking up sharply, "But not with Rob!"

"Not with Rob?" Elizabeth said, surprised.

"No, Beth! I told him I'd not bed him without marriage, and I'll not go back on it."

"Then why are you going, Rachel?"

"So I can see Rob whenever I want . . . without feelin' your anger against me or him."

A wave of relief came over Elizabeth. Rachel's leaving was a matter of control . . . of her feeling free to do as she pleased! Yes, she loved Rob, wanted to be with him, but the *real* thing was control. Well, Elizabeth thought, better far this than that Rachel live with the scoundrel. Perhaps she *could* stay out of his bed after all. But to Rachel she said softly, "If not with Rob, then where?"

"A room he found for me near the wharves—not far from where he lives. I haven't seen it yet, so as I say, I really don't know quite where I'm going. So I'd like to leave the clock here, at least for a while."

"Of course you may leave it," Elizabeth said warmly, then smiled. "I'm not sure we could sleep without its gonging away the hours."

Rachel's reserve broke and she smiled. "Thank you, Beth," she whispered, then slowly turned back to the room that had been hers for a year and a half. The sunlight coming through the hall window made the auburn tints in her dark hair glow.

Elizabeth looked after her with longing. "Rachel?" she blurted.

Rachel stopped and turned, her expression questioning.

"Rachel . . . we love you, Drew and Sabina and I."

For a moment Rachel said nothing. She held her chin high

and fixed her dark eyes at a meaningless point on the wall. "I know you do, Beth," she then replied quietly. "Truly I do. And I love you . . . I'll miss you, all of you . . . especially Sabina." She looked directly into Beth's eyes. "I have to do this, Beth. I love Rob. If I'm wrong, I must learn it for myself, not from someone trying to tell me what to do."

Elizabeth smiled faintly. "You've always resisted being told what to do, Rachel. It's part of you."

Rachel's new room was near the wharves and just south of Frampton's Brewery, so that now, as she and Rob entered the ancient building together for the first time, the yeasty smells of fermenting grain floated on the humid air.

"Follow me close," Rob said as he led her up the narrow stairway. "Don't catch your foot on a tread. I'll nail the loose ones down tomorrow. The cursed old woman who owns the place hasn't done a thing to it since her husband died. She lives on the lower floor—too old to climb stairs, so she has no idea the shape things are in up here."

"It *is* dark," Rachel whispered. "What's that at the top of the stairs?"

Large black outlines loomed above them as they climbed.

"Old boxes and furniture—stored for who knows how long," Rob answered. "Don't catch your skirt on the corner of that crate. Here we are at the door."

He turned the knob, and as he laid his shoulder to the old panel, the catch yielded and snapped, the door squeaking open on unoiled hinges. The room was brighter than Rachel had dared to hope. The first thing she noticed were three wide windows in the east wall, and three more in the south wall. They looked out over the roofs of houses and low wharf buildings. A block away a forest of ships' masts stood in thin, dark pencil lines, and far beyond them she could see Windmill Island in the midst of the river.

Rachel turned toward him, laying her hands on his shoulders and looking into his eyes. In their blue depths Rachel could see disappointment, and perhaps anger.

"It's not much," he said.

"Oh, but Rob, this room is open and full of light! As long as there's light. You know me, I couldn't endure a dark place. But this . . . with the windows facing east toward the morning—everything will be fine . . . just fine."

She turned about and ran her fingers over the woodwork. It

was painted light tan, and the walls were plastered. A thick coat of dust lay over everything.

"Let's get water," she said, turning to him enthusiastically. "I'll go to work right away!"

But Rob's face was solemn. "You're going to miss them," he said. "You'll miss the fine house, and the baby. . . ."

"Don't, silly!" she said. "That's all in the past! When we're married, and when Beth and Drew see how happy I am, how well you do, things will change. And the fine house is nothing to me! Not when I think of you. I *will* miss Sabina, but we'll have a baby of our own. The important thing is that we face life together—you and I. As long as we do, nothing else matters!"

A somber shadow fell over his face, and as she saw it, Rachel felt cold inside. He turned away, his arm against the window frame, and gazed out over the housetops and through the forest of distant masts.

"Other things *do* matter," he said. "It matters what my dear uncle has done to me at the hospital. He's cut me out—stopped me dead."

With his closed fist he struck the window frame.

"But you'll show him, Rob," she said, laying her hands on his shoulders. "Drew is a good man, just mistaken. And when he sees what you're made of, he'll come to you and *beg* your forgiveness."

"That's just what I want," he hissed, his angular jaw set hard, "to see Drew Wolfe come begging."

The cold feeling in Rachel's breast deepened, making her sick in the pit of her stomach. See Drew come begging? How could Rob think it? For a long moment she said nothing, then slowly turned around, surveying the room.

"If you'll bring water," she said quietly, "I'll begin."

Next morning at eight, just as Rachel picked up her basket to go to market, she heard the sound of hurried footsteps coming up the stairs. Without a knock, the door swung open. She giggled with joy and, throwing her arms about Rob, who had come back to fix the loose treads, kissed him firmly on the lips. Hammer and nails clattered to the floor as his arms went around her.

"Rob," she breathed, not taking her lips from his. She was full of joy at his coming. How wonderful it would be when they could share the same house, the same room, the same bed.

"Rachel," he answered softly, surprised and pleased at the greeting.

It was a long kiss. Rob pulled her tighter against him, and she felt herself melting. Her lips were moving Rob as she had never known him moved before. Then she sensed his hands sliding down from the small of her back, felt him grasp her hips and pull her even more tightly against him.

"No!" she blurted, breaking the kiss. "Rob, no! You mustn't!" She reached for his hands and tried to break his grasp. He would not let go. His hands moved quickly and his lips pressed urgently on hers.

Struggling, she began to whimper with confused emotion. This was not what she had intended. She loved Rob, wanted him to love her, but she would bed him later, when it was right and proper. For now she needed only someone she could trust and feel close to, someone to plan her future with, someone to break the spell of her loneliness. But his hands on her made her want him now. Her screams of anger warred with the feelings inside herself as much as against him, feelings of rising passion that were just too overwhelming.

At last, in sudden fury, she broke loose and stood in an angry daze, confused, wiping her mouth with the back of her hand and staring with hurt into Rob's unbelieving eyes.

"Had I wanted you to bed me now," she whimpered, "I'd have gone to live with you."

"And why do you *not* want to bed with me?" he asked desperately.

"Because," Rachel said, "I don't *want* a baby born without a father to love it! Is that so hard to understand?"

"Then why did you *kiss* me so?" he breathed out hard, his hands spread empty where Rachel had been only a moment ago. "Do you despise me? You can't tease a man the way you were doin' and love him, too!"

"No!" she burst out. "I *wasn't* teasin'. I wanted to feel you close, feel I truly have you for my own!" And she began to weep.

"Well," he roared, "where I come from, they call it teasin', and no two ways about it! Listen to me, Rachel Calhoun!" He stepped toward her so menacingly that she cringed and fell backward against the window frame. "It'll be a long time before I'm ready to wed. If you want me, here I am—if not you can stay and *rot* in this room! Oh, I'll bring you food, and I'll pay that old crone downstairs, but if it's 'love and bein' close' you want . . ."

He reached for the door with his right hand while holding her riveted with his eyes.

The sound of the slamming door reverberated in her ears. She heard his rapid footfalls on the stair, and then nothing . . . except for her own gasping breaths.

"Nooo!" she cried. The truth of everything Elizabeth had said became crystal clear, and with it, the horror of her own mistake. How quickly she was trapped, and with no place to go. How could she run to Drew and Elizabeth? She could not! Rachel threw herself across the bed and heaved out great sobs until her lungs ached.

Much later, when all her tears were exhausted and she still lay facedown on the bed, she clutched her hands between her breasts and murmured hopelessly to herself.

"I'll stay," she whispered bitterly. "No matter what Rob does, I'll stay. Under God, Drew and Elizabeth will never know!"

TWENTY-EIGHT

IT was December, just before Christmas. Rachel's face seemed empty and sallow as she stood at the windows looking out over the housetops, watching the snow swirl down about the chimneys, its white mist soiled by the dark smoke ascending from their mouths. In the distance the ice-filled river had only a narrow channel toward midstream, and not a single boat or ship was moving.

Rachel's face had lost its fullness and there were circles beneath her eyes. She pulled the shawl tighter around her shoulders and shivered. Rob had not tried to touch her again, but he had brought wood and food. Yet he was always sullen and angry. He had not been up since Tuesday. Today was Friday, toward evening, and the wood burning in the open-face stove—the last of it—was nearly gone. Soon the room would be cold. Already she had put on all the clothing she had, and still she shivered.

She felt so helpless. For three days she had been ill, and was too weak to trust herself on the stairs. If Rob didn't come soon . . . she didn't know what she would do.

Rachel turned and looked about the bare room. There was no oil for the lamps, and it was getting dark. She had found some rush lights in a drawer, the cheapest kind of light possible, nothing but the stalks of rushes with the outer shell stripped away and the pith dipped in wax. They gave out a poor light and smoked terribly, but she had used them after her candles gave out.

She had once dreamed of curtains on the windows, but Rob had never given her the money, and he absolutely forbid her either to work or ask Elizabeth for the material. She shook her head; she could not have asked Elizabeth anyway. Oh, how she wanted to be with Sabina—but she could not let them see her like this.

In the market, she had seen the women looking at her, whispering behind their hands. She had overheard, quite by accident, that she was just another of "Rob's girls." At first she didn't believe her ears, but now? . . . She sank to the edge of the bed, the corn-shuck mattress rustling beneath her.

"I'll find work," she had told him. "I sew very well."

But he would not have her working. He would bring money as he had it.

At last she had admitted to herself that there must be other girls, that there was drink—and that there would be no money.

Why did she let him tell her she could not work? No man had ever told her before what she could or could not do. Rachel was vaguely aware that her thoughts were muddled. She tried to shake the haze from her mind. There had been so little food the last month, and for two days none at all.

Her gaze fell on the stove. The flames were gone and the last stick of wood had burned down to an ember, its orange light fading, gray ash spreading as it turned cold.

"Enough!" she said, abruptly standing. The blood rushed away from her head, and she reached out to steady herself. Moving more slowly, she took a hatchet from the wood box and opened the door to the crowded landing where the boxes and old furniture stood in a great jumbled mass.

Here was wood, if she could muster the strength to get it. The encroaching cold made her desperate, and suddenly she was furious with Rob. She swung the hatchet, and splinters began to fly. A chair arm here, a bureau leg there, shattered drawers from an ancient, decrepit desk. Every blow that fell was filled with fury—fury at Rob for being gone, fury at the rumors which she knew now to be true, fury that he had virtually imprisoned her here in this room, forbidding her to go and work and bring in food and fuel that he had not provided. Never before had she cowered at a man's feet—not since she was a little girl. She would not have cowered now, but she was ashamed to face Drew and Elizabeth, ashamed to hold little Sabina after having soiled herself in this terrible self-willed mistake!

She was breathing hard when she laid the armload of wood against the wall and began to pile fresh kindling in the stove. Wisps of smoke were just beginning to rise when, from far below, she heard the sound of a heavy tread on the stairs. She waited with bated breath.

When the door opened, Rachel met Rob's cold eyes with an empty stare, betraying no emotion at all. For a long time they both stood, neither speaking.

"Where've you been, Rob?" she said, the tone of her voice as flat as the expression on her face.

"Away," he said.

"I was sure of that. Away where—for three days? In the taverns? With your girls?"

The fire rising in the stove showed her that his ice-blue eyes were laced with blood, his cheeks puffed and red.

"What're you talkin' about?" he said in disgust. He stepped to the stove and extended his hands toward the climbing flames.

"You know what I'm talkin' about," she said, so low he could hardly hear her. "You've got other girls out there, and I'm not going to sit still for it."

"Oh?" he said, barely interested.

"I'm leavin' this room, Rob."

Still holding his hands to the fire, he looked slowly up. "You're what?" he said coldly.

"I'm leavin'. I'm goin' home to Drew and Elizabeth."

"This is your home now."

"So say you," she answered. "But it's not a home, I say, and it's sure not gonna be mine!"

"And you think they'll take you back?"

"They will. And if they won't, I'll beg them!"

"You never begged anybody for anything!"

"Well, I'm ready to beg now."

At this he fixed his inflamed eyes on her. "The hell you will!" he said, his jaw beginning to quiver.

"*Yes*, I will," she said. "Not what you had in mind, was it? You were gonna play the big man—Drew would come crawlin' to you. But you couldn't take care of a wife if you had one; the girl you said you loved has to go crawlin' to him!"

"If you beg anybody, you'll beg me!" he shouted.

Rob's movements were so quick and fast that she did not see his big hands coming. He towered over her, gripping her shoulders, forcing her to the floor with a pain she could not resist. Then his hard right hand came down, and all the terror of the hated past came flooding in about her.

"This way, Doctor." There was urgency in the old woman's crackling voice.

She's eighty-five if she's a day, Drew thought. He had never seen her before, though he had passed this building often on his way to and from the waterfront.

"It was just about sundown when I heard 'em," she said as she led him through her dark back rooms, "noises up above—thuds, screams, like fightin'. Then somebody come boundin' down the stairs somethin' awful, an' the outside door banged shut. I just sat and listened. They tells me I'm deaf, but I tells 'em I can hear anything I wants to hear. Next thing I knows, there was this groanin' an' cryin'. That's when I called for the boy an' sent 'im up. He come down sayin' there's a lady up there, hurt real bad."

The boy had come through the still-falling snow to fetch Drew, the only doctor he knew. He was half frozen when he reached the Wolfe house. Drew had saddled the black, and leaving the boy before a warm fire with Elizabeth, had ridden back as quickly as the snowy streets would allow.

"Eh, here we are," the old woman said. "Dark as a stack'a black cats, but if you take my lantern, you'll find your way. Be careful of the boxes an' things at the top."

As Drew took the tin lantern in hand, its hundreds of tiny holes cast points of light on the stairs and walls and through the mist of their frozen breath.

"I'll see what I can do, Mrs. Barclay. You wait here."

"Cain't do nothin' else but wait," she said, "too old to climb them stairs."

When Drew reached the top, he found the door to the room standing open. He held the lantern above his head and looked about.

The room was desolate, half empty. Shivers of glass lay about, and snow was blowing in through the broken window, eddying into little drifts on the floor. Sticks of broken kindling were here and there. He knelt over one and picked it up; its end was covered with blood. The fire in the stove was long dead—nothing but white ash—and the room was bitterly cold. The only furniture was a wooden table and a disreputable bed.

He held the lantern over the bed, searching for the woman the boy had told him about. The sheets were rumpled badly, and spattered with blood, but no one was there.

Then he saw—the bed was moved out from the wall, and the sheets were pulled down on that side. He stepped around quickly. There she was—a young woman wedged between the bed and the wall, unconscious, lying very still. Carefully he lifted the bed out and eased her to the floor. Then, taking up the old woman's lantern, he held it above the girl's still face.

Seeing the battered face before him, Drew's composure broke. How could he have let this happen? He had determined to stay away from Rachel and Rob, to let her work out her own life, to let the fires of anger cool. What else could he have done? Elizabeth had seen Rachel in the market, and Rachel had evaded her questions about where she was living. Until the moment when he looked into her unconscious face, he had not once dreamed that this was the place, or that she had been living like this.

Very tenderly, with tears running down his cheeks, he picked her up and laid her on the bed. He pulled the table close and set his lantern on it. Then, with skillful hands, he pressed carefully here and there, searching for broken bones.

The bleeding had come from a gash on her shoulder, and had long ago congealed. Rachel was cold to the touch, very cold. Having lain long and unmoving in the freezing room, death was not far away. He jerked his coat off and laid it over her, then, with great tenderness, slipped his arms beneath her. Lifting her up and taking the lantern, he started toward the stairway.

Suddenly he stopped. There was a figure standing in the

door—a tall, slender man whose features he could not make out in the lantern light. Yet Drew knew who it was. For an instant they regarded each other wordlessly. Then the figure turned to run.

Andrew Wolfe stood, breathing hard, Rachel in his arms, as Rob clattered down the stairs. Suddenly it seemed he had found the proper target for all the hatred he had ever known. Then he remembered his burden and carried Rachel quickly downstairs to the old woman's rooms.

Wrapping the almost dead girl in blankets, Drew ordered the old woman to prepare hot broth. He stepped out the door and hailed a boy off the nearly deserted street.

"You there!" he called out. The snow was falling heavily, and the street was eerily silent, muffled by the thick blanket of white.

The boy turned and looked his way.

"Yes! You."

The boy came on the run.

"Listen," Drew said, "as quickly as you can, go up the street to this address." He handed the boy a paper. "Can you read?" he asked.

"Yessir, I can read." The boy held the paper up, and by the flame of the streetlamp behind him, read, "Israel Bowman, corner of Black Horse Alley and—"

"Yes, all right, that's enough. If you will take that message to that man, I'll see you have a pound note in your hands tomorrow."

"Yes, sir!" the boy said, and with wide eyes, turned and ran pell-mell through the falling snow.

An hour later Drew and Rachel were in a carriage pulled by four iron-grays. It rolled through deepening snow up the hill overlooking the Schuylkill River. When the carriage stopped, Israel Bowman jumped down from the seat and took Rachel from Drew's arms.

"My thanks, Israel!" he said.

"Glad to help," Israel replied. As the big man reached the door, Elizabeth opened it.

"Israel! Drew!" she said with alarm. "Who is that?"

Then she knew something horrible had happened, and pulled back the corner of the blanket.

"Oh!" she gasped. "No! Dear God, no, please!"

All that night, Drew kept a fire built in the small fireplace of Rachel's room. Gradually they brought the temperature of her body up until the blueness left her skin. Once, Drew thought she was gone. Elizabeth sat on the edge of the bed, holding Rachel's limp hand and bathing her forehead with tepid water.

"I never really knew how much Rachel meant to me until now," she said, biting her lip as the tears ran down.

Drew turned away, overcome with emotion.

"The wind, trying to blow out her light . . ." Elizabeth murmured.

"What, Beth?" he said, scarcely able to speak. "What did you say?"

"Nothing, just thinking of her dream, the light carried in her hands, the wind trying to blow it out. Perhaps this was the meaning."

Drew said nothing, but he pondered the words. Perhaps, just perhaps, he thought, this world has another side after all. At the moment all he was certain of was his own pain and confusion.

By evening the next day, crisis past, Drew went heavily down the stairs to his study below. Rachel had opened her eyes and smiled at them, but he was sure she did not know where she was.

He entered his study and sat down at the desk, feeling much older than his twenty-four years. He rubbed his eyes, then inserting a small key, unlocked a drawer from which he took a slim portfolio. He opened it and drew out two sheets of white paper.

Torn with emotion, he began to read what he had written three months ago, when Rachel went away.

Dearest Rachel,

This is a letter you can never read. I write it for my eyes alone. I expect to add to it, perhaps until the day I die. It will be a confession, Rachel, a confession of feelings, and I hope most sincerely that in writing, I will find an answer, telling me how to live with the terribly wonderful thing that makes its home in my heart.

Rachel, I cannot help myself, for I've fallen in love with you. It happened that day on the slopes of MacLaren Mountain when you kissed me. Strange as it may seem, I love Elizabeth equally well.

How humiliated I would be if you should read this! What a terrible flaw in my character it reveals! Yet I cannot escape it. . . .

There was more, much more, but Drew's pounding heart and flushed face would not let him go on. Once, twice, he started to crumple the sheets, but he could not bring himself to do it.

He knew Elizabeth would never look into the portfolio. But what if it were stolen, or what if he were to meet with an accident and die? Even so . . . He put the sheets back in and tied the string that held the closure.

Taking a deep breath, his elbows on the desk, he buried his face in his hands. Then, sensing someone behind him, he looked up.

"Poor Drew," Elizabeth said as she laid her hand on his shoulder and began to rub softly. "You've had a terrible night. The snow is too deep for you to go out today. Why don't you go up to our bed and sleep for a while? I'll watch over Rachel."

His mouth went dry, and he swallowed hard, "I didn't know you were there, Beth," he said breathlessly. Inside, he was churning with guilt. "Maybe you're right. I think that's just what I'll do."

She laid her head on his shoulder and put her arms around him. "I love you, dearest," she said. "You are truly a good and compassionate man."

He stood and took her in his arms, his cheek in her hair, holding her desperately, wanting never to let her go.

"I was wrong about him, Beth," Rachel said several days later. "So terribly wrong." She paused. "But you mustn't tell Drew I admitted to it!"

Rachel lay looking up from her pillow in her own room—a room with curtains and clean sills and a fire in the fireplace. She could hear the wind moaning softly around the cornice and see the icicles hanging from the eaves outside her windows. Beth smiled in a lovely, pleasant kind of way. She was that sort of woman, the kind whose anger cooled quickly and who would never dream of saying "I told you so."

"It's all in the past now, Rachel," Elizabeth answered. "The best we can do is forget it ever happened. The important thing is you—Drew has said again and again that he's never seen anyone recover who was so close to death as you were." She paused. "But, dear, why not tell Drew how you feel? He knows perfectly well what's happened. Wouldn't it be best if you simply said to him, 'Drew, I was wrong'?"

"No!" Rachel said sharply. "I can't let him know. Drew is *al*ways right—and sometimes I almost hate him for it!"

"*Ra*chel! What a thing to say!" Elizabeth exclaimed. "Drew has never had anything but your best interest at heart. You were simply blinded by love. He knows that and thinks none the less of you for it. Why in the world would you resent his being right?"

"Beth," Rachel said, "I cannot *bear* to have a man tell me what I must do. And I certainly don't want any man lording it over me! And Beth—you must never tell *any*one this—when Drew insisted I not be with Rob, I deliberately chose to do it just to show him I could."

Elizabeth sat quietly, her pale skin a shade paler, nervously sucking on her lower lip as she thought of the girl lying before her.

Rachel's fingers were long and slender, her hands beautiful and very dark. Elizabeth thought of the perfection of her face, how Rob had marred it with his violence. There were dark bruises, a laceration above her left temple into her hairline. Drew said it would leave a scar, but that as time went on it would become less noticeable.

"I'm thankful to be alive," Rachel said, breaking the silence. "You were right. I was very foolish to trust Rob, just as Mama was foolish to fall in love with Daddy. But I'm sure of one thing—I'll never fall in love again, not ever!"

"Now, Rachel!" Elizabeth remonstrated.

"I won't, Beth! There's not a man in this world I could ever trust my life to."

"You fell into the wrong arms, Rachel, that's all. Foolishly, yes. Spitefully, yes. But Rob and your father don't represent all men." She paused, then, trying to change the subject, "I'm glad Rob left Philadelphia. Everyone is talking about what he did to you. And Willa Godfrey—well, you know Willa. She's been over here every day since it happened."

Rachel held her sides and tried to stop laughing at the thought of Willa Godfrey. Her sides were bruised and at least one rib broken. The very mention of Willa was a constant source of merriment in the Wolfe household.

Not much older than Rachel, and unmarried, Willa was the

neighborhood gossip. Generally she was harmless, for everyone took her babblings with a grain of salt.

"Dear Willa!" Rachel said softly as she settled back into the pillow. "I suppose she wanted all the terrible details."

"Like a leech drawing blood," Elizabeth said. "And she wanted to know where Rob had gone."

"And you told her?"

"Yes. I said he'd gone north. Drew believes he'll join the Regulars—as a physician of course. He'll tell them he's studied at the Philadelphia Hospital. They'll be glad to have him."

Rachel began to cry again.

"What is it, Rachel darling? Are you crying for Rob?"

"No. Oh, no! Not for Rob, Beth. But when I think of what Drew did for me, I feel so small, and so cared for."

For a long moment Elizabeth simply stared at her. What contradictions! she thought. What a world of mixed and tangled feelings this girl held in her heart!

TWENTY-NINE

"Back to Scotland? Surely, Beth, you can't mean . . ." Drew was stammering, for he could not believe his ears.

It was an evening in July. The sun was down, but in the fading glow of twilight, one could still see the landscape. Drew and Elizabeth were sitting alone on the front lawn, both Rachel and Sabina having gone to bed early. The house was dark.

"Just Sabina and I, Drew," she said, leaning forward and taking his hands. "We'd be gone a few months at the most." Her voice was soft and pleading.

"A few months?" he said incredulously, searching her face with troubled eyes. "Beth, I'd shrivel up of loneliness. And the crossing—such a dangerous thing! Beth, if something were to happen to you . . ."

"You do understand, don't you, Drew? I once had such hopes of bringing Mother and Father here to live in Philadelphia. But their health being what it is, they'll never come. I *long* to see them just this once more before they die, and they *must* see their little Sabina—their *only* grandchild! Please understand, darling. Please!"

Drew paused and looked up, as if to find his troubled thoughts collected somewhere in the branches of the trees.

"I do understand, Beth," he said at last, reaching out to tenderly caress her arm. "But Beth, the risks! An ocean crossing. You'd be gone almost a year!"

"But I must, Drew! I must!"

And Elizabeth began to cry.

As the day came near for Elizabeth and Sabina to leave, it became harder for Rachel to face the departure. When the September sailing day dawned, she woke with a clutching in her breast, the same kind of helpless feeling as when her mother was near death, a feeling they were all being led to a place where they did not want to go.

The big Quaker gunsmith, Israel Bowman, and his wife Rebekah had come down with Drew and Rachel to see them off. Standing beside her outsized husband, the diminutive Rebekah seemed even smaller than she was. It had been Rebekah who invited Rachel to stay in the Bowman home while Elizabeth and Sabina were away.

With baggage aboard, passengers settled in their private cabin, and all standing on deck, it came time to say good-bye. It was a cool, airy morning, which sent a chill through clothing too thin for the day. Up through the spars and yardarms, one could see wispy mare's tails whipping against the washed-out blue. Inside, Rachel was miserable, thinking how even the weather had conspired to make the morning feel empty. She was crying softly when at last Elizabeth turned to her and they fell into each other's arms.

"I'll miss you so, Rachel!" she whispered tearfully in her ear.

Rachel could only sob in answer. Little brown-haired Sabina stood clinging to Rachel's skirt, looking up and wondering at the fuss. Rachel grabbed her up, hugging her tightly.

"Tears?" the child said, touching the wetness on Rachel's cheek with the tip of one finger. "Why you cry, Rachel?"

Rachel laughed through her tears.

"Because you're goin' away," she said, "and my heart is hurtin' somethin' terrible!"

At this Sabina looked puzzled, but threw her tiny arms around Rachel's neck and squeezed tightly.

"Steady, dear," Drew said, laying his hand warmly on Rachel's shoulder. She looked up to see him struggling with tears of his own, but smiling a forced smile of encouragement. "All our hearts are hurtin' today. But we'll do fine!"

Then he drew Elizabeth to himself, holding her tightly for a long while, as Rachel and the others looked on.

THIRTY

In the spring, Rachel had made a decision of her own. She must make her own way, rather than depending on her place in the Wolfe family. Donald wrote often of how he enjoyed teaching, and she realized that her years of voracious reading had prepared her to teach as well. She had told Drew and Elizabeth of her intentions, and had run a notice in Franklin's *Pennsylvania Gazette* for students.

Parents who wish to begin their children in reading, writing, and cipher, should please note that Miss Rachel Calhoun, lately of Scotland, will begin classes on the same this September. Her charges will be reasonable. Please see her at the home of Doctor and Mrs. Andrew Wolfe, where classes will be held.

It was a week after Elizabeth's sailing, a Wednesday, when Rachel was to gather her students for the first time. Elizabeth had insisted she hold classes in the house, just as they had planned from the beginning. Drew would be away most of the time, and the southeast room, with its many windows and the bright morning light, would be perfect.

When the day began, Rachel's heart was in her throat, but as the hours passed, her confidence increased. The last student was gone and Rachel was tidying the room when she became

aware of movement behind her. She looked around to see
Drew standing in the doorway.

"How's the teacher?" he asked, smiling.

"It was a good day," she said. "The children seem to like
me."

"I knew they would," he said confidently.

She walked among their seats, looking at their slates one by
one.

"Jack Hold," she said, "he's the son of one of your doctor
friends—a quick learner, I'm sure of it." She paused and
looked thoughtfully at Drew, her head inclined slightly to one
side. "And you, Drew, how are you?"

He shook his head and gazed absently out the window. "You
can't imagine how I miss them," he said quietly.

"Time will pass." There was a smile in her voice. She was
gathering her things. "Besides, we can't possibly do anything
but wait."

As she passed down the long incline toward High Street, the
kind of sunlight that only September can bring filtered down
through the diminishing leaves.

"Poor Drew," she said lightly. She felt true empathy with his
loneliness. Surely, though, he did not miss Elizabeth and Sabina more than she. But loneliness was not fatal, and it would
pass. As she went along, a delicious, careless feeling came
over her.

Drew's an attractive man, she thought. Maybe he didn't
have Rob's flair, but Rob . . . She shook her head, trying to
forget he was ever a part of anything she had known. And
Drew was more interesting than the "boys" of Philadelphia.

Suddenly she caught herself and blushed. She looked about,
as if to see whether her thoughts had been noticed. She herself
had not noticed them until the words were in her head.

"You can't let yourself *think* like that!" she said aloud, her
face burning with embarrassment. She paused, then continued
under her breath, "How *fool*ish of Elizabeth! If I were married
to a man like Drew, I would never go away and leave him
alone . . . not ever!"

Rachel did not notice the anger in her words—and if she
had noticed, she would not have immediately understood why
she was angry, nor with whom.

Drew had been afraid of Elizabeth's going for reasons other
than loneliness and bad weather.

In June, three months before Elizabeth left, the packet *Hannah* had left Newport for Providence. The armed British revenue schooner *Gaspee*, looking for contraband, had given chase. *Gaspee* had run aground at Namquit Point on Narragansett Bay. That night, men from the shore had burned the British ship to the waterline. It was now conceivable that *Gaspee*'s burning would bring on the war Israel had predicted.

Nevertheless, despite other incidents, when the white snows of winter melted and the spring of 1773 finally came, there were no British troops at the colonists' doors, and no imminent clouds of war. Israel had been wrong, and Drew, now breathing easily, watched daily for Elizabeth and Sabina's return.

With May came the rains.

This morning, in a small upper bedroom of the Bowman house, Rachel woke to the pleasant growl of low thunder from across the river. She stretched lazily in her bed, feeling warm beneath the light goose-down comforter, then raised her head slightly from the pillow and looked out the dormer window. It wasn't raining, but low clouds marbled the sky.

The realization that she'd overslept brought her fully awake. For a long moment she lay very still and listened. There was movement in the kitchen.

"Rebekah should've called me before now!" she said with irritation, throwing back the covers. Her feet touched the pine floor—it was cold. She hugged herself and shivered.

As Rachel came racing down the stairs, Rebekah Bowman was stooping at her fireplace, stirring a pot of morning chocolate. Rebekah looked up.

"Why in such a rush?" she called pleasantly. Rebekah had a delicate face, big eyes that seemed naturally sad, and a narrow mouth with a pronounced overbite. Rachel had already learned how very absentminded Rebekah was.

"Surely thou'rt not going out this morning?" she said. "There's lightning about, very close."

"Oh yes, I'm going," Rachel answered impatiently. "And I've *got* to hurry, or my students will think I'm not coming." She reached to a peg near the door for her cloak.

"Can I not first do thy hair?"

"No," Rachel snipped, buttoning the hood below her chin, "there's no time."

The pewter plates standing against the cupboard wall rattled faintly with the growing sound of thunder.

"Rachel," Rebekah pleaded, "the lightning!" But before her words could die in the air, Rachel slammed the door behind her and was on her way down Second Street.

Great trees overarched the wide street west toward the Schuylkill. As she walked hurriedly beneath their overhanging branches, going as in a frantic daze, she saw nothing. Somewhere between the top and bottom of Bowmans' stairs, Rachel had set to work out the puzzle that had eaten at her all winter. One thing she knew: Drew Wolfe was at the heart of it.

A light breeze swept down from the boiling clouds and brushed her cheek with small drops of rain, but she paid it no mind. Up in the treetops, the wind tossed the thickly grown leaves with a rushing sound that somehow heightened the restless fear in her soul. Quick lightning flashed and fresh rolls of thunder rumbled and clattered disconsolately about in the dark clouds above her head.

"What is the *matter* with me?" she whispered into the wind. "How can a grown woman feel this way! I'm no light-o'-love. I'm not a man-crazy little fool." She thought of Rob and blushed. "Am I?"

She had seen Drew alone too many times, had given too much thought to his loneliness, and day by day had felt her closeness to him growing.

A terrible thought seeped into her consciousness.

A duplicate of my father, that's what she was! How horrible! How could she be like him, so shameful, so disgusting!

But what else could she conclude? Good women did not think thoughts like those milling about in her mind these weeks. She shivered and walked a little faster.

When had this fascination with Drew begun? Eight months ago when they stood on the quay saying good-bye to Elizabeth and Sabina? No. Long before. The affection she was so sure she had driven from her mind had only gone underground, somewhere so deep she had believed it no longer existed.

Did she think Elizabeth might not return? Was it not true that she loved Elizabeth so greatly that she could never admit—even to herself—that she also loved Elizabeth's husband? She did not know. At the very least it *ought* to be impossible for her to think such things when Elizabeth was her truest friend.

And going deeper: Why, after all, were she and Elizabeth so close? Because they "liked" each other? Yes, but more perhaps. Perhaps it was because of the thing they both held in common . . . a love for Drew, Elizabeth's open and good, Rachel's hidden and . . . and perhaps evil.

What terrifying thoughts! Dare she share them with someone? But who? Rebekah? No, Rebekah would be horrified! Drew? No! He would never trust her again. He would not understand such feelings, and he would hate her utterly.

She came to the foot of the hill, and looking up, saw the house in the distance. It was here that the cobblestone of the street gave way to dirt. No matter—the rain had not begun and the ground was dry.

When she was halfway up the hill, Rachel became aware of a sudden change in the atmosphere. The day had grown much darker, and the wind was whirling with such intensity that she could scarcely stand. She drew her hood tightly beneath her chin, the weave of the cloth biting into her jaw. She squinted against the flying dust.

Suddenly, when she was but steps from the house, the whole world about her glowed radiantly white. A clap of thunder slammed against her eardrums and snapped her spine straight, jolting her teeth together. No one had ever accused Rachel Calhoun of overcaution, and she could not remember a moment of real fear from physical danger. But now she was certain she'd been struck, that in reality her body lay back in the road and only her spirit hurried on.

Large drops of rain quickly dispelled this notion. Great, cold splats falling thick and fast, until, by the time she came to the house, she could not see three feet ahead.

Looking out through the open door, Drew saw Rachel run out of a gray sheet of rain into the shelter of the porch. He stepped out and pulled her quickly inside.

"What are you doin' out in this storm!" It was not a question, but a rebuke.

Rachel pulled back her hood, shook her head so that her long hair came free, and unbuttoned the cloak. As she reached behind to gather the cape into her hands, Drew felt—only faintly, but with pleasure—the tautness of the bright blue satiny cloth about her upper body. Rachel's face was still wet. She stepped back to the door and vigorously brushed the remaining drops from the front of her full skirt. She was short of breath, and answered hurriedly.

"My pupils!" she said. "I *had* to come."

"You'll have *no* pupils in such weather," he said. At that, a hot bolt of lightning flashed through the nearest tree, and a great limb came crashing to the ground.

"And your students will have no teacher if she insists on going out in storms like this!"

She turned back into the room, looked up at him and laughed, lightly, breathlessly. "Yes, I guess you're right."

As the sound of her laugh died out, she thought of the mask she was wearing, to laugh when she felt as she did inwardly.

The darkness having fallen only moments before, there were no lights in the house. Drew stepped to a table against the east wall and from a tinder box on the mantel took flint, steel, tinder, sulfur-tipped matches, and struck fire to the twin wicks of a whale oil lamp.

The wind moaned down the chimney; the room grew cold. He placed fresh wood in the fireplace and, from the lamp, lighted a long, thin sliver of wood. Shortly, the fire blazed up and the room began to grow warm.

All the while, Rachel stood watching him light the lamp and lay the fire, and as she did, all the feelings of which she was so afraid came rushing in.

Could it be after all that he felt as she did? No, she thought, never. And if he did, he would never let her know it! She was only a younger sister to him; that's all she'd ever be. Their talks, their laughter, their walks along the road—like a sister.

She remembered sudden moments when she had turned to find him gazing at her, smiling in an unselfconscious way. But not once had she detected in him the slightest illicit wish. No. She was sure of it: the feelings were all hers; he felt nothing for her. She was half relieved, half disappointed by this conclusion. But her secret was safe. In his innocence, he would not suspect.

Outside, the wind blew harder. Now and again a limb cracked sharply and came crashing to the ground. The joints of the house creaked in the gusts, and the rain beat furiously. Water overflowed the gutters and ran in sheets over the glass planes. The lawn was awash. But the fire blazed high. Drew stood at the window, his back to Rachel, who was standing near the fireplace warming her outstretched hands over the flames.

"I've always loved the storm," he said. His Scots accent seemed thicker and he rolled the r in "storm." His masculine voice resonated evenly through the room, relaxed and low.

"The thunder makes me feel secure . . ." Again, she thought, the rolled *r*. ". . . and the lightning," he said.

At the sound of his voice, like coals grown bright in the wind, a sudden desire seized her. Rachel wanted to run across the room like one possessed, to reach her arms around him, lay her face against the back of his broad shoulders, and pour out her heart; to cleanse herself by making him her confessor. She knew her own impetuous nature, knew how in the grip of emotion she sometimes acted stupidly. She knew the outrageous folly of it, and yet she found herself moving toward him against her own will.

Just then, as suddenly as it had come, the rain stopped, its pelting staccato trailing off to tap randomly against the window. The darkest clouds moved on and the sky lightened to an even, bright gray. Sunlight flooded through the dripping trees. Drew's hands were still clasped behind his back as he turned toward her. There was blank surprise as he saw her coming toward him with purpose in her eyes. He started backward ever so slightly.

Without a change in tone of voice, he said, "The worst of it's moved on northwest, into the hills . . ." He hesitated, seemed suddenly confused, looked down at the floor and in a softer, more subdued voice, "In another hour or less, it'll hit Allentown."

Rachel froze before him, knowing the blush of shame burning on her face had already betrayed everything. She clapped her hand over her mouth and, sobbing, her long dark hair whipping behind her, Rachel bolted from the room.

As her soft-soled shoes scurried over the wooden porch and off into the soggy grass, no cry broke from her lips. Drew Wolfe did not call after her, but stood staring into the fire, the color drained from his face.

THIRTY-ONE

RACHEL was far beyond the bottom of the hill before she stopped running. Even then she walked as rapidly as she could. She had left her cloak behind, and now the damp chill made a shiver pass across her shoulders. The full skirt of her blue cotton dress and her long sleeves were covered with small dark spots, light sprinkles from the sky. Mud covered the hem of the dress, and she was carrying her too-slick shoes in her hand, going down the brick walkway barefoot. Her face was a maze of emotions. As the tears ran down her cheeks, she sucked hard and bit on her full lower lip, yet did not feel the pain. An older man who knew her, coming down the other side of the street, wondered at her haste, wondered that she did not speak, and noticed that every few steps her shoulders convulsed.

Just as she approached the street where the Bowmans lived, a carriage came rattling over the cobblestone going west. Harnesses squeaked loudly and chains rattled against the doubletree. The coachman cracked his long whip and four large horses lunged forward, rushing for their destination before the rains could return. So preoccupied was Rachel by her own humiliation, and by the fear that she had ruined her life completely, she gave the carriage no notice at all. And she did not hear a voice from the coach loudly calling her name.

When Rachel opened the Bowmans' door and entered a few moments later, she was glad to find that Rebekah was in another part of the house. She closed the door quietly behind her, ran up the stairs, and fell across her bed. There she lay, tears wetting the comforter beneath her head. She sobbed bitterly at her own horrible frailty. At last emotional exhaustion overcame her and she slept.

Much later, through the haze of sleep, Rachel heard a distant knock at the front door. She opened her eyes. As the soft webs gradually cleared from her mind, a cry from the throat of

Rebekah Bowman pierced the air. Instantly Rachel came fully awake and, looking out her window, realized that it was mid-afternoon of the same day. The sky was yet covered with clouds, and the light had begun to decline. She went fearfully to her door to listen. At the bottom of the stairs Rebekah was standing at the banister, trembling, her face hidden in her hands.

"Oh, Rachel," she said, looking up, "thou wilt never, never believe it!" Rebekah's eyes were wide with terror.

"Believe what, Rebekah?" Rachel descended the steps slowly.

"She was so *close* to home! *All* that way safely, only now . . ."

The color drained from Rachel's face. "And now *what*, Rebekah?" She gripped Rebekah's shoulders, then saw Israel standing somberly in the doorway, his broad-brimmed hat in his hand. He walked toward them. "There's been an accident, Rachel," he said, his deep voice quivering.

"Who! Oh, who?" Rachel's voice was small with fear.

"Elizabeth, Sabina. About noon. Right after the rain. Their coach hit mud at the bottom of the hill, one of the horses stumbled, the others fell, and the coach overturned into the ditch on the north side of the road."

"But they're all right! Oh, do tell me they're all right!"

"No. No, they're not. For a few moments Sabina seemed unhurt. But then her breathing stopped and they couldn't revive her. Elizabeth's badly injured . . . to the death, I'm afraid. The driver wasn't even hurt."

"And Drew," both women asked weakly, almost in unison.

"The driver didn't know Drew to be a doctor, and went running to James Miller's house for help. Miller, he sent for me; I was the one who told Drew."

Rebekah, trembling, reached into her pocket for a handkerchief. Quietly she asked, "And how did he take the news?"

"Stunned for a moment, wild with terror the next. He ran out and down the hill, going like a madman through the field to Miller's house. That's where he is now."

It was eight days later when Elizabeth's eyes fluttered open for the first time. Drew fell down beside her, grasping her hands in his, sobbing out his gratefulness.

"Drew?" she said weakly, her mind filled with cobwebs. Her

voice felt rough in her throat. She looked wonderingly at the faces looking down from about her bed.

"Right here, my darling. I'm right here."

His unruly sheaf of dark brown hair had fallen unheeded across his forehead.

"Drew," she asked slowly, "why am I here?"

"An accident, Beth," he said softly, "a terrible accident in the coach."

"I remember hiring a coach," she said. "I even remember its starting to turn up our lane. I was so glad to be home, but . . ."

Drew buried his face in her counterpane and his shoulders began to shake.

"You thought I would die!" she said to him. "Oh, Drew! My poor, dear Drew!"

She softly caressed his hair while scanning the little group of friends—Rebekah and Israel, Esther Miller, Dr. Giltner, and Rachel.

"Why're you so gloomy?" she said. "I'm going to be well. Tell them, Dr. Giltner."

"Oh, Beth!" Rachel sat down on the bed beside her, and bending over her face, broke out sobbing.

Suddenly Elizabeth knew. "My baby!" she cried. "Oh Drew, my baby! Where is Sabina?"

Elizabeth grew weaker from that day on. Giltner thought it was hidden blood loss. Forrester said there was a "seepage in the brain," and wanted to trepan her skull to relieve pressure.

"Absolutely not!" Drew said, refusing the horror outright. "She's dyin' because her child is gone," he said. "She's dyin' of love."

While Elizabeth lingered, Drew stayed beside her. He read to her; they talked. He moved his study to the room next to hers. And when it became clear they were approaching the end, Drew refused to believe it.

It was early morning, their closest friends gathered about in the room where Elizabeth lay—the room where Rachel had held her classes, the room with many windows so full of light. She had lain unconscious for the last two days. As they watched with sadness, Elizabeth's chest rose farther with each breath, until it seemed near bursting. Every pause was longer than the last.

By mid-morning the exhausted Drew could bear it no

longer. He rose unsteadily from his chair and turned toward the door, repeating brokenly, "Terrible, terrible, terrible!"

Rachel, sitting by the eastern window, watched him go. All her hope was gone, and the cold finality of approaching death had left her face lifeless.

When the door closed softly behind Drew, Israel looked sadly from Rebekah to Rachel and shook his head. Esther Miller stared at the floor. Rachel could hear Drew in the next room, pacing out his sorrow, sobbing in anguish.

Suddenly they all looked in terrible anxiety at one another— the next breath had not come. Elizabeth was gone.

Rachel stood slowly and gazed down on the face of her friend. The sunlight on her pale lips, closed now forever, made her seem only asleep. With unspeakable sadness, but without tears, she smoothed Elizabeth's blond hair and cradled the still-warm face lovingly in her hand.

Slowly, Israel Bowman rose, opened the door quietly, and went out. Drew lifted his eyes and saw his friend. The big gun-smith placed one powerful arm about Drew's shoulders, held tight, and said simply, "Drew, she's gone."

When Drew crumpled, Israel swept him up like a child, carried him to his bed, and laid him down.

It was much later when Rachel came into the room where Drew lay, his right forearm covering his eyes. He reached out and took her by the hand, gripping it so tightly she almost cried out.

"What am I going to do, Rachel? Whatever am I going to do?"

Rachel felt her heart breaking in two. And suddenly she knew that for the first time in her life, her heart was breaking not only for her own pain, but for the anguish of another.

Almost in alarm she looked about the room, absolutely certain that Elizabeth was there.

THIRTY-TWO

As the weeks dragged on, autumn's warm rich sun faded into the pallid light of winter. The hills about Philadelphia were covered with wide swaths of dull oak brown, pointed with maples of crimson fire. The smell of wood smoke filled the tangy air. It grew cold, then colder, until by the third day of November the icy air stung most bitterly.

And then there came an unexpected reprieve—eight resplendently warm days together, like star sapphires on a string. The sun in the south shone brightly, the remaining songbirds sang songs as sweet as on any summer morning, and the air enfolded Philadelphia in its endearing arms.

It was the third such day, in the early afternoon, when Rachel had finished her classes—temporarily being held at the Bowman home. By now her younger children were doing simple sums and the older ones were reciting from Aesop, while she herself had taken a sudden interest in Roman history and Greek mythology.

Nothing in all her life had devastated Rachel as had the events of the summer past. Shortly after Elizabeth's death Donald had come up from Wilmington to be with her, and to offer what solace he could to her and Drew.

"My life has become one long succession of deaths and separations," she had told him tearfully. "I'm beginning to wonder what makes it worth living."

But today, after the children were dismissed, Rachel tried to throw off her sadness by borrowing one of Israel's horses and riding out of town until the road north became a path along the crest of open bluffs above the Delaware.

She had ridden for perhaps twenty minutes before coming to an overlook. For a while she sat on the horse forlornly, gazing over the river valley, and then swung down from the saddle, breathing deeply. The air was fresh and clean in her throat, and the ride having alerted her tired mind, she began to feel she was waking from a long half sleep.

The fresh breeze rustled in the dead leaves of the oak grove behind her. The grass here was the color of straw, brittle to the touch, springy underfoot. Rachel dropped the horse's reins and lay down, stretching out on the grass. In the intoxicatingly hospitable warmth, she began to feel the tension of months draining away.

"Why wasn't it I who died?" she whispered into the air. "Elizabeth and Sabina, they had more good in them than I ever shall . . . and they had someone who will miss them so."

Rachel had come to this place for a reason. It was this very overlook where they had all come one Saturday afternoon a year and a half ago. Beneath these trees they had eaten and Sabina had played. What a happy day it had been! It was just before Rob came so close to destroying their life together.

"If ever anything happens to me, Rachel," she remembered Elizabeth laughingly say that day, "you must take care of Drew, for he can't take care of himself."

That long-ago day, Drew had prepared the lunch, even to baking the bread; and the center of the loaf, not quite done, was still doughy. Rachel could feel it in her mouth yet. He had laughed good-naturedly and had winked at her. Then they had taken a path to the foot of the bluff, and sat in its cool shade to watch the great river flow by.

"A river is a road to anywhere," Elizabeth had said, "to the sea, then to home and to Scotland. But what a treacherous road it is!"

Elizabeth could not have guessed, Rachel thought now, that the river and the sea would lead her safely home and back again, and that a simple path on the face of the land would destroy her world.

But over and over Rachel kept hearing Elizabeth's words: "If something happens to me, take care of him."

Elizabeth had been right, for Drew certainly needed caring for. Rachel was worried about him.

"He's withering of melancholy," Israel had said yesterday. "He sleeps in that study next to the room where she died . . . refuses to go back to their bedroom. He keeps Sabina's room just as it was before they went away. He hasn't shaven for days, and doesn't see his patients at all."

At this Rachel had wanted to weep. It was several moments before she could ask, "Is he eating well?"

"He hardly touches the food we send him every day," Rebekah had said.

For a moment Rachel contemplated the gray breast of a sea bird hovering overhead. Then her mind returned to that day last year.

Of course Elizabeth had only been teasing Drew when she said Rachel should care for him if something happened to her. She had not meant it at all. But something *had* happened, and why should Rachel *not* care for him, and why should she not tell him that she would? Because he would only think me an irrational child, she thought, that's why. And her mind returned to the morning before Elizabeth's death.

"What a fool I made of myself," she whispered, "a terrible fool! I'm a grown woman, and acting like a trollop!" And her face grew red at remembering.

Strange how neither she nor Drew had ever mentioned that moment again. Or perhaps not so strange, with all that had intervened. The cruel afternoon had made her forget, and it had made Drew forget as well. Else how could he have held her hand for comfort when Elizabeth died? But perhaps he had not forgotten. Perhaps . . .

The shadows had grown long without Rachel's notice. The whole gray face of the river was overcast by the bluff's dusky shade as the sun descended swiftly behind the western hills. A flight of white sea birds played in the reddish glow, swooping down and lighting on a sandbar at the river's far side. Rachel felt the air's sudden chill, and with the chill came a wild impulse to act.

Her heart beat fast, and a faint hollow feeling rose beneath her breastbone. She fought against it for a moment—but she had never been good at fighting such things. Within the span of a minute Rachel had risen from the grass, called the horse to her, and was riding rapidly back down the road toward Philadelphia.

She came at last to the drive up the hill to Drew's house. She hesitated, and a lump came into her throat.

"Perhaps I shouldn't," she whispered.

She swung down, tethered her horse, and stood breathless in the gathering shadows. The light of day was almost gone, twilight casting its rose hue across the lower third of the western sky. There was a twitter of birds going to nest in the branches. I would not *do* this if my head were clear, she thought, growing angry with herself. But how can I not go to him? she asked. Shouldn't I go? Isn't that what Elizabeth wanted? But there will be better ways, she thought, better times!

She stood still, feeling there was something dangerous in the moment, dangerous not because she wanted to help Drew, but because she wanted to go and gather him up in her arms, to confess her love to him one more time. Dangerous because, just as he had turned her away at Elizabeth's first coming, he would likely turn her away at Elizabeth's memory.

Still . . . how could she resist?

But she must not be discovered in the attempt. Think of the humiliation it would cast on them both for her to be found going to him at this hour.

She heard the growing clip of horse hooves down the drive at a brisk pace, and held the muzzle of her horse lest he whinny at the other's approach. From the shadow of a large sycamore, she watched as the horse went by in the gathering darkness. There was the figure of a man—the head of the horse and the man's upper body silhouetted against the evening sky, his form rising and falling easily, his large hat a distinct outline. It was Israel. He passed on down the road; Rachel eased and turned her eyes once again toward the house.

In the front windows of the lower story, a light burned, then glimmered, dimmed, and the windows went black. The air was still, and but for the faintest rustling in the branches above her, the birds fell silent. The darkness deepened. Rachel lay her hand against the sycamore, felt the smoothness of its trunk beneath her palm, and with complete resolve started on foot toward the darkened house.

The boards of the porch squeaked faintly beneath her soft tread. The door's brass handle, so familiar to her hand, turned, and the catch clicked. For a moment she hesitated.

"Drew . . ." she whispered into the darkness.

No answer.

He was there—she knew it from the lights she had seen go out—but more, she could feel him there. She wanted to go to him—bidden or not—to slip softly in to where he lay in the darkness and cradle his head on her shoulder, to comfort him.

Rachel reached down and slipped out of her shoes. The wood of the floor felt smooth and warm to the bare soles of her feet. She moved quietly toward the study where Israel had said he slept.

"Rachel . . ."

The voice sent a sudden thrill down her spine. She cried out, and in mid-step stood still.

"Drew?" She spoke into the darkness to her right, scanning the blackened room.

"Here," he said, "near the window."

Then she saw him, almost hidden in the darkness, slumped low in the rocker, his feet propped on the sill of the large front window.

"I saw you comin' up the drive," he said, his tone unchanged.

Rachel could not find her voice. "I knew you were here," she said at last. "I saw the lights go out."

"Why've you come?" he asked.

"I was worried about you, Drew. Israel said you're not eating, you're withering. I couldn't stand the thought of it. I . . . I wanted to be near you," she confessed at last.

There, she had done it again. And now she caught her breath, waiting to hear what he would say. The terrible risk of humiliation and rejection gathered like a whirlwind about her. For a long moment he said nothing.

"I've wondered why you didn't come to me," he said at last. His tone was flat, void of emotion.

She could think of no answer.

"I've missed you, Rachel," he said, then was quiet again.

Missed me? she thought. Her head whirled. He had *thought* of her, had *wanted* her here!

Suddenly she was embarrassed by, of all things, the bareness of her feet.

"What must you think of me, coming here in the night?" she whispered.

"Rachel," he said, ". . . come to me."

It was not a command, but a plea. She felt the shoes slip from her fingers, heard them fall softly to the floor, and felt all the foolish courage rise in her heart again. She knelt at his side, her arms around him, his hands clasping her shoulders. She had waited for the feeling of his hands for *so* long.

"You're all I have left, Rachel." His voice was husky with sadness. "They're gone . . . all gone. And now you've come. Rachel . . ." he said, without changing tone, "I do love you. I have always loved you."

And on her bare forearm she felt the cool dampness of a falling tear.

Here at last, the answer to the question she asked more than

four years ago. Rachel felt the old courage rising in her heart.
It was all right—she had come to him in his aloneness, and
found that he had wanted her to come, had wondered why she
had not. Daring and foolish as it was, she had done the right
thing after all.

THIRTY-THREE

AFTER that Rachel went to him every day.

"Let Willa Godfrey think what she will!" she huffed to
Rebekah one early morning a week later.

Rebekah turned away to hide her smile. It was as if Rachel
had suddenly a whole new reason to live. She was making it
her own private crusade to bring Drew out of his massive
depression—and she would do it, or know the reason why!

"I heard he went out yesterday," Rebekah said.

Rachel had run a long-handled spatula into the mouth of the
stone oven of Bowman's great fireplace and was bringing out
a steaming fresh loaf of bread.

"Yes. Bathed and shaved, and went down to the hospital. I
think he even saw a patient or two."

"Thou hast done a good thing, Rachel. No matter what
Willa Godfrey says."

"Someone had to do it, and—" Rachel began.

"Others had tried. Thou wast the only one who could. Apparently Drew's feelings for thee went much deeper than any
of us suspected."

"I've always known . . ." Rachel said under her breath.

"What?"

"Nothing, Rebekah," Rachel answered, laying the fresh loaf
out to cool. "I spoke out of turn."

An hour later, as the autumn sunlight came beaming over the
floor of the porch, Rachel again turned the handle of Drew
Wolfe's door. On her right arm she carried her white split-oak
basket. The aroma of warm bread and good German sausage

wafted easily through the thin linen coverlet. She entered without hesitation, without stealth this time, and he met her before a glowing hearth.

Drew could not suppress a smile at her appearance. She'd a crisp white cap on the back of her head, tied with a white tie under her chin. Her long dark hair was over her right shoulder, and her slightly-too-wide mouth with the playfully upturned corners was smiling up at him. She fancied herself an actress, but Drew now clearly understood that day by day she was teasing him out of himself, inviting him to be happy again.

She took him by the hand, quickly led him out onto the porch, and pointed upward through the trees at the open blue sky.

"Look at it," she said brightly. "It's a cool, clear mornin'. Oh, Drew, I want to see you look up into the sky and laugh at bein' alive!" She fingered the loosened tie string of his cotton shirt, ran her hand lightly over the fullness of his billowing sleeve. "Go on," she said, gripping his arm and giving him a little push. "Get your light blue waistcoat. The day is goin' to be beautiful again, and I've a lunch for us!"

They saddled horses, and she led him to the bluff overlooking the Delaware. She spread a white tablecloth just inside the oak grove, and they sat down, one on either side. As the warm breeze blew around them, a flock of white gulls, on sharp, taut wings, wheeled over the bluff's edge.

"Drew," she said, seeking out his eyes, "I don't know what to say to you. We've lived so near to each other for so long . . . and now everything has changed, and so quickly. How can it be?" She lowered her eyes to the white linen spread between them.

"I don't know," he said, "but it is . . . and I want it to be." He reached across the cloth and took her hand. With a touch of surprise, he said quietly, "I've never seen your eyes like this before."

"Like how?" She blushed.

"Blue sky reflected in deep brown," he said.

She looked into his eyes, smiling at a stray lock fallen across his forehead. The mellow light of the grove softened the masculine angles of his face. He went on.

"Your eyes are very deep, and so dark. I think . . ." He paused.

"*What* do you think, Drew Wolfe?" she interrupted, smiling. No one had ever in her life spoken this way to her.

"I think a man lost in your eyes would be lost forever."

She laughed suddenly, not from embarrassment this time, but with genuine amusement.

"You're makin' fun of me," he said, a sudden hurt look coming across his face. "You're *laughin'* at me."

Amid her laughter she opened her basket, laying out pewter forks and Pennsylvania German stoneware—gray-glazed plates with cobalt flowers in scalloped tracings.

"No. No, I'm not!" she said. Then, pausing, Rachel became very tender. "You take me so seriously, Drew. No one has ever done that before . . . and no one has ever thought me beautiful."

"Oh, Rachel," he said, shaking his head vigorously, "how wrong you are! The young men of Philadelphia—I've watched them looking at you. They think you're ravishing! With my own ears I've heard them *say* it." He paused, looking for a moment at the strand of grass twirling between his fingers. He looked into her eyes again.

"No one who ever *mattered* thought me beautiful," she said. He took her hand again. She felt herself enfolded in something new and wonderful. Then quietly she said, "Drew . . . Elizabeth told me I should care for you."

He smiled and let his eyes fall from hers.

"Yes. Elizabeth did say that, didn't she?" He paused. "She loved you, Rachel."

"And do *you* love me, Drew Wolfe?"

"Yes," he said quietly. "Yes I do."

"And will you let me care for you?" Her eyes were smiling and there was mock seriousness in her voice.

"Do you want to care for me?" His tone matched hers.

"What a fool you are to wonder," Rachel said. Rachel rose to her knees in the dry, crisp grass, reached across the white cloth that separated them, lifted her face to his, and kissed him, breathing as she did, "You are an *incredible* fool to wonder!"

THIRTY-FOUR

"WELL, it's happened! Just as I told thee it would!" Israel Bowman's bass voice fairly boomed.

It was the eighteenth of December, and Bowman was in the back of his shop, cranking at his boring machine. Drew had just entered, and before he could stamp the snow from his feet, was greeted with these words.

"One of your I-told-you-so moods, uh." Drew reached for the door handle. "I just remembered something else I have to do."

Israel laughed and kept boring. "But hast thou heard?" he asked. "Hast thou heard?"

"Well, I suppose not. Tell me."

"Boston Harbor, two nights ago. A mob dressed like Mohawks, a thousand citizens at Griffin's wharf boarded the *Dartmouth*, the *Eleanor*, and the *Beaver*. For three hours they hatcheted an entire cargo of East India Company tea and dumped it into the harbor!" Israel said all this with an undertone of laughter.

"You're joking!"

"I am not! More than three hundred chests, worth eighteen thousand pounds sterling, and a whole harbor full of the saltiest tea ever!"

Drew stood for a moment, smiling with mild shock, shaking his head slightly from side to side. "I'm surprised," he said, almost under his breath, then louder, "England has not been all that unreasonable to us. We've got friends in Parliament who plead our cause and ease our load. Somebody in Boston is just trying to pick a fight!"

"I've told thee before," Israel interrupted, "in this country we've governed ourselves for a hundred and fifty years, and now, with France out of the way, we want legal separation from England. And—I think thou'rt right—we *are* picking

fights ... for the sake of stirring up public favor for separation."

"Israel, how in the world can a Quaker—"

"Well, he can't!" Bowman dropped the crank and turned
suddenly solemn. "The truth is, Drew, that several Friends of
my persuasion may soon be disfellowshiped."

"I'm sorry, Israel. Truly I am."

"Well, a man has to think for himself, doesn't he?"

"Yes ... he does." Drew paused. "Then you believe war is
on our doorstep."

Bowman was turning the crank again. "Ah," he sighed, "I'm
neither a prophet nor the son of a prophet. We'll just have to
wait and see."

THIRTY-FIVE

"GENTLEMEN, as men of medicine, your powers of observation
are everything! Your patient's symptoms will often be quite
subtle, and it will be entirely up to you to discover what they
really are."

Dr. Stephen Giltner's voice droned above the heads of his
listeners—a small group of doctors gathered in a corner room
of the Philadelphia Hospital. It was late March, but an unsea-
sonable heat wave made the room insufferable.

Drew Wolfe fought to hold his eyes open, but his head nodded unsteadily. A large fly that had undoubtedly wintered in a
crevice above the fireplace had been coaxed back into activity
by the heat. It buzzed about heavily, then lit on Drew's neck
and bit—he slapped at it, missed, and the fly droned away.

Drew took a deep breath and sat straighter, trying to concentrate, but his thoughts were far from the lecture. What was it
Giltner just said about observation? He couldn't remember, but
he was sure Giltner had noticed his inattention.

Pacing slowly across the front of the room, Giltner eyed
Drew suspiciously, then picked up a pottery bowl and held it
where all could see.

"I want to know what you can tell me about the liquid in this bowl," he said slowly, and then paused for effect. "Observe: I dip my finger and taste.

"Now, ahhh . . . Dr. Wolfe," he said. "Repeat my experiment, please."

Guiltner walked directly to Drew and extended the bowl. Drew, fully awake and trying to be nonchalant, dipped his finger in the bowl and tasted. Instantly his lips twisted and he spat explosively.

"Astringent!" he sputtered. "Pure alum water!"

"Very astute, Dr. Wolfe," Giltner said, smiling wryly. "But your powers of subtle observation have failed you totally."

Still wiping his lips with a handkerchief, Drew cast a puzzled look upward at his instructor.

"Had you truly been observant, Doctor," Giltner said, "you would have noticed that I dipped the tip of my forefinger into this delightful brew, and tasted the tip of my *middle* finger!"

From all around came a burst of laughter. The nearest doctor slapped Drew on the shoulder. Drew saw his only route of escape and joined in, laughing awkwardly with them.

The following afternoon, Drew pushed away from the medical book lying open on his desk. With a long sigh he leaned back in his chair and stared out the window into the trees. His inability to stay awake yesterday during Giltner's lecture came from being out so late the night before with Rachel. All the doctors had known that, of course.

Four days ago Rachel Calhoun had turned twenty. Four years had passed since he first met her, a little less since that snowy night in Scotland when she had come to them, beaten and shorn. What a world of things had come to pass since then. Her hair had grown out and was now longer than before, reaching down to her waist.

Rachel's image hung before him in the air, her dark hair framing the olive skin of her face as the sunlight glinted in her eyes. What an alchemy it worked in his mind. She had become a woman, and the beauty of both her face and form took his breath as nothing in all his life.

He smiled as he thought of the boys of Philadelphia, how they had pursued her and she had not even seen. How one day a note had been hand carried to their door. An anonymous Scottish suitor had written some lines from Annie Laurie.

Her brow is like the snaw drift;
Her throat is like the swan;
Her face it is the farest
That e're the sun shone on—
And dark blue is her ee;
And for bonnie Annie Laurie,
I'd lay me doun and dee.

For certain! he thought. Like Annie Laurie, of whom the only truth known was a haunting painting in a Scottish castle. One having seen Annie Laurie, one could not forget her, and having seen, one could never forget Rachel Calhoun.

Once again he pulled the medical book toward him and began to read. But still the vision of her hung in the springtime air. He closed the book, and locking his fingers behind his head, leaned back and sighed deeply. What would Elizabeth think? he wondered. He would never know, of course, but somehow he thought she would approve.

"Israel," Drew said the following day, "Rachel and I have finally decided."

"So when is the wedding?" Bowman did not look up from his work—engraving the patch box of a rifle due within the week. The tone of his voice seemed flat, so matter-of-fact that Drew knew instantly his friend did not approve of the marriage.

"Why so reserved, Israel?" he asked, a little hurt.

Bowman looked up from his bench. His gray eyes seemed troubled.

"I'm fearful," he said, "of how things will go for thee with this girl."

Drew cast his eyes about and held his spread hands palm up in a gesture of confusion.

"Israel, this isn't the whim of a moment! Rachel and I have lived within the same walls for four years! I know her far better than I knew Elizabeth when we married."

"And?"

"And there are no mysteries left to me about Rachel."

At this Israel laid his graver aside and slowly lifted his eyes to Drew's. A smile spread across his face.

"Elizabeth must have been an unusual woman!" he said wryly. "But mark it: Rachel Calhoun has treasure enough laid up to keep thee surprised for many and many a year! I myself have seen enough to know she can never be broken to bit and saddle. She's of too passionate a nature to make what one would call a 'normal wife.' "

"That should make life very interesting!" Drew responded.

"Interesting is not the word, friend! She will keep thee guessing every day of thy life!"

"Well, I'll only love her the more for it. Besides, I'm not without passion myself."

Israel shook his head and picked up his graver. As he set its point to the pattern, he raised his twinkling eyes to Drew once more and a chuckle rumbled deep in his ample throat.

Their wedding was the last Friday in November, more than a year after Elizabeth's death, and the church was thronged. Music of a string quartet filled the air as Rachel stood waiting beside Donald.

"Look at them, Donald," she whispered. "Can you imagine it—all these people for *my* wedding!" And she laughed quietly.

"They've heard the bride is the most beautiful woman in all Pennsylvania!" he whispered.

Rachel squeezed his arm with her gloved hand and smiled. Donald was amazed at the aplomb with which she carried herself among these people. She held her head erect, chin thrust forward, her dark eyes flashing. He chuckled to himself as first one man and then another found his eyes uncontrollably drawn to her face. Then, quite suddenly, he saw a shadow pass over her features and her eyes take on an empty, contemplative stare.

"Something wrong, dear?" he asked quietly.

"It just occurred to me," she murmured, "how strange my dearest friend's death opened the way for my greatest joy!" She began to fight tears.

"Hush!" he said, lightly slapping the gloved hand on his arm. "You mustn't talk so today! I declare, Rachel, your melancholy turn frightens me sometimes."

But Rachel's melancholy evaporated as Drew entered the room. She watched him looking about for her. Then he found her in the crowd and smiled broadly.

The day was cold, and deep snow covered the ground. When the ceremony was done, the church doors burst open and Rachel and Drew emerged, hundreds of warmly bundled, laughing guests pouring out behind them.

As they climbed into the enclosed carriage, Rachel was ecstatic, but her laughter was lost in a cacophonous uproar of good-natured banter.

"Well, *his* loneliness is over," said one. "She's a *lively* one, to be sure."

"Yes," returned another, "it's so, but I'm so glad for the girl. She's lived a hard life, and Andrew Wolfe will take *such* good care of her."

"Good-bye!" called dozens of voices.

"Did you see how the Edwards boy kept his eyes on her? The entire time! Everyone said he had been sending her notes, but she paid him no mind. Now we know why!"

Rachel smiled and waved as the coach drove away amid a shower of good-byes and fare-you-wells. She turned toward Drew. Her eyes were misty, her face glowing.

"Oh, this is too much!" she said breathlessly. "No one, *no* one has ever looked at me as these people have today . . . It's as though they adore me!"

"Of course they adore you! Why wouldn't they?"

"But it's all so strange to me . . . being a doctor's wife! Respected! My head is spinning."

"You'll get used to it," he said, drawing her close. "I know you. You're strong. You'll take to this life—mark my word on it."

That night in bed beside Drew, Rachel lay with his arm about her, her head on his chest, passion abated after the most exquisite hour of her life.

"I couldn't've dreamed it," she said quietly, "that you and I would ever 'lie naked abed' like this."

"We came close to dreaming it once," he said, and pulled her softness tighter to him.

"I was only a child then," she said, "and you . . . you were simply too wonderful for words."

He laughed an embarrassed laugh.

She continued in that low, smooth voice, "The very sight of you has always made me feel such a . . . such a *wanting*!"

He laughed the same laugh, and murmured some awkward thing. Puckishly she lay her thigh full across his and, smiling, propped her chin on his shoulder. "You're blushing!" she teased.

He put his hand on the back of her head and hugged her to him, as much to hide his embarrassment as to feel her close. How different she was from Elizabeth! Elizabeth . . . so modest even when they were in each other's arms. But Rachel? Rachel was as bold as she was impulsive. And she was as passionate and unashamed as Elizabeth was reserved. Drew had not even guessed, and now he simply did not know what to say.

She began to snicker, and they burst out laughing together. When their laughter subsided, she took his hand in hers, smoothing the rough skin, feeling the strength of his fingers.

Suddenly she propped herself up on one elbow, her long dark hair falling down over his bare chest.

In the candle gleam her hair seemed to him almost · black, the auburn tones hidden in the softness of such light.

"My *father's* hands were large like yours," she whispered, "but much rougher. . . ." She searched his eyes thoughtfully. "I know how you feel about my father," she said. With her right forefinger she traced a thoughtful pattern through the dark hair of Drew's chest.

"He was a powerful man," Drew said quietly, "but you're right, I despise him for what he did to you."

"You talk as though he were dead," she said.

"He is," Drew answered. "We'll never see him again. So far as you and I are concerned, he is as good as dead."

Rachel winced. Drew shouldn't've said that, she thought. *She* might say all the bad things about her father that she pleased, but Drew should not say them. She breathed quietly for a moment, letting the twinge of anger pass.

Drew resented Bartlett Calhoun's intrusion into their wedding bed. But he knew that all Rachel's emotions lay just beneath the surface, and that at the slightest cue, she would bring out events long dead, rehearsing them over and over to anyone who would listen. Still, this was not the time, not with her soft body against him and her thigh lying so deliciously over his. His hand made warm circles on her thigh as she talked on.

"When I was little," she said, "the thing I wanted most in the world was to make Daddy proud of me . . . and he never was." A great sadness came into her voice. "He said I was stupid, and I believed him. Drew, I'll never forgive him for that!"

He stopped making the circles, gripped her thigh tightly in his hand, and said nothing. He felt her nuzzle closer, as if she were seeking shelter, then felt the wetness of a tear on his chest.

"He would say," she continued, " 'Rachel Calhoun, if I

could beat some sense into those brains of yours, whatever brains you have! Good God!' he'd say, 'how like your mother you are!' " Rachel paused, trembling with anger. "But Drew," she said, "I know now that I'm *not* like my mother! No! I'm like *him*! And Drew, that *frightens* me! I don't *want* to be like Daddy!"

"Rachel!" Drew broke in as he squeezed her bare shoulder, drawing her deeper into the hollow of his arm. "Those were lies, all of them! Just a bitter man filled with bile! You're a wonderful, brilliant young woman, and you must never forget it!"

Rachel took in the breadth of his shoulders and the gleam of the candlelight on his skin. She lifted her eyes to Drew's, and the calm of his light gray eyes brought her back into the present. She hugged him to her. "Oh, help me forget, Drew. Love me until I know what you say is true!"

Very softly, he began to laugh.

She looked up at him. "Why are you laughing?" she asked, fear in her smile.

He looked into her eyes and ran his fingers through her hair. "I was seeing you as I saw you the first time," he said softly, "on the shore of Lochredfern: the tall grass about you, a boy's cap cocked above one eye, your hair over your shoulder, and a big smile on your face!"

She smiled at the memory.

He laughed. "So theatrical!"

"Theatrical!" she repeated.

"Yes, but you were wonderful! Oh, Rachel . . . you're right. We never dreamed, did we," and his laughter became a warm smile, "that one day we'd be together like this."

She rose from his shoulder and pressed her lips against his. How pleasurable the feel of his lips! How intoxicating! How she loved this man! Her kisses were soft and quick, until the sweet pressure of their lips would not let them go. His left hand cradled the back of her thigh and pulled her to him. In that moment all Rachel's thoughts of the past were smothered in a love that somehow she had always known could be hers.

Early the next morning, Rachel came to the foot of the stairs and found Drew rebuilding the fire. About midnight the weather had turned bitter and the wind had risen.

For a long moment she stood on the stair gazing down at him. She was dressed only in her thin silk gown, a plaid shawl about her shoulders, hugging herself tightly. Her lovely feet were bare, and she leaned against the banister as Drew lay fresh logs in the open fire. Sparks snapped onto the hearth at his feet. He looked up and smiled.

"Cold!"

"Very cold." She smiled, shivering softly.

"Look at the windows," he said, nodding toward them.

Golden light had just broken over the wooded land east of the river. Below, the city still lay in shadow, but the sun's rays flooding in gave the frosted windows a glorious yellow fire.

"Oh, how wonderful," she exclaimed in awe.

Every pane was scrolled with long frosty vines and slender needles of ice. The fire on the hearth began to crackle softly and cast its warmth into the room. Rachel's eyes filled with tears of gratefulness.

"Home," she said, "*my* home! Oh, Drew, how very wonderful!"

The days raced by, and soon Rachel was thinking of Christmas. Philadelphia was ablaze with holiday illuminations.

But amid the celebration, everyone was chattering about the trouble in Boston. Parliament had ordered that no goods be shipped in or out of Boston Harbor until the tea destroyed a year ago was paid for. Lobsterbacks were again in the streets, forcing the people to house and feed them.

THIRTY-SIX

IT was six months later, a day early in 1775, and the air was full of spring. Except for a few long, high clouds wisping down from the northeast, the skies above Philadelphia were clear and blue. But below, true to Israel Bowman's prediction, the colonial pot had come to a rolling boil.

"In rebellion! The British say we are in a state of rebellion!" The speaker's strong baritone echoed from the back walls and into the surrounding balconies of the Presbyterian meeting house. The sanctuary was full, every seat taken, every standing place.

Rachel Wolfe sat crowded against the end of a pew near the front. That morning when she awoke, her heart was aching for her mother, yearning to feel close to her. If there's a way to be close to the dead, she had reasoned, it has to be through spirit. Rachel did not know about God, but believed in spirit, and so had Bess. Perhaps if she could slip unnoticed into a church somewhere, she would feel her mother's presence there.

"Drew," she had said, "I think I'll go to the Presbyterian meeting house, the one on High Street near Strawberry Alley. Would you like to come with me?"

"No," he had said slowly, shaking his head. "That wouldn't be honest of me, Rachel. You know how I feel about religious matters—superstition, wishful thinking."

So she had gone alone.

As she listened, Rachel wished Drew were there, for he would have wanted to hear what the Reverend Robert Tasker, a first generation American from Scotland, was saying.

"Many—perhaps *most* of you," he said, sweeping the congregation with his eyes, "recall the shores of England, its green hills and craggy headlands. As for me, it is farther north where my memories lie. No more than two weeks ago Ann and I gathered with other Philadelphia Scots to recall the old country. And when our host brought out a set of pipes and set them skirling, there was not a dry eye among us. We looked away and swallowed hard. It was a night of the tartan and the haggis, a night of laughter and the good Scots tongue, a night to be remembered as long as we live!

"But in our native land all those beloved things—the tartan and the pipes, the kilt and the speech, as you well know—lie under a ban. And it is the English who have banned them. For that reason alone, there is many a Scot on this shore that would gladly kill himself an Englishman! And, the truth to tell, if I would but allow it, I, too, would be tempted to draw English blood. But I keep a rein on myself.

"The dark clouds of war now hang over our heads. Forces on both sides are gathering themselves for the conflict. King George is sending fresh troops. Our countrymen up and down the seaboard are gathering powder and arms. Many say that war is inevitable. I do not know. I pray it may yet be averted. I do *not* wish to see the sons and fathers of this congregation lie bleeding and wounded on some dusty field of death."

Tasker paused while his words sank in. The congregation was utterly silent; there was neither titter nor murmur nor cough. Tasker continued, his voice quieter.

"This is Easter Sunday. And most especially in our present circumstances, it is well we remember the resurrection of Christ—Christ who came not only to save us from death, but to save us from ourselves. And God knows, we need to be saved from ourselves, from our unreasonable passions and our hatreds.

"As for myself, regarding what may be an approaching war, I am as yet uncertain. Ought we to withdraw and become a nation apart? Or ought we to work valiantly for some noble compromise?" His words began to come more rapidly now. "Which is the way of Christ? I do not know.

"But this I do know: Whatever it may be to which Christ is calling us, the road will not be an easy one. Worthy compromise can only be hammered out on the anvil of self-sacrifice. But to bring forth a new *nation* would require the white-hot forge of a much *deeper* sacrifice: the sacrifice of sons—and of daughters, too—and of homes, and friendships.

"Do the offenses against us really call for the shedding of blood? For we do have friends in Parliament—influential friends, they are—pleading our cause. And I often wonder is it not better to be ruled by one tyrant who lives three thousand miles away than to be ruled by three thousand tyrants at a distance of one mile? I confess that I fear mob rule and these . . . 'democratic' choices.

"It is my hope that whatever our course, and however fiery the trial, God will bring from the trial a resurrection—a new form to old governments—a form in which men may choose from many options to make for themselves and their families the kind of life that suits them best. And, if such a form does come forth, I pray it will be built not on the shifting sands of self-accomplishment and unguided self-determination, but on the firm structure of the will of God and of Christ! For it is He who first created freedom for men, and it is He who will lead men in their way if they will but let Him.

"No man can make our choices for us. You must choose, even as I. As your spiritual leader, I can only commit you to God and pray that you choose well."

Here Tasker paused, appeared to struggle within himself for something more, and then, with abrupt finality, said, "May God be with you all!"

The whisper of men and women rising from their seats and the murmur of subdued conversations began to fill the room. Feet shuffled along the aisles toward the doors. But Rachel Wolfe sat quietly, lost in her own deep thought and conflicting emotions. Tasker's forceful declaration had stirred her. But she sat brooding over the division that seemed to exist between herself and Drew. Five years in the rarefied air of this country had made her an American. Now she believed freedom from England was worth any cost. Her countrymen could not be truly free until every English soldier and sympathizer was driven from these shores.

But Drew? He appeared to lean toward reconciliation more than toward independence. What this would bring between them, she could only imagine. But as the worshipers shuffled past her, she did something she had not done since she was a child. She silently addressed her mother's God and begged Him to preserve the happiness she had so belatedly found.

In the small hours of Monday morning, Drew Wolfe woke from a sound sleep to hear Rachel whimpering and moaning beside him on the bed. Her voice was slurred, indistinct. He listened.

"No," she said insistently, "please *no*." Her inflections were childlike, a little girl pleading. She rolled over, and as she did, her hand brushed his shoulder. She pressed with her feet against the bed, and her voice rose to a crescendo. "Come back!" she called, "come back!" then bolted upward in the bed.

"Rachel!" he said, grasping her hand. "Wake up! You're dreaming!"

She grabbed his arm and pulled herself to him. "Oh, he's gone! He's gone! Drew, bring him back! Please bring him back!"

"Bring who back, Rachel? Who is it that's gone?"

"I don't know . . . oh, I don't know." She held him tightly, shivering with emotion, breathing hard. "Daddy maybe . . . or you . . . I . . . I think it was Daddy."

Her head began to clear.

"Ohhh," she breathed at last. "Drew, it was so real. I was little, and in a town somewhere. It was night. There was loud music, and the smell of whiskey, and people I didn't know. Then across the room I saw him. It *was* Daddy. His head was shining under the lamplight, and he was . . . what was he doing? He was playing cards—and he didn't see *me*. I called out to him—oh, it was so *real*," she said again.

"And did he hear you?" Drew stroked her hair and held her close. The back of her neck was wet with perspiration.

"No. No, he didn't hear me at all. He just got up and came toward me, but his eyes were never on me, and he walked right past, right out the door. And I was crying and screaming—so afraid to be left alone." She was still trembling. "My mouth is *so* dry, I'm going for a drink of water."

"Lie still," he said. "I'll get it."

He went to the nightstand and, from a stoneware pitcher so white that it could be seen even in the darkness, poured water into a glass tumbler.

"Here," he said.

"Thank you," she said, feeling for the glass. As she drank it down, he held her free hand.

"You're still trembling. Let me hold you close."

As she lay with her back nestled to him and his arms about her waist, her trembling began to subside.

"I hope that never happens again!" she said. For a long while she lay thinking of how real it had seemed. And two weeks later, she had the same dream all over again.

THIRTY-SEVEN

THE late spring day was ending. It had been hot, and the air seemed thick, uncommonly still. At the corner of High and Second streets, the very center of downtown Philadelphia, a large crowd had gathered about a pro-independence speaker on the courthouse steps. With the sun sinking, and torches flaring up in the street, the throng punctuated his speech with loud shouts of approval.

Drew and Rachel had ridden out into the cool of the evening, and having just left the crowd's edge, were going north on Second. In no hurry, they allowed their horses to saunter.

Stone buildings lined the street, some of them reaching to

four and five stories. Two lamplighters—one on either side—
were moving from lamp to lamp, leaving a twin trail of illumi-
nation behind them.

"Well, the man back there knows where he stands!" Drew
exclaimed. He shook his head and sighed. "And he may well
be right. Independence may be the only way. I only wish I
were as certain."

"You and the Reverend Tasker!" Rachel chided, smiling.
"You see both sides of every issue, and neither of you can
make up your mind on the most simple things."

He smiled. She was right, indecision was a weakness. But
how could one make good decisions unless he had the facts?
Even so, Rachel's mind was at rest now. Each had too much
stake in the other to let the question of independence come between them.

Continuing north, they passed Coomb's alley and had
reached the corner of Mulberry and Second when, the reins
slack, Drew's horse sidled toward the water pump and wooden
trough set in the middle of the cobblestone street. The horse
bent his neck and drank slowly of the cool water. The noise of
the crowd was far behind them now. From just across the way,
laughter filtered through the open windows of St. George and
the Dragon Inn.

Abruptly, the laughter changed to angry shouts.

"Stop! No!" And instantly the report of a gun and a scream.
There was the low rumble of men's voices, then shouts imploring someone to call a doctor.

Drew and Rachel sat for a moment, transfixed.

"Bloodshed!" Drew whispered, tugging the reins sharply to
the right and kicking his horse forward. Rachel followed close
behind.

A moment later Drew stood in the tavern door. Before him,
on the floor, a man lay doubled and bleeding. Another man,
with a short beard and sandy-gray hair, was bending over
him. It was Shackleton the innkeeper.

As Shackleton glanced up, he saw Drew, and a glint of recognition unseen by the others flashed in their eyes. The bleeding man, fully conscious, moaning and weeping, was thrashing
his legs and gasping for breath.

"My saddlebags, Rachel. Hurry!" Drew pushed through the
circle of staring men. The air was thick with a white cloud and
the stench of burned powder. A short, thick-set man stood sul-
lenly to one side, held tightly in the grasp of three large men.

Drew went directly to the wounded man. Shackleton moved aside, exchanging a quick, knowing glance with Drew.

"He's shot in the lower gut," the innkeeper said. "Right side, but not bleedin' much."

Rachel returned with the saddlebags.

"Here!" Drew took command. "Four of you, lift this man onto a table—that one there. Mr. Shackleton," he turned back to the keeper, "collect every lantern in the place and hang them from the beams." He looked at Rachel. "Lay out a scalpel . . . with needles and wax thread. This man's bleeding inside. The ball cut an artery; you can see it by the florid color of the blood."

Quickly, he pulled the man's trouser band below his hips, then drew out the long shirttail and laid it over his chest.

"Who is he?" Drew asked. With his fingers he pressed around the wound. Torn fibers of cotton and wool were deeply embedded in the bloody hole.

"Forbes is his name, Doctor."

"Forbes," Drew said sharply, shaking the man's head. "Can you hear me?" he shouted. "Forbes!"

Forbes's eyes rolled furtively and his breathing grew weaker.

"He's going quickly," Drew said to Rachel. She was close at his right. "I'm going to try to tie off the vessel. You," he said, turning to a tall man in a black tricorn hat and shirtsleeves, "you and about five others, hold this man down. There'll be pain here."

"You're not goin' to cut *into* 'im, are you?" the man said, bending his head forward.

"You'll kill 'im sure!" said a tenor voice from the crowd.

"Well," Drew said, "he'll not live five minutes this way!"

The tall man in the black hat stepped back.

"Who's not afraid to do this?" Drew called out.

One by one several men filtered from the crowd and took hold of Forbes. Suddenly aware of what was about to take place, Forbes screamed. Rachel handed Drew the scalpel.

"No!" Forbes shouted, "no!" And he began to weep and thrash hysterically.

"Are you with me?" he said to her.

"I'm with you," she whispered, smiling slightly.

And he drew the scalpel's sharp edge over the white hairy skin above the man's lift hipbone, directly through the wound. A thin red line appeared in its trail. At the second cut, a layer of fat parted.

"We're cutting into the right iliac portion of this man's abdomen." He spoke to Rachel as if they were the only two in the room.

Every man about them was quiet. One after another they turned their eyes away from the scalpel's deepening cut. Several turned toward the door. Rachel looked steadily on.

Following the narrow tunnel of tissue destroyed by the bullet, Drew separated the muscle of the abdominal wall. Blood suddenly welled up and overflowed the incision. The man's struggle stopped.

"He's fainted," she said.

"Good!" Drew responded.

Systematically he explored the man's gaping side with his fingers.

"I've got it!" he whispered, and pinched off the half-separated vessel. "Clean cloth, Mr. Shackleton! Quickly!"

Rachel plunged the bunched cloth into the wound, soaking blood until Drew's fingers appeared—the artery pinched between them.

"Now," he said to her, "the crooked needle, is it threaded?"

"Yes," she said. Her breath was even and her voice calm.

"While I hold the torn spot on the artery together, sew it shut, but only on the side. If we stop the blood flow to his leg completely, he'll die anyway."

She inserted the needle near Drew's left thumb, took it under and out near his right.

"Again . . ." he said. "Now tie it." She looped the thread as if sewing a dress.

"No," he said calmly, "if you tie it like that, the knot will loosen and the bleeding begin again. Use a *surgeon's* knot."

Rachel lifted her eyes in question.

"Like this," he said. "Bring the two ends about and around each other once . . . yes, just that way . . . then twice—then back around as in a hard knot. Exactly!"

Afterward they rode side by side along the street toward what people were beginning to call Wolfe Hill. On either side the streetlamps drove back the shadows.

"*You* should be the doctor in this family!" he said to her, chuckling.

She smiled, but said nothing. There, in the middle of the cobblestone street, beneath a lamp, he reined in his horse and wheeled it about, facing her, his right knee touching hers. They joined hands, and she noticed that even in the dim lamplight, his face was aglow.

"You were absolutely superb!" he said. "We saved that man's life tonight, you and I."

"If he escapes infection," she said, concern written across her face.

"Yes, if he escapes infection. But if he dies, it will be no fault of ours."

She pursed her lips, arched her brows slightly, and smiled. "I like it!" she said.

"Rachel," he said, nodding his head and grinning, "I do believe you've found a new calling!"

A week later Rachel dismissed her students for the last time. Her final decision had come one evening with an urgent knock and a message carried by a breathless farmboy from across the Schuylkill.

"What is it, James?" Drew asked the boy in the doorway.

"Mama needs you now, Dr. Wolfe, real bad. Can you come?"

Drew turned about. "I may need your help on this one, Rachel."

With a mixture of dread and excitement, she ran after Drew to the stable, and within minutes the flying hooves of their mounts were clattering across the wooden span over the river. They caught up with the boy on his plow horse just as they reached the house. As they entered, a woman's voice called out.

"Eli? Eli! Did you find 'em? Are they comin'?" Her words were followed by a low-throated growl that ended in an almost terrifying yell.

"They're here, Mama! They're here. Dr. Wolfe'll help you, Mama. I'm just sure he will!"

Josey Hartman was stretched on her back crossways on the bed, sweat pouring from her face and a fine sheen on her bare arms and shoulders. Her palms and spread fingers moved nervously over the great swell of her abdomen.

"Go on outside and wait, Eli," Drew commanded. "Go now, hurry!"

Drew went directly to Josey. Rachel reached for a clean white linen cloth and dabbed the sweat from Josey's forehead. Josey said nothing, but Rachel's gaze caught and held her eyes for a moment. Through the contortion of her features, Josey's eyes seemed to say she was glad Rachel had come, too. Then the lines about her mouth and eyes began to ease as the pain passed.

"Will I lose this one, too, Dr. Wolfe?" She was breathing hard.

"We hope not, Josey," he said, then to Rachel, "Josey lost her last baby. The cord was wrapped around its neck, and he died before he was born."

Rachel felt her heart beating faster as she continued to dab. A life was depending on the three of them, and, irrationally, she felt it counted on her alone.

"How long will it be?" she said calmly.

Just then another contraction gripped Josey's belly and she cried out. It was a long, throaty cry that climbed in pitch and volume.

"The pains are close," Drew said. "Her time's here."

He reached into the saddlebags he had carried in over his shoulder and took out a flat wooden case. Rachel watched as he opened the hinged lid. There, lying in their respective compartments, were his obstetric tools, all gleaming steel: long-handled scissors for snipping—also for cutting the umbilical, she supposed—and there were forceps—which she had heard about, and distrusted.

"Hold on," Rachel whispered to Josey, giving her her hand. "Just hold on!"

Drew placed Josey's feet flat against her bed and cast a sheet over her knees. "This baby has already crowned!" he said in amazement, reaching toward the open case.

"You're going to use the forceps?" Rachel whispered in alarm. "Must you?"

He shot her a disapproving glance.

"Well, are you?" she repeated as his hands closed about their handles. "Drew, forceps?"

"Find the hog lard, Rachel, and be quick."

Rachel stood staring and didn't move. "Hog lard!" she cried. "For what?"

"So the forceps will go in more easily! Now get me the hog lard!"

"Drew, women have been having babies forever without forceps and hog lard. And you said it's already crowned."

Rachel stepped around where she could see, nudging Drew slightly to the side.

"You don't need the forceps, Drew," she said. "Look," and

she reached, gathering the emerging head in her hands and beginning to guide it out. Drew stared slack-jawed, stunned into immobility. This was a man's world, and he was in charge here. Rachel had never attended a birth in her life. Where did she get the idea she could . . . ? Suddenly, Josey was racked by another contraction.

"Wonderful, Josey!" Rachel called. "Push a little harder! There! Its shoulders are free. The cord is right this time, Josey. I'm drawing the child out. Yes! It's a little boy. Drew, move over just a little, and be ready to cut the umbilical."

Drew was in shock. Apparently he was wrong about who was in charge.

As they rode home through the dark, Drew could feel the smile on Rachel's face, and he knew what it meant. She was feeling the pleasure of discovery—the discovery of something that came to her as naturally as a bird takes to the air.

"I never dreamed how it would feel," she crooned softly. "Drew, can you believe it that with my own two hands I brought life into this world?"

Silence.

"Drew?"

Silence.

"Drew, did I do something wrong? Are you angry with me?"

"I brought you along to help me, Rachel. You ignored my orders. You took over in there. What if it had been something you weren't able to handle? Have you thought of that? But I'll tell you, Rachel, if I ask you to help me again, I expect you to keep your head and take orders."

"Drew?" she said.

"Yes."

"You're right. I wouldn't've known what to do if the baby had been breech, or if the cord had been around its neck. But, Drew . . ." She paused. "You were ready to use those forceps. Forceps should be used only to save the life of the mother. They are dangerous things!" Her voice was strong, not even slightly apologetic.

"A matter of opinion," he said.

She could tell he was very angry. They rode along in complete silence for a while.

"Drew?"

"Yes."

"Dr. Shippen's class in obstetrics ... would you mind if ..."

"If you attended the lectures?"

"Yes," she said softly.

There was a long silence, the only sound being the slow clip of hooves on the road. At last he spoke.

"No, Rachel," he said reluctantly, a residue of anger in his tone. "No, I wouldn't mind."

"Thank you," she said with uncharacteristic meekness. He couldn't hear it in her words now, but Rachel was still smiling in the dark.

The heat of summer came on, and the rains of late spring left pools of stagnant water standing everywhere.

Philadelphia was a low town, mostly level, poorly drained. Its wharves jutted out into the river, slowing the faster currents so that high tides deposited all manner of rotting things along the waterfront. The land south beyond Cedar Street was lower yet, nothing but marshes and swamps. Pools dug here and there about the city to receive runoff stagnated in the summer heat, and this year brought an early infestation of mosquitoes.

When yellow fever broke out on the south side, Rachel worked with Drew day and night. Europeans had no immunity to yellow fever. Normally there were three to five deaths every day in this town of thirty thousand; there were now thirty. Every day families fled into the countryside—common laborers, doctors, clergy.

The first time Rachel went with Drew to the pesthouse, cots of the sick and dying choked passage through every room. The smell was overpowering. For a moment, as she went among the cots, she felt herself losing control, felt her throat constrict and then gag.

"Put a handkerchief over your nose," Drew whispered.

"And make them think I'm afraid?" she answered.

She took a deep breath and bit her lower lip hard. Instantly her head cleared, and she went to the nearest bed.

A ghastly face looked up at her from the pillow. He was only a boy, no more than ten or eleven she supposed. His skin was a horrible yellow, his cheeks sunken—and sudden black vomit welled up into his open mouth.

Rachel wanted to turn and run. Instead she knelt down, took the boy's head in her hands, and turned it to the side so he would not strangle. She reached for a cloth lying on the cot's edge and wiped the rancid material from his pillow. Tenderly, she washed his face and then sat on the edge of the cot, holding his hand.

"What's your name?" she asked quietly.

The boy's fevered eyes gazed up at her, lids half closed. Did he even know she was there? Rachel wondered. Then his lips began to move, though no sound came out.

She watched, intently, said, "Bobby? Your name is Bobby?"

He nodded, and smiled so weakly that it almost broke her heart. But she screwed up her courage.

"Well, Bobby, if it's all right with you, I'm going to sit right here and hold your hand while you rest."

He smiled again, and his eyes slowly closed.

Rachel sat holding his hand as the room grew dark. Just as the sun sank below the horizon, the little boy who had smiled with such love gasped convulsively and died.

Rachel buried her face in her hands and wept.

"You were magnificent today," Drew said after supper. Neither of them had eaten much. "I didn't dream you had such courage! But I should've known."

Rachel dropped her weary eyes slightly and shook her head, setting down her mug of hot chocolate. "I surprised myself," she said quietly.

"You weren't afraid for yourself at all."

"What does it matter?" she mumbled. "Not many of us live to be fifty. Dr. Rush says that of every hundred born, in six years thirty-six are dead, and after forty-five years only ten are alive." She laughed wearily and shook her head. Never had she felt so tired—for never had she seen so many deaths in a single day.

"But you love life so!" Drew said quietly. He reached across the table and took her hand in his. "Yet you risked your life today as though it meant nothing!"

She looked up and smiled a very tired smile. "If I didn't love my life," she said, "I wouldn't know those people were worth dying for, would I?"

He gazed at her wonderingly. "You make me proud to be your husband," he said, his own tired face glowing. "Very proud." He rose from his chair, leaned across the table, and lightly kissed her pale lips. "It's time for rest," he said. "Come upstairs and let's get to bed."

Not until late in the fall did the epidemic begin to fade.

THIRTY-EIGHT

THERE was other news that summer. In the spring, up in Massachusetts, seven hundred British soldiers had marched on Concord to seize military supplies from "committees of safety." They had shot and killed eight "minutemen" at Lexington. The alarm had gone out at incredible speed, so that as the troops marched back to Boston, men and boys out of the countryside sniped at them from cover, killing and wounding hundreds along the way. Within a day sixteen thousand colonists had gathered about Boston, putting the city under siege.

The Second Continental Congress had convened in Philadelphia, appointing a Virginia planter and surveyor named Washington to lead twenty thousand men who were to be called the "Continental Army."

The night was warm but pleasant. It was ten o'clock, perhaps even later, long after nightfall. Drew was in his study, working late. In their upstairs chamber Rachel was preparing for bed when a sound from below made her pause. It had been a knock at the door. She heard footfalls, the door opening, and Drew's voice. She recognized the high, thin voice that answered. It was Jacob Shackleton, the graying, sandy-haired innkeeper. Then came a voice she did not know, very deep, very full. This time when Drew responded, he spoke so quietly she could scarcely hear. There was more whispering. The door closed. Silence.

Rachel was accustomed to Drew being called out in the night. But it did seem strange that he hadn't told her he was going. She turned back to her mirror and assessed her image in the candlelight. Removing the comb from her hair and laying it on the chest, she shook her hair down and, still puzzled, wondered aloud just where it was her husband might have gone.

* * *

"Willa, what are you *saying*?" The full skirt of Rachel's glazed cotton dress rustled as she leaned forward and looked into her visitor's eyes. Rachel and Willa Godfrey were far from being close friends, but they were neighbors, and saw each other much more often than Rachel wished.

Willa was five years older than Rachel, but had married just this spring. It was only yesterday that Drew had said Willa was lucky to be married at all, considering her appearance—her nose being much too large for her mouth; and considering how, among her not inconsiderable faults, Willa had too active an interest in the affairs of her neighbors.

"I'm not *saying any*thing, Rachel," the young woman returned in her irritatingly nasal voice, "except how strange it is that Drew, at *mid*night, would consort with a known Tory like that innkeeper Jacob Shackleton, and with a man nobody in Philadelphia knows."

"How do you know that, Willa?" Rachel asked coldly.

"Know what?"

"That no one in Philadelphia knows this man."

"Well, *I* didn't know him."

Rachel shook her head with disbelief. In Willa's mind, the few persons she knew represented everyone in the city.

"But you yourself saw this man, with Jacob Shackleton and with Drew?" Rachel quizzed.

"Yes, I did. Richard was snoring so loud I had no hope of sleep—and it was hot. So I went out and sat in the yard, inside the fence, under the mulberry tree. It was about midnight when they stopped under a streetlamp no more than twenty feet from where I sat."

"Under a streetlamp?" Rachel interrupted. "Then there was nothing secret about this meeting. They didn't care who saw."

"Maybe not," Willa snapped, nervously twisting the corner of her handkerchief into a tight little pigtail and out again. "But why hasn't he told *you* about it?"

Rachel sighed. "Willa, I do think you like to make trouble!" She paused. "But tell me, what did the stranger look like?"

Willa warmed to the task. "Well, he was more than a head taller than your husband, taller than any man here in this city—that *I've* ever seen. Rugged features, dark clothes, a deep voice. In some ways he looked like—"

Just then a kettle came to boil over the fire and began to whistle. Rachel jumped up, and as she hurried through the kitchen door, called quickly back over her shoulder, "Thank you for coming, Willa. I've got to prepare lunch now. But I'll think about what you've said."

Rachel disappeared into the cavernous kitchen and did not come out again. Willa Godfrey sat a moment longer, staring at the empty kitchen door, and slowly realized that she had just been insulted and asked to leave. She tucked the twisted handkerchief into her pocket, abruptly stood, and, with short, quick steps, scurried out the front door.

It was a week after that, very late at night, when a movement on Drew's side of the bed roused Rachel from sleep. She heard Drew's feet moving on the floor, heard the creak of the stairs, and drifted off again. Then the click of the front door latch and a new thought brought her instantly awake.

Silently she sprang up, slipped into a nightgown, went quickly downstairs, and looked out the large front window. The moon was full. The hilltop lawn seemed as bright as day to her, everywhere but in the shadows cast by the large trees. At last, when her eyes became accustomed to the contrast between deep shade and the moon's silver light, she saw movement among the shadows. Not more than thirty feet from where she crouched were three men—no, four—standing, talking, and Drew was among them.

There again was Jacob Shackleton—she could see more clearly now. And there was a short, stocky man she did not know, and—yes—the tall stranger about whom Willa had spoken last week. The stranger, obviously the center of the conversation, was moving about in the shadows, gesturing.

A daring plan formed in Rachel's mind. She would slip out the back door and come around in the shadow of the house, where she could listen. No sooner had she resolved to do it than the man stopped directly in front of Drew. Drew nodded, and the man reached out, grasped Drew's hand, and shook it with firm resolve. Instantly the three visitors turned and walked through the shadows to where their horses were tethered. Drew hesitated a moment, then came directly back to the house.

Rachel lay in the bed with her face toward the wall, panting for breath. She had run wildly up the stairs and was trying desperately to suppress her labored breathing. She heard Drew's feet on the treads . . . now on the landing . . . She heard the whisper of his clothes as he laid them aside . . . Now he was drawing back the coverlet. The bed gave beneath his weight. His foot touched hers, his left arm went around her shoulder and pulled her tightly to him. Rachel held her breath. He lay his head on the pillow, and soon she felt the slow, even movement of his chest against her back, and knew he was asleep. In the darkness, she clasped her hand softly over his, but her thoughts disturbed her far into the night.

Rachel entered Israel Bowman's gun shop at the corner of Black Horse Alley and Second Street the following afternoon. A strong smell of linseed oil and beeswax, which she thought not at all unpleasant, filled the air.

She had never been to Israel's shop before, but immediately she felt at home in the ordered disarray. Israel was, typically, perched on his high stool near the front windows, rubbing a warm oil and wax mixture into the shining stock of a new long rifle.

"No, Rachel," he said in answer to her query, "I haven't seen or heard of anyone like that. But there are a good many who pass through the city that I never see." He reached into the small clay jar for more of the mixture, then chuckled slightly. "I think thou ought not be too troubled about Willa Godfrey's notions."

"But Israel," she pled in confusion. "It's so unlike Drew not to confide in me. And Jacob Shackleton *is* a Tory, and Drew—"

"Drew has been on the fence too long," Israel interrupted solemnly.

"Yes," she answered, "and he's made no secret of his indecision. Israel, I'm actually *afraid* for us!"

Israel stopped rubbing. With the polished wood standing upright in his lap, its butt resting on his heavy cloth apron, his hands gripping the forestock, he gazed for a long moment out the window.

"Tell me again how the man looked," he said.

"He was tall, very tall. He wore a large tricorn and a long dark watch coat. His white shirt was open at the throat, and he wore breeches, not trousers. For a little while I thought he had on riding boots, but then I made out that they were leggings— out of leather, I think. His shoes were moccasins."

Israel thought for a moment. "Most likely from the interior, probably from the north." After another pause he continued quietly, "The feeling for independence runs deep in Philadelphia. Drew doesn't realize how deep . . . nor how dangerous it is to straddle the fence." He turned his piercing green eyes on her.

"Why not simply ask him what he's about?"

"Because, Israel," she said, "I'm actually *afraid* to ask."

"I've never thought of thee as a fearful woman, Rachel. Indeed, I supposed thou hadst never known fear."

"Oh, Israel," she sighed deeply as she turned to gaze out the window, "I have many fears, and the worst one is that I may lose Drew."

THIRTY-NINE

"RACHEL, I'd rather not talk about it."

Drew spoke calmly, but she could see that his mind was set.

It was evening, and they were strolling hand in hand beneath the trees about their house. The sun was descending through high orange clouds, standing just above the dark western line of the earth.

Rachel had taken Israel's advice, and now wished she hadn't, for Drew refused to tell her. Neither yellow fever nor blood nor danger had made her afraid, but now she felt real fear, and it was written in every line of her face.

"You won't *tell* me?" she said, turning to face him, feeling her mouth go dry.

"No," he said quietly. "It's best you not know."

"Drew, there's nothing about you that I shouldn't know!" Her voice grew tight. "Nothing you can hide if you truly love me!"

She felt her heart beating a staccato rhythm, desperation rising in her breast. This was more than wanting to know, it was a test of her place in his life. Rachel's lower lip began to quiver against her will. She tried to blink back tears, but they ran down, making rivulets on her cheeks that gleamed in the light of the setting sun.

She stood looking at him, her eyes shifting from one of his

eyes to the other, the muscles of her jaw contracting and relaxing, contracting and relaxing. What is he doing to me? she thought. Something's taking my place. The terrible truth is that he doesn't love me! Well, she would not *let* him do this to her! She had trusted him with every last shred of her life. Now his silence was like a knife, cutting away at the trust that bound them together.

"*Tell* me!" she whispered, stepping close and laying her hands on his shoulders. "You've *got* to tell me. Who is that tall man . . . and what has he to do with you?"

Drew turned his head away and stared determinedly at the red disk of the sun, now half hidden below the horizon. Struggling within himself, he turned his eyes back to hers. The orange light gave the dark skin of her face such a lovely hue that for a moment he forgot what he was about to say, but the emotions at work there frightened him into remembering. Still, he must remain steady. Reaching up to where her arms rested on his shoulders, he took her wrists tenderly in his hands and spoke with measured words.

"Rachel," he said calmly, "somehow you've got to trust me. Please don't ask again!"

As he spoke, he unknowingly gripped her wrists tighter than intended—a signal from the past that sent alarm racing through Rachel's mind. She began to tremble. An overwhelming rage of frustration overtook her, so that her tears stopped and a terrible anger took control of every line of her face. Unknown to her, she was being transformed before his very eyes, a transformation reflected in the sudden blank wonder of his own expression.

"Don't *do* this to me, Drew Wolfe," she hissed. "I'll not *have* it!"

With his hands still about her wrists, she began to beat on his chest. Her breath was coming hard and fast.

"I will not *let* you do this to me," she shouted, beating harder.

He gripped her wrists like a vise.

"Let *go* of me!" she shouted, and wrenched free, stepping quickly away from him.

Never in all his life had Drew Wolfe witnessed such a transformation in a human face. From tender light and loveliness to wild, furious contortion, as though the spirit of Rachel Wolfe had been exchanged for some malignant spirit out of the realms of darkness. Drew's heart was in his throat as he watched her back away.

"I should've *known!*" she breathed, crouching and glaring at him with eyes fired by anger. "All your words about love, and how you care for me, and now you do this!"

"Rachel ..." He stared unbelieving, searching for words that wouldn't come.

"No!" she shouted. "I won't hear another lie!"

She turned about and ran toward the house, leaving him with his heart beating hard and sickness rising up in his chest.

When she reached their room, she locked the door behind her and threw herself across the bed.

"I *hate* him!" she said to herself. "I gave up everything to comfort him, to marry him, and now I see he doesn't love me at all!"

The coverlet beneath her face was wet with a profusion of tears, and her voice was thick with weeping.

What was she to do? she wondered. Then, unaccountably, she felt the turmoil in her mind beginning to settle and a great weariness coming over her. "Maybe it's me," she whispered between sobs. "So little rest, and Willa! Why did I ever listen to Willa!"

Her breathing was easing up, the tears coming more slowly. She sniffed, then rose to her elbows, reached for a handkerchief on the nightstand, and blew her nose—hard.

"Sleep," she said to herself, "that's the answer. Maybe it won't seem so bad in the morning."

Drew knew it was no good to follow Rachel, so he stayed in the yard, pacing back and forth between two great maples. He could not imagine why she would behave so—everything she had said and done was utterly out of proportion to the circumstances. Either he was losing his mind or Rachel was losing hers. Why did keeping this secret affect her so? Couldn't she believe that he was doing it for her own good? He didn't know the answers, but it was clear that whatever it had to do with, it could destroy their marriage.

He sat down on the edge of the porch and tried to think, then rose and began pacing again. The fear inside would not let him rest.

"Israel!" he whispered to himself, and stopped still. Then, going quickly around the corner of the house, he headed for the stable.

* * *

The two men stood in the darkness outside the Bowman house, Israel's face somber in the faint light from the window.

"I can't explain it, Israel," Drew said. "Nothing I said or did could've made her act so!"

"Unless," Israel broke in, "what thou didst do and say reminded her of her old father."

"God have mercy, Israel! There's not a *thimble* of resemblance between me and that old reprobate!"

"Except that she loves thou both, that he went back on his love and she thinks thou mightst go back on thine. And thy hands holding her so tight, as he held her and forced his will on her."

"Dear Lord," Drew said, staring into his friend's face. "So it's not between Rachel and me at all, it's between him and her. What on God's earth can a man do about a thing like that?"

Israel made no answer, but shook his head slowly.

"Well, you tried to tell me, didn't you, Israel, that she would be full of surprises."

"I'm not one for I-told-thee-so's," Israel answered quietly. "But I will pray for thee and her. I suggest that thou go and bed down for the night in another room, get out of the house before she rises in the morning, and then come home and test the water. If there's a calm on her, tell her that thou hadst no idea how keeping the thing secret would affect her . . . then tell her about the tall stranger."

Drew shifted his weight from one foot to the other, then lifted his eyes to Israel's.

"You're right," he said reluctantly, quietly. "It's the only answer." He sighed. "Well, I've troubled you long enough, Israel. I'll go along and let you get back to your family."

"No trouble, friend," the big Quaker said, "Good night."

"Good night, Israel." And Drew turned and took up the reins of his horse.

"Andrew?" Israel said.

Drew turned back. His friend's expression was as somber as ever.

"Yes?"

"What *is* thy secret?"

"Oh no!" Drew said, smiling slightly. "I'll not get into that with you!" And nudging the pony forward, Drew rode away with Israel looking after him, a troubled expression on his face.

* * *

Next morning, Drew left the house early. Returning that evening, he found Rachel sitting on the edge of the porch in the twilight, waiting for him. As he rode up and stopped, she stood and, reaching up, took his hand, not meeting his eyes with hers.

Drew felt her tension and, without speaking, dismounted. She laid her head on his shoulder and held him close.

"Forgive me," he said softly.

"It's all right," she answered, but there was no feeling in her voice.

He stepped back and looked into her cool eyes. The corners of her mouth had a hurt turn to them, and there was pain in her expression.

"I didn't know my keeping this from you would hurt you so," he said.

He hesitated, struggling with the words. "So I'll tell you . . ."

He expected her to stop him, to say, "No, Drew, it's really all right. You must do what you must do." But she didn't. She just kept looking at him with those wonderful but cool eyes. Now he had no choice.

"The tall man is the general's chief aide," he said.

"The general," she repeated flatly. Rachel could feel the anger coming back.

"Yes," he said, "the general."

"And how did *you* come to the attention of a British general?"

Her voice dripped with sarcasm. He took a deep breath and went on as though she had said nothing.

"*Not* Howe," he said patiently, "Washington."

For a long moment nothing registered in her eyes, then she began to see.

"Washington!" she whispered, and her expression slowly changed to shock. "The tall man is . . ."

"On Washington's staff," he said.

Rachel dropped her hands and turned half away, taking in all the air her lungs could hold. She closed her eyes and a flood of relief beginning at her toes rose through her body, tears coming to her eyes. In a split moment of shame—which she felt she must not let him see—she hugged him to her again.

"And Washington?" she asked, her voice barely above a whisper. "What does *Washington* want with you?"

She could not believe it. For the last ten weeks the name of George Washington, the Virginian, had been on everyone's lips. Some said it was he alone who stood between the colonies and Great Britain.

"It would be very dangerous for you to know," he said. "That's why I tried so hard to keep it from you."

Rachel's head swam. She was not losing him after all. He had come down on the Patriot side, on the side of independence, on *her* side. His silence had only been a cloak to protect her.

"Rachel—" he began.

"Shhh," she said, and placed her hand over his mouth. "As long as the war can't come between us, I don't need to know anything more!"

She laid her head again on his chest and they stood there, rocking silently to and fro.

"Rachel," he dared quietly, "never in my life have I seen anything like what came over you last night—"

"Shhh," she said, lifting her head and gazing into his eyes. "I want to forget it all . . . I want you to help me forget."

With that, she felt his gaze grow tender and, closing her eyes, lifted her mouth to be kissed. Drew didn't hesitate, and his lips were on hers, the softness engulfing her, her arms going around him. When his large hands gripped her waist and pulled her to him, her breath came fast. It had been days since they had bedded, her distrust robbing her of a dozen opportunities for pleasure and love. Oh, how she had missed his touch!

When Drew's hands went down to knead the swell of her hips and cradle her there, she felt a whimper of pleasure rise and escape from her throat.

"Oh, Drew," she sighed, "how you do make me want you!"

"Oh, Rachel," he moaned, "how you do con*fuse* me!"

But she had no time to think of confusion—not now, as they crumpled to the grass. For a moment they lay with his strong right hand under her head as she gazed with longing into his face. The last light of the sun winking through the trees made the gray of his eyes seem so pale, so deep. It shone on the firm angles of his chin and jaw, making the texture of his face more lovely than she had ever seen it before. Then the sun was gone and darkness rushed over them.

She pulled his head down, meeting his lips with hers again,

the sweet ache of longing in the pit of her stomach driving her on. Quickly she sat up and peeled off his waistcoat.

"Unlace me!" she said urgently as she laid the coat aside.

"Right here?" he asked with delight.

"Yes, right here!" she answered, turning about and offering him her lacings. She pressed him to his back as he unlaced her and pulled the dress forward from her shoulders. "Right here," she smiled wickedly, "where I can think of the fit nosy Willa Godfrey would have if she saw us!"

Together they dissolved in laughter, and then Rachel pressed her full lips over his, as his wonderful hands slipped smoothly over her bare softness and the cool of evening descended over them.

Months went by, the summer blending into autumn, autumn into winter. Then came February 1776. Rachel sat in the parlor of their home, watching a drama unfold between Drew and Israel Bowman.

"I simply cannot under*stand* thee!"

Bowman's big right fist pounded hard into his left palm. He was pacing back and forth, his booming voice riveting Drew and Rachel to their chairs. He stopped and stared hard at his friend, determination burning in his green eyes.

Rachel understood Israel's fervor. He himself was going through fire for the Revolutionary cause. A Quaker in favor of armed resistance, he had been put out of the Society of Friends, a terrible blow for both him and Rebekah. Having paid so dearly to espouse Liberty, Israel simply could not comprehend why his friend, who had no scruples against war, should come down—as he had said—firmly on the side of England.

Rachel hoped Drew would drop his cover and tell Israel the truth, that he was in fact a Patriot, but she watched as Drew followed Israel with his eyes and made no answer.

"Wilt thou at least read this?" Israel pressed, and fished a pamphlet printed on off-white paper from the pocket of his old-fashioned waistcoat.

"Paine's pamphlet?" Rachel asked.

"Yes," Israel said, "published only six weeks ago. Already it's won tens of thousands to the side of independence."

Drew waved it away. "I've read it," he said dryly. "Paine's wrong."

Drew rose and laid another log on the fire. Israel followed him.

"And Franklin!" Israel exploded. "Is Franklin wrong? Certainly he's no wild hare amongst the bushes. This very city bears the mark of his character. He founded the hospital in which thou doest thy work. And he is no young hothead. He is all of sixty-five years old—"

"Seventy," Drew quietly interrupted. He had never seen Israel so worked up, his voice so demanding and loud.

"All right then, seventy. My point is made. He is a man of respect and experience. And *he* supports independence! He says the colonies must fight. Does that not impress thee?"

"Franklin is a good man, but he's only a man," Drew replied, still calm.

Rachel was fascinated by the way Drew was playing his game of intrigue. True to her word, she had asked no more questions, and Drew had not revealed the nature of his connection with Washington's staff. But she did know that, at least for a time, it required secrecy—even from Israel Bowman.

As she watched the game unfold before her, she began to wonder. How long can we endure this? she thought, Drew having to deceive so many of their friends. How long would the war go on?

Washington's siege of Boston was now in its tenth month, and Arnold's invasion of Quebec had failed. At any moment the British could break down upon them from Canada. If it did not end soon, it might cost them everything.

Israel's manner suddenly eased, and his voice became almost imploring.

"My friend," he said, "in New England, Patriots are driving Tories from their homes and taking their property. These rumors of midnight trysts with Jacob Shackleton—a known Tory—and with some mysterious stranger . . . many believe thee to be not only a Loyalist, but a conspirator! I *fear* for thee.

"And what of thy work?" he added. "Last week Matilda Goodman turned thee away from her door and refused thy help for her husband. She coldly informed thee that they had engaged Dr. Hodge. And Rachel," he said pleadingly, "last month alone, three young mothers-to-be sent word to Rachel they would look for the services of another midwife.

"And yesterday, Edith Bratton, who has sold thee all thy pharmacopoeia, passed Rachel on the street without speaking.

She simply turned her head, and when Rachel spoke, Edith did not answer. We appear to be thine only friends, and thee places even that friendship under great strain!"

Drew slowly looked up from his chair by the fire. "I thank you, Israel," he said quietly, "but I'll not be moved. Not by you, or by anyone else. And there's an end."

The big Quaker stood tall, linked his hands behind his back, and let out a great sigh. "As thou wilt," he said. "Rachel, I thank thee for thy hospitality. Do what thou canst to change this stubborn mule's mind."

"Thank you, Israel," she said softly. "But Drew's determined, and he must do as he sees fit."

"To be sure!" Israel said. "I'm a firm believer in a man's following the light that's in him. Good night, Rachel. Good night, Drew."

"Good night, old friend."

And the door closed behind him.

FORTY

THE hills west of Philadelphia turned green with spring. The earth, fresh and damp, smelled of sprouting grass, and robins hopped lightly about within the city.

The British had evacuated Boston in March and sailed to Halifax. Washington and his Continental Army of nineteen thousand, having come south, were entrenched on Manhattan Island, waiting for Howe's next move. If Howe were to descend on the city of New York, overnight the war would be within a hundred miles of Philadelphia. As nervous agitation in the city grew, the clamor for independence increased and the supporters of Liberty multiplied. Toleration of dissenters—no longer called Loyalists, or even Tories, but "traitors"—was growing dangerously thin.

Tonight the weather was warm. A damp spring breeze was blowing from across the river and over the city, bringing with it the faint sound of music. From where Rachel stood in the open door gazing southeastward toward the heart of town, she saw torchlights flickering among the trees and along the streets.

"Drew," she called, "can you come here?"

In a moment he was standing beside her, his hand on her waist. He looked in the direction of her gaze. "What is it?" he asked.

"Music," she said, "and voices."

"A mob gathering around the State House, most likely," he said.

They watched and listened. Suddenly Drew turned, stepped from the porch, and started toward the stables.

"Where're you going, Drew?" she asked.

"To see what's going on," he answered.

"Then I'm coming with you."

Within moments their horses were cantering along tree-arched, lamplit High Street.

"You were right," Rachel said. "It's coming from the State House grounds."

When they reached the corner of Chestnut and Sixth, they could see it all. Under the trees, flaming torches and flickering lamps illuminated a mass of humanity, milling and flowing toward them like a great wave. The clamor of voices was growing louder; the lively melody of a fife and steady drumbeat was more distinct. Above the music and the rumble piercing shouts cut the air.

"Kill 'im!" came a voice, followed by the crowd's roar.

"Traitor! Damned traitor, that's what he is."

Much of the noise was laughter.

"We've got 'im now."

"If he'd like to leave, why don't he just flap his wings and fly!"

Drew and Rachel reined their nervous horses from the path of the oncoming mob and backed in among the trees. There, in relative safety, they sat gazing over hundreds of heads as the throng surged past.

In the center of the mass a two-wheeled cart drawn by a plodding ox lurched slowly forward. In the cart, on a pile of straw, stood a man, his hands tied behind his back. He was covered with white, and his face, half hidden in the floating shadows, was contorted with terrible pain. Rachel could not yet make out what this "white clothing" was.

Then, as the cart wheels creaked and clanked over the cobblestone, she caught a strange fragrance—pungent, biting.

"Pine tar!" she whispered. "Drew, it's pine tar," she said out loud, unable to take her eyes away from the figure in the cart. "They've *tarred* that poor man. He's covered with *goose* feathers!"

Drew reached across and touched Rachel's shoulder. She turned . . . He raised his finger to his lips. Instantly she understood their danger. They must not draw the attention of the crowd. Silently Drew pointed back to the man, whose face had just come full into the torchlight. It was Jacob Shackleton!

At that moment a man from the crowd jumped up into the cart. He touched his torch to one feather and then to another and another; the fire ran up the feathers to the pine tar, and it began to blaze. Shackleton screamed and thrashed against his bonds. A burning feather fell into the straw at his feet; instantly it blazed up! A second man sprang from the crowd into the cart's bed, pushing the first man violently over the right wheel. He threw his own coat about the agonized man and stamped at the burning straw. When the flames were out the man turned, and gazing angrily down at the first man, he roared, "Enough's enough!"

Instinctively, Rachel and Drew backed farther under the overhanging trees; then, quietly and as unobtrusively as possible, they dismounted and led their horses slowly into the darkness.

Back on their hill, the horses stabled, Rachel and Drew ran into the house, where they sat huddled in darkness on their bed, going over and over what they had just seen.

"I prayed God it wouldn't come to this!" Drew said.

Rachel was breathing heavily. "Drew," she said at last, "many people know Shackleton is your friend!" She paused as the thought sank in. "Oh, Drew," she said, her breath catching, "are we next?"

"I don't know," he said.

"Maybe we should go away," she said. "I think we should, Drew!" Her words were coming rapidly now, as if a spring of panic had broken to the surface. "I think we should leave this place . . . before sunrise."

"And go where?" he asked, holding her tightly.

"To the south, perhaps? The war is coming down from the

north. Donald's letters say nothing of fighting in the Carolinas."

Drew thought for a long while in silence, but his breathing was shallow and tight. "I would do it in a minute, Rachel," he said, his voice strained.

"But?" she asked, her hands suddenly tense on his arms.

"I'm needed here," he whispered.

Suddenly Rachel felt closed in. Of all the feelings in the world, that was the one she hated most—to be forced into a corner, for someone else to determine her fate.

A knock at the door sent a sudden shock of fear through their bodies, and for an instant they sat rigidly in each other's arms.

"Don't go!" she whispered.

"Someone may need me," he whispered, and breaking from her arms, stood to his feet.

"No, Drew, don't!"

"I'll look out first," he said, tugging free. "If it's someone we don't know, I'll not answer."

"But if it's a mob and they think we're in here, they'll burn the house over our heads."

But before she could finish speaking, he was out of the room and she could hear his feet padding quickly down the stairs. For a long moment Rachel sat paralyzed on the bed. She heard the door open, then voices and steps and scraping on the floor, followed by heavy noises. Then she heard Drew's voice from the foot of the stairs.

"Rachel," he called, "it's all right! It's Israel and Rebekah with poor Shackleton and his wife! Come light the lamps."

When the light from Rachel's lamp fell across the scene before her, she caught her breath and let out a little cry. There was Drew, his unruly brown hair down across his forehead; massive Israel Bowman, his calm face flushed with anger; and between them, his limp arms about their necks, the agonized Jacob Shackleton, his body still coated with pine tar and feathers, his face absolutely beyond recognition. Of all the horrors Rachel had witnessed in her life, this was the most repulsive and barbaric.

"Here," she said, "this way!" Rachel led them into the kitchen. Margaret Shackleton was leaning heavily on Rebekah Bowman as they followed behind.

"Can he lie down?" Rachel asked. "Oh, of course, it's the

only way! Lift him onto the table, Drew. Let's get some lauda-num into him."

Shackleton was sobbing and moaning with hideous pain.

"Forgive us, Jacob," Drew said tenderly as he and Israel lifted him atop the great trestle table.

Israel Bowman, in his deep voice, was mumbling to anyone who would listen. "Revolution or no," he said, as he unlooped Shackleton's arm from around his neck, "we don't treat even dogs the way they've treated this man! There's no justifiable cause for this!"

"How in God's name did you get him out of the mob's hands?" Rachel asked, her eyes wide with wonder.

"Well . . ." Israel hesitated, then a slow smile broke over his face, "as you say—in God's name. Philadelphians still have a certain respect for a Quaker."

Jacob Shackleton's bloodshot eyes stared wildly at the ceiling above him, his whole body quivering violently. His short, sandy-gray beard was severely singed on the left side, his entire face blistered red.

Shackleton was in his fifties, the same quiet little man Rachel had first seen that night of the shooting at St. George and the Dragon and had since seen talking with Drew among the shadows. Shackleton was a softly professed Tory. Because he was an innkeeper at a stop for stages in and out from the city of New York, many in Philadelphia believed he was a British spy.

Shackleton lay on the large table, moaning and shivering with shock-induced fever. Drew had returned with a bottle of laudanum while Israel had built a fire in the fireplace and put water on to boil. Rebekah Bowman had pursuaded Margaret to lie down, and was now covering the windows with quilts and blankets to make the house appear dark to anyone passing on the road below.

"Jacob," Drew said quietly, "take this for me." From a large spoon he let drops of laudanum fall between Shackleton's quavering, cracked lips.

Rachel stood with her right hand resting lightly on the suffering man's head in a gesture of comfort. She felt the quivering stop and his breaths become slow and even. He closed his eyes.

"The laudanum's taken effect," she said, turning her eyes toward Drew. Her hair was loose about her shoulders, and the lamplight reflected brightly in her large eyes. Her voice was very low and calm.

Drew thought of how wonderfully this crisis had focused Rachel's mind, how different she was from the woman who cowered with him not ten minutes ago in the darkness.

"I don't know of any other way to take off the tar," she said, "than to peel it off. From his scalp to his soles, the only place they left untarred is his face. Even the top of his poor bald head, the tender back of his neck, across his shoulders, his underarms . . . his groin!"

As she and Drew peeled the tar away, much of Shackleton's skin came away with it. The blisters burst painfully, and the white fluid made his body glisten.

Rachel glanced up to where Israel stood beside Drew. His kind eyes caught hers and held them for a moment. The plight of poor Jacob, there before her, and the presence of big, brave Israel—so uncompromising, so compassionate—touched something within her, and great tears began to run down her cheeks.

Israel saw it and came around the table. He laid his hand on her shoulder as she worked.

"Steady, Rachel," he said in his deep voice.

She moved quickly but carefully. What remained of Shackleton's skin was shriveled, blazing red, or swelled up with great blisters.

The water in the fireplace had begun to boil.

"Israel," Rachel said through her tears, "we need soft cloths. You'll find some in the chest against the east wall. Soak them in boiling water, then wring them out and bring them to me."

Suddenly Shackleton opened his eyes and a faint smile crossed his lips. He lifted a hand to touch Drew, and his lips began to move slowly. Drew leaned down close.

"Yes, Jacob?"

Shackleton's voice came out, hoarse and weak. "Will it be . . . worth it . . . Wolfe?" he asked.

Drew set his jaw tightly and clenched his teeth. "I guess a man's got to decide that for himself, Jacob," he said tenderly.

"Well . . ." Shackleton said, a faint smile crossing his cracked lips, "I think . . . I think . . ."

"Yes, Jacob," Rachel said, leaning nearer. "What do you think?"

At the sound of her voice, Shackleton turned his head slowly, until his eyes found her face. He smiled at her, a sweet smile that tore at her heart.

"I think . . . I think it *is*," he breathed, and his eyes fluttered closed again.

Sunup found Drew, Rachel, and Israel sitting around the heavy oak table where Shackleton had lain in the night. A fire burned in the fireplace, and the smell of frying ham filled the room. Rebekah Bowman was pouring batter onto a sizzling griddle, tending the pot of water boiling for coffee—a drink that had gained in colonial popularity since the imposition of taxes on tea. Margaret Shackleton was in Drew's study, where Jacob lay on a cot resting under heavy doses of laudanum. The strain of the hideous night was written in every face.

"He won't live, will he?" Rachel said quietly.

Drew shook his head slowly. "I don't see how he can, all that skin gone."

Israel had risen to gaze emptily out the window. Rebekah sat down again, covered her eyes with her hands, and sighed with exhaustion. Agitation and anger rose in Rachel's face. She closed her eyes and bowed her head.

"What will they do when they find we've treated him?" she said without looking up, a sharp edge to her voice.

"I don't know *what* they'll do," Drew answered.

"And I don't think you should stay around to find out," Israel broke in quietly.

Drew glanced up at his friend. "I have to stay," he said firmly. He rose from his seat, walked to the kitchen mantel, and poured himself a fresh mug of coffee. He held out the pot to each of the others. Rachel declined; Israel and Rebekah held out their mugs, and Drew filled them.

"I have to stay if they burn this house over my head," he said, a new tone in his voice.

Israel sensed it and looked up at his face, then toward Rachel.

"But not Rachel," Drew said, shaking his head firmly.

Rachel's head snapped upward. "Not Rachel what?" she said.

"We've no reason to put your life in danger," he answered quietly.

"You're reason enough, Drew Wolfe!" she said, tears rising in her eyes. "You're a *thou*sand times more to me than this Revolution! Or than Jacob Shackleton's love for George Rex, for that matter!"

"Jacob's one of us," Drew said quietly.

Rachel's eyes widened with surprise.

"One of who?" Israel Bowman asked, leaning forward. He suddenly realized that he was in the dark.

But Drew did not answer him. "You just have to go, Rachel," Drew said, his voice tender but firm, his expression sad.

"And just where would you have me *go*?" She awaited his reply with her lips closed tight and the sound of her breathing loud in the stillness.

"You answered that last night," he replied.

"South? To Donald?"

"South, to the Carolinas," Drew said, turning to Israel, whose face was filled with puzzlement. "Things are calm down there, no major military objectives for the British. Donald, her brother, is at Wilmington. It would be perfectly natural for her to go and see him."

Israel nodded dumbly and shifted his eyes back to Rachel.

Rachel struck the table with her fist and stood so quickly that her chair clattered to the kitchen's stone floor. "I won't *do* it," she shouted. Her eyes snapped with fire. "How can you *think* of sending me away? How could you bear it, to have me leave you, to leave this house where our lives together began?"

"I want you safe, Rachel—the war won't last long."

"You're so in *love* with this war! What of me? What's become of your love for *me*?"

For the second time in their married life, Rachel was changing right in front of him. Her eyes began darting rapidly from side to side. Her breath came rapidly, the muscles of her jaws flexing as the dark skin of her face began to flush. Israel and Rebekah watched dumbfounded as she picked up the upended chair and slammed it back to the stone floor.

"It's the same old thing!" she shouted, her face twisted grotesquely. "How can you say you love me? You *keep* things from me! You *risk* our lives! You *break* up our home!" She began to cry. "Drew Wolfe, I wish to God I had never married you! I give my love to you, and what do you do but throw it right back in my face!"

Drew's heart was pounding like a hammer in his chest. "Rachel, please . . ." he said quietly, lifting his hands in a gesture of helplessness.

" 'Rachel, please' nothing!" she shouted, turning and bolting up the stairs. Halfway up she turned and looked down at the little knot of amazed faces. "I'll *leave*," she thundered. "I'll leave you to your Revolution, and to your friends who don't care any more about their lives than you! I hate you, Drew Wolfe! I hate you with all my soul!" She stood for a long, terrible moment, breathing hard, staring steadily into his eyes, her lips compressed tightly.

When she disappeared from their sight, the three stood breathless and stunned, the only sound Rachel's heavy tread above them.

Drew sank into the nearest chair with his elbows on the table and buried his face in his hands, his emotions a terrible boiling mix of sorrow and humiliation. He realized that he was trembling, then felt a huge hand on his shoulder and heard a deep voice breathe, "Never in all my life have I seen the like!"

"Oh, Drew!" Rebekah exclaimed, her eyes clouding with tears.

"Drew," Israel said, "perhaps you should do as she wants. Pack your things, today. Take Rachel and go south *with* her."

"I'm committed to the Revolution, Israel," he said, turning and looking up at his friend. "I've promised Tench Tilghman—"

"Tilghman!" Israel exploded. "*I* know Tilghman—he's Washington's chief aide. What's he to do with all this?"

"I'm in Washington's service," Drew confessed. "A spy, for want of a more palatable word."

Israel let out a long, slow breath, dropped his hand from Drew's shoulder, and walked back to the window.

"I *knew* a piece of this puzzle was missing!" he said. "I knew it! Thank God!"

BOOK FOUR

Buchannon Hills
1776–1777

FORTY-ONE

RACHEL went feverishly about the room, throwing this and that into the trunk that stood open at the side of their bed.

"Just another damned man!" she fumed aloud as with quick movements she folded her best brocade and laid it in place. "Self-centered, independent little gods!" Suddenly she plopped down on the edge of the bed and looked around at the room she was so rapidly emptying.

" 'Rachel, go south!' " she mocked. "Who does he think he is to tell me what I must do?"

A shadow in the doorway made her look up. Drew was standing there, leaning against the doorframe, his arms crossed over his chest as he looked at her, a world of hurt in his stern gray eyes.

"I suppose you've been standing there all along!" she bristled. "Listening to everything I've said."

"For a while," he answered. The life had gone out of his eyes, and his mouth with its sagging corners reflected the hopelessness in his heart.

"Well, I suppose you got your ears and eyes full," she spat.

He said nothing for a moment, the sadness in his eyes deepening. "I love you, Rachel," he said, in an uncombative tone.

"You have a strange way of showing it," she answered, "putting me out of our—"

"I don't want to hear any more of that, Rachel!" he said, quickly cutting her off.

Strangely, she fell silent, but kept her eyes steadily on his, each shallow breath falling abruptly. Her mind had been whirling, and somehow the calmness of his voice caused the whirling to stop. The warmth of love flickered through her anger, leaving her speechless.

"I only want you to be safe," he said quietly, "until I can come for you and bring you home."

Arrogant words! she thought, flaring again. Symbols of his

lordship! The nerve they touched was raw. "You needn't worry," she flashed. "I'm leaving." And with that she was up and packing again.

"I can see," he said. The emptiness of the room made his heart sick. The bare top of the clothes chest caught his eye. "Your mother's clock—you're taking it with you."

"Of course I am! If this house burns, I don't want Mama's clock burning with it!"

"I'll come to you as soon as I can," he said.

"Don't bother!" she fumed. "The law makes you my master, but I will show you very plainly that you are not! I go of my own choosing, and I'll come home the same way—if I come home at all!"

"Rachel," Drew said, his heart beating wildly, "it *doesn't* have to be like this!"

She cast a terrible glare in his direction, and shot past him out the door. "Israel!" she called down the stairs.

Israel Bowman appeared at the banister. "Yes, Rachel?" he said, his voice and face as expressionless as he could make them.

"Israel, please help me carry my things down to your buggy. I'm taking them to St. George and the Dragon. I'll stay there until the next stage south."

Hesitating, Israel looked past Rachel to Drew, as if to ask what he must do next. Drew shrugged and Israel started obediently up the stairs.

After two nights at the inn, Rachel left Philadelphia. It was on the first day of summer, when the Schuylkill, below their home, was flowing with fresh rains and sparkling in the sunlight.

The coach was rolling along south of the city, Rachel crowded in with four other passengers: a girl of ten, the girl's mother, and two men, all strangers to one another.

"Thank you, gentlemen," the mother said brightly, "for letting us ladies face in the direction of travel." She appeared a little old to have a daughter the age of this one. "Agatha here gets sick to her stomach when she rides backward." The mother smoothed a curl on the child's forehead, and the girl cut her eyes toward her disgustedly.

Rachel eyed the woman, picturing what it would be like to travel in this rocking conveyance with a child vomiting all over everything! Then, turning her face to the window, she shut out the woman's incessant chatter and became lost in her own thoughts.

Even Israel had tried to interfere with her going, she thought. And he had tried to tell her that if she insisted on going, she should go by boat. What business had it been of his? She didn't *want* to go by boat. It was too expensive, and she must conserve every penny. But she had put a stop to his meddling.

"When I want your advice, Israel," she had said, "I'll ask for it!"

Israel's eyes had gone suddenly blank. He just shook his head and hushed. Good! There was a time for even good friends to hold their tongues. She didn't need *any* man telling her what to do.

Gradually the woman's unending stream of words drifted back into her consciousness. Rachel sighed. Will her talk never end? she wondered.

"Where will we stop for the night?" Rachel said, interrupting, as much to shut off the flow of words as to hear the answer.

"Oh, my dear," the woman said without pause, "we won't be stopping anywhere . . . not for the night. This coach goes straight through."

Rachel caught her breath and the color drained from her face. She had assumed they would stop each night at an inn. The stunning news silenced her entirely.

They were in a low valley, the coach rocking along on its thick leather springs, bouncing through ruts cut during last week's rains and since hardened under the summer sun.

"Business keep your husband in Philadelphia?" a high voice with a nervous chuckle asked. It came from the tall, paunchy man in the far corner of the coach. His gray hair was curled and powdered. On his lap lay an immaculate hat of a gray slightly darker than his hair, with a white cockade sewn to each of its three upturned sides. His nose was narrow and long, pointed above a pleasant mouth.

"Yes, business," she replied, and looked back out the window.

"Going to Baltimore?" he pressed.

"Wilmington, North Carolina," she answered, still looking away.

"Wilmington, North Carolina!" he exclaimed. "Why, young

lady," he leaned forward and chuckled excitedly as he spoke, "Wilmington . . . you'll be two weeks getting to Wilmington!"

"Five hundred miles?" she said. "Two weeks, day and night?" Rachel's throat tightened.

"Five hundred? Well . . . as the crow flies, yes. But young lady, these roads wind like snakes. The builders make them rise and dip, rise and dip—they say it rests the horses on the downgrade—and they curve around all the higher hills. You put all those curves and ups and downs and windings in, and Wilmington is probably *eight* hundred and *fifty* miles by road . . . and what a road south of Baltimore!"

"Hit's true, ma'am," said the short, lean man directly across from her. "Last winter I myself come upta Baltimore from Williamsburg. Stagecoaches is supposed to make about twelve miles to the hour, but not on *that* road." He cackled. "Nosir. That road's no more'n hacked through them pine woods. The coach wheels go all antigoglin—logs havin' been throwed into the sand and bogs to make the corduroy'n all. Driver slows the horses to a piddlin' walk, jist to keep from breakin' axles. And them wheels, they just go up over one log and drop hard down onto the next, clump, clump, clump, an' ever' clump jars your spine from top ta tail till you think you're plumb broke in two!"

"And if it rains," the tall man broke in, "the road's a river of mud. You'll ford streams you'll swear are about to float you away. God help you, young woman! If you must travel long distances in America, never go by road if you can go by boat . . . either by coastal passage or by canal. Smooth going by canal. The land just drifts by."

Rachel's heart sank. "But when I heard the road was open and good now from Boston to Charles Town—"

"Why, yes, it's true," the first man blustered while the second laughed a rude laugh, "a wonderful advance—open just this year. But good? Dear heaven! That's stage line propaganda!"

"And by ship?" she asked quietly. "How long would it have taken by ship?"

"All d'pends," the small man answered. "Even on a fast packet, contrary winds kin pen ya in fer weeks. But good weather, fair winds? Jist 'bout three days, mighty fast, and a heap smoother than this lumber wagon." He paused, and then offered, "Ma'am, if you're going to Wilmin'ton, you really oughta ship out at Baltimore. Be lots easier on ya."

Rachel eyed the passing countryside coldly. "I can't," she said. "I've spent most of my money, and no matter how long it takes, I'll have to finish the way I started." The anger in her voice made the men fall silent.

Just then they crested a hill, the road smoothed out, and on the hill's downward side the coach picked up speed. Rachel sat staring at the trees racing by, running the fingers of her right hand over the sill of the coach window, feeling the once smooth wood, now roughened by long exposure to heat and wet. She was angry with Drew for forcing her to go south, angry with herself for going by coach just to save a little money.

She'd gone off half cocked, she thought. If only Drew hadn't pressed her so!

The eyes of the woman and the gentleman and the tradesman were riveted on her, watching uneasily as she clenched her jaw and stared unwaveringly out the window. Gingerly, the two men turned to each other, and their voices droned on as Rachel's mind turned back to Philadelphia.

The day wore to noon, the air grew close, and the sweat of unbathed bodies became oppressive. The only sounds were intermittent snoring and sighs, the squeak and rattle of harness, and the constant beat of sixteen hooves on the roadway. Rachel could see it now: every mile was going to be a solemn test of endurance.

It was twelve days later when the coach rolled smoothly up a broad avenue lined with magnificent elms. Where the avenue looped around, the coach creaked to a stop. It was mid-afternoon on a sweltering day.

"Buchannon Hills, ma'am," the driver said as he opened the coach door. "Right to the very front step!"

Rachel sighed a long sigh and patted her gathered hair at the back of her head. The farther south they had come, the drier and dustier the roads, and the hotter and thicker the air. One morning north of Williamsburg she had pinned up her long hair to get it off the back of her perspiring neck and to keep the dust out of it. Great drops of perspiration were running down her arms and down the small of her back. She looked at the driver, standing there holding the door for her, and gave him a tired smile. It was the best she could do.

As she stepped from the coach, the muscles of her back and legs ached as if having recorded every jolt between there and Philadelphia. The last two hundred miles had pounded and

tossed her beyond the patience of a saint to bear. She could not
remember how many times she had gotten out to "put her
shoulder to the wheel" and help the horses drag the coach out
of some muddy creek bottom. And sleep? She had slept while
the coach lurched over stretches that seemed impassable, had
awakened with her head on the shoulders of people she had
never seen before and hoped to heaven she would never see
again.

Well, thank God, it was over! She was at last at Buchannon
Hills. The driver got down to unstrap her baggage from beneath the great leather apron on the coach's back.

Rachel pulled a handkerchief out of her sleeve and began to
mop the moisture beaded on her face.

The driver snickered under his breath, shook his head, and
turned again to her baggage.

In spite of her aching bones, the house standing at the head
of the circle only a few yards away suddenly claimed all Rachel's attention. It was absolutely unlike anything she had ever
seen before. This was *not* a great Georgian mansion copied
from the London pattern books. The last of those were up in
Virginia. The farther south they had come, the fewer houses of
any kind they had seen. It was a sparsely settled country, and
what houses were there were hidden within deep forests of
enormous pine.

Oh, this was a large house all right, she thought, and built
in a lovely place—right on the crest of a forested hill where it
could catch any breeze that should blow in from the sea. But
the house itself was hardly beautiful—functional, rather, obviously for this damp coastal plain. In form, it was almost
square, three stories tall, of North Carolina pine and weather-
boarded with yellow poplar. It stood on a hewn stone foundation the color of straw.

The most striking thing about it was that the first and second
stories were completely surrounded by wide verandas—which,
she was soon to learn, were called by the inhabitants of these
southern forests "piazzas"—something she had always thought
of as a courtyard—or "galleries," which she had always
thought of as a place to display art.

Perhaps it was because of these "galleries"—vacant in appearance, shading the face of the house as they did—that it instantly gave her the feeling of age, of something musty, empty,
yet old and honorable.

Magnolia trees of great height grew across the sloping lawn, their large white blossoms redolent in the evening air. From the arms of ancient oaks beards of gray moss touched with the faintest cast of green hung down to sweep the lawn.

With her feet firmly on the ground, Rachel straightened her shoulders and arched her aching back. The hill was high, overlooking all the surrounding countryside. Forest forever, except for small marks on its face that she assumed to be clearings. She turned about, gazing in every direction, the moist breeze momentarily reviving her.

The heat of the heavy air, the unhurried quietness, the well-entrenched order and harmony that lay over the entire hill, all these soaked into her tired arms and legs. The earth felt firm beneath her feet, and as she breathed deep, the mingled scents of Japanese honeysuckle and magnolia blossoms seemed almost too sweet for her senses.

She patted her skirt to straighten it, and a cloud of powdery road dust puffed into the air. She rubbed her fingers across her forehead and felt the grime roll up on her skin. At this moment she could think of nothing she wanted more than water and soap, and rest in a clean room.

"Ha-oop!" she heard behind her, and the rattle of harness and the creak of wheels as the coach pulled away. She turned and looked after it as it rolled down the hill, following the wide avenue that wound for half a mile down to the gate, disappearing among the long-leaf pines. As the sounds of the coach died away, a kind of empty feeling stole through her. Without realizing it, she had come to think of the coach as her last link with Philadelphia—and with Drew.

Drew . . .

He would be finishing at the hospital about now—if some wild mob hadn't already done to him what it did to poor Jacob Shackleton. She felt tears rising in her eyes at the thought. She missed Drew; really she did. She felt enormous guilt at leaving him there in the midst of danger. But he had forced her to this separation. Her tears subsided quickly, dried by a wave of hot anger.

She looked westward down the long slope of the gentle hill, and saw that the forest was broken by a wide river that, even from here, seemed to lie heavy and indolent among the trees.

"The Cape Fear," she whispered. Donald had written to her many times of the Cape Fear, of floating along in a skiff on its lazy current, hauling in heavy lines, fighting great catfish of sixty or a hundred pounds into the boat. And alligators—great

aquatic lizards with armor, lying like logs on the riverbanks.
She shuddered at the thought.

While she was lost in this reverie, the door of the great
house eased soundlessly open.

"Miss, may I help you?" a kind and soft voice said.

Startled, she looked around. Standing ramrod straight on the
veranda's near edge, entirely within the shadow, was a Negro,
very dark, with a full head of silver hair. He was slender and
old, the picture of dignity and decorum.

"Miss?" he repeated after a long silence. "May I help you?"

"Oh . . . well, yes!" she said, self-consciously smoothing her
dress and dusting at her sleeves. "I'm Rachel Wolfe," she
coughed, choked by dust, ". . . from Philadelphia. Donald
Calhoun—my brother—he lives here." She seemed confused.
"But he's not expecting me. Is he here? How can I find him?"

"Oh, he's expecting you, Mrs. Wolfe!" The man brightened
and smiled. "I'll send a boy to fetch him right away!"

"Rachel!" Donald called as he came running up from the edge
of the pine forest. His house was down there, beside a little
plot of ground where every year he raised a garden. As he approached she noticed that the knees of his breeches were covered with dirt where he had been kneeling; pulling weeds from
the okra, he told her later. His face was wreathed in smiles,
and he was laughing. As he came to her, he reached out hands
smudged with fresh soil, then threw his arms around her and
swung her about. Feeling his strong arms and her feet leaving
the ground, her angry mood broke and she laughed and hugged
him tight.

"You *knew* I was coming!" she said. "How?"

"A letter from Drew," Donald answered, setting her down.
"It came by packet over a week ago. Of course I had no idea
when you would arrive."

"Neither did I," she flushed. "I'm afraid I would've been
much better off to've taken the packet!"

"I'm surprised you didn't." He smiled, but she made no reply to his implied question.

"What did Drew say in his letter?" she asked carefully.

"Only that the war fervor was heating up in the north, that
he believed you would be safer here, and that you had agreed
to come. He said you'd had a narrow scrape that night before
you left. And he said to tell you not to worry—that things in
the city had quieted down some."

Within, she breathed a little sigh of relief.

"Rachel, it's wonderful to see you," he said, gathering up her hands in his again and looking into her weary face, "but you must be absolutely exhausted. It's selfish of me to keep you here talking when you could be having a bath and—"

"You think I *need* to bathe?" She laughed.

He touched the skin of her forehead and rubbed his fingers together in front of her eyes. "No doubt about it," he said, smiling. "Quincy!" He looked up at the old Negro still standing near. "Have Mary prepare a hot bath for Mrs. Wolfe. Mistress Buchannon has a room waiting."

"Yes, sir," he replied, and disappeared through the doorway.

"When you're fresh, Rachel, I'll introduce you to Abigail, and then we'll have a long walk in the flower garden while you tell me all that's happening in the north!"

By the time Rachel had bathed, put her things away, and met Abigail Buchannon, the sun was dipping rapidly toward the western horizon.

At last she walked with Donald along a narrow pavement that wound through a lush garden of shrubs and flowers. Thickly leaved trees fluttered in a faint breeze, and the fragrance of roses made the air sweet and languid. The sun cast a gold light over the hill, about the houses, over the gardens and the dark skin of slaves coming in from the fields. The air was cool enough to be pleasant. Donald had changed into an evening suit of clothes, off-white linen shirt, white satin vest, and white breeches. There was a cravat at his throat, and he wore a russet waistcoat that set to advantage his flaming red hair.

"It was a terrible thing!" she said as she told him of Jacob Shackleton's agony. Donald shook his head somberly.

"I forgot to tell you," he said. "Shackleton died two days after you left."

Rachel caught her breath. In her heart she had known it already, but to hear it spoken . . . well, it was so final, so bitter.

"There was a loneliness about Drew's letter," Donald said, "something that made me feel he hardly knew how to mark out his day without you."

She said nothing.

"You're angry with Drew, aren't you?" he asked quietly.

"Yes," she said, without looking up, "very angry . . . but I do miss him."

"Did you part peaceably?"

"No," she said. "No, I'm afraid we didn't. He tried, but I was trying to hurt him, determined to make it as hard for him as I could—his forcing me to leave and all. I put on quite a show." Her voice was a little sad, but she looked up at him and smiled.

Donald did not smile in return. "Rachel, sometimes I believe you really think your little demonstrations are charming. . . ."

A chill ran across her shoulders and down her spine. She caught her breath and ignored his commentary. Of all things, she didn't want Donald starting in on her now. Forcing down her anger, she broke in with hurried words.

"But what about you, Donald? I worry about you."

He smiled self-consciously. "Why do you worry about me?" he asked.

"That you're so alone in the world—that you've found no one to love."

"Well," he laughed, "sometimes I worry about that myself."

"Isn't there anyone?" she asked, genuine concern in her voice, and marveled at how quickly she had gotten hold of herself.

Donald blushed, then plucked a leaf from the rosebush and began nervously to pick it to pieces.

"Well," he said, "there's one, but there are barriers."

"Barriers?" she asked. "What kind?"

"I'll tell you about it someday," he said. The sinking sun cast a halo about his red hair as an embarrassed smile crossed his lips.

They ambled in silence for a while. Coming to a Japanese honeysuckle growing in a sculpted arch over the walk, Rachel stopped and plucked a single yellow blossom. She contemplated the tiny flower, twirling it slowly between her fingers.

"I once thought, Donald, that one day my sad times would end, that when I got away from Daddy, I could live a happy life." She paused, gazing at the flower, not seeing it, then looking up, tossed her head. "But the last five years I've had more pain than ever. More death, Rob, now the war . . . and Drew's insistence on my coming here."

A small phoebe flitted down and caught a fly buzzing lazily about the roses. The bird's gray crest was gold in the setting sun.

"I had found someone to make a life with. And now he's

gone." She paused for a moment and then laughed mockingly. "What is it, Donald? Is there a curse of some kind on me?"

"You're tired, Rachel," he said. "All these melancholy feelin's and doubts will pass when you're rested."

"It's the most terrible thing!" she said. "On Easter Sunday morning I actually went to church—can you believe I did that? And that I, your sister, actually prayed? I prayed I might keep Drew. And, true to form, now he's gone!" Rachel's eyes took on a hard look, a defiance at her misfortunes.

"Some things are beyond us, Rachel—in God's hands, really. We've got to remember what our mother used to say. 'The Laird is the licht a' my salvation, I'll binna feared for what man can do tae me.' "

Rachel said nothing, but Donald thought he saw a tear rise in her eye. He was not sure whether it was a tear of tenderness or a tear of anger.

"Rachel," he ventured, turning toward her, "it's that you're *angry*, and that's a kind of curse. For you there's no takin' life as it comes and makin' the best of it. You've always got to be puttin' the blame on somethin' or someone."

He took her reluctant hands in his and looked into her eyes. "You're not fightin' against Drew, Rachel. You're fightin' against yourself, and against Daddy."

"Donald . . ." she began, a steel edge to her voice.

He released her hands and took her by the shoulders, his blue eyes looking keenly into hers. "You've got to forgive that old man, Rachel! You've got to get the poison of hate out'a your blood! Remember, Rachel, how Mama used to pray?

"Forgie us the wrangs we hae wrocht,
    as we hae forgien the wrangs we hae dree'd;
and sey-us-na sairlie, but sauf us
    frae the Ill Ane."

"Save us from the Evil One," she repeated bitterly. "But God didn't save her from Daddy."

"He did, Rachel! He gave her the strength to bear him no hate, and it saved her in life and in death! Her heart was not eaten by her own bile while she lived, and when at last she died, it was not the Black Gate she entered! He saved her from becoming *like* him. *That* was the important thing!"

"Let go of my shoulders, Donald." She said it quietly, but with such determination that he relaxed his hands. "Mama taught me *one* thing," she said, "and Daddy taught me another. Sometimes I think Daddy was more right than I gave him credit for. And that terrifies me!" She bit her lip and tossed the blossom onto the grass. "It's a terrible world we live in. It has no meanin', and my heart pains me every day for it!"

"Rachel!" he almost shouted, looking around to see if anyone heard. "Rachel," he said softly, "it's your own hate that creates your misery! Forgive Daddy and be done with it!"

"Forgive him? Donald, do you know that I still *dream* about Daddy in the night? He took everything away from me. And he didn't care!"

"Perhaps he didn't," Donald said, "though I've always wondered if his bluster was a front for his own hurt and anger."

"That was no front! That old man was Daddy through and through!" she fumed. "And besides, what if it was a front? It was all the same—whatever the cause, he did what he did!"

"You're right about that. Perhaps . . ." He paused, then went on. "It's a terrible pain we feel when someone who should love us does not. The glory comes when we rise above the pain. But before you can rise above it, you must forgive Daddy, else he'll pull you down forever."

"What comes over me!" Rachel said aloud to herself.

It was dark. She sat alone in her second-story room, half reclining on the settee, her arm on its back and her cheek propped despondently against her half-closed fist. They had given her a corner room with large windows on two sides; deep windows that started at the floor and went nearly to the ceiling, with inner shutters folded open to catch whatever night breeze might stir. The moon was just past full, flooding her chamber with light. Outside her windows, beyond the edge of the veranda, the gently waving branches of an ancient long-leaf pine had a mesmerizing effect on her mind.

"A whole year away from Donald," she said sadly. "Then I come and we fall into it like that!"

She sighed deeply, and letting her arm drop in a gesture of disgust and deep weariness, resolved to sleep. She rose slowly, went to the high bed, and folded back its covers, plumping its down mattress. It would be her first night in a bed in almost two weeks. Then she turned back toward the window and, bathed in moonlight, unlaced the back of her dress. With her bare arms extended, she let the dress fall forward from her shoulders and then to the floor.

"No more," she said to herself. "Whatever it takes, I will not fight with Donald again. 'And there's an end,' as Drew would say. I can be as determined as my husband and brother."

Stepping up onto the little stool beside the bed, she climbed in, slipped between fresh sheets so clean and cool they were a dream in themselves, and filled with weariness, was at once asleep.

FORTY-TWO

RACHEL woke to brilliant sunlight pouring through the open windows, and to the strong but gentle cooing of doves in the trees outside.

As she lay there, gazing about the room, the cool spaciousness of the house made her feel wonderfully serene. She passed her hand over the sheets; they were crisp, the best cotton, carefully ironed and wonderfully smooth. The ceiling was high, a pale green, trimmed with wood molding; the door and window frames, the wainscoting and louvered shutters, all mint-green. A great pine beyond the veranda whispered in an early breeze.

The rich sunlight passing through the great pine's needles glistened in the irregularities of the upper panes, spreading out across the bed, its warmth creeping through her coverlet.

The sun! How bright it seemed, and how peaceful the whole world, and how clear her mind! Oh, how clear her mind—for the first time in weeks! She stretched and arched, luxuriating in the perfect freshness of every muscle. What a contrast to the long hot days of her journey; how different from that frantic night in turbulent Philadelphia. Here everything created an atmosphere of deep spiritual peace.

"Perhaps Drew knew best," she whispered. This was where she should be. She hadn't seen it clearly before . . . but she resolved not to tell Donald how wrong she was.

The crisp sheet made a whisking sound as she threw it back, and the deep feather mattress yielded pleasantly as she swung

her legs over the side of the bed. For a moment she sat very
still with her feet resting on the stool, sensing something foreign, unusual . . . an uneasy feeling in the muscles of her
throat, a bitterness seeping onto her tongue from the corners of
her jaw, a spinning in her head, a sudden violence in her stomach. The room began to blur, and she fell back on the bed.

As she lay there, the room gradually stopped whirling and
the sickening ache subsided. What in the world? Twelve days
in that miserable coach! That, and a night of deep sleep. If she
could just lie there a little longer, then rise more slowly. Rachel
rested her right forearm over her eyes to block out the light,
then dozed back into sleep.

Half an hour later she was up again, her brief sickness
nearly forgotten. She dressed, brushed her long hair, and descended the staircase to a late breakfast.

"Am I fit for such an occasion?" Rachel whispered nervously.

She and Donald were crossing the wide lawn from his cottage to the big house where the Buchannons were giving a dinner. The grass yielded pleasantly beneath her soft-soled shoes;
just that afternoon a half-dozen black servants had swarmed
over the grass, swinging scythes with curved blades glittering
on long wooden handles. Now, with the sun going down, it offered up a sweet fragrance into the evening air. With darkness
upon the Cape Fear valley, random carriage lights glimmered
along the lower road and up the drive like fireflies ascending.

"You look wonderful!" he assured her, squeezing her hand.

Rachel's hair was upswept in back, tied with a light green
silk scarf that flowed down over her left shoulder. The white
lace over her bosom was tight about her slender throat, and her
deep green sacque gown of ribbed silk, close at the waist,
trailed large box pleats grandly behind. It was her newest
dress, bought only days before that terrible night when Jacob
was so cruelly treated. She ran her slender fingers over the
silk, took comfort in its newness and in remembering that
Drew was with her when she chose it.

As they neared the house, the darkness was punctuated with
graceful tapers shining in the windows and with the fine hush
of talking voices and laughter. Two young men riding on either
side of a low-slung chaise drawn by two spirited white horses
bantered light-heartedly with the young ladies it carried. At the
front steps the young men handed the girls down, committed

the carriage to the servants, and disappeared through the front door just ahead of Rachel and Donald.

As they entered the foyer, the buzz of conversation became louder, a cacophony of polite sound from the crowded dining room. In the center of the room a long table set with fine white plates and silver stood waiting beneath a great crystal chandelier that sparkled brightly onto the milling guests.

Rachel could not remember Edward Buchannon's face from their brief meeting six years ago, but she recognized him instantly. She had remembered only that his shoulders were very broad, and that he was taller than Donald. She remembered, too, that his hair had been wavy and black. Now it was streaked lightly with gray, but had lost none of its fullness or its wave. Rachel judged Buchannon at about fifty years, perhaps a little more. His height, principally in his torso, gave the impression of great power. His face was ruggedly handsome, but the bulk of his build made him seem out of place in his red brocade waistcoat with flowing ruffles at his throat and wrists. He would have been more at home in linsey-woolsey, she thought.

His wife Abigail was beside him, and they were moving among their guests, greeting first one and then another. As she watched, Rachel felt his personality to be larger than the house in which he lived.

"Mr. Buchannon," Donald called, "I want you to meet my sister, Rachel."

"Yes!" Buchannon said, and turned to face her.

Buchannon's black brows were heavier than she recalled, and grayer, wide arcs over light blue eyes that were alive and friendly. His easy smile showed a full row of white teeth, perfectly even except for an upper front tooth slightly chipped. Something about the entirety of the man—the warmth of his smile, an unprepossessing gentleness that belied his stature—made his presence overpowering. Instantly Rachel felt that she wanted to know Edward Buchannon, to have him as a true friend.

Buchannon's big hand swallowed hers. Standing very straight, his chest swelling out, he laid the other hand on her right shoulder and looked directly into her eyes. "Mrs. Wolfe—" he began.

"She'll not be happy unless you call her Rachel," Donald said, and chuckled.

" 'Rachel,' then," Buchannon said, his eyes twinkling. His

voice was strong, not deep, but pleasant, very kind. "Rachel," he said, "all day long folks have been telling me what a beautiful woman you are . . . so that I was just beside myself to meet you. They didn't stretch the truth a bit!"

Rachel blushed and glanced at Abigail, whose eyes were on her husband, and full of merriment.

"No, really now! You *are* a lovely girl." He laughed heartily. "Rachel, we just think the world and all of your brother. If you're anything like Donald, you'll be welcome in our home for a long time to come!"

"Thank you, Mr. Buchannon," she said, recovering her composure, "but I'll be going back to Philadelphia as soon as my husband feels it's safe. He insisted I come down here until the war frenzy blows over. He thinks I'm some sort of hothouse plant . . . obviously!"

He chuckled. "Well, from what I hear, you are definitely not a hothouse flower! And we hope the 'war frenzy,' as you call it, passes quick enough. But until it does, you just think of yourself as one of our family."

He squeezed her shoulder and turned away to other guests.

"Let's stroll about," Rachel said, taking Donald's arm again.

In the next room tables were prepared for games of lanter-loo, whist, and quadrille. The chairs about the tables were empty, but a cluster of gentlemen in the southwest corner were talking earnestly among themselves, something about how the war would affect the South's trade with England. In the billiards room a larger cluster of men lounged about a huge table.

As they reentered the dining room, Rachel stopped abruptly. Donald, feeling the tug on his arm, looked about to find her staring ahead with rapt fascination.

"What is it, dear?" he said.

"Donald, that girl! What is she *doing* here?"

Donald followed her gaze across the room to where a young woman was mingling freely with the guests. She had an air of great aplomb, a commanding presence that equaled Edward Buchannon's. Perhaps the girl felt their gaze, for suddenly she looked their way and smiled.

"That's Salali." He spoke the name slowly, and in such a way that Rachel looked up at him and wondered. They returned Salali's smile and nodded.

"Salali?" Rachel echoed to get the sound of it. "What an unusual name," she said, but it rolled pleasurably off her tongue, the *a*'s sounding like "ah," and the last syllable a long *e* that rose in pitch. "Sa-la-lee," she murmured again.

"Edward's daughter," Donald murmured.

"His *daughter*!" Rachel said in a shocked whisper, holding her hand in front of her mouth so others wouldn't hear. "But she's—"

"Don't!" he muttered, gently pushing down her hand. "There, you see! She thinks you're whispering about *her*!"

"Well, I am! I want to know how—"

At that moment the sound of a fork tapping on crystal rang through the room and silence fell over the crowd. Rachel stopped in mid-sentence, exchanged a withering glance with Donald, then turned her eyes reluctantly toward Edward Buchannon, about to speak.

"I'll tell you later," Donald murmured.

"Folks." Buchannon lifted his voice. "Nabby—Mrs. Buchannon—and I welcome you. As you know, with the outbreak of this war, the Continental Congress in Philadelphia has forbidden 'every species of extravagance and dissipation.' These are hard times. Our men in the field need everything you and I can scrape together to survive. The Wilmington–New Hanover Safety Committee has passed a resolution interpreting Congress's act against extravagance and dissipation as forbidding horse races and cockfights and balls.

"You know, of course, that Nabby and I give a ball about this time every year. In the past we've served every kind of wine we could get our hands on—and good lemon punch, plenty of cider, all the meats and breads and sauces you can find room for. Well, this year we have some punch and a little cider. The table is not loaded with *all* the good things we'd like, and there will be no dancing. Such merriment with our soldiers in the field would be more than unseemly.

"But tonight, when you sit for a game of whist or 'loo, all your winnings will be gathered up and sent by next packet to Philadelphia for the army. If you don't fancy a game, a simple contribution will do as well. And . . ." he paused for effect, "there's not a man-jack among us who'd have it any other way. And if you would, I don't know how you got invited here tonight."

"Hear! Hear!" the crowd roared, and broke out laughing. Edward had filled a glass and was about to lift it in a toast when from somewhere in the crowd a man spoke.

"*I* was *not* invited!" he shouted.

A hush fell over the room. Rachel felt Donald's hold on her arm tighten. She craned her neck to look about. A ripple of questioning voices murmured through the crowd. The man pulled up a chair and stood on it, raising himself above the crowd. Rachel could see his face clearly. He was tall and lean, with a short red beard and eyes that burned under thick brows. His voice was bold and demanding.

"Sir!" Buchannon said, nodding toward the man.

"*I* was not invited," he repeated slowly, "and I don't agree with a word you've said."

"What *is* your mind, sir?" Buchannon's voice rumbled low with restraint.

"Of the mind that says rebels be damned!" the man answered.

A roar rose from the crowd. Buchannon motioned for silence.

"Say on," he urged.

"And," the man shouted, "of the mind that Alan MacDonald be returned unharmed to his wife from whatever stinking hole of a prison you've sent 'im to!"

"Alan MacDonald's a prisoner of *war*, sir!" a woman shouted.

Rachel felt Donald's hand clamp on hers.

"Salali!" he whispered.

Across the room the young woman had taken a chair of her own, standing above the crowd, her black eyes shooting a bold, almost insolent gaze at the bearded man, a gaze that transfixed him like an arrow from a bow.

Rachel's mind whirled. How was it possible that these people would permit even the *presence* of this girl, much more that they let her speak? For as Salali stood above the crowd, the light from the chandelier and a dozen sconces reflected brightly on her dark-hued features.

"Alan MacDonald was taken in the act of marching against Wilmington!" she cried. "Had it not been for the man in whose house you now stand and whose hospitality you have accepted—and four hundred like him—MacDonald and his Highlanders would've made blood flow in the streets of Wilmington!"

"Yes!" roared many voices from the crowd.

"Pull 'im down! Put 'im out!" cried others.

A dozen hands grabbed the man and, his arms and legs flailing wildly, passed him above the crowd, depositing him outside the door, then slamming it and locking it behind him. Shouts and roars shook the walls.

Edward Buchannon gazed across the room and smiled with approval at the girl, who then gracefully descended from her makeshift stage.

Buchannon motioned for silence.

"We know where we stand!" he shouted above the roar. He motioned again, and the crowd quieted. "We know where we stand," he repeated. "And until this war is over," he raised the clear crystal glass, "a toast to Washington, to the Sons of America, and to their success in the field!"

When they sat down to dinner, Rachel hardly noticed the food passing before her, but clung to every word from busy lips all about. Amid the clink of silver and rustling of silk sleeves and pouring of drinks, the buzz of conversation centered on the man's brash appearance. Gradually Rachel began to understand.

"War? Here?" she breathed. "I thought—"

"Oh, I'm afraid someone's misled you, young lady," said a man across the table. "There's already been fighting in the South!"

"You bet!" said another. "We've had our share of the war down here. Every able man drills monthly in Wilmington. A year ago, fifteen hundred of us marched to the mouth of the river and burned Fort Johnston to the ground. Burned a few plantations along with it. Likely as not, we'll have a good bit more of the war before it's done!" Then, poking a three-tined fork in Donald's direction, "Why don't you ask your brother there?" The man chuckled. "He's been right in the thick of it!"

"You, Donald?" Rachel looked about in alarm. It was impossible for her to imagine Donald with a gun in hand, shooting at living men.

"Yes," Donald answered. "I helped burn the fort, and I drill with the militia. But our one real battle was about five months ago—late February." He laid his fork down, his eyes taking on a fire as his voice rose. "It was a rout! Fifteen hundred Highlanders—Tories down out of the Piedmont to take Wilmington!"

"But you never told me!"

"I wanted to spare you the worry. But I would've told you—after you'd settled in. You've had enough troubles of your own."

"Where did this battle take place?"

"The bridge on Moore's Creek—just about fifteen miles from here."

"And I thought the war was entirely in the North," she whispered. Her swarthy face turned pale, as though the blood had drained away.

"Well," she heard a strong voice behind her say, and at the same moment felt a big hand on each of her shoulders, "the North is where the armies and the generals are." She recognized Edward's voice. "And the *big* fights," he continued. "Up till six weeks ago, our little tussle at Moore's Creek was our only battle . . . other than a few random skirmishes."

"Were many killed at Moore's Creek?" she asked, fearing the answer.

"A good many," he said. By now everyone in the room was listening to Buchannon. "We laid ambush this side of the creek. Took the planks off the bridge before the Highlanders got there, is what we did, and soaped the beams—then hid in the trees along the banks. Sure enough, here they came. We could hear 'em off in the distance long before we saw 'em—the skirl of the bagpipes cuttin' through the mist that lay in the creek bottom. Made the hair on your arms stand on end! Didn't it, Donald?"

Donald nodded, and Rachel could see a shiver go through his shoulders at the memory.

"At last we saw 'em," Buchannon went on. "Hundreds of 'em! Pipers swingin' along through the mist, an' Alan MacDonald ridin' at the head."

"Why Scots fightin' for the *Crown*?" Rachel burst in incredulously.

"The Royal Governor's curried Scottish favor hereabouts for years," Donald answered, "knowin' such a time as this might come."

"Well!" said Buchannon, "here they came. MacDonald took one look at the bridge and ordered 'em across on the bare timbers! It was a sight! They no sooner hit the soap and grease in the middle'a that bridge than their feet slipped first this way and then slid that—and they begun to fall!"

Rachel looked about to see Donald, his elbow on the table, the hand across his mouth hiding a smile.

"Then's when we opened up on 'em," Buchannon went on. "Rose right up out'a the grass, smoothbores boomin', rifles crackin'! Some died before they hit the water," he said in a little softer tone. "Some jumped . . . some crumpled down across the beams and just hung there. We shot 'em like fish in a barrel. Those on the far side turned and ran."

"Like hog-killin' time," Donald said quietly, "only they were men, and when you killed one, you know you'd taken somethin' away that could never be got back."

Buchannon's brows narrowed. "We thought we had put an end to the whole thing right there! But . . ." He left the sentence hanging in midair.

"The first of June," Donald said, "about seven weeks ago, a British fleet down from New York attacked Charles Town by sea. Only a hundred and sixty miles southwest of here."

"And?" Rachel asked anxiously.

"Failed. Fort Sullivan at the harbor's mouth—its walls are palmetto logs, spongy, backed by sand, and the British cannonballs just sank in. Two ships ran aground. Resistance was strong, so they turned and headed back north."

"You see, Rachel," Buchannon said, "the South is as divided as the North. Strong feeling on both sides. Moore's Creek showed that. Those of us who own a good bit of land in the Tidewater want independence. But you go back a hundred miles into the hill country, the small farmers in the Piedmont hate us Tidewater planters. So just to spite us, lots of 'em are Loyalists—Scotch-Irish in the main—men still mad because they got to this country and found the best land taken."

"Then there's the 'Over the Mountain Boys,' " Donald put in, "those out *beyond* the Piedmont, in the Blue Ridge and farther west on the Nolichucky and Watauga rivers. They're out there in violation of English law—across the ridge of the Appalachians, over the 'Line of 'Sixty-three.' "

" 'Line of 'Sixty-three'?" Rachel asked.

"King George's line," Donald answered. "Everything beyond the crest of the Appalachians is Indian land, and we're to stay out of it. Makes a lot of folks mad as a meat axe. They don't give a hang about Cherokee land, just thumb their noses at the line, not gonna be told where they can live.

"Boone's been out there for years, killin' deer and packin' out their hides. Now he's goin' out for Henderson's Transylvania Company, to the part they call Kain-tuck-ee. No tribes living in those parts, so they figure it's up for the takin'. Henderson says he bought it from the Cherokee, but the Cherokee didn't own it, they just hunt there, and so do the Shawnee.

"What it all boils down to is that they're mad at King

George and his Line of 'Sixty-three, and that makes the Over the Mountain Boys in *favor* of revolution!"

As the talk ran on, it became clear to Rachel that in coming south she had simply jumped from the frying pan into the fire. Then, once again, as had happened many times throughout the evening, she caught a glimpse of the dark-skinned girl across the room. Each time she saw her, for a moment Rachel became oblivious of everything else. There was something about the girl that was irresistible. It was the exotic beauty of her face, and far more: it was the very mystery of her presence.

When the last guest was gone and the great clock on the staircase landing struck eleven, Rachel and Donald walked onto the second-story veranda. As soon as the door closed behind them, she turned about and faced him.

"Now!" she said almost breathlessly, "don't put me off another moment. You know I can't stand the suspense. Who is that fascinating girl you call Salali?"

"I told you," he repeated, "she's Edward's daughter."

"But not Abigail's?"

"No. Abigail's, too," Donald said.

"But Donald, that girl is not *white*!"

"No," he said, "obviously she isn't. She's half white, part black, a good bit Cherokee."

"How in the world . . . ?"

They walked to the railing and leaned against it. The air was fresh and moist. Trellised honeysuckle filled the night with sweet fragrance. From here they could see the faint outline of the plantation barns against the night sky and the pine forest's black silhouette, a few dim lights glimmering in the slave quarters.

"It happened many years ago," Donald said. "Edward had a sister—"

"Had?"

"She died when Salali was small. Her name was Kathleen. Kathleen was a little older than Edward, maybe two or three years. She grew up right here on this place. Men came calling when she was of age, but she never married. Seems she had fallen in love with the plantation overseer—a man one-quarter black, three-quarter Cherokee. They had three children; Salali was the only one who lived. Salali is really Edward's niece, but everyone thinks of her as a daughter."

"Well I never . . ." Rachel said wonderingly to herself.

"North Carolina common law says the child always takes the mother's status, and that means Salali was born free. She inherits a sizable part of this estate from her grandfather." He chuckled. "It's all a different twist. Lots and lots of children are born to white men and black slave women. And just the same way, the child takes the status of the mother, so *those* children are slaves. Kathleen just turned the whole thing around on everybody." He chuckled again.

"But the obvious acceptance! As though she were as white as any woman there!"

"Buchannons are well-connected. Makes all the neighbors color-blind."

Rachel's head was spinning. Obviously she had much to learn about this complex and often contradictory southern society.

"I want to meet her," Rachel said quietly. "Anyone with the courage to stand and speak out as she did tonight . . ." Her voice trailed off as she remembered.

"You'll meet her soon," he said. "Well, Rachel, I must get some rest. Big day tomorrow."

"I think I'll stay here and enjoy the stars a little while," she said as she gazed out through the darkness to the lights in the forest. "Good night, Donald."

She turned just as his silhouette disappeared through the doorway, then leaned against the rail, lifting her eyes heavenward. The Great Bear glittered white overhead. Rachel followed its pointers to the Pole Star and gazed north. Somewhere, she thought—hundreds of miles away in the northern darkness—Drew might at this very moment be gazing at the same star.

She slapped the rail sharply with her small hand. "But what consolation is that!" she said in disgust.

Sighing deeply and fingering the smooth silk of her gown, she turned about and retired silently to her room.

FORTY-THREE

It happened again. For the fifth morning in a row Rachel was overwhelmed with dizziness and nausea. When Mary the slave girl entered her room, Rachel was on her knees over the chamber pot, vomiting. As she lifted her head, her face pasty-white and her lips trembling, she felt she was about to cry. The girl stood startled in the doorway.

"Not a word about this to anyone, Mary!" Rachel rasped weakly, the tears starting down her white cheeks.

"Oh, Miz Wolfe," the slave girl pled. "Is you sure? Doesn't you want 'em to know you're sick so they kin he'p you?"

Without answering, Rachel sat back on the floor and leaned against a leg of her bed. She began to count on her fingers, then looked up intently at Mary.

"Twenty-six days . . ." she said aloud.

"What you talkin' 'bout, Miz Wolfe?"

"Oh, Mary, never mind." She had thought the girl would know immediately. It had been twenty-six days since her last time with Drew.

"I may be about to have a baby," she said at last to the girl.

"Now? Oh, Miz Wolfe, I'll run and git—"

"*No*, Mary! Not *now*. Ohh," she groaned. "Surely it could *not* be, not after all those days over corduroy roads through the forests of Virginia and North Carolina! It just can't!

"Mary . . ." Rachel pursed her lips and steeled her eyes. "Do you understand? Not one single word to anyone!"

"Yes ma'am. I understands."

FORTY-FOUR

FRIDAY, July 12, was a burning hot day. The heavy Tidewater air held in the heat of the sun like furnace walls hold the heat of a fire.

At two in the afternoon Buchannon ordered the slaves in from the fields and woods. Donald turned his students out— the boys racing down and plunging into the river, while the girls, their chintz no longer crisp and linen wilting as if never touched by starch or iron, sought out shaded seats on the front lawn.

Rachel followed Abigail and Salali slowly up the stairs to the second story, where two broad hallways ran the length and breadth of the house, opening at each end onto the piazzas, to catch whatever breeze that blew. The servant girl Mary had preceded them and hung hammocks on iron hooks set in the walls of the hallway.

"Did you *ever* feel such heat?" Abigail Buchannon said as she unlaced her dress.

"Pennsylvania was insufferably hot," Rachel said, "but this is unspeakable."

When Abigail had undressed down to a single muslin petticoat and short gown, she stretched out on a hammock and picked up a fan made from palmetto frond. Salali and Rachel followed suit.

"There's not a breath of air," Salali said, dabbing at her face with a handkerchief. "See the sweat rolling down."

They lay languidly, fanning themselves slowly as the perspiration beaded on every inch of skin, running down, dampening the fabric of the hammocks.

"Are you sure the men won't come up and find us like this?" Rachel asked uneasily, looking down at herself. Her chemise was damp and her skin glistened.

"What would it matter?" Salali chuckled. "In heat like this, one never gets improper ideas."

Abigail stopped fanning momentarily and listened.

"Even the birds haven't strength to sing or stir," she said. "Visitors from the North think us lazy when they see how wild the land still is, so much of it uncleared. But who could labor in heat like this? And with the turpentine works and the saw mills so deep among the trees . . ." She fell silent.

Rachel's hammock was nearest the piazza door. Gazing out at the hard blue of the eastern sky, she pulled the hem of her damp chemise up to mid-thigh and began to fan her legs.

Rachel had been there only ten days, and already felt perfectly at home.

"The heat is much worse upriver," Salali remarked.

Indian and black or not, Salali's voice *sounded* as white as any southerner's, strong and pitched low; Salali stared up at the ceiling, her coal-black eyes glazed from the heat.

"That's why Grandfather built the house so near the sound," she said. "If there's a breeze anywhere, it will be here, and the tides moving in and out seem to stir the atmosphere a little. Those who live inland a few miles suffer from all sorts of disorders of the still air, ague and such. I'll forever be thankful to've been born here . . . unless, of course, I could've been born in the mountains."

"I miss the mountains," Rachel said, almost in a whisper.

"You lived in the mountains?" Salali asked.

"The Highlands of Scotland," Rachel mused, "where the air is never too hot to breathe. The trees there are few, and don't hinder the ocean winds from bathing the hills in the most delightful way." She paused. "I doubt, though, that I'll ever lay eyes on the hills and heather again." She became suddenly aware of the ancient musty feel of the cavernous house, how it blended with her mood. She sighed a long, deep sigh.

"Is it Scotland you miss," Salali ventured, "or something that only feels like Scotland?"

Rachel paused, touching her cheek with her fan. When she answered, her voice was as low as Salali's. "You're right," she said, "it isn't really Scotland I miss."

"It's the hardest thing in the world to be away from one you truly love," Salali said.

Rachel wondered how Salali could know, but thinking it imprudent to probe, only asked, "This terrible heat can't last long, can it?"

"A day like this is a weather breeder," Abigail answered. "Perhaps there'll be a change very soon."

Later Rachel would wonder why Salali wished she had been born in the mountains, having never lived in them—if it was simply a childhood dream, if she had heard stories of their beauty, or if there was some deeper reason. But right now it was too hot to think, too hot to sleep, too hot to talk, and so they drifted into a somnambulant stupor in which none of the three had any higher ambition than to draw their next breath and feel the cool of evening come.

When evening did come, the heat hung on. Clouds of mosquitoes came swarming up from the river and fields. Abigail ordered Mary to bring out yards and yards of gauze for mosquito canopies over their beds. But far to the west the sun was sinking into an ocean of rising thunderheads. As the clouds neared, a sudden cool wind came whipping through the tops of the forest trees, rushing through the hallway; as it did, it took the terrible heat and insufferable clouds of mosquitoes with it.

At the approach of the clouds, the men and boys came up from the river, the girls came in from the lawn. The women, still lying in their hammocks, began to breathe again, and to talk and laugh. Abigail rose and went down to the kitchen to supervise preparations for the evening meal. Rachel laid aside her palmetto fan, got up from her hammock, and slipped back into her dress. Together, she and Salali went out onto the west piazza.

"The clouds!" she exclaimed, gazing toward the hills. The entire horizon lay beneath a bank of towering black thunderheads that seemed to be marching across the land, lashing the face of the sky with forked whips of lightning as they came. Below, they saw Edward Buchannon down by the stables, bringing in the horses. Black slaves were closing barn doors and barring shutters against the coming storm.

And when it reached the far side of the river—an impenetrable gray wall of water moving toward them, curtaining everything off from sight as it advanced: the hills, the forest, then the river itself. On the gray curtain came, across the valley, past the road, over the lowlands, up the hill, and then they were engulfed. As the rain pounded on the roof, Rachel and Salali drew back from the piazza rail, smelled the cool air, and felt the splatter of the drops. The sound on the roof was deafening. Frequent blinding flashes made the gray deluge glow instant white, then darkness plunged in again, followed quickly by thunder that made the clapboards of the house vibrate and the glass panes rattle in their frames.

The sun had set, and when the lightning passed over, advancing out onto the ocean, there was only blackness, and the pounding of rain all through the night.

At dawn the sun appeared again, rising amid the last fleeing clouds. The chirp of birds, the lowing of cows, the voices of men calling horses to feed and children calling to the chickens and the clinking of pans and dishes—all blended wonderfully in the damp, cool morning air. With the fields too wet to work, the day would be given to other things.

It was nine o'clock when Rachel and Abigail first came out of the house. Donald was with them as a shining calèche came rolling up the winding drive, the horses' hooves clipping along in the damp sand.

The grass, the trees, the stones of the walks and the gravel of the drive—everything was washed clean. As Josiah, the black driver, reined the team in, Edward Buchannon jumped down and handed the women up, Abigail first, then Rachel. Abigail chose to ride facing backward, and Donald sat beside her, while Rachel and Edward took the forward-facing seats.

The carriage was rolling down the drive, nearly to the gate, when Rachel noticed a brightening in Donald's face and at the same moment became aware of hoofbeats coming up to her right. She looked about and heard a strong young voice from behind.

"Uncle Edward! May I come with you?"

"You bet!" he called, looking over his shoulder at Salali, mounted on a large black stallion. He waved her on.

Rachel looked at Donald and began to smile to herself. His eyes were riveted on Salali as she rode up even with the rear wheel of the coach. There was such a happy look in his eyes that Rachel began to wonder.

Salali's brown face shown in the sun, tinted wonderfully with crimson highlights on high cheekbones. Everything about her was regal, her face clear and fine. She wore an open-throated blouse of white, crisscrossed with beige plaid, the collar of which she had turned up stylishly to the back of her long, graceful neck. On her lower body she wore doeskin knee breeches, well-tailored. From foot to knee her legs were sheathed in tan silk stockings, and she wore thin-soled leather shoes.

Rachel's eyes locked with Salali's. Rachel smiled and reached out over the carriage wheel to grasp her hand and squeeze it affectionately.

From the moment they met, there had been something good between Rachel and Salali. Donald smiled to see the rapport between them. He had thought often how much Salali Buchannon was like Rachel, outspoken and fiery. But Salali was steadier, not so likely to lash out at those she loved. He was smiling to himself as Salali glanced his way and her eyes caught his. Rachel saw him blush and look away quickly.

Edward Buchannon turned to face Rachel.

"Salali is the daughter we never had," he said above the sound of hooves and wheels on the rain-beaten sand. "Nabby and I think of her as our own—but she's really my sister's girl."

"Donald told me," Rachel said.

Abigail smiled with pleasure.

"When my daddy died," Buchannon said, "I gave her father his freedom, and he went back into the mountains where he was born. But Salali chose to stay with us."

Rachel glanced up at the mention of Salali's father and the mountains. Perhaps this was what she had meant yesterday about its being hard to be away from someone you love, and why she longed for the western mountains. Rachel looked at Buchannon's face. His blue eyes twinkled with pride as he gazed at Salali riding alongside.

Salali smiled and reined her cantering mount to the right, away from the carriage wheel. The road dropped sharply into the river bottom, the carriage picked up speed, and Salali's mount fell in behind.

Edward Buchannon leaned back in the carriage seat and smiled to himself. Rachel noticed with fascination how the wind played in his short beard.

"You love the Tidewater, don't you?" she said to him, as quietly as she could and still be heard.

"Love it? You bet I love it!" he answered. "Born right there where the big house stands now. My daddy came over from Scotland in 'thirty-one. Oh, I've been north to Philadelphia and west into the mountains . . . but this is home."

"And *I* love the *sea*!" Abigail broke in. Abigail had intelligent eyes and a friendliness one could not resist.

"Oh, so do I," Rachel breathed. "But I've not seen the ocean in six years, not since we came to Philadelphia."

"It won't be long now," Buchannon said and, reaching over, patted her on the shoulder.

An hour's ride over smooth roads, a ferry to the barrier island, and the carriage broke from the oaks and pines to top a grass-covered dune beyond which lay the rolling ocean. Rachel stood in the carriage and gazed seaward. The breeze was blow-ing in strong and fresh. Great breakers were crashing on the beach: breaker, pause, another, pause, and another, ceaselessly, never resting, their wonderful roar rising to her ears. Out be-yond, the ocean itself was a deep, translucent green. The feel-ing of its power overwhelmed her, and she sank down to the seat with a flutter at the base of her throat.

"Oh, how wonderful!" she said.

"Yes! Isn't it!" Abigail answered softly.

At that moment Salali, who had reached the shore ahead of them and had been walking the black stallion in the surf, came leading him up a rabbit path through the tall salt meadow hay, the waving heads of sea oats brushing against her legs as she approached.

"And what do you think of the light?" Salali called above the sound of the surf and wind.

"Light?"

She pointed. "There, south, just above the dune."

Rachel turned her face to the south. Wind-whipped strands of long hair lay across her face. For a moment she searched the horizon. And then she saw it.

"A lighthouse!" she exclaimed. "Here on the cape? Of course, why wouldn't there be?" Then, like the child she really was, Rachel turned to Buchannon.

"Can we go to the light?"

"You want to go?"

"Yes!" she exclaimed. "More than anything!"

"There's an inlet between us and the light. We'd have to row across in a bateau staked down on the sands there . . . but, yes, we'll do it!"

The inlet was simply a break in the great barrier dunes that stretched for hundreds of miles north. From Ocracoke on to the mouth of the Chesapeake, they were called the Outer Banks. Here, they were simply barrier islands that protected the main-land from the beating of the sea.

The inlet's water was rough and choppy. But for the com-bined power of the men's oar strokes, the bateau would have quickly wallowed and sunk in the incoming waves. It was a flat-bottomed and flat-ended boat of native wood, raked at stern and bow, with sides flaring amidships. Ten minutes of hard rowing, and the bow of the boat was sliding up onto the soft sand of a small cove.

As quickly as Rachel's feet touched firm ground, the great tower of the light claimed all her attention. Donald and Edward pulled the bateau up onto the beach. Buchannon, delighted to share his surroundings with anyone who would love them as he did, watched Rachel closely. Her eyes grew distant with a feeling of mystery as she scanned the great tower, and a smile stole softly to her lips.

The light stood a hundred yards from the ocean, elevated on the little island's highest rise. The tower was tall and round, a massive thing, all of great stone, broad below, tapering gracefully, gently upward. Its blocks, rough-hewn in northern quarries, had been brought here by ship. The side of the tower that faced the sea was scoured bright by blowing sands, but on the land side the stones were spotted with moss and the mortar had grown black with the collections of time.

Sixty or more feet above the island, perched on the tower's shoulders, was the great lantern itself, a round room with walls of glass, capped by a low roof and surrounded with a catwalk and a railing of iron.

All gave the impression of being sunk—as indeed it was—in mother rock, built to withstand the passing of time and the heat of the southern sun and the howling of great hurricanes that rampaged out of the Caribbean. Even had it been only a tower—without a light—its existence would have been justified by the very strength it made one feel.

"The keeper," Buchannon broke into her thoughts, "Old Spaun, we call him—he's away for the day. But he'd not want you to miss going up into the lantern. Shall we?"

Rachel looked at him in amazement. "Of course we shall!"

Within, the hollow tower was cavernous and dark. A wooden staircase clinging to the stone walls spiraled upward in darkness through three wooden floors. With the entrance door standing open, the wind moaned softly, drawn irresistibly upward like the draft of an enormous chimney. When Buchannon shut it behind him, the moaning suddenly became a thin whistling of air. With Edward, Donald, and Salali, Rachel climbed the creaking risers, their whispered voices echoing.

"Why do we whisper?" Salali asked half seriously.

"Because it *feels* like we should!" Donald answered in the same tone.

When they reached the lantern, the sun—freely admitted through the walls of glass—made them shield their eyes from its glare.

"The lantern is so much bigger than it seemed from the ground," Rachel whispered.

A wide panorama of sea and coast lay neatly arranged below, mile upon mile of far-stretching dunes and glistening breakers.

"And this is the light," Salali said, turning to the center of the glass-walled room.

There, arranged in tiers before a tall, deeply curved sheet of gleaming brass, stood two dozen thick candles, their wicks ready for the falling of night.

"Old Spaun did his morning work," Donald said. "Smell the spirits of wine? He used it to wet this," and he pointed to a soft chamois that hung over the back of a chair. "He wipes the reflector down with it every day."

"How far out can sailors see the light?" Rachel asked.

"It stands all of eighty feet above the face of the sea," Buchannon answered, "when you consider the tower and the hill and all. I've been on the water at night, and I've seen the light's glow *way* out there. I've heard said fourteen miles or farther. And I guess it must be so."

Next to the light tower and attached to it was a low cottage of randomly shaped stones with a roof of gray slate; Old Spaun's bachelor quarters, ample space for a man alone.

A broad lawn of thick, short grass anchored the surface of the sandy hill, and across the lawn was a scattering of gnarled oaks, a cluster of which grew at the tower's base, between it and the sea.

Among the oaks the little group spread a flowered white cloth, ate a leisurely lunch, then stretched out on the grass, some sleeping, others talking. Suddenly Rachel and Salali got to their feet.

"We're going to walk along the sands," Salali announced.

Donald began to get up.

"For some woman talk," Rachel said, smiling.

"Oh . . ." he said, sitting back down, and with an expression of disappointment on his face watched them as they walked away toward the surf.

When the two women reached the water, Salali slipped the stockings from her legs while Rachel hoisted her skirts about her knees. Their bare feet left rounded prints in the firm, wet sand, and behind them the foaming surf boiled in to wash the prints away.

Rachel looked up to find Salali looking admiringly at her. Salali blushed and, smiling nervously, dropped her gaze.

"Forgive me," she stammered, then, feeling that somehow she must explain, "but everything about you fascinates me." It was a bold beginning, but Salali was not one to temper her speech.

"I? I fascinate you?" Rachel said, laughing. "What is there about me that should make you feel so?"

"Many things," Salali said. A thin sheet of glistening water washed up and began its retreat into the sea, leaving behind a suddenly exposed and badly confused crab. Salali squatted down and reached for it, but it scurried quickly to meet the next incoming wave. Without rising, she looked up, her black eyes shining. "Donald says you're quite as good a physician as your husband. I admire that. And you're young, no older than I, I expect." She paused. "And I admire your beauty . . . as well as your pluck."

For a long moment Rachel stared quietly at the sand. She knew how it felt to have men admire her for her appearance; but, gratifying as it was, that sort of admiration was such a superficial thing. It was quite another thing to be admired by another woman—and for all the right reasons. Rachel looked up and smiled. "Thank you," she said quietly. "In fact, I feel the very same about you . . . and for most of the same reasons," she added. "You were magnificent that night at dinner. You refused to give that man a single inch."

Salali made no answer at all, but simply continued her upward gaze, smiling to think of their mutual admiration, warmed at the idea of so close a friend. Her clear eyes sparkled. They were intelligent eyes, the inner corners hidden under folds that imparted an almond shape. Her brows were dark and evenly curved. Her lips inscribed a firm, determined line where they met, in spite of the mischievous smile that played about her mouth. With the sudden realization of friendship, the two burst out in gentle laughter, paused, and not knowing what to say next, laughed again.

A breaker washed higher than before, wetting Salali's legs. She sprung up and brushed the sand and water from her haunches.

"The tide's coming in," she said.

They ambled on, mesmerized by the breakers spreading their thin sheets higher on the sands.

"Your name," Rachel said, turning to Salali, "it's so beautiful. Does it have a meaning?"

"Yes," Salali answered, smiling. "It's a Cherokee word. Moments after I was born, my father saw a gray squirrel make a long, graceful jump from one high limb to another."

"Salali—gray squirrel. Is that it?"

"Yes," she said.

"Your father . . . he's gone into the mountains?"

Salali paused. "My father is dead."

Rachel felt utterly stupid. "I'm sorry," she apologized, "I thought he'd only gone away."

"He did go away," Salali answered, "after my mother died, though it tore his heart out to do it. He would have taken me with him, but the Real People were in trouble. It was dangerous, no place for me to be, and he said he had to go to them. Of course I was just a girl at the time."

"What kind of trouble?" Rachel asked.

"The whites were driving his people—*our* people," she corrected herself, "farther and farther toward the mountains. It was impossible for them to resist, partly because so many had died when the whites brought smallpox into the villages forty years ago. *Half* the Real People died then, including my father's father and mother. Before he was grown, whites captured him and brought him out of the forest. Uncle Edward's father bought him. He was bright, a good worker, and eventually got to be overseer."

"What was his name?" Rachel asked.

"Teesatuskie," Salali answered thoughtfully. "He was killed ten years ago by whites."

"Once he went away," Rachel said, pity and caution in her voice and eyes, "did he ever return?"

"Yes, he came to see me, and to see Uncle Edward and Aunt Nabby. Sometimes Uncle Edward would go to the beloved village, Chote, and join him. They went together on long hunts that kept Uncle Edward away for months at a time. They were great friends."

There was a long pause as Rachel thought of how different their lives were.

"My father is still in Scotland," Rachel said, her eyes very sad.

"And you miss him?" Salali asked.

"No. No, I don't. We fought. He beat me. Once he took me down and sheared my head as he would've one of his sheep."

It was Salali's turn to feel pity. She saw the hurt in Rachel's face, then let her eyes follow the length of Rachel's long dark hair. Salali envied the auburn tints gleaming in the descending sun. In contrast, her own hair, almost as long as Rachel's, was an absolute black.

"I'd like to ask you something," Rachel said.

"I'll answer if I can," Salali responded.

"On the way here, I saw something in my brother's eyes when you rode up. It was there every time he looked at you, every time you spoke."

Salali smiled. "You're asking if there's something between Donald and me," she said. "If there is, he's never told me."

"And if he did feel something for you?"

Salali's smile grew wide. "I don't know," she whispered. "Perhaps . . ."

"Enough said." Rachel smiled.

Just then a gigantic breaker crashed around their feet, sending them into spasms of laughter.

They walked on for a long while on the wet sands; from the island's south end they saw the tide stand and begin to ebb as they spoke confidingly. At last, when the sun fell behind the clouds, the green sea turned a mournful, heaving gray. Far in the distance half sails reached above the watery horizon, the ghosts of fishing boats with their catch, returning to the mouth of Cape Fear River.

"I'm glad you've come to Buchannon Hills," Salali said.

"So am I," Rachel answered. "You and I—we'll be close friends. I'm sure of it . . . unless . . ."

"Unless what?" Salali asked, surprised.

"Unless you grow weary of me."

"And why should I grow weary of you?"

"I'm very hard to like at times," Rachel said. There was pain in her soft eyes. "And sometimes cruel to those I love the most—and sometimes I feel very sorry for myself. You'll not believe the things that go through my head. I'm a grown woman who has delivered children into the world—who's

mended terrible wounds." Rachel's hand moved to the lower
bodice of her dress, and her voice dropped to a near tearful
whisper. "And at other times I'm nothing but a resentful,
spoiled child!"

Salali stopped and reached for Rachel's hand, then embraced
her. For a long while neither spoke. At last Salali stood back
and looked Rachel full in the face. The last glinting ray of the
sun lighted Salali's copper-brown skin for a moment, then sank
behind the trees of the mainland.

"You know what I think the difference between you and me
is, Rachel Wolfe?" Salali said.

"No, Salali Buchannon," Rachel said as the darkness fell.
"What do you think the difference is?"

Salali could see the underlying sorrow in Rachel's eyes. "I
think," she said, her voice full of intensity, her eyes welling
with longing to comfort Rachel, "that when you were a little
girl, you hadn't a father to love you and make you feel safe
. . . and now, when you're afraid, you still feel you've no place
to go. Oh, Rachel, when one has felt loved and safe, she can
stand up to anything—and she can love in return."

Rachel did not know what to say, but holding her tearful
eyes steadily on Salali's, she felt overcome by the other woman's tender understanding.

Salali's eyes shifted to something beyond Rachel's shoulder.
"Old Spaun's back," she whispered.

Rachel looked around. There, up on the crest of the grassy
dune, stood the lighthouse, all in shadow. At first she saw
nothing but its massive stone and dark lantern. Then . . .

"He's lighting the lantern," Rachel whispered.

There was a quavering flicker, a gentle glimmer slowly
growing by degrees as one by one Old Spaun lighted the candles. When he was done and all the candles were aflame, the
lantern sat glowing high above the dune with a calm and
steady brilliance.

Its soft light stole into Rachel's heart. "Oh, how wonderful!"
she said.

Just then, from the opposite bank—where the others stood
with the chaise and horses—came a smaller glimmer, unnoticed by Rachel and Salali. Nabby called down, "Girls, Josiah
has the carriage lanterns lighted. We'd best be going."

"We'll be right up, Aunt Abigail," Salali called.

With hands joined, Rachel and Salali found their way to the
skiff. The inlet had calmed, and soon they were across. Shortly,

the cool air of evening was rushing about them as the carriage
sped back toward Buchannon Hills. This time Salali was in the
carriage beside Rachel, as the stallion trotted along behind.

FORTY-FIVE

THE carriage rolled through the night, gently winding along the
river road, the high lanterns quavering with a bright yellow
light. The voices of the passengers droned comfortingly amid
the sounds of beating hooves and the calèche's easy sway. The
cool air of the bottomland smelled pleasantly of flowing water
and river mud. As the carriage came around the last bend, the
lights of Buchannon Hall winked through the trees from its
distant hill. Rachel, riding between Salali and Donald, had
drifted off to sleep with her head on Donald's shoulder.

They were yet a quarter-mile from the turn when a commotion arose. Rachel, roused from sleep, opened her eyes and listened. A voice was shouting from somewhere in the darkness
ahead. She sat up and looked. The carriage lights shone on the
backs of the horses and illuminated the road for a short distance. Suddenly, the form of a man on horseback appeared in
the twin circles of light—and Buchannon shouted at the driver
to halt the carriage.

"Mr. Buchannon, sir!" the rider called.

The squeal of stressed harness, the clatter of tongue and
doubletree, and the sudden stop jolted Rachel into full wakefulness. Edward Buchannon stood in the carriage.

"Tom!" he cried. "Is there trouble?"

"No, sir!" the man said. "Not trouble—news! Fast packet
from Philadelphia sailed into Wilmington two hours ago. Sir!
We've snapped off the yoke! They've declared us independent
from England!"

"Done!" Buchannon shouted. "By the Almighty, it's done!"
The big man snatched his hat from his head, and the carriage
rocked with the stamping of his foot. He looked about at the

others, his face alight with excitement, and then back to the messenger.

"When, Tom?"

The young rider's horse skittered beneath him. "Nine days ago, sir. It was on a Thursday. Bells, cannon, mobs . . . like Resurrection Morning, they say."

Rachel's imagination went wild. She was in Philadelphia again, part of the surging crowd on High Street in front of the State House. She could see Franklin's bulk on the steps and hear the bells pealing and cannon booming. But where was Drew?

"Oh Lord . . . Drew?" she said aloud as she turned to Salali. "They'll take him for a traitor, put him in prison, or . . ." Her heart was in her throat. Salali looked from Rachel's face to Buchannon's.

"And the war? What news of the war?" Buchannon's words snapped Rachel again to attention.

"Not much action right now. The British are still in New York, sir, on Staten Island. The harbor's choked with their ships. Howe has thirty-two thousand troops there! London's decided to take this war seriously!"

Rachel gasped. Buchannon's mouth dropped open and he sank into the seat.

"And Washington?" he asked, subdued.

"He's holding Manhattan Island with nineteen thousand men."

"God help us!" Buchannon said. Then, remembering independence, he jumped to his feet and with a mighty "Hoorah!" threw his hat sailing through the air. Laughing with glee, he sat back in the carriage.

"Tom," he said, "give that wife of yours a hug for me. And thanks for the word!"

"Josiah," he called out, "drive on."

As they pulled away, Rachel heard him chuckle quietly to Abigail. "That was a good hat I threw away. I'll have to come back in the mornin' and hunt for it."

"I'll not sleep tonight!" Rachel said to Salali as they swept up the stairway.

There was anger in the way she held the front of her long skirt high with one hand and the brass candle holder with its lighted taper in the other. Her feet struck the treads sharply. "I was *wrong* to leave him. He *made* me do it, but I left in such a fury!"

"Have you answered his letters?" Salali asked quietly. Letters had come from Drew at the rate of one every three days since her arrival, and she had treated each one as she had the ones that preceded her to Buchannon Hills.

"No," Rachel answered sheepishly, "I wanted him to suffer awhile."

As they reached Rachel's door, Salali shook her head. The wavering candlelight revealed the sympathy in her eyes. There was kind firmness in her voice. "No good," she said. "This is war now—no time for children's games. The packet will sail from Wilmington on Monday. If you wrote tonight, he could have a letter in five to ten days."

"Yes! He could, couldn't he?" Rachel exclaimed.

Once inside, Rachel lighted two tapers in wall sconces, set the candle on the red mulberry wood nightstand, then paused and stood thinking. Her eyes were clouded with tears, then they brightened. The packet that could carry a letter could also carry her!

"Or *I* could be in Philadelphia!" she said. Her eyes moved excitedly over her friend's features. Salali's face was blank.

"Yes," Salali said slowly, "if there's room. . . ."

Rachel was filled with excitement. "I'll do it," she said. "I'll go to him, on Monday!"

As abruptly as she'd brightened, her face fell. She walked slowly to the window, raised the sash wide, and gazed out. The sound of dogs barking in the distance floated into the room on the still night air. Below, an occasional lamp lighted the paths through the grounds; otherwise, all was darkness.

"Salali," Rachel said. Her voice was small and frightened.

"Yes?"

"Salali . . . I'm with child."

"With child!" Salali whispered.

"Yes, I'm sure of it. Drew would feel differently if he knew. He would want me to come home to him!"

"Yes," Salali said quietly, "he might. Or . . . he might want you here all the more."

"I've *got* to go to him," she said, turning to face her friend in the candlelight. Her voice was determined. "I'm *cer*tain that's the way he would want it!"

* * *

The next morning was Sunday. Wilmington's parish church was filling rapidly when Donald and Rachel arrived with the Buchannons and several of their slaves. It was forbidden that slaves be baptized in North Carolina churches, but the law was regularly ignored, and there were a number of blacks in the congregation. As Rachel and the others were threading their way through the crowd toward the Buchannon pew, Tom Cramer handed Edward Buchannon a letter.

"In the excitement, I forgot about this, Edward. It came on the packet yesterday . . . addressed to Mrs. Wolfe."

Buchannon looked at the folded sheet. It was sealed with the blue wax and stamp that he had come to know as Drew Wolfe's. He looked about. Rachel, who sat ahead of him, had not heard. He slipped it into his pocket.

It was much later, at home and with dinner over, when everyone had risen from the table, that Edward took Rachel aside and handed her the letter.

When her hand touched it, Rachel's heart leapt in her breast. Feeling the need to be alone, she fled to the front lawn. Sitting on the thick carpet of grass under the outspread arms of a great magnolia, she broke the wax seal, unfolded the pages, and read.

Dear Rachel:

I've lost count of the times I've written, yet I've heard nothing from you in return. I know you, Rachel, better than anyone one else in the world; and I know you're letting me suffer. But I also know that you love me.

Rachel, I miss you terribly. There are days—and especially nights—when I'm sure I did wrong in sending you away. But Rachel, I could not bear to think of you caught in the crossfires of war. I know all too well that at times fears rule my mind. This may be one of those times. If I have done you wrong, then, dearest Rachel, please forgive me.

In spite of my frequent misgivings, I *am* sure of this: that you and I are part of a cause greater than the sum of our two lives. Whatever the cost to us, a favorable outcome will be worth whatever the price—if not to us, then to all the thousands who follow in coming generations.

And now, dearest, there is something I must tell you, something very hard. My work for "our tall stranger" continues, and I have enlisted with the British forces as a medical officer. By the time you receive this letter, I will no longer be in Philadelphia, but with Howe on Staten Island, or in the interior, perhaps up in the northern theater of war; I do not know where. And of course it may be that I will not survive this war. It is at least possible that neither of us shall.

Yet I confess, Rachel, that I fear your anger more than I fear the war itself! There is duty, however, and I cannot forsake it. Until we are together again, I must say that I am glad you are safe far away from the front. How contradictory this all sounds! Yet how typical of my feelings in these terrible days! When you write, as I hope you soon shall, send your letters to Israel. He will know where I've gone.

Good-bye, Rachel. May you always be safe.

Your loving husband,
Andrew

A bitter acid taste filled Rachel's mouth, and her chin began to quiver while shining tears brimmed her eyes. She rose slowly from the grass and walked aimlessly away from the house. Never had she felt so helpless as at this moment. She was crying uncontrollably, the thoughts of Drew's going away, her failure to answer his letters, the child she was now certainly carrying, and that Drew did not know—all rushed in at once to overwhelm her.

By the time she reached the gate at the bottom of the hill, she was running. Crossing the road, she descended through tangled brush into the wooded river bottom. At last she stood on the river bank, her heart beating like a rapid hammer, until it seemed it would burst.

With the afternoon sun glinting off its face, the wide gray river rolled by at her feet. Overhead, great sycamores stretched their gentle arms and wide green leaves, giving her weary heart shade. A willow dipped its long narrow fronds over the water, their tips making little swirls where they touched the current. For a long while Rachel stood swaying, feeling everything, noticing nothing, weeping. The river swirled as her mind was swirling.

Would there never be an end? Would she never see him again? Why should this happen now, of all times? She laid her hand on her belly, which had not yet begun to swell, imagining how soon she would be able to feel the beat of the new heart she knew was there.

A white sharp-winged gull hung bobbing low over the wa-

ter. The smell of fresh mud and green grass grew stronger as
the afternoon disappeared—Rachel took no notice that her
head had begun to ache. All was covered in shadow before her
mind was clear again. She remembered Salali's words: "This is
war now—no time for children's games."

Her friend was right—she must toughen up. She must stop
fighting life and get on with living, no matter what. She must
be honest with Drew; indeed, she must be honest with herself!
Now she had no way of finding him—no way of being sure
anything she wrote would reach him! Here she was, and here
she must remain—for however long it took.

F O R T Y - S I X

RACHEL knew her letters might never reach Drew, that they
might not be saved or forwarded to wherever he might be. But
it was the only way she had of feeling close to him—and she
wanted more than anything else in the world to feel him close.
She could not bring herself to write in so many words how
sorry she was for the way in which she had left, but thought
that perhaps he would know anyway.

Mostly, her letters were filled with the new and overwhelming land to which she had come. For the South that Rachel
found waiting for her was unlike anything she had imagined it
would be. Pennsylvania had been forested with oak, maple,
and sycamore, a land of dark earth and rolling hills. But here
the earth was dead white sand, light, low and level. Long-leaf
pine made up most of the forest, but there were countless other
kinds of trees, many of which matched the beauty of those in
Pennsylvania.

It was the last Sunday afternoon in July, an unusually cool
day, when she sat on the front lawn, her feet tucked beneath
her and her skirt spread wide over the finely clipped grass. She
had a bottle of ink at hand and was twirling a sharpened quill
between her fingers as she thought. Above, somewhere in the
branches of a great magnolia, a chorus of cicadas hummed a

lively tune to the soft summer breeze. With a mixture of love and sadness in her eyes, she dipped the quill and set it to the fine white paper, drawing her letters in dramatic loops and flourishes.

My Dearest Drew,
    How I wish you were with me!
    This is a truly wild but lovely land! Even as I write, I'm sitting on soft grass at the foot of a great tree called a "magnolia." I'm sure it is quite unlike anything you have ever seen in all your life. Imagine, if you can, a perfectly shaped oak with huge, glossy leaves, and covered with white roses larger than your two hands together! If you can see it, you will have the magnolia in mind, both in appearance and in fragrance.
    I arrived just in time to see the wild petunias in their last days of purple bloom. In the fields the rice is whitening, the indigo is ready; and the cotton fields are little seas of white flowers on green plants tall as a man's thigh.
    The plantation is "down on the sound"—as the inland folks say. The sound is the seaward edge of land that lies between the Cape Fear and the Atlantic. It's separated from an endless line of barrier dunes by long, narrow sea-fed stretches of water.
    The house, and the lawn on which I now write, sits on a high point of the sound. We are surrounded by forest, hacked through with terrible roads that lead to the plantation's saw mills on the little creeks, and tar and turpentine camps deep in the woods. There are also indigo fields here, but the rice is planted farther inland. Salali says the summer houses are built on the sound to escape the heat, but it's even truer to say they're built here to escape the smell of the flooded rice fields. Oh, Drew, that is one odor you can simply not imagine. It utterly *putrefies* the air! More like *soured laundry* than anything else I can think of.

Rachel looked up from her writing to see that the sun had sunk behind the house, muting the light. She stretched her fingers. They were growing stiff, and her legs had gone to sleep. She dipped the quill again.

    I must lay my pages aside for now, dearest. But I promise to take them up again tomorrow.

Early next morning, as soon as breakfast was done, Rachel was at the red mulberry wood desk in her room, the letter spread before her again. "Dearest Drew," she wrote . . .

It is Monday morning, very bright here, but the cool of yesterday lingers blissfully over us. I slept well, and hope that you did also. I was telling you about the Buchannon plantation.

It is really quite small when compared to some of the others, especially those up in Virginia. There a man might own thirty thousand acres in parcels scattered from the coast up through the Piedmont. The Buchannons—Edward and Abigail and Salali—have about a thousand acres of nearly level timber and crop land, half of it on the sound, and half in the inland rice fields.

They tell me that the "big house" was built in the fifties, and yet somehow it seems much older to me. Perhaps it's the great hollow rooms and hallways, and the piazzas on every side, so deep and shady. Or perhaps that the wood, though freshly painted, already shows the weathered marks of the thick salt air and the wet winds.

There's a large kitchen on the southwest side—the side nearest the river. One reaches it through a passageway called a "hyphen." The servants are busy in the kitchen every waking hour, for the preparation of meals for such a household is a never-ending affair.

Out behind the big house are the working buildings: stock barns, a house for the indigo vats. There's a smithy, and a little distance from it are the stables.

Yonder, on the other side of the barns, it is like a little village, another world of houses, scattered willy-nilly among the trees in the edge of the forest. I went there for the very first time only yesterday with Salali. The slaves' houses are small, though no smaller than the cottages Daddy led us in and out of in Scotland. But they are much more drab—unpainted, rough-sawn timber on beams hewn square.

They are sturdily built, though—each with a fireplace, some with more than one room, and a few with wooden floors. But in most, packed earth serves for the floor, the same kind as the white settlers' cabins up in the Piedmont, they say.

It takes a hundred able-bodied slaves to keep the plantation going: a few house servants, groomsmen, a blacksmith, some overseers; but most are field workers.

You may well wonder, my dearest, how I can express such affection for a man who owns human flesh. These human chattels were part of his father's estate when he died a decade ago. True, North Carolina law permits a planter to manumit his slaves, but it also demands that with manumission, the planter post bond guaranteeing the slave can make a living on his own, and so not fall back on the parish for support. And this Edward simply cannot afford to do.

I have heard him say that *one* day, if he ever can, he will free them all. His four reasons seem very sincere. First, he believes every man is born free and equal. Often he says this is the thing he likes most about the Revolution. Second, he says his conscience condemns him for keeping human beings in servitude. His third reason is the golden rule—which seems very important to him. He says he would not wish to be kept in slavery himself. I shall quote his last verbatim. He says, "I want to die with a clear conscience, so that I may not be ashamed to appear before *my* Master in the future world."

Oh my dearest, how I long to know your whereabouts! How I long for you to know our secret—that in a few months I will bear your child. My one hope is that you shall receive my letters and that soon I shall be reading pages from *your* hand.

I will close now. Josiah is driving into Wilmington in the morning. He will deliver this to the captain of the packet leaving for Philadelphia with the next tide.

Your loving wife,
Rachel

FORTY-SEVEN

SALALI often went into the forest's edge to mingle with the slaves, and often Rachel was with her. Today, a blustery Sunday afternoon in late September, they wandered together along the path that led down to the little gray houses. The trees about them, having never been cut, were enormous, their crowns reaching above a hundred feet over the young women's heads, their densely bunched needles brushing and whispering in the wind.

As they walked down the dirt path strewn with reddish tree bark and sawdust, Salali took a sidelong look at Rachel. "You're beginning to show," she said, and smiled.

"I'm surprised you're just now seeing it," Rachel answered. She swept her hand down over the now perceptible swell. "Has anyone else noticed?"

"No one has said anything to me. Does Donald know?"

"No."

"Well, I've told no one, but you won't be able to hide it much longer."

They were coming up on the first house at the edge of the clearing. There was an air of order and cleanliness to this house that many of the others lacked. On its front step sat a woman with a red neckerchief about her hair, knotted behind her head; so frail was she that it seemed the wind itself could carry her away at any moment. She had a gray blanket thrown about her, beneath which the slight humps of her sloping shoulders utterly disappeared. She seemed little more than a frail old head perched upon the blanket. One faded hand held a clay pipe near her thin lips. Her eyes, glazed over with milky-white, looked toward the sound of their steps.

"Who dere?" a crackling voice called out.

"It's Salali, Aunt Martha," she answered, her voice louder than usual.

" 'N' somebody else, too," the old woman responded testily.

"My eyes may not be no 'count, but I kin still hyear putty good."

Salali laughed, and plopping down beside the old woman, hugged the narrow shoulders warmly, then spread her skirts out on the step.

"What's this I hear about you, Aunt Martha?" Salali asked.

"Do know! What you think you hyear?"

"That you've been poorly of late."

"Oh, dat! Yeah, it so. But what a woman like me ought to 'spect, bein' ol' as I is?" She puffed on the pipe and smiled a smile as rich as vanilla. Her paper-thin eyelids blinked slowly.

Rachel perched herself on the lowest step and stretched her feet out before her. "You've been sick, Aunt Martha?" Rachel said.

"Who want to know?" the old woman demanded.

"This is my friend, Aunt Martha," Salali said. "Her name is Rachel."

"You needn't talk so loud, girl," the old woman said. "I told you, my ears is still good."

"Aunt Martha is the only one on the place that was born in Africa, Rachel." She lowered her voice to more conversational tones and squeezed Aunt Martha's shoulders tighter. A self-satisfied grin spread over Martha's thin face.

"How many years ago did you come to America?" Rachel asked.

"I cain't count dat high!" the old woman crackled. "But I come over 'tween the decks of a slave ship when I was young 'n' putty. Dey couldn't han'le me, though—I'se too wild fer 'em. Dey hed to chain me on deck to keep me from fightin' wid de othas." She chuckled low at this ancient memory. "I ain't wild no mo', I tell ya," she said. "Ain't putty no mo', neitha."

"We all get old, Aunt Martha," Rachel said wistfully.

"No, no we don' all git ol'," the woman said. "Ony dem 'at *lives* gets old. 'N' you. I kin tell you ain't old. Sich a putty young sound you makes; I bet a putty young face goes with it!"

"It does, Aunt Martha. Rachel is one of the prettiest girls you've ever seen."

"She got a man?"

"Yes, but he's in Philadelphia," Salali answered.

"*You* de young woman whose man sent 'er down hyere to git away from de wa'!"

"Yes, Aunt, that's right," Salali said.

"I jumped the broom oncet, lotsa years ago," the old woman said.

Rachel's eyes turned to Salali.

"A slave marriage ceremony," she said to Rachel. "Some slave owners don't allow Christian weddings, so the couple jumps over a broom stick, and that constitutes their marriage." Turning to Martha, Salali inadvertently raised her voice again. "But we don't do things that way here, do we, Aunt?"

"No," the old woman said. "No, Mistah Buchannon's too good a man for dat. He eitha does the ceremony hisself or he calls for a minista to do it for 'im."

"But you've been ill, Aunt Martha?" Rachel ventured again.

"Not 'been,' *is*!" Martha answered.

"Can you tell me what's wrong?"

"Rachel is a doctor, Aunt. She might be able to help you."

"A doctah!" the old woman exclaimed. "Well," she said slowly. Then she turned her white eyes toward Rachel. "Sumpin' eatin' away at me," she said. "Ain't gonna be nothin' you kin do fer me."

"Where is it eating at you, Aunt?"

"Hyere," she said. Her bony fingers went to her collar buttons. She laid open the bodice of her loose dress. Rachel's face turned sad, and she shook her head ever so slightly. Suppurating sores larger than Spanish dollars gathered on the old woman's left breast. Rachel recognized immediately the utter hopelessness of her case. Salali read it in her eyes. Rachel pressed about the withered breast with her fingers. More of the foreign growths lay deeper, just as she knew they would. No doubt they had also entered her body and would soon begin to show elsewhere. After that, death would not be long in coming. There was strained silence, then Rachel spoke.

"I can't make you well, Aunt Martha," she said. Another pause. "And the sores won't go away. But I will come down every day and help you keep them clean. Are you in much pain?"

"Not a heap," she said. "Oh, it don't matter no how. I'se old and sick all over. But then, I done okay for lotsa years. Cain't ask God for mo' time than what He's a'ready give me."

"No," Rachel said. "You really can't."

Together Rachel and Salali dressed the old woman's sores, rebuttoned her dress, covered her shoulders with the faded blanket, and left her on her step, smoking her pipe as peace-fully as when they had come.

The afternoon lengthened, and the sun, like a yellow spark, was already entangled in the top branches of the tall pines as Rachel and Salali ambled slowly back to the big house. They were talking in low, sympathetic tones about Aunt Martha when, without warning, a shrill scream cut through the humid air.

"Kill 'im! Kill 'im, I tells ya!"

There were other yells, and dull thudding noises.

Rachel and Salali stopped and stared at each other, their eyes wide with wonder.

"It's Ruth!" Rachel said. "She's found Anthony with Mary again! She'll kill him sure," and she turned and started on a run back down toward the cabins.

The screams seemed to be coming from the west edge of the village where the ground descended rapidly toward the creek.

"It must be a terrible fight!" Salali said as they ran. "Just listen! Lots of men's voices . . . and what is that terrible groan-ing sound!"

"Kill 'im! Kill 'im!" the voice said again as they stepped into a small clearing. Rachel had been right; it was Ruth, the slave girl. There she stood, a white cloth wrapped about her head turban-fashion, with one hand holding up the hem of her full skirt, her bare feet dancing on the damp-packed mud, while with the other hand she was jabbing her finger deter-minedly toward something writhing on the ground. A dozen men surrounded the writhing object, each stepping lively as it came first toward one and then another. All about and under their feet the ground was littered with white feathers.

"He's done stole the last goose he's *evah* gonna steal from me!" Ruth shouted again. "Kill 'im, I says!"

Suddenly the crowd of men parted in their direction. Rachel, totally unable to believe her eyes, threw her hands up to her face, grabbed her skirt, and stepped back in terror.

"Salali! What *is* it!" she shouted.

"Alligator!" screamed Salali, who bent forward, her hands on her knees, eyes dancing as she began to laugh at the frantic scene.

"Oh, Miz Buchannon!" Ruth said excitedly. "I hyeard this ungodly commotion in my poultry yard and come running out. It uz this hyear beast slitherin' back into the brush with my best goose honkin' and flappin' in its big ol' mouth! I picked up a pole as thick as my wrist and hit it ez hard as I could, aimin' fer its eyes, but it let go the goose and riz up on its legs and come for me, its mouth open, ready to take my arm off up the elbow! The men, they got hyere jest in time!"

Salali was nearly doubled with laughter, but Rachel was horrified.

The terrible blows raining down on the beast's body were bouncing off its tough armor, but others, aimed at its vulnerable eyes and at a spot under its throat, were making it roar with pain and anger. It whipped its terrible tail about and raised up on its legs again as its body cleared the ground, the horrific jaws plunging and snapping at the men. Never had Rachel seen such a maw, the force of its jaws surely enough to sever a leg.

"Kill dat robber!" Ruth screamed above the roars of the beast and the shouting of the men, as she kept dancing and jabbing the air like a boxer in a London ring.

Then one man with a pole knocked out the creature's remaining eye as another flung himself forward and plunged a long knife into its throat. The knife entered with such force that the man's hand followed it into the pouring gash.

Rachel wanted to cover her eyes, but stood riveted to the scene. The beast's screams cut into her like the knife that had just severed its throat. And all the while, the dying creature was emitting the most terrible musk—making her sick. She could hold it back no more, and bending at the waist, began to retch and vomit.

When at last the great carcass lay nearly still, twitching only slightly, and most certainly dead, Rachel felt the pastiness of her own skin. By this time Salali had composed herself.

"You're white as the feathers on the ground," Salali said.

Rachel was breathing hard, wiping her lips with the back of her hand.

The goose was limping about on a torn foot, dragging its left wing, broken, next to its body. Not wanting to see it suffer, Ruth quickly grabbed the goose up by the neck and, biting her own tongue between her teeth, cranked her arms in a circular motion, wrung the goose's neck until the head separated from the body and the body went somersaulting off into the trees.

The heavy alligator musk lingered as the men stepped off the great body from nose to tail.

"Eighteen feet!" cried the man who had done the pacing.

The others smiled and laughed at their victory. Wiping the sweat from their faces, they grabbed the beast by its taloned feet and dragged it away to be butchered.

That night, Rachel wrote to Drew, describing the scene in her closing paragraphs:

Strange—with every new scene that comes before my eyes, I think of you and how you would delight to see it, and how much more I would enjoy the discovery of this wild and wonderful land if you were with me! I can pour my heart out to you in my letters, but I cannot even know if they will ever reach you. How bitterly alone and sad this makes me feel!

Almost every day thereafter, Rachel came down to Aunt Martha's house. Two nights in October she stayed with Caleb, an eight-year-old boy who had stumbled and plunged his arms into his mother's boiling laundry kettle. She put salve on his burns, gave him laudanum, and comforted the boy's mother and father.

In November she delivered the fat twin boys of a doe-eyed girl whose name also was Rachel. When Rachel asked the father's name, the girl sat with her lips tightly pursed. Finally the boy came forward and there was a wedding.

Then winter came. When the living weight in Rachel's belly grew large, pulling at the muscles of her abdomen and at the joints of her back, her movements became slower, her breathing more labored, and the humid air more of a trial. Even so, she kept her daily vigil down among the little gray houses, sometimes only to sit and make the hours pass more lightly for Martha. And the work took her mind off her discomfort and off her separation from Drew.

As Rachel's face grew rounder, it glowed with the unmistakable aura of health—a ruddy glow matching the auburn highlights in her hair.

Salali could see in Rachel's face how it hurt her to be away from Drew, but she also saw the lines there becoming softer, somehow happier, perhaps because she was thinking less of herself, more of the sadnesses down in the little village, of Donald's continued loneliness, and of the poor soldiers fighting in the north.

Twice each week she continued to write. And at least once a month came a reply from Israel, saying always that Drew was in the northern interior where the letters could not reach him.

One morning in late November, Rachel and Salali were alone together in Rachel's room. A fire was burning in the fireplace; Salali was doing cross-stitch, and Rachel was standing at the south window, staring emptily through tree branches toward the road beyond which lay the Cape Fear. It was a gray day, a cold mist having blown in from the sea, and the windowpanes were glossy with wetness. Rachel murmured something, almost under her breath.

Salali looked up from a new piece of cross-stitch.

"Today is our anniversary," Rachel said again, still so softly as to be scarcely heard. "Drew and I were married two years ago, on the twenty-fifth of November."

"No wonder you're so quiet this morning," Salali said softly.

"And he doesn't even know we're expecting a baby," Rachel whispered.

Rachel stepped slowly back from the window, and gazed at her profile in an oval, full-length mirror. There was the faintest hint of a smile on her otherwise expressionless face as her eyes ran up and down her image.

"A child without a father—just as I was . . . or am," she said.

The hem of her brief "shimmy" hung higher in the front than in the back, by several inches. Through the thin material she could see that her breasts were changing. She spread her hands over her growing belly. Her petite body appeared perilously overbalanced, since carrying the baby high made her seem even larger than she really was.

"But it's going to be all right," she breathed, patting her abdomen firmly and straightening. Salali thought there was a look of near arrogance on Rachel's face. "Mama made me happy before Papa came home," Rachel declared, "happier than we ever were again. I can do the same, and someday, when Drew does come, you will have a father.

"Oh!" she made a quick intake of breath. "Salali, come feel!"

Beneath the palm of her right hand a little bump moved slowly across. Suddenly came a kick so violent she recoiled with pain.

Rachel took hold of Salali's hand and guided it to the place where the last movement had been. She waited only a moment when they both felt it, then looked at each other, warm smiles in liquid eyes. Rachel pulled the fabric tighter and pointed, watching as two lumps moved randomly about.

"You really are there, aren't you?" Rachel laughed. "Well," she said, smiling at Salali, but speaking to the invisible child, "we're not alone, you and I. And we're going to make it just fine!"

FORTY-EIGHT

WHEN the following March swept in, the days were cold, then warm, then cold again. Moisture-laden winds fell across the Tidewater, and days of rain, until it seemed the peninsula between the ocean and the Cape Fear would float away. Horses and men trod muddy roads and barn lots to do work that had to be done, feeding stock, hauling wood for cookfires—but it was impossible to get into the wet fields.

On the twenty-second of March rain had been falling for three days. For two of those, Rachel had kept to her bed, the signs all saying her time was near. She had no lack of attendants: Abigail, the servant girl Mary, and Salali—especially Salali. Salali had stepped out, and for the moment Rachel was alone.

As she lay momentarily at ease, gazing out the window, the rain was coming down in gray sheets, beating loudly on the piazza roof. How empty the outside world seemed, she thought, and how the creeks must be running full and the river carrying every low thing before it. She wondered if it was raining in Philadelphia. What matter? Drew was not in Philadelphia, otherwise he would be sending letters, and she had not heard from him in seven months. Strange, how her love for him had changed to a different kind of love, deeper, more gentle. She felt that Drew was truly a part of her, and this morning her love glowed like the fire burning on her hearth.

Rachel felt the muscles in the sides of her upper abdomen tightening again, felt the pressure building and her back muscles tense in anticipation of the pain. Then it was gone, just as quickly as it had come.

There was a soft knock on her door.

"Come in," she called, and turned her head on the pillow to see. Donald peered around the edge of the door. Her heart grew warm at the sight of his smile and the bright redness of his hair. There were not many bright things on this rainy spring day. She smiled back at him.

"Feel like talking?" he said.

"Yes. It would help pass the time."

"You're glowing," he said, noting the perspiration standing out on her head.

"I'm sweating!" she countered. "A pain just came and went."

He sat down by the bed and took her hand. "Closer now?"

"Closer—five minutes about." She was looking at the face of her mother's clock on the chest. The sound of its ticking was subdued against the beating of the rain.

"You and I both were born with that clock looking on," he said. "No doubt Mama timed her pains by it just as you're doing now."

Rachel smiled at the thought. It was a small point of continuity between her mother and herself. Suddenly the smile disappeared and her eyes grew large.

"Another?" he said, squeezing her hand.

"Yes!" she said, and her body began to stiffen. "Sooner than the last."

"I'll go for Abigail."

"No," she said. "The first child always takes . . ." But her voice trailed away into the mounting pain. She squeezed her eyes tightly closed, clenched her teeth, and her fingers gripped his tightly. New beads of perspiration popped out on her forehead. She opened her eyes and looked around nervously, panting and sucking air.

"That was the strongest yet," she said, swallowing hard. "I started to say that the first child takes longer to come. If this were my second or third . . ." And she felt the powerful grip coming again—almost no time between it and the last, much harder, an insistent pressure in her lower belly that turned to excruciating pain. Against her will she screamed out.

"I'm going for Abigail!" he said, rising quickly and prying her fingers from around his hand.

Mixed with her pain, Rachel heard Donald's feet going hard

down the stairs and, at the same time, his muffled voice calling for Abigail, Salali, and Mary. The force of her muscles was still growing, and she could not keep from pushing. A sharp, severe pain beyond all she had ever imagined tore hard between her thighs and she screamed again.

When Rachel's scream rang through the house, Abigail was running up the stairs, Salali, Mary, and Donald all behind her.

"Go down to the parlor and wait!" she ordered Donald.

"No!" Donald answered. "I've got to be close by. I'll wait right outside the door."

Mary the servant girl turned and looked reproachfully at him.

When Abigail opened the door, the sight before her eyes stopped her in her tracks.

"What*ever* . . . ?" she said.

Salali gazed wide-eyed and open-mouthed over Abigail's shoulder. Mary was near to fainting. Before them, Rachel, upright and bending forward in the bed, was slowly bringing the child into the world with her own hands. Abigail bolted forward.

"No!" Rachel screamed. Her loose hair was forward over her shoulders, strands of it matted in the sweat that was pouring down. Her face was drawn with agony and she spoke in gasps between clenched teeth. "I want . . . to do this!"

When Donald started down the stairs on shaky knees, Quincy was waiting at the foot of the landing.

"Mr. Donald," he said in a quiet voice filled with concern, "is she all right?"

"She's all right, Quincy. She's just fine. So is the baby."

"Oh, thank God," Quincy breathed. "I don't think I could bear to see her suffer one more thing. It's so hard for her, her husband not bein' here for the birth of that baby."

Donald made his way through the hyphen separating the big house from the kitchen. There a fire blazed on the hearth, and two women servants were busily at work, one cleaving a smoked ham on the big wooden table, the other stirring a pot of vegetables over the fire. Near a large window on the room's back side sat Edward, waiting patiently.

When word had reached the slave quarters that Rachel's baby was coming, a half-dozen had come up to wait with the others. "Aunt Mart'a want to know," a soft-spoken girl of nineteen or twenty had said, "soon as it happen."

"How is Martha?" Buchannon asked.

"I cain't tell," said the girl. "But she ain't been out'a bed for two, three week now. Rachel been comin' down, feedin' 'er wid a spoon. She was down dere ez late ez yestiday a'tanoon. But Aunt Mart'a, her min' still clear, 'n' she want to know when it happen—jes ez soon ez it does."

"It's come," Donald said as he entered the kitchen.

"Is Rachel all right?" Edward said, his black brows arched, his keen blue eyes searching Donald's face.

"Fine, fine," he said. "A big boy, about nine pounds, Abigail guessed—sound and healthy."

"You look tired," Edward said, "subdued, maybe."

"Rachel delivered the child with her own hands," Donald said. There was a catch in his voice. "She told Salali how our mother had done that very thing when she was born—our daddy refused to help."

He sat down in a dark straight-back chair and leaned forward, his elbows on his knees, and ran the fingers of both hands through the red hair of his bowed head. Buchannon saw a sudden tiny splotch of wetness on the dark red flagstone floor over which Donald leaned. He reached out one big hand and laid it on Donald's shoulder.

"That girl's got guts," he said quietly. "She'll make it through. And you 'n' I, we'll help 'er all we can."

By ten o'clock the next morning, Rachel lay propped against a huge down-filled pillow, the baby nestled in her left arm. She felt happy, deeply serene, the sunlight in the room illuminating the natural shine on her face.

"Sho a beautiful chil', Miss Rachel." It was the young slave Rachel who spoke, the one whose twins Rachel herself had delivered four months ago. "We so happy for ya," the girl said, tears in her eyes. As the line of slaves filed through her room, Rachel beamed at them out of tired but contented eyes.

That afternoon, when the sun had begun to decline and the air in the room felt close, Rachel's spirits began to fail her. Salali's crisp form appeared in the doorway, a pitcher of fresh cool water in her hands. She set it down on the table by the bed and opened a window. Soon a cool stir of air broke up the late afternoon mustiness. When Salali returned to the bedside, Rachel was gazing longingly at her baby, her eyes beginning to mist.

"Rachel, dear, what is the matter?" Salali said tenderly. She knelt down by the bed, looking first at Rachel, then at the baby, and back again.

"Life is such a mixed-up thing, Salali!" Rachel said when she could speak. She stroked the baby's forehead with the tips of her fingers. "You would think I'd be perfectly happy today, wouldn't you? My little boy here in my arms?" She sighed. "But it always seems happiness is just beyond my grasp. Life is such a mixture of sorrow and joy. The baby, all these friends—and Drew not here to see his little boy born!" She shook her head and smiled at the baby through her tears.

Salali smoothed back Rachel's hair and rearranged it on the pillow.

"It's true," Salali said, "but if the joys of life weren't *worth* the pain, the birth of a child would make us weep rather than laugh."

She reached out and touched the baby's open hand with her little finger, and the baby's fingers closed around it.

"I think of Aunt Martha," Rachel said, gazing up at the ceiling, "old and dying. She's seen more sorrow than most will ever see. But when they told her my baby had come, she laughed and slapped her knee with happiness. Is it a secret of the old, Salali, that life's joys *are* worth all its pains? We must pity those who can't see it. We must pity them more than all the other sad creatures in this world."

FORTY-NINE

FIVE days later Rachel left her bed for the first time. She looked down on her baby lying asleep in his cradle—a cradle built especially for him by one of the slaves. His hair was dark and plentiful, and Rachel had combed it so that it lay over his forehead just as Drew's stray lock lay over his. She smiled and then, pulling a gown about her shoulders, made her way unsteadily across the room, opened the window, and sat down at the desk.

There she spread a blank sheet of white paper on the red

mulberry wood and, not knowing how to begin, sat staring out the window. Strange, she thought, how so simple an act as opening a window to the fresh air was an expression of hope. As the smell of white, twelve-petaled magnolia blossoms drifted in, she reached for a freshly sharpened goose quill, dipped it in the pewter inkwell, and began to write. Her letters, full and round, flowed easily.

March 27th, 1777

My Dearest Drew ...

It's been weeks since I've written, it all seemed so useless, not knowing where you are. But Salali and Donald say I must choose to be happy. They are right, of course, and I'm going to try very hard.

Drew—oh my dearest—we have a child, you and I. A little boy, born on the 22nd, just five days ago. He is a big baby, perfectly healthy, and he awakens only once in the night for feeding, so he's very easy to care for.

In one of my letters in the winter, I asked you what we should name our baby. But no answer has ever come. I could scarcely bring myself to name him without your help, but it would not be fair to make him go through his first days without a name. So I named him for your father— James, and I call him Jamie. It's a good strong Scots name, and I think you will be glad for it, since you've always loved your father so.

Each night I kiss Jamie—very tenderly, just as I know you would do if you were here—and I tell him that it's from his daddy. And, Drew, I take my brother's advice and pray. It is the only hope I have. I pray that we will soon have you with us, Jamie and I.

I send you our most tender affection. Do keep safe, my darling!

Your loving wife,
Rachel

FIFTY

In October a long procession of whites and blacks, all intermingled, trudged a narrow trail to a little cemetery deep in the woods and buried Aunt Martha.

As the column went, the blacks raised an African wail and leaped frenziedly about. An eerie fear ran through Rachel's frame. It was a scene from hell, a thick mist of hopelessness and despair that dissipated only when Edward Buchannon began to read the Christian rites of burial.

An autumn breeze whirled the leaves down about them. Hammer blows rang through the woods, fixing the coffin lid tightly in place. The hammer's sound raised an old vision for Rachel of a wet November day eight years ago when she had watched her mother being buried beside the kirk in Lochredfern.

That night, in her second-story room, she dreamed of her father.

She was back in Lochredfern, standing at the top of the little road that ran down to the harbor. A man was climbing out of a dory and drawing it up on the shore. As he turned and started slowly toward her, she saw it was Bartlett. He came on steadily, saying nothing, his eyes avoiding hers, almost as if she were not there at all. But when he reached her, he suddenly extended his hand as if to take her by the arm. Terrified, she drew back. A great sadness came into his eyes. His hand touched her arm, tenderly; there was a tear in his eye, an unspeakable sorrow. Then it was no longer her father she saw, but Drew's face. He shook his head, turned about, and walked away.

Rachel jerked upright in panic, tears running down her cheeks. As if still in dream, she called after him. He had been right there; she knew it! Then a thin cry pierced the haze, Lochredfern's harbor fading into the shadowy walls of her room. She got up, went to where little Jamie lay in his cradle, wakened by her cry, and scooped him into her arms. She laid the tiny bundle on her shoulder and patted his back softly.

"Shhh ..." she said. "Shhh, now, don't cry. Everything's going to be all right."

He grew quiet, content to be in her arms. She sang softly to him, standing before the window, watching the faintly brightening sky. She was fully awake now, but her heart was still beating so rapidly she could feel it in her throat. If only she could put the past behind her and simply live in the present! A man was able to do that; he could walk into the future and never glance back! Anger flared within her: anger at Drew, anger at the Revolution, anger at whatever directed the fates of men into paths as cruel as those she had known.

BOOK FIVE

The Search
1778

FIFTY-ONE

IT was one year later, a warm northern morning in mid-May.

Drew Wolfe, sleeves rolled to the elbows, was wiping his hands on a white linen towel when a sudden bump came from outside his marquee tent. He looked around to see two men pushing the flap aside, dragging a third man between them. Thick blotches of blood stained the third man's shirt and white stockings; his face was white, his breathing shallow. He was unconscious.

"Over here, soldiers!" Wolfe said to them. Around the inside perimeter of the large tent, a dozen men lay on folding cots. "Put him over there, against the east wall. Good."

One of the man's arms dangled over the cot's side, and his fingers bounced limply as he came to rest. He groaned with pain.

The face of thirty-year-old Andrew Wolfe was etched deep with the worries of war. After months in this hospital tent, or slogging along on night marches through rain and snow, or watching in the red glow of some grim dawn as men fell before musket and artillery fire or died on bayonets, he was unspeakably weary.

Sir William Howe's army had wintered in Philadelphia, and with the occupation Drew had at last returned to the city. His medical tent was erected on a high point of land at the city's north edge, beside the road to Germantown, just behind British redoubts.

"What happened to this man, Private?" Drew asked firmly as he unwrapped a long white bandage from the man's upper body. "There's no fighting today."

"It's hard to explain, sir," one of the men answered.

"Try," he demanded impatiently.

As the bandage fell clear, blood began to run again, dripping rapidly from the young man's fingertips.

"Here, hand me that basin," and he placed it on the ground

307

to catch the dripping blood. "Well, I'm waiting! How did he get these wounds?"

"We were foraging, sir." It was the older of the two men who spoke. He was blond, with a receding hairline, a sharp nose, and an accent that marked him as being from the north of London. Drew had seen him about the camp before and always thought him arrogant. Drew ripped impatiently at the wounded man's shirt, tearing it from cuff to shoulder.

"Foraging . . . for some poor farmer's cow, I suppose."

"Yessir . . . well, not exactly, sir." The private took a deep breath. "There was a girl, sir."

Drew looked up. "A girl? What has a girl to do with this?" He lifted the young man's arm and pointed to three wounds in a straight line near his shoulder. "Or with this?" Another straight line of evenly spaced wounds went from the soldier's shoulder to the middle of his back. Around each were wide borders of purple surrounded by a sickly yellow. "These are puncture wounds," Drew said, "*deep* puncture wounds!"

The wounded man coughed hard, and a sudden stream of blood poured from the corner of his mouth. Drew grabbed his shoulder and turned him onto his side, to keep him from choking.

"Private, what kind of instrument made these wounds?"

"A pitchfork, sir."

"A pitchfork!"

"Yessir. It was in a barn. He . . . he was bending over the girl. The girl's mother caught him from the back with her pitchfork."

Wolfe stared hard at the two young men. "And where were you that you didn't stop her?"

"We didn't see her, sir. We . . . we were holding the girl down for him, and we didn't hear her. The girl was screaming."

The wounded man's chest was rising high, his breath intensely labored.

"Soldiers," Drew Wolfe gazed up at them from the cot side, "in just a few moments your friend here . . . what is his name?"

"Miller, sir."

"Your friend Miller here . . . in just a few moments is going to drown in his own blood. And there's not a thing on God's earth I can do about it. That fork punctured his lungs, both of them. But," and he stood up, his bright gray eyes flashing bitterly at first one and then the other, "I feel no pity for him. And I feel no pity for you. It's the likes of you and your petty commanders that's made this army stink in the nostrils of every man, woman, and child in this countryside!" Drew's face was livid and he was shouting at them. "It's freedom from this kind of atrocity that these Americans are fighting for." He paused a moment. "How badly was the girl hurt?"

"Not at all, sir."

"You *think* not! Now you listen to me: this is an order. I want complete directions to that girl's home! I'm going out there and see what I can do for *her*!"

A thick gurgle escaped from the young soldier's throat. The three men looked down. His limbs were quivering, then his eyes opened very wide as a mighty convulsion wrenched his body. When it passed, he lay utterly still. Drew turned back to the two privates.

"Get out of my sight!"

With blanched faces they turned and left the tent. Immediately the flap lifted again, and this time a large man in black entered, an old-fashioned broad-brimmed hat in his hand.

"How long have you been standing out there?" Drew asked, his voice quiet but tight with anger.

"Long enough to hear what happened," Israel Bowman answered, his eyes resting on the cot where the dead man lay. "Did you know him?"

"Never saw him before—but this army's full of the likes of him." Drew stepped out and called a guard. "Private, I need burial detail in here."

"Yessir!" And he snapped a sharp salute.

It was noon when Israel and Drew rode out on the Germantown road to find the girl.

"We're taking our lives in our hands," Drew said. "This red coat could draw a cloud of farmers out of those hills like a nest of hornets."

"Franklin was right," Israel said. "Howe didn't take Philadelphia. Philadelphia has taken Howe!"

"Washington's treated the Tories well," Drew said, "and demanded good behavior from his army. A good many Loyalists are losing interest in this war."

"*Washington* may treat Tories well, but a host of his fellow Patriots are not so kindly disposed," Israel said. "I shudder every time I think of what they did to Seago Byles in Delaware."

"Seago Byles?"

"Patriots caught Byles stealing arms. Tried and sentenced by a court in Delaware."

"And?"

"Hanged by the neck, but not until dead," Israel said. "Taken down alive, bowels cut out and burned before his eyes. Then beheaded and his body cut into four parts."

A strange discomfort seized Drew's own bowels. He rode another quarter hour before the feeling passed.

"Well," he said, "I knew the risks."

For a little while they continued in silence. At last Israel spoke. "Hast thou heard again from Rachel?"

"Yes," Drew answered. "Two letters a week, and I write at least one every week. She's well."

"And the little boy?"

"Jamie's well, too." Drew's face was inexpressibly sad. "Israel, I never dreamed a man could miss a woman so much!"

"Rachel's full of fire," Israel commented. "She made thee feel alive." He paused. "Has she forgiven thee for sending her away?"

"Yes." Drew exhaled slowly. "Yes, I think she has." He paused. "You know, Israel, a man can never fully discharge his duty to a cause like the Revolution. But when I think of Rachel, and of Jamie, my own little boy whom I've never even seen, then I'm tempted to throw cause to the wind and run to them as fast as I can go."

They were now a mile beyond the redoubts, their horses sauntering, no one nearby. Drew quietly asked, "Do you have anything new for me?"

"Perhaps," Israel said. "Judge for thyself."

"All right," Drew said, nodding.

"You know that every day, two or three lobsterbacks come into my shop. But Howe's loose-tongued aide—the one who commissioned the fancy pistol before Christmas—he comes in every week to loiter with one or two of his friends—always a little drunk. I've worked on the pistol as slow as I dared, just to keep him coming in. He was there this morning.

"Howe got word from the war ministry yesterday that his resignation had been accepted. Parliament is badly shaken that the French have entered the war. Clinton's been appointed to replace Howe. And there's rumor that when Clinton comes, he'll evacuate Philadelphia."

"Evacuate? Why?"

"To free troops for campaigns in the Caribbean against the French fleet."

"Absolutely amazing . . ." Drew stood full height in the saddle and shook his head in wonder.

"You're amazed they plan campaigns in the Caribbean?" Israel asked.

"No. I'm amazed a Quaker Whig can uncover so much that a British medical officer never suspected!"

They found the girl's house off the Germantown road, back east on a narrow lane looping through a meadow lush with new grass. It was a large stone house, neatly kept. Nearby stood a great barn, banked into a hill, covered with stone to the weather, but all wood to the south. A copper stallion above a barn gable, weather-streaked with green, ran before the day's light breeze.

"That's where it happened," Drew said, nodding toward the barn. They were nearing the house. Suddenly the sharp crack of a gun rang out and a fleck of leather from Drew's pommel went flying into the air.

"Down!" Israel shouted.

Crouching low in the saddle, they lunged forward, jumping to the ground behind a rick of fire wood.

From the house came a barked command: "Go home!" It was a woman's voice. "You hear me? Go home!"

The men, covered with dirt and old leaves, stared at each other. Another shot thundered across the yard. Slivers of wood leaped high from the wood rick near Israel's right shoulder.

"Doctor!" Drew shouted. "I'm a *doctor*!"

Silence. The men waited, then ventured to call again. "I'm a doctor, and I've come to help your daughter."

"Show yourselves!" the voice said.

Slowly they stood, hands up, palms forward. There she was—on the porch, a long rifle in her hands, the cock drawn back, ready to fire. They advanced slowly, tentatively. In the absolute silence, Israel heard the tiny click that meant the woman had set the rifle's hair trigger.

"Far enough!" she said.

She was a tall woman with a fine face, thirty-five perhaps. Her hair was done up at the back of her head, and her long brown dress flowed to the ground. Her lips were quivering, and her eyes darted back and forth between the men.

"Believe me, Missus . . ." Drew waited for her to supply the missing name. She said nothing, and he went on. "I've come here to help your daughter."

"What do you know about my girl?" the woman demanded in a quavering voice.

"I know that three British privates came here this morning, that they assaulted her. I know you killed one of them."

"Killed?" The woman's face blanched.

"He died about noon. Your pitchfork went through his lungs." Fear rose in her face. "Don't worry," Drew said. "He needed killing. My only interest is to help your girl."

The woman bit her lower lip, and swinging the rifle muzzle, motioned them into the house.

"Dear Lord!" Drew breathed.

The girl was no more than a child—thirteen at most—eyes timid, tear-rimmed and sad. Her hair was red, like her mother's, her face freckled. There was nothing about this girl to inflame the passions, she had nothing with which to tease.

"This is Malinda," the woman said, her voice softening.

"Malinda," Drew said gently.

The girl's eyes were riveted to his, like the eyes of a cornered animal. Then she looked at his red coat. Suddenly she burst into tears and ran from the room, her bare feet flying beneath her long skirt.

"Malinda," Drew called after her, "we want to help." Their hands were still in the air. He turned to the woman in silent appeal.

"What did you expect?" the woman said. "Did you think she'd want the help of a bloodyback doctor?"

Exasperated beyond endurance, Drew snorted, and disregarding the threat of the cocked gun, clapped his hat firmly back on his head and turned to go. Israel stood a moment longer, his kind eyes fixed on the woman; he was profoundly moved by the pain in her eyes.

"Friend," he said calmly. The woman looked at him as though seeing him for the first time. "Friend, if thou wilt not allow this man, Dr. Wolfe, to help thy daughter, perhaps thou wouldst let my wife come and talk with her. The words of a woman—someone other than her mother—might be a great help just now."

The woman's expression did not change. "A traitor is a traitor whether he wears British red or Quaker black," she said sternly.

"I'm no traitor to the American cause," he said, shaking his head. "Many Friends favor the Revolution. And my friendship with Dr. Wolfe began before the war."

Her brows narrowed, then the lines of her face eased. She held the rifle steady, but her eyes misted slightly.

"If your wife would be so kind as to come and help Malinda and me," she said quietly, "we'd be grateful."

"She'll be here in the morning. Thou can count on it." Israel paused. "Where is thy husband?" he asked.

"Beyond the Schuylkill, at Valley Forge," she said. Then, as though her strength had given way, she let the gun drop and stood it against the wall. Lowering herself heavily into a straight-back chair, she began to weep out her pain and frustration. "Why don't they just go back to England and let us alone!" she cried.

Israel looked compassionately at her. "Perhaps sooner than any of us dare believe," he said, "for whatever small comfort it may be to thee this dark day."

Drew removed his hat again, and the girl reappeared in the doorway.

The sun was lingering just above the forested hill and barn when the two old friends closed the farmhouse door behind them. Once out of the lane, they spurred their horses to a brisk canter and soon came again to the Germantown road. Drew reined in and spoke with firm resolve.

"Israel, I'm not going back into Philadelphia tonight."

The big gunsmith looked carefully at him. "And where *wilt* thou go?"

"I'll follow this road on down to the Schuylkill."

"And run into Continentals for certain."

"I'm counting on it."

"And in that bright red coat they're likely to shoot thee dead."

"No," Drew answered, "they'll ask questions first."

Israel looked at him skeptically. "Thou'lt be back by morning?"

"Sometime tomorrow. But tonight I must find Tilghman."

"Washington's aide," Israel said, half to himself.

"Washington may know already the British are leaving Philadelphia, but I have to assume he hasn't heard."

"And what will I say if someone comes asking?"

"Tell them . . ." Drew thought for a moment, then with a

breath of resignation, "Tell them I stayed the night to help this girl our brave private raped. Tomorrow Rebekah and I can ride back together."

A great feeling welled up in Israel Bowman's massive chest. This was his friend who was riding purposely into danger. Prolonging the moment, he asked, "How many times will this make?"

"Six," he said, "in as many months."

"One of these nights thy luck may run out."

"A Quaker speaks of luck?" Drew asked, chuckling.

"Only in jest, friend." Israel grinned. "Only in jest. God go with thee!"

As the hooves of Drew's horse clambered away into the evening, Israel Bowman sat in his saddle, watching after him. The moon stood full above the horizon behind him, and the sun was almost down. The tiniest edge of its disk remained, a spark among the trees beyond the river. At the place where the distant road emerged from a timber-covered draw, the brilliant red of his friend's coat emerged, and then faded rapidly into the gathering darkness.

FIFTY-TWO

It was late afternoon the next day when the door of Israel's gun shop opened abruptly, the bell jangling, and Rebekah Bowman burst in. Israel looked up and saw deep concern written across his wife's oval face.

"I've just come from Malinda Putnam's. . . ." she said.

"And?" he said sharply.

"Oh, Israel." Rebekah touched her cheek with her left hand and shook her head sadly. Her eyes swam with tears. "She is such a sweet, innocent child! Those men . . . God help me Israel, I almost *hate* those men for what they did to her!"

"Some men are worthy of hatred, Rebekah."

"But the girl took to me, I think. I'm certain I can help her.

Her mother was very grateful. Poor woman . . . so defenseless against those young animals!"

"She wasn't defenseless against Drew and me," Israel said, squinting, as with his oversized fingers he fit a tiny screw through a lock bridle.

"But Israel," Rebekah leaned across his workbench and spoke with greater urgency than before, "Drew didn't come back to the encampment last night. I stopped by to talk to him about the girl. No one has seen him since yesterday when you rode away together. Now they're out looking for him."

Israel's mouth suddenly went dry.

Rebekah went on. "Last night there were terrible rains upriver—thunderstorms after midnight, to the northwest. From toward the Blue Mountains and down the Schuylkill as far as Norristown there were cloudbursts. The Schuylkill is swollen. From where the two of you parted, I could see the Wissahickon running among the trees' lower branches."

"He couldn't make it back across!" Israel exclaimed under his breath. "What in the world can we tell them when they come looking?"

It was toward evening. Before the oil lamp that hung above Israel's workbench, two British officers cast long shadows across the west wall.

"A Continental patrol," Israel said. "We ran into it in the dark, and they arrested him on the spot."

It was the hardest thing Israel Bowman had ever done—to lie—a Quaker's word was his bond. He wondered if the twitching fingers of his right hand would give him away, and tried to make the muscles of his face form a believable expression.

He was holding a brass template in one hand and a bright piece of newly filed steel in the other. He rested the heels of his hands on his widespread knees and looked them straight in the face. The lamplight glinted in his green eyes as they went calmly from one officer to the other.

"But you did not report it?" The older of the two men eyed him suspiciously.

"I did report it, to the first officer I met, a lieutenant whose name I do not know."

"You're lying, Bowman," the younger man said, shifting his weight from his left leg to his right.

Israel could do nothing but return the officer's icy stare.

When at last the shop door closed behind him, Israel breathed a long sigh of relief. It was possible Drew had been shot by a Continental patrol, but more likely the flood had prevented his return. So where could he be? Surely he won't try to return to camp now, Israel mused. "No. No," he said to himself. "He wouldn't dare.

"But Rachel . . . oh God, help Rachel!" he said. "Two years the girl's been away." Most of that time, she hadn't known where Drew was. How could he tell her? he wondered. If only he could write and say how many lives he'd saved! But he couldn't—it was too risky.

That night at home, Israel Bowman sat down with Rebekah, and they wrote a letter of another kind.

Fifth month, sixteenth day, 1778

Our Dear Rachel,

We are sorry to tell thee that last night Drew disappeared from the British regiment. We do not much fear for him, for we believe he is in the hand of God and safe.

Rebekah and I are in good health, having taken William Howe's occupation of Philadelphia in stride.

Drew misses thee greatly, Rachel, though I am quite sure he has told thee so. Thou art the great love of his life. He is indeed lonely and pines daily for thee and Jamie.

Please rest in Drew's love, Rachel, and find peace in God, for He, too, loves thee and watches over thee and thy little one.

> Thine own friends,
> Israel & Rebekah Bowman

FIFTY-THREE

"I can't bear this any longer," Rachel said. Her voice was quiet but firm.

She handed Israel's letter to Salali. Donald had just returned from Wilmington and brought it directly to her room. Salali had heard him going up the stairs and come to investigate.

"I've had enough of not knowing whether Drew's alive or dead," she said, "and enough of loneliness. Enough of my baby's not knowing his father!"

Rachel turned to her chest, yanked open the drawers, and began pulling out armloads of clothes, laying them on her bed.

Salali cut her eyes at Donald and handed him the letter. Her expression was somber.

"If your Quaker friend Bowman doesn't know where Drew is," Donald asked cautiously, "how can *you* expect to find him?"

"I've no idea." Rachel was working faster and her words were becoming clipped, her tawny face growing dark from her exertions. "But find him I shall!"

"And if he's on some sensitive mission, won't it be dangerous for you to intrude?"

"Mission!" she huffed, pulling her trunk from the wall and throwing open its lid. "This war has us acting parts we don't know and can't possibly be any good at! I'm *sick* of it!"

"So there's nothing we can do to stop you?" Salali asked.

"Nothing," Rachel said, slamming down the cover of her hat box.

"You will come back . . . when you find him and set your mind at rest?" Salali spoke with such affection that Rachel stopped in the midst of laying out her russet dress. As she looked at their eyes, tender with pain and concern, the impetuous anger faded from her face. She looked first at Salali, then to Donald. She was leaving the dearest friends she had ever known.

"Back?" she said softly. "Yes . . . of course I'll be back, and I'll bring Drew with me, if I can."

"And Jamie?" Donald interrupted, his pale blue eyes filled with concern.

"What *of* Jamie?" Rachel asked, startled. At the sound of his name, Jamie looked up from the corner where he was playing contentedly with a little iron horse Donald had given him. He was just past fourteen months, fat and healthy, toddling everywhere, and learning to talk. He made the iron horse gallop across the plain of the floor and over the mountains of his chubby legs.

"The trip will be too much for him," Donald said. "Let us keep him here. There's no telling where your search will lead."

"Oh, I couldn't . . ."

"Donald's right, Rachel," Salali said. "It *would* be best."

"But Drew will want more than *anything* to see Jamie."

"I'm certain he will," Donald said, "but you can't tell where your search will lead—places perhaps where Jamie can't go. Leave him here with us, Rachel."

Rachel held the russet dress up in her hands, looking but not really seeing it, mumbling unintelligibly.

"You're right, of course," she said at last. "He'll be much safer with you."

Next morning the springtime sun, just above the trees, was shining off the broad breast of the Cape Fear at high tide when the packet from Wilmington to Philadelphia came under full sail around the river's bend. Rachel was waiting, seated comfortably amidships in Edward Buchannon's longboat.

When the vessel rounded the bend, a murmur went up from the little crowd standing on Buchannon's landing. In the long-boat, six black men bent their powerful backs and arms to the boat's oars, and it shot out to intercept the packet's course. Rachel sat beneath an awning of blue and white striped canvas, Donald beside her, her baggage in the stern.

The oarsmen's bare arms flashed in the early sun as the steersman, speaking in plantation Creole Rachel could not understand, chanted cadence. With every stroke, the men called back in a chorus of deep voices. Rachel felt the excitement of swift water and rapid motion, knowing it gave the slaves an illusion of freedom they could find in no other way.

"Good-bye, Jamie," she called above the chant and oars, waving at the small figure on the edge of the pier. Salali, her long black hair blowing in the morning breeze, was behind Jamie, her hands on his shoulders, smiling fondly.

Rachel felt a warm sensation in her breast at the sight of Salali, as she thought of how Donald had at last spoken his mind to her and how they would marry next spring. Last night she had told Salali that if anything happened to her, she wanted them to take Jamie and raise him as their own.

A lump rose in her throat as Jamie waved his little hand confidently and his voice came to her, thin and distant, over the water.

"Good-bye, Mommy!"

Wiping tears, she looked at Donald and smiled bravely, and he smiled back—a solemn kind of smile. Her eyes turned to the blue and white awning's scalloped edge fluttering in the breeze, and she listened to the powerful voices, smelled the fresh morning fragrance of the forest's flowering vines mixed with the heavy odors of the river.

Then, so softly that only Donald could hear, "Good-bye, Jamie," she repeated. "One never knows. . . ."

"You'll be back." Donald smiled reassuringly. "I feel it inside," he added, and tapped his chest with a closed fist.

"Oh, you and your intuitions!" She laughed and took his hand. Then looking into her brother's eyes, she felt something powerful rise within her. "I love you, Donald Calhoun," she said quietly and with great intensity. "I'll miss you almost as much as I'll miss Jamie." She was thinking of all the times Donald had stood between her and disaster. "Where would I be without you to keep me on the straight and narrow?"

He laughed and, leaning forward, kissed her on the cheek.

Abruptly, the cadence of voices stopped and there was just the clatter of oars as the shadow of the packet fell across them. With both ship and boat in forward motion, the men stood and grabbed the gunnel of the larger vessel. The black helmsman called out to hold steady as Donald lifted her up to hands reaching down from above. Then came her luggage. The next thing she knew, she was standing at the ship's rail, gazing fondly down at Donald and at the grinning slaves.

Once more they had picked up the cadence with their booming voices and, dipping their oars, were propelling the longboat in a race with the packet for the open sea.

It was a hard voyage north. Battered by adverse winds, the packet did not enter Delaware Bay until the fifteenth of June. Two days later they had ascended the river, reaching Mud Island. Then the scarred battlements of Fort Mifflin came into view, then British batteries on the northwest shore, and Fort Mercer on the southeast.

"This is where the British broke Washington's siege last December," the captain said.

That night, within sight of Philadelphia itself, the little ship lay anchored in the middle of the wide river just above Windmill Island, waiting to be cleared for docking. As the sun went down, Rachel stood at the rail and gazed at the distant shoreline. She could make out the spire of Christ's Church, thinking that less than a block from it was Israel Bowman's gun shop. She felt her heart trip at the thought Drew might be nearby.

When the sun set and the world was growing dark, Rachel was still at the rail, watching the lights on Swanson Street come on, from south to north, each one a glimmer and then a steady glow, as the invisible lamplighter made his rounds. The lights shimmered across the Delaware's current, giving an illusion of peace in the midst of war.

At last she went to her cabin, but for a long while lay with her eyes closed and a thousand thoughts racing through her mind.

Next morning at sunrise, when murmuring and exclamations filtered through her cabin window, Rachel got up quickly, pulled on a dressing gown, and went on deck. The entire crew was gathered at the rail, looking northwest. The rising sun to their right made a blinding glare on the water. Small fishing sloops dotted the river, their spread sails catching the first golden light as sea gulls swooped and bobbed over the water's face. The city lay low to their left, church spires pointing heavenward above the long maze of buildings, the wharves a dark line at the water's edge. She gazed about, puzzled at the crew's rapt attention.

"What is it?" she said to no one in particular, her sleepy voice husky in her throat.

Simultaneously, two of the men turned about and, seeing her, pointed.

Upriver, where Cooper's Ferry ran, flashes of sunlight on wet oar blades caught her eye. Hundreds of them in a great line, from the waterfront docks on the west across the broad expanse to the Jersey shore, and among the flashes, tiny flecks of red, as many as the oars—it was Clinton's British army.

"Evacuation," said a small middle-aged sailor. "They're quitting Philadelphia."

FIFTY-FOUR

EARLY the next morning, Friday the nineteenth, Israel and Rachel rode on horseback out of Philadelphia. They had talked of taking a buggy, but not knowing what lay ahead, decided on the greater freedom of horseback.

Their destination was Washington's encampment eighteen miles northwest, on a ridge overlooking the Schuylkill near the little town of Valley Forge. The Grand Army had headquartered there since December, the ridge being easy to defend, and there being abundant water and plenty of wood for building and fire. Besides, the site stood between occupied Philadelphia and York, the town to which the Continental Congress had fled.

True to Rachel's nature, she hated conventional riding dress for women, floor-length dresses with trousers underneath. Such attire was unbearably hot, and riding sidesaddle was awkward and uncertain over rough terrain. Today she rode out of town dressed in a silky white blouse with billowy sleeves and full lapels above form-fitting knee breeches, knee-high stockings, and low black shoes. She smiled to herself, for every time they met passersby, a dark crimson blush crept across Israel's face.

By the time they reached Valley Forge, the day was sweltering, one of a whole string of hot days that bred thundershowers, each day hotter than the one before.

Washington's encampment sat on the crest of a hill, the foot of which was encircled by great earthen fortifications. As Rachel and Israel approached the great earth berms, they reined in their horses and scanned the scene before them. The forested hills of the encampment appeared pleasant, even hospitable, but the strong network of redoubts forbade entry. Israel stood to his full height in the stirrups, searching for signs of movement.

"I'm surprised," he said. "I expected to be stopped a half-dozen times by now, but there's not a sentry or guard in sight!

Well," he sat back in the saddle, "let's move on. They can't do more than stop us."

They spurred forward and, finding an opening between the great mounds, rode in unchallenged. Inside, they gazed about in wonder, for only emptiness greeted them, and hard-trodden earth, and the hollow windows of squat log huts. Silent and open-mouthed, each looked at the other.

"Whoever yer lookin' fer's gone," a voice called out.

Startled, Rachel spun about.

"There," Israel said, pointing toward the nearest hut. A figure was standing in the door's shadow.

"Why, it's a woman!" Rachel exclaimed.

The woman ducked her head and emerged from the low door and straightened. She held the neck of an empty canvas bag in one hand, and with fists on her ample hips, looked directly at them.

"They're gone, I tell ya."

"The army is gone?" Israel asked.

"Who else would I mean?" she answered impatiently.

Rachel stared at her. The woman, clutching a man's sagging felt hat in one hand, wore a full bodice with faded yellow spots and a striped apron tied with a cotton string over a torn and patched linsey-woolsey skirt. She might have been fifty years old, and she might have been much younger. These poor farm women, Rachel thought, almost always use themselves up early. She became aware that the woman was gazing back at her with an equal intensity, eyeing her from head to foot.

"Say now! Ain't you sump'n," the woman said. "Darlin', you do cut a mighty pert figger, all decked out like that! Can't say as I seen anything like it in all my days."

Rachel felt her face flush as she wrestled with the impulse to return the compliment, but she said nothing. From the corner of her eye she thought she saw a smile creep across Israel's lips. The woman took a deep breath and looked about at the emptiness.

She cackled. "I'se jest here seein' what they mighta left behind." Then, with an exasperated shrug of her shoulders and a laugh that exposed her shining gums, "Didn' leave nothin'! No sir, they took it all!"

"Took it where?" Rachel asked, leaning forward.

"North!" the woman spat. "Crost the Schuykill at Swede's Ford. Headin' on to Coryell's Ferry to git acrost the Delaware."

"Going after Clinton's army!" Israel said under his breath.

"Goin' after 'em, I reckon! Lord! But they did look good—like a new bunch'a men, anxious they was to ketch ol' Clinton." She spat on the ground. "Ol' von Steuben done 'em a bunch'a good. They looks like *soldiers* now, they does!"

The big Quaker sat shaking his head. "Who would have thought it?" he said. "That they could go out, lusting to fight after a winter like the one they spent here! Eleven thousand men—three thousand perished of starvation, exposure, typhus!"

Rachel saw from the faraway look in Israel's eyes that he was deeply moved at the resurrection of men who a few months ago were so close to annihilation.

"And all for a people who wouldn't even sell them food and clothes!" he breathed.

"Wouldn't sell to the army?" Rachel said.

"Our army pays in Continental currency, the British in sterling! Beeves and poultry and grain raised hereabout went to Philadelphia."

"Well, me'n my man, we sold 'em what little we had," the woman boasted. She paused, looking around. "Ya know," she said, "fer weeks men was a comin' from everwhur, jest *flockin'* in here to join up."

"Washington, they'll do *any*thing to please Washington," Israel whispered reverently, then realized that Rachel wasn't listening.

Her eyes were focused on the ground, bitter disappointment in every line of her face. Hundreds of miles she had come—only to find a deserted camp. "We've missed him," she said softly, "and by only a day."

There were tears in her eyes, and Israel was afraid she was about to cry. "I'm truly sorry," he said, his voice deep and consoling.

Rachel took a deep breath and looked up, her jaw set firmly, determination in every feature. "We can follow," she said. "We can overtake them before they reach Clinton's army. We can find Tench Tilghman somewhere in New Jersey, at Princeton, maybe."

"Ohhh, Rachel," Israel breathed, shaking his head slowly. "That could be like walking into the mouth of a furnace!"

The old woman began to cackle. "Feels like a furnace to me already, these hot days. Hunnerd degrees, people says. An' it don't 'pear there's gonna be no change!"

* * *

Rachel and Israel had come provisioned for only one night. Israel would be willing to pursue Tilghman, he said, if first they returned to Philadelphia, to tell Rebekah. And they must pack food—for the army going before them would most certainly strip the country bare. In spite of herself, Rachel saw Israel was right and agreed.

"But we can't go back to Philadelphia in this heat, Rachel," he went on. "It would kill the horses."

"But Israel, we'll lose them!" she pled.

"Clinton's army will go slowly across New Jersey," he reasoned. "All the bridges that way were burned or cut down. With fifteen hundred baggage wagons, he'll have to rebuild them as he goes, and Washington will cut across his path before they get very far. And even at that, it may be eight or ten days before it happens. Believe me, there's no hurry."

So they unsaddled their horses, and each found a soldier's hut in which to sleep. But soon vacuous, somber feelings of loneliness came over Rachel.

As the afternoon waned, clouds gathered, until a great anvil-shaped thunderhead obscured the sun. The air grew cooler and it began to rain. There, alone on the deserted hill of the Valley Forge encampment, Israel and Rachel fed their horses and ate their evening provision as the storm blew over.

As night fell, Rachel went to her hut, slipped the shoes from her feet, and wrapping herself in a gray wool blanket, lay down on the hard ground. She felt a deep bone-weariness creeping into her body. For a long while she turned this way and then that, trying to escape the unyielding earth.

When at last sleep settled down on her mind, dreams came creeping. There in the mists were the men, thousands who had walked and lain beneath these trees, laughing, talking, anticipating battle. They milled about the wide parade ground and along the roads and paths intersecting the camp. Her sleeping mind wandered from hut to hut, watching them prepare to be suddenly gone. Her spirit wandered beside one morose soldier to a place where there were graves, thousands of graves spread out before them. One of the crosses seemed to draw her, and she began to walk slowly toward it, a terrible apprehension rising in her heart.

"An easy path to follow!" Israel Bowman exclaimed as they pursued Clinton's army northeast out of Philadelphia.

Thousands of imprints of feet and hooves in mud and sand marked the way, as well as the absence of cattle and livestock in the fields, the felled trees at creek and river crossings, and the animated gossip of travelers who had met the army.

The trip was hard. Every afternoon, the thunderstorms came, leaving the air thick and muggy. Deep sandy roads exhausted their horses and slowed progress.

The sun, directly above, bore down without mercy on their heads. Where the stockinged calves of Rachel's legs touched the saddle's skirt, the sweat, running down to puddle in her shoes, made the leather slick and unbearable.

Sunlight filtering through the straw weave of Rachel's wide-brimmed, low-crowned hat cast a pattern on her face. She'd taken a red ribbon from among her things and gathered her long hair just above her neck. Still, the little trails of sweat were running down between her shoulders to the small of her back.

Even Israel had asked Rachel to put his own free-flowing hair into a braid. He loosened the ascot at his throat, and stuffed his black coat into his saddlebags.

"Men *can't* march in such heat!" she exclaimed.

"But they are marching," Israel answered, "and many will die for the effort."

The horses went heavily through the deep sand, too slow to stir any coolness out of the air. Israel, mopping his brow every few moments with a white handkerchief, began to wonder if he himself could survive.

At noon on the ninth day, they reached a place three miles south of a junction where the road to Englishtown crossed the roads to Middletown and Amboy, a junction called Monmouth Courthouse.

"Ho!" Israel said, tugging his mount to a stop and raising his hand for silence. Instantly Rachel obeyed and strained to hear.

The sound came from far away, a dull, concussive sound, so low they felt rather than heard it. Then silence. Then another concussion . . . and another.

"Cannon!" he exclaimed, turning in the saddle toward Rachel. "Washington has overtaken Clinton!"

They urged the sweating horses on, not rapidly, but as fast as they dared.

Rachel felt her heart accelerate. She looked about. Hills and woods, all interlaced with ravines, marshes, and creek bottoms.

"Trees deaden sound," she said. "We may be nearer than we think."

A road turned off to the left; the undisturbed sand in its bed would be firmer and make for easier traveling, they decided. Soon the sounds were coming from their right, growing louder. They could hear it clearly: at ragged intervals, the hollow roar of artillery. Another mile and Israel put spurs to his horse, suddenly leaving the road and plunging into the forest, with Rachel close behind.

Riding low and dodging limbs, they beat their way through the trees and up a slope so thick in moss the horses' hooves slipped, bringing them again and again to their knees. At last they were at the edge of the woods, on high ground overlooking a long ravine through which ran a small creek flanked on either side by low, marshy ground. To their left, across an arm of the creek, stood a bare-topped hill where the midday sun glinted from polished bronze. As in a dream, ragged puffs of white burst sporadically into the air, followed moments later by dull thuds. In the valley below were thousands of men.

"The Grand Army!" Rachel exclaimed.

Her eyes scanned the valley northward. From the east, a yellow road descending the face of another hill stretched along the spine of a causeway across the marsh, then dipped into a low ravine before rising again to continue its way to Englishtown.

They were too far away to distinguish anything but color, masses of blue coming from the west. Ahead of them, a thin blue line already formed across the road. Coming toward the blue from the east was a sea of undulating red—jagged lines advancing, breaking, scattering back, regrouping to advance again, all amid puffs of white and sharp little cracks of sound.

Rachel and Israel sat their horses unmoving, entranced as a thick pall of gray smoke settled in the lowest ravines and spread across a marsh that moments before had been bright yellow with wild buttercups.

Rachel's horse stamped, then swinging its head down, began to crop grass. The dusky skin of its shoulder rippled beneath her hand. A startled butterfly winged upward past her head, so close she waved to shoo it away.

Without a word the two of them swung down from their saddles, tethered their horses in the timber, and coming back, stood in the shade of a tree to watch. All about, the grass was lush and green, dappled with purple flowers of wild ginger and red gatherings of columbine. And yet, amid this resplendent June, roared the distant thunder of guns. Among the masses, tiny points of red and blue were falling and lying still.

"How strange," Rachel said softly, "to watch men dying far away."

As the sweltering afternoon wore on, the red line advanced and broke, and advanced and broke again. But though the blue lines changed shape, they remained firm and gave no ground. Then, suddenly, the red line broke into fragments that went scurrying down the ravine's slope, back across the marsh and into the sea of red from which it had come. And after that, the red line did not return.

Israel reached into his vest pocket, pulled out his watch, and clicked open the case. It was five o'clock.

"Is it possible," he said under his breath, "that these are the men that got whipped at Brandywine and Germantown?" Then louder, "The old woman was right. The German von Steuben made them into an *army!*"

"He's not there," Rachel said, lost in her own thoughts.

"Von Steuben? Of course he is."

"Drew," she said.

Israel studied her face in puzzlement. "How can thou be sure?" he asked.

"I can't," she said. "It's only a feeling, a terrible fear." She paused, staring tiredly ahead. "But I've got to go down, Israel—to search, to help with the wounded."

"How would we reach the field?" he asked, genuinely puzzled. "The creek appears impassable from here, and it would be a long loop to go back to the main road. Besides, to reach the American lines, we would have to cut right through Clinton's army. No," he said, "we'll have to wait to see what morning brings."

Down on the battlefield, white flags of cannon smoke kept bursting out sporadically, then gradually died away into nothing, and both the red and the blue made camp exactly where they had fallen in their exhaustion.

The sun was sinking. Its slanted saffron rays threw gray shadows across the scarred expanse. Its red disk sank behind the hills, and the world went dark. Below, scattered cooking fires sprang up, dotting the black field, and overhead the stars came out.

As she sat across their own fire from Israel, Rachel was silent. Then, abruptly, she stood up.

"I can't *stay* here!" she said, and tucked the remaining loaf and chunk of ham back into their canvas bag. Israel did not move, but sat staring at her over his half-empty tin cup of coffee.

"You're going to try to get down there, aren't you?" he said.

"I can't do less," she answered.

"All right," he said, knowing he had lost. He pitched the rest of his coffee into the fire—the coals hissed and steamed—and got to his feet. Quickly they saddled their horses and mounted.

"Which way?" he queried, willing to yield to her judgment.

"Follow me," she said, and urged her horse forward over the edge.

"No!" he warned.

But already he could hear hooves sliding down in the darkness.

Then, all at once, he was with her, sliding directly down the steep slope into the ravine. At the bottom the horses fought and slogged through the blackness, through marsh-grass reaching above their heads, water lapping at their bellies, mud sucking at their hooves. Rachel's heart was beating hard. Perhaps she had been wrong. Perhaps they would not make it through the marsh.

It was a hard hour later when the campfires became visible through the tall grass. Israel tugged his mount to a stop.

"We mustn't go in there," he said firmly.

"Why not?" Rachel whispered.

"We've lost our sense of direction. We've no idea whether that's the American or British camp."

"What's the difference? There're wounded men to care for."

This was Quaker logic Israel could not resist, and shrugging his shoulders, he moved forward.

Above a chorus of crickets and the deep, constant croaking of frogs came sounds from about the campfires: moans and cursing mixed with prayers that punctuated the night. At last the hooves of the horses began to be borne up by higher ground, a little farther, and they lurched upward out of the marsh. Rachel's eyes went momentarily to the sky. There, brilliant Arcturus pointed the tail of his kite, and the great dipper upended its cup.

The wounded and dead lay everywhere before them. There was movement on the ground to Rachel's left. The leather of her saddle creaked as she dismounted and knelt down beside a fallen boy. Israel was behind her instantly, grabbing a lantern

from a nearby tent, holding it just above her head so she could
see.

Dried blood from a deep saber cut across one ear lay thick
on the boy's neck. His left sleeve was torn and his arm was
still oozing blood. The boy looked up at her face, tawny in the
firelight, and at the reflection of campfires glowing in her large
dark eyes. Her gathered hair fell long over one shoulder and a
strand of it brushed his lips. The moment her soft hands
touched the skin of his forehead and arms, tears rose in his
eyes and ran down the side of his face. "Thank you, ma'am,"
he said. "Oh, thank you, ma'am. Thank you!" Reaching beneath her dress for the edge of her petticoat, she tore it in strips
and bound him up.

All night long Rachel moved from camp to camp, Israel beside her, stanching bullet wounds, suturing gashes, salving abrasions, always working her way to the rear.

FIFTY-FIVE

IT was two in the morning when Rachel and Israel, aching
with weariness, spread their blankets at the edge of the battlefield and lay down. For hours Rachel slept fitfully, then lay
fully awake, gazing up through the branches of the tree that
overspread her pallet. A few feet away Israel lay snoring
loudly. Out of all the black sky, one bright star seemed caught
in the branches directly overhead. For a long time she lay
looking at the star, startlingly white, twinkling through the heat
waves of earth. So beautiful, she thought, but so far away,
somehow comforting, yet so impersonal, so indifferent to the
field of death on which it shone.

After a while she rose, then, having brushed out her hair,
she sat, simply sat, gazing through the darkness to the east
where the sun would rise. The black sky turned dark blue, then
slowly to fairer shades, until she could see clearly. A flock of
sea birds winged in low from the east. From somewhere in a

thicket came the harsh caw of a crow, and from a clump of
bushes the sounds of a scampering rabbit.

Gradually the black of silhouetted trees became dark green
and the face of the marsh was again a field of faintly glowing
buttercups. Details of light began to emerge from the night,
and Rachel could make out spots of white on the British side
of the field.

Suddenly she tensed, then stood. Where were the tents?
Where were the wagons and stacks of arms? Was she looking
in the wrong direction? No, that was impossible. Every moment the valley was growing lighter, and with the clarity of
light, she became certain.

"Israel!" she whispered excitedly.

The snoring stopped.

"What? Somebody call?" he asked thickly.

"Israel, get up!"

In an instant he was at her side, rubbing his eyes and trying
to focus in the direction she was pointing.

"Israel, look!" she said.

"What . . . why . . . the valley's *empty*!"

"Yes," she said. "They've gone! The British have run
away!"

It was true. Under cover of darkness Clinton had silently
moved his army out. The meadow where he had been was littered with unmoving figures in red and white—the dead he'd
had no time to bury. When the sun's leading edge touched the
horizon with its spark of flame, every able Patriot was looking
eastward in quiet awe toward the empty field. By the time the
sun's full disk was up, the Americans were shouting and dancing in each other's arms.

Rachel's heart leaped within her to realize that now her
search for Drew could begin.

"Your hospital tents," she called to a soldier standing near a
fire with breakfast plate in hand.

"Straight ahead, ma'am," he answered.

Amid an electric air of victory, Rachel and Israel rode
through camp, the soldiers hooting and laughing about them.
Some fell silent as she passed by, raising their eyes to watch
her, some respectfully touching the brims of their hats. Again
and again from the camp's far corners came cheers: "Hoorah
for Washington! Hoorah for Washington!"

"Look at these men," Israel said, his plump cheeks flush with excitement. "What a victory!"

"Why, Israel," she smiled tauntingly, "you wish you'd been at a cannon's breech last night, don't you?"

"The world, the flesh, and the devil!" he said, laughing nervously.

Just then, through the maze of pitched canvas, three marquee tents came into view. The tents of the common soldiers had steeply sloping walls that made them look like a wedge of pie stood on end, but the "markees," usually reserved for officers, had high walls, a peaked ridge, and scalloped fringe hanging down around the eaves. These three "markees" had been converted to hospitals, and on the ground all about them the wounded lay on pallets.

Israel dismounted, lifted the flap of the first tent, and motioned Rachel before him. Inside, doctors and their aides were working among moaning men, rewrapping wounds, splinting legs and arms, probing deep into flesh for lead bullets.

"No doctor in this regiment by the name of Wolfe, ma'am," an officer said to her. "I know 'em all." Rachel felt suddenly tired. "You might ride on to Freehold Church," the man continued. "Another regiment's usin' it for a hospital."

"Hospitals are the sinks of human life in the army," Israel said as they rode away. "Not just the wounded, but the diseased. Disease takes ten of our soldiers where the sword takes one."

Rachel made no reply. She knew these things already, and her mind was elsewhere. Israel could see by her face how the tension was mounting.

At Freehold Church the story was the same. All morning long she went from regiment to regiment, searching, knowing each time she entered a tent that she might come face to face with Drew and each time emerging more disappointed, a little sadder.

But once that morning, for a short moment, she forgot her mission altogether. They were near the center of the camp when a tall man emerged from the uplifted edge of an officer's marquee. The man looked toward her for an instant, smiled and nodded politely, never pausing in his step.

"Look!" she had whispered to Israel. Somehow she knew instantly who the man was.

Both Rachel and Israel sat holding their horses in check, watching after him as he walked away. High-topped riding boots accentuated his masterful stride. His canary-yellow uniform shone brightly in the sun, and the large cocked hat rode easily on his head at a confident angle.

"Never once did I think to see him with my own eyes," Rachel whispered.

All too soon the man was out of sight. When Rachel looked around at Israel, the great leveler, the man who took off his hat for no one, was sitting with hat in hand, tears streaming down his cheeks.

At last they found Tench Tilghman. When Rachel saw him, a world of memory flooded upon her. She was face to face with the shadowy image she first saw in the night three years ago.

With an exclamation of pleasure, Tilghman offered her his most comfortable folding chair and nodded at Israel. As Tilghman took his seat behind his campaign desk, he gazed at her intently.

"Why do you look at me so, young woman?" he said. "Have we met before?"

"No, Mr. Tilghman," she said in a level tone. "But I've seen you, in the moonlight, in my yard under the trees, three years ago."

"Well." The bachelor laughed, making no connection with any memory. "I'm certain that had I met you in the moonlight *any* number of years ago, I would recognize you instantly!"

Rachel's eyes were solemn. "I said we didn't meet, Mr. Tilghman. I saw you from my window. It was in Philadelphia, early spring of 'seventy-six. My name is Rachel Wolfe."

Tilghman's expression went blank, then memory dawned and a troubled look fell over his face.

"Rachel Wolfe," he said quietly. "Drew Wolfe is your husband."

"Yes, Mr. Tilghman! Yes!" she said, sitting forward on the edge of the chair. She felt her hopes shoot skyward at Tilghman's use of the present tense. "That's why I'm here. I was in the south, near Wilmington, where Drew had sent me to escape the war. A little more than a month ago Israel—my companion here—wrote saying my husband had disappeared one night when he took information to you at Valley Forge. We believe high water cut off his return to the British regiment. It is true, isn't it? He is with you?" Her words were coming so rapidly they fell each over the other. Tilghman's gaze fell from her eyes to the top of his desk. Her heart sank again.

"He *did* return! He is here, is he not?" Her last words trailed weakly away as she looked at the man's face. Tilghman rose and stepped around to sit on the edge of his desk.

"Mrs. Wolfe," he said, "your husband's work was very valuable to us. It was he who first brought us word that Clinton was about to abandon Philadelphia. But . . ."

"Yes? 'But' what?"

"But we were just as surprised as you when he disappeared. It was a great loss to us."

Rachel's eyes went wide and she settled back weakly into the chair. "He's not here?" she whispered.

Israel stood behind her and laid his large hands on her shoulders.

"Would to God he were!" Tilghman said. "We could certainly use another physician this day! We've got dozens of men wounded, forty dead of heat stroke from the hard march between Valley Forge and this place. Others suffering from heat prostration." He paused, looked tenderly at Rachel, then leaning forward, said with quiet intensity, "But no, Mrs. Wolfe. Your husband left Valley Forge the same night in which he came to bring us his last message. The flood waters *could* have cut him off at the ford . . . he could have met a British patrol. But whatever happened, he didn't come back to us."

Back in Philadelphia, Rachel searched desperately for some trace of Drew's fate; someone who might have seen him, a scrap of identifiable clothing, lingering gossip of a body left on a sandbar after the river's flood subsided. Toward the end of the first week, her hopes sank desperately when word came of a new grave downriver near Penn's Grove. She went to see. The disinterred body was not Drew's.

Gradually her hope gave way to doubt, and doubt to utter discouragement, until at last she knew she had reached a cul-de-sac. At the end of July, Rachel, saying a sad farewell to Israel and Rebekah, sailed for Wilmington.

FIFTY-SIX

It was late—well past midnight—and Drew Wolfe was riding hard to the east, back toward the Schuylkill, the great earthen redoubts of Valley Forge having long since disappeared into the darkness behind him. He'd yet a dozen miles to cover before crossing the river to the Germantown road, and miles beyond the crossing before he would reach the British encampment.

Neither dawn nor the British must catch him on the road. He could tell British patrols that he had been tending the girl their fine soldiers had raped, but a suspicious mind might easily uncover the fact that he had been to Valley Forge. Every muscle in his body was tense, and he held the reins with a sweaty grip that was so tight his hand ached. The warm night air was rushing against his face, his mount's hooves beating against the dirt road. The mare was breathing hard, her sides heaving between his legs. A fleck of foam from the horse's mouth flew against his cheek. He was pressing her too hard. He eased back, straightened in the saddle, and reined her to a steady canter.

The moon—full and past its zenith—was standing in the sky over his shoulder, so that the road lay clearly visible, a long waving ribbon of moonlight before him. For that much at least he could be grateful. As long as there was moonlight, he could hold this pace and be asleep in his tent at sunrise.

Then it happened. A sudden flash made the full moon grow pale and whitened the forest and fields about him. Another flash followed the first, and another, while deep thunder rolled down the valley of the Schuylkill. Within a moment clouds had smothered the moon, and the road had disappeared in blackness. Immediately Drew reined in his horse. The mare's sides were heaving, and he could smell the familiar aroma of her sweat in the thick, still air. He turned in the saddle and looked back to the west.

Back above Valley Forge a massive thunderhead towered

upward into the night, a black, silver-edged hand shutting out the moon. For a moment its ethereal beauty made Drew forget everything else. White flashes were playing deep in its recesses, flickering bursts of light intermingled with blackness. Suddenly the entire cloud whitened in a flash that blinded him, and in seconds deafening waves of thunder rolled down upon his head. A gust of cool wind touched his face, breaking the air's stillness. The storm was near. He shook his head bitterly—he could not reach the camp, not before sunrise, not with utter darkness blocking his path. His shoulders slumped and he sagged in the saddle. It would be futile to hurry. Indeed, he *could* not hurry. And it was no use trying to outrun the storm.

Half-heartedly he tugged the reins to the left, weakly kicked the mare's still-heaving sides, and began picking his way slowly through the blackness.

Another mile and it began to rain, a few drops at first, then a shower, and then a cloudburst. With his canvas rain hood drawn over his shoulders and head, Drew rode bowed through the downpour. Both horse and rider could scarcely breathe. "Never supposed I'd drown on horseback!" he mumbled to himself.

Time after time the little brown mare, unable to find the submerged track, stumbled and slipped on its edge. First they found themselves in the right borrow ditch, and then among trees, with the limbs dragging at their shoulders and heads. At last, with the heavy drops driving against the broad oak leaves until all the world was aroar, they stopped with Drew hunched forward and the horse standing helplessly.

But the rain poured on and on. Drew's heart was aching. Yesterday's anger at the soldiers, his frustrated effort to reach camp, his growing desperation to go to Rachel and Jamie—all gathered in his breast like an overpowering leaden weight.

As he sat in the thick leather saddle, the rain's roar in his ears, his poor horse soaked beneath him, hope gone, he remembered Rachel's eyes, and he remembered her tawny arms about his neck. The vision was perfectly clear. There had been fear in those liquid brown eyes that night when he told her she must go. She had gone—angry, yes, but willing to please him. Two years . . . two years! She had made an incredible journey, borne their child alone, worked with unbending determination among the sick. She had given eveything—but so had he. The difference was that he had forced the choice upon her.

"It was wrong!" he shouted into the rain, drawing out each syllable. At the sudden sound of his voice, the horse shifted her weight and stamped the watery ground. His heart was bursting within him. He had thought he was right. But someone else could have done what he had done. Was he sure of that? No, he was not sure.

How could he make it up to Rachel? He ached for her nearness. One after another there came to his mind visions of her loveliness so wonderful that they blotted out the pouring rain. He had held this woman in his arms, he had caressed her face with his fingers, had stroked her softly with his hands; so that now the memory of her smoothness came alive to him. Night before last he had dreamed of her. She had been in the bed with him, in his arms, and his hands had cradled the curve of her hips. In abandon, he had burrowed his face into the softness of her breasts. And now, as he sat here in the rain, he remembered; in his mind he saw, with his hands he felt, and he wanted her . . . oh, how he wanted her again! He felt her tugging at him irresistibly across the hundreds of uncrossable miles standing between them.

And still the rain poured down, and the roar in the trees went on mercilessly unabating.

After a long while, just an hour before dawn, as suddenly as the storm had begun, it ended, the clouds moving on east to lose themselves over the distant ocean. Drew and his little horse emerged dripping from the woods in which they had become entangled. There was the road, slippery and deep with mud. In the west the full moon was low, casting its silver light over newly washed earth. But Drew found no heart for the beauty of the predawn landscape. He urged the horse forward toward the river.

Perhaps he could tell his commander that the storm had detained him. At least that would not be a lie, and they would believe it. His mood had made him think his predicament worse than it really was.

Then he came to the place where he must cross the Schuylkill. It was a low place where two roads met at the river's western bank, one road going east across the river, the other going south, following the river's west bank. He looked across. The morning was about to break and the low river lay clearly before his eyes. What he saw made the heart go out of him again. The storm had raised the river. Above the boiling surface of the flood waters, all that was visible were the king posts of the bridge! Sadly he shook his head; he could not cross, and there would be no way to explain his presence on the Schuylkill's west bank. They would know.

Wearily he turned the horse back west toward Washington's encampment.

"Ah well," he said to the little mare, genuine relief in his voice. "It'll be good to live the truth again." It had been such a long while since his real allegiances had been known.

Then he stopped, looked at the long muddy hill, the beginning of his journey west, and thought again of Rachel. He had more than one allegiance, didn't he? That sagacious Quaker, Israel Bowman, had said so, and Israel was always right. I've given everything to my country, Drew thought, and left my wife and son to shift alone. His heart sank into his belly. He was torn with indecision. In all his thirty years, he could not remember such pain. He had a wife whom he had failed, a son he had never seen, and a country at war. Suddenly, he slapped his heels to the sides of the little horse and pulled the reins sharply leftward. He would follow the river south.

F I F T Y - S E V E N

WHEN the sun broke over the horizon, Drew Wolfe was straight west of Philadelphia. He was still riding in his rain cape, not because it was raining, but to hide the brilliant red coat he wore underneath. He could not hope to dodge all travelers, not if he rode in the day. So, when a thick woods loomed on the road's right, he looked about for watchers, and seeing none, rode in among the trees. Deep within, he staked his horse where she could graze, then beneath the overspreading limbs of a low-grown cedar, rolled himself in his blanket and slept the sleep of exhaustion.

The first thing Drew did the next morning was to bury the telltale red coat in the soft earth—so deep in the woods it would rot to tatters before being found.

Then on he went, traveling at night. During the days, he snared rabbits for food, even sparrows, grubbed edible wild greens, drank from streams and rivers, and slept in random wooded hideaways.

He had wound his way beyond Baltimore, but was still somewhere in Maryland—though perhaps in Virginia, he thought. Always he angled sharply inland, away from the western bank of the Chesapeake. The country was rolling upward here, great hills reaching away in every direction, all thickly wooded, uninterrupted by any farmer's field. The deeper into the western country he came, the more secure he felt, the more certain that given time and caution, he would succeed in reaching his little family.

Two weeks after he set out, after traveling all night, at earliest light, Drew found himself picking his way along the edge of a deep chasm. Because of rocks and steep terrain, the night's going had been nearly impossible. He knew nothing of where the animal trails were leading, but he did know by the stars that he was going south. After several nights of blackness, the moon was returning. Last night it had not gone down until about midnight.

He brought the little mare to a stand. They were on the north edge of a valley, atop a natural wall of rock, like palisades, that dropped straight down fully three hundred feet. The sun had not yet risen, and in the half light a mist rose up from the deep chasm. In the chasm's depths he could make out the white rushing water of a river flowing north, curving abruptly back west and disappearing north again. On the river's other side a single point of light shone, probably from the window of a wilderness cabin.

He looked around. "Hah!" he said to himself. Having avoided every soul for so long, he had become perfectly accustomed to talking to himself and his little mare. "A perfect place. Valley in front of me, trees behind, almost empty wilderness. We'll be safe here." Wearily he swung his leg over the horse's rump and stood down.

At that moment sunlight touched the treetops above him. He looked up and took a deep breath. Then he felt his eyes drawn irresistibly back to the light of the settler's cabin so far below. He worked his tired shoulders about, loosening knots and kinks that had formed during the night's ride. The mare was cropping grass, huffing gently, and there was the sound of grass tearing as she ripped it with her strong teeth. The sweaty sheen on her chestnut-brown flank glistened. She was faring well, he thought. Every night they had camped in good grass, and water had been abundant. She was tired, but sleeker now than when they had set out two weeks ago.

"Too bad I've not done as well," he said under his breath. With both hands he felt his own ribs. What fat he had in reserve at the beginning was pretty well used up, and yesterday he hadn't eaten at all. His last full meal had been at Valley Forge. At first it was Rachel who tortured his sleep with the dreams that had been driving him on. But yesterday, as he slept on a mat of leaves beneath the roots of a great sycamore, he had dreamed only of food. Before him had been a table and great plates of Virginia ham covered in brown sugar glaze and melted butter. There were side dishes of steaming bread and pound cake smothered in sweet clotted cream. Never before had food displaced a woman in his dreams, but never had he been so hungry.

He looked back down at the point of light. The valley's gray depth was becoming visible, and he could see that the light was indeed from a house. From its chimney ascended a wavy line of white smoke. Right now he could imagine nothing but fresh venison dripping on a spit in an open fireplace.

"Breakfast," he said.

The mare's grazing had taken her to a clump of brambles. A quick movement, and she snapped her head back. A small, cotton-tailed rabbit jumped frantically up and scurried into the woods, and Drew looked about just in time to see the puff of cotton disappear. For a moment he chewed on the inside of his lower lip, all the while slapping his left palm thoughtfully with the ends of the reins.

"Can't resist it," he said, and in another moment he was astride the little brown horse, winding along the ridge of the palisade, looking for passage into the valley.

By the time the great palisade was shining in the sun, Drew was at the foot of the rock wall, leading the mare through the river's treacherous rapids. He stood dripping on the other side, emptying his boots and looking toward the cabin that stood amid the trees not more than a hundred feet away. In reality it was not a cabin, but a house of solid hewn logs with a shake roof, not the crude thing he had expected. Someone with skill and determination had carved this place from the wilderness. Near the house was a log barn to shelter the stock and hay. He did not approach unannounced. A livercolored, rawboned dog at the edge of the trees was barking fiercely.

Drew advanced and stood. "Hellooo the cabin!" he called. His voice echoed from the palisades and lost itself among the pines. He waited. There was no answer, but knowing by the smoke that the house was inhabited, he called again. "Hellooo the cabin!"

"State your name and what you're doin' here!" a voice from too near called back.

Drew looked around. The voice had not come from the house, and the echo from the rocks confused the source, but he was certain the voice was female.

"Who *are* you," the voice called again, "and what'd'ya want?"

Drew addressed his answer toward the house. "Wolfe is my name," he called, "Andrew Wolfe. I'm on my way south, toward Wilmington, and I need food."

Silence. Then movement among the pines caught his eye, and a woman stepped from the trees. At waist level she carried an aimed rifle in her hands. It struck Drew as an unpleasant coincidence that in the space of two weeks two different women had held him at gunpoint. A product of the war, he thought, the need to be suspicious of everyone. Carefully he came forward, until less than two rods lay between them.

"Far enough," she said firmly.

He obeyed. From here he could see the intensity of her eyes and made out that the gun in her hands was not a rifle, but a big smoothbore pointed exactly at his middle.

"I won't miss," she said, her voice very calm and even.

"I believe you," he answered, his voice as even as hers.

She was not a mere girl, of that he was sure. He could not tell the age of the back-country women, though, and she might be younger than she appeared. Even so, he judged she was somewhere in the middle of her childbearing years—a handsome woman, really, with black hair, a slender nose, and strangely dull brown eyes.

"Would you please lower that fowler, ma'am?"

"Convince me," she said.

Drew was at a loss. "I can only tell you that I'm harmless—and very hungry."

"Hungry I can believe," she said, looking him up and down. "You're as gaunt a man as ever I've seen. You'll not weigh more than twelve stone, little enough for a man tall as you."

"I expect you're right, ma'am. But two weeks ago it was thirteen and a quarter stone. I've eaten nothin' but what I could snare along the road and trail."

"You're not armed, then," she said. And her eyes softened. Still she held her finger on the fowler's trigger, a fact that did not escape him.

"No," he said, "not armed. I'm a doctor. . . ."

"An *army* doctor," she said, "a *British* army doctor, by the cut of your clothes and the saddle on your horse."

He had not expected her to be so astute. He opened his mouth to tell her he was not British at all, but in Continental service. But he stopped. How could one convince a perfect stranger that he had been serving Washington as a spy? And after all, he did not know this woman's loyalties. She could as well be Tory as Whig. The wrong word and she would kill him as easily as she could wink one brown eye. He closed his mouth, bit the corner of his lip.

"Yes," he said quietly.

"A man's got no index but his face," she said, then, releasing a long breath, "and I believe you'll do me no harm." She lowered the gun's cock to half notch, and with its barrel motioned him toward the house. "Besides," she said, "a doctor might not be bad to have around here for a little while."

He saw then what he had been unable to see before; saw it in her heavy movement, saw it in spite of the thick indigo surtout she wore against the deep valley's cool morning. The woman was with child.

She did not invite him at first, but entered alone. It was a two-story house, not new, for the hewn timbers were already weathered a dark gray. He sat in the yard, on a stump sawn cleanly off at knee height. In a little while she returned with a wide pewter plate in her hands. It was heaped with meat—ham, he knew by the smell—and bread.

"Can't give you butter or milk," she said. "Buttercup's gone dry. Bred her in April. Sorry."

"Ma'am, hungry as I am, I'll not miss a little milk and butter!"

He took up the knife in one hand and three-tined fork in the other, quickly noted they were silver, and ate voraciously. When he was done, his concern turned toward the woman, who, after bringing a bag of oats for the horse, had sat nearby, obviously as hungry for human companionship as he had been for food. Gingerly he approached the subject.

"You said you'd be needin' a doctor soon. . . ."

She was sitting on an outcropping of granite, her legs wide beneath her long dress and surtout, the heels of her hands resting on her knees. She looked down at her large belly.

"Soon, I *hope*!" she said.

"How long?" he asked.

"Two weeks more," she said with certainty.

"You're sure?" he questioned.

"Certain," she said. "Conceived the night before Ethan went away to the war, in the soft grass yonder by the river." Her eyes got a faraway look in them. "That was on the twenty-ninth day of September, a warm night, and the sun was down beyond the mountain yonder."

"You've been alone since?"

His question broke the spell, and she looked directly at him, new fear in her eyes. It was a suspicious question, and he could not blame her for feeling afraid.

"I'm sorry I asked," he said. "You don't need to answer."

She hesitated, then said, "Yes, alone but for trips into the settlement."

"Settlement?" he asked. "So where am I, anyway?"

"Virginia," she said, "fifty miles west of the Shenandoah and the Blue Ridge, and the river here is the Potomac."

Hedda Conners's story was a simple one.

"We met four years ago in Baltimore," she said that evening as they sat near the fire after supper. "He went there looking for a wife. He had come out here and cleared this place ten years before I met him, said the wilderness is full of what a man needs to feel alive. I said that if we married, I'd come here with him. So *we* did, an' *I* did, an' now I'm as in love with this valley as he is." She paused and looked down at the narrow band of gold on her finger. "Then, in October," she continued, "Ethan left to fight with the Grand Army."

She admitted the loneliness was hard, that it was having its effect on her. "Couldn't'a stayed on without the animals," she said. "Two oxen, the dog, a milk cow. Had to take the cow clear into the settlement, twelve miles from here, just to breed her. But we needed the calf. Can't use an ox for breeding. Did you know that?" she said, her face brightening at her recent discovery. She didn't wait for his answer. "They're castrated, raised for work, not breeding."

He chuckled to himself. She seemed completely unembarrassed. As he watched Hedda, Drew felt her curious charm taking him in its web. She was a handsome girl—city-raised, out here in the wilderness—twenty-five years old, she admitted to him. But he was worried for her. Should he choose to stay till her child was born, what would folks in the settlement say, knowing she had a man here with her?

"How will they find out?" she asked.

"You'll tell them," he said. "You're a transparently honest woman."

"Let 'em say what they will," she said with a shrug. Then, abruptly, she changed the subject. "Ethan fought at the Brandywine last year," she said. "Do you know about the Brandywine?"

"*Oh* yes," he said. "I know about the Brandywine!"

"We almost won that one," she said.

"Yes, we almost did," he answered. She did not notice this incongruity, for her mind was on her husband. A smile rose from her heart into her face. "Ethan's an ex*cit*ing man!"

Drew sat in his rocker, looking intently at her firelighted face, musing as to whether he should go on his way or remain to help her. The urge was strong to be up and ready to go when tomorrow's night fell. But what would another two weeks be in exchange for Hedda's gift of food, safety, and a place to rest? And how could he possibly begrudge two or three weeks of his time to a woman pregnant and alone? He could not, not when she had shown him such kindness. Besides, he was a doctor, and it was simply his duty to give aid wherever he found need.

She was right to the very day. On the twenty-ninth of June, a Monday, Hedda Conners gave birth to a baby boy and named him for his father, Ethan.

Hedda had grown on Drew, not in a romantic way, but tenderly, as a man sometimes feels for a woman with whom he is not in love but in whose happiness he has a deep emotional interest. In fourteen days of waiting in this valley, evenings spent in quiet talking, neither having had contact with another living soul for so long, there was a bonding between them. Now that his work was nearly done, he was loathe to leave her to her lonely life. Though he had not fallen in love with

Hedda, he had fallen in love with Hedda's valley—thinking every day as he gazed beyond its palisades and pines at the blue sky above, how wonderful it would be to bring Rachel here when all was done. Wilderness folks need doctors, too. Perhaps they *could* return. The land would not cost them greatly, and it would be a place to begin again.

It was the following Friday when the rapid hooves of a single horse came thudding in the distance. Drew heard the sound while it was yet a great way off, and he was standing at the door when a pudgy man of medium height on a dapple horse reined to a stop.

"Where's Hedda?" were the man's first words, but his small black eyes were full of suspicion. From a leathern pouch he pulled a letter.

"Everybody in the settlement wants to know what's goin' on with the army," he said to Hedda as she came out, babe in arms. She handed the child to Drew, opened the seal, and unfolded the single sheet. All the while the short man on the dapple was sizing Drew from head to foot, a faint look of displeasure on his face.

"Oh, Drew!" she said, blanching at first, then tears of excitement rising in her eyes. "It's from Ethan. The British have left Philadelphia. Washington chased them. There was a battle, and our Continentals won! Oh, Drew, they won! They won!" She was delirious with happiness. Then, still reading her letter, she walked off to be alone with intimate details intended for her eyes only.

The rider sat gazing down at the babe in Drew's arms.

"Four days old." Drew smiled awkwardly.

The man said nothing, his eyes shifting back and forth between the baby and Drew's eyes.

At last, feeling compelled to explain, Drew said, "I'm a doctor, happened here on my way south. Hedda wanted me to stay and help with the child's birthing."

"You're a Scot," the man said, stony-faced.

"I am," Drew said.

"And those are his majesty's boots you're wearin', and his majesty's britches."

Drew bristled. "I'm as much Patriot as any man!" he said, not wishing to explain.

"Well, mister," the rider said, "if I'uz you, I'd make certain folks could tell it by lookin'!" And unconvinced, the pudgy man wheeled his horse and rode away.

FIFTY-EIGHT

It was nearly two weeks later, Thursday, the sixteenth of July, when Drew was finally satisfied that Hedda could do for herself and the baby. As evening shadows darkened the valley of the South Potomac, he said his good-byes to mother and child, swung into his saddle, and under cover of darkness began to pick his way along the forest trail southward.

Drew's heart was light as he started off.

"My soul!" he exclaimed to himself. "What bravery for a woman to live out here alone—and with a newborn!"

Then his thoughts leapt ahead. In his imagination he saw himself riding up to the Buchannon mansion and, beneath great magnolias, swinging down from his horse and running to sweep Rachel up in his arms. He was in ecstasy at the joy he envisioned on her face and the tears of gladness running down her cheeks. In his imagination their little son was beside her. He folded the little boy in his arms and held him tightly. Never had he loved Rachel as he did at this moment! He was in love with the very dirt of the path that was leading him to her. He could not restrain himself from prodding the horse into a gallop, and the dark trees went flying rapidly by. He would stay inland, he reasoned, behind the mountains, until he reached the James, then break through and travel the lowlands to the headwaters of the Cape Fear River, which he would then follow to Wilmington and the coast.

He had been riding for three hours, having slackened his pace to a canter. It was nearing midnight, and the trail had become a narrow road bordered on the east by overhanging trees and on the west by the winding riverbank of the Potomac. There was a half-moon shining above the trail. The river had narrowed, and its noisy rushing all but hid the hoofbeats of Drew's horse. Swarms of mosquitoes up from the eddy pools buzzed loudly around his head and kept him slapping and scratching continuously. It would be all the same if he stopped, perhaps worse, so he kept going.

Then, far ahead in the moonlight, he could make out that another road crossed his. "The road to the settlement," he said to himself. For a moment there seemed a shadowy movement in the open space where the two roads met. He halted and rode in among the trees at the roadside, watching, listening.

Yes, there it was again. A dark figure on horseback, venturing out from the cover of the trees. No doubt whoever it was had heard his approaching hoofbeats and now wondered why they had stopped. The figure looked about and, seeing nothing, motioned to others hiding among the trees. A half-dozen riders sat now in the crossroads, gazing toward him.

"Can they see me?" he whispered to his mare. He could not tell. They started in his direction, kept coming. He leaned forward, clamped his hands tenderly but firmly about his horse's muzzle. They rode past him. He could hear them talking, angry words like "lobsterback," "traitor," strings of words like, "can't let him get away."

He let out his suspended breath as they moved slowly down the road in the direction from which he had come. They went a short distance and stopped. One man dismounted and, crouching, examined the sandy soil of the road in the moonlight. There was a whispered conversation, and simultaneously two of the men pointed back up the road. Slowly they began to move toward him. Cold sweat broke out on Drew's forehead. He felt a constriction in his chest and a tension that he could not bear.

He braced himself, then suddenly lashing with the reins and kicking with his heels, he shouted and burst from the trees onto the open road. He could scarcely hear the frantic shouts that rose behind him, but he knew the riders were coming. He was crouched low, his head close by the little mare's lunging neck. The crossroads passed behind him. Quickly the hill dropped, and the mare's hooves splashed wildly through the stream at the bottom of a hollow. He was outreaching them; he was sure of it now. There was a chance.

Suddenly above the clambering of hooves, there rang out the sharp report of a gun. He actually heard the lead whiz past his right ear. They had stopped. They were taking careful aim. Another report, and a burning concussion to his left shoulder. He was not down. He could go on. But the next shot might . . . and with this thought he pulled so hard on the reins that the little horse went to her haunches in the sand. Drew fell backward, landed on his feet, and turned. With his one good arm uplifted, and the wounded one hanging limply to his side, he stood facing his exultant captors.

BOOK SIX

Civil War
1778–1781

FIFTY-NINE

It was early afternoon, the first week of January 1780. A sudden pounding of hurried hooves, feet mounting the front stair, and a sharp knock at the door roused Edward Buchannon from the paperwork spread across his desk. He tossed his horn-rimmed half glasses on top of the papers and listened as an urgent voice spoke his name. Moments later Quincy, a black servant, appeared in the doorway.

"A gentleman from Wilmington to see you, sir," and the man stepped in.

"Tom!" Buchannon said. "What's the trouble?"

"A fast packet from Philadelphia, Edward. Clinton's sailed from New York! At least fourteen ships of the line in his fleet, and nearly a hundred troop transports, more than eight thousand on board! He's headed for Charles Town."

Buchannon, drawing in a slow breath, settled back in his chair. "England's given up in the north," he said. "They're lookin' to their southern Tories to fight the war for 'em!"

"Yes," the man said, "I expect that's about it."

"Tom, when will they pass Wilmington ... given fair weather?"

"Another two days, maybe three," he answered.

"We have a little time," Buchannon said thoughtfully, perching his feet on the desk corner. "They'll try first to occupy Charles Town ... and think about us later." He looked up sharply. "On your way in—did you tell anyone in the house about this, Tom?"

"No sir, I did not."

"That's best," he said quietly. "A lot can happen to a fleet in a thousand miles. Let's don't frighten the ladies till we're certain."

It was the next day—a day uncommonly warm for midwinter—a damp warmth one ordinarily felt only with the ap-

proach of spring. Rachel stood looking from the open window
of her room, down to where the clouds of naked gray trees
crowded the riverbanks. Puffs of wind were blowing her hair
about, and she had just fingered a strand back in place.

"Just feel the air!" she said to Salali.

There was a lingering sadness in Rachel's eyes, but a mild
excitement in her voice, for, little by little, she was learning to
live again. She leaned against the window's deep casement,
luxuriating in the touch of the breeze on her face. She could
not get enough of the sensuous air.

"I woke this morning thinking it was spring," she said. "But
the only sign is in the air. There're no buds on the trees, and
the grass is dull, and the rosebushes in the garden seem so
sad."

Salali sat on the floor in the middle of the large multicolored
hooked rug. She'd tucked her legs up behind her and was leaning on her right hand, as with her left she scooted one of
Jamie's lead soldiers toward him. The little boy was delighted,
and brought a cannon into position.

"Pshhh! Pshhh!" He made explosive sounds with his mouth,
imitating gunfire. He would soon be three years old.

"Yes!" Salali answered. "It *is* like spring. A wonderful feeling!"

"Cape Fear winters are warm," Rachel said, "but what little
cold there is cuts deep." She hugged herself, shivering. "A day
as warm as this is such a wonderful reprieve!" She paused and
looked toward the south. "I think we'll have storms tonight.
There're banks along the southern horizon—just as in spring."
Overhead, high wisps of windblown clouds were streaming
northward.

She turned about, and for a while stood gazing at her friend
and little son, smiling at Jamie's happiness. There was an inter-
lude in the battle of the toy soldiers, and Salali looked up.

"Smell the *ocean*!" she exclaimed.

"Salali!" Rachel paused, suddenly excited. "Let's go down
to the ocean—to Spaun's light. Jamie can play in the sand and
we can watch the surf roll in. Jacob would be glad for the
company."

They reached the ocean dunes in early afternoon. Little Jamie,
on Rachel's shoulders, waved a white handkerchief wildly in
the air to draw Jacob Spaun's attention, and soon he was row-

ing toward them across the inlet. The wind was in their faces, and they could hear Spaun's voice as he came.

"Heeeee!" he called happily. "Come to see Old Spaun, did ya!"

Jacob Spaun was seventy if he was a day, and until back in '64 had been a blacksmith in Wilmington. That was the year Cape Fear fishermen and merchants set out to erect this light, and hired Spaun to do the iron work. He built a smithy right on the dune, forged every piece of iron—made the great bolts and anchors tying the stone tower to bedrock, right up to the cap of the roof.

By the time the light was done, he had become so fond of this grassy bar of sand—and so fond of the light—that he had applied to be keeper. From that time on it had been "Spaun's Light."

Spaun sprang to shore on short legs, badly bowed from a childhood case of rickets, and jerking the boat firmly onto the sand, turned and reached for Jamie. Spaun was a short man, Rachel's height, but he was broad through the shoulders and thick through the arms and body. His face was squarish and very rugged. He had only a few wisps of white hair on the top of his head, but on the sides and back it was thick and bushy. He walked with a strong side-to-side rocking motion.

Jamie laughed and squealed as Spaun pulled him from Rachel's shoulders, then held him in one arm and hugged first Rachel and then Salali with the other.

"Th'older a man gets," he often said, "the more he 'preciates the fine clear beauty of the young folks!" He loved Rachel for the courage he saw in her eyes. "She's got *sand* in 'er craw!" he often exclaimed.

He and the boy had gotten to know each other when Jamie was less than a year old. Up and down the island they had gone together—hand in hand along the surf. "Birrr! Birrr!" the little boy had called out, extending his finger and pointing to the gulls that flew close on their starched gray wings. Then Jamie would run over the firm sand with his little bowed legs so like Spaun's old bowed ones, chasing the gull in its flight or running after the foaming sheets of water retreating back into the great ocean. And Spaun would laugh and grab the child up, his heart warm, thanking God that he had lived to hold blooming life in his aging arms once again.

Rachel's fascination with Spaun's beloved light had endeared her to him. Indeed, in the last two years, the light had become a refuge to her, and very like the meadow pond in Scotland, she came here often "to bind up the raveling threads." Spaun had even taught her to tend the light. Jacob knew that he himself would not be able to do the work much longer, for around the brown disk of each iris, a milky-white ring was growing in his eyes, and one day soon his sight would be gone.

While Jacob and Jamie walked along the sand looking for shells and beached jellyfish, Rachel and Salali sat under the trees a little way from the light, talking. The afternoon flew pleasantly by. About four o'clock Rachel spotted sails—far out. In slow motion she stood, her left hand on the trunk of the palmetto palm beside her, her eyes never leaving the horizon.

"What is it?" Salali asked, her dark eyes fixed on Rachel's puzzled expression.

"Sails," Rachel said.

"So?"

"Not fishing boats."

At this Salali came to her feet and gazed seaward. "Warships," she said.

At the word, Rachel turned about and ran toward the light. Throwing open the heavy tower door, she bounded up the steps two and three at a time. Once in the lantern, she grabbed up Spaun's old telescope, brass, bound in brown leather, and pulling it to its full length, raised it to her eye. A breeze from the sea made the glass walls about her hum. She was breathing heavily from the climb, and for a moment the round image in the scope was only a blur of dark blue sea and light blue sky. As the image sharpened, she held her breath and steadied the scope.

"The Union Jack!" she whispered. Her deep brown eyes reflected the details of the lantern as she gazed. "What can it mean?" she wondered. A fullness rose in her chest as, with a series of clicks, she compressed the telescope and returned it to its leathern case. She opened the door, stepped out onto the catwalk surrounding the lantern, and called down to Salali, who by now had been joined by Spaun and Jamie.

"British sails!" Rachel called down. "Two ships on a southern course. The wind's against them, but they're making fair time."

Very gradually the ships disappeared over the horizon.

Evening fell on an almost normal sea, the gray swells only a little broader, the breaks a little larger, and their roar on the beach a bit louder. Whatever storm the southern wisps of cloud foretold would miss these dunes and the mouth of the Cape Fear altogether—or so Jacob Spaun predicted.

Night came on. Rachel ascended the tower once again, poured spirits of wine on the chamois, and gave the reflector a final polish. Then lighting a single taper, she held the flame to the wicks of the highest candles and one by one lighted them all. About her the great lantern was glowing, guiding fishermen away from the sand shoals north of the river's mouth. But Rachel was thinking—knowing in some mysterious way that the sails they had seen in the afternoon were Clinton's fleet on the way to Charles Town.

And if he did take Charles Town, what then? She knew the answer. Every Tory in the South would come to his side, every Patriot would rise to arms. The prospect was horrible: death and burnings, neighbor against neighbor, occupations of towns and cities! Oh, Lord, when would it end?

That night—unknown to all but the men at sea—a storm from the south struck the vanguard of Clinton's ships off Hatteras, driving them onto Diamond Shoals, sending some to the bottom, scattering others across the Atlantic. A ship loaded with Hessians washed ashore on the coast of Cornwall, England.

Yet, within three weeks, the fleet regrouped and anchored off Tybee Roads, where they made repairs and sailed for Edisto Inlet, thirty miles south of Charles Town.

At last, on the twelfth of May, stormed by sea and land, Charles Town fell to the British.

S I X T Y

SPRING was in full bloom. The grass was green, birds were singing, and the air about Buchannon Hills was full of the smell of resurrected life.

Once Rachel had believed the lot of a plantation mistress was one of unconcerned ease. Abigail Buchannon had set that

misguided notion to rest in less than a week. Abigail had little
time for fashionable embroidery, reading novels, or, except in
the hottest weather, for afternoon naps. Up at six each morning
to meet the kitchen servants as they came in from the quarters,
she watched over every detail of their appearance and work.
Rachel watched Abigail with a mixture of mild amusement and
considerable admiration.

"Joanna, who in the world fixed your hair this morning!"
Abigail would say. "Here, let me take a comb to it. It'll only
take a moment."

"Sarah, that apron is wrinkled and soiled; have you worn it
a month? Here. Let me have it and you get a fresh one!"

"Joel, when you bring in the breakfast ham, stop by the
springhouse and get fresh butter."

Every day but Sundays Abigail went hurriedly through the
house, inspecting for dust and cobwebs, opening windows to
air each room. Once in two weeks she ordered the beds carried
out and sunned. All through the winter months she saw to it
that the chimneys were swept down every day, and once a
month—always choosing a rainy day—had a roaring fire built
in each fireplace to burn accretions of soot from the chimneys.

Since the servant girl Mary was efficient with washed and
ironed things, Abigail let her have free hand. Occasionally she
would say, "Remember, Mary. Never put Master Buchannon's
shirts away with buttons missing, or his stockings with holes in
them. And be sure his drawers have strings! Think how short
his temper is when he starts the day with strings missing from
his drawers!"

"We have no right," she would say to Rachel, "to expect
servants to be more attentive to details than we are willing to
be. Here," she said, handing Rachel a fistful of candles, "you
clean the drippings from these while I polish the candlesticks
. . . and oh yes, when you're done, take the cloth and shine
those sconces on the south wall. Did you notice how smoky
those candles burned last night? Replace them with the pretty
green bayberry candles—you know, the ones we made last
winter with wax myrtle? And be sure to use the spermaceti
candles in the parlor."

Today the entire plantation stood on tiptoe, waiting for "Abigail's spring flurry" to begin, and she was about to oblige.
With the breakfast table cleared, Edward gone to the rice
fields, and Donald on his way to classes, Rachel and Salali

were busy in the kitchen, waiting for Abigail's onslaught. They heard her voice as she came through the hyphen to the kitchen.

"Rachel!"

"In here, Abigail."

Abigail entered as Rachel was placing the white stoneware plates back into a triple-tiered rack near the fireplace.

"Rachel, do you think they'll need you down in the servants' quarters today?"

"No." Rachel shook her head. "No, Abigail, I expect to be working right here all day long."

"And Mary can watch Jamie?"

"Yes, I'm sure she would."

"And you, Salali?"

"Of course." Salali sighed, smiling mischievously.

"Good!"

There was a scraping of feet on the stone hearth behind her. Abigail turned about to face the servant Augustus, who had just come in from the well, a yoke bearing two wooden buckets of water across his shoulders. The well was situated just beyond the kitchen porch, under a covered arbor in the middle of a kind of quadrangle. About the edges of the quadrangle were the smokehouses, and on the northeast corner the springhouse. Next to the springhouse was the weaving room where most of the "Negro cloth" was made.

Augustus was a middle-size man, a house servant, dressed this morning in dark blue breeches and gray stockings. The string ties of his open shirt collar hung down untied, a thing Abigail permitted of the servants engaged in heavier work.

"Augustus," Abigail ordered, "when you've filled the kettle, make up a large batch of whitewash."

Augustus, an Ibo from Nigeria, lacked the normal quota of energy. Suddenly his face went blank with dismay, but he recovered quickly.

"The usual proportions," she said, "two bushels of unslaked lime, slack it with boiling water and whiten it with two gallons of flour paste. Put in a little bluing. And, Augustus, on your way out, send in some of the older boys and men Master Buchannon excused from the field."

Then, turning a triumphantly beaming face to Rachel and Salali, she said, "Now we can begin!"

That day all the carpets on the top floor were taken up and carried into the yard. Every piece of furniture, oil paintings, lamps, draperies, and decorations accompanied the carpets out under the trees. Then all available hands took up brushes and began to coat the upstairs walls and ceilings with fresh white-wash.

"Once a year!" Abigail exclaimed to Rachel at least a dozen times that day. "A bright house is a happy house! Tomorrow we begin the second floor, and the last three days of the week we'll do the downstairs—weather permitting!"

When evening came, all was back in place in the glistening rooms of the upper story, supper had been eaten, and most of the servants were "off task." Rachel was going to her room when she smelled the familiar aroma of vanilla-flavored to-bacco burning somewhere nearby. She searched and found Edward on the upper piazza, his straight-back chair tilted and his feet propped on the rail. He was watching the sun as it de-scended toward the trees. With his back to her, he didn't see her there. Deep in her heart Rachel felt the serenity of the mo-ment. Edward had become to her the father she never had—and with Drew gone, he had become the central towering male figure in her life, the one whose wisdom and strength she con-stantly relied upon.

For a long moment she stood there, not wishing to interrupt his thoughts, enjoying the sight of him sitting just as he was. At last she stepped out, and he heard the brush of her soft sole on the worn floor. He looked around.

"Rachel!" he said, between teeth tightly clamped to the stem of his pipe.

She came and laid her hand on his shoulder, saying nothing. It was a powerful shoulder, broad and muscled. Edward reached around and patted her hand affectionately and, as he did, looked up at her face.

"You're tired," he said, taking the pipe from his mouth.

"It's been a busy day," she replied, a touch of weariness in her voice.

"That Nabby's a whirlwind, ain't she!" Edward chuckled, returning the pipe to his mouth and sucking; the pipe had gone out.

Rachel smiled back. "That she is." She slipped her hand from his shoulder and came around to the rail. The afternoon heat lingered momentarily before a cooling breeze just sprung up from the sea. She perched on the railing beside Edward's feet, her back to the open yard, smiling down at him. The blue smoke from his pipe wafted up and curled about, sweetly flavoring the evening air. Her feeling of security deepened.

She glanced quickly up as the door opened again. It was Mary with a silver tray. Bowing slightly at the waist, Mary held the tray out first to Edward, then to Rachel. On it were two tall glasses of iced liquid in which sprigs of mint were floating. Rachel smiled her appreciation, took a glass, and sipped the faintly green contents. It felt cool and good on her tongue. Her arms were sore from the day's work, and her back and legs ached with weariness as she gazed out over the evening landscape, her thoughts a mix of the busy afternoon and the night before.

"Gonna be a hot summer, feels like," Buchannon broke into her thoughts. "We laid in more ice than common—and if we're careful, it'll last through fall."

Rachel said nothing.

"Why so quiet tonight?" he asked cautiously.

For a long moment she struggled, trying to find the words. She felt his inquisitive gaze searching out her expression.

"Maybe I'm pryin'," he said, trying to appear indifferent.

"No! Oh, no. Not at all, Edward," she said.

"Thinkin' about Drew?"

"Always," she said. "Drew is never far away from me. I've no reason to believe anything but that he's dead, but whether dead or alive, he seems close. When I look at Jamie, I see the way Drew's eyes crinkled at the corners when he smiled. And then I think of our time together, the wonder of it, the danger of it, how he touched me, how . . ."

She bowed her reddening face and touched her forehead with splayed fingers, embarrassed at having been so bold as to talk about her dead husband's touch.

"I'm sorry," she stammered.

"No need to be," Edward said. "I've been up and down the road many a time, and I know the things a man and woman feel for each other."

She lifted her eyes and collected her thoughts. "Edward . . . I've never even told this to Salali. But there are days when if it weren't for Jamie, I would just walk away and die. Perhaps if I did, Drew and I would be reunited in another world. Sometimes I wish the war would come and carry us all away."

"Rachel . . ." Buchannon broke in quietly, great sadness in his eyes, "you can't *mean* that."

"Oh but I do," she said earnestly. She paused for a long moment and looked away. "But it isn't Drew or death that troubles me just now."

"Then what?" he asked.

"A dream," she said. "A dream I had."

"You're dreaming again?" he asked.

"Again," she said.

Buchannon nodded.

"It was two nights ago. I dreamed that you and Donald would be goin' away. It frightens me. I can't get it out of my mind."

"Well," Edward said, blowing a ring of smoke into the air, "it's a sure bet *that* dream'll come true. We'd be gone a'ready if it hadn't been for the plantin'. Most o' the men are."

"But this was one of *those* dreams," she said, "the kind that feels as though it has meaning. And there was somethin' else . . . In the dream, I went with you."

"Well, you can mark that part off as nonsense. We'll go for sure, but for you to come along, now *that's* not even poss—" He stopped mid-word as some movement far out on the dusty road caught his eye. Rachel saw it also.

"Someone's coming," she said, standing and shielding her eyes from the lowering sun.

"A rider, hard from the west," he said. Edward let his feet fall from the railing to the floor. When the front legs of his chair struck the boards, he was already standing, peering expectantly into the distance. "Too hot to ride that hard," he exclaimed. "He's gonna kill that horse if he don't slack off!"

Up along the edge of the fields the rider came, hoofbeats gradually becoming audible, and at last he was close enough that his face could be seen.

"Who is he?" Rachel asked.

"Never saw him before. It's a stranger."

As the rider came rapidly even with the stables, Buchannon waved his arms above his head. The rider caught sight, and reining abruptly left, horse and rider lurched up the intervening rise of ground.

"Waxhaws!" he cried, swinging down even before his lathered horse had stopped.

"Waxhaws?" Buchannon asked impatiently.

"Place up in the Piedmont," the man said, nearly breathless with exertion and excitement. "Colonel Buford's Third Virginia Continentals on their way to aid Lincoln at Charles

Town. Hit with about three hunnerd Britishers, some of 'em
the Seventeenth Dragoons."

"What losses?" Buchannon bellowed, now excited.

"Bad! Real bad!" the man said. "Buford told us to hold our
fire till we could see the whites'a their eyes. But that don't
work when it's cavalry chargin' ya. They rode in, slashin' and
skewerin' men everwhur, whuppin' us so bad Buford ordered
up the white flag. But the Britishers never had no mercy, jest
kept on ahackin' and thrustin' with their swords." He strongly
pronounced the *w* in sword, reflecting his Highland descent.
"Only a hunnerd of the three hunnerd 'n' fifty got away. I'uz
one of um, an'ay sent me out to spread the word. Ever'body's
a sayin' now that if we ever meet 'um agin, we'll give Tarleton's Quarter right back!"

"Tarleton?" Rachel asked, glancing at Buchannon. "Who's
Tarleton?"

By now the entire family had come out to gather at the rail.
Jamie had come running with them and tugged at Rachel's
skirts till she gathered him up in her arms. Jamie peered down
over the rail at the man below, widest-eyed of all.

"Tarleton?" the man spat. "Damnest little banty rooster of a
Britisher ya ever seen—but so blasted quick with them Dragoons o' his'n, caint *nobody* stand in front of 'um!"

" 'Tarleton's Quarter' . . ." Buchannon repeated thoughtfully.
Then shaking his head, " 'Tarleton's Quarter!' " and he struck
the railing hard with the heel of his hand.

"They's callin' fer everbody kin come," the man went on
excitedly, "even the women!"

"Women!" Buchannon returned. "Why the blazes do they
want the women to come where there'll be fightin'?"

"Nurses," the man replied. "Washin'ton's sent out word that
he's so short of doctors and nurses that he'll pay any woman
willin' to come into the army same as he'll give a soldier.
That's how desprit he is!"

All night long Rachel struggled in her sleep, dozing and waking, dozing and waking. Twice she drew back the covers and
rose to stand over Jamie, asleep in his own little bed, the
moonlight showing so pale on his face . . . his expression perfectly serene.

A mighty war was being waged in her breast. She went silently on bare feet to the window and looked up at the moon.
Its beams were filtering down through the branches of longleaf

pine, leaving thin shadows on her face. Her big eyes reflected sadly in the moonlight. Why did she want to go with the men? she asked herself. A sense of duty, of course. After all, she was a trained physician, and here on the plantation she had learned even more about her craft. She sighed so deeply that Jamie stirred in his bed.

Part of her said she was needed there in the battle lines where men would be wounded and dying. Another part said she should be here with the slaves. And with Jamie. What about Jamie? With his father gone, how could she think of leaving him? She didn't know, but she could leave even Jamie, if she decided she must.

And there was the dream. Hadn't her dream said that she would go? And if she did not return, it would be because she had been shot down, sharing the glory of this Revolution with all the others who had died. Wasn't there honor in that? And if she were shot down, or died of dysentery or some other malady so common to war, wouldn't that mean ... She hardly dared think it. Mightn't that mean she would be rejoined with Drew?

Nearly all night she struggled with her conflicting desires: mother, patriot, lover—which would it be?

When the sun rose at last, it came with the promise of more intense heat.

Outside the stables, Buchannon, Donald, and Rachel were packing their horses, the family clustered about to say farewells.

Rachel had announced her intention to go with them at breakfast, leaving everyone looking at each other in slack-jawed shock. Buchannon and Abigail had taken her aside and privately implored her to stay, but her mind was made up. Salali, she had told them, loved Jamie almost as much as she, that he would be safe with her, and that her place was in the war.

Buchannon, who was absolutely disgusted with Rachel's logic and bull-headedness, became angry and distant.

Rachel had curried her own horse, blanketed and saddled him, and was just buckling on the saddlebags. She was dressed in her favorite garb—sleek black knee breeches and billowing white linen shirt, pure white ribbed stockings, and black leather shoes.

Salali could hardly take her eyes from Donald. Until the war moved to the south, they had planned to be married, but when Donald saw it coming, he said they must wait. There was love in her eyes, love that made them brim with tears. Now and again Donald's gaze locked with hers. Rachel saw these exchanges and knew their hearts were breaking for each other.

Rachel forced herself to think about Tarleton, and about bleeding wounds and sutures and splints. It had to be that way, or she would not be able to ride away from this place, from these people, from Salali and from Jamie. It was almost more than she could do to finish her preparations. She stooped to pick up her chest of surgical tools and medicines. "Here," Donald said, bending down beside her, "let me help you with that."

It was a wooden chest, covered in black leather and buckled securely. In it were scalpels, a curved amputation knife, an amputation saw, a screw tourniquet, bullet probes, and many other things besides the medicines.

Together they lifted it into place atop the saddlebags and buckled it down with straps cut long ago to carry it about over the countryside.

Everyone was grimly silent. Buchannon, fuming over the turn of events, was talking to himself while the others listened in.

"So that's the way it's gonna be!" he said. "White flags won't mean a thing now—not to either side! Well, by the Almighty, Tarleton's started more than he bargained for."

He lifted the saddle up onto the back of his favorite white mare, the "Wonder Horse," he called her. "Always wonder what she's gonna do next," he explained to strangers who didn't know.

He was dressed differently than Rachel had ever seen. His hat was low-crowned felt, white turned gray with long use, and the cuffs of his buckskin trousers—soiled from past excursions into the wilderness—came down over his center-seamed, Shawnee-styled moccasins, made new just last night. His upper garment was a red felt shirt whose style was hidden beneath a long, fringed buckskin jacket, as soiled as his trousers. Around his neck he wore a heart-shaped bag, pierced with the stem of his short pipe and filled with tobacco. The little pouch was beaded about the edges with red, blue, and white beads, and tied at the opening with a thin leather thong. While he packed, he kept rumbling under his breath to anyone who would listen.

"Clinton's got outposts from the coast of South Carolina to

the Blue Ridge now," he said, pulling the cinch firmly up under the mare's belly. The big man's heavy dark brows were drawn down and his face was a thundercloud. "Fort Ninety-Six on the Saluda," he rumbled under his breath, "Granby on the Congaree, Motte at the Wateree, and God only knows where else!" His movements were angry and quick. "All of a sudden every other damn fool in the Carolinas and Georgia says he's *against* the Revolution, because he thinks it's gonna fail!"

Nabby Buchannon watched nervously as Edward threw the bedroll over his mare's rump and saddlebags and pulled the leather saddle straps tight around it. Not for one moment had Abigail Buchannon thought to ask Edward not to go. She knew where his duty lay as well as he. This was work that had to be done. Yet her heart did ache. He seemed so invincible, but she knew a .75-caliber ball from a British Brown Bess could take Edward Buchannon's life as easily as it could an ordinary man's.

"And Clinton," Buchannon rumbled on, " 'You southern rebels just lay down your guns, and I'll give you amnesty,' he says." Buchannon weighted the word *amnesty* with heavy sarcasm. "And so here comes every Patriot and his dog, crawlin' out of the woodwork, and promises to be good. It's enough to make a man puke! And then Clinton tells 'em that to *get* their amnesty, they've got to fight for the Crown! *We'll* give 'em amnesty! Many a man would've stayed *out* of the fight if he'd let 'em be neutral. Now he's stirred up a cloud of hornets John Bull won't be able to brush off his neck!'"

Rachel was ready. She stood silently watching the others, listening to Edward ramble on as her heart raced to begin.

Uncomprehending, Jamie played about with the children just inside the stables. When he ran too close to the heels of Donald's horse, Rachel reached out and pulled him back, for a moment holding him against her legs. But he tugged away and went running off again.

"Edward," Rachel broke in. She could barely control the tone of her voice. There was an uncharacteristic quaver in it.

He turned and looked at her, the disapproval still in his eyes.

"Edward," she said quietly, "is Tarleton likely to reach Wilmington?"

It was the question that had been in his mind all morning. Everyone waited in perfect silence for his answer. He took off his hat, fingered the brim, and gazed gravely around into the eyes that were looking to him. He spoke firmly.

"If you hear of Tarleton bein' near Buchannon Hills," he said solemnly, weighting every word, "if there's *any* warnin' of a raid, scatter into the pines. Don't *wait* to see if it's him."

"How would we know Tarleton if we saw him?" Nabby asked.

"He's a stocky little redhead, not thirty years old," Donald answered. "Quick and cocky, they say."

"And rumor has it he's as ruthless with women as he is with men," Buchannon added. He shook his head and turned to his horse, readjusting the girth strap.

There was no more excuse to linger. Salali's eyes were brimming with tears as she threw her arms around Rachel. They stood there a long time, softly crying, rocking in each other's arms.

"I'll take good care of Jamie," she whispered, "even to giving my life!"

"I know," Rachel whispered. "And I'll take good care of Donald."

"Do," Salali said. "Oh do!"

Salali loosed Rachel and went to him, looking up into his eyes, taking his hands and placing them on her own waist. She laid her head on his chest, and he stroked her long black hair.

Buchannon turned to the women, placing his big arms around each in turn and hugging them tightly, whispering warm assurances of a soon return and words of affection.

"Oh be careful, Edward," Abigail said as she held his big shoulders. "Come back to me safe!"

"I will, Nabby," he said. "You count on it."

SIXTY-ONE

THE fourth day out from Buchannon Hills, boredom set in. It was mid-afternoon. The sun was in their faces, pouring down a pure southern heat more intense than anything Rachel had felt at Monmouth Courthouse.

Then they entered the forest again, tall and thick, barring all movement of air. When an hour ago they had dismounted to rest the horses, they stepped down into deep, hot sand that blistered their feet through the soles of their shoes. Beads of perspiration stood on Rachel's upper lip and ran in rivulets down the small of her back. Neither she nor Buchannon nor Donald had spoken a word for the last half hour.

The going was as dangerous as it was uncomfortable. They met few travelers, but when one did appear, there was no way to tell his loyalty without asking outright. And there was no way to know whether the infrequent clearings with log huts along the roadside were inhabited by Tory or Whig, whether some nervous finger might be tightening on the trigger of a gun aimed at one of them. Only one thing was certain: Whig or Tory, every man and woman they met was as suspicious and on edge as they, and all the more dangerous for it. It was best not to ask anyone who they were, or what they were, or where they were going, and best not to tip your own hand. So every traveler was greeted by a faint smile, a cautious wave of the hand, and with a feeling that made the hair on the back of their necks stand on end.

Two days ago the land had begun to ascend steadily as flat Tidewater turned to gently rolling hills. Yesterday the hills had become small mountains and the going steadily more difficult.

In silence, the horses plodding slowly through the heated sand, Rachel was thinking how she envied her two companions. Edward was riding ahead of her, the tail of his white mare swinging at flies that buzzed continually about her white swaying rump. Donald was coming along behind. Edward had left his Nabby, and Donald his Salali, but neither had left a child dependent on him for love and nurture. Besides, she thought, women feel these things more deeply than men. All a man has to do is turn his mind toward some task and it fills his whole world, blotting out everything else. Not so with a woman. Jamie was constantly in her thoughts, and her heart was aching. But she knew she must get those feelings under control, or be worthless among the wounded.

As late afternoon came on, light on the forest trail began to soften, and the heat let up. The trail became narrow and turned down the western slope of some nameless mountain. No longer was the soil sandy, but dark and loose, mixed with fractured rock that made it slip beneath the feet of the horses. The trail itself must have been hundreds of years old, first beaten by the moccasined feet of ancestral Cherokees. Above their heads the treetops had grown together, and from somewhere in the forest came the sounds of a falling stream.

"Fresh water for the horses," Donald said.

"And for us!" Buchannon added. It was the first flowing stream they had been near in two days, and their canteens were dangerously empty.

The banks of the stream were gradual, an easy crossing, and a good place for the horses to drink at their leisure.

Without a word to the others, Rachel swung down, perched on a rock, and pulled off her shoes and stockings. Feeling gingerly for her footing, she waded in to midthigh. First she drank, then abruptly plunged her head into the water, only to jerk it back into the air, her long hair streaming down and her breath coming in spasms from the chilling cold.

"Oh!" she exclaimed, her shoulders shivering uncontrollably. "Oh how *good* it feels!"

Donald sat watching, his hands resting on the pommel of his saddle, too weary to think of anything at all but how it would be to have the grime of the road washed away.

"Don't see why she oughta have all the fun, do you?" Buchannon said, interrupting Donald's thoughts.

A moment more and Edward had taken the plunge, with Donald close behind. A while later all were reclining in soft grass beyond the brook, the horses grazing among the trees.

"Edward ..." Rachel was propped against the trunk of a great beech, drying her hair with a towel.

"Um?" Buchannon answered. He was lying with his right leg crossed over his left knee, hands clasped behind his head and hat tilted down over his eyes.

"Why not camp right here tonight?" she asked. "There's water and grazing and the cover of the woods."

Donald, who had been lying on his side, rolled over and sat up, looking around. "I don't think so," he said.

"Why not?" Rachel asked with surprise. "It seems perfect to me."

"The stream," Donald answered. "The noise would cover the sound of anybody comin' up on us. Not safe."

Rachel wound the towel about her head turban-fashion, saying nothing, but she understood that Donald was right.

"We prob'ly oughta move on a little ways yet tonight," Buchannon said, not stirring from beneath his tilted hat. Then he heaved a great sigh and raised himself to a sitting position.

As he did, he was facing up the trail in the direction they would be going. The expression on his face froze.

"What . . . ?" he said, and came up onto one knee.

Rachel followed his gaze. "What is it, Edward?" she said.

"I'm not sure," he whispered. "Somethin' unnatural up there beside the trail. Somethin' that don't fit."

"I see it," Donald said, as the three slowly got to their feet.

About a hundred yards up the long narrow corridor of trees, in the place where it widened a little, something was out of place, something unlike the boughs of the trees or their bark or leaves. Where the arm of a spreading oak reached out over the trail, a dozen feet out from the thick, knobby trunk, something hung suspended above the ground. Edward picked up his smoothbore, thumbed the frizzen forward, found the priming good, clicked it into place, and walked slowly forward. Donald and Rachel, each pulling rifles from their saddles, followed. Halfway there, the image lost its mystery, and they went heavily on.

At last they stood with weary faces gazing upward.

He had been a young man, perhaps not more than twenty-five years old, but it was hard to tell. His lips and eyes were puffed grotesquely and his face was ashen-gray, his neck pinched by the rope that held him, absolutely unmoving in the forest stillness.

"Dead for two or three days, I'd guess," Buchannon said. Edward's voice seemed absorbed by the forest, deadened somehow. The stench of decay made Rachel take a kerchief from her pocket and hold it over her nose. With the other hand she clutched Donald's upper arm, and stood shaking her head slowly. Crude letters carved deep into the young man's bare chest told the story: *Traitor!*

Edward silently turned, went back down the hill to their packs, and returned with two spades. "Here," he said, driving his blade into the ground directly beneath the body. "The less we handle 'im, the better off we'll be."

"I wonder what he'd done," Rachel mused, looking away, letting her eyes wander among the upper branches of the trees. Her voice was muffled by the handkerchief.

"No tellin' even what side he was on," Donald said as he marked an outline for the grave.

"That's sure!" Edward exclaimed. "The Tories say we're traitors and we say they are. Only God knows which he was."

The two men were now digging in earnest, forsaking talk as

they labored. Donald's breath was coming harder, and pouring sweat had made great damp spots on the blue denim of his shirt. The ground was clear of rocks here, and the two spades slicing in made a mellow chuffing sound, sometimes together, sometimes in dreary syncopation.

"How deep, Edward?" Donald asked.

"Pretty deep," Buchannon replied, "so the wolves an' bears don't smell 'im an' dig the poor fella up. He's had hard luck enough already."

Edward drove his shovel into the building mound of earth, thumbed off his suspenders, and peeled the shirt over his head. Rachel had never seen Edward without his shirt, and for a moment she stood looking. She could still see the massive musculature of his arms and shoulders that left him the unchallenged captain of any group of men in which he happened to be.

At last the grave was done. Donald put his right foot into Edward's palm and felt himself being lifted easily out, then he turned and pulled Edward up after him.

"Rachel," Edward called.

She had wandered back down toward the stream to escape the smell. She turned at his call.

"I think the best way to do this," he said, "is for you to ride your horse up here, so you can lean in close enough to cut the rope. Donald an' I'll lower 'im into the hole."

Soon Rachel was urging the nervous beast closer to the grave and to the body than the horse wanted to be.

"Here." Edward handed her his long sheath knife. "Watch it, it's like a razor."

She leaned toward the body, holding her breath against the stench, and steadied herself with one hand on the limb. The keen-edged knife sliced easily through the hemp, and as the last few strands began to snap and unwind, the two men took hold and lowered the young man down.

Soon the body was covered over and the soil smoothed until it appeared undisturbed. But darkness was setting in.

"Let's get to higher ground," Edward directed.

By the time they topped the next rise, the sun had set and the trail was obscured by darkness. This rise was not as high as the last, and provided no place to pitch. Ahead, the way dropped quickly down into another hollow. Absolute blackness closed in until the only way to tell the trail was the fireflies floating motionless between the trees. Their lights were long and slow, and imparted an eeriness to the trail's narrow world.

From somewhere came the voice of a whippoorwill, and close by, two owls were calling back and forth. They rode slowly along, depending on the horses to pick their way.

"Don't wanta pitch right on the trail," Edward murmured again. "We shoulda picked a spot while there was light." His voice was quiet, his ears alert for any signal of danger.

"I couldn't've stood it to stay in the clearing near that grave," Rachel said emphatically.

"Don't tell me that, Rachel," Donald chided. "I've known you to lay down in a salty hold where rats ran over your feet an' go off to sleep like a baby."

"That was a long time ago—"

"Well, look at this!" Edward said, and the sound of hooves stopped.

"The fireflies, you mean?" Rachel asked.

"Lightnin' bugs they're callin' 'em now," Buchannon chuckled, "but whatever you call 'em, you can see by where they are we've come into a wide openin' in the woods."

It was true. Off to their right a thousand hovering lights dipped and blinked, all unimpeded by a single tree. And above the blackness of a distant, uneven line of trees was the distinct blue-black sheet of heavens sprinkled with stars. It was the first time in two days they had seen the open sky.

"A meadow," Donald said, his voice hushed.

"Could be," Edward mused. "And even if there's not a level spot on it, that's where we'll bed down. I don't wanta go any farther tonight."

Carefully they turned into the clearing, again letting the horses pick their way. They found it was indeed a meadow, and that the ground was rolling and grassy.

"How about here?" Donald suggested.

Without waiting for an answer, he got down from his horse and began to feel about in his saddlebag. Edward and Rachel, still mounted, heard the scraping sound of flint on steel, saw sparks flying from Donald's invisible hands, and the growing fragment of orange light in the char. Within the minute, Donald had lighted a small pierced-tin candle lantern. He held it up, and it threw the light in a thousand fragments around them.

"This look all right, Edward?"

"Douse the light!" Rachel demanded.

Instantly, without question or word, Donald blew through the lantern door and darkness swallowed them again.

"Look toward the Great Bear," she whispered, ". . . then come straight down. Do you see?"

In the dark sky sat the Great Bear with its tail to the west. Beneath it, under the line of trees, was a small flickering flame. For a breathless moment they watched. The flame enlarged, sprang higher, and across the wide meadow came the faint, thin sound of screaming followed by a growing concussion that could be felt in the earth—the beat of approaching hooves. Edward grabbed the bridle and muzzle of his horse and the others followed suit.

Suddenly, stormy silhouettes, men on horses, came thundering, their yells of triumph and hatred filling the air! Rachel cringed, certain they were about to be run down . . . but the riders went by, leaving them untouched, and faded unknowing into the night.

"Good Lord!" Buchannon whispered, "we nigh had a battle right here!"

Rachel loosed the muzzle of her horse and looked back over her shoulder.

"Edward! Donald! Look!"

When they reached it, everything was swallowed up in blaze—a cabin of logs with only the dovetail-notched corners protruding from the conflagration, and the flames crawling rapidly across the shake-shingle roof. The heat was too terrible to come within a hundred feet. A short distance away, a barn was also burning, with a roar that equaled the roar of the cabin. Glowing cinders rushed upward in the heat-made wind, carrying sparks out over the wide meadow.

The three looked about in the glaring light. Small bundles of feathers that proved to be chickens with their necks wrung lay about the clearing. A milk cow with her throat cut was stretched in a blood pool. The zigzag rail fence had been pulled down. Smashed dishes and crockery littered the cabin yard.

"We're all wondering the same thing," Rachel said quietly.

"Yep," Edward said as he searched about with his eyes, "whether there's anybody in there."

"If there is, there's sure nothin' we can do to help 'em," Donald remarked.

"Not a thing," Rachel said, "but let's look around."

After a while they all reemerged into the light of the fires, each seeing in the eyes of the others that they had found no one.

"Well," Edward said, "let's go over, make up a place in the edge of the woods, and bed down. That thing's gonna be too hot for us to sift through, but we can look around some more in the woods tomorrow an' see then if anybody's still alive."

S I X T Y - T W O

THE three hid themselves, scattering into the woods. If some wandering band of marauders stumbled onto one, the other two might escape. Rachel crept in among a thick stand of bushy cedars near the edge of the clearing. There she spread her bedroll on the hard ground and slept the sleep of exhaustion.

When first light melded over the meadow and seeped into the edge of the woods, Rachel stirred and stretched her travel-weary limbs. Then, eyes suddenly wild, she listened. What *was* it that woke her? The happy chirp of small birds sounded in the limbs above, and the cawing of a crow winging his way across the meadow. But there had been something else. She was sure of it. Still she listened. Nothing. Perhaps it had been the falling of a cabin timber to the ground. Twice or three times in the night a crash from the fire had momentarily wakened her—or she had dreamed it. For a moment longer she lay, examining the night for dreams, just as she always did. Again, nothing.

The air smelled of burned wood, but other than the popping and crackling of the fire, and the birds singing their morning songs, all was silent. She raised up on her right elbow and peered out from beneath the low cedars. Above the clearing hung a white, smoky pall that obscured the tops of the encircling trees. The light of the sun cast slanting rays through the pall. One corner of the cabin was standing, otherwise only two ashen and glowing heaps marked where it and the barn had been. But in all the clearing's expanse, nothing moved.

There! She heard it again. A small, weak cry, but yes, there was no doubt—it was the cry of a child. Quickly she scrambled out of the bedroll, poured a little water into a cloth, washed her face and hands, pulled on her riding boots, and found a place to relieve herself.

She emptied the priming in her pistol and replaced it with new from the delicate horn tucked in the dark leather pouch on her belt. With the pistol at the ready, she crept out and began to circle the clearing, slowly, cautiously, from north to west, staying just within the shelter of the woods.

The dewy grass was quiet beneath her tread. Even at so great a distance, intense heat beat against her cheek from the heaps of char and ash. On the west side, with only a few slender saplings of hickory shielding her movement, she entered a wide patch of knee-high weeds that instantly soaked the thighs of her breeches with dew. Silently she moved on, until, in the midst of the weeds, her foot struck something soft yet so firm she stumbled and started to fall. As she caught hold on a sapling, a sudden chorus of thin, bewildered chirps came up out of the grass. Rachel regained her balance and spread the weeds to see.

On the ground, by the wet toe of her boot, lay a strange mass that she did not recognize. Her impression was that it had once been white but was now charred black as coal. About the blackened mass scurried a dozen chirruping chicks, bright yellow against the springtime grass and dark ground.

"Ohhh," she moaned, when meaning suddenly dawned, and with gentle respect, she nudged the mass over onto its back. There, uncharred, were the feet and underfeathers of a brood hen. As the chicks scrambled over the toe of her boot, Rachel could not instantly tell why, but her heart began to beat quickly and tears stung her eyes.

"She covered her chicks with her own body," she said under her breath, "saved them from the fire, and somehow reached this grassy place before she died!"

Jamie's face came full into her mind, and her heart felt near to bursting as she suddenly wondered what in the world she was doing here, hundreds of miles away from her little boy.

A sudden down-dropping of smoke bit her already tear-filled eyes and she began to cough. Stepping forward, she unexpectedly found herself on a path into the woods, and turned to follow it.

The trees among which the path meandered were a blend of

hardwoods and loblolly pine, very tall, their high branches spread wide above her head, the early morning light filtering brightly through the hazy smoke. The deeper Rachel went, the more ghostlike wisps of smoke came down to meet her and cloud her vision.

The path, well-worn at first, dissipated into an unmarked forest floor that began to ascend among old fallen trees and rocks grown thick with bright green moss.

Then she heard it again—the faintest whimper, stifled— somewhere to her left. She laid her hand on the scaly bark of a huge fallen tree whose spidery roots were spread wide in the air, her eyes flickering about as she listened, searching. Carefully, slowly, Rachel eased around the splayed roots, the pistol raised in both her hands, its cock drawn back to fire instantly.

There, beneath the trunk, was a huddle of five dirty children, hands clasped in terror over their own mouths. Cowering behind them shrank a woman, so horrified she could not speak.

At the same instant came the distant voices of Edward Buchannon and Donald, calling her name.

"Skeered? Not a bit of it!"

They were back in the clearing, the children gazing despondently at everything they had in all the world, consumed into ashen shambles. But Sebetha Seiver had shaken off her terror.

"No, sir!" she said. "It was sundown when they come bangin' on our door. Lord, it didn't scare me none! I've had neighbors come knockin' at all hours fer help, with me all alone, and I ain't never turned *none* of 'em away.

"Rousted us out like we was a bunch a wild hogs! Lined us up on the edge o' the clearin', threw pine-knot torches around the walls, and let 'er burn! I shouted at 'em till my throat hurt ... told 'em that if my boy Jim was here there'd be hell fer 'em ta pay! But they jest laughed an' called us names I couldn't never say, bein' the godly woman I am!"

At the mention of her boy, Rachel winced and Edward looked up, catching Rachel's eye. Sebetha Seiver ran steadily on.

"Soon ez I see the far spring up in the shingles, I know'd they wad'n no hope, so I grabbed the young'uns an' broke an' run into the woods like ol' split foot uz after us. It uz then we got to the place whur the young lady found us. But, oh Lord! We could hyear the roar'a them flames and the screamin'a the animals."

Edward broke into her steady stream of talk. "What about your husband, Mrs. Seiver?"

"He's off to the war, sir," she said, her chin coming up and her teeth clenched. "He's afightin' fer Lord Cornwallis off in Charles Town. Tryin' 'is best to put down this damned rebellion!"

"Your boy," Edward pressed on. "You mentioned a boy."

"Lord, yes, I got a boy! A fin'un, too. He—"

"Off to the war with his daddy?"

"No. His daddy told 'im to stay to home an' be a help to me. But he's been off huntin' for four, five days now. Bucks an' doe in these parts is gettin' harder to come by all the time."

"How old a boy, ma'am?" Donald said quietly.

"Old? He'uz twenty jest last month. Or so I think. Sorta lose track of time out h'yar."

She caught a glimpse of the question in Edward's eye, and her lower lip began to tremble. "Why?" she said, spreading her lower lip wide. "Why do ye ast?"

Rachel laid her hand on Sebetha Seiver's shoulder. "Just last night," she said softly, "we found a young man down the trail."

"And?" The woman's eyes were wide with fearful anticipation.

"He was dead," Rachel said, as tenderly as she knew how.

For a long moment Sebetha only stared, then she bowed her head and began to sob.

There was nothing to be accomplished by lingering. At their mother's command, the children gathered up the chicks and bundled them into the oldest boy's shirt. Rachel, Edward, and Donald filled their canteens from the well, helped Sebetha Seiver and the children onto the horses, and, themselves walking, led the little group out of the clearing and back onto the main trail.

The sun was about to set that evening when they came to the next cabin. There they ate, spent the night, and rose early, leaving the burned-out family behind.

SIXTY-THREE

WHEN the little party of would-be warriors forded the Catawba, or the Wateree, or the Santee—what it was called depended on where you were when you crossed it—what sky they could see through the towering treetops had been gray with clouds for days. They had ridden all yesterday in the rain, but it had slacked off in the night. That afternoon, when they found the Patriot encampment, large drops had just begun to splat down again, beating a slow tattoo on the broad leaves. It was the tenth of July.

"Mrs. Wolfe," said Captain James McClure with enthusiasm, "the only medical man I've got in this outfit is an old fella who learned his 'doctoring' about as far back in the woods as you can go. And he's rum-sotted more than half the time." McClure, a tall, wiry man of middle age, smiled warmly. "Ma'am, I'll see to it you have a shelter to yourself— one where you'll have privacy, and all the space you need to work."

He led her into the supply tent and pointed toward a bundle of canvas lying in the corner.

"It's a marquee tent, ma'am. Vertical walls, a peaked roof held up with a couple of poles. The roof on this one has scalloped edges trimmed in scarlet. Lots of room."

"Yes, Captain McClure," Rachel responded, "I'm acquainted with the marquee. I saw many of them at the Battle of Monmouth Courthouse."

McClure cocked his head and looked her full in the eyes.

"You were at Monmouth Courthouse?" he mused, admiration in his voice.

"Yes," she said, a look of sadness clouding her expression. "I was there looking for my husband. We were separated at the beginning of the war."

"I'm sorry," McClure said quietly, then turned to the men who had followed them. "Colonel, have your men pitch this marquee wherever Mrs. Wolfe chooses. See if you can have it set before the rain gets heavy again. And be sure there's good drainage so she won't have a river running through it!"

"Where will my brother and Mr. Buchannon be?" she asked.

"On the north side of the encampment. There's good ground there for the marquee if you'd like to be close."

"Yes, Captain, that's exactly what I'd like."

In less than five minutes a half-dozen young partisans were unrolling the dry canvas, and in another three had raised it, staked it down, and spread a ground cloth. Rachel lifted the flap and stepped into her new dwelling. Because of the gray day, the inside of the tent was dark. She walked about, then stood, holding to the pole lofting the tent's west peak. As she listened to the rain beating on the roof, she began to envision the things she would have to do within these canvas walls.

All about her, men were coming and going, bringing in her gear, laying her saddle in one corner, the bag containing her clothing in another. But to Rachel it was as though they were not there at all. Out of the heavy, wet air, she thought she heard the moaning of wounded men, and stood transfixed, heavy with the pain. It was not hallucination; it was real—and its time would come. The sounds faded.

"Mrs. Wolfe," the corporal in charge of the detail said, "are you all right?"

"What? Oh . . . yes. I'm all right. Thank you, Corporal."

"But you're white as a ghost. Are you sure . . . ?"

"Quite sure, Corporal. Quite sure."

The young man looked down at the heavy object in his hands. "Your stove, Mrs. Wolfe. On a day like this, it can take some of the damp out of the air. You'll be glad to have it."

With that he set the black iron box against the back wall. Soon it was crackling with a cheerful sound, and two glowing pierced lanterns cast a warm light about. There was also a folding bed that the men had brought and erected for her. For the first time in a month she lay on something raised above the ground. The grass-stuffed mattress crackled beneath her as she lay down and pulled up a warm wool blanket. Soon she fell into a deep sleep.

When Rachel awoke two hours later, it was to the sound of a thick stick of wood being slipped as quietly as possible into the stove. She looked toward the foot of her bed and found Donald closing the stove's iron door.

"Sorry, Rachel," he said. "But I thought you'd be glad for the warmth when you woke." The fire began to roar as the rush of hot air ascended the pipe.

"It's all right," she said, her voice hazy with sleep.

Edward was sitting cross-legged near the stove, making small circles on a gray pocket whetstone, sharpening the slender blade of his rifleman's knife. He glanced up at her and smiled. Rain was now beating down hard, and they had to raise their voices to be heard.

Donald sat back on his haunches, the palms of his hands open to the stove. Buchannon turned back his sleeve and tested the blade on the hair of his arm as Donald watched.

Donald smiled. "Shaves clean."

"Yep." Buchannon chuckled and wiped the hairs from the blade. Then he slid it into its sheath and put the whetstone back into the small leather bag. He looked up at Rachel, who was still blinking sleep from her eyes.

"Say, you really *rate*, 'Doctor'!" he teased. "Your brother an' I were just sayin' we think you oughta let *us* have this tent, an' you go over an' bunk with those smelly men they threw us in with."

Rachel smiled, but the smile faded quickly. "Men will die in this tent," she said slowly, her voice tempered with awe.

Edward and Donald exchanged glances.

"They will, Edward," she said. "When I first came in, I heard them moaning. There's going to be fighting, lots of wounded, and some will die . . . right here."

Both men dropped their gaze and nodded.

"How many men in camp?" Donald asked, trying to change the subject.

"Bratton told me about four fifty," Edward said. "Most volunteers right out of the Catawba wilderness."

Donald began to laugh for no apparent reason.

"That hit your funnybone, Calhoun?" Edward asked, surprised at what seemed an inappropriate change of mood.

"Our 'Carolina Gamecock'!" the younger man answered, half choked on his own laughter. "When Tarleton burned Sumter's *own* plantation, the Gamecock got on the move!"

Buchannon chuckled. "Sumter's quite a man . . . Cherokee fighter, peacemaker, traveler, now brigadier general and partisan commander."

"Before this is over, Tarleton may wish he'd stayed away from Sumter's place," Donald said flatly.

"Sumter was with Braddock on the Wilderness Road, wasn't he?" Rachel asked. She still lay on her bed, the wool coverlet pulled up over her. Her travel-stained riding boots stood by.

"He was there," Edward said. "But that was twenty-some years ago, and he's had a world of experience since."

"Did he know Washington?" she asked.

"Can't say," Buchannon answered, "but it could be he did, bein' in the same campaign with 'im."

"He'll be a good man to serve under," Donald said. "Sumter's got the experience, and he'll take us where we can hit the British hardest—the stronghold at Rocky Mount is next, I'm told."

The rain was coming down harder than ever, the roar on the tent roof louder. Buchannon paused, looking around and sniffing the air. "You know," he said, "it's rained so long, I think my beard's begun to mildew!"

Donald Calhoun lay back and laughed till the tears rolled. A smile broke across Rachel's face.

Then, above the sound of the pouring rain, they heard the beat and splash of a horse's hooves. Buchannon got up and looked out.

A rider on a large black horse, coming in from the north, reined up. The stallion's wet coat glistened and steam was rising from its neck and flanks. Instantly the rider was on the ground, calling out.

"Captain James McClure!" It was the voice of a woman. "Can you tell me where he is?" she said, catching sight of Buchannon in the tent door. Before answering, Buchannon threw on his rain cape, stepped into the downpour, and took the skittish horse by the bridle, stroking his neck and speaking soothingly to him.

"Now, boy," he said. "Settle down."

The woman's face was young, framed in a rain cape of black wool lined in red satin. Random locks of abundant blond hair were plastered to her left cheek. She was pretty, but her features were contorted with anxiety and with the exertion of a desperate ride. Rachel broke from the tent door, having pulled on her boots and cape.

"Captain McClure's tent is this way," she said, starting in that direction.

"I'll tend to the horse and be right along," Edward called after them.

"You're drenched," Rachel said, searching the young wom-

an's face, judging her to be several years younger than herself,
"and desperate!"

When they reached an officer's tent, Rachel called out for
permission to enter.

"Mary!" McClure jumped to his feet. "What are you doing
here?"

"Daddy! Oh, Daddy," she wept breathlessly, grasping his
arms.

"She just rode in, Captain," Rachel said quietly. "From the
looks of her horse, she came a long way."

"Thirty miles . . . if she came from home. Did you, Mary?
Did you come from home?"

"Yes," the girl choked out. "Daddy, British regulars and partisans, dragoons from Rocky Mount, at our house. They were
coming here. They burst in on James and Edward while the
boys were pouring bullets. Oh, Daddy, they're going to *hang*
them in the morning! And, Daddy, when Mama pleaded for
their lives, their commander *slapped* her across the face
with the flat of his *sword*!" At this the girl broke down and began to weep. "And they've ransacked Colonel Bratton's house,
too. You've got to hurry, Daddy! You've got to hurry!"

It was three in the morning before the rain finally eased off.
Nonetheless, James McClure's column of partisans picked their
way through the darkness and mud toward his home. Edward
Buchannon and Donald Calhoun were riding near the column's
head. Rachel, with her medical chest, rode near the middle of
the command, with Mary McClure at her side.

When bright candlelight appeared in a distant window, the
column slowed, advanced with caution, and found that the enemy was gone. McClure and his daughter dismounted.

"Mrs. Wolfe," he said, looking up at Rachel. Light from the
candle in the window made her features visible. "I'd like to
have you with my wife right now; but they may need you
more down the way."

"Then I'll go on with the column, Captain McClure," she
said.

Donald, who was close by, heard his sister's calm tones and
marveled. It was clear she felt at ease with danger. She was
growing steadier all the time.

"Bratton, you and Lacey take the men and go on," McClure
ordered. "Send out an advance of three before you move beyond Lacey's house; don't stumble into a fight tonight if you

can help it. As long as we've got the advantage of surprise, there's a good chance we can take this bunch where they sit."

"Yessir," Bratton answered. "Men, let's go!"

With that the column moved forward, the only sound the squish of thick mud around the hooves of the horses. It was a moonless night, and thick clouds had shut out even the ambient light of the stars, so that one could not see the rider in front or to the side. All was done by feel and listening.

"We're pretty close to my house," said a voice out of the darkness ahead. Rachel recognized it as Lacey's.

"Buchannon," Lacey said as they drew nearer, "I want a dozen men posted as guards around my place. I'd be glad if you'd go in with me."

"Why guard your own house, Lacey?" she heard Edward ask.

"My old daddy," the younger man said. "If ever there was a wild-eyed Tory, Daddy's one. When he sees us come through that door, sure as God made little guineas, he'll break and run to the British camp! Ho," he whispered, "we're there."

Rachel heard the creaking of wet saddle leather as a half-dozen men dismounted. She saw a light glimmer to life inside, the shadowy profile of a man outside the window, and suddenly there was shouting. Impetuously, and unnoticed, Rachel climbed from the saddle and was in the doorway when there came the crash of shattering glass.

Young Lacey and Edward Buchannon had entered the room together. It was a small clapboard house of three rooms where Lacey lived with his wife and father. Lacey had struck a flame and lighted a candle. As the glow spread across the room, there in the bed lay Lacey's young wife, cowering in terror. She had heard the squeaking of leather, the soft blowing of the horses, and every creak of the boards as the two men had entered. Lacey raised his finger to his lips, but she had cried out in relief.

The next thing the two men saw was the elder Lacey, standing framed in the doorway to another room. Dressed in a long white nightshirt, he was a grizzled man with large watery eyes and a firm-set mouth.

"What're you doing here, boy?" he asked firmly, his voice deep.

"The raid, Daddy. Mary McClure brought us word. She said they're gonna hang young James and Edward in the morning."

"What traitors to the Crown should expect!" the old man shouted.

"Depends on how you look at it, Daddy," young Lacey said, and added, "and you and I sure look at it different!"

Instantly, before either Buchannon or Lacey could react, the old man slammed the door between them and bolted it. There was the sound of bare feet running across the boards, then the shatter of glass.

Rachel pressed her back to the doorframe as young Lacey ran toward her.

"Get him!" Lacey screamed through the front door. Outside a shout rose. "Get him!" "There he goes!" Then sounds of a struggle.

Rachel moved quickly aside as four strong rebel partisans came through the front door, one behind the other, the old man laid across their shoulders, kicking his sinewy old legs, his nightgown riding up to the point of indecency as he screamed to be let loose.

"Quiet him down!" Lacey said under his breath.

Snatching the plaid shawl from a nearby wall peg while the guards held the old man, he tightly gagged his father's mouth. The old man's eyes flamed and his skin glowed red in the candlelight.

"Sorry to do that to you, Daddy, but we're here to save lives tonight. It may cost Tory lives for us to do it, but we're gonna give it all we got!"

Rachel watched the spectacle, feeling very small in the milieu of men pitting their strength against the feisty old Tory as he stood struggling, his eyes big with burning rage. A tear ran down young Lacey's cheek, and for a moment he turned away. Buchannon took a firm hold on the older man's arms.

"Let go of 'im, boys," he said to the partisans.

"Handle him easy, if he'll let you, Buchannon," the younger man said, and then, after a pause, continued, "but take him in and tie him to his bed. We can't have him runnin' loose."

Rachel stepped forward, entered the bedroom with them, and stood by the spread-eagled old man. A young private brought rope from outside and began to loop it around the man's wrists and then about the bedposts.

"You've got it too tight!" she said sharply.

He looked up, ready to tell her to mind her own business, but her glowering eyes made him hesitate. He loosened the rope. The old man mumbled something through his gag that sounded very much like " 'amn oo aa ta 'ell." When he said it, he was looking as furiously at Rachel as at all the rest.

"They're bivouacked along a high stretch of road near Williamson Plantation . . . between the rail fences." James McClure had rejoined the column and received the intelligence. He sat his horse in the darkness, plotting with Bratton and Lacey while the others listened. "It's Huck," he said flatly. "We didn't even *guess* he'd come this way!"

"Huck! I heard 'um talkin' about him yesterday," Donald explained to Rachel and Buchannon. "Christian Huck's a cavalry commander. He leveled an iron works near Camden just a few days ago. Un*god*ly profane man!"

"Profane enough!" McClure huffed. "Says that God Almighty's turned rebel, but if there were twenty gods on the Patriot side, the British would conquer them all!"

"How's Mrs. McClure?" Rachel asked.

"Shaken—a bruise the width of a sword blade across her cheek." He shifted tensely in the saddle. "By heaven," he said, "I'll see Christian Huck pays for *that*!"

"They're gonna make it easy for us, Jim," Bratton said, "bedded down along the road like they are. First light's no more'n an hour and a half away. Let's lay our plans and get ourselves in place!"

The trees were still dripping when the eastern sky began to glow over Williamson Plantation. As the light crept slowly through the gray clouds, the tents of the dragoons gradually became distinguishable from the high grass and the trees and the rail fences behind them. Beyond the fences, on the edge of the woods, horses grazed. In the high grass the Patriots lay waiting.

The wet ground beneath her seeped through Rachel's leather coat, through her black linen breeches, and her elbows sank into the grassy mud.

Edward had tried to stop her, told her she was more valuable back out of danger. What would she be able to do for the wounded if she had a bullet in her own head?

She knew he was right, but reasoned she might be able to move about among the wounded and thus save lives that would not otherwise be saved. Edward had insisted, but she had done as she pleased. It was the only thing to do, she felt, when you were arguing with a man.

On a leather strap over her shoulder hung a medical bag—bandages mostly, several simple straps for tourniquets, to stop bleeding in the field. But her saws for amputation, the bullet probes and such, she had left at the Lacey house. That's where she would set up hospital after the battle. But for now she would concentrate on saving life in the field.

She carried no rifle or musket, just a pistol, loaded and ready. She had already decided not to fire it unless personally attacked at close quarters. Her long hair marked her clearly as a woman, and it was at least possible that simply because of her sex she would be left alone.

The field was hushed, the dragoons blissfully ignorant that the grass held anything but rabbits and toads. Edward and Donald lay ahead of her, one to her right and the other to her left, both prone in the grass. She could see the tension building in Donald's body, the readiness in Edward's movements. She could feel her own pulse pounding in her temples and her breathing trying to run away with itself.

She watched Edward as, with his right hand, he pushed up the front of his dirty broad-brimmed hat for a clearer view. She saw him lick his right thumb, wipe the frizzen of his rifle, and check his priming. The grass about them was full of men, but none made a sound. Above, in the limbs of the tall pines, grackles, black as night, clamored harshly for the sunrise.

At last it came—the thin notes of a bugle somewhere in the encampment, sounding reveille.

Those hidden in the grass watched.

A moment more, and here and there men stuck their heads from their tents and looked about sleepily at the morning. Others stepped out stretching and yawning. Stiff from another night on the ground, they ambled awkwardly off into the woods to relieve themselves. Cooking pots and mess dishes clanked and banged. Thick wisps of smoke rose up from reluctant, damp wood. Then, in the tall grass, rifle locks clicked as they were drawn to full cock. Rachel saw Buchannon push up again on the brim of his hat, saw him carefully pick out a man kneeling over a small fire, and gaze down the barrel of his rifle. She knew exactly the one he was aiming for, and her body, tense as a harp string, began to quiver. In a moment she would see human life taken in a premeditated, deliberate manner. She laid her own pistol in the grass, lest her trembling hand set it off and all advantage be lost. A thousand thoughts raced through her mind. Jamie . . . where would Jamie be at this moment . . . and Salali, what would Salali think if she could see—

"Fire!" The hoarse scream shattered her thoughts as four hundred fifty rifles boomed a ragged staccato, erupted flame, and a sudden pall of white smoke leaped out of the grass to cover the meadow. She could not see what had happened to Edward's man—the smoke was too thick. Not one among them knew if his target had fallen.

What next?

Up, all of them, the pounding of feet and four hundred fifty voices screaming as they bounded toward the encampment. Rachel was amazed to find herself running through the tall grass, screaming as loud as she could.

Among the Loyalist tents and over their fires, men had crumpled straight down or pitched forward on their faces, while others dove for cover and for their own muskets. McClure's men were covering the ground like madmen, Rachel in their midst. Out came the defenders to meet them, bayonets fixed and lifted. But suddenly the Loyalists hit the rugged rail fence, and it stopped them as if they'd hit a wall.

Across the field, from the door of the Williamson Plantation house, the Tory leader Christian Huck belatedly rushed out to rally his scattering men. He had run a dozen paces when a rifle's crack cut him to the ground.

And it was over . . . just that quickly.

Rachel was standing in the grass, bewildered. What could she do next? She searched the field with her eyes for wounded Patriots. There was one pitched forward over the rail fence. She ran to him, struggled to lift him up from the fence and stretch him out on the ground. Then she knew—he was dead . . . a man not quite as old as Edward, one she had never seen before. She closed his eyes with her hands.

She looked about for others, and found that there were none—not another Patriot dead, not another wounded. She climbed over the rail fence that had been so decisive in the battle, and walked boldly out among the enemy dead and wounded.

They were everywhere—draped over the fence, lying dead in the campfires, the smell of their burning flesh blending horribly with the smell of burned gunpowder. Some had been cut down in the doors of their tents. Others had run into the forest; she had seen them going as hard as they could.

All around her Patriots were shouting orders to Tories who

had thrown down their guns and were holding their hands high in the air, hundreds of them.

She knelt beside a man who was still alive, and her hands were bathed in his warm blood as she tried to stanch a wound in his side. Nothing she could do would stop the flow.

Suddenly she heard herself chanting:

"And when I passed by thee, and saw thee polluted in thine own blood, I said unto thee when thou wast in thy blood, live; yea, I said unto thee . . ."

All the rest of Rachel's day would be taken up with the wounded—bandaging, probing little tunnels of flesh for bits of lead, giving orders . . . amputating, spending every ounce of her strength. When evening came and she had done what she could, she fell wearily down on her open bedroll, gazing up at the blue of a clear summer day. Donald and Edward were resting a few feet away.

"What's going to happen now?" she wondered half aloud.

Donald chuckled. "With a victory like this, there'll be volunteers comin' out'a the woodwork," he said. "I'll bet you that in two days this little army'll more than double. They'll come by the hundreds, volunteers from all over the Catawba District to fight for the Carolina Gamecock!"

"Just the beginning," Edward said quietly. "There'll be no rest for anybody in the Carolinas till this thing's done. The hate's just boilin'! There're gonna be battles an' raids, neighbor against neighbor from now on. God help us, Calhoun, Rachel. It's gonna be a dark time!"

SIXTY-FOUR

THAT same day, nearly a thousand miles north by road, the abrupt hills of Connecticut were overspread by a blue and creamy sky. It was an extraordinary afternoon. Wherever one turned, the hills were rich with green, the air still, perfect for lolling about on the grass, or standing and trying to find the line that divided the blue of the sky from the blue of the distant hills. Up over the face of the sun, the sky had turned white with high clouds.

On the near crest of one of those hills—called the Turkey Hills—stood a small but strong house, built on rectangular stone blocks. Just outside the house's two doors there were men walking about with a lackadaisical air, as though it was something they did every day, and that while they were doing it, nothing ever happened to bring them to attention. Each of the men carried a military musket in the crook of his arm. Occasionally one would step to the door of the stone house, look about inside, and then come out again to resume his aimless pacing.

Inside the blockish little house was a single room with a wooden floor, once brown, but now worn by the passing of many feet, until the stain remained only around the room's edges. The floor was worn most in the center, around a three-foot square of flat, heavy iron. The entire scene, in fact, gave the impression that the house itself had been built exclusively for the purpose of surrounding and sheltering the iron square.

On closer inspection it was clear the square was a framework of heavy iron bars, fastened closed by two massive padlocks of brass. Between the bars, a narrow shaft went straight into the earth, its walls dark and in places exuding a vomitous green corrosion. From somewhere in its depths came the orange flickers of a burning pine knot.

Drew Wolfe lay on a hard wooden bunk in total darkness, listening to the slow drip, drip of water, its hollow echo making a metallic ring down the adjoining corridor. From the blackness came the sounds of men coughing, whispering, shuffling about.

Drew was far from sleep, but his last candle was gone and his spirits were low—so he just lay in his bunk with a single blanket drawn up about his shoulders, thinking. What else was there to do but think? It would be a God's blessing if they still allowed them to dig the copper as a part of imprisonment, but for one reason or another they would not. It would at least have given them something to do, and they could have made use of the muscles that were atrophying to flab.

Drew's feet were getting cold. No wonder; the blanket was barely long enough to reach from feet to shoulders. But it was a heavy wool blanket, thank God, not like the pitifully thin thing poor Taylor in the next alcove had.

It was strange, Drew thought, that this blanket and he had become intimate friends during their months together. While sitting at his pine table, he wrapped his shoulders in it, and while walking through the corridor that led to the lower spring. And, of course, when he slept. And yet he didn't even know the blanket's true color.

He had seen it only an instant in the light, when it was thrown down to him before the rusty iron grate clanged over his head. He had almost lost his balance on the ladder trying to catch it. Later he had examined it by the poor light of the prison's hog lard candles, and it looked to be a dingy blue with a black stripe the width of a man's hand across each end. But in the darkness why should it matter what color it was, as long as it kept him warm? He didn't know why, but it did matter.

It had been more than a year since that night when the back-woods Patriot band had ambushed him on the south branch of the Potomac. There had been blood streaming from the gun-shot wound in his left shoulder, but they had thrown him facedown in the sand, and so roughly bound his wrists that the stiff hemp rope had torn the flesh till it burned like fire.

There had been a hasty trial in which no one had believed his story. If not for the cool head of one sensible old man in the settlement, they would have hanged him. As it was, they had cinched him tight, and three of the village men had es-corted him eastward across the Blue Ridge. On the banks of the Shenandoah they met a Continental patrol that took him off their hands. Then a circuitous route on water and land brought him to this place, where, they said, he would wait out the re-mainder of the war.

"This place"—it was, they told him, not far from Hartford, an old copper mine whose deep shafts the local inhabitants had turned into a prison before the war. General Washington had chosen New Gate—for so they had named it, after the infa-mous London prison—as a holding place for Loyalists and Tory raiders, as well as for court-martialed American soldiers.

Lord! It seemed he had been here forever!

"Wolfe?"

"What!" he said, startled. Lost in thought, he hadn't heard the approach of Samuel Collins.

"Saw you were in the dark," the coarse voice said. "Thought you might enjoy a little light."

Collins had nursed his weekly candle issue with greater care than Drew, and came carrying the lighted one in his hand. Drew roused himself to a sitting position on the edge of his bunk and looked up in Collins's face.

"Come on in, Sam," he breathed. "It's good to see some light."

Collins was a likable man, one of the few of his fellow prisoners Drew enjoyed. He was a Loyalist from up the coast, a British spy—taken in the very act. He was above forty years old, a tall man with a narrow face, an especially long distance between his nose and upper lip, and a hairline that had receded nearly to the top of his head. His front teeth were crooked, but he had a warm smile, and eyes that shone bright with intelligence—even in the light of these hog lard candles. He had won Drew's friendship the instant they met.

Collins sat down in the cell's only chair, held the candle up over the center of the table, and fixed its base in the drippings. Then he leaned his lanky elbows on the table and stared at the flame, a pleasant expression on his face.

"Precious commodity, light," Drew said.

"This is my last candle," Collins replied. "There won't be a new issue for at least two more days."

Drew sighed. He was surprised to find sudden tears swimming in his eyes. He wiped hard at them, embarrassed, and turned his face away toward the seeping wet wall and its green tracings of copper ore.

"It's a far harder life than I dreamed, Sam," he said. His low voice rang hollow. "Pretty bitter thing to do without light. . . ."

"But worse to be without a wife and baby," Collins finished for him. "I'm lucky," he said. "My children are grown, and Maggie can take care of herself pretty well. So it's not so bad for me."

"Well," Drew said, "I'm feeling sorry for myself."

"No, Wolfe," Collins said, smiling. "That's not your way, to feel sorry for yourself. You feel bad for your wife and boy—just like any good man would in your circumstances. Besides," he said, "Elijah himself sat under the juniper tree for a while. And like Elijah, you're only a man."

"A disappointed man!" Drew answered. "You know, Sam, I've always prided myself on being able to adapt. I left the country and adapted to the city. I left the city and adapted to the country again. I adapted to America, to the loss of my wife, then I adapted to another wife. But I cannot bear having my path to Rachel and Jamie blocked!" He rose to his feet and began to pace the narrow cell. "Every hour I sit here and chafe and boil and fret! I've written letters to Rachel, letters to Washington, letters to a Quaker friend in Philadelphia—but I never hear a thing back. It's inconceivable to me that no one would respond. It can only mean that my letters are never posted! Now why? Why in God's name!"

He laid the fingers of his right hand over his mouth. They began to shake, and his lips began to quiver.

"Rachel can't know where I am! She thinks I'm dead. So does Bowman." He turned abruptly to Collins and, crouching forward, spread his hands on the table. "Collins, I've got to get out of here! I've *got* to!"

Collins drew a deep breath and let it out slowly, all the while looking Drew steadily in the eyes.

"Don't try it, Drew," he said.

"You mean you're not with me!" Drew said, anger rising in his voice.

"We've been over this same thing a dozen times before," Collins answered. "Now, Drew, you're a sane man . . . most of the time. And in the moments when you're sanest, you know it can't be done—not without the loss of life, even your own. Think of William Crawford, that horse thief, and his friend who tried to dig their way out. Both of them lie buried where their escape tunnel caved in on them. And the men who saved all the charcoal from their fuel allotments. They built a fire against that boulder, hoping the heat would crack it and they could get through to the outside. Instead the smoke filled the mine and three of them died of the poisoned air. Besides, every opening is bound with iron. If you try to force your way out, you'll wind up like those men; and then what your wife probably *thinks* is true *will* be true. You'll be dead, and never see them again. So, as you like to say, 'There's an end!' Don't let this obsession kill you."

Drew paced back and forth. Collins was right. He clasped his hands behind his back, stood to his full height, and breathed deeply, collecting himself.

"Take my advice, Wolfe," Collins said. "Time'll come when you thank me for it."

At last Drew turned to stare emptily into the candle flame. "Hope, Collins. That's what it takes to stay sane—hope. If I had just a little of it left."

Collins's candle had burned down to a stub and the flame was beginning to flicker. Both men gazed at it with longing.

"My wife and boy have borne the burden of my choices," Drew said. "Jamie is three years old, and I've never held him! Oh, Sam, if I had only known, I never would have gotten involved with this war."

"Listen to me—" Collins said.

"Do you know that right now my wife has probably not only given me up for dead," Drew went on, "but that she may have married somebody else! That my little boy is calling somebody else 'Daddy'!"

"Wolfe, get hold of yourself! Now think. All you say may be true, but for your own sake, you'd better learn to think a different way. If your wife is half the woman you tell me she is, every day she reminds that little boy what a courageous man his father is . . . or was. You've got to believe it, Wolfe. You've got to say it to yourself over and over again until you know it's true!"

He reached out with his huge sinewy hand and gripped Drew about the wrist. "Do you hear me?"

Drew took a deep breath. "I hear you, Sam," he said quietly.

The spent candle wick wavered in the pool of melted lard . . . and then darkness.

SIXTY-FIVE

IT was the eighteenth of August, mid-afternoon. In the five weeks since Williamson Plantation, Donald had become weary of killing. He and Edward had taken the lives of at least twenty men, and had come close to losing their own.

After the battle, hundreds had come pouring out of the Catawba District to Sumter's flag. Flush with victory, they had ridden down on Rocky Mount, where, after eight hours of hard fighting that got them nowhere, they had withdrawn. Then, twelve days ago they had attacked the British outpost at Hanging Rock, killed two hundred enemy, and lost a dozen of their own. They had done this boldly, within grabbing distance of Camden, a stronghold of more than two thousand British.

Horatio Gates had been sent to command the southern army, and had come marching down from Charlotte to attack Cornwallis at Camden. Before the attack, Sumter and his partisans had taken three hundred of Gates's men and ridden off to Wateree Ferry to cut British communication lines between Camden and Charles Town.

Wateree had been like taking candy from a baby. They had captured eighty-six loaded supply wagons, three hundred head of cattle, a few sheep, and more prisoners than they could take care of.

But the morning after Wateree, on their way through the bottomlands to rejoin the main army, they heard the sounds of battle. Suddenly a rider had burst out of the trees, going away from the noise like a bat out of Hades. He reined in and gave Sumter the story. Gates and Cornwallis had blundered into each other in the night. Patriots were being cut down like wheat under the scythe.

When he heard it, Sumter's face had turned to ashes. He had wheeled his column and the wagons around, starting north for the safety of Charlotte.

Night and day they had worked their way through the bottomlands on the west side of the Catawba. What with the cattle and wagons and cannon and prisoners, going had been slow and miserable. Sumter was not about to leave all the plunder for Cornwallis, and certainly not the prisoners to fight again. But forty miles—that was all they had made—in forty hours.

At last, a little while ago, they had reached Fishing Creek —or Catawba Ford, as some said—and Sumter had called a halt. He had posted a rear guard a way back. It wasn't likely, he said, that Cornwallis even knew they were near. Everybody was exhausted, and it was time to rest.

Sumter had ordered the horses unsaddled, teams unhitched from the wagons, prisoners guarded, and all arms stacked. Then he had set the example by spreading his own bedroll, and in a few moments had dropped off to sleep.

All tension disappeared, and the whole camp—like a great sail when the wind drops down—had gone limp. Here and there men built cooking fires. Some went right down to the water, stripped, and began to bathe. Others, like Donald, had laid down to sleep. A few, like Edward, were nervous about the whole business, and stood watch, rifles in hand.

Just before Donald closed his eyes the last time, he raised his head and looked down along the creek bank. Rachel was there, tending a young man wounded at Wateree Ferry. Rachel glanced toward Donald and smiled.

The wagon in which she had ridden the last forty miles had been drawn up under a spreading oak at the water's edge, and in it lay the wounded soldier. Rachel stood on the ground at the wagon's end, slowly unwrapping his bandaged right shoulder.

At Wateree, right in the midst of battle, she had come upon this boy lying in a pool of his own blood. She had knelt over him, pulled his shirt away from the wound, and stanched the bleeding by pressing a strip of cloth into it. Then she had bandaged it over, desperately hoping infection would not set in. The bullet must have been nearly spent when it struck, for there was no exit wound, which meant the pellet of lead was still inside. But there had been no time to probe for the bullet then; she would wait until after the battle or, if worse came to worse, until they had rejoined Gates.

Riding in the wagon beside him, Rachel had looked down at his young white face, her heart aching for him. He was some mother's child, some boy who came into the fighting not knowing what he was getting into. When news of the slaughter came, and the wagons had wheeled about to begin to run from Cornwallis, she had held his head in her hands to keep it from bouncing about on the hard boards. She had winced whenever he cried out, had bathed his dry lips with cool water, and had learned that his name was Toby Johnson, only fourteen years old.

The air beneath the great oak tree was still, and as Rachel unwrapped his shoulder, perspiration rolled down her arms.

Toby woke up. Rachel looked down into his eyes and cupped the palm of her hand over his forehead. He was hot to the touch.

"I'm hurtin'!" he whispered through his parched throat.

Without speaking, Rachel reached for the wooden canteen hanging on the end of the wagon, uncorked it, and with one hand placed it to his lips while she raised his head with the other. When she lowered the canteen, the boy reached to pull the spout back to his mouth, crying out at the pain. Rachel lifted it again and the cool water flowed over his lips once more.

"Slowly now . . ." she said. Her voice was relaxed and low. "You mustn't take it too fast . . . there. That's enough for now."

She lowered his head gently, and he turned his eyes toward her, searching out her face.

"Who are you?" he asked weakly.

"I'm Rachel," she said.

"Rachel? Oh, Rachel," and tears began to roll down his cheeks, "what am I gonna do? I hurt so bad."

Rachel looked about at the soldier who had just come up beside her. He was a short, stout man with kind eyes.

"Can I help, Mrs. Wolfe?" he asked.

"Perhaps you can, Mr. Compton," she said softly. "I must take the bullet out of his shoulder, and it's going to hurt him like the fires of Hell! If you and some others could hold him while I work . . ."

Compton went away to find help, and Rachel turned back to the boy.

"Toby . . ." she said.

He had been drifting off, but her voice startled him back into wakefulness. "Yes!" he said abruptly.

"Toby, do you have a mother?"

"Yes'm, I do," and he began to weep again.

"Where does she live, Toby?"

"Up in Charlotte," he said, half dazed. "She didn't want me to come, but I wouldn't listen to her. When General Gates put out the call, I just naturally had to come. O Lord!" he said amid his tears. "I wisht I'd 'a listened to 'er. She'll be heartbroke when she hears I've died!"

"Hush, Toby! Don't talk so. You've not died!" She leaned over very close to him, so close she could smell his rancid breath, and for the hundredth time in two days smoothed back his hair with her hand.

"But I'm goin' to. Ain't it so? Ain't I gonna die?"

Rachel felt her heart breaking inside. She could not lie to the boy. Death was not the time to be lied to.

"I don't know, Toby. I just don't know whether you'll live or die."

He turned his face away and his chest began to heave. Suddenly he caught his breath. "Oh, it hurts!"

At that moment Compton and four other men returned. One

was as burly as Compton, another was a giant of a man—
Tanner, she thought she heard them say—and the other two
were of ordinary size, but appeared uncommonly strong.
Compton had chosen well.

"I'll need you to hold him as still as you can," she said to
them. "I'm going in after the bullet."

"Why don't you just leave it in, ma'am?" one of the
ordinary-sized men asked. "Ain't you likely to make 'im start
bleedin' all over again?"

"Because he's fevered, Mister . . ."

"Stewart, ma'am. M'name's Stewart."

"Because he's fevered, Mr. Stewart. If there's infection in
the wound—as there probably is—it might help to have the
bullet out."

Reaching into the chest of surgical tools open on the ground
beside her, Rachel drew out a pair of small forceps, a device
somewhat like scissors or pliers, but long and very narrow,
with little cups on the end that would just fit themselves about
a lead ball.

"Mr. Compton . . ."

"Yes'm?"

"I need a bullet. Is there one nearby?"

Compton laughed. "There'd better be, ma'am. An army
camp where there ain't no bullets 'nearby,' as you say, is a
pretty sorry—"

"You know what I mean."

"Yes'm." His face fell, and he reached into a pouch on his
belt and handed her a ball of pure lead.

Rachel weighed the bullet in her hand for a moment, eyeing
it. It was of about fifty gauge, or .45 caliber. Rachel thought
how little good it was really likely to do, but she looked down
at the boy.

"Toby . . ." He opened his fevered eyes and mouthed her
name, but no voice came out. "Toby, I want you to take this
ball in your mouth . . . Can you hear me, Toby?" She raised
her voice. "Take this ball in your mouth and clamp down on
it with your teeth!"

His eyes widened. Toby had heard of this kind of thing, and
had prayed to God it would never come to him.

"What're you gonna do, Rachel?" he asked, lifting his head
up from the wagon board. There was fear in his voice.

"I'm going to take that bullet out of your shoulder," she
said. "Bite down on this ball for me, as hard as you can. It will

keep you from gnawing your tongue in pain, and it'll help you not to cry out."

Reluctantly he opened his mouth. With her fingers, she placed the lead ball between his teeth, and he clamped down. Rachel nodded to the men, and they gently but firmly took hold of the boy. Compton held him at his hips, the two average men were at his feet, the other burly man held Toby's right arm, and the giant vaulted up into the wagon and laid one great hand on the boy's shoulder and took Toby's left hand in his own.

Rachel was impressed by the kindness she saw in the eyes of the giant. She had seen him about camp many times, but hadn't met him until now. She looked down at Toby, who was looking about wildly, then up to the giant, who nodded he was ready.

"Ready, Mr. Compton?" she said.

"Ready, ma'am."

"Bite down, Toby!"

She spread the wound with her fingers, quickly inserting the cups of the bullet extractor. Toby pulled at his arms and screamed between his teeth.

"Bite hard, Toby!" she said, and thrust the extractor half its length into the wound. The boy raised at the waist with all his might, but Compton laid the weight of his considerable body across Toby's, holding him immobile. All the while, the giant with the kind face was pressing hard on the boy's upper body and whispering reassurances in his deep voice.

Rachel felt her own heart pounding like trip hammers in a mill. Perspiration poured down into her eyes so she could scarcely see. Still she had not reached the bullet. Suddenly Toby's jaw parted and the lead from between his teeth fell to the wagon floor. Rachel glanced down for an instant. In the few moments she had been at work, he had flattened the bullet so that it was only a thin, irregular sheet of lead. He was throwing his head from side to side wildly, his mouth fully open and his screams tearing at the midday air.

She felt the movement in his shoulder wrenching the instrument almost from her grasp.

"Mr. Lewis! Hold his head still." And she thrust the instrument deeper.

Abruptly, she pulled her hand smoothly backward, withdrawing the extractor's full length all at once, and held it up.

"There it is, gentlemen," she said, smiling. "Just what we

were after. Had we only known just where to cut, we could have reached it more easily through an incision in the back of his shoulder."

Compton, still leaning over the boy's body, looked at her and grinned admiringly. She was holding it out toward the kindly giant for him to see, smiling as she did, when a distant crash rang out from behind. The giant's head jerked back, his eyes widened for an instant, and a rush of red blood spurted from his forehead and splashed down across Rachel's hands. Then the giant fell headlong across the boy's body, down to the ground between Compton and Rachel.

Stunned, Rachel looked at Compton. His eyes were darting about when there came the instant thunder of hooves and the sound of "Huzzia! Huzzia! Huzzia!" from a band of furiously riding horsemen.

S I X T Y - S I X

IN shock, Rachel jerked her head around, staring at the place upstream where Donald had been sleeping on the bank. His bedroll lay empty. Edward was there, the brim of his hat pushed up as he shot at the oncoming charge, using the willow trunk as a shield. Then she saw him drop to a crouch and come running along the creek bank toward her, firing behind him as he came.

"Follow me, Rachel!" he shouted. "We'll make a stand downcreek a ways!"

"I can't leave this boy, Edward," she screamed after him. But he didn't hear, and quickly disappeared. Rachel looked about to discover that the unconscious boy and dead giant were her only company.

She glanced down at the boy. Compton was right; the disturbed wound had begun to pour blood, and a pool, fresh and red, was widening across the cracked boards of the wagon floor. Charge be hanged! As the first horseman came rushing past, her own duty was clear.

Squatting by her surgeon's chest, she took up suture material and the proper needle—a curved one that could dip into the flesh easily and come up and out again. Knowing that hesitation or unsteadiness could cost the boy his life, she lifted the needle up and slipped the thread through the eye on the first try.

Then she rose, squeezed the wound together, and coolly plunged the point into the flesh at the edge of the wound. The boy did not flinch this time—a godsend, for all her helpers had fled. Three quick stitches, then four, the proper knot, and it was done.

Rachel took a deep breath and again smoothed Toby Johnson's brow. Thank God he had passed out from the pain as she had withdrawn the bullet.

Rachel was not even slightly aware of the thunder of hooves rushing around her, even when a bullet tore a man from his horse and he thudded and rolled to a rest near her feet; nor of the clatter as stacks of arms were run down and scattered over the encampment; nor of the strewn bodies of men. But then a sudden voice brought her to her senses.

"Captain! Arrest this woman!"

She looked up to find herself overshadowed by a man in British commander's attire. He was young, with flashing blue eyes and flaming red hair, and aback a skittering, lather-flecked horse. He was not a large man, but there was no mistake about it, he was in complete command.

A memory sprang into Rachel's consciousness. Was it possible? Yes, somehow she was sure it was he!

Before his subordinate could respond to the command to arrest her, Rachel had reached smoothly beneath a neatly folded towel that had remained untouched throughout the operation, withdrawn a pistol, and leveled it at the young commander's face. In the excitement, she did not even hear the smooth click as she drew the hammer with her thumb, but the red-haired commander did.

"Brigadier General," she intoned evenly—he smiled, acknowledging her words—"I am a doctor, and this young soldier is my patient. I stay with him."

"And if not?" he asked calmly. His mount skittered about. He raised his hand, signaling the captain to hold.

"If not, you will not live to know it," she said.

"Madam," he said, guarded amusement in his face, "you've no idea how *big* the mouth of that pistol appears to me at this moment. I would be grateful if you would aim it in another direction."

She was gazing down the steady barrel, the blade sight fixed on the center of his head.

"Do I stay with the boy?" she said.

"Look around you, dear lady. You have many duties to perform before the sun sets."

"And you will let me tend them?"

"You may attend both your wounded and mine," he said.

Rachel held the pistol steady, considering. The captain stood at bay, his eye on the commander.

"Is the word of Bloody Banastre Tarleton any good?" she said slowly. "The man who boasts he's raped more Patriot women than any other soldier in the British army?"

His smiling lips made a fine line of contempt. "Your choice is simple," he said. "Lower the pistol and see, or kill me and be killed. But if you make the latter choice, of what good then would you be—either to your people or to mine?"

He was right. Her only hope was that his men needed medical assistance as badly as the Patriot fallen. Slowly she lowered the pistol, letting it fall to half cock, and held it toward the captain, who then rode forward to receive it.

It was night, and the flames of a hundred torches and campfires beneath the trees cast circles of light on the banks of Fishing Creek. In the center of the encampment stood a hospital tent. The soldiers walking about outside could see its warm lamplight and Rachel Wolfe's shadow moving on the walls, growing large and then receding as she worked within.

And there were voices, some groaning, some weeping, some only the raspy sounds of labored breathing. These were the voices of her vision five weeks ago.

The yellow light glistened on a sheen of sweat covering Rachel's face. Her sleeves rolled above her elbows, she used a rod to lift a cotton cloth from a copper kettle of boiling water, held it to let it drip and cool, then twisted and wrung till it was only damp. She turned to the man who had just been carried in. Though the fighting had been over within minutes, this man had not been found until now. He was unconscious, but his groaning had led searchers to the place where he had fallen. With the wet cloth she began to clean his terrible wound.

"There's no way for this man to live," she said to the litter bearers who stood looking on. "Look at this. Shrapnel from an exploding shell has torn into his bowels, flung the filth all through his abdominal cavity. It will be a God's mercy if he never regains consciousness. Take him out and bring me someone I can help."

The litter bearers didn't move. She glanced up at them to find them staring at her. She could see the shock of death's presence on their faces, that and a trace of admiration for herself.

"Could you men bring in more water?" she asked kindly.

"Yes, ma'am," they said, and immediately bore the dying man out.

Rachel pressed both hands into the small of her back, breathed deeply, and looked around the tent. She wiped the sweat from her forehead and pushed back a stray lock of hair that had fallen before her eyes.

What a pitiful sight this was. It clearly had not taken Tarleton long to finish his work once he'd begun. Of Sumter's men, he had killed a hundred and fifty outright, and taken three hundred prisoners of war—of whom she was now one. Somehow—she did not know how—the others had escaped and taken some of the wagons and supplies with them. "Bloody Ban" had recaptured forty-four of the wagons taken in the last week, and all the cattle. Well, at least we won't starve, she thought. All of Sumter's Catawba Indians had escaped, fading like smoke into the forest. It's certain we'll never see them again, she thought. They know this country, and they owe loyalty to no one.

At that moment she looked about to find a girl standing in the shadows of the tent door.

"Betty," Rachel said, "come in."

Betty Morgan was a camp follower—the young wife of an equally young soldier, and had been with them since the week before Hanging Rock. As the girl entered, Rachel saw that her eyes were red and swollen from crying.

"Betty, what is it?" she asked.

"I can't find him!" the girl sobbed. Rachel noticed then that Betty had a tin lantern hanging down dejectedly in her hand, the candle burned very low.

"Jim? You can't find Jim?"

The tears burst from the girl's eyes again, and without speaking buried her face in Rachel's shoulder. Rachel took her in her arms, patting and stroking her back comfortingly.

"We'll find him, Betty . . . for better or worse, we'll find him. But it's too dark for you to go looking anymore tonight. And whatever you do," she added, holding the girl at arm's length, "you must not go out looking alone! These men are not like ours. If they catch you, they'll take you out and force you. The only reason in the world that I'm safe is that they need what I can do for them.

"You must go back to your tent now and try to get some rest."

Rachel ushered her to the door and watched after her as the girl went slowly across the encampment to her tent.

"Dear Lord," she mumbled, "what's to become of us? And where are Donald and Edward?"

Tarleton gave his men three days to rest, and on the twenty-first, with cattle in tow and wounded loaded in the wagons, he ordered them forward. Another four days of slow moving and they reached the stronghold at Camden, where the very next day a contingent of troops started all prisoners on the road to Charles Town.

Rachel was in one of the hospital wagons with the rebel wounded. There had been no room to leave them at Camden. There were already a thousand sick and wounded British regulars unfit for duty there, and the place certainly would not bear any more.

The ruts of the road were deep and hard, for the weather the last few days had been dry, so the wagons jostled and pitched without mercy. Never mind, she thought, I'm accustomed to the "little inconveniences of military life." Strange how one got used to it. After being without a roof over your head for a month or more, a dark rainstorm became hardly more than the passing of a light breeze. She realized she'd learned to pay no attention to the sun and to the knocking around horses and wagons gave her. She rubbed the tips of her fingers together— her hands had grown rough with the work—and laughed silently to herself. She had always prided herself on the smoothness of her hands.

"How hard life is on our vanities!" she said, unaware that she had spoken aloud.

"What was that, Rachel?"

Rachel looked at Betty Morgan, who sat across from her in the jostling wagon. Betty had found her Jim, but he was badly wounded, and it had become Rachel's duty to amputate his right leg. He had screamed out in protest when he learned

what they were about to do—but it was either take off the leg
or let him die a terrible death.

"Nothing, Betty. I was talking to myself."

Rachel watched the two as Jim lay with his head in her lap,
suffering written all over his face. Betty was proving stronger
than Rachel had believed possible.

It was an open wagon, and as the sun climbed higher it began to beat down on the men's faces. Rachel got up and went
from man to man, arranging little shelters of cloth to shield
their eyes from the sun.

Rather than sitting again, she braced herself against the side
board and, shielding her own eyes against the sun, gazed up
and down the long column of wagons, watching guards as they
passed. The one riding past now turned to her and smiled, but
it was not a smile that she liked. It seemed to her that these
men had a hard and reckless look in their faces. They were
professional soldiers—thousands of miles from home and family. The best the army could give them was adventure, a little
glory perhaps, and the opportunity for a random conquest. She
did not return the smile.

At Fishing Creek, Rachel had searched for Donald and
Edward, going among all the bodies awaiting burial. Neither
had been among them. So still there was hope, and for now
she was quite willing to settle for hope as the best she could
find.

S I X T Y - S E V E N

IT was midwinter, early February of '81, one of those "in-
between days," too warm to freeze, too cold to be comfortable,
and it was damp—bone-chillingly damp. Above, the skies
were clear, a pastel-blue that only made the damp seem colder.

This morning, while there was still a light touch of frost on
the grass, a man came riding hard up the road to Buchannon
Hills. The old house servant, Quincy, heard him coming and
stepped out. Up the drive the rider came, the brim of his hat

turned up by the wind, furious little clouds of steam pouring from his horse's nostrils. Quincy was at the edge of the piazza when the man reined to a halt.

"May I help you, sir?" Quincy asked.

"Quincy, tell Mrs. Buchannon that the British have taken Wilmington!"

Quincy's face went blank with shock. "Oh no, sir, it just can't be!"

"But it is, Quincy. You tell 'er, now! I've got to spread the word."

And he was off again, leaning forward in the saddle as Quincy ran to tell the mistress.

"Quincy, have Josiah hitch the iron-grays to the calash!" Abigail Buchannon ordered.

"Ma'am," the old man returned, pleading, but retaining all his composure, "you surely don't mean to go into Wilmington with British soldiers there!"

"That's exactly what I mean, Quincy. We'll be safe enough, I think. And we may get news of how the war's gone up in the Piedmont!"

As Abigail walked hurriedly out of the room, Quincy turned to Salali and shook his head.

"It's all right, Quincy," Salali said as she gathered herself up. "I'm going with her. I'll say nothing to Abigail about it, but there may be prisoners."

In a matter of minutes the calash drawn by the team of four iron-grays was racing toward Wilmington. The narrow road of white sand lay before them, and the forest's green walls were rushing by on either side. Salali sat silently, wondering if after all Quincy might have been right—that she and Abigail had taken leave of their senses. At the last moment, God only knew why, Abigail had decided to bring Jamie. However safe an occupied Wilmington might be, it wasn't safe enough to bring a child along. But what was done was done.

"With Edward away," she said, "I have to keep my ear to the ground."

Salali only listened, her dark eyes gazing first at Abigail, then at the empty expanse of road disappearing behind. Jamie was in the seat between them up on his knees, facing ahead. The folding top of the calash was down, since it faced ahead and would only have acted as a wind scoop. The old landau would have been better on a cold day, since it had a top that folded from both front and back, but Abigail had sold the landau only two weeks ago. Money was getting tighter all the time, and when a wealthy planter up near Castle Hane had offered her a good price, she had snapped it up. So Salali and Abigail sat with their backs to the wind, cape hoods pulled up over their heads, a bearskin robe tucked warmly about them. But it worried Salali the way Jamie was snuffing up the wind.

"Jamie!" she said, an edge to her voice, "turn around and get your face out of the cold air! You're going to make yourself sick."

Jamie immediately turned about and snuggled himself into the seat between the two women, pulling the thick lap robe up under his chin, meanwhile casting a baleful glance up at Salali. Salali believed in the Cherokee way of raising children: give an abundance of love, never spank, never shout, but restrain the child when necessary. Abigail thought this method totally wrong, but kept her advice pretty much to herself.

Salali sloughed off Jamie's glance and returned to her thoughts. It had been four months since their last letter from the Piedmont, and she was nearly frantic.

There had been both good and bad news of the war. In October nine hundred North Carolina Militia and Over-the-Hill men wiped out a thousand Loyalists under the command of Major Patrick Ferguson at King's Mountain. The battle was a great loss to Cornwallis, and an enormous boost to Patriot morale.

Then Congress had given command of the southern army to thirty-nine-year-old Nathanael Greene, Washington's best. Last month Greene had sent veteran Daniel Morgan into the field, and Morgan had promptly wrecked Tarleton's legion at a place called Cowpens.

Victory did at last seem to be swinging toward the Patriot side, but the capture of Wilmington would surely bring terror to the Lower Cape Fear.

Wilmington had roads running out in five directions. The road from New Bern entered from the northeast, then crossed the river on a long bridge to continue down the coast. Another came from Castle Hane to the northwest, another went downriver to Brunswick, and yet another ran to the sound. It was the road to the sound that led in from Buchannon Hills.

It was noon when at last the steady beat of the hooves slowed to the rhythm of a walk, and the singing of thin iron tires cutting through sand fell to a hum. Jamie had dropped off to sleep, but when the carriage slowed, he awoke, and looking around, found that they were in Wilmington. The upper part of the city was on high ground that dropped off quickly to the business district which crouched down on the banks of the Cape Fear. Above the buildings, one could see the tall masts of a dozen ships, their brightly colored pennants snapping in the chill wind.

"Look at the people!" Jamie shouted as they rolled toward the wharves.

"A crowd at the docks, ladies," Josiah called back. "Looks like a ship's about to moor."

Salali stretched her neck to gaze over the heads of the gathered throng. Sailors on the yardarm were furling the mainsail of a ship flying the Union Jack as it glided gently toward the wharves. There was the sudden clank of the windlass, and the heavy splash of an anchor as it dropped into the river.

A black boy came running past, and catching his eye, Josiah called out, "What port's she from?"

"From Charles Town!" the boy shot back, hardly hesitating in his run. "They say she's got prisoners on board!"

"Oh my Lord!" Abigail said with disgust. "Prisoners of war! What more do we need—to make Wilmington a prisoner of war camp!"

"I've no idea why they would bring them here," Salali mused, "unless . . ."

"Unless what?" Abigail questioned.

"Unless they were prisoners from the Lower Cape Fear . . . being released to their families."

Abigail was thoughtful. "If there were such people on board, and if we could just talk with them . . . Josiah," she said, "let the horses rest while we watch."

From where Josiah parked the calash, the women could see everything that was happening on deck. After a long wait, while the ship's boat was lowered to bring the captain ashore, a Royal Marine emerged from the ladderway, bringing prisoners up behind.

When the first man came blinking into the bright sunlight, Salali caught her breath and started from her seat. He was a young man with flaming red hair.

"Donald!" she whispered, and put her hand to her mouth.

He was the same height, the same build, but no, it was not him.

She sat back in the calash, covering her eyes with her swarthy hand, bitterly angry with the darkness of war, not caring to look further.

Abigail called out to Josiah and Jamie, who were carrying an oaken bucket of water to the horses, "I'm going to talk to the captain."

Josiah quickly set the bucket down, to help her from the carriage. She was approaching the stocky man in a captain's uniform on his way up from the dock, when she heard Jamie's voice behind her.

"Mama!"

Salali looked up and Abigail whirled around.

"Mama!" he shouted again, and he ran down toward the dock.

"Oh, dear Lord!" Salali whispered, "it is! It really is!"

As Rachel came out on deck, she winked in pain at the blinding sun. She had been in the hold of this ship for two weeks, all but three days of which had been spent anchored in the strait within sight of old Fort Moultrie. Before that she had spent four months in the stinking hull of a prison ship anchored within Charles Town Harbor. Four months of darkness and gloom, close bodies—some of them dead for as much as three days before being taken out and thrown weighted into the sea.

The wind snapping the ship's pennant up above struck a chill deep into her bones, but in spite of its blinding light, the sun felt good on her face. And there was the air—the fresh, clean, crisp air! After the close, smelly hold, this was heaven.

When the ship had left Charles Town, no one told them where they were going. She was afraid it would be New York or Canada, where she would be confined for the rest of the war. She was sure that, like thousands of others, if she had to wait out the war in the dank hull of a ship, she would never see Jamie again, or anyone else she loved.

When her eyes became accustomed to the light, Rachel looked toward the docks and the little town above them.

Suddenly she knew! This was Wilmington!

She had been in this very spot in Edward's longboat, during one of their wonderful excursions up and down the river.

"What are we doing here?" she asked of the Royal Marine nearest her.

"I've no idea, miss," he said, hardly turning his head toward her.

Suddenly she heard a small voice calling out above the murmur of the crowd. It struck fire in her heart, and she looked across the water. There he was, running and pushing his way frantically along the dock and through the crowd.

"Jamie!" she screamed. "Oh, Jamie!" And she began to sob as though her heart would burst.

"I'm free! Oh, Jamie, I'm free!" Rachel sat weeping in the calash, the bearskin lap robe thrown about her thinly clad shoulders, arms about Jamie, who lay in her lap with his cheek pressed against hers. His right hand held her close. Rachel's face and arms were thin, and she had grown pale.

"Paroled!" Salali said in astonishment.

"Yes," Rachel answered in spite of her tears. "Paroled on my word that I'll take no further part in the war."

With her free hand Rachel reached out for Salali and pulled her close. For a long moment she held her, both women weeping for joy. Then she reached out to Abigail, then down to Josiah, and stroked his dark brown cheek. As she did, she smiled and her eyes sparkled through her tears.

"How wonderful," she exclaimed, "to again touch those you love."

"And you didn't know you were to be paroled?"

"No—not until it happened."

"Rachel . . . ?" Salali felt a tightness in her throat. "What about Donald? Is he alive?"

Rachel looked her friend full in the eyes. "I don't know, Salali," she said, shaking her head. "I just don't know. I saw him last at Fishing Creek . . . Edward, too. They were there, and then suddenly they weren't. The best I can say is that they were not among the dead or the wounded."

"Thank God! Oh, thank God!" Salali dropped her head forward and began to cry softly, and Abigail took a deep breath, looking away.

"I'm exhausted," Rachel said. "It's as though every ounce of strength has been drained from my body. Months of confinement, now freedom—how am I to take it all in?"

"You must lie down," Salali said, wiping at her own tears.

"Here, move over to the back seat of the carriage, and we'll cover you with the lap robe."

"Josiah," Abigail said, "we must take her home."

"Yes'm!" Josiah answered, smiling broadly.

Rachel felt the softness of the plush leather and the warmth of the robe as Salali's hands tucked it up under her chin. She felt the warm tears coming to her closed eyes all over again. The very first time in four months she had felt the loving care of another human being, and the sensation was overwhelming.

She felt the carriage sway as Josiah climbed to the driver's seat, felt movement as he turned the team onto Third. She heard Abigail and Salali talking softly as they settled into the front seat. For a moment she opened her eyes and saw Jamie looking lovingly at her from his place between her two wonderful friends.

They had almost reached the corner of Market and First, when Rachel sensed the coach was slowing.

"Is something wrong?" she asked without opening her eyes.

"Somethin's happenin' up the street," Abigail said quietly.

From less than a block away came the thunder of hooves as a troop of men came galloping in. They were leading a riderless horse.

"Who . . . ?" Abigail asked.

"British soldiers!" Josiah exclaimed. "Whoa," he said to the team, and reined them in right in front of the Burgwin house. The Burgwin house was a white mansion, the finest in town, but the owner was away in England and the house had been inhabited only by Burgwin's servants. Rachel opened her eyes to see Salali pointing ahead.

"Abigail, look!" Salali said. "That riderless horse . . . there's a man tied across the saddle!"

"That's Cornelius Harnett!" a strong voice broke in. A tall, gray-haired, well-dressed man who appeared to be in his late forties had reined up beside them. By now a crowd had gathered, a murmur of surprise and disapproval rising from a score of throats.

"Harnett." Rachel's eyes went wide and she pulled herself to a sitting position. "I remember Jacob Harnett," she said. "He read the new Declaration of Independence to the crowds five years ago, right here in the streets of Wilmington." Rachel could see it in her mind, the excited crowd lifting Harnett to their shoulders, carrying him jubilantly through the streets, shouting and singing. Now she caught sight of his helpless form.

"He's dead!" Salali exclaimed.

"No," said a voice from out of the crowd. "He's alive."

They were close enough now that Rachel could see him clearly. Harnett was trussed hand and foot, riding on his belly across the back of the cantering horse. She could hear his sharp gasps as every bounce knocked the breath from his lungs. Harnett's long graying hair, unbound, nearly swept the ground with every downward motion of the horse. His mouth hung open, his reddened face contorted with pain.

The laughing troops reined up in front of St. James Church in the next block, and a flock of startled white geese, honking and flapping their wings, scattered before them. Quickly, a soldier came about and cut the rope holding Harnett to the saddle. He slid and dropped heavily to the ground. Two redcoats yanked him to his feet, then dragged him limp and gape-mouth up the steps of the church.

"Why Harnett?" Rachel wondered aloud.

"Our most popular Patriot," the unnamed man at their side returned. "Wilmington's Committee of Correspondence, member of the Wilmington–New Hanover Safety Committee, and our man in the Continental Congress in Philadelphia. Now he's a British prize . . . an object of choice humiliation!

"Poor devil!" the stranger went on. "Harnett's a sick man. They marched him on foot all the way back to Wilmington from Spicer's place out on the north road, where they found him. When they got to the edge of town, they threw him over the horse and galloped him in." He shook his head slowly. "He'll not last long."

Near the front of the crowd a woman screamed, and the crowd drew back. At the top of the church steps two young soldiers, their coats off and sleeves rolled to the elbow, were swinging a fine oaken pew between them. They let it go, and it came crashing down at the crowd's feet. The soldiers burst with peals of raucous laughter. Before their laughter could die away, two more soldiers emerged with another pew on their shoulders. With one continuous motion they ran and threw it with all their might. This one landed beyond the first, scattering the crowd farther. The second team of pew-throwers raised their fists into the air and broke into cheers of victory.

To the side of all this at the top of the steps, his arms folded over his chest, a young officer stood, smiling confidently. He was enjoying the ransack of St. James Church as much as his men.

"Tarleton!" Rachel spat. "Banastre Tarleton!"

"That little man?" Salali exclaimed.

"That *little man*," Rachel answered, "is Bloody Ban."

S I X T Y - E I G H T

A gray, rain-washed light fell through the large west window into the parlor where Rachel sat alone. Cupped in the palm of her hand, a small tabby kitten only a few weeks old, all fur and curiosity, lay beneath her breast, batting Rachel's moving fingers with its paws. Then, tiring of the game, it lay with head and ears raised, its eyes wide, looking about.

How wonderful the old house seemed to her now. Two months of exposure to wind and rain, riding and plodding through mud and southern August heat, following, always following, on a course of death. And then long imprisonment within coldly indifferent walls . . . Yes, the old mansion was heaven, a place of friendship and love that she wished never to leave again.

Three days in bed and plenty of good food had restored most of Rachel's strength, yet somehow she felt as though she could sleep for a month.

On the hearth at her side, behind bright brass andirons, a fire of oak burned. The fireplace was framed in black marble which in turn was framed with a carved white frieze beneath a wide mirror. Altogether the fireplace and its ornamentation rose to the ceiling in a tower of marble and wood that ended in a grand joining of column and entablature.

Perhaps it was the fire's warmth, she mused, that gave her this feeling of security; a *false* security, she amended. And the rain, pouring so hard, the world so awash in every direction, that not even Tarleton's legion would be out working mischief. So she burrowed down deeper into the cushions of the Queen

Anne chair, stroking the kitten and watching the blessed rain as it spattered on the panes of the tall window.

Then behind came a quiet footstep that broke softly into her reverie. Without turning, Rachel spoke.

"The rain's still coming down," she said quietly.

"Beginning of a long spell," Salali answered. "It might last a whole month." Salali breathed a long breath that contained a world of sadness. "I've known Februarys when we never saw the sun," she said.

"There were just such months when I was a girl in Scotland," Rachel said as she watched the gray water wash down. "Many more such days than we have here."

"More?" Salali asked, incredulously.

"Oh, much more," Rachel answered. "Perhaps twice as much. I loved it . . . and I miss it. But the rains of Carolina make me feel at home . . . more at home than I felt in the North."

The kitten chose that moment to bound out of Rachel's hands, and with two leaps was in Salali's lap, startling her, but she began to stroke it, almost immediately feeling the deep throb of its purr.

Rachel looked at Salali, at the sadness in her eyes. It was a sadness they all felt these days, the men being gone, but she felt especially sorry for Salali, Donald's disappearance coming so soon after their having fallen in love.

"Oh, Salali," Rachel blurted, "for your sake, I pray Donald is alive. He will make you a wonderful husband!"

In the long silence that followed, the only sounds were the beating of the rain against the window, the slow deep tick of the great clock on the landing, and soft breathing through tears.

Then a loud pounding on the front door interrupted their thoughts. Rachel whirled about, startled. The roar of rain must have drowned out approaching hoofbeats.

Once again the pounding came, harder and louder this time. Both Rachel and Salali dabbed at their tears, waiting, hoping the knock had nothing to do with either of them. At last Quincy reached the door and there were hurried voices.

"There's a young woman here who's a doctor!" someone asserted.

"Where have you heard this, sir?" Quincy's polite old voice carried clearly through the hall into the parlor.

"Well, is it true or not?" The stranger's anger was rising.

"I cannot say, sir," Quincy answered discreetly.

"Damn you!" the stranger shouted, followed by the sounds of pushing and stumbling.

"Salali, don't follow me!" Rachel whispered as she hurried out. "Just listen and be careful!"

Framed in the entryway, poised and in command, Rachel saw Quincy leaning awkwardly against the foyer wall, where a soldier had pushed him.

"You're looking for me?" she asked, her voice calm and even.

In spite of his urgency, the young man was struck dumb at the sight of Rachel. For a moment he simply stared. He had expected someone who dabbled in herbal medicine and midwifery. Then, coming to himself, he stood to his full height and reached out a hand to help Quincy, who was ruffled but unhurt. Quincy ignored the offered hand, yanked his vest down into place and stood, ready to intervene.

"Our captain has a knife wound," the soldier said. "I'm told you have certain skills. . . ."

For an instant Rachel hesitated. Why should *she* who had just returned from the iron grip of a British prison help British injured and wounded? But instead she asked, "How badly is he hurt?"

"Ma'am, that's what we want you to tell us!" There was more than a touch of acid in his voice.

"Then don't stand there, soldier . . . bring him in," and Rachel turned about. "Bring us blankets, Quincy," she said as she stepped toward the fallen man.

Then she bent over and gazed into the wounded captain's pale, ashen face.

Suddenly, as if she had seen a dead man, Rachel reeled and braced herself against the wall. She passed a hand over her eyes and stood straight again, trying to steady herself, struggling for breath.

"Ma'am," the young soldier said, "if you can't bear the sight of blood, you're no good to *us* as a doctor!"

Rachel was breathing rapidly, her face pale as death. Quincy returned with the blanket and, catching sight of Rachel, hesitated. Rachel steadied herself.

"Quincy," she said quietly, "get my medical things. Soldier, bring this man to the kitchen."

The bleeding captain's fellow soldiers lifted him onto the blanket and, with a man at each corner, followed Rachel as she hurried through the house. They had gone no more than a dozen steps when blood soaking through the blanket was ready to drip to the wooden floor.

Rachel led them through the hyphen that joined the great house to its separate kitchen. Her heart was racing, but not from exertion. What must she do now? What in heaven's *name* must she do now!

The kitchen was darker than the parlor, and it took a moment for eyes to adjust.

"Mary!" Rachel demanded, "light as many candles as you can and set them around this table . . . and open all the shutters."

The plastered stone walls were white, and the wide pineboard floor creaked under their hurried feet. From a beamed ceiling hung bunches of spices and baskets of grains, as well as three newly killed chickens intended for the evening's pot and a hock of smoked ham. Rachel was sorry the soldiers had seen the food, fearing they would take it.

At the far end of the kitchen stood a fireplace so enormous that one might easily walk into it and never stoop. On its stone face hung all manner of iron utensils: tongs, ladles, large forks, pans, and on a crane in the fireplace cavity, a great iron kettle under which one of the servant girls had just built a blazing fire.

"Hot water, Agatha!" Rachel said to the girl. At the sudden appearance of soldiers, the girl stumbled back to the wall, badly frightened. "Hot water, Agatha!" Rachel repeated. "Step!"

Agatha recovered and swung a small black pot over the rising fire.

"Here," Rachel said, turning to the soldiers. They laid the young man, blanket and all, on the great trestle table. The soldier who had been giving the orders faded awkwardly into the background as Rachel took command.

At that moment Salali revealed herself, entering from where she had been standing just outside. She took one look at Rachel, on the opposite side of the table from her, and silently moved around until she was near enough to speak softly into her ear.

"What's wrong?" she whispered, laying a hand on Rachel's shoulder. "You're white as a ghost."

Rachel whispered back, "I'll tell you later. Just help me."

Quincy entered the room at an awkward trot, a medium-size chest covered with black pebbled leather in his arms. He set it on the table and opened it, laying out its trays one by one. Mary returned with a basketful of candles in their holders and quickly arrayed them on the edges of the table, while the girl Agatha followed behind with a taper, lighting them.

The captain lay with perfect stillness, his head thrown back, palms up, fingers splayed. Rachel pressed the tips of her fingers against his throat. She could scarcely feel the faint rapid beating of his heart. His breath was coming rapidly, and suddenly he began to thrash his arms about.

"He's dying," she said firmly. Then, as if disregarding her own words, she said, "Hold him still." For a moment longer her unbelieving eyes lingered on the wan face.

Moving quickly, she took scissors from the chest, cut away the leg of the man's trousers, and split his shirt's long tail.

"There it is," she said. "The knife went through the inside of his left thigh. It just missed the bone."

Without an instant's hesitation, she tightened a tourniquet around the man's thigh, between his heart and the wound, then, with her scalpel, she widened the knife's cut, following the hidden muscle lines. Flesh and fat split easily before the razor sharpness, then the muscle, and in a short moment her fingers were probing the deep incision, sponging blood with clean white cotton cloths.

Salali, standing behind Rachel's left shoulder, watched every movement of her hands, and saw calm returning to Rachel's face.

"The artery . . ." Rachel said as she felt inside the wound. "It's completely severed . . . disappeared into the tissue. I need a tenaculum."

With bloody fingers Rachel reached into the tray and removed an instrument about the size of a pencil.

"Salali," she said, "move around to the other side of the table and hold a candle up where I can see . . . yes, there, that's good."

Peering into the wound, she inserted the tenaculum, and feeling carefully, captured the artery's end on its delicate hook, pulled it out, and pinched it closed with her fingers.

"This is a small artery," she said, a faint smile crossing her face. Her movements became slow and very deliberate. "I can tie it off, and he'll be no worse for it. Quincy, cut me a length of the heavy thread. And if our tie holds . . . and if infection doesn't set in . . . If . . . if . . . if, always if!"

A sudden chill ran down Rachel's spine and her mind began

to race. For an instant she looked up and found Salali's eyes staring intently into her own. Salali knew what she was thinking, but not all.

I hold this man's life in my hands, Rachel thought. He's the enemy. I could save his life or I could take it from him. If I let him die, they'll burn the house over our heads. And if I save him, he will go back to battle and kill again. But it's a surgeon's duty to save life—regardless of circumstances. And if I save him, I save Buchannon Hills from burning.

But there was more ... more that Salali could not possibly guess. She had no way of knowing that this soldier was the one man in the world whom Rachel hated as badly as she hated her father. He was a man worthy of death.

Then, as she was slipping the thread around the end of the severed artery, Drew's voice came to her; from a day in the distant past when she stood beside him in St. George and the Dragon Inn in Philadelphia. Clearly she heard him say, "If we tie this knot in the ordinary way, it might fail and the artery re-open. We would not know he was bleeding again until he was dead. So we tie it with a surgeon's knot, crossed and looped, pulled tight, that's it. Again. Again. Perfect!"

A sudden shock went across her shoulders and into her arms, right down to her fingertips. Yes, of course. She could make them think she was doing everything to save his life, and yet kill him with a carelessly tied knot. No one would be the wiser. The plantation might be saved out of gratitude for her efforts and an enemy disposed of in one stroke. But then, she thought again, there is duty ... to life ... and to man. "Love your enemies," she heard her mother's voice say, "do good to them that hate you, and pray for them which despitefully use you. ..." The words rang in her ears. But what good had such advice done her mother?

A cold sweat broke out on Rachel's forehead and her hands began to perspire. She glanced at Rob Wolfe's ashen face. Rachel looked again at Salali, saw her smile the faintest smile, felt some unspeakable thing pass between them.

She tied the knot securely—a surgeon's knot—and began to close the wound.

SIXTY-NINE

RACHEL was tying the last suture when she looked up to see Abigail come through the kitchen door. Abigail's eyes went fearfully from soldier to soldier, then to the man on the table, then to Rachel's eyes.

"Where shall we put him?" Rachel asked matter-of-factly. "He can't be moved from the house."

"The middle room on the northwest side," she answered quickly, "on the third story."

That night Rachel and Salali sat in Rachel's room. A fire was burning in the little fireplace, and an occasional puff of steam would rise as an errant drop of rain found its way down the chimney. Rachel sat on the settee, her legs drawn up in front of her and her arms around her knees. She was staring emptily into the fire and telling her hidden story.

"You *know* him?" Salali had said in amazement, then jumped at the most plausible explanation. "You must have met him in Charles Town—while you were in prison!"

"No," Rachel answered quietly, not taking her eyes from the fire. "No, Salali. It was in Philadelphia, ten years ago."

"Philadelphia!"

"He's Drew's brother's son."

Salali drew a quick breath. "Rob?" she exclaimed.

Salali's dark eyes flashed with surprise and she could feel her own heart beating. "What a strange, mystical thing!" she said. "Rachel, Rob didn't come here by chance! There's *meaning* to this."

"No meaning I care to know!" Rachel retorted.

For a few moments Salali reflected on the implications of this peculiar reunion.

"I thought Rob was a doctor," she mused.

"He was. I don't understand, either," Rachel said. "All I know is that it's Rob, and that he's the one man I hate as much as I hate my father."

"It's a miracle you didn't kill him," Salali said in a solemn whisper.

"That," Rachel answered with emphasis, "was a glorious opportunity! But I couldn't . . . it would have been desperately wrong."

"All's fair in love and war," Salali answered, "and this is both love *and* war."

"Perhaps . . ." Rachel said with a faint smile. "More of hate than war, though."

"What will you do when he wakes up and recognizes you?"

"I don't know. For now, he's just another man struggling to live. It's my duty to help him do that. It's not so hard now, seeing him as he lies near death, helpless as a kitten. But when he regains consciousness and his old personality comes to life . . . well, the sooner he's out of here, the better off we'll be!"

For three days after the blood flow from his veins had been stanched, Rob Wolfe lay silent and unknowing. For two days his pulse tripped rapidly, his breath racing quick and shallow. In spite of the hate Rob had ground into the grain of her being, Rachel refused to let anyone else watch over him.

The first day, as she had sat staring at his face, pallid in the lamplight, common sense told her she had nothing to fear from his sudden reappearance. But her heart was in turmoil, like a kettle boiling over the fire, bringing up the crust and scum of old emotions. It seemed just like yesterday that Rob Wolfe had abandoned her in those squalid rooms near the wharves in Philadelphia; like it was this very morning he had beat her senseless and left her for dead. And the anger she felt was fresh and exquisite.

It was the fourth day, early morning, when, for the sixth time since midnight, Rachel entered the room where Rob lay. The rising sun was casting its first rays brightly across the coverlet and over his face, making his pasty skin appear lifeless. For an instant, in fact, Rachel thought he was dead. But when she touched him, the warmth of his skin told her he was not.

Quietly she turned back the covers and drew the nightshirt borrowed from Edward Buchannon's wardrobe up until the bandages about his left thigh were exposed.

Rachel had been removing the bandage every day, watching closely for putrefaction in the wound; knowing that if rot set in, there would be little she could do, short of amputation. But she had already made up her mind that no matter how rotten

the wound became, she would not amputate his leg. She had
amputated more than a dozen times during the Catawba campaign, and later in the prison, and it always left her on the
verge of despair. No, Rob's life was not worth that to her.

This morning the flesh around the sutures was an angry red
in the soft white of his thigh, but she could see that it was
mending. She pressed gently about the incision. Then, for the
first time since the operation, he stirred and his eyelids began
to flutter.

Suddenly he began to thrash his shoulders about. If he tore
the sutures . . . Rachel took him by the shoulders, trying to
force him back against the bed, but he was too strong for her.

How could a man in his condition have such strength?

His eyes opened wide and he stared wildly, first at the ceiling, then at the walls . . . and then his eyes fell on her. He
raised his head from the pillow and grabbed her wrist, gripping
it with a strength that seemed impossible.

Instantly the blood rushed from her face and she twisted violently away, opening her mouth to scream. The wildness in
his eyes was the same as on that night ten years ago, and the
grip around her wrist was the same grip that had held her
while he bludgeoned her senseless.

She did not scream, but wrenched free then stood back,
breathing hard, the line of her lips thin and white as she
clenched her teeth and the muscles of her jaws stood out. She
looked down on the irrational man before her, rubbing her
wrist, hatred boiling in her eyes.

He raised up on his elbow, his eyes wide, confused. Rachel
took one deep breath, then another, and boldly approached the
bed again.

"Shhh," she said soothingly. "Rob . . ." The name felt
strange on her lips. "Lie down."

But once she was within reach, he fastened onto her arm
again. She flinched, closed her eyes, and bit her lower lip, but
did not twist away.

"Rob," she said, calmly prying his fingers loose, "you must
let go of me. There . . . now lie back."

His eyes locked on to hers. There was no hostility there,
only confusion. Once free, she cradled his head and laid him
back.

"Who . . . who are you?" he said with great difficulty.

How weak his voice sounded. Good! The last time she had
heard that voice, it had overpowered her with fear, and she

had sunk into unconsciousness with his vicious words thundering in her ears.

"I'm your doctor," she said quietly. She had not said, "Rob, it's Rachel." No, she couldn't bring herself to do that. There was no reason. Rather, she added, "You very nearly died. You've got to lie still. Rest, and get well."

He lay back, his lips moving without sound. At last the words she had spoken seeped into some small place of consciousness. "Died?" he mumbled.

"Nearly," she answered.

"Oh," he said without emotion. His eyes closed the second time, and he drifted back into sleep.

Rachel laid her hand on his brow; it was hot. His fever was climbing, making him sleep, making him see things and dream dreams. To her surprise, she felt the smallest pang of compassion for him. She hesitated a moment, then reached out slowly and brushed back his sandy hair.

She had forgotten the color of his eyes—an ice-blue that was always striking. Ten years had made a great difference in his face. Two years older than she, he would soon be twenty-nine. She shook her head.

For a young man who wanted money and women as Rob had, how could he have spent ten years as a common soldier? Perhaps as a captain he had just enough power over other men to satisfy him, and enough freedom to keep him happy.

For several moments she stood contemplating his features. Then she knelt down beside him, rebandaged the wound, tugged the cover up over him, and slipped quietly from the room.

SEVENTY

It was the day after Rob first stirred—the last Tuesday in February.

Rachel was standing on a chair in the parlor, returning freshly cleaned candle sconces to their places on the wall. The day was cold, and the servant girl Mary had just added a fresh armload of wood to the open fireplace. The logs had already begun to crackle in the blaze as Mary swept up the bits of bark and dirt that dropped as she brought them in.

"Mary?" Rachel said.

Mary looked up from her sweepings.

"Does this sconce hang crooked?"

"Yes, ma'am, it does," Mary returned. "But if you move the bottom a little to the right . . . Yes, ma'am. There, that's just right."

A sound from somewhere high in the upper part of the house caught Rachel's attention, and she gazed upward, as if trying to look through the ceiling.

"Whatever could that be?" she said, looking quizzically at Mary.

The quick sounds grew louder.

"Somebody comin' down in a hurry!" Mary answered.

Salali appeared at the top of the last landing. She was bounding down the stairs, holding both hands over her mouth, crying and laughing all at once. She ran through the parlor past Rachel and Mary without seeing them, and burst outward through the front entrance.

"What on earth?" Rachel exclaimed. "She didn't even stop for a cloak!"

Rachel stepped down from the chair, running after her as far as the door, and looked out.

The temperature had plummeted the night before, the sky was heavy gray, and snow was falling. The big white flakes plummeted through the windless air, settling on the big magnolia leaves, sifting down through the long pine needles. Salali's footprints in the snow marked a straight path across the lawn. Rachel stood in the door, pulling the wool scarf about her neck tighter, watching after Salali as she ran. Mary came up and gazed over Rachel's shoulder.

"Where is she going?" Rachel asked.

And then she saw. A lone figure on foot had left the winding drive and was trudging through the trees, coming toward the house. At that moment Salali reached the figure, who dropped a gun from his hand and opened his arms wide to receive her. Like an electric shock it came over Rachel.

"Donald!" she whispered, and lifted her hands to cover her mouth. "Donald . . . oh, Donald!"

Rachel started across the piazza, then stopped abruptly,

panic in her eyes, and turned around. She ran back into the parlor, grabbed up a platter of fresh tarts, and bounded up the staircase. When she reached the third-floor landing, she stopped to regain her composure. She took deep breaths, adjusted her hair, and rearranged her skirt. But her heart was beating fast when she entered the place where the British soldiers sat, keeping watch over their captain in the next room. She held the platter of tarts out to them.

"Breakfast was a long time ago," she said, smiling, consciously making her eyes sparkle, and at the same time keeping her breathing even.

The two soldiers who were playing cards looked up and smiled. Then they glanced at each other, wondering at the sudden burst of hospitality.

"What are you playing?" she asked.

"A game a 'loo," the younger man answered. His blond hair fell down in a boyish way over his forehead. A fire was blazing in the small fireplace, and both men had laid their red coats over a chest beneath the window.

"You mind if I sit down and watch for a while?" she asked. "I've never understood lanterloo. Perhaps you could show me how to play."

"Why, you'd be welcome as rain in the spring, Mrs. Wolfe," the older man said, pleased to have a feminine presence at their table. "You see," he said, holding out one of the cards, "the aim of 'loo is to . . ."

Rachel's eyes were riveted to the card in the man's hand, but her mind was not on his words. She was hoping against hope that Salali was taking Donald down to the slave quarters where he would be safe against discovery.

The man's voice droned on. She knew lanterloo as well as if she had invented the game herself. The only one on the entire plantation who could beat her was Edward himself.

"Do you see, miss?"

She glanced down. The younger man was holding out another card to her.

"See?" she said. "Oh, yes. Yes, I *think* I do!"

"Mrs. Wolfe?" It was Mary's voice. She appeared in the doorway, and the men looked around.

"Yes, Mary?"

Rachel's eyes locked with Mary's and a look of understanding passed between them.

"Mrs. Wolfe, they needs you downstairs. Somethin' about

what Agatha should do to mend that little tear in your taffeta dress, I think."

"Oh ... well, thank you, Mary."

Rachel stood and started toward the door as the two men looked after her with disappointment. She looked back.

"Thank you for showing me about the game," she said. "And I do hope you enjoy the tarts ... they're cherry. Abigail—Mrs. Buchannon—made them. She makes the very best cherry tarts you've ever eaten in your life!"

With that she was out the door, hurrying down the stairs with Mary.

Just as they reached the main floor, Abigail came scurrying in from the rear entrance. Rachel searched Abigail's face for answers. Abigail cast furtive eyes up the stairway.

"He's hidden," she whispered excitedly. "Down in Aunt Martha's old cabin."

"I'm going to him," Rachel declared. Her cheeks reddened as if she were about to cry.

When Donald had seen Salali running toward him down the long snowy drive, joy welling up inside made him laugh and brought bright tears to his eyes. He did not think of how he looked, his eyelashes and the red beard of his face white with frost, ice glistening on the barrel of his fusil and crown of his tricorn hat. His brown knee breeches were ragged, and the tan hose were snagged and thin. He limped as he came, the moccasins on his numb feet wrapped in castoff rags. Beneath his linen rifleman's frock he had on three shirts; even so, he was shivering when she reached him and with a cry came into his arms.

They held each other desperately, Salali whimpering and sobbing with joy as he kissed her frantically. She did not notice the ice in his beard as it brushed her tender cheek. With her finger she wiped away the tears running down his face, then kissed him full on the lips, a long kiss as they held tight to each other.

When they broke the kiss at last, Salali looked back over her shoulder. "We've got to hide you!" she whispered.

"Hide?"

"Yes! British soldiers!"

She took him by the hand and they ran across the lawn into the forest. Once in the cover of the trees, they embraced wildly again, then, running hand in hand, hurried toward the quarters.

"Rachel knows by now it's you," she said, looking back over her shoulders. "She'll do something to keep them back!"

Rachel left Abigail and ran down the winding tree-bark path so quickly that once she fell headlong, scraping the heels of both hands as she caught herself. When she burst through the door of old Aunt Martha's deserted cabin, a blanket of warm air met her. A fire was blazing in the fireplace, and Salali was pouring steaming water from a heavy iron teakettle into a basin that sat on a weathered old table near the fire, where Donald stood warming himself.

"Donald . . ." She wept as she ran into his arms. "Oh, Donald!"

As she held him, she felt a deep tremor racking his body every few moments.

"You're shivering!" she said, and gripped his hands in hers. His hands were roughened from long exposure, and were cold, so cold.

She cradled her brother's face in her hands and looked up into his eyes, red-rimmed and watery blue. He smiled weakly, then closed his eyes and held her tightly.

"I'm so glad you're home!" she whispered.

"And you, dear," he said. "I thought never to see you alive again! I thought you'd died at Fishin' Creek."

"I was captured," she said, "by Tarleton himself! You know how I am, nothing but the best for me!" She laughed through her tears. "They brought me with the other prisoners back to Camden and on to Charles Town. But you, Donald . . . oh, how I've hoped!"

"At the first shot," he explained, "Edward shouted for me to save myself. I never got up off my blankets . . . just rolled down the creek bank and into the water. I dove under and swam to the other side, then slithered up through the mud into the trees."

"Let me wash your face and hands," Salali's low voice interrupted. "Come sit down."

Donald sat at the table while Salali placed the basin before him and, taking his hands tenderly, immersed them in the warm water. He winced.

"Scalding!" he exclaimed.

"No," she said. "It's very warm, but not hot. It's just your poor, frozen hands."

"But Fishing Creek was six months ago!" Rachel broke in. "Where have you been?"

"I joined the North Carolina Militia in October. We wiped out Ferguson and his Loyalist command at Kings Mountain."

Salali's smooth hands were bathing his slowly with a white bar of hard soap and a gentle cloth.

"You were at Kings Mountain?" Salali exclaimed. "The turning point of the southern war!"

"Yes," he said, "and four weeks ago I was at Cowpens. We gave Tarleton his comeuppance there. Then, when we heard Wilmington was occupied, Edward thought I should come on—"

"Edward!" both women chorused. Salali stopped in the midst of bathing his hands, and Rachel sat staring.

"Edward's alive?" Rachel exclaimed.

"Alive and well—and determined as ever that we'll win this war."

"Oh, thank God!" Salali buried her face in her wet hands and turned away. Rachel sat breathless.

"What we have to be grateful for this day!" Rachel breathed, gazing up at the old rafters. Wet tear paths on her cheeks glistened in the firelight, and her chest heaved.

That night secret visitors crowded the little log house to welcome Donald home. Salali had stayed, but Rachel had slipped back to the big house to keep up appearances. Everyone had to take great care in going and coming, because one part of the path was clearly visible from the window of the upper room where the guards were staying.

As Donald looked about into the clutch of surrounding faces, the yellow light shone in his eyes. Salali sat close by, her hand on his as he recounted to the little assemblage the wearisome defeats and thrilling victories of the last eight months. He told of friends lost, buried hurriedly in ground to which no one would ever come to lay a wreath or plant a flower, and how it felt to fire point-blank into the face of a man you have no reason to hate, or even dislike. He told of bone-breaking marches and countless nights on hard ground, and petty jealousies, but most of all of the loneliness, the unmitigated loneliness. Here he enclosed Salali's hand in his own. The children giggled when they saw it, but the older heads nodded knowingly.

The next morning, just after sunup, Rachel went back to the

slave quarters. Salali was with her, bringing Donald a loaf of bread freshly baked in Abigail's kitchen, along with hoecakes and slices of fresh ham. They watched the pleasure on Donald's face as he devoured the plentiful food.

"This British captain I'm hiding from," he mused as he ate, "will he live?"

Rachel hesitated a moment, not meeting Donald's eyes. "Yes . . ." she said slowly. "I think he will."

"Well," he went on, "some will think you're a British sympathizer."

"No, Donald," Salali broke in. "Rachel's only doing what she must. You should have seen her face as she worked to save him. I knew what she was thinking—how his life was in her hands. I knew . . . but I didn't know all."

"All?" Donald looked up quizzically.

Rachel cast a hurt look at Salali, as though Salali had betrayed her.

"Well, he has to know sometime," Salali said.

"I thought perhaps he *didn't* have to know," Rachel answered quietly.

"Know what?" he asked, looking from one to the other. "What are you women talkin' about?"

Rachel looked directly into Donald's eyes. "Donald, that captain is Rob Wolfe."

Donald stopped breathing as his eyes grew wide and the hand lifting his fork with a bite of meat on it sank to the table.

"Rob Wolfe?" he said slowly.

"Yes," Rachel answered.

Donald felt his chest tighten and his heart begin to trip. Slowly he sat back in his chair, looking from Salali to Rachel and back again.

"I want to see him," he said solemnly.

Rachel's eyes began to shift. Donald had never met Rob Wolfe, but he knew what Rob had done to her before she married Drew. Rachel could see that the war had changed Donald, and she was afraid.

"I can't let you," she said quietly. "He's regained consciousness only once before today, and right now his awareness comes and goes. I just can't let you see him."

Donald took a deep breath, rose from his chair, and walked to the little cabin window, his hands clasped behind his back. How many times had she seen him turn away in exasperation in just that way. She could hear his heavy breathing.

"All right, Rachel," he said quietly. "I'll not bother the man—not now. But I remember what he did to you. To forgive is right, and to forget is good, but you've got to protect yourself. And such a man's got to face up to himself. At the moment I'll stay away from him . . . and wait till later. But when he's up and around, I want to see the man face to face."

"Donald." Rachel stood and looked at him, determination in her eyes, her jaw set. "Believe me, I hate Rob Wolfe more than anyone in this world hates him. I would like to see him dead. But both now and later, you must leave Rob alone. The war has put a jagged edge on us all. We resent the British right now, and you . . . even you, Donald, want someone to vent your anger on. But for me, please leave him alone. I can't bear another fight or another killing!"

S E V E N T Y - O N E

THE next morning, when Rachel went into Rob's room up on the third story, carrying fresh towels, she found him lying awake in bed, for the first time aware of his surroundings.

When he saw Rachel's face, his mouth dropped open and he stared at her, astonished, as if he'd seen an apparition. She was just inside the door when he recognized her, and she stopped to return his stare, a strange, twisted smile on her lips.

"Hello, Rob," she said.

The sound of her voice confirmed that it was indeed Rachel. He gasped and his face went even paler than before.

"Rachel . . . Rachel Calhoun," he whispered, his confusion absolute.

Her twisted smile deepened at the perverse pleasure she felt.

"Rachel," he murmured weakly, "where am I? What happened? What are *you* doing here?"

"One question at a time, Rob," she said quietly. She went to the chest, pulled open a drawer, and put the towels away. "You're at Buchannon Hills, a plantation on the Cape Fear. You've been given shelter here until you're well." Her voice was cold and detached. He was no longer a dying man, and there was anger in her words.

"When I woke this morning," he said, "I knew I was sick . . . and weak, but I couldn't tell why."

Rachel looked at him, searching his face. He sounded different somehow, as though he was meek and ready to hear. Rachel stood beside the bed, looking down at him, and unfolded the story. As she talked, she looked directly into his eyes, forcing him to shift his gaze to the wall. She could see his discomfort and was relishing every moment of it. He lay and listened with all the strength he had, once or twice passing his hand over his eyes.

"And my name is not Calhoun," she said as she finished the story.

"You've married, then," he said, looking directly at her.

"Yes, I married your uncle Drew."

"And Elizabeth? What happened to Elizabeth?"

"Dead," she said, "a coach accident."

"And Drew is here?" A look of panic flashed across his face.

For a moment Rachel was silent and deep sadness crept into her features. "It's a long, long story, Rob," she said. "Drew is dead, and I'm living on the plantation near my brother. Buchannon Hills is my home now." She turned from the chest and started for the door. "Enough of this," she said, a sharp edge to her voice. "You've got to have rest."

"Rachel," he said. She stopped, still facing the door. "Ten years has made you more beautiful than you were at seventeen."

She took a deep breath and felt the color rising to her face. "Thank you, Rob," she muttered, without turning back, and left.

When Rachel reached the parlor, she felt her knees go weak. She dropped down onto the last stair and put her head in her hands as Salali came in from the study.

"Rachel!" she said. "What happened?"

Rachel sat looking at the floor, her hands clasped at her temples. "Rob's awake."

"And?"

"And he knew me. He asked questions . . . and I answered them."

Salali sat down beside her and laid her arm comfortably around Rachel's shoulders.

"You're trembling," Salali said.

"It was just all so unsettling," Rachel answered. "When I looked into his eyes, I saw Drew. The bridge of Rob's nose is exactly like Drew's, and the cut of his chin. Drew had such a strong face."

Salali said nothing, but listened quietly, her dark Cherokee eyes full of compassion. Today her hair was in one thick braid tied by a scarlet ribbon. The braid fell forward over her left shoulder and was touching Rachel's arm. Rachel fingered the scarlet ribbon absently as she spoke, and slowly shook her head.

"It's the strangest thing in the world to me," she said. "Rob is like Drew, but he's also like my father. Drew was tender and handsome. Daddy was handsome and cruel." She lifted her eyes to Salali's, and as she did, her own long dark hair fell down unfettered over her shoulder. "Salali," she said, "I'm just shocked into breathless . If ever I hated anyone, it's Rob. But for just a moment, as i was talking to him, I felt a twinge of tenderness," she paused, "and that frightens me!"

"Rachel," Salali said, "it's not Rob you feel the tenderness for. It's Drew. You see Drew in Rob's face. That's all. And the hatred is for both Rob and your father."

"Perhaps," Rachel said.

Salali thought for a moment. "You know," she began, "there's a very strange thing. You've seen how Abigail's little lap dog makes the life of that new kitten so miserable? She chases him and rags him about—but if the dog ignores him, the kitten comes up to her and rubs against her and purrs. And before long, the dog is doing all the old things the kitten hates. Some people are like that, Rachel, drawn to the person who abuses them, as though they want to be punished for what they are."

"A moth drawn to the flame?"

"Exactly!" Salali's tone was low and earnest. "You must *not* let your feelings get tangled up with Rob again. For your own sake. And Rachel, you know Donald would simply not stand for it!"

Rachel drew a deep breath and straightened. "You're right," she said. "Absolutely right. I must be kind to Rob, though. As kind as I can bring myself to be."

Rachel smiled at Salali and squeezed her hand.

* * *

Rob Wolfe felt so safe at Buchannon Hills that he dismissed his bodyguards to return to Wilmington, telling them that as soon as he was able, he would join them there.

Soon Rob was sitting in the sun on the second-floor piazza, a patchwork quilt draped warmly about his shoulders. The rigors of his majesty's service had made him resilient, and his strength was coming back more quickly than Rachel had thought possible. But he was not yet strong enough to take meals downstairs, and the wound in his thigh made him walk with a cane.

Today was a bright morning in March. The sun was well up, and the little family, including Donald, had gathered for breakfast in a small room with blue walls and many white-trimmed windows.

"What a lovely morning!" Rachel exclaimed.

Mary, the servant girl, bringing in a platter of Indian hoecakes, smiled at Jamie as Rachel tucked a napkin into his open collar.

"Did you know," Rachel chatted on, "that the first day of spring is only two weeks away?"

Abigail and Salali glanced at each other. It had been a long time since Rachel had bubbled like this. Midway between the hoecakes and dried apple pies, Jamie looked up from his mug, a thick ring of white milk on his upper lip. For a moment he sat gazing into his mother's face.

"You're happy today, Mama!" he exclaimed.

Rachel paused with her fork uplifted. "I guess I am," she said, "and I really don't know why." Then she smiled. "But this is just the way one should feel on such a wonderful day."

Jamie accepted the explanation without further questions, and bit into another piece of pie. Almost imperceptibly, Salali shook her head and glanced at Donald.

After breakfast, Rachel hurried up the stairs, unaware that she was singing as she went, some happy tune circulating through the colonies. She didn't know the name or any of the words, only the melody. Something she had heard from one of the slaves, perhaps.

On the second flight, Rachel overtook Agatha, the kitchen servant, on her way to Rob Wolfe's chamber. Agatha had a breakfast tray in her hands.

"Here, Agatha," Rachel said as she went past and took the

tray, "I'll care for that. I have to look in on Mr. Wolfe anyway. You go about your other chores."

Rachel came singing down the hall, then rounded the corner into the sun-flooded room and stopped short.

Rob Wolfe was up. He was standing with his back to her, looking into a mirror perched on top of a small chest of drawers, feeling the smoothness of his chin. In his right hand he held a razor, and on the night table at his elbow stood a porcelain basin and a silver mug of lather. His cane was propped against the chest, within reach. His shoes were still under the edge of the bed, and he stood there in his long stockings of light green and a pair of beige knee breeches—both stockings and knee breeches borrowed from one of the servants. He wore the breeches in fashionable style, the waistband a little below the hipbone and laced tightly in back. His shirt still lay on the blue and white checked counterpane of the bed. To his left the window stood wide, and the fresh March air made the room seem alive, though faintly chill.

For a shocked instant Rachel stood gazing, holding the tray, mildly aware of the pleasure she felt at seeing Rob's fine muscular back. He had not heard her enter, but he smelled the heady perfume she always wore. Without turning, he spoke.

"Wonderful morning, 'Doctor'!" His voice was strong and full of life, not the voice of a man so recently in the arms of death.

"Rob Wolfe!" Rachel scolded. She set the tray down and hurried to the open window, slammed it closed, then with one hand on the sill and the other hand on her hip, stared at him disapprovingly.

"What's the matter!" he asked, laughing and stropping his razor. "I thought fresh air was good for the sick."

"Only if the sick are dressed," she spat. "As you most assuredly are not!" Notwithstanding the rebuke, Rachel was smiling. She picked up the white linen shirt and threw it at him. "Here," she ordered, "put it on before you catch cold and die . . . or haven't you come close enough already?"

The flying shirt struck him and fell to the floor. His face was all alather now, and he held the long straight-edge blade poised near his right cheekbone.

"I thought perhaps you'd show me about the plantation today," he said. "It's a pity to spend a month here and see no more than I have."

Rachel felt suddenly panicked. She had counted on confining Rob to the third floor until he was well enough to leave, thereby avoiding a confrontation with Donald.

"You're not quite ready for such a trek," she answered confidently.

"Nonsense!" he said with force. "I've lain in that bed too long!"

The brilliant light, untempered as it was by any drape or even a gauzy curtain, so illuminated his swarthy back that Rachel simply stared. She felt breathlessness rising in her throat. For days now she had been having a hard time with her promise to Salali.

"All right, Captain," she answered slowly, careful not to relinquish medical command. "In another day or two I'll show you the plantation."

Two days later, with Donald safely in Wilmington on business that Rachel had created to get him off the grounds, she led Rob about the plantation. In the warm March sun they walked slowly through the gardens and under the great magnolias, occasionally stopping for Rob to rest on his cane. Rachel pointed away, toward the river, and then took him down to the stables, where he admiringly stroked the backs of a fine pair of Arabians.

"I'll show you the smithy," she said next.

They were halfway between the stables and the smithy, Rachel walking a little ahead of Rob, when he reached out and took her hand. She turned about sharply, her eyes flashing anger, and pulled away. He smiled, but said nothing, and they went on. Rachel also said nothing, but she could hardly sort out the feelings battling inside her.

The smithy was a sturdy building of hewn logs, with a big open door facing south. As they entered, a large Negro man, standing at the forge shirtless—with sweat glistening on his massive shoulders—was tugging down on the rope above his head. As he tugged, a bellows breathed thunderous life into the intense fire before him. Rachel and Rob came up behind the man and watched as, with his free hand, he adjusted two glowing pieces of iron among the coals.

The man turned about and, with averted eyes, smiled at Rachel.

"Rob," she said, "this is Clayton Walker. Clayton's the plantation smith, one of Edward's most dependable men. Clayton, this is Rob Wolfe."

Rachel saw an immediate change in Rob's manner. He took on a sudden air of superiority, staring right through Clayton Walker with those icy-blue eyes and saying nothing.

"I'm pleased to meet you, Mr. Wolfe," the slave said. Rob made no response, just as though Clayton Walker was not there. He continued to stare until Clayton turned back to his forge. It was not Rachel's imagination that suddenly the fire in the forge was roaring louder than before.

With a pair of tongs, Clayton took the two pieces of a broken plowshare from the coals, each glowing with a light so intense Rachel could scarcely keep her eyes on them. Clayton touched the pieces together. They were tacky and pulled apart reluctantly—just hot enough for the weld. He laid them together on the anvil, then, with rapid, careful blows, hammered them into one. Gradually the iron's yellow dimmed to a red glow, and the red dulled to blue. He held the dark iron up to the light.

"Perfect," he whispered with satisfaction. "Just perfect."

"You're a good workman, Walker," Rob said.

"Thank you, sir," Clayton answered.

"We could use a man like you in the British army right now. In fact, you ought to volunteer to serve Tarleton's legion, quartered down in Wilmington. Lots of horses to shoe. You might even get to see battle if you worked it right."

The effect of the proposal was electric. Clayton Walker lifted his eyes directly to Rob Wolfe's.

"Bloody Ban might have a place for me, sir, but I have no place for Bloody Ban!"

Rachel's heart leapt into her throat. A sneer crossed Rob's mouth, and he started to speak; then, just as suddenly, he thought better of it. Even if he were well and strong, he would be no match for this man in a hand-to-hand fight.

Just then they heard the sound of children shouting at play and coming toward the smithy. Rachel turned about, glad for the distraction, and looked out through the wide doors. Mixed with the shouts were screams of anger and the honk of a goose.

There they came, up from the stock pond, a whole band of children with Jamie Wolfe in the lead, running with all his might and shouting angrily as he came. The other boys and girls were cheering him on.

Running ahead of him, her feet barely touching the ground, ran the bane of Jamie's life.

"I hate you, Betty!" came the little boy's shouts. "You're the meanest, hatefulest goose in the world!"

Betty always guarded the pond as though she owned it. Now she was running for her life, honking and waving her wings wildly in the air. As the furious little boy closed the gap between them, the goose settled into a dead run, left the ground, reached for altitude, and glided in a long, graceful arc back over the pond and away toward the lower meadow.

The red-faced little boy stamped the ground furiously, fighting back tears as he watched her descend among the distant meadow grasses. She had escaped him again! Jamie Wolfe would have killed the creature had he caught her. The other children ran in a group to some new adventure, but Jamie, catching sight of his mother, came toward her with a disgusted stride.

Rachel reached down and swept Jamie into her arms.

"*Look* at this, Clayton," Jamie cried, and pulling down the band of his breeches to uncover half of one small buttock, he displayed a spot of flaming red. "I'll *kill* her someday," he wept, his eyes red and running, more from anger than pain.

"Oh, Jamie!" Rachel said sympathetically. And she put her arms about him, hugging him tightly.

"And who is this?" Rob Wolfe asked.

"This, Rob, is the little boy born to Drew and me," Rachel said proudly. After all, she thought, other than Donald and herself, the man before them was Jamie's only living relation.

"Well I'll be da—" He caught himself. "So I've got a cousin, have I?" And he laughed, but it was a hollow laugh.

Rachel looked closely at him. "Rob," she said, "you're getting tired. I can see it in your eyes. It's time to go back to the house."

"Maybe you're right," he answered. Tiny beads of perspiration broke out on his forehead and he leaned harder on his cane.

Jamie squirmed down from Rachel's arms and ran out of the smithy, back to his friends.

Clayton Walker was pumping the forge billows again and did not so much as look in Rob's direction as Rob walked away. Rachel caught Clayton's eye, smiled at him, and followed after Rob.

"Mama," Jamie said that night as he lay in his bed.

"Yes, Jamie?" Rachel had just reentered the room after going for a fresh pitcher of water to leave on Jamie's bedstand. She came and laid her hand on his shoulder.

"Donald and Salali," the little boy said, rubbing the counterpane nervously, "they love each other, don't they, Mama?" Without waiting for her answer, he said, "I'm just sure of it!"

Rachel smiled and squeezed his shoulder tightly. "Yes, Jamie, they do," she said after a thoughtful pause.

Jamie loved to hear his mother's voice. It was a feminine sound, but low, so warm and reassuring. She smoothed his forehead with her soft hands. The delicate lace flowing from the cuff of her sleeve brushed his cheek.

"Yes," she said again, "they love each other very much."

"Donald and Salali picked me up and hugged me between them yesterday, Mama." He was not sheepish about it. He could tell his mother anything. "And Mama, it felt so good."

Rachel smiled again, but felt sad inside. How she wished she and Drew could have raised Jamie together!

"Mama," he said, with a question in his voice, "why don't you have someone to love you?"

For a long moment Rachel was silent and her deep eyes searched his face. "I did once, Jamie," she said. "Like Donald and Salali, your daddy and I loved each other very much. But then the war came between us. There's just never been anyone else."

"But, Mama, I don't even remember my daddy," he pled. "For me, it's like he never was."

"I know," she said, gripping his hand reassuringly.

"Isn't it hard for you to be alone, Mama?"

"Of course it is, Jamie. It's always been hard—and hard to see you growing up without your daddy."

Jamie lay there, loving the touch of her hand as she stroked back his long hair. "Their arms felt so good around me, Mama." An uncertain boyish smile crept across his face. "And I was thinking . . . wouldn't someone's arms around you make you feel good?" He laughed an embarrassed little laugh at the possible silliness of what he'd said.

Rachel bent down and hugged him up from his pillow. "Your arms are the only ones I need!" she said. "They make me feel just wonderful!"

With Jamie in her arms, she went to the window and gazed out. For a long time she stood there with him, each clinging desperately to the other.

* * *

Later, when Jamie finally lay sleeping, Rachel stood in her window looking out over the descent of the moonlit hill. The night was so bright, she thought she could see the river's meandering face. As she stood there, one knee resting on the window's deep casement, the moonlight whispered through the thinness of her nightgown. Rachel loved to stand at this window, especially on moonlit nights. Its depth made her know the thickness of the mansion's walls and gave her a feeling of security. How could she have made it through these years without the strong emotional shelter of this house?

But her thoughts were not now on the river, nor on the house, but on Jamie's words. They were echoing in her mind, as though he had spoken them that very moment—she was hearing them over and over again. "Wouldn't someone's arms around you feel good, Mama?" And she let her thoughts run before her long-denied emptiness.

SEVENTY-TWO

IT was a warm mid-morning, Salali and Rachel in the garden alone, ambling slowly along the flagstone path that wound among the rosebushes. The bushes were beginning to take on a cast of green, the first cautious buds swelling. An aroma of spring was in the air, and somewhere among the trees a turtledove cooed.

"I think," Rachel was saying with hesitation, "that I could forgive Rob for all the terrible things he did to me."

An unintentional sigh escaped Salali's lips. Rachel looked up sharply. Her love for Salali had grown manyfold these years, and she cared what Salali thought, but this sigh touched a nerve.

Dismayed that she had given away her hidden feelings, Salali looked apprehensively at Rachel. "I'm sorry," she said. "It's none of my business."

"But you disapprove of my forgiving Rob." Rachel was

searching Salali's face, framed beautifully by the long black hair, which shone so brightly in the sun.

Salali turned her eyes to the path and broke a twig from a nearby hydrangea bush. "Disapprove of forgiveness?" she answered softly. She looked directly into Rachel's eyes. "Never! But Rachel, Rob doesn't *want* your forgiveness. He has no conscience whatever. I disapprove of Rob . . . and I'm terrified to think you might become entangled with him again. The man nearly killed you once, and he broke your heart. You mustn't per*mit* him to do it again!"

"Rob will never have the chance to do again what he once did to me," she said. "And yet . . ."

"Yet, what?" Salali asked, her eyes flashing.

"Time and experience do change people, even people like Rob."

Salali shook her head. "I don't think so, Rachel. There's something about him—his face is too perfect, his smile too easy, his manner too smooth."

"You're imagining things," Rachel responded. "His eyes— they have something that makes you feel he's gazing right through you—something that disarms you when he's near. That's all."

"Un*dresses* you, is more like it," Salali exclaimed quietly. She put her hands on Rachel's shoulders. "Look, I don't want anything to come between us, but I must tell you, I think you trust him too much. You want Jamie to have a father. I know Rob makes you think of Drew. But I think you're only asking for the most terrible unhappiness you've ever known."

"No!" Rachel huffed and looked away. Salali was imagining things. There wasn't the slightest chance she could love Rob again, but somehow she did want things healed between them.

"You and Rob are not the *same*," Salali went on. "There's something deep and sensitive within you. But Rob cares for nothing but himself. Two spiritual qualities as different as light and dark. Be*lieve* me, Rachel, I know about these things—and the two of you are not for each other." She hesitated a long moment. "Besides, Rachel, you should be thinking of Edward and Abigail now."

Rachel looked up in surprise. "What have they to do with this?"

"You're forgetting that we have neighbors who don't understand your saving the life of a British soldier!"

"Doctors can't turn away from dying men," Rachel answered.

"Yes, and you've done your duty by Rob. But Rachel, a Patriot woman *can* turn away an enemy lover!"

Rachel blushed. "I told you, Salali, we're not lovers! And we will never be!"

"But do our Patriot neighbors understand that? Rachel, it's time the man went back to Wilmington. He's strong enough, and everyone—including me—would rest much easier if he were not here."

Rachel sighed and looked at the almost-spring clouds floating serenely in the mid-morning sky.

"And Rachel, if Rob had changed, he would see the danger he's putting you in . . . and he would already be gone."

"Abigail," Rachel said one day in March, "what in the world is going on?"

"What do you mean, dear?" Abigail answered.

"The servants," she exclaimed. "They've been whispering among themselves all day . . . as though something's about to happen; something they don't want us to know."

Abigail smiled. "I've seen it," she said. "Something's afoot, but I know better than to ask what. It's best not to know some things."

Salali smiled knowingly while Rachel stared at them, puzzled.

Toward evening all the servants but Quincy and Mary left the house. Quincy was watching through the main door that opened on the rear piazza, and saw them drifting off toward the unused barn that stood down over the brow of the hill. Just as Rachel came up behind him, he shook his head condescendingly and frowned.

"Where are they going?" she asked.

"Miss Rachel," he said, smiling slightly, "you just don't want to know."

As Quincy walked away chuckling to himself, Rachel stood with her mouth open, looking after him and wondering what it was that could be such a secret among the slaves. With a quick huff of exasperation, she stepped out on the piazza.

The sun was setting beyond the forested horizon, its light in her eyes. Unexpectedly, she found herself in the presence of Rob Wolfe, who was leaning idly against a pillar of the piazza, his arms folded across his chest.

"Where are all the darkies drifting off to?" he asked when he saw her.

"Don't call them by such names," she said, casting him a disapproving glance. "Their lives are hard enough without thoughtless insults." "Darkie" was a new word for Negroes, always disparaging.

"Oh, I don't know," he answered with a smirk. "Seems to me they have it pretty good, especially these house servants."

He looked around just as Mary, the kitchen girl, came out. Mary glanced at him and smiled. As she walked across the yard, he followed the sway of her hips with his eyes. Rachel felt a pang of anger.

"After all," he went on, "how many whites back in the Piedmont live as well as the blacks here?"

"That's not the point, Rob. The point is the same one we're fighting this Revolution for. . . ."

"You think too much," he huffed.

Then, hearing shouts from the distant barn, Rachel softened, and thought finally to answer his question about where the slaves had gone. "I don't know what they're about," she said. "I was just going to see." She glanced toward him. "You can come along with me if you'd like."

"I thought you'd never ask," he said.

Twilight was settling over the river valley as they went toward the edge of the hill. Rachel wished for something to ward off the evening chill. Underfoot the ground was soft from the few snows and many rains of winter. One could smell a dampness in air laden with new life. In the twilight, beyond the river, lay the flat blue shadow of the earth's circle, timbered but without hills.

As the two approached the barn, she felt the brush of Rob's hand against hers. Had he intended to touch her? Yes, no doubt about it, he had. Then she felt his fingers folding about her hand, warm and strong. She did not want that, and yet she did, as an electric thrill went through her.

They came to the place where the ground fell suddenly down. Below, in the semidarkness, stood the old tobacco barn that predated even Edward's father, perhaps by fifty years. The barn had gone long without paint, and the elements had roughened it by wearing away the soft parts of the wood's grain. It stood dull gray, coated in patches of green lichen, but in the gathering night it seemed only a somber black. Through its myriad cracks and crevices, the yellow light of many lanterns and torches poured into the damp night . . . and the constant murmur of talk and laughter.

"Strange," Rachel said as they came near, "but I've not been in this old barn for more than a year." Her mind was not on the barn, but on her hand in his.

Rob chuckled. "Can't imagine why you'd *want* to go in such a place," he said.

Salali was right, she thought. She and this man were as different as night and day. Ancient barns, like ancient houses, were full of mystery—the smell of old straw and of horses, and echoes of men pouring out their lives in labor. Rachel could always feel those things; but it was obvious that Rob did not.

As they reached the light of the doorway, she looked directly into his eyes, smiled slightly, and withdrew her hand.

Three of the younger slaves were standing there, and as Rachel and Rob brushed past, they looked at her, grinning sheepishly, their eyes and teeth flashing in the torchlight.

Rachel looked about at the cavernous interior. The barn's frame was of hand-hewn beams a foot square on which the rough exterior planks had been nailed up and down. It was built on stone pilings, open around the foundation for the free flow of air to dry long racks of tobacco leaf. In long-ago days when the barn was in use, the airflow could be increased by lifting a few of the vertical planks that swung outward from the bottom on wooden hinges. The air would enter beneath them, then rise and escape through a vent that ran along the roof's crest. Even now the faint smell of ancient tobacco lingered in the musty air. All around, dozens of pitch-pine torches stood out from wrought-iron holders in the walls, their dancing flames casting a yellow light over the crowd of people that packed the room.

"Everything's changed!" Rachel exclaimed when she saw.

"How changed?" Rob asked over her shoulder.

"The drying racks—they're gone . . . and that pit—it wasn't there a year ago! Why, Rob, the servants have made this into a—"

At that instant a roar of approval rose from the crowd as two men, sweating with the heat of excitement, entered a wide pit from opposite sides. The crowd was made up of blacks with a sprinkling of white men among them—some well-to-do, by their attire—some of whom Rachel knew as prominent men from surrounding plantations.

The pit, widest at the uppermost, sloped inward until it was about twenty feet across at the bottom. Around the sloping sides men, women, and children sat thickly in tiers of seats. The two men who had just come into the little arena held in their hands what appeared to be small bundles of brilliantly colored feathers.

"A cockpit!" Rachel exclaimed, but in the deafening cheers, no one heard, not even she. "Rob." She turned away. "I want out of here!"

The noise drowned her words, but Rob read her lips and face clearly. He only smiled and shook his head. Rachel started to leave, but he caught her by the arm, turning her toward the pit. Then curiosity overcame her and she wedged herself beside Rob onto the wooden bench to watch what was about to unfold.

Edward had forbidden cockfights at Buchannon Hills, and she could not believe these loyal blacks would do this.

Rachel had never seen the two "pitters" before. Perhaps they were slaves from upriver, or from lumber or turpentine camps deep in the woods. The pitters came to their feet, facing each other from across the pit, and began to circle for advantage. The light played across their skin and made their slow movements seem eerie in the sudden silence. Then, abruptly, with a thrust of the men's glistening black arms, the birds were in the air, hurtling toward each other. The crowd rose as one, screams and shouts instantly ringing from the dark rafters.

The cocks collided in midair, flailing and slashing with outsized spurs. Back they fell to the ground, marking a tight circle, each about the other, sidestepping, neck feathers bushed out menacingly. Up they rose again, flying at each other. Suddenly there was blood! The crowd came to its feet, roaring with delight. One cock limped as it circled. The other pressed its advantage, and they met in the air once more, the fallen, limping cock dragging a wing in the dust. From the pit's edge the owner shook his fists and paced, shouting encouragement to his wounded champion.

Up they rose again, flailing, slashing, then tumbled back into the dust as the roars of the crowd thundered around them. Rachel clasped her hands over her ears and momentarily averted her eyes. What in God's name? she screamed inside. Is there not enough misery in this world without creating more! What is there that makes us love cruelty!

Then it happened—high in midair the lightning slash of a

spur, a tumbling down, and the bird which an instant before had held the advantage lay a rumpled heap of blood-soaked feathers in the midst of the cockpit.

It seemed to Rachel that the barn would come tumbling down about them under the force of the roar. She could see wide mouths pouring out moans for their fallen hero, and wails of agony for dozens of lost purses.

Then very close in her ear, a voice unrecognizable for its huskiness, "The birds have no feeling, Rachel." She looked up. Rob Wolfe was flushed and great drops of sweat were running down his glistening face—a profusion far out of proportion to the warmth of the crowded barn.

She gazed at him in shock. Her lips framed a question. "What—" she began. And then it came to her. Rob was intoxicated by the shouting, by the slashing spurs and spilled blood, by the lifeless form. Even his hand on her shoulder trembled. His half-wild eyes darted up and down from the scoop of her bosom to the wave of her hair.

"Did you ever *feel* such exhilaration!" he exclaimed, turning his strange eyes back to the spectacle in the pit.

In utter revulsion she looked away from his face back to the arena. The losing pitter had picked up his bird, and with the dead mass overflowing the palm of his right hand, was going toward the edge of the cockpit. Two more contestants were waiting to begin.

"Let's get out of here!" Rachel said, rising as she spoke. The oily torchlight revealed the energy that snapped like lightning in her dark eyes.

"No!" he whispered hoarsely. He gripped her shoulder and pulled her back into her seat. "I've got to see this!"

She wrenched free and pushed past him through the crowd. For an instant he hesitated between what was happening in the arena and following her. Then he got up and caught her in the dark just outside the door.

"You *love* it!" she said incredulously, trying to squirm loose again.

"Yes, I love it!" he hissed. "Why do you think I'm a soldier?"

"Because you believe in England, I supposed!"

"England be hanged!" he shouted. "I don't give a damn who wins the game, it's the action I want. We're not all alike, Rachel," he said breathlessly, "loyalty, glory, money—but I like the *action*."

She stared at him with sudden loathing. "The *blood*, you mean!"

"All right!" he shouted. "Blood. My God, Rachel, you should've seen us at Paoli!"

"You? At Paoli?" Her face grew dark. General Mad Anthony Wayne's lookouts had failed him at the Pennsylvania village of Paoli. A British contingent had attacked at midnight, guns unloaded and bayonets fixed.

"Yes, I was at Paoli!" he rattled. "Right in the thick of it! I stuck 'em like so many pigs, right and left, till their blood ran out the touch hole of my musket and into my hands!"

Rachel looked down at his hands. They were still trembling, and so were hers, but hers trembled at the memory of how his bloody hand had felt in her own a short hour ago.

"And Waxhaws," he went on unbidden. "Oh how the blood ran there! 'Tarleton's Quarter,' they call it," and he laughed with excitement at the memory. " 'Bloody Ban!' Oh how I love the way that man fights! Tarleton's a genius!"

In a rage of revulsion, Rachel pulled away. He started after her, only to find his way blocked by the massive figure of Clayton Walker, Clayton's eyes staring coldly into his, Clayton's massive hand gripping his arm. Rob craned his neck to look over the big man's shoulder.

"Where're you going?" he called after Rachel.

"Back to the house," she said, not turning around. "I've made a terrible mistake."

"I guess you have," he shouted. "If your stomach's made of water, you have no business here!"

She turned to face him through the expanse of darkness. "That's not the mistake I mean," she shouted, then came back to within a few feet of him. Clayton's grip on Rob's arm was tight and she felt safe. "I mean the one I made when I saved your life!" she said. In the darkness her lips were tight and the muscles in her slender neck like the strings of a harp. "You were dying, Rob! Rain-drenched, blood-soaked, and dying! In *spite* of what you did to me, I saved you! Well, Rob, you weren't worth it!"

For a moment her pupils darted as she stared into Rob's smoldering eyes. Then, confident of Clayton's power to restrain him, she turned and started up the hill toward the big house.

When she reached the hilltop, she glanced back. Clayton Walker still held Rob where he stood, the two figures framed in the yellow light of the barn door, defiance written even in the silhouette of his form.

SEVENTY-THREE

IT was a few hours later, just before dawn, when Donald Calhoun came riding rapidly down from Wilmington. The chill of the damp night air was in his face as he came at a gallop along the river road, a brown wool scarf blowing about his neck, his tricorn hat clamped down tight on his head. The scarf did not cover the tops of his ears, and they were stinging, just short of going numb. He sat the running horse easily, holding the reins loose in his right hand, his left dangling at his side.

Since Donald had returned from the war, he had been in and out of Wilmington a dozen times. And it was Rachel who had found reasons for every trip he'd made—all a pretext to keep him away from Rob Wolfe.

Finally realizing her motive, Donald decided he had had enough of it. How dare Rachel keep him from Salali for the sake of this man! After all, he and Wolfe could not avoid each other forever. If Rachel was going to play the fool and trust him, then a confrontation would be inevitable.

Salali. Every week that passed, he found himself more deeply in love with her. How foolish to have waited so long to speak his mind. But she had been his student, and even after she was grown, he had wanted to avoid the appearance of impropriety. He thought lovingly of her as he rode along in the darkness.

It was dangerous to ride through this volatile country at night. He had expected his business in Wilmington to be complete tomorrow. But in the early morning hours, Donald had seen that he must leave immediately, or trouble brewing in Wilmington might prevent his leaving at all. And, if he must ride in the night, at least he had the moon in his favor. It was one day from full, and low to his right, making the sandy road shine before him like a white satin ribbon unrolled through the forest.

Three hours ago he had been sleeping peacefully in an upper room of the inn, when the sound of hooves and shouts woke him. He had opened his eyes to see the ceiling of his room aglare with torchlight from the streets below. Instantly he had risen and gone to the window to look down on a gathering crowd of hastily dressed men and women.

He had thrown on his clothes, bounded down the stairs, and slipped unobtrusively into the street.

"Three days ago," a man in the crowd told him, "Nathanael Greene beat Cornwallis at a place called Guilford Courthouse."

It had happened in crop-bare fields and heavy woods. Greene's riflemen had broken up Cornwallis's formations and fought hand to hand. In desperation, Cornwallis had cannonaded both armies with grapeshot to break up the fighting, killing as many of his own as he killed of Greene's. The Americans had run, but Cornwallis lost more than a quarter of his command and now was in full retreat, coming straight toward occupied Wilmington. Another day and the countryside would be so full of British soldiers, it would be impossible to move about.

Donald was almost there, the drive leading to the big house being just ahead, at the place where the trees from either side of the road met above it to form an arch. The moon sifting through their leafless limbs cast a spiderwork shadow on the road's deep sand.

He slowed the horse to a trot and turned him to the left. His mount's hooves struck hollow sounds from the short wooden bridge spanning the roadside ditch. As he crossed, about to pass between the great rock gateposts, glinting moonlight caught his eye. There was something in the ditch at the end of the bridge.

"Whoa," he commanded, reined in, and swung down.

With the leather lines still in hand, he stepped down a grassy sward into the declivity. The thing lying there was all dark, except for the small object catching the beams of the declining moon. He drew close—a human form, a drunk probably, from one of the turpentine camps.

He reached down to lay his hand on the small shining object, and as he touched it, a chill shot through his body. For beneath it was a mass of soft, black hair. The object was an ivory hair comb.

Donald's heart stopped as he took the form's shoulder and gently rolled it over until the body was lying faceup. By now his eyes had grown accustomed to the shadow, and to his utter horror he saw that the form was Salali's. The moon's light falling through naked tree limbs fell across her face, making her skin glow blue and pallid.

With a cry bursting from his throat, Donald scooped her up in his arms, climbed the bank, lifted her into the saddle, and swung up behind her. Holding her tightly and spurring the horse into a run, he headed for the house.

When Donald burst through the front entrance, he was carrying Salali in his arms.

"Quincy!" he shouted. "Rachel! Help us! Bring light!"

His desperation-filled voice rang through the house, followed by the sounds of bare feet hitting the floor, then by faces appearing in the parlor where he laid her down on the dark maroon couch.

Quincy, running with the peculiar gait of an old man, came dressed in nightshirt and cap, barefoot, carrying a lighted candelabra in his hands.

"A fire, Quincy!" Donald demanded as he knelt across her, holding the warmth of his body to hers. "And comforters, Mary! As quick as you can!"

He felt soft hands on his shoulders and looked up.

When he saw his sister and felt her presence, Donald suddenly lost his composure. His blue eyes went wide with terror. "Oh, Rachel, look! Just look what they've done to my Salali!" And he began to sob.

"They, Donald? They who?" said Rachel, tears welling in her eyes. She held Donald's shoulders tightly and leaned down to touch her dear friend's face. "So cold!" she exclaimed.

"Is she dead, Rachel?" Donald asked.

Rachel placed two fingers against Salali's slender throat. Donald looked up at her pleadingly. From about the couch came muffled sobs, and from the kitchen hallway echoed the commands of Abigail Buchannon for hot water and plenty of towels.

"A pulse," Rachel whispered. "There's a pulse. It's faint, but she's not dead."

"Thank God!" he said.

Mary came running, her arms full of comforters, and began to spread them one by one over the unconscious form. Rachel felt about Salali's head and withdrew her hand. Her fingers were smeared with blood.

"She hit her head," Rachel exclaimed. "Perhaps she fell from her horse."

"At this time of morning?" Abigail broke in. Abigail was standing, arms akimbo, her lips trembling, a terrible scowl of suspicion on her face. "Whyever would she have been riding this time of night?"

"You're right, Abigail," Rachel said. "The blood hasn't clotted, which means that whatever happened, it wasn't long before Donald found her."

Mary placed a porcelain basin of hot water on a stand at Salali's head.

"Her clothes," Rachel said to Mary, "let's get her out of her clothes."

As Rachel began spreading the wet, warm cloths on Salali's forehead and bare limbs, she saw the bruises, on her face, her arms, her thighs—most especially on her thighs. Donald could not bear it, and rose to leave.

As Rob Wolfe carefully closed the door of his third-floor room behind him, a sack of hastily thrown-together belongings in his right hand, he was grumbling quietly to himself.

Too bad he had misplayed his hand last night. Another week and he would have had Rachel in bed. Rotten shame to miss a chance like that, but sometimes you win and sometimes you lose. There was no point in pushing his luck with her; she was too unpredictable, too much temper. And if she was as sorry as she said for having saved his skin, no telling what she would do next. Besides, that blacksmith was all too willing to defend her. The last thing he needed now was to tangle with a buck like that one.

He started down the stairs, so lightly that the treads did not creak beneath his feet.

Ah well, if he couldn't have Rachel, the tussle with that Indian girl partly made up for it. Sheer luck to have run into her in the stable an hour ago. He had gone down to choose a horse for an eventual escape. It was the least likely time to run into somebody—but there she was. Said she hadn't been able to sleep and had come out to curry the black stallion that was such a pet of hers.

There had been fear in her eyes when she caught sight of him—no mistaking that. And when he forced her, she fought like a cat. The sting of a long claw mark on his cheek kept him thinking about it. But then, he liked them better when they fought. That girl had needed taking down, uppish as she was, altogether too uppish for him. He couldn't figure how a half-breed like her had any right to put on airs. Anyway, it was time to go before they found her.

When Wolfe reached the second landing, he drew back in surprise. There was light at the foot of the stairs. And what was the commotion? Could it be that somebody had found the girl already? Yes! And they had carried her body into the parlor. He reached the bottom of the stair and slipped into the dark hallway.

Confound the luck, what now? He could go back to his room before somebody saw. If they caught him on his way out, they'd know he had done it, and he wouldn't have a prayer. He stood a moment longer in the darkness, listening.

He barely overheard Rachel whispering, "A pulse. There's a pulse. It's faint, but she's not dead."

How could that be? He had been absolutely sure she was dead. His heart quickened and he stepped deeper into the shadow, his breathing suddenly shallow and quick. If by some miracle that girl woke up . . . For a moment he stood in panic, then, his mind swimming, he turned quickly toward the door.

As Donald stepped from the parlor, he heard movement in the hallway, followed by the click of a latch.

"Strange," he said to himself. "I wonder who . . ." And going immediately to the door, he opened it and looked out.

The parlor clock chimed six just as the sun broke over the horizon, and at the same moment Salali opened her eyes.

"Salali!" Rachel cried. "Oh, Salali, thank God!" Rachel stroked her cheek softly.

Salali tried to focus her eyes, first on Rachel's face, then on the dozen flickering candle flames of the chandelier above. Suddenly she began to scream.

"No! No!" she shouted as she lifted her shoulders from the couch. "Let me go! You can't!"

Rachel pressed her back to the couch. "Salali!" she whispered. "It's me. It's Rachel. There's nothing to be afraid of. You're going to be all right!"

Salali raised up on her elbows and looked with wild eyes from Rachel to the others gathered about. "Rob," she whimpered. "Why did he *do* this to me?"

Rachel's face went white. "Rob?" she whispered, and straightened up, staring ahead. Then she looked about, suddenly aware that Donald had not come in when Salali shouted.

"Where's Donald?" she asked no one in particular, then jumped to her feet and ran out.

As Rob headed toward the stable, he stepped lightly so as to make no sound. In spite of the cool morning, his face was beaded with sweat. If that girl wakes up and tells . . . well, that would be that, no question about it. He was cursing himself for going back into the house after doing the girl in. What a stupid thing! Nothing in the bag was worth the risk.

Rob did not notice the high feathery clouds blowing in from the west, the sky was clear and the air bracing. His breath was coming in short, shallow jerks as he willed himself toward the stable. Three minutes—that was all he needed to take a horse and be gone. He reached the stable door and slipped inside.

Good! There in the third stall was that black devil of a horse the Cherokee wench had curried. The great horse stepped back as the stranger came toward him. He lifted a fine, silver-trimmed bridle from its peg on the north wall and, reaching out, grabbed the animal's nose.

"Settle down, you black—" In spite of the tossing head, he forced the halter into place. No time for a saddle. He would not go back to Wilmington. He was tired of the army, and this was a good time to leave it behind. No, he would head inland, swing north, and work his way toward Delaware or Pennsylvania—some coastal city. For certain not back into the miserable wilderness of the Blue Ridge.

Very quietly, he led the beast from under the low roof, gathered the reins in his left hand, and looped his right over the horse's neck to pull himself up.

"Rob."

A calm voice came from somewhere behind him. With his foot still lifted slightly from the ground, he turned slowly and looked over his shoulder. He was instantly blinded by the rising sun as it filtered through the branches of a long leaf pine. He shaded his eyes.

Then he saw her; Rachel standing in her nightdress, barefoot in the dew-wet grass. There was a red-haired young man just behind her and to one side. Rob Wolfe's heart went cold. Then he saw something else, and his heart froze hard as ice. In Rachel's hands was a long fowling piece, the cock fully drawn.

"Rachel ..." he said, lifting his hand, splayed fingers up and palm out in a gesture of protection. He started toward her.

"Not another step, Rob," she said calmly.

He stopped. "Rachel," he said in a voice that shook in spite of himself, "I was going to ride in and report myself fit for duty. Clayton said I could borrow this stallion."

"You're lying, Rob. That's Salali's stallion, and you're stealing him. You do *know* Salali, don't you, Rob?" she said, her voice dripping with sarcasm. "Salali is my best friend, the girl my brother intends to marry."

He stepped back, shifting his gaze pleadingly to Donald.

"This is my brother, Rob—Donald Calhoun, the man I've protected you from these last weeks."

"Calhoun," Wolfe said pleadingly as he moved back another step, "tell her ..."

Donald said nothing, but shook his head slowly, never taking his eyes from Rob's.

"What do you intend, Rachel," Rob said, "to execute me? The law looks down on that."

Rachel shook her head slowly. "What difference does the law make to a man like you, Rob? You're a ravager of women. You thought you'd killed Salali. Why should you live?"

"Rachel," he said, smiling nervously, "you saved my life once. How can you ..."

"I told you last night, Rob, *that* was a mistake! I thought I had to save your life then. But what's done is done, and I certainly can't have it on my conscience to let you go free!"

"Rachel," he said, the cool sweat on his forehead beginning to run, "remember the plantation. If something happens to me, Craig will send Tarleton out to burn it to the ground. He's let it stand this long only because you took me in." He turned to Donald. "For God's sake, Calhoun! You know war. Tell your sister she'd be crazy to—"

"Wolfe," Donald said in an even voice, "I was going to kill you myself for what you did to Salali. But Rachel stopped me, said she had first claim. I had to admit she was right. Whatever she does to you will be good by me."

"Rachel," Rob said, turning back to her, gulping air and trying to gauge the look in her smoldering eyes. "I'm going to turn and walk away from here ... very slowly, on foot. I won't even take this horse." He dropped the reins. "Save yourself and let me go."

A large bead of sweat rolled down and burned in the corner

of his right eye. His smile faded and his lower lip quivered. Without taking his eyes from hers, he lifted the yellowed canvas bag to his shoulder and stepped away from the horse.

Rachel shook her head and smiled. She had taunted him with fear long enough.

"I'm not going to kill you, Rob. Not that you don't deserve it. We're going to keep you right here under lock and key until we can get justice. One thing certain, Tarleton wouldn't give us justice if we took you to him."

In a split instant Rob ducked down and was on the other side of the stallion, grabbing the reins and throwing his leg up, intending to ride out with the horse shielding him.

Rachel raised the gun, looking for a clear shot. She would not let him leave the plantation! Suddenly the horse spun wildly and Rob was in full view.

Across the fields, over the early morning dew that lay golden on dead winter stalks and glistened on the green of coming spring, the boom of her gun echoed, once from the walls of the big house, again from the stables, and once again from the edge of the forest where the slave cabins clustered.

SEVENTY-FOUR

WHEN the gun rumbled and bucked hard in Rachel's hands, a cloud of white smoke billowed out before her, stinging her nostrils and blotting Rob from her sight. Slowly, as the smoke dissipated, the firm black outline of Salali's stallion appeared again, his head lowered as he snuffed curiously at a dark something on the ground.

When Rachel saw the jerking form, a tremor went through her body. A moment ago she had been full to the very brim with anger, and the anger had borne her up. But with Rob Wolfe stretched helpless on the ground, all the strength ran out of her as water runs from a lake when the dam bursts. She felt empty, and weak, very weak.

She realized then that she had truly forgiven Rob for all he had done to her years ago. With that realization, she felt the strength returning. She would have let him walk away unscathed, if not for what he had done to Salali, and what he would do to God only knew how many others. That's what had made her do what she'd done.

And what was it she had done? She had ordered him to stay to face justice; she would not have killed him if he hadn't tried to run. With Salali's pain fresh and clear in her mind, she had no regrets.

As the smoke dissipated into the clear morning air, Donald ran to Rob's side. Rachel looked down at herself, suddenly feeling very vulnerable in her long white nightdress, shining in the early sun.

"Oh, Lord, no!" came a cry from behind them.

When the echo of the gun came rolling through the doors of the house, Abigail had jumped to her feet and run onto the piazza. She bolted onto the lawn and reached Rachel just as Clayton Walker, the big blacksmith, arrived from the quarters.

Abigail grabbed at Rachel's hands. "What have you done!" she breathed. "What in God's name have you brought upon us?"

"He raped Salali," she said, her voice even and quiet.

Abigail caught her breath sharply.

"And he tried to run," Rachel finished.

"Then you did right," Abigail said firmly, "no matter what it brings on us."

A circle of servants, already gathering two deep, stood solemnly quiet. Clayton Walker stepped down to where Rob Wolfe had fallen, and the little crowd followed.

"I want to see him," Rachel said. There was not the sign of a tear in her voice.

"There's no need . . ." Donald began, but she paid him no mind.

Rob lay before her, perfectly still, his eyes open and staring sightlessly at the sky. Blood was seeping slowly from points on his vest, running down and darkening the ground.

"Clayton," Abigail ordered, "get that sorry devil out of sight."

With one sudden motion, Clayton scooped Rob Wolfe's limp body up and went running into the stables. Quincy followed, pulling the doors together behind them. Rachel stood looking quietly down at the pool of congealing blood.

"Come back up to the house with me, Rachel," Abigail said

quietly, but firmly. "There's nothing you can do here, and Salali's going to need you."

Donald slipped into the stable and stood beside Quincy, looking down on Rob Wolfe's body.

"Buck and ball," Clayton muttered up at him in the stable's darkness. One by one, with the index finger of his huge right hand, the slave touched six small holes in Rob's shirt, each dark with blood, then inserted the entire finger to the second knuckle into one very large hole. "She loaded that gun with buck and ball!" he exclaimed. "Certain to kill!"

"If she hadn't, I would've," Donald said quietly.

"Nobody on this place gonna blame you, Mr. Calhoun. Nobody's gonna blame her."

Murmuring voices filtered into the stable from beyond the closed doors. Without a word, Quincy went to the door, opened it narrowly, and slipped out, then stood with his back against it. Donald listened as the old man spoke firmly to the gathered blacks. In the intensity of the moment, and out of the need for secrecy, Quincy abandoned English altogether, speaking in his Wolof language, a Niger-Congo speech of Senegambia. Quincy was the one man on the plantation who, in addition to Plantation Creole, spoke an African tongue, a thing that added to his stature in the eyes of the slaves. Though not one of them spoke it, they understood the speech very well.

"Been a man killed here this morning," Donald heard him saying slowly, though he could not make out the words.

Quincy cast his eyes over the crowd. Even so early, there were small children between the legs of the grown-ups, their morning-fresh eyes searching Quincy's face innocently.

"Do you love Master Buchannon and the mistress?" he asked tenderly, quietly. His eyes locked with the eyes of one and then another. He seemed to expect an answer. A murmur of affirmation ran through the company, and a nodding of heads.

"Then say nothing!" His voice was intense and his sagacious eyes burned. "Say nothing," he repeated, "or the British will most certainly come and burn this place to the ground," for a long moment he let his words sink in, ". . . and take you with them!"

There was not the slightest movement. They all knew the fate of those blacks who had cast their lot with the British at

the Revolution's beginning. English promises of reward had
gone unfulfilled, and those who went over to the other side
would have been far better off to have remained with their
masters.

"Hannibal," Quincy looked directly into the eyes of a short,
stout man, "give me your word."

"You have my word, Quincy."

"And you, Delilah?" She nodded. "And your children?"

"And my children; I swear it."

"Good," and Quincy, without turning or taking his eyes
from theirs, opened the door behind him, slipping quietly back
into the stable.

The day was a nightmare of anxiety. Rachel ordered Salali carried to her own room, where she and Donald sat watching over
her.

When full dark had descended, Clayton, with three trustwor-
thy men, took Rob Wolfe's body from beneath a pile of straw
in the stable and bore it down through the pines to low ground
where great cypresses towered above the creek bottom. There
they lowered the defunct captain into a deep grave, tossing in
the bag containing all his belongings. Over the grave they
spread dense tufts of four-tooth moss, working carefully by the
light of two tin candle lanterns, until the ground appeared as
though undisturbed since the day of creation.

There was nothing to do now but wait.

By the next morning Salali's mind had cleared. She lay with
her head cradled in a deep pillow. There were swellings and
bruises on her face, until one could hardly tell it was her. Rachel was holding Salali's left hand, while Donald sat holding
the other.

"Yes," Salali said weakly, but without tears, "I remember
everything. He took me at gunpoint down to the little creek beyond the gate." She let her gaze wander over the ceiling, and
swallowed before going on. "When it was over, he picked up
a broken limb and struck me with it. He must've thought I was
dead, because when I woke up, he was gone. I tried to reach
the house, but from what Donald says, I got only as far as the
borrow ditch by the gate."

"Thank God he didn't shoot you," Donald breathed. He
stroked her hair gently.

"He couldn't risk the sound of a shot," Rachel said.

At the touch of Donald's hand in her hair, tears began to well up in Salali's eyes. "You've risked everything for me," she said.

"Nothin' we could risk for you would be too much," Donald said.

"Salali, you've got to remember how we love you. You mustn't hold your feelings in; if you do, they'll burn you like fire. We'll talk, you and I, until all the feelings are gone and life can go on."

Salali squeezed Rachel's hand and smiled through swollen lips. "Dear Rachel," she said. "We share more now than ever we did before. Truly, you're my friend!"

"And you are mine," Rachel whispered, leaning down, embracing her tenderly.

It was three days later, just about sundown, when Rachel sat with Abigail and Salali in the parlor.

Salali had drawn her feet up on the settee, and was nearest the fire. The single braid of her long black hair lay over her left shoulder, and the orange light of the blaze flickered over her features. Today the bruises on her face seemed a bit lighter and the swelling was nearly gone. She had even walked about, trying to regain strength.

Six tapers cast their light over Abigail's shoulder onto the white fabric she was cross-stitching. Rachel had been reading, but her eyes had grown tired, and her book lay open facedown on her lap. Their conversation was guarded. Rob Wolfe's name had not been spoken among them since the morning he died, as though everyone thought that by power of conspiracy, he could be willed never to have been. But yesterday an officer had ridden out from Wilmington to see if Wolfe was able to return.

"Do you think he believed us?" Abigail asked for the third time within the hour.

"I don't know," Rachel answered quietly. "Desertions aren't uncommon. I can think of no flaw in our story. Yes, surely they believed us. They have no reason to believe anything else."

"But these are not reasonable times," Salali said, her voice smooth and low.

Suddenly, from the kitchen passageway, came the sound of footsteps, which each recognized as belonging to Mary, the servant girl. She was in a hurry, and when she burst into the parlor, their eyes were turned toward her, waiting.

"Mrs. Buchannon!" Mary said in alarm. "Oh, Mrs. Buchannon, do come! I think there's redcoats on the river road! I seen 'em from the kitchen door!"

Rachel rose instantly from the Queen Anne chair and went to the window. She saw them, out beyond the rose garden and down the hill, just visible in the failing light.

"Men on horseback! Dozens of them!" Rachel said, her voice tense.

Salali started up from the settee, but Abigail, who had put her cross-stitch aside and was on her way out, laid her hand on Salali's shoulder.

"Wait here," she said. "Mary, you stay, too."

On the brow of the lawn where it broke over and fell toward the river, Rachel and Abigail stood watching. The riders had come as far as the gate to the long drive, waiting, as if for final orders. A pinpoint of light appeared, and then another, as though flame was being passed from torch to torch.

"Oh, Rachel, it's all over," Abigail said. "They've come to fire the house!"

"Warn the others!" Rachel cried, and began to run.

Donald came walking at a leisurely pace up from the stable.

"Donald!" she screamed. "Redcoats! Torches! Tell the slaves to hide themselves! Jamie, where are you?"

Donald turned in his tracks and, cupping his hands about his mouth, hollered down to Clayton Walker, who bolted toward the edge of the pines where the slave dwellings stood. Jamie came running from the stables where he had been with Clayton. Donald grabbed him up and ran with Rachel directly to Salali, who sat waiting.

"What's happening?" Salali said when she saw their faces.

"They're coming!" Rachel said. "With lighted torches!"

Donald scooped Salali up in his arms and started out. Jamie looked around and, not knowing which way to turn, began to cry. Rachel grabbed him by the hand. "Stay right with me, Jamie!" she ordered, and started out the door behind Donald. Then she heard Salali call back frantically.

"The stallion! Someone save my stallion!"

"We'll get the stallion!" Donald said over his shoulder, and turned toward the stable.

Rachel was trying to think of what must be done. It was hard to think with the house servants screaming and running about as though they were chickens with their heads cut off. She was on the edge of the piazza when she thought of them— her mother's clock and Drew's letters. Why must she lose those? There might still be time.

"Donald!" she called. He was nearly to the stable, with Salali at his side. He spun around. "Take Jamie with you!" Rachel shouted. "I'm going back for Mama's clock and some letters."

"No!" he thundered.

"Yes!" she answered, and without hesitation turned and disappeared through the doorway.

Donald, on the verge of panic, called to the confused little boy. Abigail came running out, her arms filled with the precious little she could gather. Quincy was at her side, a pistol in his hand. He was pulling her on, ready to defend her with his life.

"Jamie, follow me as hard as you can go!" Donald said, and disappeared with Salali into the stable.

When Jamie reached the stable door, Donald and Salali were coming out, both on the back of the stallion. Donald bent far over, grabbing him by the hand and lifting him up. An instant later they were galloping toward the edge of the dark woods.

Back in the house, as Rachel reentered the parlor and made for the staircase, the faint light of distant torches was dancing furtively on the deserted walls. Lifting her skirts high, she bounded up the steps three at a time, ran down the hall, and came to her corner room. Instantly throwing open the trunk at the foot of her bed, she scooped up a small sheaf of letters. Hurrying to the chest of drawers, she opened the glass face of her mother's clock, removed the pendulum, and grasped the clock to her body.

The thud of many hooves came to her ears; pausing, she went to the window to gaze out. There they were, their torches flashing in little bursts of light, coming in a cluster not one hundred yards from the house. She turned about and one last time looked upon the room where she had found such welcome haven. Then she ran out, down the stairs and across the darkened lawn, toward the towering pine forest.

As she ran, the sharp insistent pain of breathlessness stabbed into her side. The clatter of hooves was on the upper drive, and felt nearly upon her. Torchlight brightened the budding leaves and gray bark of the trees that lay ahead. Surely they saw her, she thought. Surely within moments one would ride up behind and with his saber cut her down!

The rough ground descended suddenly beneath her feet as the dark woods towered only yards away. Suddenly she was among the trees.

"Which way?" she whispered. It was hard to think. She stood still and looked around. Everyone else had disappeared. She knew where they had gone: to a place agreed upon months ago, a ravine deep in the forest, thick with pine and undergrowth, hard to find and harder still to penetrate. Could she find the place alone in the darkness? She would be safer there, and she could comfort Jamie, who must be frightened out of his mind by now. But what if she could not find it? She could wander lost in the woods for days.

Then she saw it. Only a few feet away, festooning the limbs of one of the great trees, a bower of wild grapevine hanging down. Its vines were laden with Spanish moss. Grasping the clock tightly to her body, Rachel went down to her knees, and with voices and hooves clambering over the hilltop behind her, she crawled in among the vines and moss.

On the cold earth she lay facedown, breathing hard, gripping her side in pain, not daring to look. Then curiosity overpowered her and she lifted her face. Peering out from beneath the thick beards of black Spanish moss, her heart pounding in her throat, she watched.

Beyond the buildings of the plantation a blanket of dark gray clouds overspread the sky from horizon to zenith. Ignited by the low-lying sun, the clouds were a deep and brilliant orange. The great house with its grand piazzas stood tall, silhouetted resplendently amid black magnolias and pines, the gentle glow of candlelight still glimmering in its tall windows. That house, for Rachel, was a place of refuge, and after all these years, more her home than any place on all the earth.

The soldiers' shouts died down, and in the silence Rachel heard the hollow clomp of boots on the front piazza, heard a fist pounding on the door and a voice ringing out. A pause of utter silence. A shout, "The house is empty." Then, with a hundred pitch-pine torches blazing bright yellow in the deepening black of night, the shouts rose again. She watched them, men swinging down from saddles, clambering onto the piazza, heard doors broken down, glass smashed and tinkling to the floors; and then, to be burned forever into her memory, thrown torches making bright yellow arches of light. From the empty windows light flared—then silence, broken only by the crackling of draperies and hot wood hissing out long-trapped resins, little flames bursting forth. For breathless moments the flames grew on the drapes, until every window of the mansion was filled and the crackling became a roar. Then came crashes as plaster split in the heat and glass chandeliers fell, as fire from the clouds above seemed to descend on the fire below.

In the firelight she could see them clearly. These were British, all right, but not redcoats. Every man was dressed in the green of Tarleton's legion. Then her eyes focused on him—standing closer to the flames than all the rest, a stocky redhead in tight white breeches, black riding boots, and a black plumed hat.

"Tarleton!" she spat. Here again was the man she had met face to face at Fishing Creek, the man who gazed coolly down the bore of her pistol. Would God she had killed him!

Then, as suddenly, she forgot Banastre Tarleton. For the upper stories of the house had begun to burn and heat was reaching out. Silhouettes of tall pines were bursting with a roar into light; their crowns were torches raining down fire. Wonderful magnolias shriveled in the blast, igniting the honeysuckle-twined gazebo. The circle of soldiers widened and moved back to places of safety.

The night was cold, but the heat of the flames reached out to the forest, and beneath the beards of moss came a blast of heat. The light of the flames glistened in the sheen of sweat that broke out on Rachel's face and in the tears of disappointment and rage running down her cheeks. With her mother's clock resting at her side, she struck the ground with her fists and wept out her frustration.

Had justice on the head of Rob Wolfe been worth this? No! her mind screamed. This house was not hers to offer to the god Vengeance!

"Oh God!" she whimpered, "why did I bring this on them?"

Then from somewhere deep in her mind came a thought: The British are firing houses and barns and stacks of hay throughout the Cape Fear Valley. They know nothing of Rob Wolfe's fate.

For a moment Rachel caught the thought and held it, but quickly she let it go. Imprisoned in a cage of guilt, she was certain that she and she alone was to blame.

The flames, roaring to twice the height of the house, illuminated the hilltop from the smithy to the stables and the forest's distant edge. Below, on the road to Wilmington, a bewildered traveler found his way as clearly as he might have at midday.

Rachel watched the fire climb the pillars of the piazzas and the piazzas buckle and come crashing down. Then followed the magnificent roof, folding inward, shooting geysers of flame and belching sparks upward.

Had Sebetha Seiver felt as she now did when she watched her little wilderness cabin burn? Perhaps, but of all the aches of Rachel's heart, this was among the greatest.

It was midnight when at last the soldiers rode away. Rachel saw them go, heard the beat of horses' hooves fading away into the distance, but she did not move. Every fiber of her body was exhausted. There was no place to go, and it was not long before the weariness overcame her and she slept.

She awoke just before dawn. Even with the heat of the blaze, the cool ground on which she had lain chilled her through and through. Aching in every joint and muscle, Rachel crawled slowly from beneath the vines and moss. She straightened, ran her fingers through the tangled strands of her long hair, and then, alone, ambled slowly toward the still flaming ruins of the house. Only the hulks of four great chimneys reached upward from the burning mass. The towering old trees that stood about were charred and smoking.

Sorrowfully, she wandered from ruin to ruin. The smithy lay leveled to the ground, nothing but its blackened anvil and stone forge standing out of the ashes.

Then she found herself at the stable, standing on the very spot where she had fired the fatal gun four days ago. Lying among the stable's charred beams were the half-burned bodies of horses that had had no one to lead them from the burning barn. With unspeakable pain Rachel remembered how she had lain helplessly listening to them scream as the stables burned around them.

Just then she felt a warm hand close about her own. Frightened and startled, she looked about.

"Donald," she exclaimed.

"Rachel, we thought you were gone," he said, and gathered her close. "I came to find you."

"And the others?" She looked up pleadingly.

"Safe," he said. "Clayton came up with me to the edge of the woods, and he's gone back to bring them out."

She turned to look over the glowing ruins, then laid her head against his chest. "We did this," she said quietly.

Donald breathed deeply. "Perhaps," he said.

The sun was rising as the little band of refugees emerged from the forest. From everywhere, one could hear them weeping over the ruins. Only the little gray huts of the slaves, hidden among the pines, stood sound.

A heavy pall of white smoke lay over the hill, perfectly still in the unmoving air. The puzzled dogs sniffed about, little concerned, and Jamie and the other children were more fascinated by the burning than saddened by it.

Abigail came walking slowly over what had been her front lawn. The white smoke gathered in layers about her like a thick fog, and she wheezed a little as she spoke.

"I loved it more than I knew," she said quietly to Rachel. Even so, there were no tears in Abigail's eyes, and she smiled a little.

"Oh, Abigail," Rachel said, bowing her head, "what *can* I do? This," and looking up, she waved her hand over the smoking scene, "this is my doing. I tried to make him face what he had done to Salali . . . and I've pulled everyone down with me!"

"*Non*sense, girl!" Abigail said. "It was your presence among us that kept them from burning the place weeks ago!"

"Oh, how I want to believe that!" Rachel said.

"You must believe it, dear," Abigail returned, placing her arms about Rachel. "You absolutely *must* believe it!"

S E V E N T Y - F I V E

SHUT away from the sun as he was, Drew Wolfe found it hard to keep track of day and night, let alone of the months, but he calculated today as Friday, the eighteenth of May.

He jotted down the date in the worn leather journal he had carried since the beginning of the war, noted the number of days he believed he had been here—one hundred ninety-six—

then reached over and pinched out the flame of his candle. Light was precious, better saved till there was a face to see or thoughts to be put to paper.

"Collins," Drew had said last night as they sat in their stone dungeon, the candlelight glimmering on his prisonmate's unshaven countenance and in his watery eyes, "when a man's got three hours of light a day, even your ugly face is a sight to behold!"

In absolute darkness Drew went unerringly to his bunk, lay down, and pulled the blanket up about his head to shut out the clammy cold. Even the blanket seemed damp, but it was warm. Drew was starved for sound. Through this endless night, all he heard was water dripping incessantly from the walls, plinking with a metallic sound into puddles, that and the rasp of his own breathing, and voices drifting in from other parts of the mine.

As of today, the mine's stone bowels imprisoned thirty men—exactly thirty—and Drew had written down the name of every one. There was John Young, who called himself Mattick, and Ebenezer Hathaway and William Smith, both of whom were privateers caught in British service. There were three American soldiers—court-martialed, sent to New Gate by Washington himself; "flagrant and atrocious villains," Washington had written.

All the other prisoners were common felons; all, that is, but Samuel Collins, his Loyalist friend from upcoast, a British spy—taken in the very act. Collins was forty years old, pleasant, easy to get along with, and believed in England's right to rule the colonies. Since Taylor's death, Collins was the only man here Drew cared much about.

Taylor had died suddenly, about a month ago; some respiratory thing that ended in pneumonia. It was a wonder anyone survived in here, Drew had concluded. He had grown accustomed to the smell of mold in his clothing and thick beard, but one thing he hadn't got used to was the buckets of human waste that sat for hours before being hauled up on ropes. An infestation of smallpox would be hell down here.

When he thought about Rachel and Jamie, it drove him to distraction, so he tried not to think of them at all. Those days when he could not help himself, the inner pressures built to the point where he paced up and down the stone corridors until men in adjoining cells shouted for him to stop. Then he would stand, breathing hard in the darkness, tears cascading down his cheeks. He had never wept much before—not when his mother died, not when he left his father. But here he had learned; it was either weep or go mad.

He had also learned to occupy his mind with trivial things—counting the number of drips that fell in an hour from the corner ceiling of his cell into the puddle on the floor. He had removed the crystal of his pocket watch, so as to feel the hands. At first the dripping irritated him, but at last had become his companion. He counted the days of his life—twelve thousand, three hundred and ninety until today. He went through—in minutest detail—the performance of dozens of surgical procedures. For a time he would project himself out onto the ocean's face, sailing in a packet boat. But he had to give that up. Always the packet would turn uncontrollably toward the south, toward Rachel and Jamie.

Lying with his head covered, he tried to blot everything from his mind.

Suddenly, a sharp sound rang down the ladder shaft and through the corridors; iron on iron, someone banging the trapdoor. He listened. Hinges creaked, and a voice called out.

"John Young!" Pause. "John Young! Come to the head of the corridor. Your wife is here to see you!"

That would be Samuel Lilly's voice. Lilly was second-in-command over the prison guards. Soon Young's feet came shuffling past in the corridor.

Drew Wolfe listened, wondering why Young's wife should visit him at such an hour. Was it not night? He was sure of it, having felt the hands of his watch before pulling the blanket over his head. It had to be at least nine in the evening, perhaps even later. Drew followed Young's progress in his mind—through the corridor, to the foot of the vertical shaft, then step by step up the ladder. For a moment he thought he could actually feel a night breeze on his face, and then he imagined new leaves coming on the trees, and how they shone in the sunlight. Yes, above all, the sunlight! It would no doubt blind him after these months, but oh, Lord, how he longed for it!

"Wolfe!" came a whispered voice.

Drew threw the blanket from his head and looked about in the darkness. The voice came from the door of his cell. He had not heard the approach of Samuel Collins.

"Wolfe, did you hear that?"

"Hear? Sure, I heard Young going up the ladder shaft. What of it?"

"Nothing, maybe." Collins's voice was a whisper. "Could be my imagination, something I felt more than heard ... but I thought it was men going along the corridor, several men ... toward the ladder."

Drew held his breath and listened. He heard his own pulse thumping in his ears, and nothing else but the scraping of Young's shoe soles on the ladder. Then, abruptly, there was the sound of other feet, many of them.

"There's something afoot, Collins," Drew said quickly, rising on his right elbow. "Too many men in the ladder shaft!"

Then it came! The squeal of dry hinges, a shout, the explosion of a pistol, harsh voices of men shouting.

"Collins, it's a break!" Drew whispered hoarsely.

Instantly Drew was up, out of his chamber and crouching beside Collins in the blackness. Both strained to listen. Fighting—the vibration of heavy objects striking walls and of gunfire and men screaming. Then stillness.

The voice of Ebenezer Hathaway came down the ladder shaft.

"Stemson! Wolfe! Collins! The rest of you men, get up here!"

"Dear Lord, Hathaway! What do you think you've done!" Drew Wolfe was kneeling over Thomas Shelton where he lay on the guardhouse floor. Shelton was a prison guard.

"What do *you* think I've done, Wolfe?"

"I think you've lost your mind."

A large red pool spread out on the rough planking about Shelton. His shirt was blood-soaked from shoulder to waist, and his breathing came rapidly.

". . . and," Drew went on, "I think you've killed this man."

"Oh, dear God, John!" The voice belonged to Abigail Young, John Young's wife. She had retreated from the light and was standing in a dark corner of the guardhouse. Her shoulders shook and all she could say was, "Oh, dear God! Oh, dear God!"

Shelton's chest rose in a great gasp for air, and sank for the last time.

When Samuel Lilly had opened the door for Young to see his wife, the others, clubs in hand, had poured out of the shaft behind Young. Shelton, awakened from sleep, had come running and fought hard, but Hathaway had snatched up a gun with fixed bayonet and run him through.

Other guards lay wounded across the floor. Immediately Drew moved on to the next.

"You haven't got time, Wolfe," Hathaway said. "Let's go!"

"I'm staying," Drew answered without looking up. "Mrs. Young, get me some bandages!"

"Where?" the frightened woman sniveled.

"Tear your petticoat into strips if you have to!"

Hathaway snorted with disgust and turned toward the door.

"Risk our lives to get you out'a this hellhole, and like a fool, you say you're gonna stay!"

"Don't you want your own wound tended before you go?" Drew asked.

"No!" Hathaway shouted, and with the others he disappeared into the night.

"Where to now, Wolfe? Back to New York?"

It was the end of the first week in June, and the two men stood outside the guardhouse, basking in the delicious sunshine that spread its light across the woods and meadows of the Turkey Hills. Every tree was full green now, resplendent in summer foliage. It had been two weeks since the escape. Of the twenty-eight who fled, sixteen had been captured within six days. Prison authorities, grateful to Wolfe and Collins, had released them to go where they would—no questions asked. Drew breathed deeply and looked about him. He had missed winter entirely. Over his shoulder was a canvas bag that contained all his belongings.

"To my wife, Collins. I'm going to my wife and son. I've given this war everything I've had. More than was mine to give. Now the only thing I want is to live."

"You know, don't you," Collins said, "that the colonies will likely win this war? The Loyalist cause is lost." He paused, shielded his eyes from the sun, and gazed around at the distant Connecticut hills. "And we have to decide how to survive in a country that's come to hate us."

Drew smiled inwardly, not at Collins's misfortune, but at having kept his own secret so well. Even in prison, the one man he genuinely liked did not know. He could not say it to Collins, but he felt true sympathy for him, and for thousands like him, if, as they saw it, worse came to worse. Indeed, what would his kind do? There would not be many choices. They could return to England or go to Canada. There was talk of Halifax, land grants for the Tories from the Crown. Or they could restrain their tongues on political issues, stay where they were, and fit in as best they could.

There's no reason to tell Collins the whole truth, Drew thought. Better to part with good feeling between them.

"Well, Collins," he said, extending his hand, "this is good-bye." Drew looked into his friend's eyes, smiled, and shook his hand hard.

"God be with you, Andrew."

"And with you, Sam."

Then they had simply turned and walked away, one toward the south, the other toward the sea.

For two weeks Drew Wolfe avoided every human contact. He would not make the same mistake he had made last summer. Once again he traveled at night, not even daring to cross a road in the daylight. He had come a long way, having successfully bypassed New York without detection, and was deep in the pine forests of New Jersey. Soon he would find a place where he could cross the Delaware. To go by ship would have been faster, and infinitely easier, but his pockets were empty, and there was the ever-present risk of recognition or challenge.

Today the morning was sweet and his heart was full. Deep within the pines, he dropped beside a stream to drink. He lay facedown, his head and arms extended over the bank of a creek, lapping from his cupped palms. As the water touched his tongue and filled his mouth, its fluidity seemed to Drew Wolfe like the coming again of life. On the lowest limb of a wide-spreading oak, just above him and a little to his left, a barn swallow perched, its buff-colored throat swelling as it called gregariously, verse after rapid verse, "sweeter-sweet, sweeter-sweet, sweeter-sweet," ending each verse with the comic little chorus, "quiz-z-z-zeep, quiz-z-z-zeep!"

Drew chuckled, and then, in spite of himself, broke into laughter. He raised to his elbows. Below, through the stream's clear water, a small school of sunfish swam slowly past, the morning light shining brightly in the golds and blues and greens of their backs and fins. After a while Drew rolled onto his back and gazed off through the foliage toward the blue sky spread out overhead. For the first time in three years he was on his way to living again, and this cool creek bank with the sun-fish below and the twittering birds above was a promise of what he would find farther south.

The creek was the south branch of the Rancocas, but he did

not know that. And it did not matter that he did not know. He knew the direction of North Carolina, and he knew that, once again, he was free.

BOOK SEVEN

The Light
1781

SEVENTY-SIX

WHEN the great house fell in, all traces of aristocratic life at Buchannon Hills disappeared. Easy days of contemplation and school and music and cross-stitch were now only yearned for—impossible in the quest for simple survival.

It was mid-morning on a day of bright sunshine, and Rachel was sitting with Salali on the steps of the cabin that belonged to Mary the servant girl.

The warm sun filtering brilliantly through the long pine needles snatched away the chill of the glade and cast a patch of sunlight about them. Across Salali's face one could see, broadly written, the strokes of Rob Wolfe's treachery, and on Rachel's the burden of guilt.

"Salali," Rachel said, "if it hadn't been for me, Rob wouldn't even have been here. You would all be a thousand times better off had I never come!"

"Nonsense!" Salali said, taking Rachel's hand and holding it warmly. "Not one of us feels so. Why, Rachel, you and Jamie and Donald have added more to our lives than ever you could take away. Rob deserved what you gave him. No one can say why Tarleton burned us out, but we're not the only ones, and you've no right to blame yourself for being among us. Besides, dear, I can never forget that you did what you did in my defense. Please don't trouble yourself so!"

"Thank you," she whispered. Then, with an air of determination, "I can't go back and undo it, I can never replace the house, but what I can do, I will do."

"No one doubts that, dear Rachel," Salali said. "We know you all too well to believe anything different!"

Early the same afternoon, Donald and Clayton led crews of men and boys into the woods and began felling trees.

"We can cut enough timber in a week to build cabins," Donald said.

469

"And in another week," Clayton added, "we can have the cabins up."

Two weeks later, six new cabins built of unhewn logs stood on the open flat between ruins and forest.

When Rachel first stepped into her own cabin, her eyes dimmed at the memories of childhood. Floors of packed earth, a good roof to turn the rain, windows to let in the sun, and shutters to close out the wind. This was better than the little Scottish crofters' cottages, she thought, for rather than a circle of stones in the midst of the room, at one end was a fine fireplace. And over the top of its cavernous mouth, made of thick, rough-sawn plank, was a mantel.

Clayton Walker entered behind Rachel, bearing in his hands a hastily built box the size of a trunk. In it were all Rachel's earthly belongings.

"Set my things over there, Clayton," she said, "at the foot of the bed."

"Yes, ma'am," he answered.

The bed, as hastily constructed as the box, and just as sturdy, stood against the south wall beneath the open window. Clayton placed the box on the dirt floor at its foot as Rachel sat down on the corn-shuck ticking sewn with her own hands. The tick rustled and crackled as she sank into it.

A thought struck her, and she sprang up, going directly to the box. Clayton himself had built it, and as she opened it, he stood back and looked on appreciatively.

"This will go there," Rachel said, nodding toward the mantel as she lifted out a bundle wrapped in water-stained linen.

Gently she unwound the cloth and held its contents lovingly before her eyes. Her rescue of her mother's clock at the time of the soldiers' approach was now being rewarded. It was among the very few surviving treasures of the plantation.

"Set it in place for me, won't you, Clayton," she whispered.

"This old clock means a world to you, don't it, Mrs. Wolfe," he said as he took it gently in his big hands.

"More than I can say, Clayton. The feel of the wood and the quavering old chimes bring back memories of my mother and Scotland . . . and of Drew." She paused thoughtfully. "Drew loved to hear it ring out in the night; and early in the morning, while it was still dark, he would count the hours by its strike."

Clayton set the clock in the center of the mantel and looked questioningly toward Rachel.

"Perfect, Clayton," she said softly, then reached into the box again to find the pendulum and key. Even in the cabin's shadow the pendulum's silver disk shone as she rehung it and set it swinging. Once again came the rapid clicks of the old wooden gears as she wound it. With hands set, the clock immediately began to chime the hour.

"Time goes on, Mrs. Wolfe. Nothin' we can do to stop it."

Food was hard to come by. Deer—killed wholesale for hides shipped to England—had been dwindling in the coastal woods, until one might hunt for days and never once see the twin-pronged impressions of their feet in the soft earth. But Tarleton had not burned their grain store, and the Cape Fear, the swamps, and the Atlantic herself could yield food enough to pull them through: catfish and eel from the swamps, clams and crabs from the beach sands, and whatever could be brought up from the sea.

There was a mountain of debris to clean away. Endless sifting for treasures impervious to the firestorm; iron kettles and trivets and cranes from where the kitchen had stood, all pulled from deep ashes, shaken, wiped, and washed.

A pile of ash marked the spot of the majestic black marble fireplace. The marble had crumbled as it would have in a lime burner's kiln. Shapeless lumps of tarnished brass lay where the melted chandeliers had run down.

The foundation of the house had survived, and the chimneys, though there were dark gaps where stones had exploded. With borrowed horses, the men pulled the chimneys down, and with iron scrapers they leveled the hill and made it clean again. The black-charred trees, once loved for beauty and shade, were sawn and pried from the ground, and the earth smoothed over. Within a year or two grass would inch its way over the scars, erasing every sign that the house had ever been . . . every sign except its memory in the minds of those who had loved it.

In the midst of all this, on a day late in May, a cumbersome two-wheeled cart rattled up the drive behind a half-starved ox, driven by a man who lay propped against the cart's side. The ancient conveyance reached the hilltop without anyone realizing it was there. For a long while the man stood gazing, biting the inside of his lower lip, his eyes hollow with hurt, a little misty, shaking his head slowly from side to side.

"Dear Lord," he murmured, "what can a man say to a sight like that?"

Just then Jamie Wolfe rounded the corner of a cabin, saw

the ox, the cart, the man, and stopped still, his eyes growing wide. The little boy lifted his right foot, lowered it again.

"Jamie!" Edward Buchannon called.

"Grampa!" Jamie answered, and running hard, climbed the side of the ox cart and threw his arms around Edward's neck. Edward held him close, and Jamie buried his face in the big man's shoulder.

"Your mother?" he questioned at last, breaking the spell. Jamie looked about and pointed toward the cluster of little houses.

"Mama's in our cabin," he said, and twisting free, bounded down. Suddenly he stopped and stared at Edward's right leg.

"What's the matter, Grampa?" he said with a quaver in his voice.

Edward's knee was bent sharply, his foot tucked in an old slipper that had been nailed to a thin piece of board. A leather strap attached to the back end of the board was tied to his upper leg just above the knee, holding the knee flexed and the foot extended.

"Well sir!" Edward chuckled. "A fella I didn't see whacked me with a sword—right in the back of my leg, and cut a tendon clear in two."

Jamie continued to stare, fell silent, the image of a man with a razor-sharp sword looming before his eyes.

"Are you gonna get well?" he asked, his eyes very large.

"You bet!" Edward said, smiling broadly. "But I gotta wear this rig till that tendon heals." He paused. "Now, Jamie," he said, "let's see if we can find your mother and Salali and Grandma Buchannon."

And with a light snap of the whip above the head of the ox, the beast stepped forward and the wooden wheels began again to groan.

When Rachel had heard Jamie shout "Grampa," she had risen from her mending and looked out the door of her cabin. It had been a whole year since Edward had gone away. Even across the yard she could see that he was different. The fleshiness of his face was gone and his body had slimmed down—and yet there was still the power and strength about him there had always been. As she ran to meet him, her large brown eyes met his gaze and found that the bluish-gray she had always loved was more piercing than ever.

His wonderful smile broke the spell that had fallen upon her, and she ran out crying, "Abigail, Edward's come home!"

Rachel reached Edward just as he was hobbling out of the cart to the ground, and threw her arms about him.

"We missed you so!" she said, her cheek against his.

His big hand felt warm and good on her back as he held her.

"Oh, Rachel, you'll never know," he said.

With Edward steadying himself on her shoulder and leaning on a crutch fashioned from a white oak sapling, they started for Abigail's cabin just as his Nabby ran screaming to him. Rachel stood back as Abigail came into his arms.

Finally, Abigail looked into Edward's face and laughed. "You're brown as a hickory nut," she said.

"Isn't that what dried-out leather's supposed to look like?" he joked.

The skin of his face and hands was weathered from months of uninterrupted exposure to the sun and wind, heat and cold, and his black hair was grayer than before. But as he held Nabby, looking over her shoulder at Rachel, the old quick, easy smile spread over his face, and his smooth row of upper teeth glistened white in their warm and friendly way.

"I see you built me a brand-new house," he said quietly as he hugged Abigail close.

When Rachel heard his words and saw the strength of his resolve, she began to cry.

"Oh Edward! Edward!" Abigail wept. They were the first tears Rachel had seen in Abigail Buchannon's eyes since his going. "I did the best I could," she said rapidly. "Oh Edward, hold me!"

"You did *good*," he said, as his arms tightened about her. "You did *real* good!"

In spite of his injury, Edward Buchannon took charge of everything on the day of his return. For eleven months the plantation had been like a body without a soul, for he was the kind of man who leaves a large empty place when he's gone. He began by standing in the midst of the leveled site where the mansion had stood, his arm around Abigail's shoulders, looking about at the emptiness.

"It's worth it, Nabby," he said. "Our part of the price for a new nation."

That afternoon, Edward rode out to look at his fields and to order the planting of the crops.

* * *

It was a warm morning in early summer as Rachel emerged from her cabin with a small palmetto frond basket on her arm. Edward was sitting in a wicker-back chair under the shade of one of the great magnolias that had survived the fire. His hickory crutch lay across his lap, and his temporarily crooked leg was stretched out before him. Clayton Walker had just spoken to him and was now heading toward the barns.

As Rachel passed under the magnolia on her way to the lilac bush, the tree's large white blossoms let down their fragrance about her. Her path led behind Edward's chair, and as she went by, she patted his shoulder warmly.

The lilac bush, taller than Rachel, was covered in fragrant pastel clusters. With a small pair of scissors, Rachel clipped one, smelled its sweetness, and reaching over, laid it on Edward's shoulder. He smiled, took it between his fingers, touched it to his nose, and breathed deeply.

For a moment the only sound was the snipping of Rachel's scissors as she clipped bunches of lilacs and placed them in her basket, that and the coo of doves from a tall pine.

"Clayton tells me the planting is done," Edward ventured.

"I overheard," she answered, her voice soft and quiet.

He was looking over his shoulder, watching her closely. "Rachel . . ." he said tentatively.

"Yes?" she answered.

Obviously Edward wanted to draw her out. She knew the expression on her face was neutral, neither a frown nor a smile. Sometimes these days she didn't feel much like smiling, but she was content. She waited for him to speak, and snipped the last bunch of lilacs to fill her basket.

"Rachel," he dared at last, "you've been different since I came home."

She turned about and her large brown eyes met his gaze. "We're all different, Edward," she said. "That's what war does to people."

She left the bush, walked slowly toward him, and sat down on the grass near his feet. Quietly she began to arrange the flowers in her basket.

"You mustn't blame yourself for what happened here, Rachel," he said, waving his hand over the hill.

"So everyone tells me," she answered. "But it's hard not to."

"I know," he said, laying one large hand discreetly on her

shoulder. "And all this just adds to the load you've carried for years. You've had too many troubles—all of them hard—and it's been too long, the war, your husband . . . and now this."

With the little basket on her knees, Rachel cupped her hand over the blossoms, patting them gently into an oval dome. Silently she shook her head—slow little movements. She set the basket aside and looked out over the distant river.

"It has been a long war, hasn't it," she said, with slightly more expression than before.

She looked down to see an inchworm alternately arching and stretching its way up over the hem of her dress, a pale green worm whose color blended with the deeper green of the cloth. She reached down and extended her finger. The worm attached itself to her fingertip and inched its way onto her palm.

"Measuring me for my coffin," she said, with a little laugh.

It was a thing often said lightly, a minor superstition. Even so, Edward winced inwardly. "Don't talk that way," he said.

"You think I've given up on life, don't you, Edward?" she asked, looking directly into his eyes. "But I haven't. Oh, Rob made a fool of me, and I'll never again trust a man with my love. Maybe that's what you see in my face—the end of my hope for a man's love. But I haven't given up on life, so don't you worry."

Edward smiled a little. "There's nothing a man can say to that," he said at last, his voice very quiet. "You know we all love you, Rachel, but you're talking about a different kind of love . . . a kind none of us can help you with."

He fell silent again. A light breeze ran by, stirring the leaves of the magnolia above them.

"Rachel," he said at last, "I'm going to say something to you." He hesitated, as though struggling. "I don't know what you think of the way I live my life. It doesn't really matter what you think, I guess. I'll probably go right on living it the way I do no matter what anybody thinks." He looked down at her, smiled his familiar smile, and chuckled. His heavy brows arched, and there was kindness in his gray-blue eyes.

"You probably don't think I'm a praying man," he went on. "But Rachel, I do pray. A man can have a world of land, a big fine house—like Nabby and I had—a good family. And I've had the best . . . absolutely the best! But Rachel, no matter how good life is, disaster is always only a hairbreadth away.

And so—even though you can't tell it by looking at me—I do pray."

He picked up his crutch and jabbed nervously with it at the ground, obviously uncomfortable with this self-revelation.

"When the reg'lars charged us in the woods at Guilford Courthouse, you can bet I prayed then. I asked God to get me back home. And ... I prayed for my family. And for you. You're part of my family, have been from the first night I met you."

Rachel laid the inchworm down and watched it arching and stretching its way through the grass.

"In the end, Rachel," he said, "life will be what you make it. But I'll tell you this," he leaned forward, arching his brows and looking directly into her eyes, "you're a better woman now than when you first came!"

Rachel blushed and lowered her eyes, smiling—the first real smile he had seen on her lips in days.

"God—whoever, whatever you think God is," he added, "He works on us, Rachel. It's the way of life. He puts us up against the hard things and makes us learn our lessons. And when we've learned one, we go on to the next, and the next, and the next. If that sounds high-toned comin' from me, I got it from your brother when we lay in the mud together back on the Congaree."

Rachel laughed. "Then I guess I've had lots of lessons to learn, Edward," she said. "But I think you're right; I am a better woman than when I came to the hill. Less selfish, a little slower to speak my piece."

"Careful you don't make yourself sound like some old woman!" He chortled. "You got lots of fire yet to tame."

Rachel laughed and patted the lilacs again. "And we just never know where it's going to flame up next, do we?" she said.

"No, Rachel," he said, smiling, "we surely don't!"

SEVENTY-SEVEN

DREW WOLFE dragged the black tricorn hat from his head with one hand and wiped sweat from his brow with the other. In front of him, another tidewater creek lay blocking his path. In spite of early July heat, the water didn't look a bit inviting, spread over as it was with green, scummy algae, broken limbs sticking up, hung heavy with Spanish moss. He wondered if alligators lived this far up the coast, though he really had no way of knowing how far south he had come.

Picking his cautious way down the seaboard, he had come to an occasional narrow, sandy road, never yielding to the temptation to see where it led. Whenever he had found the forest thinning or spotted a farmhouse, he angled a bit back to the east. That kept him among the thickest forests, but on terrain that was hard to travel.

Now, he stood looking down at the scummy water. No telling how deep it was. Three feet maybe, maybe ten. He hooked his thumb under the strap of his "new invented haversack," swung it to the ground, and looked around for something to float it across on, but nothing suggested itself. The sack held his eating utensils—a cup, a spoon and fork combination, a few roots scrounged from the forest, and food that he had stolen from an unguarded house. His blanket—the one that had kept him company in the copper mine—was rolled up and strapped inside the haversack, sagging out at each end. Every night he lay on half the blanket, covered with the other half, and used the sack for his pillow.

His eye fell on a dead sapling leaning against a nearby oak. Taking it up, finding it dry and sound, he hauled back and swung the sapling hard against the oak trunk again and again, snapping off pieces as long as his arm. Then he yanked down handfuls of Spanish moss, and with its strands, bound the broken pieces of wood into a miniature raft.

With hat, haversack, and shoes piled on the raft, he pushed

it out across the water and stepped in after it. The oozy mud squished warmly between his toes, then the bottom fell away and he was swimming, pushing the raft before him. The water, hot as the heavy air, gave him no relief from the heat.

Drew compressed his lips tightly as the stinking scum lapped nearly to his nose, and he held his breath to keep the fetid air out of his lungs. But the creek was too wide, and at midstream he lifted his head, gulped a deep breath, and plunged on.

A broken treetop, snapped eight or ten feet above the ground but never wrenched free from its trunk, lay angled with its crown in the water. Strips of bark, rotted and shaggy, hung limply, unmoving in the motionless air. Drew was passing through the shadow of the broken trunk, scarcely aware of the log's existence, when he cut his eyes upward. There, on top of the log, warming its cold, thick body in the afternoon sun, was a snake. It was still, unmoving. Drew tensed. Even from low in the water he could see that the viper's head was wide and its body marked with dark, ragged-edged stripes. Then the snake's eyes came alive, it started and began to slither down. An electric shock went down Drew's spine and his blood turned cold.

The serpent slithered off the side of the log and dropped heavily into the water beside him. Drew kicked hard, trying to lunge for the shore. Slimy ground slid under his bare feet as he grabbed at roots and vines to pull himself forward. Scrambling up the bank, his feet went out from under him and he fell hard on his face, his hand coming down on a broken limb. He grabbed it up and turned about, ready to swing, but the snake had disappeared.

It had not followed him after all, but he saw it, rapidly winding its way through the water, cutting the green scum, its wide head planing the surface. It reached the bank not ten feet from where he stood, gliding up and into the damp fallen leaves, seeking cover in the underbrush. Drew lunged savagely forward, striking the thick body just behind the head with his club.

The snake curled back around, its yawning mouth a white, puffy cavern, its two long yellow fangs unfolded to strike. With all his might Drew whipped the club sideways, pinned the snake's head to the ground, and, laying all his weight on the upper end of the club, ground the creature's neck into the dirt. Its thick body flopped and twisted and looped furiously about the club as a raspy hiss poured from its open throat. Then thin red blood came oozing out, staining the white, cottony mouth, and the violent flopping slowed to nothing. But Drew pressed harder, his teeth clenched, pouring sweat blinding his squinting gray eyes.

Whole minutes went by before he slowly took his weight from the club. With it, he nudged the thick body until he knew beyond all doubt it was dead, then reached gingerly down, picked it up by the tail, and, holding the tail above him, observed that its head still dragged the ground.

"Bigger around than my arm at the biceps!" he said aloud.

He drew the knife given him when he left prison, and pried the snake's mouth open, watching as the yellow fangs folded down. He propped the mouth open with a stick, and with the knife tip nudged the soft cottony tissue.

Having satisfied his curiosity, he laid the neck across a log, severed the spine, cut off the wide head, and made a shallow incision down the long belly. The entrails he tore out with his fingers, and staking one end of the body to the log, peeled the scaly hide back from white, fresh meat tinged faintly pink.

When the job was done, he dropped down to sit on the ground, but not before making sure no other dangers lay beneath him. He saw, then, that his hands were shaking. He lifted his right hand up and tried to hold it steady, but it shook as though not his own. His nails were ragged and dirty, and black dirt filled the crevices of his skin.

Steady at last, Drew got up and retrieved his things from the raft, which still lay in the water's edge. He pulled the worsted stockings from the shoes where he had stuffed them, slipped them over his feet and up his calves, shaking his head in dismay. The stockings were full of holes torn by brambles in the pine barrens, but at least the raft had kept them dry.

Since leaving the copper mine, he had made certain there was nothing on or about his person that bore even a suggestion of the British army. His shoes, badly scuffed and worn down at the heels, were perfectly ordinary. His tan breeches and white shirt were sun-faded and stained. He tucked the tops of the stockings up under his breeches, knowing full well that within a hundred yards they would be sagged down around his shins.

Anxious to get through the swampy ground, he threw the snake's body into his haversack, swung the strap up onto his shoulder, and headed out, cheered by the thought that tonight he would have real meat.

Drew felt reasonably sure that he was headed in the right direction, for even among the tall trees it was easy to keep the sun before him. And always on cloudless nights he guided himself by the north star.

As he trudged onward, he thought again of his destination. It was the one thought that kept him fighting day after day through this interminable tangle of forest and undergrowth: that he would find Rachel and Jamie. Again and again Rachel's face came before his eyes. He could see her just as she was in their brightest hours. Instantly his spirits soared and strength surged into his tired back and legs.

On he went, slashing at vines and fallen limbs, until, with the sun sinking into the west, he came to a place in the forest where the ground rose up in a hill. On the hill's slopes the trees seemed to thin out a little. There was a hospitable feeling here—as though at some time or other, perhaps in the long distant past, something of humankind had tarried on this spot. The hill's gentle bank was covered with thick, green moss, deep and spongy, the kind a man could lie down on and almost feel he was in bed. A small spring of fresh water ran noiselessly out of the earth near its crown and down a narrow cut, to gather in a little pool at its feet.

Dropping down, Drew cupped his hand and lifted the water to his nose. It even *smelled* clean. Weary almost beyond endurance, he stretched full length and plunged his head into the cool water. When he rose, he spread his blanket over the deepest moss and put his things in order. He gathered wood, struck a fire, and cut a young green limb. Soon the slender limb was lying across two forked uprights, with half of the snake's body spitted over the flames.

The meat was sweet and good. When at last Drew stretched out and pillowed his head on his haversack, his stomach was full and he felt at ease. Tomorrow he would have the strength to resume his quest for Rachel and Jamie.

That night Drew slept soundly. He awoke just as the morning sun brightened the uppermost tops of the trees above him. Today was the fifth . . . the fifth of July. He was certain of that, because on the day he left New Gate, he had cut a fresh green stick half as big around as his little finger and twice as long.

Every morning since, before doing anything else, he had notched the stick, making a wider notch for Sundays.

Drew raised up on his elbow, fished the stick from his haversack, and carefully cut today's notch. As he tucked it away again, he became aware of a faint sound somewhere in the woods—the noise of feet moving, whether human or something else, he could not tell. More than once he had been fooled into thinking some wild thing was human. Instantly he sprang up, snatched his blanket and pack from the ground, and plunged into the brush. Hunched down and hardly breathing, he listened as the crunch of feet came nearer, then stopped. There was a long moment of silence. Then the bushes parted in front of his eyes, and he found himself staring down the barrel of a French musketoon in the hands of a Continental soldier.

They *believed* him! He told them he had served Washington in the north, had been captured, freed, and now was headed south to find his family.

"We're Lafayette's command," a soldier said, "playing tag with Cornwallis!"

They sat cross-legged outside the soldier's tent, the same soldier who had spotted the tail of Drew's blue blanket sticking out beneath the bush.

"Lafayette! Cornwallis!" Drew exploded. "In the south? Where are we anyway?"

"On the peninsula," the soldier answered, "a few miles outside of Williamsburg. Benedict Arnold's been making raids into Virginia. Washington sent Lafayette down to stop him. Cornwallis got enough of Greene in the Carolinas, and came up here to beat Lafayette; thought he could 'trap the boy,' but so far 'the boy's' proved too slick for 'im."

"Lafayette," another soldier broke in, "*he* says we're not strong enough even to get beat!"

Drew's head was in a whirl. "Does he expect to en*gage* Cornwallis?"

"Harassment mostly, but it looks like Cornwallis is about to cross the James—maybe tomorrow. Lafayette's gonna dog 'im all the way. Who knows, maybe we can catch 'im straddlin' the James."

Drew's interest rose quickly. This might be his chance at last—his chance to fight openly on the side he believed in. He leaned forward, his eyes fixed on the soldier's face.

"Can Lafayette use another doctor?"

The soldier returned his gaze with surprise. "Always!" he said.

"Well," Drew said, "lead me to your chief medical officer!"

SEVENTY-EIGHT

ONE morning when summer had given over to mellow September, Rachel sat alone in front of her cabin. She was on the grass, cross-legged, with the skirt of her gingham dress spread about her. She was leaning so intently over an open book that she did not hear Salali approach.

"The book must be good!" Salali said.

"Oh!" Rachel started, and looked up.

Salali was standing over her, arms akimbo, smiling. Rachel smiled back.

"It's a wonderful book," she answered, and held the embossed leather cover up for Salali to see. *"Macbeth."*

"Ohh," Salali exclaimed.

> "This castle hath a pleasant seat; the air
> Nimbly and sweetly recommends itself
> Unto our gentle senses."

"You know it, then!" Rachel was pleased.

"Only a little—but the lines I know happen to fit the day," she said as she sat down facing Rachel.

A mild breeze from the southeast gently waved the hand-size leaves of a nearby magnolia, imparting the slightest feeling of autumn. While Rachel was looking up, the wind flipped three or four pages in her book.

"Where's Jamie?" Salali asked. The sun reflected warmly on the dark skin of her forearms and face.

"With 'Grampa Buchannon.' " Rachel chuckled. "I think they've taken each other to the river fishing."

"Good," Salali said. "Everyone's worked hard, and we need

rest." She looked at Rachel again, this time at the weariness in her eyes. "And you've worked hardest of all," she said.

"I owe it," Rachel answered.

"Still thinking they burned us out because of you," Salali responded.

Rachel dropped her gaze to the grass. "It's hard to think another way," she said.

Salali shook her head and smiled. "In any case," she went on, "we've confined ourselves to these dreary little houses and the labor of setting things right for too long! What would you say to our riding down to the light? We could stay the night with Spaun. Jamie's well-tended, and Donald's busy with his students. We'd hardly be missed."

Rachel looked wistfully down at the pages of her book, then up through the pine tops at the morning sky, where light feathers of cloud scrolled a rich blue. It had been many months since they had been to the light. Warm sand would feel good beneath bare feet, and the salt air and the sound of gulls crying in the wind. Besides, there was Old Spaun; she had neglected Spaun too long. She looked back at Salali.

"Yes . . . yes," she said. "I'd like that."

When their cantering horses topped the last rise and the ocean came in view, it was early afternoon. Spaun's light was visible to the southeast. Just as Rachel had envisioned, the seas were running high before a strong breeze. The smell of salt air was in her nostrils, and out over the breakers the gulls were crying.

"You see," Salali said loudly above the surf's roar, as they reined in on the rise above the beach, "the ride has done us good! We *have* to feel better with our blood pumping again!"

Rachel tossed her head, her long hair, gathered and tied to flow down the center of her back, whipping out before the wind. In her eagerness, she was hardly hearing Salali's voice. Rising in the saddle, Rachel gazed toward the ocean's great horizon, scanning it from south to north. Her face was shining and her eyes glistening as she drank in the power of the surf, feeling the old pull. There was something in the rhythm of land, sea, and sky that was more than the cold mechanics of a great cosmic machine. It was almost as if it were alive. And sometimes she was certain it was speaking to her. That was what she liked most about Salali. Salali shared that feeling with her.

It was their nature, in the midst of the dreariest rain, to seek

out the most dismal, dripping forest, and in the wind to find
the windiest hill, or to come here where the surf was fierce and
wild.

"It takes my breath away!" she called over the sound of
breakers and gulls. "And you were right, it was time to come
here again. I need to feel it—the power, the freedom, the wind
on my face and in my hair!

"Look!" Rachel shouted suddenly, pointing over the dune.
"Look! Oh, Salali, look!"

Above the dune, reaching high into the air, was a vortex of
hawks.

"Never in my life have I seen the like!" Salali exclaimed.

"No," Rachel whispered in awe. "Nor have I."

There were almost two hundred hawks forming the perfect
vortex, each bird wheeling about the center, the lowest perhaps
fifty feet above the ground, and the highest, at the vortex's
wide crest, much, much higher. All were drifting as one to the
south as though following the line where water met land.
When the vortex came over the tower of Spaun's light, it
paused, and then moved on.

Both young women sat staring.

"It has meaning," Rachel whispered, her gaze fastened to
the gathering of hawks as it grew fainter.

"Surely it must," Salali said. "Come on," she shouted,
breaking the spell and kicking her mount's sides.

Together they plunged forward over the sandy ridge and
down through the wind-bent sea oats, to where pounding water
met hard sand. Hooves splashed wildly in the rolling silver
film as on and on they raced, southward, parallel to the sea.
Euphoria surged through Rachel, her heart pounding more rapidly than the sea. She could feel it in her chest and hear it in
her ears.

When they reached the point, before her mount had come to
a stop, Rachel swung down and Salali followed suit. She
slapped the rumps of the horses, sending them galloping back
to graze higher up among the grasses and sea oats; then forgetting the horses altogether, they turned to face the sea. One after
another the breakers, white-capped, stretched out to where the
water was deep and the dark green rollers ran, parted by wide,
dark hollows.

"Shall we?" Rachel shouted, looking at Salali and grinning.
With her hair whipping about into her face and eyes, she laid
one hand on Salali's shoulder, pulled the high-topped riding

boots from her feet and the stockings from her legs, then tossed them aside and ran into the breakers.

The water surged about Rachel's feet and ankles, then rose and suddenly broke chest high, sending spray over her head. A laugh burst from her lips as she reemerged, shaking a spray of water from her hair and wiping her eyes. Just then Salali, too, ventured into the crashing surf, and running out, took Rachel by the hands.

"*Feel* it!" Rachel said, standing thigh deep in the boiling foam. "The *life*! The excitement!"

Then, looking back over her shoulder, she screamed to see a breaker coming that stood gigantically above all the others. In an instant it was upon them, irresistibly bearing them up, passing on and leaving them as they rubbed their eyes and spit saltwater amid wild laughter.

Farther out they ventured, until forced to swim with all their strength when the mountainous, emerald waves crashed like thunder about them. One by one each rolling green swell passed on to the shore, leaving them in a great trough, shutting the land from sight until their entire world was one mountain of translucent green after another.

Rachel felt sudden awe as great as if God Himself had come to stand before her.

"It *draws* me so!" she breathed, the water running down her face. She pulled back her hair with both hands. They were out beyond the roar now. "I could plunge into the next crest and swim out forever and ever!" There was a look of longing and a strange distance in her eyes.

"Don't talk so!" Salali said, feeling a sudden pang of fear. About their legs they felt the irresistible outward flow.

"We've gone too far!" Rachel said with alarm. Instantly the next unpredictable roller bore them up in its arms.

"*Now* we swim!" Salali shouted.

And with all their might they pulled for the shore.

It was not until an hour before sunset that Spaun became aware of their presence. He saw them standing across the inlet, waving and calling. With his hands high above his head, he waved back.

"I'm coming," they heard him call. The inlet was quieter than the exposed beaches, and over the distant roar, they could hear the gladness in his voice.

He came down the grassy hill in his bow-legged run. Overturning his dory and shoving it out, he jumped in and, his back toward them, began to row. Ashore, he bounded out, embracing first Rachel and then Salali.

Rachel saw a tear in the old man's eye, and he turned away to hide it, motioning them into the boat. Once on the water, Rachel gave herself over to the undulation of the boat riding the crests, the first feeling of pleasant languor she had known in months. They had dried themselves in the evening sun, and Salali sat leaning against the gunnel, trailing her finger in the water. Rachel watched her, thinking of how Salali's race once came to these bars of sand for clams and fish, and how the Europeans had driven them inland, decimated their nation, and cut them off from the sea. At the moment, her friend's face reflected the same inner peace that she herself felt.

The trio tugged the boat up onto the sand. Rachel, running ahead, was first to stand at the foot of the light and gaze seaward.

Darkness was coming rapidly on, the sea growing calm as Rachel mounted the tower steps for the first time in many months, and lighted the candles one by one.

As the lantern glowed with warmth and light, it seemed to Rachel that it was sympathizing with the warm ache in her heart. Now that there was nothing left for her in the north, this coast, this light was truly home, especially the light; there was something about the stone tower, so indestructible even in the fiercest winds. It gave her a feeling of safety and a sense of peace in spite of the war, stalemated in the north, but violent as ever up in Virginia where the armies were, and in the little skirmishes that flashed here and there across the Carolinas and Georgia.

The light blue western sky shrank rapidly before the gathering darkness. With the lantern lighted, Rachel leaned her shoulder against the glass and gazed into the night, seeing an occasional blinking star, and tiny lights where distant fishing boats rode homeward on the breast of the deep.

Morning came. The rising sun broke through unsettled clouds; grays, both light and dark, mottled with patches of distant blue. There was a fresh wind blowing in from the sea.

Spaun sat with elbows on the table, his empty breakfast plate wiped clean. Salali knelt at the fireplace, rolling fresh wood from her arms onto the fire while Rachel sat across the table from the old man.

"Jacob," she said, a question in her voice, "we saw something on our way here yesterday. And last night as we lay in bed we wondered if ever you had seen anything like it."

"What'd ya see?" he asked.

Salali came over and stood nearby, listening as Rachel told Spaun about the hawks circling in a vortex over the light. The old man shivered and grinned.

"Never seen nothin' like that!" he said. "Most hawks I ever seen in one place was about twenty, all out settin' in a field. But two hunnerd, and all aflyin' around like that? No, never did."

Rachel looked up at Salali and smiled.

"It means something," Salali said.

"Maybe it'uz a weather change," Spaun said.

"No," Salali said, "something more."

"Well, *some*thin' uncommon in the air!" Spaun said. "They's a weather change acomin', hawks or not."

"I've noticed," Rachel said. "A storm?"

"Can't tell for certain, but I think so," he answered absently. He paused, rose, and went to the window. "Long as you're here to see to the light," he said as he looked out, "think I'll go in for supplies. Coffee's low, and I been waitin' for a fresh bunch'a candles to come down from Philadelphia."

"No one expects us home until tonight," Salali put in. "If Rachel doesn't mind leaving Jamie with Abigail another day, I'd like to stay." She looked questioningly at Rachel.

"We'd be glad to keep the light, Jacob. Go and bring us news from town."

In moments he was gone.

Salali went out to walk the dune in solitude, while Rachel sat with *Macbeth* open on her lap. At the beginning of scene five her concentration wandered for a moment as she noticed the climbing whine of the wind about the eaves.

Rachel had been alone for perhaps two hours when she heard feet scraping outside the door. With a burst of wind behind her, Salali entered, slammed the door and stood with her back to it. She was breathing hard, less from exertion than from tension in the air.

"Oh!" she exclaimed. "The wind: it's roaring across the sand, and the swells are like mountains!"

"I heard," Rachel answered. "Jacob was right—a storm is on its way in." Rachel laid aside her book and got up. "I'll do the lantern chores now."

"I'll come along and help," Salali said.

"No ... if you don't mind," Rachel said, "I'd like to do them alone."

Salali looked at her quizzically.

"There's nothing wrong," Rachel said in response to the look. "I just need the time by myself. I'll come down in an hour or two."

The wind made the glass of the lantern hum, and it whistled about the eaves, but the tower did not so much as quiver in the gale.

With a pair of scissors, Rachel carefully trimmed the wick on every candle, then, with fine-powdered rouge on the soft chamois, polished the great brass reflector and bathed it with spirits of wine. The cabinet beneath the reflector proved to be full of candles, but the ones in place would last at least another night.

She examined the eight tall glass panes, faintly clouded with salty condensation. A catwalk ran completely about the lantern, and there was an iron rail for protection—but when she opened the door, the blast of air drove her instantly back. It took all her weight and strength to force the door closed.

As she stood with her hand on the latch, something suddenly came over her—a feeling first of panic, then of fear, for out on the water a ship had appeared. It was as clear as anything she had ever seen, and yet she knew perfectly well that it was not there. And there were voices—faint screams coming from across the waves. Then they were gone—both the ship and the voices. Rachel's heart pounded hard in her chest and she was hardly breathing.

She sat down heavily in Spaun's dark-stained chair. What could it mean? she thought. There was not a ship on the horizon. The sun was shining brightly, though there were scattered dark clouds torn in pieces by the wind, scudding in from the southeast.

"What does it mean?" she asked aloud for the second time that day. There was no answer but the moaning of the wind.

It was late afternoon when Spaun appeared on the opposite shore. For the last hour, both Rachel and Salali had watched for him. Together they ran down to the beach. There he stood across the rough water, frantically waving both arms, gesturing that the inlet was too rough to cross.

"That settles that," Salali said, waving back. Her voice was nearly lost in the wind. "Without Jacob's boat, we can't cross."

"Well, it's all right," Rachel said. "We knew this could happen ... it is hurricane season." She peered across the inlet. "What is he saying now?" she asked. "I think he's trying to tell us something."

"Whatever it is, he's excited about it," Salali exclaimed.

"He's pointing to the open sea," Rachel said, turning about, but from her vantage point she could see nothing other than the light and the dune on which it stood.

Spaun kept pointing, gesturing excitedly. He tried shouting, but the roar of the surf and the wail of the wind drowned out his voice.

Rachel turned and ran into the tower while Salali remained on the ground below. Two steps at a time she ascended the spiral staircase in the darkness, breaking into the lantern compartment. From high above the dune, she swept the ocean's horizon with her eyes.

Yes! There they were! White sails spread wide and reaching hard to the north. She yanked open a chest drawer, took out the leathern case, and removed Spaun's telescope. She extended it, focused on the nearest spread of sail, and instantly understood his wild animation. On the stern flagstaff of the ship, whipping boldly in the driving wind, were the red and white crosses of Saint Andrew and Saint George, the Union Jack of England!

Rachel bounded down the steps three at a time, running back to Salali.

"What is it?" Salali asked.

"British ships headed north!" she answered, at the same time waving to Spaun that she had seen it.

When Spaun was certain they understood, he waved again and turned. The last they saw of him, he was going up through the wildly waving oat grass to higher ground with his peculiar, bow-legged walk, to seek shelter.

Salali started back up the rise, realizing when she reached the keeper's house that Rachel was not with her. She looked back to see Rachel walking very slowly, her head lifted to the wind, obviously in deep thought.

"What's the matter?" Salali called.

"Nothing," Rachel answered, her voice sounding far away. "Nothing at all," she whispered to herself, but she knew there was something, something she did not understand. Did the ship

bound north have something to do with the vision that had
flashed before her that morning?

She could do nothing but wait and see.

SEVENTY-NINE

THE sun sank in the west, darkness fell over the sandy dune,
and the wind's force grew.

Inside the keeper's house Salali busied herself preparing a
supper of salt pork and cornmeal mush. In the fireplace a small
kettle hung on a crane over a blazing fire, and in a skillet on
the grate two pieces of meat popped and sizzled. When the
door opened, a swirl of wind entered, and Rachel followed.

Salali looked up. "All done?" she asked.

"All done," Rachel said. "The lantern's alight."

Rachel found Spaun's favorite whale-oil lamp, lit it, set it on
the table, and sank into a chair. She spread her hands on the
table and stared blankly at them.

"I don't know why you're so worried," Salali said. "It's not
as though we never saw a British ship before."

"It's not the ship," Rachel answered. If Salali could only
know her struggle at this moment. ". . . at least not *just* the
ship. Lafayette's in Virginia, and that ship is headed for the
mouth of the Chesapeake. . . ."

"And a great sea battle," Salali said.

"Yes," Rachel answered, then paused. "Salali . . . this morning . . ." Should she tell her friend about her vision? Would
Salali think her insane? No. No, Salali's people understood
things such as these. Their lives were full of mystery—spiritual
mystery that had guided them through thousands of years.

Salali looked up when Rachel paused. "This morning,
what?" she asked.

"This morning I *saw* something," Rachel burst out,
". . . something that wasn't there."

Salali stood with the kettle lid in her hand as a chill ran
down her spine. "What did you see?" she asked quietly.

Rachel paused, searching for a way to answer. "I saw a ship," she said in a whisper. "A British ship . . . just off shore, and I heard men screaming." She compressed her lips and looked at Salali. Rachel's large brown eyes, reflecting the yellow flame of the lamp within their depths, were full of intensity.

"Anything more?" Salali asked quietly.

"No. Nothing more," Rachel whispered, "but when it disappeared, my heart was pounding and I could hardly breathe."

A darkness came over Rachel's features.

"Salali?" she said, her eyes fixed on the flame of the lamp before her. "Salali, do you know what this war has done to you and me?" Rachel felt enormous tension building in her breast, a feeling as though she would explode, as though something in the surrounding room was in command of her emotions and that she was a vessel too small to contain it.

Salali laid the lid back on the kettle, and came quietly to sit at the end of the table, never once taking her eyes from Rachel's face.

"First," Rachel went on, her voice calm but intense, "it took away my husband. My baby is four years old and has never seen his father. Year after year we've lived in fear of raids in the night. It took Donald away from you, and Edward has suffered wounds. It burned our home from over our heads. Salali, I *hate* this war! I want it to end!"

Salali had seen Rachel like this before. She said nothing, but gazed intently into Rachel's eyes.

A bitter taste rose in Rachel's mouth. "I don't know what's come over me," she said, cradling her head in her hands and staring at the table. She looked up. "I'm going up into the light."

"But I've fixed supper," Salali remonstrated.

"I don't have time," Rachel said, getting to her feet. "I've got to go up in the light," and she headed toward the door.

"Then I'm going with you," Salali said, swinging the kettle's crane from over the fire and sliding the sizzling skillet to the side of the grill.

High above the dune, the lantern room, filled with the mellow pungency of melting wax, glowed eerily about them. Outside, the great dome of the sky darkened as the Atlantic sank into midnight blackness. For a long time neither Rachel nor Salali spoke, and the only sound was the terrible wind.

"What are we doing here?" Salali whispered at last.

"Looking for running lights, I suppose," Rachel answered.

"You suppose? Don't you know?"

"Call it intuition," Rachel said.

"That's not what *I* call it—" Salali began.

Then suddenly, far out in the southern blackness, they saw a gleaming pinpoint of white.

"There," Rachel shouted. No sooner had she spoken than another light appeared behind the first.

"More British war ships," Salali murmured.

"I felt they would come," Rachel said. "No, I didn't just feel it, I knew it. There wasn't a single doubt." Am I making sense? she wondered. No matter. She turned about to face the four and twenty candles flaming brilliantly before the great brass reflector. Its concentrated light made her swarthy face pale and shadowless.

"What are you doing?" Salali asked in alarm.

Rachel had picked up the candle snuffer and was dipping it over the wick of the first candle on the highest row. Its flame went out and a curl of black smoke wafted upward.

"The light . . ." Rachel answered quietly as she went to the next candle. "Tonight, for the very first time, Spaun's light will be dark."

Salali was stunned. "But the shoals!" she said.

"The shoals . . ." Rachel answered. "I'll not give the British fleet the light of a single candle to avoid the shoals!"

Candle by snuffed candle the light dimmed, then all was black. Rachel and Salali stood in the darkness, listening to the wind moan around the cone of the roof and the humming of the glass. There would be no moon tonight. The wind had only grown stronger, rattling palm branches down below and throwing sand against the stone tower. The surf on the shore was crashing like thunder, and a bank of clouds from the south was shutting out the stars.

As they watched, the distant point of light grew brighter, came nearer, but within the hour passed far out to sea.

"Gone," Rachel said, her voice full of disappointment. "The shoals, no light, and yet he kept his course." She shook her head.

"You did your best," Salali said.

"Maybe not," Rachel whispered. It was an ominous sign. She fell silent, and when she spoke again, it was with excitement. "There *is* something else!" she said.

"What more could there possibly be?" Salali asked.

"I'll show you," Rachel answered, groping in the darkness for a tinderbox that always stood on a table near the door. "Follow me," she said, and quickly started down the stairs into the tower.

On the highest landing she paused, feeling about until her hand fell on a lantern hanging from a hook on the cold stone wall. It was a large wooden lantern with glass windows and a door. Rachel opened the door, and as the candle caught, the light revealed her determined expression.

Then, with a sharp echo answering each step, and the lantern casting massive shadows, she descended the cavernous tower, Salali trailing behind.

Out on the dune the wind tore at them, flinging sprays of sand hissing against the lantern window and stinging their faces.

"Where are we going?" Salali called after her, her voice ragged in the wind.

"You'll see!" Rachel called back.

Within moments they were panting up the crest of the great grassy dune south of the light, the highest point of land on the bar.

"Watch the horizon," Rachel whispered. They stood close in the wind-whipped silence, Rachel's heart racing, Salali wondering.

"There! A glimmer." She waited. "Now," she said, and holding the lantern high, its light casting deep shadows in their eyes, Rachel began to walk back and forth along the dune's crest, lowering the lantern, raising it again, pacing, forward and back, forward and back.

"Woman!" the stupefied Salali said as Rachel passed in front of her, "what on earth do you think you are *doing!*"

"Just look to the ship!" Rachel answered, the yellow light revealing her determined smile. "There! Now! Do you see?" Rachel's heart tripped.

"I can't believe it!" Salali gasped.

Suddenly, two lights had appeared in the blackness, running together in tandem.

"We can see both her lights. That ship's coming *toward* us—toward the *bar!*" Salali said.

Rachel called out over her shoulder, "The helmsman thinks my lantern is the hinder light of another fleet ship rising and falling on the waves."

"Rachel, you're going to *wreck* her! You're going to kill hundreds of men!" Salali caught her by the shoulders. "Stop this thing! This is revenge!"

Rachel turned to face her, her dark eyes flashing in the lantern light.

"Not revenge," she shouted above the wind. "War. I'm fighting a war. For every man who does not reach Cornwallis in Virginia, some American will live! Some home will not burn. Some father will return safe to his children!"

Rachel turned away and continued to pace, raising the lantern and lowering it, raising and lowering.

Salali said nothing.

Tears were running down their sand-stung faces. Weariness pulled down on Rachel's uplifted arms as her feet beat a firm path in the sandy crest of the dune, and the lights came slowly toward them.

"It won't be long," she said, "it won't be long!"

Then it happened—of a sudden. The pinpoints of white light jolted, twisted upward, and behind them rose a single light as white as Rachel's lantern. Up it went with agonizing slowness, higher and higher, while the forward lights descended, disappeared, and all was dark.

"Gone," Salali breathed.

"Gone!" Rachel repeated. On the wind came the thin sound of terrified human voices and screaming horses going down in the waves.

EIGHTY

"QUICK! They'll be on us in minutes!" Salali pulled frantically at Rachel's arm. But Rachel stood unmoved, staring through the darkness, the wind whipping her hair about her face. The glowing lantern hung by her side.

"Do you hear me?" Salali shouted.

"Who'll be on us?" Rachel said, her voice distant, as though she was in another world.

"The sailors, the marines, whoever survives that wreck!"

Rachel looked toward Salali. "You're right," she said. Instantly she held the lantern up, opened its door to the wind, and the candle went out.

"To the light," Salali called, then stopped and looked back. She could barely make out Rachel's form in the darkness. "Rachel," she shouted, "come on!"

High in the stone tower, sick with fear, they stood peering out through a seaward window. The hours dragged by with the wind whining above. At last the faintest light of dawn began to spread over the face of the sea. Far out in the shallows wallowed a black, burdensome silhouette, like a dead sea monster heaving before the wash of the waves. As the light came on, scattered debris appeared on the beach below—torn sails, broken masts, shattered railings . . . and rolled by breakers onto the sand—bodies, their arms and legs tossed about grotesquely in death.

Rachel felt herself breaking and slumped against the cold stone wall. She let her body slide down until she was sitting on the steps, then dropped her head into her hands.

She sighed. "When my emotions take over, I don't think things through to the end, do I?"

"No, Rachel." Salali sat down and slipped an arm about her shoulders. "You never do. You just settle on what looks right to you and you do it. But you've got to keep telling yourself just what you told me, that this is war."

"Leaving Drew, killing Rob, now this," Rachel sobbed. "It's all the same. Oh, Salali, please forgive me. I may have killed you as surely as I killed Rob."

"If you have, we'll die together," Salali said quietly.

For several minutes they sat, Salali rubbing Rachel's shoulders, speaking soothing words, trying to comfort her. Suddenly the whistling in the lantern dropped down . . . the wind had slacked.

Rachel gathered herself together, peered again out the tower window. A quick intake of her breath made Salali jump to her feet.

The light of the sun had melded across the face of the ocean, its blinding brilliance broken only by the roughness of the waves and by the bulk of the upended ship. Rachel clasped her hand over her mouth and Salali gasped.

Out beyond the wreck, straining at anchor in deeper water,

almost hidden in the glare, was a British man-of-war. Against
the dawn, Rachel and Salali caught glimpses of sailors crawling about her yardarms like ants, reefing her sails. Boats were
being lowered, and already, a party having reached the hulk,
men were climbing about on the steeply slanted deck. It could
not be long before they came ashore.

"How well do you swim?" Rachel quietly whispered, wiping her nose and growing very calm.

"I'd never make it," Salali answered. She had gone to a
window on the landside to appraise the channel's width. "But
if *you* can do it, you must try."

"And leave you here to take the blame?" Rachel said firmly.
"Never!" She thought for a moment. "Salali," she said
brightly, "if we could find places to hide, they'll see Spaun's
dory on the other side of the inlet and think we've left the island. They'll give up and go away."

"But where can we hide on this dune?" Salali asked frantically. Quickly she crossed back to the seaward window and
looked out. "They're coming!" she said, her eyes charged with
fear.

Below, a longboat filled with men holding muskets upright
before them was battling with surf. Desperation neared panic.
Rachel pressed hard against the wall, closing her eyes and biting her lower lip. Her mind raced over the island, through the
house, through the light, trying to find places to hide.

"The cistern!" she said suddenly, her eyes opening wide.
"Salali, you go to the cistern. I'll hide in the storage space
under the lantern floor! If they discover me, I'll say I acted
alone. You can stay in hiding till they're gone and Jacob comes
back. Then you can tell him what's become of me." She
paused. "And if you're found, I can do the same for you."

Sunrise was pouring through the tower window, its partitions
casting a cross of light on the opposite wall. For a moment Rachel's eyes locked with Salali's, then Salali began to nod her
head in a rapid yes.

They heard the distant, hollow sound of oars being stowed
away, and instantly Salali plunged down the spiral stair as Rachel ran wildly up to the lantern.

"Calm yourself, Rachel Wolfe," she said as she tugged desperately at the hatch.

Beneath the boards was a storage space between the joists of
the lantern's floor, but she could not get her fingers into the
crack to pull the hatch up. At the last moment she found pur-

chase with her nails and breathlessly lifted. It gave! The space was close and dark, just large enough as, lying on her side, she squeezed in. Reaching out, she lifted the hatch and dropped it into place, plunging herself into immediate darkness.

Wiggling about, she pushed and pulled at wooden crates and small boxes, molding herself in. Doubled on her side, she tried to quiet her heaving lungs, and waited, listening. All was quiet, the only sound the diminished wind moaning softly about the great glass lantern.

From somewhere far below came the squeak of the heavy tower door swinging open, the shuffle of feet, men's voices murmuring, quick steps on the stair, louder, louder, nearer. The upper railing creaked. The brush of clothing, boot soles shuffling and clambering inches above her head! Rachel fought to slow her breathing. Male voices filtered through the floor and into the darkness.

"The island's empty," said a smooth masculine voice. "There's the keeper's dory on the far shore. He got away."

"You didn't ex*pect* him to stay, did you now, lad?" said a guttural voice that Rachel imagined to be that of a common seaman.

There were curses.

"Look at them!" said another voice with a hard edge to it. "Scattered on the beach like driftwood! Good Englishmen, wasted to a wrecker!"

"And but for a few survivors, we'd not know it was a wrecker," the coarse voice said. He paused. "We'd think the keeper just darkened his light while we sailed past."

"Damn it all!" said the voice with the hard edge. He stamped the floorboards above Rachel's head, cutting loose with a stream of profanity so thick she wanted to stop her ears. Suddenly, amid the cursing, came a crashing of glass and a tumbling of a dozen heavy candles bouncing on the floor.

"Torch it!" the hard-edged voice shouted.

"Torch it, sir?" came the smooth voice. "But the light will be of use to us."

"I said torch the blasted thing!"

Then came the murmur of reluctant agreement, and a clamor of descending feet on the stairs.

"Trapped in a chimney!" Rachel whispered. Certain at last that the tower was empty, she threw off the hatch and squirmed out of her cramped quarters.

Hovering near the floor so as not to be seen, she pondered her situation.

"Oh, God," she breathed aloud. "What am I going to do? Do I burn or surrender?" If she surrendered, she'd hang ... or more likely, and worse, be raped by one woman-starved seaman after another!

She remembered the stories filtered down from the north; women raped by British soldiers, women who had done far less than she to provoke wrath. But would it not be better to be raped than to burn?

Perhaps there was another way. Perhaps while they went for torch wood, she could run undetected to the inlet, swim across, and come back for Salali when all was over.

The decision was made, and in an instant Rachel was on the stairs. Down she plunged to the highest landing, then to the next. Then she heard it, the heavy tower door swinging open, the splashing of liquid, a sudden whooshing sound followed by the shouts of men.

Almost instantly there came the smell of burning oil and wood. Leaning against the rail, Rachel peered cautiously through the stairway hatch to the lower chamber.

"Oh, dear Lord!" she gasped, and her throat tightened with fear.

The tower's lower wooden floor, coated with oil, had been set ablaze. Already the flames were climbing the railing. Instantly she reached for the door to the hatch and slammed it, hoping to cut off the draft and buy a little time. Within moments black smoke was seeping up through the cracks in the floor, and with it came the crackle and hiss of burning wood. The air, thick with heat and smoke, was suddenly hard to breathe, and she began to choke and cough.

When the soles of her shoes grew warm, she knelt to touch the floor and found the boards blistering hot. Desperately she turned to the nearest tower window—perhaps she could force it open and jump. Then through the window she saw them, dozens of men gathered about the tower, waiting for the flames to appear, men she feared more than she feared the fire.

There was only one direction to go—back up into the lantern.

"There's no way out!"

She threw herself down onto the floor of the lantern compartment, whispering frantically to herself. "Oh, dear God, don't let me die this way!" And she began to cough as the air of the lantern grew hazy with smoke. "But I can't give up." The tower was stone, she thought. *It* won't burn! But the wooden floor of every landing would . . . and the wooden stairs. If she stayed here, the floor would collapse under her, and she would fall into the fire.

Now a growing hot wind began to sweep up through the hollow tower, pushing upward at the closed hatch and rattling the tall glass panes. Within minutes it would be a rushing heat—like a furnace, and impossible to bear. Five minutes and it would all be over; but oh what suffering in those five minutes!

"The walkway," she choked. A little longer to live, a few more breaths of air, and when the lantern caught, she'd jump. Death, but not so terrible as burning!

When Rachel burst onto the catwalk, she found herself staring far down into dozens of startled faces, British sailors and marines waiting to see the flames explode into the lantern.

"A woman!" she heard them scream.

"Where?"

"At the top! On the catwalk!"

Rachel lunged forward and grasped the rail as, with eyes hungry for life, she scanned the horizon one last time.

"The wrecker!" one whispered in sudden realization.

"Let 'er burn!" shouted another.

"No!" said a marine. "You can't let a *woman* burn to death!"

"What else can you do? There's no time to save her," said the first.

The marine swung his musket from his back, primed the pan, and raised it to his shoulder.

At that instant, Rachel remembered, and a wild plan sprang full-grown into her mind. The sequence of thought ran like lightning: Spaun's store of gunpowder, three kegs, fifty pounds to a keg, the light's formidable stone tower might contain such an explosion, and if the wooden stairway and landings would be blown away, the fire could not reach her. But the risk! The flames at this very moment might be licking up the rail within feet of the powder store. Just as the front sight of the marine's Brown Bess lay on Rachel's heart, she bolted through the door and again entered the lantern.

The powder was stored on the highest landing, in a wall chest, heavily barred. The withering air swirled like a storm about her, the smoke growing thick like a cloud. With lungs burning and head whirling, Rachel shoved the bar upward. Stuck! Again she pushed, with all her might this time.

With a clang the bar flew into the air, rebounded, and struck her full across the face. For an instant she stood stunned, then staggeringly grasped the chest door and swung it open.

There they were. Three kegs of the most volatile thing known to man—and the most powerful.

She felt the hot floor blistering her feet, but it did not matter. Quickly she knelt, wrestled a heavy keg to her shoulder, then tottering dangerously under its weight, bore it up the stairway into the lantern. Down again, and once more. Done!

Now she must work carefully, quickly. The kegs must roll down the spiral staircase, one upon the other. And before they could plunge into the flames, she must reach the walkway again.

She laid the kegs on their sides, one behind the other, and leaning hard against them, pushed. She turned, heard them bouncing on the stairs, and threw herself through the lantern door out onto the catwalk. Hugging the low stone wall beneath the tall glass panes, she buried her face against it, held her breath, and waited.

In quick succession three thunderous shocks rocked the tower, its rough stone striking Rachel hard in the face. A vast rush of roaring power flew skyward like shrapnel from the barrel of a giant cannon, bits of shriven glass by the thousands, the lantern roof rushing away through the air.

And the stone tower, shuddering under the force, quaking . . . held.

Burning debris rained down—shingles, fragments of hot iron, burning splinters falling down on the beach, dropping and hissing into the water of the sea.

Then silence. Dust and smoke hung in the air. For a long moment all was still, the only sound coming from within the tower, down in the lowest chamber: the fire growling on, hungrily consuming stair timbers that had fallen into its maw.

Gradually the hailing debris softened to a gentle rain, pattering down about Rachel where she lay on the catwalk, and onto the leaves of the palms below. The explosion's roar was still echoing in her ears, the inside of her head was swirling as her vision faded. Weakly, she reached for the railing and tried to draw herself up to look over the side.

Down on the grassy dune, men had flung themselves headlong onto the sands, arms wrapped defensively about their heads. But one open-mouthed marine stood transfixed, musket in hand. With her hand on the rail she pulled herself to her knees, then to her feet. It couldn't matter that they saw her now.

Still the smothering hot wind rushed up out of the tower's yawning mouth, so that again she fell to the floor to escape its searing heat. There was nothing more she could do.

EIGHTY-ONE

RACHEL lay facedown on the catwalk, her right arm dangling loosely over the edge, her eyes closed. Inside her head a whirling vortex bore her down into darkness. Nausea crept up in her throat. As the furnace roared below, its withering heat on her back, a breeze from the sun cooled her forehead and cheek.

The men stared in amazement up through the clouds of settling dust. Instinctively they knew what Rachel had done, and a wave of admiration passed over every man. They picked themselves up from the sand and, with resounding shouts, sailed their hats into the air.

The marine who a moment ago had thought Rachel's death the only way ran across the sandy beach to the boat and scooped up a grappling hook and line. Mightily he threw, and with a clang hooked the tower's walkway. Quickly, while a dozen sailors held it tight, hand over hand he ascended the line.

Though unable to open her eyes, Rachel sensed the man's presence, felt his powerful hands turning her over, felt the rough rope being tied beneath her arms and her body swaying gently as he lowered her, down, down, down into the hands of those waiting below. Within moments she was being carried toward the water and into the ship's longboat. Then came the violent upward heave of surf and the boat's surging forward under the force of many oars. But before the oarsmen could reach *Indomitable*, she fell into deep unconsciousness.

* * *

"*Nasty* bruise across her face!" she heard someone say in a voice that seemed far away. A pair of masculine hands was feeling gently about her body and limbs. "Lighter bruises on her shoulders," the voice said, "some lacerations on her arms and face, soles of her feet blistered proper enough, but no serious burns. Not a singed lock in that long hair. Amazing!"

"I sware to heaven, sir," another voice said, "I wish you coulda seen 'er. What that woman done! Savin' 'erself by blowin' the guts out'a that tower. I tell you, sir, there was men with tears runnin' down their cheeks. If the rebels had a hunnerd like 'er, we'd be ruined already!"

"Ahh," the first voice sighed, seeming farther away, "I think we *are* ruined, Ensign. Everyone but Germain's War Ministry knows that by now." The voice paused. "Don't let anyone disturb her," it said. "There'll be time to question her later."

While Rachel slept, the wreck's remaining dead were being buried on shore, and salvage operations begun, munitions and livestock mostly. Though most of the ship's chickens and hogs had drowned and been washed away in the tides, surviving horses had swum ashore and gathered in a small herd in the island's south end. A contingent of men had gone in to round them up and swim them out to the ship behind longboats.

At a quarter past three in the afternoon, with the sea rising lightly and the sun rapidly declining, the wreck's sixty-four cannon had been loaded onto jury-rigged rafts and were under tow, some to be craned aboard *Indomitable*, the rest to be sunk in deep water.

The first raft was just reaching the ship when a geyser of water shot up behind it, drenching every man on board. Then came the dull concussion of a single cannon shot. Shoreward, on a rise of ground beyond the dunes, there appeared men and horses. The ship's burial parties took to their boats and fled before musket fire kicking up sand and water. In the tow boats the crews, shrinking beneath bursting artillery shells, cut the tow ropes and pulled for shelter. Free of their tethers, the cannon-laden rafts wallowed in the surf and crashed in piles along the beach.

With men scrambling to her shelter, *Indomitable*'s gun ports swung up, heavy iron barrels thrust outward, and smokebursts and thunder roared from stem to stern.

It was that tremendous concussion of the guns shuddering

through *Indomitable*'s massive frame that woke Rachel. She opened her eyes to a gray room in the ship's bowels, a large wooden lantern swinging gently from a hook in the beam directly above her. She lay on a narrow bed next to one of the ship's great curved oaken ribs.

"Miss, we've orders to take you to our captain when you awake." The man spoke kindly to her.

Rachel turned her head and two men came into focus.

"There's no hurry, Ensign." It was the voice she had heard earlier. "Plenty of time. Besides, I think our captain will learn nothing from this young woman. She acted alone."

"I have my orders, sir," the ensign answered.

"Yes, I suppose you do," her defender said.

The ensign was young, no more than twenty, while the other man appeared in his forties. The older man had a gentle face, and when he looked directly at her, Rachel saw compassion in his eyes.

"Are you in terrible pain?" he asked quietly. The slightly muffled roar of a cannon one deck above drowned out his voice, and he repeated his question.

Slowly, licking her dry lips and turning her head, Rachel lifted a hand and ran it through her long tangled hair. She closed her eyes again. Exhaustion penetrated deep into every bone and muscle of her body.

"No," she whispered weakly, "not much pain. But I can hardly move. I . . . I'm exhausted."

Another cannon spoke, and the lantern above Rachel's head swung in an inverted arc.

"Little wonder," the man said. "You need rest, lots of it, but as soon as you can, we'll have to take you to our captain. He has many questions for you. Sleep now . . . if you can."

Two hours later Rachel woke again. For a while she lay while her head cleared gradually. The cannon were still booming, but from somewhere farther away, and not as often. The ensign and another young sailor sat nearby, both watching her carefully.

"The captain wants to see me?" she croaked, her throat husky from sleep and weariness.

"That he does, ma'am. As soon as you're able."

Slowly Rachel turned back the single sheet that covered her. Her boots were gone, her lower legs were clad only in white, knee-high stockings, and a long rip in her black riding breeches revealed a shallow cut up and down her right thigh.

She had been unaware of the torn flesh, and only now did she feel its sting. Looking up, she blushed to notice the ensign's eyes fixed on the bare swatch of skin. Abashed, he quickly looked away.

Rachel rose up on her right elbow, determined to get to her feet.

"Where are my riding boots?" she asked, looking about. Then she saw them at the foot of the bed. "Help me, Ensign."

Anxious to please, the youth reached for her hand, but once Rachel was on her feet, her blistered soles forced her to her knees.

"Shall we carry you, miss?" the second ensign asked gently.

"No. No," she said, biting her lower lip, "I'll try again."

The men were gentle. Each took an arm and bore part of her weight as she limped toward the ladderway.

As they passed upward through the gun deck, a cloud of acrid white smoke stung her eyes and made her nostrils burn. The thunder of cannon beat at her ears like hammers. A barefoot boy of ten or twelve with a cartridge of gunpowder tucked under his arm darted past, almost knocking her from her feet.

Up the forward ladderway they went, and out onto the main deck near the belfry. A light breeze was keeping the deck clear of smoke, and Rachel took a deep breath of the clean air.

Instinctively she looked toward shore, saw how the sun was dipping toward the horizon, the light of day very nearly lost. Where was Salali? Had she escaped from the cistern to summon the men whose guns were puffing white wisps from the rise? Or had Spaun gone for them?

A haze of gun smoke had gathered on the face of the sea, and reaching above it was Spaun's light. Thanks to me, Rachel thought, no longer a light. The decapitated tower, pitifully empty, yet strong against the setting sun, seemed to say to her, "Don't give in!"

Beyond the tower a small cloud of white smoke puffed out; then came an artillery shell whining through the rigging above her head, without effect.

The ensign urged her forward, past the ship's great wheel, beyond the quarterdeck, to the door of the captain's cabin.

The captain was standing by a starboard window when she entered, his hands clasped behind his back, watching the action on shore. The dull, deep voice of cannon firing from the lower gun deck intruded like distant thunder. Rachel drew into herself a little as he turned, his bright brown eyes regarding her with obvious interest.

She glanced about. The floor of the cabin was a pattern of large black and white checks, the lines of which ran diagonal with the cabin walls. There was a couch against the port wall, in the middle a dining table surrounded by chairs, and a desk. Against the starboard wall, beneath the windows, sat a dark oak stand with the top recessed to hold a wine cask. In spite of the cabin's refined appearance, even here there were gun ports and cannon. Obviously, in a matter of moments, the cabin could be transformed into a fighting deck.

Rachel took in all these things in a moment, but the central object of her attention was the captain himself.

The ship's master was a ladylike little man with thin face and narrow nose, sharp along its ridge. He had long slender fingers, on one of which he wore a plain wide gold ring. His long-tailed coat of a very dark color, trimmed in heavy gold thread, contrasted sharply with hair of pure white, very full. His shining forehead reached halfway up his crown, so that his entire coiffure grew behind an imaginary line reaching across from ear to ear. In spite of his size, this delicate little man's piercing personality transfixed Rachel instantly. As he sauntered toward her, his dark eyes bore in.

Rachel swore to herself that he would not intimidate her. Squaring her shoulders and forgetting the pain in the soles of her feet, she stood firmly and fixed him with her large dark eyes.

He saw her intent, and smiled. It was a smile in which the straight line of his thin lips widened, curving only where the corners turned down. It was an unconventional smile, yet warm, and to Rachel's surprise, it set her at ease. A backward motion of his hand signaled the guards to leave them alone.

Rachel returned his smile with closed lips, and looked the little man over from head to toe.

"Well, well, young lady!" he said at last. His voice was pleasant, not high, as she had expected, but rather full and masculine. "This is something of an honor for me!" Here was pure British speech such as she had not heard for a long while, with all the peculiarities that made it sound so . . . so arrogant to American ears. When she said nothing, he continued.

"It isn't every day I meet a stripling girl, who—if we surmise correctly—has sunk one of his majesty's ships-of-the-line, and in one blow slain several hundred good Englishmen!"

At the mention of the dead men, his smile disappeared and the shade of Rachel's skin lightened. She stared unflinchingly into her host's eyes.

"I am Captain Thompson," he said, "but I suppose my subordinates told you that. May I call you by name?" He motioned to a chair.

Rachel did not move.

"Your name?" he said again.

"Rachel," she answered at last, her voice low and relaxed. "Rachel Wolfe. And you *surmise* correctly," she said, "that I wrecked your vessel of war."

Now it was the captain's turn to ponder *her* speech. Rachel's Scots brogue was of a kind the English despised as ignorant rusticity, back-country hill talk, yet it was tempered by a decade of living among Philadelphia German and Irish, and flavored by ancient English from the Tidewater south. All this made Thompson's smile return.

"Well, Rachel Wolfe, you have put me in a peculiar strait. It is quite normal to summarily hang such as you from a yardarm. In fact, it would be completely in order if I should do that very thing about now, while the sun is going down."

"Then do it," she said flatly, her eyes steadily on his.

He watched her face for signs of breaking. There was nothing but boldness. *"But,"* he continued, "I am afraid you have won the admiration of the men on this ship. They admire your courage . . . as, frankly, do I. Besides, they have not seen such a display of pyrotechnics as you gave them in all this miserable little war." He paused, then went on. "And I'm told the sentiment among them is to let you live."

"Then you'll set me free." Her words were slow and measured, without a hint of begging; but she was thinking of Jamie.

"Most assuredly not!" He laughed. It was his eyes that did the laughing. "You have cost us too dearly. To simply return you to your pursuits would obviously be quite dangerous. No, but I will put you in hold for the conflict's duration. Certainly it would be proper to keep so formidable a warrior as yourself a prisoner."

"I have a son," she said, "a little boy who needs me."

Thompson's eyebrows rose. In the background the ship's cannon continued to rumble. He watched her face carefully, and thought he saw a slight glaze over her eyes and a dampness in her lower lashes.

"Mrs. Wolfe . . ." The captain's tone was almost intimate. For a moment she felt he was speaking to her as a good father might. "Mrs. Wolfe, one ought to consider one's relationship to his or her family *before* engaging in acts of war. Don't try to take advantage of my admiration. I want to spare your life, but I cannot allow you to—"

A violent shock jolted the ship's frame. Thompson's face turned one shade paler. He murmured something unintelligible, stepped quickly to the door, and threw it open. Beyond the mizzenmast, billows of smoke were pouring from the hatch.

"Explosion in the forward magazine!" came a jumbled shout.

Thompson turned toward Rachel. His straight smile had disappeared altogether now, and the corners of his mouth turned down menacingly.

"Young lady," he said, "you have this day cost his majesty's navy more dearly than you can know. I think your fate is not yet decided!"

The door slammed heavily, and she heard his key click in the lock.

Alone, Rachel looked about the cabin again. How strange—she felt not an ounce of fear, but a surrounding, enveloping peace.

"Jamie!" she whispered with determination. "I must go to Jamie!"

It was settled—nothing else mattered. The time for escape had come. With rapidly beating heart, she pondered the dark oak stand with its cask of wine.

With a few steps she went to it, jerked opened the bung, and upended the cask, pouring half the red wine out onto the cabin floor. Then, snatching up a chair, she threw it with all her might through the nearest window, bursting the glass out over the face of the sea. With the half-full cask under her left arm, she crawled through the jagged opening, perched with one foot in, the other out, and looked down.

The cool night breeze and darkness on the water's face sent a chill down her spine. The waves twenty feet below were illuminated darkly by light from a lower cabin. She gathered her courage, took a deep breath, and, refusing to think the worst, dropped the cask into the semicircle of light. With her eyes riveted to the bobbing object, she jumped, feet first, down into the sea.

* * *

Down Rachel plummeted, the night air rushing about her, her stomach in her throat. Her body knifed smoothly into the waves, plunging deep, the water driving up into her nostrils, her long hair trailing above her. Down and farther down she went . . . then stillness . . . slow ascent through watery blackness, rising forever and ever until her lungs were near bursting.

The surface! All at once she was sucking air and water, coughing and choking, sweeping her arms and kicking her feet, riding the swells and troughs up and down and up again, her long hair floating lightly on the dark water. The taste of brine was in her mouth, and her nostrils stung like fire. But the wine cask. Where was the wine cask? Had it drifted away?

Indomitable rose above her like an immense mountain—so close she could touch it, only to be denied the safety of its oaken slopes. Where the cabin lights cast their gleam on the waves, the cask was nowhere to be seen. The water was warmer than the night air, and for this she was grateful. She thrust herself forward, if only to touch again what had moments before been her ark of dubious safety. What of the ship's fire? The only sounds were her own breathing and waves sweeping at the hull.

Then the tip of the middle finger of her extended hand brushed something in the water. She kicked, turning herself about to see. There it was, the empty wine cask floating half out of the waves. She reached, clasped it under her arm, and, treading water lightly, looked about.

Indomitable's great hull brushed the back of her head. Then she realized that the anchored ship was slowly swinging out with an ebbing tide—a tide that would easily sweep her to sea. She must try to reach land now.

The ship's bow was her only hope—swim around the bow and let the outgoing current press her against the hull until the tide changed. She hugged the cask with her left arm, and with her right reached out. Stroke . . . stroke . . . stroke. Long minutes passed; she gained midships and rested, breathing hard. With her free hand she gripped the ship's lower sidestep below the entry port. She swam again. The bow at last. High above, the long, upward-sweeping bowsprit pointed toward the land, and beneath it an outsize man bore in his hands the royal orb and scepter of Great Britain.

From the shadows ahead, standing at an angle out of the water, emerged the mammoth cable that bound the ship to its five-ton anchor. If only she could reach the cable and rest. But as she came even with the bow, the land breeze caught her, sweeping her back. No matter how hard she stroked, the anchor cable was fading into the darkness—the ship was moving away, tide and wind conspiring against her. A terrible weakness went through Rachel's whole frame. Her heart beat like a hammer, and fear made her mouth go dry.

Within moments, *Indomitable*'s profile stood out in the darkness, lantern lights on deck reflecting from her masts and rigging, men going about here and there with no hurry in their steps. It was like a dream, points of light moving away, a universe of darkness closing about her—an intense irrational reality, a vision of approaching death.

Indomitable disappeared altogether. The sea's rolling troughs enclosed Rachel in darkness, as above, the stars burned white and close. In the north Cassiopeia was at its zenith, and the Northern Cross lay overhead. There was the Milky Way— "where the dog ran"—spread diagonally across the sky. She smiled, remembering the night when Salali had told Jamie the old Cherokee legend.

Jamie . . . oh, Jamie! He would be in his own bed now, warm covers tucked about his chin. He would be dreaming. Dear God, she had never been so alone—never, never had she dreamed that one *could* be so alone!

But for the stars above and the faintly luminescent plankton floating just under the fluid translucence, all the world was black. Little jellyfish brushed by, their nettling tendrils setting her skin on fire.

There was only Rachel, with her half-empty cask, rising slowly up and falling back again, her arms desperately weary, and beneath her feet, the fathomless deep.

Sorrow and panic rose like acid from the pit of her stomach into her breast and throat and head. This was death, separation from all the familiar things, all the places, all the sounds and smells of life, and the people. She would not see Jamie grow to manhood, would not see him wed and have children of his own. Tears mixed with the wetness on her face. How stupid to have placed herself in the arms of the pitiless sea! How unrepentable!

Weariness wrapped her in its arms until she could do nothing but hang between the sky above and the deep below, her legs and feet swept about by the currents, as though detached from her body, her numbing arms grasping the cask however they could; both at once, one at a time, first with this arm, then with the other.

An abrupt jerk shot through her body. She had dozed and snapped awake again. Sleep, how she ached for sleep. Stars and waves and darkness blended into a dream, and her weakening fingers began to loosen their hold. A sudden rap of the cask against her head and a terrible bolt of fear jarred her spine again.

"Oh, God!" she cried. "What can I do?"

As in answer, without the slightest hesitation, a new thought came to her mind. Her billowy blouse—perhaps she could capture the small cask in the front of her blouse and in that way bind it to her.

Struggling with her free arm, she pulled the long shirt from her riding breeches and, with great difficulty, scooped the cask inside. Her arms quivered and shook with weariness, then hung limp at her sides. Suspended on the face of the sea, she surrendered to exhaustion and slept.

E I G H T Y - T W O

IT was night again when Edward Buchannon with his forty men and two cannon drove the last landing party into the sea, then forded the inlet onto the dune. Before them in the darkness stood the hollow tower. Seaward, *Indomitable*'s lights were fading to the north, and with them every hope of recovering Rachel.

It was Spaun who had ridden for help. When he had seen that it was impossible for him to reach the light, he had sat against the trunk of an oak, wrapped in his wool greatcoat, watching the drama played out on the dune's windswept stage.

And now it was Spaun, a coil of rope over his shoulder and a wooden lantern in his hand, who went directly to the open cistern. As he leaned out, fragments of old rock from the edge dislodged, their pebbles falling and pattering down the side to the dry bottom. He held the lantern high and peered into the pit's dimness.

"Salali!" the old man's voice echoed.

"Jacob!" she answered. "Oh, Jacob! Is it truly you?"

Hand over hand they pulled her up, threw a blanket about her shoulders, and eased her down onto the grass.

"She's dead!" Salali whispered, her voice hoarse and her eyes swollen from weeping.

"Rachel's alive, Salali," Edward said quietly as he knelt over her. He took Salali's hand in his. "At least she is if they haven't hanged her." He gripped her hand tightly and looked seaward just in time to see *Indomitable*'s stern lights disappearing over the horizon.

Donald Calhoun was riding in from Castle Hayne when he met a party of horsemen about to enter the gate to Buchannon Hills. In spite of the darkness, he recognized Edward's voice and knew immediately that something was amiss.

"Edward!" he called. "It's Donald. Where've you been?"

"Had a run-in with the British down at Spaun's light," Edward answered.

Donald rode up beside him, wishing he could read the expression on Edward's face, but it was too dark.

"Bad?"

"Pretty bad," the big man replied. "Let's ride on up to the cabin and light some lights so we can talk."

Donald sat leaning forward, his forearm resting on the edge of the rough-hewn cabin table, his fist clenched. The same yellow lantern light that washed out the red of his hair blanched the already pale skin of his stern face. His blue eyes were hidden under the shadow of thick brows.

"It's hardest of all on you," Abigail said to him, her voice quavering and her right hand rubbing his shoulder comfortingly. "Your sister gone and Salali suffering as she has."

Donald reached up and squeezed Abigail's hand.

"I can't believe Rachel's gone," he said lifelessly. Then he looked across the table at Edward. "I'll go down to the light and to Salali now."

"She'll be sleeping," Abigail said.

"Nabby's right, Donald," Edward put in. "She hasn't slept for two days. We tucked 'er into Spaun's bed, and before we left she was sound asleep. You don't wanta bother 'er now."

"I won't wake her. But I can't sleep, and it'll help just to feel her close by." Donald stood and pulled on his coat. "I'll go down and get a fresh mount."

He ducked his head and went out.

Riding along the road toward the dunes, Donald gazed upward into the sky. The air was warm for an autumn night, but the stars seemed so cold, their beauty lost in bitterness and sorrow.

Poor Rachel! How could God allow one person to suffer as she had? Visions of her childhood rose in his mind. There were the two of them playing beside the little valley stream. Her laughter had been the most beautiful sound he had ever heard, and her trust had been complete. The sweetness of her face lingered before him as he rode.

Likely the British had hanged her, he thought, so that now her troubles were over. But what a horrible end!

But he would take comfort where he could find it. He would be there for Salali when she woke—and in the dark hours before dawn, he would walk the dune's sands, and be in the last place Rachel had been seen by someone who loved her. Perhaps even to feel the presence of her spirit, he thought, if spirits lingered a little while to say last good-byes before departing this world.

It was three in the morning when he crossed the inlet and felt the sand of the dune scrape beneath the dory's bow. What was left of Spaun's light stood directly above him like a heavy shadow—a headless stone hulk outlined against the distant stars. The still-burning coals within cast an eerie red glow through the empty windows and upward into the faint cloud of smoke rising from its hollow mouth.

Donald bowed his head and walked very slowly toward the tower, feeling the soft sand beneath his feet, his heart aching, his spirit praying, reaching out for his sister.

Then he stood below it, and a bitter laugh broke from his lips. Here his sister had fought an entire battle of the war, had withstood hundreds of men, had dared a thing only the bravest—or the most foolhardy—would dare. And she had paid dearly for her act—as would they all.

The palm leaves whispered in the sea's steady breeze, and the uncaring stars shone down, oblivious to all the pain in his heart. But even in the darkness, the massive stones of the tower seemed to offer comfort. They had withstood the terrible blast, and still within them the fire burned. He could hear it quietly cracking, interspersed with the rhythmic roar of the surf.

He reached out and spread the palm of his right hand against the rough stone, bowing his head and leaning against it. It was hot to his touch, but he did not flinch. This was the place, he thought, and a sudden burst of unspeakable sorrow heaved upward into his chest.

"Oh, God," he shouted, "have mercy on my sister, Rachel!" And dropping to his knees, both hands gripping at the tower, he touched his forehead to the hot stones and wept.

EIGHTY-THREE

WET silk cutting into the skin beneath her arms forced Rachel out of a drugged sleep. A deep paralyzing ache had settled between her shoulder blades, and the muscles of her tortured back were burning like fire. She woke to find it was still night, but that hours had drifted by. The Great Bear was just rising out of the northeastward sea, and "where the dog ran" was gone. A sudden lunge of water caught her full in the face. She spat and coughed in spasms, racked by the rawness of her throat.

How far to sea was she? There was no way to know. Was life "past praying for"? A sudden, violent spasm shook her body from head to foot, and her teeth chattered uncontrollably. Then, as quickly as it had come, the spasm passed. A minute went by, and another spasm seized her. Her body was growing colder than it could bear. She began to long for the sun to rise with its warming light.

How long before death would come to release her? Hours? Chilling nights and blistering days? No, surely blessed death would come before long.

A startling thought bounded into her mind. How easily she could be rid of the cask that bore her up, and once free from it, how quickly she would slip down into the deep. A surge of happiness swelled up in her breast. She would do it. A merciful God would not hold her accountable for such an escape. She reached for the cask and began to nudge it from under her blouse. How good it would feel to rest in death!

When the cask was ready to spring free of the confining blouse, she paused. One more time she would look upon the stars, one more time feel the wonder of the universe. Directly above, the square of Pegasus hung where the Northern Cross had been, and in the southern sky, dim, watery constellations unknown to her spread themselves.

How she had loved the earth and sea and sky, but with the stars overhead, the earth far away, and herself carried in the ocean's arms, she saw clearly that the love was not returned, saw how hard and indifferent all the natural world was to her existence. The sea cared nothing whatever about whether she lived or died. Always she had felt it was somehow aware of her, that it was her friend. What cruel self-deception!

Her mother had said that God loved her. But God had not saved Bess from misery. God's love was her *mother's* self-deception. Was He, if He existed, any *less* indifferent to the plights of her life than the stars and earth and sea? Surely He had exhibited a stony silence through all her life—a silence that spoke either of nonbeing or unconcern. No, she had never been able to settle it in her heart that He existed, much less did she find it in her heart to love Him. Though, if He did exist, she thought, and if He were different than she conceived, to know and love Him would be her highest delight.

At that, when, for the first time she saw clearly how impersonal all things were, a strange thing happened. A warming wind rose on the face of the sea and the troughs deepened. From where would a wind so warm rise in the night? she wondered as she held tightly to the cask.

Then, as the water fell suddenly away beneath her, as she plummeted downward, two images leaped at the same instant into her mind. One was the image she always saw whenever thinking of God: an old man with long, flowing beard of white blowing in the wind, borne along in the arms of naked, baby-faced cherubs—the God of unconcern for whom she felt nothing. But the other image held the stronger place, and all at the same instant: God who was not a man at all, without form, more like the warm wind blowing over the face of the rolling ocean. A God without form who knew all there was to know, who had always been, who rode on no one's arms, and wonder of wonders, who loved her.

Her heart leapt up. For this God she would gladly live—or just as gladly die—and inexplicably, she knew with the knowledge that alone is knowing that she could not live without His presence, nor without loving Him in return.

This was the One toward whom the aching love of sea and sky and earth had been pointing all her life; the One meant when the heather-covered hills of Scotland had said to her, "Look at me! What do I make you think of?" At last she had found the object of her longing. I Am had come.

She felt a melting ... as if, as Donald had once said, she were made of ice. The melting began—she could not tell where—but the ice began to trickle and meld with the waters of the ocean. And when the melting was done, the barrier that had stood between her and Him was gone.

For a long time Rachel rode on the crest of peace, in which nothing mattered but this that had been discovered to her.

And then, in the deep of night, she saw it, far to the west—it had to be west, since the pole star was to her right—a point of light on the horizon, very steady, very clear, visible only when she was on the crests. The light felt alive, and it seemed to know. She heard a voice, the voice of Israel Bowman. "Look to the light, Rachel. Always—look to the light. It will never guide thee wrong."

And slowly lying over on her side, the cask still buoying her up, she began to stroke toward the light.

It was morning. Donald, after a night of agony, sat with his feet drawn up before him, his hands linked about his knees, watching as the red sun climbed up out of the ocean.

More than anything he wanted to go and bang on Spaun's door, to wake Salali and sit beside her, smoothing her hair and holding her hand, but he would wait for signs that Spaun was up.

The tide was coming in, its thin sheets of foam rolling nearer and nearer to his feet while the little quick-stepping sandpipers waded by, plucking out snails or whatever new tidbit washed in. But his thoughts were far away from the sandpipers. His immense melancholy distracted him from any notice of the incoming tide.

He was staring down at his hat, the brim of which he held crumpled in his hands, then back up to a blinding sun on silver breakers. How he wished he could see her again, laugh with her one more time, hear her tease him about his hair—red as copper—and the dapper little bows he wore in his plaited queue. If only he could look into her eyes again, so dark, yet so full of light. Donald bowed his head in his hands and tears rolled between his fingers, dripping down onto his linen shirt.

A vast breaker caught him unawares, snatched him up and sent him sprawling on the sand. As the water rushed back into the sea, he lay for a moment—stunned. Then, above the roar of the surf, he heard another sound—the shrill whistle of a hawk. Startled, he lifted his head from the sand and looked about. There it was, the hawk, perched atop something just washed up on the beach. Another body from the wrecked ship, facedown.

He looked again. This was no soldier, it was a *woman*! A woman with long hair highlighted auburn by the morning sun.

"Rachel!" he shouted. As he jumped up from the sand, the hawk spread its wings and lifted into the air. Donald ran to her side and rolled her over.

"Rachel!" he shouted, and groaned pitifully, "ohh, Rachel!"

He touched her face, her poor face, blue and cold and lifeless. Then he bent down and embraced her, pressing his cheek against hers, his body shaking as he wept.

"Donald?" Like a bolt of lightning her weak voice went through him.

"Dear God!" he whispered. "You're alive!"

He jumped to his feet and scooped her into his arms, then ran, his feet sinking cumbersomely into the sand, toward Spaun's house.

"Jacob! Salali!" he bellowed.

Before he reached it, the door swung open, and Old Spaun, freshly shaved, stood looking out.

"What? Donald Calhoun! And . . . no! It can't be!"

"What is it, Jacob?" Salali said from within.

Donald burst through the door with his burden.

"Who?" she exclaimed, seeing the form he bore. "Rachel!" she shouted with joy, and turning toward Spaun's bed, "Quick, Donald, put her down here. Oh, she's so blue. Is she alive? However did she escape? Water, Jacob, hot water!"

Spaun ran bow-legged to the fireplace, grabbed up a towel, and took the kettle from the fire as Donald lowered Rachel to the bed.

"She's alive!" Donald said. "She spoke my name!"

"She's so cold," Salali said, passing her hand tenderly over

Rachel's cheek. "And what is this?" she exclaimed, reaching beneath Rachel's blouse and tugging on the object.

"The thing that saved her life," Donald said, taking it from her.

For a long moment the three looked at the cask in his hands wonderingly, as though it were a holy thing.

"Donald," Salali interrupted, as he looked up. "If you and Jacob would go out now, I'll get her out of these wet things, bathe her in warm water, and bundle her in the covers."

"Of course," Donald answered haltingly, Jacob chiming in.

Spontaneously she reached out to Donald, and they came into each other's arms. "Just hold me close!" she whispered.

"Oh, Salali," he breathed. "When they told me what you've been through! I nearly lost you!"

"I'm strong," she whispered, "and I have you." Salali pulled away gently and looked toward Rachel. "Go now," she said.

"The war is over."

These were the first words Rachel heard when she awoke days later. The shock of near-burning, capture, and exposure had taken her to a precipice; she had lain for days near death. The first three weeks of October 1781 were totally lost to her memory, but during those weeks the world had changed forever.

Two hundred miles north, on the Virginia peninsula, the allied armies of Washington and de Rochambeau had penned General Cornwallis in by land, and Admiral De Grasse with his French fleet had blocked him by sea. Cornwallis had tried to cross the Chesapeake, but a violent storm had beaten him back. On the nineteenth he surrendered his entire command to Washington, one-fourth of all British strength in America. The Revolution was virtually over.

EIGHTY-FOUR

As Rachel leaned against the doorway of her cabin, the warm, luxurious air was sweet with the smells of autumn. Today was the first of November, a day of Indian summer stillness, the sun's milder light glinting through radial spires of longleaf pine. She was watching the approach of many guests as they wound their way by carriage and horseback up the drive.

Her waist-length hair was gleaming auburn in the sun, her arms contentedly crossed. The hem of her wonderfully blue brocade dress swept the ground, and the most delicate white lace encircled her wrists. There was a tiredness in her body, but a happiness, too. She understood that it would be a long while before her strength fully returned, and that was all right; she could be patient. Yes, if experience had taught her anything, it was patience.

She knew she had changed since that night in the ocean's arms, the night of which she had confided to no one but Salali.

"Somehow He came to me there on the waves," she had told her, "and for the first time in my life, I knew."

Salali's dark eyes had burned with interest, and she had nodded in understanding.

"But above everything else, Salali," Rachel had said, "more than the unspeakable peace, more than not being at odds with life anymore, there is this wonderful intimacy. Absolutely, it is the most exquisite pleasure I have ever experienced, more delicious even than our friendship—yours and mine. There is no way I can describe it to you."

Salali had nodded again and dropped her eyes. "If you could describe it," she had said knowingly, "it would not be as wonderful as you say. If you could tell just how you came by the discovery, you would kill it. It would break from your hands and go to a simpler heart."

Yes, Rachel thought as she looked up at the hard blue sky,

Salali understands. She and I are like the same soul in two bodies.

The delicious experience had repeated itself more than once since that day. And there had not been a moment when it was not somewhere in her mind, very near the surface, creating an atmosphere of joy, through which she moved. Even today's wedding was not so important to her as her new life had become.

The wedding. No sooner had Donald and Salali realized how close they had come to losing each other than they had set the date, and now it had arrived.

As carriages rolled up the drive, their wheels crisping in the sand, friends called out and waved to each other. The chattering crowd grew. There were women and girls in colorful gowns, men in Revolutionary uniforms, sabers for which they no longer had any use hanging at their belts. There were food and drink and laughter, an atmosphere of relief and true joy.

Just then Jamie peeked cautiously out between the doorframe and Rachel's skirt, his brows furrowed and his round little face dark as a thundercloud.

"I don't wanna go out there!" he fumed.

"Go on now, Jamie," Rachel urged, smiling and giving him a little push on the shoulder. "Join your friends. Let them see your new outfit!"

He cut his eyes up at her. "I don't want 'em to see my outfit!" he muttered. "And my feet hurt!" He pointed down to a new pair of shining black leather shoes with silver buckles.

"Go on, Jamie." Her voice was harder this time.

She laughed to herself as he took a deep breath and slipped out. She loved his white shirt and the ascot at his throat, and especially the lace at his cuffs. But she knew that if Jamie did as he wished, he would take them off and throw them away. His bright red jacket, all trimmed in blue piping, matched his hat . . . Where was his hat?

"Just a minute," Rachel called after him. "You forgot your hat, Jamie."

She found the low-crowned hat on the chest at the foot of her bed. It had a narrow brim that turned up in front and back. It was blue with red piping, to match his jacket. She fit it carefully on his head and adjusted the angle.

"There," she said, "that's better."

She smiled as she watched him slowly ease out, sullen under the cocky little brim, hoping no one would see. But Abigail, standing at the edge of a gathering crowd, spied him immediately.

"Oh, there he is!" Abigail said excitedly. "Jamie, come show these folks the new clothes we've made you! Look, everybody," Abigail called, "red, white, and blue! A fitting suit of clothes for our new beginnings."

"Would you look at that!" Edward Buchannon roared. "Say, Jamie, is it you gettin' married today?"

The sound of sniggering made Jamie turn about. Two neighbor girls—also dressed to the nines—peered at him from behind their mother's skirts. Rachel was horrified to see him stick his forefingers in the corners of his mouth, cross his eyes, and pull a frog face at them.

"Jamie!" Rachel scolded.

Laughter ran through the crowd.

"Jamie!" Rachel repeated, coming out and taking him by the hand. "You stand by me. The ceremony is about to begin."

A string quartet seated beneath a great magnolia began to play, and a white-haired man in a long black gown and with an ascot at his throat stepped forward. These were the signals for which everyone had been watching, and quietness fell as Donald, resplendent in a new russet suit, took his place. Then, from the door of the Buchannon cabin, Salali stepped out, wearing a gown of satin and holding a bouquet in her hands.

When the ceremony was over, Rachel came to Salali and took her in her arms, each brushing tears from the other's cheeks.

"They're tears of happiness for you," Rachel said, smiling.

"I know." Salali hugged her tightly.

Jamie, who had managed to loosen his ascot and lose his coat, smiled up at them.

"Donald will be a wonderful husband," Rachel said. "I know he will."

"Yes, and nothing between you and me will change," Salali answered.

The music's tempo picked up, filling the autumn air with rustic country tunes. Within a moment the lawn was filled with men whirling their ladies about.

"Dance with me, Rachel," a voice from behind her said.

Rachel turned from Salali. Donald was standing there, a broad smile on his lips, blue eyes glinting in the sun, russet coat accenting his flaming red hair. He extended his bent arm. Rachel hesitated. She had not danced since she and Drew parted, and she felt that such gaiety might in some way profane his memory.

"Do me the honor," Donald pled tenderly.

Rachel smiled into her brother's eyes, took his arm, and for the first time in years danced to a joyful country reel. When it was over, she curtsied and smiled again.

"I loved it," she said breathlessly, "but . . ."

"But if you go on, you'll overdo," he said with happy understanding.

"I'm afraid so," she answered. "It's time for you to dance with Salali again."

For a while Rachel moved about, chatting with first this guest and then that. But soon another feeling crept over her.

"If you would, please excuse me," she said to the cluster of guests.

"Of course, my dear," a matronly woman said, "you must be weary."

"Absolutely," echoed a young man whose enthusiastic attentions had made her more than a little nervous. "It's going to take some time for you to recover, after all you've been through."

"Yes. Thank you," Rachel said demurely, and backed away.

Alone, she ambled to the place where Abigail's rosebushes had begun to grow again in the summer. Their faded foliage, contrasting starkly with the yaupon and holly whose shining leaves and red berries surrounded them, was ready to fall. The music and shuffling feet seemed far away as Rachel mindlessly followed the old flagstone walk, lost in thoughts of what had been and what was yet to be.

She knew that in a little while, amid much fanfare, Edward Buchannon would break ground where the old house stood. He would announce that, weather permitting, they would soon begin to build again. Life does go on, she thought, looking down the long hill toward the Cape Fear.

The British still held Wilmington and Charles Town and Savannah, but rumor had it that Craig would quit Wilmington before the month was out. Tories were leaving the south by the hundreds, many of them heading for Canada, some on their way to England, some sailing for the Caribbean. A good many had rewritten their own histories, suddenly transforming themselves into Patriots, and were settling in to stay.

Yes, she thought, life will go on, for the country, and for me. Twenty-eight is, after all, not too old to have made the greatest discovery of one's life. And with an energetic boy of five to care for, she would never be bored. What if a man should happen to come along, one who really cared for her? But no, there had been enough of that. Jamie and the practice of medicine would fill her life to the brim.

Scenes from bygone times came one by one before her eyes: Elizabeth's death, Jacob Shackleton's tarring; little Jamie's being born into the world with no father; her own search for Drew—a dream never to be realized; and there was that night, horrible beyond words, when the flames of Buchannon Hall leapt up, a blinding light in the forest's darkness. And, as always, there was the image of her father—that terrible, wrathful man—hovering, overshadowing her all these years.

Yet, that night on the face of the sea, images were softened and all those transformed somehow. She had at last learned that when one *gives* grace, one *receives* grace; for to forgive another is to heal oneself.

And there were good memories. The look on Drew's young face when first she saw him that bright morning on the banks of Lochredfern. A little laugh broke from her throat.

Even their tempestuous times brought a smile to her face. And there was Donald's unfailing love, and the friendship of the Buchannons ... and there was Salali. What more could one ask than to find a good and honest friend like Salali!

Rachel took a long, deep breath and gazed peacefully toward the autumn-brown trees in the river bottom. The sun, lingering an hour above the horizon, shone through air that was crystal clear, casting a copper tint on all the tan grasses and on the limbs of the leafless trees. The Cape Fear was a good place to be. She would stay here forever.

A movement on the river road interrupted her thoughts. She shaded her eyes. It was a lone horseman, riding unhurriedly along, perhaps a straggler coming for the dance or for the ground-breaking. The rider was too far away to make out clearly, but the evening sun cast a kind of sheen on his roan horse. He was obviously a military man, for even at this distance she could make out flecks of color that suggested a blue waistcoat and buff trousers—the Continental uniform. She could even see that he held a dark tricorn hat in his hand, which rested easily on his left thigh. No matter. If he was coming here, they would know soon enough who he was.

Her mind turned from the rider to her own deep thoughts, only to be quickly interrupted again. By the time the rider reached the great stone entrance to the plantation grounds, she could see him much more clearly. He reined in his horse, looking up at the gate as though hesitating, indecisive. But he suddenly tugged the reins sharply, walked his horse through the gates, and with certainty put spurs to its sides until the roan was racing up the winding road. For a moment she lost him in the trees, and yet something, she could not tell what, had quickened the beat of her heart. Something familiar about the way the man sat his horse. Then it leapt into her mind, the unthinkable thought. Oh dear God, her heart was playing tricks on her. It could not be! And she did not wish to think it if it was not true! Her hands went to her mouth as the man reached the last rise and burst from the trees. She suppressed an uncontrollable sob.

"It is!" she screamed. "Dear God, it is! It's Drew!"

She broke out running across the grass, and he saw her. All hesitancy gone, his face shining, he left the drive and spurred the roan toward her. Heedless of the galloping horse, she met him, reached up to his arms, and felt herself lifted bodily to the saddle's pommel. Her arms went about his neck and her cheek to his.

"What are we doing here?" Talaii whispered at last.

AUTHOR'S HISTORICAL NOTE

No one would quarrel with my mother's maiden name, Robertson, being Scots. Maybe that's why I wanted this story to begin in Scotland. Of course, that bold little country holds mystery and fascination for other reasons: castles and moors and bagpipes and that wonderful way of talking. But those are only symbols of the spirit of the place.

If you look at a map of Scotland, you see it resembles the British Lion standing erect, clawing at the North Atlantic. That's the way the people of Scotland have always been: fighters, independent, defiant. Even when the Romans tried to invade Scotland centuries ago, they ended up building a wall from sea to sea, and crouching behind it to keep the Scots from invading *them*.

But Scotland finally lost its independence one bitter, rainy day at Culloden, a moor in the country's far north. It was in 1746, when the Lowland Scots conspired with England against their Highland brothers. Until that day, it was the Highlanders who had successfully devoted themselves to remaining free from English rule.

When you come right down to it, when we speak of Scotland, it's the Highlands that most of us are thinking of, a great mountain fastness that lies northwest of a line from Aberdeen through Loch Lomond, a place of breathtaking mountains and deep glens, swept by heavy rain and high winds. The breast of the Highlands is cloven in two parts, from Culloden to the Isle of Mull, as if by a giant claymore in the hands of God. It's the home of names like McDonald, Duncan, Robertson, Buchannon, and McClure—people who wore the weave of their tartans as a family badge.

But following the Highlanders' defeat at Culloden, the weave of the tartan quickly unraveled, for England was determined to stamp out their way of life. To prevent further uprising, every sword and dirk was confiscated. To help break down family solidarity, England forbade them to wear their beloved tartans. Gaelic was banned and English wedged into its place. And the bagpipes were taken away—said to be an instrument of war. If you've ever felt the skirl of the pipes go down your spine, you'll understand that. It's a sound that has pierced the smoke of many a battle, electrifying Highlanders till they've fought like very devils.

By 1755, Culloden's tragedy was bearing bitter fruit, and the Highlands were in a sad state of affairs. It was in the 1760s—when Rachel was a little girl—that Samuel Johnson toured the Highlands. But he said he had come too late—that their glory had already passed away. In place of glory he found poverty and purposelessness, and a mighty emigration to places that offered hope—places like the American colonies.

Partly as a result of that outpouring, Benjamin Franklin estimated in 1760 that the city of Philadelphia was a third English, a third German, and a third Scots, Scots-Irish.

When Rachel arrived in the colonies, she found a country slowly approaching war. But she also found a place bursting with activity, and a place where in spite of the advantages held by men, women were active participants in business, the arts, in medicine, and in war. Most businesses were home-based in those days, so that husband and wife worked together. That didn't change for another forty years or more. So when Rachel came, there was a good deal of opportunity for women. For example, when Congress wanted the Declaration of Independence printed for distribution to the thirteen states, they gave the contract to Mary Katherine Goddard, who was a printer in Baltimore.

The Quakers of Philadelphia held a special interest for me. They found the Revolution a hard time, for they differed among themselves about whether it was right to become involved, and some were put out of the Society of Friends for their views.

About the time I began to write Rachel's story, I rented a copy of the old movie *Friendly Persuasion*, with Gary Cooper. I was puzzled at what I saw—or heard. That movie was set during the American Civil War, and Gary Cooper—a Quaker—spoke with many "thees" and "thines," but without a single "thou." Why were there no "thous"? Had Quakers actually dropped the use of the subjective singular by the time of the Civil War? If so, did they still use it during the time of the Revolution? A detail like that is important to historical fiction.

A friend of mine (who is also a Friend), Elaine Maack, is curator of the Quaker Room at Friends University Library in Wichita, Kansas. Elaine was kind enough to search until she found the answer, and told me that "thou" was dropped among Quakers in the late 1700s, before the Civil War, but after the Revolution. Now I knew that when Israel wrote to Rachel reassuring her of Drew's love, he would not say to her, "Thee is the great love of his life" (as Gary Cooper would have said a hundred years later), but "Thou art the great love of his life."

Anyway . . .

In Rachel's story I've included a few quotations in Scots, with some words you and I simply can't recognize. I've taken these directly from *The New Testament in Scots*, translated by William Laughton Lorimer, a book which makes *wonderful* reading if you love Scotland. If you like, try this from the *Book of John* on your tongue:

Ane o the Twal, Tammas, at wis caa'd "The Twin," wisna wi them whan Jesus cam; an whan they tellt him at they hed seen the Lord, he said tae them; "An I seena the sted o the nails in his haunds an stapna my finger intil the place, an my haund intil his side, I s' ne'er believe sic a thing!"

A sennicht efterhin his disciples wis inbye again, an Tammas wis wi them, whan Jesus cam and stuid i their mids, for aa the doors wis lockfast, an said, "A blissin on ye!" Syne he said tae Tammas, "Rax here your finger an luik at my haunds, rax out your haund an stap it intil my side; an binna misdoutin nae mair, but believin."

Now, about the Revolutionary War in the South. Though popular history focuses on the northern theater, the South saw atrocities perhaps even more terrible than the North. Not everybody in America agreed the colonies should break off with England. Someone has estimated that loyalties were divided into thirds: one-third Patriot, one-third Tory, and one-third neutral. It was the large Tory presence in the South that, toward the end, made some Englishmen believe they could make a stand there and still win the war, letting their Loyalists do much of the fighting. So the southern war became an especially vicious civil conflict in which neighbor was hating and fighting neighbor.

Of course, even apart from the war, the South had a very different flavor. North Carolina was far behind the northern colonies in industrial and agricultural development. The climate and soil were unlike that of the North. Crops grown there demanded a different approach, and of course there were more slaves in the South. I have tried to understand and capture this difference of flavor, and part of that difference had to do with the presence of Scots there.

Many Scots had come down from the North because America's own southern highlands, the Great Smoky Mountains, reminded them of their ancestral home. Many of them liked the isolation they found there—and used it to advantage both then and later, to hide the Scots invention they brought with them— the stills in which they made *uisge beatha*, "the water of life." But there were also Scots who came directly from Scotland into the Carolinas through a southern port.

To tell the truth, one of the reasons I chose Wilmington is because of the ominous sound of "the Cape Fear." But the choice was good for other reasons. Beverly Tetterton, of the Wilmington Public Library, tells me that in the 1700s, *forty thousand* Scots entered the colonies through the mouth of the Cape Fear River.

Scots fought on both sides in the Revolution. The proposed Tory attack on Wilmington that ended at Moore's Creek bridge was made largely by Scots, and led by a Scot. But of those who fought *for* independence, no doubt, many fought even more furiously because of Culloden, which by that time was only twenty-six years in the past.

One of the mistakes we make is to assume that the conditions of slavery in the South during the Revolution were the same as they were immediately prior to the Civil War. They were not the same. There was generally a kinder attitude toward slaves at that time, and more social mixing. For example, an examination of St. James Parish records in Wilmington reveals that half the membership of that parish were black, and that slaves were baptized into the church almost weekly.

I visited by phone with Dr. Jerry Cashion, a leading North Carolina historian, and he helped me a great deal. I learned that in those days a master could still free his slaves at will, the only provision being that he had to post cash bond, guaranteeing that if the slave failed in his business or trade, he would not be driven back on the charity of the parish. That limited some who wanted to free their slaves, for specie in North Carolina at that time was practically nonexistent. But sixty-some years later, in about 1839, it actually became illegal to manumit a slave at all.

Under some very special circumstances, a slave during the Revolution could even inherit his master's land—at least in North Carolina. There, slavery or freedom was passed down through the mother. If she was a free woman, the child was free. If the mother was a slave, the child was a slave. Therefore, if a child was born to a free man and a slave woman, the child was a slave. But if born to the union of a slave man and a free woman, the child was free.

Bastardy was rampant in those days, and most of the unions were between free male master and female slaves. But on rare occasions a free female who owned slaves would fall in love with one of her male slaves. If this union brought forth a child, the child was free. So it was with Salali, who was a blend of white, Negro, and Cherokee, the daughter of a free white woman and her mixed-blood overseer.

Dr. Cashion also directed me toward Janet Shaw's journal, *The Journal of a Lady of Quality*, edited by Charles and Evangeline Andrews. Janet Shaw was present in Wilmington just preceding the Revolution, and gives many wonderful insights into life there at the time.

Now, about Spaun's light. This is the one background detail of the book that I've invented. Spaun's light is fictional. There was no light built at the mouth of the Cape Fear until the Bald Head Light more than a decade after the war. *But* the British *did* try to destroy the Cape Henlopen Light at the mouth of the Delaware Bay during the Revolution. And several decades after Rachel's brave stand, a band of attacking Seminoles set fire to the Cape Florida Lighthouse, and the young keeper, John Thompson, saved his life in exactly the way Rachel saved hers!

But what of the way Rachel lured a ship to destruction? Her method is a matter of history, repeated countless times, both on North American and European shores.

As to the mystical or spiritual parts of the book, all Rachel's experiences have been known to others, and so are not spun out of nothing. As such, they have considerable meaning to me. After all, the story is about a person, Rachel, whose greatest struggle is with herself and with her understanding of what life is and what its spiritual realities are.

My feeling about Rachel is that she is a person tormented by her past, but who has enough steel in her bones to learn how to face herself squarely.

I think it's impossible for one to truly be a hero or heroine unless his or her greatest battle *is* with himself. Many people are thought virtuous who simply haven't enough character ever to have been tempted. They wouldn't know how to be anything but virtuous. Mark Twain once said, "Anyone who has had a bull by the tail knows five or six things more than someone who hasn't." Rachel's virtue was real, because within herself she had a bull by the tail, and she eventually triumphed. In my mind, Rachel is a real heroine, a person who faced life, then faced herself, and changed her mind about what is real and about what her duties to God and man really are.

My wife Linda and I live right in the center of the continent, and I've not been around the ocean very much. But I wanted to see the Atlantic from the same place Rachel saw it, and so during the summer of '89 we took our family vacation in North Carolina. Very early one morning I went down to the beach and waited for the sun to rise. I sat on the sand watching the morning light change, listening to the birds, watching the crabs scurry over the sand, letting the thin sheets of water wash around me as the tide came in. About mid-morning I ventured out into the surf, gingerly at first. But then I discovered the thrill of diving into the breakers, and in a state of euphoria, dove into one after another, until, with real fear, I realized I could not get back because of the seaward flow against my legs. I was truly near panic, and began to swim for my very survival.

Life is like the ocean, very beautiful, but when you're caught in its arms, and discover how unspeakably powerful it is, it's then that you must swim or perish.

All her life, Rachel swam.